I0763602

Praise for The Riddle Solver

"This work of visionary futurism shares an intelligence and sophistication that comes from a time that has not yet happened. Whether the author is a time traveller, seer or futurist, he somehow manages to bring back glimpses of an advanced and artful humanity. Fans of William Gibson, Terence McKenna, and Buckminster Fuller will delight at this cutting edge foray into Future Fiction."

- Delvin Solkinson, Senior Managing Editor
CoSM Journal of Visionary Culture

"The Riddle Solver embodies some deeply psychedelic threads as it weaves subcultural history into a highly creative mythology. Trippy and engaging."

- James W. Jesso, author of *Decomposing The Shadow: Lessons From The Psilocybin Mushroom*

"Shaun Friesen is a true artisan of the modern era. His visionary approach plots an aesthetic course toward our species involution as occupiers of the Nth dimension."

- Andrew Rand Brassil, author of *Portal of Creation*

THE RIDDLE SOLVER

by

Shaun Friesen

2st edition

ISBN 978-0-9949841-1-1

Cover art, interior graphics, and book design by Shaun Friesen. Back cover photography by Janis. Editing by Rachel Paul (www.lotusediting.com)

For ordering information please visit www.TheRiddleSolver.com

Free Zen Design
Calgary, Alberta, Canada

www.FreeZen.ca | www.TheRiddleSolver.com

Preface

The Riddle Solver is a fictional work written in Calgary, Edmonton, Keremeos, and Vancouver, between 2003 and 2013. The storyline reflects this highly compacted evolutionary period in culture and includes topics such as technology and communication, social commerce and grass-roots global community, along with the revitalization of human spirituality: new humanism.

The Riddle Solver uses the hero's journey, a cast of unique and familiar characters, extreme plot twists, and a visually poetic voice to explore a contemporary future of layered dimensionality, practical magic, and the functional use of meta currency. Within the far reaching implications of our present technological and environmental consumption, combined with the transfiguration of civilizations social and economic infrastructure, indeed at a time of internally recognized cultural and global unity beyond all previous understandings, it is a tale neither distopian nor utopian, but the paradoxical present-future of both.

Dedication

This work is dedicated to the
upliftment and transformation
of human consciousness
and to all those who
find themselves inside this story.

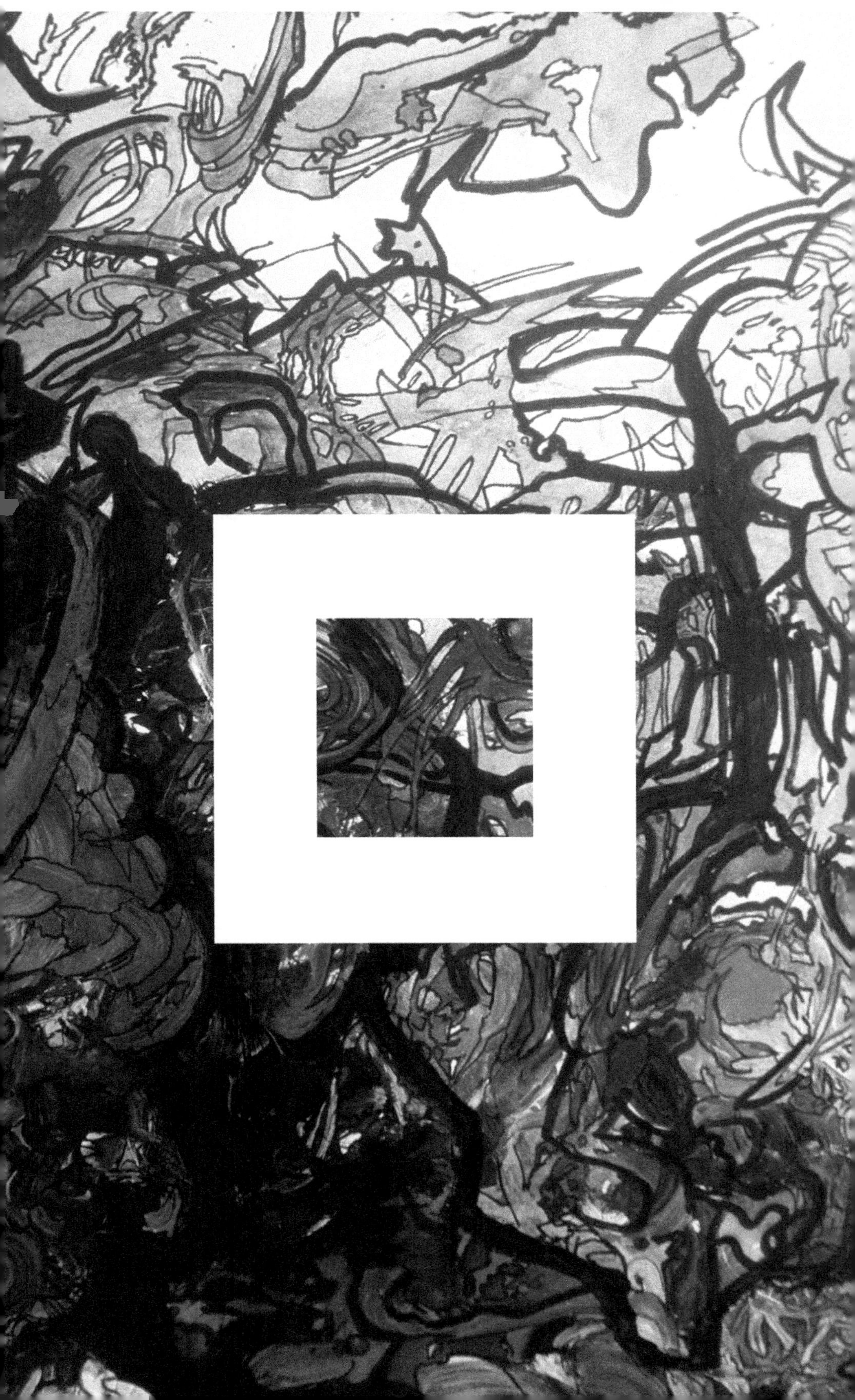

ONE

"We are between stories.…The Old Story sustained us for a long period of time. It shaped our emotional attitudes, provided us with life purpose, energized action. It consecrated suffering, integrated knowledge, guided education. We awoke in the morning and knew who we were. We could answer the questions of our children. We could identify crime, punish criminals. Everything was taken care of because the story was there…Now the Old Story—the account of how the world came to be and how we fit into it—is not functioning properly, and we have not yet learned the New Story."

—Thomas Berry

Chapter One

A sudden buzz of energy halted the chatter of the awaiting audience in the John deGryder Community Hall. Scattered gasps punctuated the hot room as a man in red entered through the main doors. Camo-clad DJs had been spinning jungle and breaks most of the night, but now sonic ambient textures slowly poured out of the speakers as the dense crowd parted for the focal performer. Taking calculated steps toward a microphone at center stage, he was surrounded by colorful dancing fairies, demons, and angels, all playing with the energy rippling from his red cardinalesque cloak. Were these creatures a visual distortion of space? An etheric fire-like by-product of his movement through time? No one in the audience could quite tell, because the priestly man moved unbothered by the creatures as if they weren't there at all.

Reaching the stage, the maestro stood in front of the microphone for a few seconds, his powerful presence extending wordlessly over the room as he tuned into the large crowd, waiting for the precise moment to begin. The fairies, demons, and angels continued to dance behind him, forming a chaotic triangle that pointed toward the entranced crowd, the man in red at the apex. The creatures suddenly calmed themselves, dim beams of light shifted in the hall, and the man spoke with a strong voice.

"Thank you all for being here, my friends, my brothers and sisters, in this time, in this space, listening to these words and feeling this emotion."

The fairies, demons, and angels pulsed in different ways now, moving to the rhythm of each word.

"As a species, we can see ourselves on Earth, our home, this vessel, moving within the infinite. However, the infinite can see our species, this Earth, the microcosm to the macrocosm, moving within its own self." The creatures were somehow transforming their mass between geometric and organic forms. "Allowing the consensual physical laws of nature to break down around us will be the first step toward our transition to quantum awareness, realizing the only rules we live by are the ones we create for ourselves." He paused. "We have no boundaries."

As if on cue, a hypnotic, low-frequency pulse was emitted from the large set of speakers, softly distorting the man's voice. The creatures integrated this sound into their movements, becoming more synchronized.

He continued, "Within a state of fluid consciousness, the structures that bind you are easily recognized and discarded, if that is what you choose. You may choose to learn from these structures longer if that is what you wish, but they will trap you if you do not recognize what they are and how they affect your individual growth."

The sonic pulsations began to rise, becoming more and more distinguished in the ocean of sound.

Using the strength of the unexpected, a man in the crowd suddenly shouted at the man onstage, "I'm waiting for death dressed in a skeleton suit to stab my third eye with HemlocX! To me, it's a holographic injection of dimensional medicinal truth I'm willing to dose with in order to reprogram the way I live!"

With this, the creatures moved in a more sporadic and unfocused style, as if the interruption was a distraction to the audience's attention—and to the flow of the unfolding universe. Remaining calm, however, the disturbance did not bother the enigmatic orator. He stood silently and listened as the shouting man went on: "Some would say I'm downright stupid to think individuals are free. I think it's stupid to let boundaries shape all that we are. We live as products in a world created for creating products!"

As the last word came out of his mouth, a character from the jumble of creatures on stage emerged, dressed in a skeleton suit. It moved down into the audience, out of sight for those in the back of the hall who were watching the events with curiosity and amazement.

Throughout the evening, the waiting crowd had been mingling and making connections to those of like mind. Gradually the social atmosphere transformed and the dance began as row upon row of black lights flickered on and the hall lights were dimmed. Accompanying the black lights was a grid of white, glowing, interwoven string. The grid was invisible with the regular lights of the hall, but reacting to the different light spectrum, it reached out across walls and beams, rounding corners and angles. It all made for an otherworldly setting, spaceship-like, especially filled with the onlooking mesmerized eyes of incarnated alien refugees, costumed trance dancers, eager social-ladder climbers, and artists. Enthralled by the new discovery of this arcane congregation of social mash, and particularly captivated by the lead preacher, the audience included an exceptionally receptive artist named Aum FreeZen.

Dressed in a 1930s vintage army jacket and black cargo pants, with thick brown-framed glasses and mad-scientist hair that stuck up in high defiance of gravity, Aum tried to maintain stoic composure within the ongoing bombardment of bouncing rainbow balls of color disguised as human beings. Eyes wide, it was his first major meeting, and he was trying to figure out whether the skeleton just popped into this dimension through the powers of the man on stage or if one of the creatures happened to have a skeleton costume underneath a devil costume. Aum didn't know, and neither did any of the other members of the watching audience. For all he knew, it could have been part of the performance, but due to the synchronistic way his week had been going, he was doubtful.

The man in red raised his arms and spoke, recapturing the attention of the crowd, "Even though the deal is done and the decision made, you still have not escaped the illusion. You have not stripped yourself of Māyā, the blinding deception described in the Hindu Vedas and Vedantas, the veil which clings dearly to the fibers of your mind."

The creatures continued to dance and move behind him as a small hint of a steady beat slipped its way into the tip of the pulsing sound. The audience stood motionless as the man at center stage continued, his voice gaining strength and focus.

"The pain you feel is entirely of your own choosing. The voyage of your vehicle through the ether around you is entirely under your control. And finding out whether you give that control to another should be where you put your awareness. Your shackles have been undone for centuries, yet you only notice now that your freedom is in…"

The music swelled, becoming an immense vibration that moved through the ocean of bodies present; the creatures onstage looked as if they were preparing for a rocket launch; intuitive audience members began to jump and yell in the exploding moment. The man suddenly dropped his hands as a dark sheet of fabric fell behind him, revealing a white fractaliean spiral, set aglow by the many more black lights that simultaneously turned on. More grid lines appeared throughout the space, creating a convergent three-dimensional form that ended in the flat two-dimensional glowing spiral. As the man dropped his arms, his hood fell back to reveal a thick red beard, wild feral eyes, and glowing sacred geometry painted on his forehead. The man's final word resounded galaxies of faith and confidence, climaxing the sonic crescendo.

"Movement!"

There came a tremendous scream from the hypnotized crowd as punishing deep sea–diving beats moved the audience in ways they never thought possible. Much like with the creatures, there was a unity on the dance floor that could happen only with shared understanding. Minutes and hours and days passed. Everyone existed only inside the moment, which was inside the sound, which was inside their eardrums and a part of themselves.

Near the back of the hall, Aum FreeZen finally noticed he was in a dancing frenzy. He was flailing arms and legs without regard for his own physical limitations, yet still in unison with those around him. He felt the intense urge to move to the front of the dance floor. There he could feel the music without distraction and really dive in. He wove in and out of the crowd, ducking beneath the waves of expression coming from the hands and feet of those dancing around him. At some points, he had to stop and backtrack because the group entrainment, the pranic soul mesh of the expressive dance floor, was too solid. It became a physical blockade, impenetrable to any who were not wielding a stronger intent. The audience was so blissfully lost inside the music that any unconnected step or gesture would disrupt the collective focus of the dance floor. As Aum realized this, he began to surrender his body to the crowd, while focusing on a position closer to the stage.

In the middle of the crowd, someone touched Aum on the back. He turned around to see Cat's striking eyes. Her short blonde pixie cut was messy and sweaty from dancing. His eyes couldn't help but take her all in. An unbuttoned white cloak flowed with her movement, opened to reveal a slice of indigo fabric that was tied at her neck and dipped to her hips. A short gray skirt dove wildly around her thighs as she danced in white knitted legwarmers. They locked eyes and began to move with each other, reacting and flowing like two lovers in a dream. Dancers in the audience began to focus their attention on the two of them as they moved together, the focus drawn away from the man in red. Aum and Cat's rhythm slowed; they danced to the atmosphere behind the fast beats, rather than letting the psytrance pulse move them repetitively. The connection between them radiated to the rest of the crowd, dancing becoming clapping and grinning becoming cheering. They were creating their own performance as onlookers began to see electricity move between them.

An hour earlier, when Aum's night began, he had entered the hall and scanned the crowd meticulously for two unknown people that he was supposed to find. He heard a familiar voice over the hum of the crowd near the back of the hall.

"I'll find you later. Don't go too wild and crazy on me."

Aum looked over to find a sparkling young woman in a buttoned-up white cloak that reached the floor. She had short blonde hair and was touching a taller man's arm as he walked away from her. Aum recognized Cat's voice from a phone message she had left him earlier in the week, inviting him to this evening's event. Aum decided to take the opportunity to thank her, even though they had never formally met. He caught her eye as he walked toward her.

"Hello Cat, my name is Jerome." Aum introduced himself, wondering where the decision to camouflage his character might take him.

"Jerome!" She recognized his voice as well. "You got the message I left you!" She checked him out, though way deeper than just attire or physique. "Wow! Fantastic."

He smiled under her microscope "I'm very grateful to be here."

"I gave the call quite a creative disguise, just as you asked. It surprises me that you made it," Cat said slyly. "You can never be too careful about who you invite to these invitation-only Riddle events. I can just imagine a first-time player walking in on this meeting and literally losing his mind because he's used to a roomful of people playing with a set of archaic figurines or something."

"No doubt," Aum said. He felt himself melting into eyes that were bright and lips that caused trouble.

"Would you like some tea?" Cat said with a daring smile.

"I would love some, thank you," the naïve Jerome replied, in place of Aum who was suspicious of the contents of the tea.

As she poured him a thermos lid full, he asked in a playful tone, "So what exactly did I ask you to do again?" Aum was curious because he in fact did not ask Cat to call him.

She passed him the tea and answered without suspicion, "I found a letter under a park bench that was addressed to Cat from Jerome. It had your phone number on it and you asked me to call you about tonight but to be creative with the particular details."

"And that you were. I probably wouldn't be here without your added creativity," Aum said sipping his tea. "How did you end up under that park bench?"

Cat laughed out loud at the question. It was a loud, boisterous laugh that made it clear to everyone that she was having a good time. Maybe she was just using the strange question to draw attention to herself, or maybe she was just stalling.

"That's for me to know and you to find out, love. All I can tell you is that there were many platonic solids produced by a plethora of pranayamic pole dancers watched by apprehensive prairie potatoes, eyes pointing the way."

Then it was Aum's turn to laugh out loud. He shouted "Yeow!"

Curious about this bizarre alliterative spectacle, he switched directions in the hope of circling back around. "So, other than pole dancing, what kinds of things do you spend your time on, Cat?" She laughed back, still flirtatious.

Aum's ulterior motive for attending this meeting returned to his mind. He had to find two players to help him with his own performance in a week's time. And after getting a strange and perverted answer from the last promising contender, a guy who was dressed in a fluorescent pinstriped suit, Aum had decided that Cat was a much more obvious choice for his quest. But then again, getting to this event was not quite as simple and obvious as a creative phone call.

"Hmm, interesting question," she said as Aum handed her back the empty thermos lid. The conversation switched to a more serious tone. "Right now, I'm reading a book on sacred geometry. I'm trying to incorporate its historical lineage of geomantic practice and study into the mandala work that I do."

"What's a mandala?" Aum asked, nodding for more tea when she motioned to him.

She filled up the thermos lid once again. "A mandala is a creative act that focuses on healing. For me, when I create them, I use natural materials: rice, twigs, rocks, things from nature. Usually I have a group of musicians play in order to help me focus, or sometimes I have prerecorded electronic music that I use. It helps me get into the creative flow while I move materials around to create patterns."

"How do you know what you're going to make?"

"I don't. I just go with the inspiration found in the moment and encourage whatever is inside of me to come out."

Aum gave her a playful grin, "I have a performance I'd like to do that you'd probably get a kick out of. Would you be interested in collaborating with me at a meeting next week?"

Aum knew that the right people for the collaboration would ask for something in exchange.

"Only if you're willing to do a collaboration with me the following week," she responded.

"Of course, but don't you think that's a little hasty? You're just assuming that I can play an instrument."

"And you're just assuming that I want you to do a mandala performance with me, Jerome. What if I want to videotape you doing cartwheels in your birthday suit while I smear my naked body with yellow Jell-O?"

"Funny, I was just asked that tonight by a guy in a pinstriped suit." Aum finished the last of his tea and stared deep into her eyes. "I'll still do it of course, but only 'cause I think you would look great in yellow Jell-O."

She took back her empty lid. “Then we’ll be in touch, love,” she toyed, walking away with a sly smile.

She was back in a matter of seconds, “Oh, by the way, Jerome, there was a high dose of psilocybin in that tea you just drank.” And with a pixie wink, she disappeared into the dense crowd.

Aum stared blankly for a few seconds “Isn’t that what you’re supposed to do at these things?” He asked it more to himself than anything.

After the tea, Aum felt something tingling in his stomach, and things started to look more detailed just before the man in red took the stage. But now as he danced in the presence of this magically attractive woman named Cat, a circle began to clear around them as space and time bent from the concentrated flow of graceful hands and limbs. With this change in focus, Aum closed his eyes and began to push himself further into the body-based vibration of drug-induced depths. The all-encompassing freedom he felt in that unlocked multisensory hyperspace distracted him from the physical dance floor, where he was approached by a circle of dancing men dressed in skeleton suits.

The men were moving toward them in a rotating counterclockwise motion, plowing and pushing their way through the dance floor like a new-age gestapo. Nobody paid any attention to the bizarre sight until the skeletons broke apart, forced Cat to the outside of the circle, and reformed around Aum in a matter of seconds.

Imagine having the time of your life, dancing with an incredibly alluring partner, closing your eyes for a second, and then opening them to find yourself surrounded by glowing skeletons—all the while hitting peak sail on the gales of astral travel. Needless to say, Aum fumbled, fully ripped, and found himself lost beyond return. He didn’t know if he was in the same building or even dimension for that matter. It was as if a magic portal had swallowed him whole, and within that portal, death awaited him.

As he was in an extremely heightened state of mind where thought becomes physical at a much faster pace than normal, Aum’s dancing became bigger and faster as adrenaline liquefied his fear and transformed him into a man of utmost certainty. There was no way he was going to be overtaken by a bunch of skeletons. No matter what dimension he was in, he just had to remember how to defend himself against the mysteries of the spirit world. He took in a sharp quick breath between beats and forced his threatened soul out of his body to blitz his attackers.

In his mind, he created walls and spears, sharp bats and boomerangs. He screamed inside, *You have no power over me!* and jumped Caporeia-like into the air.

The music faded as Aum's jump defied gravity, his body laying out and spinning on a horizontal axis in midair. As he fell back to the ground, Aum contorted himself, landing flat on both feet with arms up, as straight as a pillar. And then, for added emphasis, he let his entire body be taken by gravity to the ground.

Bending his knees and feet together, Aum's hands came down from above to slap the concrete like the great ape he was. *CRACK!* He hit the floor just in time with the downbeat as the music kicked back in.

There was only silence in his mind now. Calm. Invisible. Nothing. All the built-up energy from the night materialized in that movement which broke the consensual physical laws of nature. Crouched on the ground, Aum's head hung heavily near his balanced feet. His knees reached up passed his armpits, and he held his hands together at the end of his outstretched arms. He knew that the skeletons were still encircling him, but to Aum's surprise, they were not advancing on him, just rotating around him.

He wondered, *Did I just stop death?*

The music faded back in. Aum sat in relief and astonishment as he lifted his hands to see cracks in the concrete.

At that point, a separate circle of skeletons emerged from the crowd, rotating in a clockwise fashion. They pushed their way through the dance floor, moving toward the first circle, which continued to rotate counterclockwise. Aum looked around; not a single person was dancing. Every eye was watching the configuration of skeletons. Murmurs went through the crowd as the two circles merged into one flowing infinity symbol. There was a cheer from the crowd. The flowing infinity symbol then disengaged and became a flowing oval, and on the other side of the oval was the man in red. And he was walking toward Aum.

Aum knew he was in for something fierce when he saw the look on the man's face. He was no longer the benevolent father figure. He looked like a very angry Satan, red cloak and all. His furrowed brow distorted the sacred geometry on his forehead to create horns, and Aum could almost see a tiny pitchfork tail swooping and dipping with his movements. The man's clenched teeth synchronized with the deep dark growls in the music. His angry steps stomped beats into Aum's brain, attacking his confidence with all possible weapons. Aum tried to stand up but the man was on top of him before he knew it, pushing him to the ground.

"No! You are dead!" He scathingly hissed in Aum's ear. "I am the Riddle Solver and you are dead! You can no longer participate, nor bear witness! That is to say you are no longer here!"

Animalistic growling seared into Aum's perception as shivers crawled across his entire body like spiders, "In this world, you are no longer alive, and you no longer exist!"

Aum's eyes widened in utter disbelief. The man met his gaze with total domination. Caught, Aum calmly found a path through the powerful gaze into the costumed man himself, and inhaled a deep breath. But just as quickly as he had come, the man in red stormed back to the other side of the oval and disappeared. The skeletons closed the gap between them and morphed back into two circles, which began moving in opposite directions, separating the two men. The crowd cheered in fanatic devotion at this strange choreographed glowing skeleton dance; none of the internal goings on could be seen by the audience. In the midst of the celebration, a confused Aum retreated from the dance floor. The devil man's words still hung in his mind. *I am the Riddle Solver and you are dead!* Not quite what he expected to hear in the throes of feeling truly alive…

After hiding in the bathroom for twenty minutes, Aum decided to make his way home. There was no way he could continue dancing or even be in the community hall without feeling floods of paranoia. Once outside, Aum saw there were two girls smoking by the bike rack, talking loudly.

"I can't believe what people are missing out on by not being a part of this! Did you see all those skeletons?!"

"Yeah! Isn't the Riddle Solver soooo way cool?! He probably knows everything."

"Yeah. Like enlightened!"

Aum walked over and interjected, "Do you think I could get a drag?"

"Uh, yeah, sure," the first girl replied. "What's your name?"

"Jerome. You?"

"April, and this is Autumn."

"A pleasure," he said. "I couldn't help but overhear your conversation. This is indeed a very interesting place, but I wonder…I mean…I just need to ask, What is it about the Riddle Solver that you guys like so much? I mean…" Aum bent in and whispered, "I heard he's a real asshole."

They both turned to Aum like he was crazy. "Are you kidding! Look at the amount of time that's put into this dump of a community hall to transform it into something special."

"Yeah! Look at the number of talented DJs he brings in from all over the world!"

They fed off of each other now.

"Yeah! Look at the vast knowledge he dispenses to us about who we are!"

"Yeah man! Look at how he incorporates that knowledge into his performances!"

"Yeah! Look at the mega-synced community that has formed around him where we can just be ourselves!"

"…He hits us so hard with his power, we just want to give all, all of ourselves back to him!"

"Yeah!"

"Yeah!"

"Yeah, that's what I said! What do you say to that, *Juh-rommme* "

Aum had to keep himself from bursting out in laughter. He was in a much lighter mood after hearing this youthful enthusiasm.

"First off, thanks for answering my question. Second, I don't doubt the Riddle Solver's power," he said sincerely. "But nonetheless…" He paused. "How long have you two known each other?"

The two girls looked at each other unexpectedly, their mouths wide open, "…We…just met."

"This is pretty much the first time we've talked."

"Yeah, we've seen each other around at gatherings, but this is the first time we've really vocally connected, you know, really gotten a chance to express to each other how cool it is to be a part of the Riddle!"

Then April looked at Aum hard. "How long have you been a part of this community?"

He had to be honest. "This is my first meeting."

"Well then," Autumn responded, "I hope that you will soon appreciate the amount of effort needed to choreograph dancing spirits and marching skeletons! Let's go, sister April!"

"Yeah, let's go!"

And off they walked, showing little respect for Aum, a newborn exposed to a fresh and challenging world, unbounded by the rules of normalcy.

Just as The two girls walked back inside, Aum remembered that he still needed to find one more person for his performance next week. A streetlight flickered in the parking lot and went out.

"Why the hell would I want to play this stupid game anymore if there's an asshole cult leader running the show?" he said aloud. Then he mumbled, "I guess I just got kicked out anyway." Aum straightened his jacket, put his hands in his pocket, and began to march through the parking lot.

"It seems to me that an ancient bearded monk has reincarnated himself here and now to help and influence those around him. What do you say to this friend?"

Aum stopped in his tracks and turned to find a man with a heavy dark-green cloak wrapped around him. He had long wavy brown hair, was taller and thinner than Aum, and was smoking a cigarette in the green courtyard next to the parking lot. Behind a pair of wire-framed glasses, Aum connected with the mysterious man's calming brown eyes. This calmness was enough reason to engage in conversation.

"But you have no beard, my brother. My name is Aum," and he extended his hand, completely forgetting about his pseudonym.

With a loud laugh coming out as a jolly "Ha Ha Ha!" the stranger shook Aum's hand and said, "It's my pleasure, Aum. I am Toumai." He looked into Aum's eyes. "It looked as if you were having a little bit of trouble back there on the dance floor. Is that why you're leaving so soon?"

"Hope of Life?..." Aum responded obscurely, but then continued, "Yeah, I'm not feeling very accepted into this tight circle of Riddle Solver *worshipers*." He said the word with such frustration that Toumai was jolted in surprise.

"They're just playing you know. They reacted that way because they're frightened."

"What are you talking about?" Aum said, still frustrated.

"You're pointing out obvious character flaws in those two girls, and you're also challenging the power structure of this community with your entire being. Why else do you think he acted so much out of fear?"

"You mean the Riddle Solver? The solver of the Riddle?! How can anyone comprehend the near infinite nature of the Riddle, let alone solve it?"

"Aum," Toumai put a hand on his shoulder, but Aum continued: "And you're telling me that the person who's solved the Riddle is afraid of me?! He just kicked the shit out of me!" Aum smacked his head with both of his hands in frustration.

"Take a breath and relax. The man you call the Riddle Solver, the man in red, is named Dennis, and he is not the Riddle Solver." Toumai paused to let it sink in. "You are not kicked out of the Riddle."

Toumai continued, "Dennis is caught inside the power and the attention that comes with his role in the Riddle. And because of this lack of self-awareness, he cannot fly higher than where he sits; he believes he's completed the Riddle."

Aum looked up at him, frowning, "But then what are all those things like the giant spiral, the angels and demons and creatures prancing behind him, and even his speeches? He's the man at top, Toumai!"

"Yes, but still just a man. Dennis puts on a convincing show, and is certainly the most prominent figurehead within this community of Riddlers, but not all communities." He grinned knowingly. "Figureheads and leaders are very different. Let's just say he's on a very stubborn ego trip right now, and you came in and gave him a run for his money with your magic moves, especially with Cat, Dennis's girlfriend!" Toumai began to laugh.

"What?!"

Toumai paused. "You…you mean you didn't know Cat was his girlfriend?" He burst into such hysterical laughter that Aum could see an anime character flopping around, complete with large eyes and a circle-shaped mouth.

When he calmed down, Toumai explained, "Dennis and Cat sort of run the show together. Dennis has his crew preparing the visuals and décor while Cat has her crew preparing the drugs and medicine. Nothing hard you know, just mind expanding. For a lot of these people, the first time they've had a mind-expanding, mind-altering experience—and the only time they have it—is with Dennis and Cat. They're sort of psychedelic group leaders, bringing their flock into the vortex of the unknown, gaining notoriety as purveyors of truth and dispensers of important clues in the Riddle."

"Really?"

"Yes. And they will lovingly distribute clues to those who participate within the boundaries of *their* Riddle. Stray from those boundaries and disrupt the flock, however, and...well, you know, you were there."

"And nobody catches onto their little riddle within the Riddle?"

"I'm sure there are a lot of people who have come to realize the showmanship surrounding Dennis and Cat's events, but they are completely oblivious to that fact that there is more to the Riddle than just doing drugs, dancing, and being led through cool trippy shit." He paused for a second, "I guess that's what the Riddle can be all about if you want it to be, but the scale can go much bigger, I assure you. Fuck, most of the Riddlers here don't even know the very important history of raver culture. That alone sets them back quite a bit, at least in this branch."

Aum simply nodded. He had just finished reading a book called *Cyberia*, detailing major changes in thought during the eighties and early nineties—directly linking music, technology, and paganism.

"Shit, he must have been so mad!" Toumai continued after a puff on his cigarette. "No wonder he messed with your brain so much. Because you took such confident steps, he had to reach beyond his familiar tactics to remain in control. You were about to steal that entire crowd from him, especially because of how you were moving with Cat!" His voice got goofy, "The new magician in town! Walking in and stealing the show, with no props or preconceived plans, or extras even! Fuck! That's the best performance I've seen in a long time!" He was jumping up and down at this point.

"So what is this then? Was tonight a kind of a preliminary stage of the Riddle? To see where people's convictions lie?"

"In a way. For some it's here and for some it isn't. It's completely individual and personalized just like everything else. Nobody really knows until it happens."

"So does the Riddle Solver even exist then?"

"I don't know. The Riddle Solver is a myth, a legend. Supposedly there is an original player of the Riddle, and I guess that would be him. I bet he's like a reincarnation of Mozart or something, a master composer, a master builder—how else could the structure of the Riddle exist if there wasn't somebody to pave the way?" He took another puff on his cigarette. "But like I said, Dennis is not the Riddle Solver. I'm here to tell you this and see to it that you move on to your next level of play. What you've been doing so far is small prairie potatoes, my friend." Toumai patted Aum on the head. "And now it's time for bigger and better things; what you did on the dance floor is proof of that." He leaned back and stared up at the starry night with wide eyes.

"So why are you here? Why don't you move on instead of sticking around here, connected to Dennis' hazardous leadership?" Aum asked.

"Well. Here. Okay." Toumai seemed as though he was deciding whether to give the truth or not. "A while back, I told Dennis something similar to what I told you tonight at a meeting something similar to this, but…" He paused. "He took it all the wrong way. He didn't quite get it and I don't think he quite gets the Riddle as a whole. So, I sort of feel responsible for everyone here. I feel like I need to make sure that nobody gets catapulted into outer space and back into a malformed and confused timeline. Dennis's selfish intentions usually leak through to those in the right place at the right time, which is the case here tonight with you. And just like now, I advise them that there is more to all this, and they accept it or they don't. They usually quit playing, or continue on as if nothing happened, and sometimes they move on to bigger and better things. Frankly, I don't see why the actual Riddle Solver allows Dennis to impersonate him in the first place."

"So why should I place my trust in you Toumai, if you can redirect the path and possibility of anyone inside the Riddle? What makes your intensions at this intersection so righteous?"

Gravity washed over his face. "Because otherwise, you'd be walking down that street right now," Toumai pointed with the hand that was holding the cigarette. "You'd be thinking about how cults in society are spreading like wildfire now that consensus reality is toast and how most individuals are seeking and accepting the first answers they come across. *Lazy skin bags!* is what you'd think."

Aum's head jerked back from the street to Toumai's face as fast as light.

Toumai continued with a gentle smile. "One day you'll see what I see: an ancient bearded monk that has reincarnated himself here and now, to help and influence."

Aum's mouth dropped, and he realized Toumai was talking about him.

A man and a woman burst out of the hall doors, loud and laughing, snapping Aum out of the depth of his double shot of medicine trance and back to day-to-day reality. The couple got into a nearby car, and after some inebriated necking, drove off.

Aum was about to thank Toumai for everything and continue his journey but then remembered that he still needed to ask one more person to help him with his performance next week.

"I don't know. That's a pretty big question to ask me," Toumai answered.

"Well, I'm supposed to get two people to help me and I've already got one. I was about to leave the Riddle behind tonight, but you've given me new direction…and renewed my faith."

"How do you know that I have any performing ability?"

"I don't. But maybe this is an opportunity to escape Dennis and shred links with the structures that bind you." Toumai's eyes lit up. Aum must have said something right.

"I'll be there."

"Great. Meet me on the Boards in two days at two o'clock; we'll have about two minutes to discuss the necessities."

Aum knew that they had an infinite amount of time to discuss things, but now that he was at this so-called next level, he might as well play like it. He began to walk off.

"Aum, one last thing," Toumai tapped his shoulder. "This is for you. Congratulations, you earned it." And Toumai handed Aum a green and blue hooded scarf.

"What is this?"

"Peace acknowledged and future path manifested."

“Hmm…thanks.” He smiled and began his journey home in the dim light of a rising sun.

Chapter Two

"You got in late last night."

"Yeah. It was in an interesting evening, that's for sure."

Aum and his girlfriend Jenn were in bed, whispering softly underneath the blankets, hiding from Saturday's midday sun.

"Where'd you go?"

"I think I went to a rave."

"You! Really?! They didn't kick you out for being an uncolorful old goat?"

"I'm not that old, and I'm not that uncolourful…though I do wear a lot of dark earthen tones I guess."

"So how was it?"

"Um…lots of decoration and time put in, good music, a complex social atmosphere. There were some strange intimidation tactics happening, but also some intense learning…It's kind of hard to describe in totality."

"That sounds more complex than any rave I've been to."

"What do you mean?"

"At raves nobody really talks to each other. That's what I mean." She shifted her position in bed, "People just wander around in a drugged-up stupor, some of them dancing like death is on their heels, and some just gawking with mouths wide open."

"There was a lot of that last night, and I think death was actually there."

"If you were convinced that death was actually there, it must have been good." She tossed the covers off her long, warm body and got out of bed, "You getting up?"

"Yeah…in a bit," even as Aum said the words sleepily, his mind wove and wound its way back to the night before. Submerged in his memory, he heard his words and saw his actions. He felt the social architecture inside moments and reactions, but out of all of it, connections with Cat hit him the hardest. He felt the most stabbing desire and the heaviest weight of guilt.

Aum and Jenn had met just shy of nine years ago. It was in high school art class where Aum first noticed her. There were a lot of pretty girls in school but none caught his eye quite like Jenn. She had long chestnut hair, a button nose, and deep brown eyes. She had a naturally tanned skin tone and long, thin limbs, making her slender and delicate. And for some reason, whether from her voice and breath or voice and heart, Aum noticed that Jenn seemed to make an audible noise when she smiled. With beauty as bright as the sunrise, she wore conservative clothes—jeans and t-shirts—nothing too flashy and nothing too noticeable. Along with her teenage awkwardness and the developing artist in her, these subtleties captivated Aum. In class, he sat a few rows behind her and a few seats over. Jenn was always working on very precise still-life drawings. Her pictures of animals or nature scenes were quite a contrast to Aum's surrealist drawings, always heavy with symbolism of hell and heaven.

Aum often caught Jenn staring back at him in class—the innocent, awe-filled eyes always directed toward his self-defined oddity. He had a tendency to cause a ruckus in class. Forgetting he was in a public space, Aum usually began talking to himself, or he would attack his canvas with a paintbrush, dueling it to the death, or sometimes he took dance breaks with his headphones on. He received a lot of stares but the only ones he caught were Jenn's. She would blush and turn away. He still thought often of that surprised and coy face.

One day, a friend of Jenn's invited Aum to a house party—her parents were going out of town. Aum replied nervously, a timid teenager, saying he would only go if Jenn was going to be there. Jenn's friend smiled, giggled, and replied to Aum that she would make sure of it.

As a teenager, Aum was socially awkward. Even though not the greatest with women, he was still the ever honest and kind nice guy. His heart fluttered, his palms got sweaty, and his mental processes got sporadic while talking to members of the opposite sex. He became even more paranoid when he could tell the girl was picking up on his discomfort. It wasn't like this with Jenn though. The shy guy inside took a backseat to the confident, sure Aum FreeZen.

The day of the party arrived, and Aum was busy preparing himself, picking out his nicest outfit. He decided on a vintage ensemble that resembled one of his grandpa's old suits. (In high school, Aum had fully embraced the lingering fashions of the Seattle grunge movement.)

Later that night, the partygoers gravitated toward a pool table in one of the rooms, but Aum was more than grateful to find himself on a nice leather couch with a scotch in one hand and his other arm draped over Jenn's shoulder. She sipped a bottle of alcoholic lemonade as they sat on the couch talking about art, music and movies, political movements, bands and directors, their favorite art mediums, DJs, and actors.

"I like you Jenn," Aum said suddenly. A little more than tipsy, he confessed, "I like you a lot. I would like it if we could hang out more like this."

Jenn smiled one of those big sunshine smiles. "I don't know. I've never had a boyfriend, Aum, and...well...you intimidate me. A lot. You make me nervous, but, at the same time, there's this feeling I get inside I can't describe. I just want to...I just want to..." And she aggressively moved in and kissed Aum hard on the mouth. Surprised and happy at the response, Aum kissed Jenn back until they were interrupted by a random partygoer. The word spread instantly.

After graduating high school, they both moved on to higher education. Aum attended the local art college and Jenn the university. One night, Aum went over to visit Jenn while she did homework. He lay down on her bed with his sketchbook, switching from abstract form, to the room they were in, to Jenn herself, working at her desk. Jenn was making various noises of frustration and anger. She got up and left to go to the bathroom, practically stomping with irritation.

School had been very challenging for her. She was taking a streamlined course focused on law. This was not her choice. Both her parents were very successful professionals, specializing in law and business. Naturally, they wanted their only child to follow in their footsteps. Jenn's parents paid for her entire schooling, and whenever she expressed disapproval of this forced career path, they would tell her, "You'll be able to have a stable future, do whatever you like. It's a career path paved with abundance and prestige."

Jenn's dad, five years away from his retirement, was always at the office, getting in late and leaving early in the morning. Saturdays and Sundays were spent on the golf course or at the country club, and friendship consisted of business relationships. This left little time for family. Jenn's parents drank and fought a lot. They separated for a while when she was twelve and had managed to work it out, but very rarely did she think they were happy. She would catch them talking about her sometimes, "She just can't see right now. She'll have such a successful career in law if she just gets her degree."

Jenn usually shook her head and went back to work with a sigh, thinking about how dependent their identities were on their jobs.

"They don't actually know how to live without stress in their life," Aum would say with concern. "If they don't have enough stress at work, they create it with each other."

Jenn usually got defensive when Aum started criticizing her parents. She still loved them, but she didn't know how to get them to see who she was or even who she wanted to be.

BEEP!

"Ahhh! What the fuck do you want me to save the file as then?!" Jenn shouted at her computer screen. "It's due tomorrow! Don't you get it?" as if it was a living thing. Aum looked up to see her rubbing her temples and running her hands though her hair. She was in the midst of a midterm push. Aum walked over and in a barely audible whisper asked, "Can I get you anything, love?"

"A drink of juice would be great, Aum. Please and thanks." Some sobs also escaped.

He gave her a peck on the top of her head and went upstairs. At the same time, Jenn's mom came down the stairs and into the kitchen.

"Hey, Aum, how's school going?"

"Oh pretty good. I've got a paper coming up, comparing and contrasting artistic ideologies. It's going to be a tough one."

"So you've got two more years left then you'll have your diploma, right?" Aum could smell alcohol on her breath; she was pouring another glass of wine.

"Um, yeah. A degree, actually. Two more years." He got asked this question a lot by Jenn's parents. He knew what was coming next. In a slurred voice, she asked, "And what are you going to do once you've got your art degree?"

His answers were different every time, for every person he talked to. They usually ranged from "Work at McDonald's" to "Direct movies" to "Whatever I want to do."

"I'm moving to New York to make it big in abstracts." And he walked back downstairs with two glasses of orange juice.

Aum and Jenn disagreed a lot about her education during her first year at the university. Aum told her that she should follow her dreams and give her parents the finger. That made things worse. He eventually stopped telling her what she should do and just focused on supporting her. He tried to bring out the playful confident woman in her, getting her involved in his bizarre art-school projects.

One of these projects involved Aum sitting on a wheeled toilet dressed in a suit while Jenn pushed him around the heart of corporate downtown. Aum had volunteered himself, and in order to get her to take a break from studying every single day, afternoon, and evening, he also volunteered Jenn. He really just wanted to spend some time with her away from her intensely academic world. He could remember her smiling all day long.

While pursuing his fine-art degree, Aum learned about color, composition, design, art history, art history's relationship to politics, politics' relationship to contemporary media theory, the media's relationship to Western culture, and Western culture's relationship to Plato's cave. This formal education was set up as the groundwork for a more personally directed studio practice in his last two years of study. During those years, he could pursue whatever branch of knowledge he wanted and create whatever kind of art he wanted—even a brigade of toilets with wheels.

Aum gulped down the last of his orange juice, packed up his bag, and walked to the bathroom, getting ready to leave for the evening. He could hear Jenn starting to make popcorn. He walked out of the bathroom and heard a muddled conversation.

"He's too much of a distraction for you, Jenn."

"No he's not, Mother! He sits on my bed and draws! How is that a distraction for me?!"

"Having a boy around that wastes his time drawing rather than making something of his life is not good for your future. Tonight is the last night he's allowed over her until your midterms are done."

"Mom! I'm not a child. I'm twenty years old. I'm in my second year of university, studying law. I can decide for myself who I spend my time with. This is my life!"

"Jenn, what do you…"

Aum shut the bathroom door loud enough for them to hear and walked toward the kitchen. As if broken, Jenn ambled around the corner, holding back tears. He could hear her mom slink up the stairs without a word.

"Is everything okay?" Aum asked with concern.

She looked up at him with tearful eyes. "I can't do it anymore, Aum. It's just too much. I'm dropping out of school." She took a step closer and they embraced. She whispered in his ear, "Everyday it's the same fight."

Aum touched her cheek and she continued, "But now I know what to do. It's actually up to me. I have to tell them what they're doing to me." She laughed a quick laugh. A smile spread across her face.

"I get to choose what I want to do with my life, not them." She buried her face deep in the crook of his neck. Aum could feel wet eyelashes and a warm exhale on his skin.

"I love you, Aum. And I want to actually spend time with you when we hang out, you know?" She moved her head and looked deep into his eyes. "Do you know what I mean? I would much rather hang out and talk, listen to music, and share ideas, maybe even paint a picture together, you know? I can't do that while I'm doing homework like it's my sole purpose in life." She shook her head, hair falling in front of her face. She looked down at the floor, a whispered breath escaped from her lips, "I don't know."

"Jenn…you do know." He paused to let it sink in. He lifted her chin with his hand, looked into her eyes, and continued, "You just want to be happy, and what you're doing isn't making you happy. What do you need to change in order to find happiness in your heart?"

There was a long silence.

"Move in with you," she said quietly.

"What?" Aum said in surprise but with an excitement inside his stomach that buzzed. "What did you just say?"

They had been Dating for four years, so Aum agreed, and they made plans. Jenn was able to make it smoothly through the rest of the semester knowing that she would be taking a break from school indefinitely. Aum finished his paper and ended up doing a final project on chaos theory, converting fractal mathematics into sound. He got an A in the class. They continued to prepare for the move in together, like it held some kind of magical paradise where they could fall even more deeply in love.

"How's the packing going?" Jenn asked Aum one day over the phone.

"Good. I have to keep on reassuring my parents that I can handle living on my own. Moving in with my girlfriend, they're not too keen about."

"Yeah my parents aren't speaking to me. We had another big fight last night. They made it more than obvious that they won't be helping me out financially at all. I'm fine with that, though—proud even. I've already got an interview lined up as a server at a fancy restaurant downtown."

"That's awesome," Aum congratulated her. He was going to continue on with school in the fall and had applied for student loans to cover the majority of costs.

"Are we still going to your gallery opening at the school tonight?" Jenn asked.

"Yeah, totally. I was gonna meet some friends from school down by the river this afternoon. Would you like to come?"

"What are you guys going to do?"

"Ah, you know, play some hacky sack, have a drum circle, that kind of thing."

"I'd love to."

Aum continued packing, but all his thoughts were filled with Jenn. They got together with Aum's friend at their riverside hangout. Had they been fifteen years younger, there would be some kind of fort walls built with a sign that said *No Girls Allowed.* Now they were more than welcome. Aum had found it easy to find like-minded people at his school. Some were more reserved then he, and fewer had more extreme characteristics, yet all were generally interesting people. Most conversations revolved around the books, bands, and theories that Aum and Jenn talked about, so of course her presence was welcome every time.

"Last night I had dreams of flying vampires and superheroes and music and, well, the end of the world. And when I woke up this morning, I wrote something down the second I got out of bed. Would you guys like to hear it?" asked Aum.

There was a noise of overall agreement.

Aum stood up and began reading in his epic movie trailer voice: "The world you have awaited for is here. Do not expect to be given the knowledge of the universe and not have to rebuild it, flawless. The battles of the future will not be fought with tanks or guns or on battlefields. You will not witness it on the web or on television—these things do not exist. The battles of the future will take place in your mind. Remember always, you can never be defeated."

There was a brief moment of silence; then the group commenced in a silly round of golf claps and comments such as "Brilliant, brilliant!" "Encore, encore!" "Triumphant!" all in phony English accents. Aum took a deep sweeping bow.

Jenn usually remained quiet and concentrated on listening and usually declined any offer of pot. After a joint was passed around, Aum hopped from rock to rock until he got to the water's edge. There he remained still for a long period of time.

"What were you just drawing?" Jenn asked Aum's friend Kevin, who had just finished frantically marking up his sketchbook. He looked up at her and spoke.

"I just had an epiphany. I started drawing a circle and putting the words *Atoms*, *Cells*, *Organs*, *Man*, *Countries*, *Planets*, *Galaxies*, and *God* around the circle. The word *God* ended up at the twelve o'clock position and the word *Man* at six."

He lowered his sketchbook and looked over at Jenn to further explain: "I've been studying a lot of eastern religious philosophy and read that a square is equivalent to Man, a triangle to Nature, and a circle to the Divine. When I was just sketching there, I was trying to use these shapes to draw out a relationship between the three, while at the same time incorporating other symbols such as spirals and infinity symbols. My first attempt ended up looking like a head shape. I tried again and I drew a body. I did the same thing and it turned into an arm. I did the same thing and it turned into a finger. I realized then that the consecutive forms were doing the same thing as the words *Man*, *Organ*, *Cell*, *Atom*, and so on, eventually reaching the unknown space where God resides. I thought it could go the other way, too. I could draw Planets, Galaxies, and Universes to also find this God space…but I didn't even try."

"How come?"

"I realized that this is a very linear way of thinking. By thinking nonlinearly, one can get from any point on a linear spectrum to any other point, basically moving from a single spot in any direction and find the Divine, from the smallest atom to the most volatile country, like an interwoven mesh or inescapable web. The last design I did turned into this web. It sort of looks similar to a mandala, huh?" He showed her his sketch, "Fuck, what a crazy brainstorm."

Jenn's eyes were wide. "Yup." She picked up a small stick and started digging a hole in the soft dirt, trying to soak it all in. Jenn looked up to see Aum in shorts and t-shirt taking a first step into the crisp spring river, his sneakers and socks haphazardly thrown on top a nearby boulder. He looked back at Jenn and gave her a quick smile as he stumbled a little with his footing.

"He's one loosely tied knot, hey?"

Another friend, Jeremy, sat down next to Jenn.

"Yup, a daring knight in shining armor for damsels in distress," Jenn replied as she passed him her stick that now had an ant crawling on it. Jeremy looked at it in curiosity. The ant crawled to one end of the small stick, found nowhere to go, and turned back the other direction. Jeremy turned the stick upside down in his hand so the ant was crawling up to another dead end. He did this five times consecutively, then cleared his throat. "It's so bizarre to think that this ant can only see a millimeter or two in front of its face. It can't see me at all, or this river, or these roads, none of those cars over there…that dude on the bicycle, or anything in our reality here. It has no comprehension of the world past its own senses. All of this stuff exits and it will never even know it. Everything beyond is always a hazy unknowable existence."

"I'm sure glad I'm not an ant," Jenn said.

"Just imagine what the anthill's like," Kevin added.

"The anthill's right there!" Aum shouted, pointing to the towering downtown office buildings on the other side of the river, "So who's holding onto the stick?"

The three of them just looked at each other, not knowing how to answer.

Two of the other guys stood up, almost in a panic.

"It's ten to seven. We've gotta jet if we're going to catch the new Chuck Norris movie. Are you guys coming?"

"Yeah, totally," replied Jeremy.

"You bet your ass," Kevin replied, gathering his things.

"Aum? Jenn?"

Aum had rolled up his shorts to about as high as they could go and was halfway out into the steady current of the river.

"I think we'll probably just catch up with you guys later at the opening," Jenn replied for the two of them.

"Cool."

As their footsteps faded into the distance, Jenn sighed heavily and looked over to Aum. His innocence and curiosity caused her to stare in wonder on many occasions.

"Are you going to come join me?" Aum said, wading toward the riverbank. He took off his t-shirt and threw it toward the shore. When he started undoing his belt, Jenn interrupted.

"Aum! What are you doing?!"

"I'm goin' for a dip? Coming?"

"Naked?! I don't think so! It's freezing!"

"C'mon, you'll get used to it."

"No way!"

"Just take your clothes off and jump in! See? Watch!" Aum proceeded to pull down his undershorts and throw them onto the boulder with the rest of his clothes

"Oh my goodness!" Jenn covered her mouth to stifle her surprised laugh.

"What the?!" Two middle-aged joggers yelled in surprise as they ran passed Aum standing in the thigh-high water. Aum stood as if a deer in headlights; his face went completely red. Jenn burst out laughing, shaking her head as the joggers continued on their way.

"Maybe I should put my clothes back on."

"Um…yeah, maybe."

Jenn and Aum made it to The McCagney Gallery fashionably late. Hors d'oeuvres were already being served and inhaled by the skinny art students who had been working late in their studios. The McGagney Gallery was a small space at Aum's art college that was run by the student union as practice for larger gallery administration positions. The show this week was a fundraiser to allow the gallery to continue to operate.

"That's a nice piece you have in there Aum," said Reginald, his Interactive Sculpture instructor.

"Thanks, Reg."

"Did you use a digital printing process?" The Interactive Sculpture class was mainly about studying and building on the tradition of installation work, usually by incorporating sensors, triggered video projections, sound, and lighting, but Aum knew that Reg's own interest was in digital photography.

Aum, Jen, and Reg all walked over to the five-by-seven hanging on the wall. It was in between a large landscape painting and small television screen embedded in the wall, playing what looked like distorted video soup.

Turning back to Reg, Aum replied, "Sort of."

Pointing to some of the details on his five-by-seven, Aum continued, "It's an image of light passing through paint. I pressed acrylic in between two layers of transparency, pulled them apart, and captured the pattern that it created."

"It's amazing the amount of detail that's in there, hey?" Jenn remarked.

"You bet! When do I get to see a forty-by-sixty?" Reg asked Aum.

"When I can afford to print one that big!"

"Ah don't worry about that. I bet you could sell it straight away, maybe even make enough to print off a couple more. Keep up the good work, Aum."

Reg casually walked over to the food table while admiring the work on the wall. Other classmates and friends all greeted and congratulated Aum on his work. Once Aum and Jenn had seen everything in the gallery, they made their way out and saw Jeremy, Kevin, and the crew pigging out at the table of appetizers.

"I think the only reason they could afford to go to the movie is 'cause they skipped out on groceries," Aum said to Jenn. She laughed as Kevin walked over chewing some pita bread, cucumber dip in his scruffy beard.

"You guys coming down to the pub after?"

Jenn and Aum looked at each other.

"We should probably finish packing," Aum replied.

"Yeah," said Jenn. "I don't think we'll be able to make it tonight, Kev. Thanks for the offer though."

"We'll invite you guys over for the housewarming. Should be a stellar party," added Aum.

Jenn slipped her hand into Aum's and held it in silent anticipation of their move. They took their time wandering home, deeply in love and no longer constrained by commitments to time or space.

Aum had finally gotten out of bed, and he was Working up the steam to get started on a pile of dirty dishes before making himself lunch. The sun was shining brightly from the kitchen, catching him as he stood mesmerized by the jammed traffic backed up the hill.

"Finally out of bed? Sandra and Kay are heading over here in 10 minutes," Jenn said, walking into the bathroom. "We're going to have coffee before we go to work. Do you think you could make some lunch?"

"I guess I could do that," he said. He threw an old tea bag in the garbage and proceeded to scrub the teapot. Aum sighed heavily; the counter and sink were full of dishes still to wash. He prayed to heaven for a magical dishwasher delivery.

Sitting on the toilet with the door open, Jenn yelled, "Can you do the rest of the dishes after you make lunch, Aum?" He could hear her peeing and in a frustrated whisper responded, "I'm already on it."

Life had been rainbows and lollipops for a long time; their love was innocent and vibrant like autumn leaves rustling in the wind. A whole new world blossomed for each of them when they first moved in together. Jenn shed much of her shyness, becoming fun loving and ever addicted to the daily adventures that Aum loved to cultivate. They pursued any and all forms of creative expression; they practiced yoga and meditation; they discussed the nature of the universe and their deepest desires in life. They also practiced being silent together.

To Aum that seemed like a few lifetimes ago. Jenn got the waitressing job at the upscale restaurant, making enough money for them to get by. It allowed her plenty of time to spend enjoying life. Aum had also returned to his third year at art college but was challenged on a daily basis, finding out the discouraging statistics on art school grads and learning about the politics of the art institution—that it had very little to do with creativity. Bitterness slowly invaded his outpouring of joyous inspiration as he realized there would be much less stability once his education was complete. He managed to keep a positive outlook, however, and continued to make what others told him was groundbreaking work.

Jenn began hanging out with a girl named Sandra, a fellow waitress at the restaurant. Jenn told Aum how quickly they were drawn to each other, how well they got along, and how much mischief they got into. Not that they didn't take their job seriously or were disrespectful, but they often had many laughs at the expense of the high-class suits who frequented the lounge. They both had men regularly propose to them while they were working or offer to take them away from their meager lives of servitude. They did not realize that Jenn and Sandra were in fact the ones who were happy and content with their lives. When Sandra casually mentioned she had a six-year-old daughter named Kay, their drunken inquiries were squashed and they usually didn't return to the five o'clock watering hole.

When Jenn met her, Sandra was twenty-six, five years older than Jenn, and a single mom. This, however, did not hold her back from living her life as fully as possible. Sandra and Jenn hung out late into the evening and on weekends, hitting the bar scene after work, as well as attending different after hours parties and even a rave or two. Meanwhile, Aum often stayed at home or in his school studio diligently working on elaborate projects that were increasingly becoming more eccentric.

There was a Honk of traffic and then a knock at the door. Aum put a couple more pieces of cutlery away and walked over to answer it. As usual, Kay burst through with her normal exuberance before he could even make it to the doorknob. She ran up to him and gave him a big hug.

“Hi Aum! You know what? Uncle Roger just bought me a pair of kittens! You know what their names are? Keara and Mittens! Do you know why I called her Mittens, Aum? Do you know why?”

Aum knelt down on one knee to be at eye level with her. He shook his head a little, and his grogginess evaporated with her enthusiasm.

“No, why Kay?”

“Because she has cute little white paws and the rest of her is black. Her feet are so cutesy and little!”

“So when do I get to meet them?”

“I dunno, next time you come over, I guess. Oh no! Here comes Mom!” And in clothes that never quite seemed to fit, she was off tearing around the house. Kay’s long brown hair trailed after her as she hid from her mom.

“Terrorizing you already I see,” Sandra walked in the open door, plopped a few bags down, and they hugged. “I can’t believe the traffic out there! It’s a complete war zone!”

“I guess the city was having some power problems this morning; all the traffic lights went out.”

“That’s what I heard on the radio, too. I guess most people can’t remember how four-way stops work when they’re in a hurry to get to work.”

“Hey Sandra,” Jenn walked in from the bedroom dressed in her work clothes: a black skirt and black short-sleeved dress shirt with her hair pulled back tight in a bun.

“I thought Kay was coming with you too?” They moved in to give each other a warm hug.

“She’s here.”

“She’s hiding,” Aum whispered. He could see her poke her head around the corner with a mischievous look on her face. “Would you like some pancakes, Sandra?”

“Sure, that would be great.”

Jenn went into the living room and turned on the TV.

“Do you think Kay would like some, too?” Aum asked Sandra.

“Oh, I think so.” She quickly turned her head to hear Kay give a squeal, then run and jump on the bed.

"She's just been all over the place since Rog got her those kittens. Nothing seems to calm her down. It'll be good for her to have a little break from them."

Aum was about to ask something but was distracted by the breaking news broadcast from the television.

"...This has been the third incident of this nature in the past month. Local authorities are baffled, and citizens are equally concerned."

It cut to a curly haired woman with large spectacles:

"I just don't know what to think anymore. It must be a sign of the times, you know. It's just baffling that an overall decrease in cultural morale would result in this kind of extreme behavior."

Then an older woman in her late fifties appeared:

"It's downright ignorance! I can't believe people would use their lives to act out such horrible horrible... It's just... It's... sickening!"

Then it cut to a young man in his blue-collar construction outfit:

*"Lighting yourself on fire and burning to death for everyone around you to see...is this some kind of sick joke! I just don't (*BEEP*)ing get it!"*

It cut back to the reporter on scene, surrounded by ambulances and police cars.

"These comments were taken this morning just after the victim's remains were discovered in the middle of a downtown intersection. Some believe that it may be a protest against the new legislations passed that support further economic bailouts of the oil and gas super majors; yet other more fringe opinions claim it to be the result of underground cult activity. In each case, a final correspondence is left near the victim, stating 'I am going to New Eden.'"

All three of them stared at the screen, mesmerized by the footage of officers interviewing people in tears, unrolling caution tape, and setting up barricades.

"This gruesome and perplexing act of suicide will remain in the memories of those who were at the scene of the tragedy for some time to come. All witnesses were unable to give an interview at this time. As the pile of ash is cleared from the street and police

barricades removed, life continues to speed along, through chaos and turmoil, just as it always has. Back to you, Conner."

It cut back to the news desk.

"Indeed. Another tragedy in the city. We'll be back after the break with the second part of our five-part story called 'The Evolution of Identity Theft.' But, first, a story on little Jimmy Tucke. Do not adjust your set folks—that is his pet snake, Slimey, crawling in one nostril and out the other. Back with this hilarious story after these messages."

"Ho-ly-shit," Jenn stormed over to the television set and turned it off, "I can't even turn on the TV anymore. It's driving me bonkers! It's just too much, you know?!"

There was a long pause before anyone spoke.

"Another one, hey," Aum said to himself quietly, under his breath.

"Yeah, the downhill slide of television seems to be getting really steep and a lot quicker these days. Last night I saw a commercial with a skinny blonde in a bikini at a car wash, you know, washing her boobs, of course, and taking a big bite out of a cheeseburger. It's just like…What the fuck!"

The conversation muted as Kay entered the room.

"Aum, can I play on your computer?"

"Well…I guess so," he said playfully. "Just be very, very careful; it's the only paintbrush I own."

She gave him a look as if to say "You're weird" and left for the spare room that Aum used as his home studio. In the midst of flipping pancakes, Aum asked Sandra, "So how's Kay doing with her media time restrictions? I'm sure she desperately wants to see women in bikinis wash their boobs…I know I sure do."

Jenn hit Aum as she walked passed him to grab some plates from the cupboard.

"I've lifted some of the computer restrictions, but that's it," she said, helping Jenn with the cutlery. "I'm beginning to see things in a new light, Aum."

"Really? How so?"

"Well, her teacher told me she's a computer whiz."

"What?! No way!"

"That's what I said. Now maybe it's because I've held her back with strict parameters—so unconsciously her interest has grown—but that's not happening with the television at all. She has very little interest there, thank God! She doesn't have to see all these ridiculous reports on people killing themselves in the streets! What is this New Eden thing anyway? Have you heard of this before?"

An enormous chasm of silence opened up in the kitchen. Jenn and Aum looked at each other as if in a pistol duel at high noon.

"What? What do you guys know? What's New Eden?"

At the same time, Aum and Jenn responded.

"See, Sandra, it's like this…"

"Oh my God! No, Sandra! Don't even start him on it!"

Aum sighed heavily, plopping the last pancake down on the stack.

"Here she goes," Aum said rolling his eyes.

"New Eden is a disease! It's sucking the life out of intelligent people in our society. Like a certain somebody," her eyes blazed at Aum.

"Jenn! Chill out!"

"Holy can of worms," said Sandra to herself.

Bracing herself against the kitchen table Jenn shook, "I just…I can't…Fuck!"

Kay made a subtle noise in the bedroom. Jenn forced her anger into a container of expression that was more kid friendly and awkwardly out of sync with her truth, "It looks like we don't have any maple syrup! Great! I asked you to buy some last time you went shopping, Aum! Ridiculous!" Jenn said, about to fly off.

"But Jenn!" Sandra yelled.

"Just get him to explain the damn puzzle game!" She slammed the door and was gone.

There was a brief pause, then Aum said, "So…computer whiz, hey? Good for Kay."

"You guys haven't been doing the greatest for a while now, I can tell," she responded bluntly. With a head tilt, Sandra asked, "Aum, what's going on?"

"It's a long story."

"Well, who knows when she'll be back. We might have a lot time. Let's go sit on the couch," said Sandra, psychiatrist-like. Aum slid the plate of pancakes into the oven, grabbed a couple cups of tea, and sat down with Sandra.

Aum had graduated two years prior with High expectations of becoming a professional artist straight out the gate with his shiny new BFA degree. He and Jenn were convinced of this, and they continued to grow their life together while Aum attempted to make it big. Jenn spent an ever-increasing amount of time out on the town with Sandra, so Aum took over the spare bedroom and set up his studio. Paintings were half finished on the wall, tubes of paint were lying on the floor, and there were plenty of ink stains on the carpet. There was a corner filled with recording equipment and instruments—the most revered of which was Aum's didgeridoo. Cultural appropriation be damned, he loved to play for hours on end, creating hypnotic frequencies and ancient worldly rhythms. Most of all he loved to practice his circular breath control; it meshed very well with his meditation practice. Sometimes he recorded samples and composed multilayered songs, adding in more percussion later on. In another corner of the spare room, Aum had a computer station set up, where over the past two years, he had spent a lot of time honing his graphic design skills. He landed a few contracts here and there but had not retained a steady job since graduating. One of the things he was currently working on was a film soundtrack for a company in Japan; however, it didn't pay him anything. He was essentially doing it to gain experience.

He often worried about how the rent would get paid. Early on, Jenn was very understanding of Aum's creative drive and aural style. At one point, she thought that the Japanese people would understand it as well, even though it wouldn't pay the bills. Aum, however, had to tell himself every time he worked on the soundtrack to have confidence in himself. He felt the fringes that his artistic style resided in, most of the time, were more than people could handle.

Overall, Aum was tremendously talented, but it seemed that no one wanted to hire him for his creative talents—unless it was for a job that did not use those talents or even acknowledge him as a human being. At one point Aum tried to hold down a job in a furniture factory. He worked from 3:00 till 11:00 a.m., six days a week, packaging office furniture in cardboard. There were only six different pieces of furniture that passed through his assembly line, so after half an hour of work on his first day, he already understood the full scope of what he needed to do. The rest of the time was spent killing brain cells through robotic repetition and a lack of mental stimulation. His coworkers' conversations consisted of bragging about what they spent their money on when they got their reward for being a cog in a machine.

The line lead at his cardboard packaging job was a three hundred–pound man from the African Congo named Dregg. He was a boxer. The first day of work, Dregg showed Aum the bruises on his ribs; he even unbandaged his waist to prove it. Aum couldn't believe the irony. Dregg was a boxer by day and got boxed by night.

Aum attempted other "careers" in washing dishes, digging holes, assembling electronics, and painting houses. With each job Aum quit, Jenn became all the more disheartened. She continually encouraged Aum to apply for gallery shows or even administration positions, but her positivity dwindled. Eventually she quit her job at the restaurant and began doing secretarial work at her parents' office. After all her growth toward finding a voice for her cultivated passion, a voice that stood up to her parents and their expectations, and after taking many risks, both personally and for Aum, Jenn was spent.

"I'm starting to get really sick and tired of this, Aum," she told him one day. "I'm tired of worrying about bills. I'm tired of waiting for this big break you're talking about. I just want some stability. I want a decent paycheck. I want some nice clothes. I'm sick of looking like I'm scraping by, like I haven't eaten a proper meal in weeks."

"Okay, Jenn, I understand. But out of all places are you sure you want to go back to your parents for support?" he replied.

"It's just a job, Aum. Things will stay the same."

"Okay, love. Do what you need to do."

Aum really wanted to be supportive, but he just couldn't. Without his partner there to charge headfirst into life with him, he knew the sun would be less bright and the sky less blue.

Jenn found Sandra a position at the firm as well so they could continue with their rambunctiousness but on a bigger budget. The gap between Jenn and Aum became a little wider, and this space became the new norm. Their animosity toward each other was subtle but grew stronger as time went by. When Aum wanted to talk about a project he was working on, she would no longer pay any attention. She would suddenly have to go to the bathroom or remember to phone a friend for lunch. She no longer had time for his dreams. Once she started to cash in her much more substantial paychecks from her parents' law firm, Jenn began to realize she should have stayed at the university—that her journey with Aum had been fun but a waste of time in many ways. She became overtly critical of Aum for not having his "shit" together. Aum became overtly critical of Jenn, too. To him, she had abandoned her freedom and the creative and spiritual path she started. Every so often, just because he knew it would irritate her, he would turn up his meditation music just a little louder than usual, just enough so that she could hear it but not do anything about it. And even though he woke up to the same woman every morning, just as he had done the past four years, Aum felt lost.

And then he found the Riddle. Or maybe the Riddle found him. He was still trying to figure that out.

"So..?" Sandra asked.

"So I guess things haven't been going well since I started playing the Riddle." He lied, but just a little.

"Oh yeah, Jenn has mentioned this Riddle thing you're doing, but every time it comes up, she gets really upset and changes the subject. But…what about New Eden?"

"The two are related." His pace quickened. "Well, that's sort of speculation. No one has really gone public to prove it yet. I bet things would really start getting out of control then."

"Okay, so why does she hate this Riddle thing so much?" Sandra asked.

"Well, for one, she doesn't understand it and what I'm doing in it. I'm learning mad in-situ amounts about what's out there and how things are connected—for example, where and when intuition and synchronicity meet. But the main reason she's continually pissed at me is because it's completely divergent from developing my career path. You know, like I should go do graphic design for an organic cereal company or something—but Sandra I know, I just know, there's something important here that I need to…investigate."

"You need to solve the Riddle," she smiled.

"Sounds a bit mental, hey?"

"Yeah. A little. Who told you about it?"

"No one. During my extensive raking of the Internet, looking for job opportunities or doing research for other projects, I stumbled across this very bizarre website. www.gargantuan_artist_manufacturing_incorporated_by_suzie.org. Here, let me show it to you." He stood and stepped toward the spare room but then remembered Kay was on his computer. "Oh yeah. Well, anyways, it all begins by registering as a player on this website. The name is quite misleading because it's a huge database of communication dealing with culture and the arts. But it's like entry number 2,970 on a list of 3,000 sites when you do any sort of search on the arts." He shook his head as if he was still amazed by the discovery.

"To become a Riddler," he continued, "You fill out some of your run-of-the-mill community message board surveys—this is to best suggest a group to join that suits your creativity. The forms get more and more interesting as you go along; they are completely personalized to what your interests are, as if someone is right on the other side of that screen creating and programming new forms to fill out as soon as you're done the last."

"Really?"

"Yeah, these questions can range from whether you enjoy the comedy of Bill Hicks or more obviously conspiracy-theory-based questions that pertain to public events such as the first lunar landing or 9/11. But like I said, it's pretty much 100% personalized."

"But what is it that you do exactly?"

"Oh, you know, talk with people, discuss ideas. It's sort of like an interactive online community that extends out into the real world. The Riddle can be played as an individual, but people of like mind usually evolve into small teams or even large groups over time; we make connections at different meetings or manage to meet on an individual basis."

"Like, meet in real life?" She sounded shocked.

"Yeah, in real life. You exchange ideas, or objects, or opportunities. I heard about this guy who found a ticket in his mailbox one day. It was for a plane that was leaving in forty minutes when he lived an hour from the airport. And he did it, through pure will and most likely a cracked-out ex–race car driver at the wheel of the taxicab, he made the plane and flew across the country to meet with a group that was organizing one of the biggest gatherings that's ever been held. Most of the time, you just receive clues from all directions, completely anonymous sources, or people you've never even heard of before."

"So you need buckets of bravery and blind faith. What happens if somebody lies?"

"Yeah, it is possible to lie, but immediately the player who does is put into a situation that will verify all the information they've entered. That might be through an authoritative figure, like a police officer or something, coming to their house and using intimidation or manipulation tactics during questioning, or a player might be surprised with a strange award and have to give a public speech on the present breakthroughs in the field of astrophysics. It can all be very scary. I've heard some bizarre stories on the Boards."

"The Boards?"

"Online message boards. So if a player's information is proven to be lies, they'll be disqualified and will never hear of the Riddle again. It is, however, possible to back up those lies, whether through sheer ingenuity to defend your character from interrogation tactics or by studying astrophysics for three days straight—either will prove a player's creativity, commitment, and focus on succeeding in the Riddle community, and thus they will be rewarded for their strength or research by receiving what they want or need."

"Like what?"

"Like a plane ticket in the mailbox," Aum said. "For example. But it all depends on the situation. It could be a free dishwasher, or a check for $89.70, but rest assured, it will be the exact price of that dishwasher you're asking for."

"What? I mean…what? No wonder Jenn is pissed. It sounds like collective insanity. You still haven't answered my question either: How is New Eden related to the Riddle?"

"Well, before these suicides started being reported on television, there was a lot of talk on the Boards about this place called New Eden. I don't even know if it's real or just a rumor, but supposedly it's a modern paradise. Everyone lives in harmony with each other and the environment while still being quite technologically advanced—like a new city started from scratch. It's supposedly off the grid, self-sustained, and separate from all human contact. The opinions out there on the Boards can get really messed up, though—like this one dude thinks New Eden is a space station orbiting the Earth. Another thinks it's in a different dimension, and then there are some people who think they can only get there through death." He looked at her with concern. "Jenn is really scared that this is what participating in the Riddle will turn into for me, and I'll eventually kill myself or something. It's like, fuck! Does she really think that I'm that unbalanced?"

"Oh boy," Sandra sighed.

"But, you know, these suicides are the first events I've witnessed in mainstream media that have any relation to the Riddle at all. Interactions and meetings usually maintain complete obscurity within our culture."

"This is mad! Are you sure this game isn't going to mess you up?"

"Of course not. I find that a lot of it is just running around like a rat in a maze, delivering things."

"What do you mean? Give me an example."

"Okay, so three weeks ago, I received an e-mail to be at a certain bus stop at a certain time and wait to give a man in a blue coat one of those old eight-inch floppys."

"That's pretty strange. Who uses that archaic technology anymore?"

"I don't know, but what's even more strange is that this guy wasn't even on the bus. He just drove up in his car—a regular guy with a red ball cap, t-shirt, and dark blue jacket. He looked at me straight in the eye, and all he said was '10-4310 Dovedrive Avenue.' He gave me an envelope with a key in it; I gave him the floppy and he got back in his car and drove off."

"Sounds like playing this game is for paranoid schizophrenics who want to develop their illnesses even more," she said.

Aum continued despite her criticism or the fear shaking her voice, "I didn't have any plans the rest of the day, so I went to the address. It was an internet café," Aum said in a dramatic tone as if it was of significance. "I didn't really know what to do, so I just checked my account on the Boards. I had no new messages, so I started to walk out of the café, just to check that I had the right address. As I did, a server carrying some dirty dishes bumped into me and everything crashed to the floor. I tried to help clean it up with him, but without even looking at me, he said, 'The door you're looking for is on the roof, not the floor.'"

Sandra's head Twitched to the side in curiosity, "Really?"

"Most definitely really," Aum continued. "I went to the back of the building and climbed up onto the roof, via an old rickety staircase, only to find no door. I scanned my brain for any possible answer, hoping not to get caught trespassing, when I noticed a small safe in the brick wall near an air-conditioning unit."

"Did the key open it?" Sandra exclaimed, moving closer to the edge of her seat, her eyes growing wide.

"No. It was a combination lock."

"Oh. Too bad you didn't bring your crowbar with you; you could have busted it open," she said. Aum burst out with excitement, "I didn't have to. I busted it open with my mind!"

She looked at him in astonishment.

"Yeah, I managed to open it just by figuring out the combination."

"Was it the number the man with the blue jacket gave you: 10-43-10?"

"No, that was the first thing I tried. It took me a few minutes of thinking and a couple different tries, from the actual date, to birthdays, to the time I received the key, but then I looked at my pocket watch and realized that a combination lock looks quite similar to a clockface. I imagined 10:43:10 p.m. layered over the existing numbers, guessing the correlating digits were 43-36-7, give or take." Aum shook his head, "It was such a long shot, but for some reason, I thought if I give it this one last try—like I said, intuition and synchronicity—and…it worked," he said with a shrug.

"Crazy. What was in the safe? What did the key have to do with it?"

"Oh, there was an outline of a key drawn on the bottom of the safe with a felt marker. So I just put the key in the safe, closed it, and left." Getting up from the couch, Aum continued, "When I got home, there was a very strange message on the answering machine. It seemed like they had a wrong number, but I listened to it again and it made sense." He walked over to his desk and grabbed the phone. Aum punched in a few numbers and handed it to Sandra. She put the phone to her ear:

*"You have one saved message…*BEEP*…Hi there, this is Cat. Sorry you couldn't make it, Jerome. The game was so good! We won forty-three to thirty-six with only seven seconds left. Maybe you can make it to the next one; we could really use your skills on the floor. It's this Saturday starting at 11 p.m. at the deGryder Community Hall. You should come; it'll be good times.* CLICK*…end of message"*

Sandra pulled the phone away from her head and stared at it in disbelief.

"Wow, she's so casual about it. If you didn't get that combination right or even if you weren't paying attention, you'd think it was a wrong number, talking about a basketball game or something."

"Exactly," Aum said. "I think that's the whole point. Playing in the Riddle gets you really focused on the whole moment; it really makes you think about your surroundings in a lateral way and absorb all aspects of environmental stimulus. I think that's why I play it and practice it, and why Jenn doesn't like it. Right now she just wants the stability of a solid straight line in her life."

"And life has no straight lines," Sandra replied.

There was a pause in the conversation. Aum automatically began listening to a pattern of noise creaking out of the old house as Sandra looked up at him, "That waiter sure played an important role in getting you to the safe. He must be involved in the Riddle, too, then?" she asked with curiosity.

"I guess so," Aum responded, tilting his head. "Or maybe it was just some random expression that popped out of him. I dunno. Was he then waiting for me to arrive with the key? And if so, is he at a level where he could see how integral his word play was in helping me receive my first event invitation?"

"Dude!" Sandra shouted in playful frustration, "I think you just broke my brain!"

Aum started laughing and moved in and rubbed her head. She continued, "Whoever came up with this puzzle game is sure going to like how you think." Aum could see a light bulb turn on in her head. "I know what you should do." She looked into his eyes playfully. "You should create a riddle within the Riddle, Aum. You could get everybody playing the Riddle to think that you created it, but really it's just a riddle inside the Riddle that everybody thinks is the actual Riddle."

He looked back at her warmly, thinking of the night he had just had at the community hall, and said seriously, "Sandra, there are people already doing that." And he proceeded to tell her about his adventures with Toumai, Cat, and Dennis.

Chapter Three

Sandra and Aum were sipping their tea and letting their brains cool on the living room couch when Jenn returned with a bottle of maple syrup. She didn't look like she was doing any better. Everyone went into the kitchen, and they ate lunch in silence, except for Kay, who was the only one talking.

"So then Karen said to Jessica…" She just kept going and going whether they were listening or not.

"Alright, time to head to work. Will the dishes be done when I get back, Aum?" Jen asked, once the meal was finished.

In sarcastic monotone, Aum nodded, "Yes, dear."

"Thanks for lunch, Aum," said Kay. "You're the best pancake maker ever!"

"Why, thank you."

Jenn and Sandra gathered their things, getting ready to leave for the office, and Kay jumped back on Aum's computer.

"Oh, by the way" Jenn said to Aum, "I told Sandra she could leave Kay here with you while we go to work. You didn't have any plans today, did you?" The spite in her voice easily gave away that she was still angry.

"Jenn?" The mood of the room shifted closer to the razor's edge as Aum's agitation grew.

"What?" Jenn was still on the offensive.

"Can you give me a little more notice next time?! I was planning to work on my computer all day; you know, trying to find work, trying to make art! I may not be making fifty grand a year now, but that doesn't mean…"

"Mean what?! Don't kid yourself, Aum; you were going to waste your time on that Riddle shit again! That's what last night was all about too, I bet!"

"Jenn, just fucking go! Have fun in your anthill!"

Jenn stormed out, and Sandra left with a sincere smile and a wave. She mouthed the words "I'll talk to her." As the door closed, Aum picked up a glass and threw it across the kitchen. It shattered in the sink. "Shit!"

After taking a few breaths, he walked into his studio, laid down on the floor, and stared at an unfinished painting that was pinned to the ceiling. Kay was sitting next to him, playing some sort of puzzle game on his computer.

She was a bright kid. He had been hanging out with Kay a lot during her summer break. Aum could remember one evening a few years back when Sandra found herself a date and he babysat for the evening. Aum was apprehensive at first, but once Kay was there, he forgot all about his hesitation. She had so much energy that it was hard for her innocence and playfulness to not rub off on him.

Aum could distinctly remember a game that he and Kay played called "Monster." One person was the Monster and the other the Hero. The Monster had to walk in a pattern around the room and try to tag the Hero. The Hero moved through the room while trying to dodge in and around the Monster's arms. The Monster counted to thirty, then changed the walking pattern to something more complex, moving up to the next level. When the Hero was caught, they switched roles. Kay got so complex in the Monster role that she followed an actual step pattern. Rather than sticking to a simplistic and general route, she mapped out every step like practicing a dance routine, acting like a detailed adversary in a video game. Aum instantly recognized the relationship, yet this was something more real for her than any computer game could be.

Aum found guilty pleasure in contemplating Kay as a Riddler. With her inquisitive mind and imaginative intelligence, she would be perfect for this new type of entertainment. He had even heard on the Boards of an offshoot game being created for children. It was most likely created by a group of Riddler parents who felt their children could benefit from the game—a space where their interactions with other kids would develop new skill sets that TV would not facilitate.

"I have to get on my computer soon, Kay. You can go into the living room and watch a movie, or you can stay in here if you like...do some painting maybe?"

She was only half listening to Aum, who was still lying on the floor; she was completely zoned into her game. "Um, I'll watch a movie, Aum. I just want to finish this level."

Aum wondered if that's what he looked like when he was on his computer: wide-eyed and zombified. After a few minutes, she said, "Okay, your turn," then left to the living room and started to stream the new *Swiss Family Robinson* remake.

Aum scrambled over and sat down at his computer. It all disappeared: the world around him, thoughts, emotion, structure. It was an overly complex and highly unusual way to achieve a Zen state, where intricate cognitive interweaving merges self to the all and physical hardware becomes metaphor: global brainwaves manifested out on a screen in front of him—anything he wanted to know about, download, or buy was only a click away.

He didn't know what he was doing or what he was looking for until he found it, especially when he was in a creative mood. After exploring a number of links, Aum wove his way to a photograph database website and downloaded a picture of a leaf. He opened some image-editing software and cruised back and forth between bitmap and vector programs with ease, cutting and pasting, adding layers, adjusting color, all at lightning speed with fingers flying through software shortcuts; he had become very proficient with his pixel surgery tools.

In no time at all, the image was done—he had turned a very nice picture of a bright green leaf into a multilayered green and bright yellow lotus.

He titled it 'The Single Spark'. After thorough admiration, he posted it on a few online sites, as well as his personal page on the Boards.

Aum was just warming up.

He reached for his iced tea and spotted a stack of mail next to his computer. Jenn must have thrown it on his desk earlier. He picked up a padded manila envelope that was addressed to him and found an inscription on the back, written in black sharpie: *Welcome to the*

Towers. He opened it up and found a USB drive inside, stamped with a picture of a red key.

"No way!"

He had heard of these USBs before. They allow Riddlers access to four different communication sites linked to the Boards. These sub-site networks are called the Towers, independently constructed on the same sovereign servers that hosted the entire independent digital ecosystem. The Towers were a distinct, independent, and noncommercial space. The whole mysterious thing; the Boards, the Towers, the meeting rooms, all used a vastly different set of interface rules than the well-known Corporate Boards. The Corporate Boards were a groomed, polished, human monitoring device using the leading edge of post-psychology methods to track and understand user data, and harvest attention; corralled, cornered and milked by bit farmers and byte ranchers. It was a planned out system that was fully and unquestioningly integrated into society; as easy and as natural to learn as eating and shitting. To Aum, it felt like stepping into the deep end of a buzzing noxious hive mind gas. Nearly suffocating, it usually took him days to get all the voices out of his head. The Riddle on the other hand was user-built and open-source; and looked like it. Sparse, raw-code showing, UI and back-end together as one, and so loosely and archaically held together it looked like a gust of wind would blow it away. So far out of the norm, it was a blessing to be a part of, and witness.

The Red Tower was constructed at the same time as the Boards, or so he had heard. There was also the Yellow Tower, the Green Tower, and Aum had only once heard of a Black Tower, still under construction. Each key drive is coded to allow a player access to specific floors and rooms within the Tower. The key drive must be in a port to allow direct information transfer, unlocking different coded pathways between the PC and the remote network. Each Tower has a specific purpose, and the Red Tower allows players a communication space for coordinating events and planning Riddler meetings—such as the one Aum attended the previous night. Aum guessed that the other Towers handled other, more complex details of the Riddle, such as player information and tracking, object management, and whole system coordination.

With anticipation, Aum inserted the red key drive into a free USB port.

A swirling organic red-spectrum animation momentarily took over his screen.

"I think it's working," he said to himself excitedly.

Once the screen was back to normal, he double clicked his browser icon and typed in the Riddle website, www.gargantuan_artist _manufacturing_incorporated_by_susie.org, and logged in. There were a few new general news posts, mostly about the latest New Eden suicide, and a few new entries on the Boards he was a member of. Nothing out of the ordinary.

"Maybe it didn't work?"

Then he spotted a small addition to the site menu at the top. A new button called "Towers" had appeared. He placed his mouse over it, and a dropdown menu revealed a single entry—The Red Tower.

His heart raced a little.

He clicked it and his screen went black.

"Uh oh."

A few seconds passed and Aum was about to reboot his computer when an animation began to play. A simple single-line perspective diagram zoomed out to reveal a small box in the center and, at each corner of the screen, four much taller rectangular boxes. When the perspective of the diagram rotated to a top view and the boxes changed into flat squares, he realized it was a very simple 3-D wireframe animation. It was a visual depiction of pure information to better conceptualize, and make concrete, the ephemeral world of digital data. Led by a small spark, a moving line traversed from the center square to the bottom right square, touching its edge to bring a red grid into focus.

Slowly, the box with the red grid inside filled with color, solidifying into a red square. The color stretched beyond the box to turn the entire screen red, after which point, three white windows opened up in the middle of the screen: one contained a large X in its center; the second held a blinking cursor, reminiscent of MS-DOS; while the third, a smaller box on the left, held two lines of text:

027-01

027-56

Aum clicked *027-01*, which triggered an animation to appear in the top left corner of the screen. He sat bewitched by the visual poetry inside the binary flickering of grid moves and color washes, entering what he assumed was the first room on floor 27.

The screen once again contained the Three windows, with numerous lines of dialogue appearing in the center window:

It seems like there is so much pressure, yet this is the easiest thing to do. The pace sometimes frightens me because dreaming can be a scary thing.

But it's worth it, knowing that one day we will take to the sky as truly free beings.

Fly? Right now?

Why not?

Aum didn't know who was in the chat room, nor how many players were typing out their immediate thoughts at that moment, but it seemed to be a space for Riddlers to figure out direction and meaning through brainstorming, contemplation, and sharing. A player could sit and watch, pick up random clues for investigation, or add in comments if it felt right.

That will be how WE see it anyway. It's all just another illusion; the laws are just different.

That's why WE are here in particular. That's why WE are doing what we are doing right now. WE get to test out the extent of these new laws.

Trust is a major issue in letting those old laws fall away. But once again, it is the easiest thing to do.

No it's not.

Yes it is. It all relates to openness and the ability to communicate with actions and body language.

Being 100% comfortable with who you are.

I know myself, as I am being, came to the conclusion while taking a pee this evening that I don't think at all about what I am physically putting out into the space around me (as far as movement goes), only what I'm putting out mentally—then my physical body follows that lead.

An interesting development. Shouldn't it be the other way around? Your body moves through space, then after, you think about what you're doing?

It's good to be able to control your brain before you get to this stage.

Or maybe it's better to not use your brain at all.

The multilevel nature of reality that WE have created is becoming more and more apparent.

Reading a book, I was told that I was being reminded about the fact that I had asked to be reminded at that particular moment that I was reading that particular book. It changed my life.

Aum started laughing, "This is way too random for me." He clicked on the next line, *027-56*. The same animated process began in the top left corner, but with the spark finding a different square in the grid. The dialogue box cleared and the cursor was blinking, waiting, at the top left of the window.

Hello, he typed in. Aum waited a few seconds.

He typed some more, *Hello is anybody there?*

Nothing. "Must be a private room," he thought. Then a line appeared.

Greetings and salutations. This is Toumai.

"What?!" Aum shouted at his screen, then typed:

Hey Toumai, this is Aum. It looks like this event may get organized a little faster than I had expected. Was it very difficult to find a key to this room?

No, a man in a red hat delivered it to me in person a few minutes ago. I felt like I should check it out right away.

Awesome! Is there anybody else here?

I don't think so.

That's strange, Aum thought. *If Toumai is here, Cat should be here too*.

Have you heard from Cat at all?

No, I heard that she left town today. Some family thing I think.

That sucks. She was the other person who I had asked last night to help plan this event. Hopefully I hear back from her as soon as she gets back.

Yeah. We'll just have to do what we can until then, I guess. Maybe we can lay some groundwork right now.

Sure thing, Toumai.

Aum and Toumai chatted the length of the afternoon, between numerous Riddler-esque activities with Kay. They talked about different promotional activities they could do within the online Riddle network but also about other underground and mainstream media sources they could pulse.

They talked about Aum's idea for the performance and how it would work as an extension of the art in the space. Aum would begin with some spoken word, and slowly a mob of musicians would appear within the crowd, encouraging others to contribute in whatever way they saw fit. There was a very good chance it would be a stuffy uptight crowd, but it would be good to have a challenge. Toumai was going to play the role of Aum's polar opposite, keeping the focus contained from the other side of the audience once the performance began: holding space. This is what Toumai did for Dennis and Cat's show, so he readily accepted his role. Aum and Toumai had both been in contact with a couple of their musician friends, who were going to each bring a handful of *their* musician friends, who would in turn bring a handful of their friends. The only stipulation was that musicians must be able to conceal their instruments—hopefully there were no security pat downs at the front door.

Aum passed out flyers to all his friends and even random people on the street throughout the following week. Many of them replied and told them they would be able to make it. Kevin and Jeremy were up for attending, but Aum was still trying to convince them to be involved in the music-making aspect. He sent out group e-mails and even placed some subversive want ads in the weekly. He didn't know who might pick up on the clues, but anything was worth a shot. Aum had still not heard from Cat, but he was hoping to enroll her skills as an assistant in directing and conducting the musicians, as well as everyone else in the space. With a smile, he thought about how great it would be.

At the end of the week, Aum found himself standing nervously at the train station, lit eerily by yellow florescent lights, thinking back on the previous week's preparations. Tonight was the night and the sky was clear with a bright new moon. There were a few others waiting for the train: a woman who looked like she was headed home from the office, a couple of intense looking preteens, and a disheveled old man with graying hair. He walked passed Aum and stared at him with his beady eyes. Aum took in a deep breath to shake the mistrusting grimace that hung in the air. He tried to give the old man a smile, but it was returned with a toothless scowl. He heard someone yelling a few blocks away.

Lack of community while living with several million people could be quite a strain. For some, it was an unending search for hope while the psychological weight of televised war, persecution, and natural disaster were internalized day after day. It all added up so quickly, but the flat answers of scientists and politicians could no longer appease the majority of public. Aum could see it unfolding on the TV screens right there on the platform if he liked: riots, environmental degradation, out-of-control pollution, but he was one of few that had consciously decided to develop blinders, protections from the interruptions of regularly scheduled programs. He noticed a lot more interesting things going on once he decided to ignore TV. No one seemed to realize that the food quality available at the international chain supermarkets was quickly growing worse or that half of the things being sold in them were remedies and pills or things like aspirin apples. Aum figured the food and drug coalition was the next king in line after the oil barons relinquished the reigns of control.

Meanwhile, people still continued to drive their cars; five dollars a liter was a reasonable price, especially during the holidays. In fact, last week, Aum had been part of a discussion with others on the Boards who felt that the oil and gas industry was milking humanity's ignorance, or maybe patience, to the point of cultural revolt. One Riddler thought it would turn to global anarchy as the system crumbled in on itself. At this memory, Aum snorted a sarcastic chuckle standing on the train platform, "Oh man, I wonder what that would look like?" Everyone stared at Aum talking to himself as he turned his gaze to a poster ad for *Brainflossing: Jimmy Tucke and His Pet Snake* TV series. "Oh…"

The train whooshed past and came to a stop. Aum adjusted his glasses, stepped on, and found a seat. The transit cops would probably be out tonight and he didn't buy a ticket. With only a small amount of cash to his name, an investment in food or other supplies far outweighed the consequence of not buying one.

The train glided over the tracks, coasting over a hill toward downtown. He got off the train at the third stop, near an empty ten-story parking garage. It had over fifteen walkways sprouting out of each floor, connecting building to building to building, like a giant spider web. The concrete jungle was still tonight. Buildings loomed and the hum secretly residing inside the silence was almost unbearable, like a thousand mosquitoes swarming in a darkened bedroom. The late-night city workers drove giant insect-like vehicles down the roads, washing streets and watering the unhealthy trees that were planted in small holes in the sidewalks. As Aum walked down the street, he touched each one of them, thanking them for their half-starved endeavor to keep nature in conscious vision.

He had begun to realize it was a very tough town for an artist; coming down here during the day proved that. It was an act of bravery he did not usually attempt—for this city was the home of the oil barons. They were the engineers of hive-mind apathy, moving earth and mountains with a single handshake, giving it a new spin. Since the "trickle-down effect" from those handshakes fueled all branches of commerce, the citizens gave little or no thought to the ramification of those dubious deals on the entire city, country, or planet. Immigration was on a huge uptake, with jobs available in every sector; a hundred houses were built every day, and roadways pushed further and further into wetlands, ranchlands, and farms. Exponential growth was nothing compared to this boomtown.

Aum walked passed a wooden construction wall completely plastered with 8½ × 11 posters advertising local shows at clubs or underground bars. The multitude of punk rock bands clearly showed how intense and opposed the underground of this city was: Scorch the Earth, Inner Surge, Ex-Millionaires Club, FireWaterBurn, The Mad Cow Scramble, Red Hot Commodities, The Rules of Anarchy, and Lenin's Tomb. On the wall, there were slogans of revolution and protest, peace marches and calls for change. This is where the city's real art lived on—this one fucking wall! The last barricade of genuine cultural integrity. Aum saw a graffiti stencil of a bomb with the words *This one's for you, baby!* on it. And as he walked, Aum saw the stencil four more times, a battle cry stamped on corporate buildings, shouting *Burn this house to the ground*, *It will only sting for a second*, and simply *Earth Murderer!* He had seen this kind of work before. It came from a collective of artisan jujitsu guerrillas, all living in a single rundown crumbling house somewhere in the area. There were only twelve of them, but they easily balanced out at least 120 blocks worth of apathy.

He found the right building and followed the architectural maze though corridors and freight elevators into a small, discreet hall.

He was a bit nervous. These window displays showcased work from the top artist-run centers in the city, and his exhibit would be two months long. He was proud of himself; it was his first show since the gallery fundraiser, and he was hoping for the same support and feeling of community.

Aum opened the final door only to find the hallway empty. He was shocked. The soft display lights were on, and the slightly perfumed air pulsed past him as the same void of humming silence reached his ears—here inside the hall, just as outside of it, empty.

He had put so much work into promoting this event. The mail-outs, the ads in the newspaper, all the work he did online through the Boards…and no one. The florescent lights buzzed louder in the dead silence and, disappointedly, Aum walked over to his display window, his body stooping with a shadow of surrender. He looked at his hanging piece. Its potency was lossless.

With a combination of conscious and unconscious lines directing the viewer's eye toward detail in the underlying color, the piece included deep intricate spaces that communicated more than just the complex inner workings of Aum's brain. In the process of outlining and defining chaotic acrylic color with ink, an organic interlacing pattern formed both the tower-like point of focus and the more subtle, abstracted hand holding it.

It was a giant blue hand holding a pile of liquid fireworks, drawn and painted both on the wall and on a forty-by-sixty piece of paper. The piece had taken Aum a few months to create over the spring, and the extensions he added, flowing out beyond the paper edge onto the wall, took mere hours, months later.

It was work that stopped passersby dead in their tracks—a self-analysis of mental and physical health followed for some. For others, being dead was nothing to worry about.

The emptiness of the space pressing in on him, he inhaled and crouched in a single spot, worn out, tired, ready for enlightenment by death at the end of a sword. He let out a big sigh, and with it, waves of emotion and expectation he had built up. He let go of Toumai, who was not there. He let go of Cat, who he had not heard from since the night at the community center. He even let go of his plan to become someone or even accomplish something of importance within the Riddle. He let go of every compliment he had ever received, as well as criticism he took too seriously, about himself and his work. He blew it all out in a lung full of air and took in a fresh breath with a new outlook on life. Aum shrugged his shoulders and whispered, "All I can do is this," and he let in a feeling of peace. A slight smile appeared across his face as he rose.

From the opposite side of the hallway, a man entered, walked past Aum, and moved directly to Aum's display window.

"Is this your work?" he asked.

Aum nodded, smiling a little more. The man was dressed in a double-breasted, knee-length heavy overcoat with a black t-shirt underneath. He was the same height as Aum, with dark shoulder-length hair and a similar demeanor, but older—midthirties maybe. "What is it? What does it all mean?"

Aum's smile grew into words. "Okay…so…You're going to have to hold on here. This is going to be a hefty download and will most likely mess with your mind a fair amount."

The man looked at him seriously. "Perhaps."

Aum took this as a challenge.

"This show is called *Creation*. In the overall sense, a creation is an extension of its creator. All experiences influence who a person, or being, or creator is, affecting what they develop into and their decision-making skills in the world, not to mention the way they interpret new life path experiences. A creator is an extension of their own experience, history, and programming, and those experiences and programs are chosen according to previous experience and programs. It's all one evolution." Aum looked at the man standing across from him.

The man nodded in understanding and added to the download, "We create our own lives. We are held responsible or are rewarded instantaneously. We exist as the creators of the things we leave behind in the field of time, and we are also creations ourselves—existing infinitely in time."

Aum nodded, "Righteous." He was a little surprised by the wisdom of the stranger's response.

"Continue, my friend," the man said intensely.

So Aum did, "Now this drawing here tries to represent that concept—creation as an extension of its creator—by having similar mark making within the hand that is holding the creation and within the creation itself, as if the creation is exploding out into space from the hand." He took a breath, letting it soak in, then continued. "The object held can be anything you want it to be. It can be learning how to play a new instrument and becoming a more knowledgeable music maker, it can represent a sculpture, it can be the new car that you just bought, it can be a spoken word performance, it can be yourself, it can even represent the most grandiose thing, like the universe being created, because it's all the same process, it's all the same thing. So that drawing right there in front of you is everything."

After a pause, the man responded, his jaw firm, "Most infinite." Aum hadn't cracked him yet, so he continued his dissertation.

"Now to emphasize the concept of the infinite here in real time, I added that quote on the window there," he pointed. "It's from the Bhagavad Gita, which is one of the main source books on Yoga and a concise summary of Vedic wisdom." The man scanned over the quote:

Behold, O Arjuna, My forms by the hundreds and thousands, of different sorts, divine and of various colors and shapes! Now behold, O Arjuna, in this, My body, the whole universe centered in the One—including the moving and the unmoving—and whatever else thou desirest to see!

"Are you familiar with the Bhagavad Gita?"

The man shook his head.

"Okay. So this particular quote is Krishna talking. He's sort of a main dude—God incarnate in physical form type thing. The whole Bhagavad Gita is basically a conversation between Krishna and his student Arjuna. In this particular quote, Krishna has just shown Arjuna the entire universe in himself. He is everything that exists." He stopped for emphasis. "Everything. Even Arjuna is included in this. Another important thing is that Krishna is blue. That hand right there, that hand, is blue as well. The funny thing is, I didn't make the connection until everything was up and finished."

The man continued the line of thought, "That blue hand right there, that's the hand of Krishna?" He pointed to the hand drawn on the wall.

"Exactly," Aum laughed. "So, when the viewer stands in front of this drawing and reads the quote, the voice of Krishna can be heard inside their own head. The viewer takes on the role of Arjuna, and in front of them, there Krishna is, showing the infinite in himself to his student in the field of time, just like in the Bhagavad Gita, trying to create more creators like himself."

Aum paused. There was no response from the man. Aum began to feel strange to have explained every intricate detail about his work—like he went too deep, revealing too much of his source and spirit. He sighed and kicked the air, "It's quite ridiculous, though, on my part. Even though there are many clues and hints, without me standing here and explaining it, explaining the Bhagavad Gita, explaining who Krishna is, it's just another messy attempt at discovering worth and meaning, easily judged by dead eyes as a fucked-up, drugged-out drawing."

The man looked at him, a new glint in his eyes, "But that judgement doesn't matter to you, right? Because people will get it if they want to, if they choose to see it, and be activated on a deeper level. They can choose to be enlightened. They can choose to be inspired by your creation or pass it off as mere doodling."

Aum burst out laughing. He didn't expect to receive such support.

"Have you thought about who you are at all? Identity?" the man asked. "I mean in relationship to the concepts you're putting out there into to this world with these acts of creation."

"No, not really. I mean, I sort of know who I am, but, I dunno, it's a continual exploration I guess."

They both stared into the drawing in silence. Aum was lost in very deep contemplation of the man's question and also the excited feeling of appreciation. The plural reverberated in his mind: *acts*.

"So how do you think the art world will react to this work?" The man continued. Aum snapped back to reality; something was different though. His eyes were a little unfocused, and he knew something came out his mouth, but he wasn't entirely sure what.

"Creativity exists at all times and it is the pretentious institution of art that ruins it. The formalized hierarchy and inherent social strata defining what's good and bad, what's in, what's hot, what personalities are peaking—all of these things are irrelevant if you know what it is to be creative, to have that resourceful fire in your belly, running up and down your spine. There are lots of people out there that feel this, and hopefully they realize the institution is irrelevant. It's something to work around and in between. So to tell you the truth, I don't really give a fuck. This is not for the institution. This instruction set, and all like it, will be bypassed by those trapped inside their white-walled prisons, intent to continue their self-involved brain masturbating, feeling cocky until their funding is cut and they realized they've just fucked themselves to death. The relationship between creativity and *art* is equivalent to spirituality and religion; an oppressively binding system that takes you further from the essential human truth rather than closer."

"Yes! Absolutely! Good," the stranger responded. His words affirmed Aum's trumpeted call to arms and minds. He smiled and the man extended his hand, "My name is Zhe."

"Aum," he replied and shook it.

"Thanks for sharing, Aum. I'll see you around." He gave a low nod and walked away. Aum wanted to stop him; he wanted to get into a deeper discussion and quench a large thirst that had just been discovered. However, a moment passed and Aum remembered where he was and that he was supposed to be doing a performance right now for the Riddle, yet not even once did that pop into his brain as he talked with Zhe.

His brow furrowed and to himself he softly said, "Whaaaaaat thuuuuhh fuuuck?"

He knew no one else was coming, so he left for home. That was it. Performance done. Weird. Really weird.

The next day, Aum awoke to a phone ringing.

He made it home the previous evening a little perplexed but fully together. Jenn was in bed reading when he got there. With much trepidation, Aum asked Jenn why she didn't make it to his would-be performance. She said she was busy prepping material for presentations to East Coast clients, but pretty much anything she had to say was just an excuse to him.

"By the way, I'll be leaving town tomorrow for a week," she added. Aum did not respond, as it was the first time he had heard of this. He jumped into the shower, and when he got out, the light was off and soft snores were rolling out from her direction.

In the morning light, as he reached over to grab the still ringing phone, he realized she was already gone. The sun shone through the window, and he saw the digital read-out of 8:57. Half-asleep, he talked with an old friend from high school who was now in a moderately successful independent band. He had heard about Aum's skills though intersecting circles of friends and wanted Aum to do the artwork for the band's new album. The friend was willing and able to pay him quite well, so Aum agreed.

The week went by fast as he was constantly meeting with band members, evolving the cover concept, doing photo shoots, painting, and drawing. He was caught up in the band's success and motion. Nevertheless his mind lingered on Jenn's absence. Her week-long trip was proving to be more difficult for him than he had first guessed. He realized too many things were left raw between them, and this just added to the undercurrent of pain that grew beneath the surface of their brittle shell of love. Aum had tried calling Sandra a few times, but she wasn't answering her phone. He wanted to see if she had talked with Jenn before she left, and if there was an opening, maybe get her advice on a many number of things, including his solo performance for the mysterious Zhe.

He was walking home from the final band meeting, and his mind wandered fully back into the Riddle. *I wonder who this Zhe is? I'll have to look him up on the Boards when I get home; see if I can dig up some leads*. The band work had kept his mind occupied, but now, especially without Jenn nearby, there was ample space to ponder what had transpired in his alternate world. He sighed and cut across a grassy patch, kicking an old weathered tennis ball hiding in the leaves. Aum looked up at the deep blue cloudless sky moving to dusk and remembered his feeling of excitement at sharing the dance floor with Cat. His heart began to race. He sought out every single reason why she, of all people, didn't get back to him. He muttered to himself, "Cat, where are you? Was that night just a dream?"

He continued walking and reached a main road, letting his eyes wander, observing the architecture. He was in an old neighborhood that had just completed one of those inner-city overhauls. The insides of old brick character buildings had been gutted and modernized with hardwood floors, coats of fresh paint, and trendy new furniture. But there were still the same shady neighborhood inhabitants that had lived there the past twenty years, so the draw to the area was still small.

Aum turned the corner and saw a man halfway down a side street in front of a pizza shop strumming an electric guitar, banging on a snare drum with one foot pedal, and banging on a bass drum with another foot pedal. The snare drum had a picture of cat eyes and a diamond shape in the center. With the microphone cord running along with the guitar cord into a multitude of effects pedals, both signals finally reached inside the small amp he was sitting on as the busker sang his heart out. To power everything, he had hijacked an electricity line from a nearby telephone pole. In front of him was the typical guitar case with a few quarters and nickels. Different people flew in and out of the only pizza shop in the neighborhood, stopping only for the briefest moment to listen to or request a song.

"Do you know any Sonic Youth?" a young man asked with his trendy frosted fohawk.

The busker nodded and smiled, "Uh, yeah. I'm up for a challenge." He began softly and slowly, building up layers of guitar noise and scratchy vocals. Aum couldn't believe the sound he was able to get out of such a small amplifier. He continued to strum emotionally on his guitar, rocking back and forth, almost oblivious to the gathering late-evening dinner crowd. Gaining too much momentum, the song spiraled out of control. Squawks and buzzes, captured birds and jungle creatures, tried desperately to escape the tiny amp box. The song concluded with the man toppling his amp and mic stand in an attempt to stomp all the pedals off. Even though it came to a grinding halt, everyone around applauded in support as they chomped down their greasy pizza.

"That was fucking awesome dude!" said the man with the fohawk emphatically.

"Thanks," the busker replied, out of breath.

"Have a good one," and the fohawk walked off, still eating.

'What the hell?!" Aum thought. "He's not going to give him anything? Not even a quarter?!"

It didn't faze the busker, though. He gathered himself and started to play something more upbeat. An old and filthy weather-beaten man stumbled over before the busker could get into full performance mode.

"Hey…hey…can I sing a song?" he asked in a polite yet slurred voice.

The busker smiled big, his messy hair reflecting the setting sunlight. "Sure man, what do you want to sing?" as he kept on lightly strumming his guitar.

In an even more slurred voice, he replied, "I want to sing about how I lost my job, and how my wife left me, and how I slept on the street last night."

Without breaking a stride, the busker said, "Well let's get you set up then." He put down his guitar and adjusted the mic stand so that it was the correct height. He grabbed his guitar again, and with complete sincerity in his voice, he offered it to him. "Want to play guitar?" The man shuffled his feet, almost losing his balance in front of the mic stand. Testing the mic out, he said, "Yeah sure." He quickly backed away. "Whoa, is that what I really sound like?" As the busker strapped the guitar to the homeless hero, he nodded for him to begin.

Aum had his homemade didgeridoo wrapped and strapped to his back. He thought about joining in on the music making action, but there was no obvious opening, so he continued to observe the bizarre scene with patience.

The homeless man's eyes glazed over for a second, "Wait, I don't even know how to play guitar."

"Well…I could play along with you If you like," said the busker.

"Yeah yeah."

He gave the guitar back; the busker strapped it on, and he looked at the derelict man, waiting for him to start singing. The man on the mic looked perplexed, "I don't know…I don't know what to sing, you start, you start."

The busker played some simple chords and the man eventually worked up the courage to sing, "Oh my wife just left me and I slept under a tree by the river last last last, oh last night…"

Everyone groaned and left the scene because his rhythm was bad and he was way off key. The busker was loving it, though. Words flowed out of the homeless man, "Down the yellow brick road is the final destination, when your heart is broken and you're waiting at a station. You can stir in the sugar, 'cause the hot buns are bakin'. Don't purr in my ear, unless it's the perfect pizza you makin', baby."

The busker joined in and they must have repeated the line ten times, "Don't purr in my ear, unless it's the perfect pizza you makin', baby." Somehow the busker was managing to create a melody and rhythm that built on the strange music coming out of the homeless man. Aum was enthralled by the busker's patience, character, and infinite heart, but after the twentieth line of the same lyrics, Aum went inside and got a slice of pizza.

The two of them had packed up when Aum finally exited the shop, so he continued his meandering journey back to his house with pizza in hand. He walked past a bakery, the smell of fresh goods stimulating his nostrils. He went another block and saw a covered bus shelter with an older woman crumpled up inside, waiting. She looked downtrodden, even heartbroken.

Too weird, Aum though as he remembered the surreal lyrics he had just heard. The smell of the bakery still wafted in the air as Aum looked down at his slice of pizza midchew. His eyes moved to the bus stop and then far down the street where there was a road that hadn't received the city upgrade treatment. As the evening darkened, the streetlights flickered on, causing the old stone road before him to take on a yellow sheen.

"Final destination?" He asked aloud. And then he almost spat out his really tasty slice of pizza. He thought of the cat eyes on the snare drum and the purr reference, "No way! There's no way! But I'll never know if I don't check it out, right? Right?" He looked around. The street was deserted. He vaguely heard the sound of the bus somewhere and noticed the woman was gone. He didn't remember seeing a bus.

He took a breath and stepped forward. A jolt of lighting hit his stomach, and a frightened but curious butterfly flew up into his throat. He knew he had just stepped into something very complex, and now, fully engrossed, he felt as though finding his way out would not be as easy. "I guess this is the lead I was looking for," he said as he unstrapped his instrument, which doubled as a walking stick. He followed the yellow cobblestones to the doorway of an old warehouse. Many vehicles were parked outside. He entered and could see nothing as his eyes adjusted.

"Twenty dollars, please," someone whispered to his lower left.

Aum cursed silently under his breath. He pulled out his wallet and extended his last twenty dollars. The money was quickly snatched out of his hand, which was stamped at the same time.

The space inside was open and wide—the size of a gymnasium with a ceiling just as high. It was very quiet, and the lights were dim. There was a very distinct smell in the air. Dirt. Mulch. Pine needles.

Nature.

Aum's eyes begun to adjust to the darkness as he walked forward—a silent shadow. He began to make out forms in the complete darkness and was aware of a dense crowd of people he could not yet see encircling a lit area in the center of the building. He walked towards the light. Bleachers of spectators towered to the left and right of a well lit floor area; what looked like a large spotlight.

There was another smell in the air. In high contrast to the smell of nature was the smell of booze. There were some stragglers running and stumbling in the dark toward the lit stage area, plastic cups of beer in their hands half-full, the other half on the floor somewhere. Aum looked around as he approached the center and noticed the spectators were much older than he had expected. They were dressed in very formal attire; high-class evening wear. This must be an event for the fat cats and oil barons of the city, he thought. Some extra spectators who weren't in the bleachers crowded around the lighted area, pushing in four rows deep, craning their necks wherever they were standing so they could see.

His eyes continued to adjust and Aum could see there were eight main pillars holding up the warehouse roof, and the middle four held scaffolding and a platform between them, halfway up to the ceiling. This platform held the contents of what was usually referred to as backstage. In this theatre, backstage was a tech-fort that floated above the bare concrete floor—a blank palette of the mind. In the fort up above, Aum could see from the gleam of monitor screens a handful of black clothed A/V techs manning soundboards and controlling lighting effects. Bright white lights shone from the bottom of the fort onto the gray concrete stage, where small insect-sized mics hung discreetly, just above head height.

Because everyone was fully concentrated on the stage, Aum went unnoticed amongst the three-piece suits and ugly eighties prom dresses. He moved to the front corner of one of the bleachers where the view was clear. He knelt down to his haunches and leaned on his didgeridoo like a staff. His gifted Riddler hood was pulled over his head, covering his face, and his scarf hung down in front of him. Once again, just like at the community center, he stuck out like a sore thumb, wearing his paint-encrusted green cargo shorts, indoor soccer shoes, and black tank top that exposed his lean yoga shoulders.

The performance had started mere moments ago. Anticipation, like the musky smell, still hung heavily in the air. Aum could hear very subtle Eno-esque ambient atmospheres floating out from the speakers somewhere—a sound that he couldn't hear when he entered. This sound seemed to be the only thing holding the audience's attention.

On the square stage, there were eight piles of material: dirt, mulch, dried flowers and leaves, black beans, grains of wild and black rice, green lentils, yellow lentils, and a pile of small round stones. The piles of material were laid out as an X on the stage. At the four tips of the X shape stood a man standing with a djembe drum strapped around his shoulders, braced against his body. There were only three men on the stage, and in the position closest to Aum, there was a drum sitting on the floor with no drummer in sight.

The audience began to stir. There was movement in the very center of the X; a woman was curled in a ball at the center. Aum hadn't even noticed her. She was dressed in the same color as the material she was lying on and slowly she began to rise, turning in his direction. She had long, brown, knotted and dreadlocked hair; a brown patchwork of hand-sewn garments; and an abundance of necklaces bearing amulets and talismans.

She raised her head to look at him.

Her appearance made her seem like a completely different person, but there was no mistaking her. Aum was statue-still as Cat's penetrating eyes bore into him.

Chapter Four

"He loves you a lot. He just wants to share his passions with you."

It was a successful day, and to celebrate, Jenn and Sandra were having a drink at a five-star restaurant. It was a few nights into their business trip, and Jenn had really appreciated having Sandra with her—up until now.

Over the years, Sandra had been a big help to her at the office, and now, as a portable assistant, organizing cab rides and equipment, booking hotels, and reserving tables at quality restaurants. Sandra made it easy for Jenn to focus on her boardroom presentations and contract negotiations.

Sandra prodded Jenn again, in the austere candle-lit silence, "Well, can't you see that?"

"Yah, I know. It's just so hard when that passion leaves you a starving and dirty hippie."

"So then it's really about the money?"

"No. Well, yes. Sort of. I think it's more about stability. I guess it's the steady income that provides me with that stability—something Aum doesn't need at all. I don't even think he likes stability," she said. "He lives on a very sharp edge and he frequently gets cut. I swear he could live off of bread and water and think nothing of it. It would be normal." She looked out the window at the neighboring brick building, it's heritage bathed in the orange glow of the nearby streetlight. "I can't be there with him like that, Sandra. It's just too much."

"I've seen your ideals transform considerably since you started at your parents' company, Jenn. It' s put a lot of pressure on your relationship, and I know for sure it's been really hard on him."

"Yeah," Jenn looked back at her friend from the window.

Sandra lowered her drink and continued: "I feel like I'm watching two polar opposites moving as far away from each other as possible, but still connected for some reason. If you buy a sleek little car, he spends a few days out in the wilderness with no provisions, trying to fend for himself. You go out with co-workers for drinks and casual business discussions, and he spends time with his Riddle community. And from what I hear, they're as far out as you can get."

"But his Riddle community isn't doing anything! I'm making business deals worth hundreds of thousands of dollars and trying to understand corporate structure. He's just wasting his time. If only he applied his skills to something real, based his art on something tangible, more concrete, you know? Something that could ground him in a long-term reality."

"Yeah, but like you said, Aum likes to live on the edge. And that will never change until he decides it will."

A waiter came by and refilled their glasses of wine.

Sandra's eyes glinted with the street light. "He does have a show up right now. I know we weren't able to make it for the opening, but maybe we could take an afternoon to go check it out—it is up for a month, and it may be the closest thing he does to something tangible." She looked at Jenn, searching her eyes. "It's quite an accomplishment in the world he's living in."

"Yeah, it is." She picked up her glass and was about to take a sip. "But to live your entire life in that world? The life of the starving artist, of the spiritual renunciant in Western culture—that life's not tangible at all."

"Yeah, but maybe it won't be for his entire life. He allowed you the space to change your path, your ideals, so maybe you should show him the same courtesy. Don't you think if you just took a single step closer to him, he would take a step closer to you?"

"What do you mean?"

"Allow a little bit of uncertainty into your life, Jenn."

Jenn frowned at Sandra.

Sandra continued, "I don't know, I just think you guys have pushed each other as far away as possible, and to take a single step closer to each other would make you both a lot happier."

Jenn looked up at her, and for the first time saw the wrinkles of age in her friend's face. "Yeah, you're probably right."

***

Aum's heart raced as he and Cat shared a soul-to-soul connection in a single glance, an entire conversation happening in an instant. Her wide, liquid eyes offered joy, release, shame, apology, hope, and confirmation all at once, emotions made more palpable by her welling tears. Cat broke the gaze and looked at the unmanned drum, then back to Aum. Aum looked at the other drummers who were also staring at him, as if he was late…maybe they had been expecting him? The drummers looked familiar. Not because he had seen them before, but because they were "like" him. Between the four of them there was an air of unspoken recognition in their shared gaze of awareness, their presence, and their connectivity, even reflected physically in their clothing. Their attire paralleled his own unique style: street clothes with an added twist. One man had a green Mohawk, wore warrior face paint, and was shirtless. Another had an animal skin hat on and a long vest that went down to the floor, and the last had a brown fedora, long black hair underneath, bare feet, and jeans. For once, Aum fit right in.

He looked back at Cat. She was waiting. He felt the weight of his role in the performance, its outcome now his to decide. Aum swooped into position in an agile motion and without hesitation. As he did this, he drew the audience's attention away from Cat, so in response, he hit the center of his drum, emitting a loud bass note as he set his didgeridoo down beside the drum.

The performance began.

Cat raised herself to her full height.

Aum played a steady single heartbeat as she took full advantage of the anticipating audience:

"In this very special period of time, we must not forget the essence, the very core of human nature; an embodiment of developmental process; a breaking away from our Earth Mother. As unruly teenagers, we must learn to respect and cherish what she has given us."

The man with the green Mohawk leapt at the pause in narration and began a fast-paced but light patting on the edge of his drum. With the shift in focus, Cat began to run and dance in between the piles of nature. His drum hits became louder, more pronounced. The other two drummers filled the air with accents and pulsing rhythms, and Aum pushed the pace of the heartbeat up. Cat moved to the center once again and spun, spiraling her hands up from her body into the air, reaching for the sky. The drumming came to a peak as all musicians connected and came together. Aum dropped an extra loud heartbeat, and Cat dropped to the floor and began working magic with her hands, molding the material into a pattern.

Aum began to add in more complicated drum rhythms to the steady heartbeat. He held everyone together on the ground floor with the bass hits, but slowly began to ease off as he intuitively became aware of the unified focus shared between the performers and the audience. There was enough cohesive creative energy on the stage that the first foundational level was totally unnecessary in the performance space, and the hearts and imaginations of its occupants began to take off in full upliftment. Aum glanced quickly, smiling, at Cat as she worked, her long hair swaying to reveal an aged Inuit face—for but only a moment.

Close to the ground, her hands connected and worked with each material; the mulch of aged trees, dried flowers and leaves, and the spiritual aspect of Mother Earth that each represented. Her trance opened her up as an electrified conduit for the manifestation of a heightened awareness; a channeled thoughtlessness that impacted the audience on deep subconscious levels.

Cat moved from one pile to the next, taking single steps that seemed to stretch completely across the stage. Aum snuck another peak at her as he increased the heartbeat's pace. He saw bird feathers flying and the fur of great cats ripple as large muscles flexed under her skin.

With this bending of reality, the audience began to dip into confusion; they became malleable and loose like water. Aum could feel the breathing of the other three drummers; he could hear their strain as the connected entrainment of their fast patterned pace began to fall apart.

Holy shit! Aum thought as he drum rolled from the burgeoning complexity back to the simple, steady heartbeat. This time he pounded even louder than before, bringing back empathic focus and direction. He maintained the heartbeat with one hand and picked up his didgeridoo with the other.

As he began to play, putting his knowledge of breath work into the performance, the entire stage changed. The drumming maintained its intensity, but its tempo opened up. Like the unsuspecting target of a snake charmer, members of the audience began swaying very slowly to the hypnotic downbeat and the complex interior sound waves. The musical exploration began triggering specific synapses in brains and the waves hit nerve endings in physical bodies. Eyes watched Cat stretch her arms across the stage, moving piles of material around. The audience at the top of the bleachers could see a triangle come into formation. It was composed of dirt, stones, mulch, dried flowers, and leaves. The brown triangle's apex pointed down and south, representing the feminine Earth.

One of the drummers stopped and began clapping out flamenco type rhythms, and in response, Cat's dancing changed while she shaped the other piles of materials. Now she bounced up and down, bending at the waist, head shaking back and forth to the rhythm.

To Aum, her frame remained birdlike, a creature creating a nest for herself.

From the center of the first triangle, she formed a second triangle pointed in the opposite direction, intersecting the other. This shape represented the masculine sun and was created with seeds and beans, lentils and rice. The two triangles combined as a single symbol: a two-dimensional six-pointed star-tetrahedron.

What did I get myself into? Aum thought as he looked up.

The shape brought together the two hemispheres of the brain, as well as masculine and feminine nature. Cat brought the last four lateral quadrants of the X together, connecting them with a much larger universal nature using sheer intention; her quick flowing hands, and above all, her loving wisdom.

She stood in the center breathing very hard. She had stopped moving altogether. She was standing in the middle, staring right at Aum. *Am I supposed to do something here?* he thought frantically as he felt the immense pressure to improvise. Aum continued to didge but discontinued the heartbeat. At this, the bottom almost fell out of the performance; as they fell through the initial foundation they began with, falling into the dark basement of unconsciousness, devoid of heartbeat, into the realms of near death and wounded healers. The veracity of edge they had reached in the journey was beyond where some audience members were willing to go. They awoke from the rhythmic trance to discover their own incapacity to understand what they were seeing and, more importantly, its direct connection to what they were feeling. These ones left their seats to get more booze.

Cat stood there and jerked her arms out in a yoga-like pose and Aum did a double take as he saw black spots, grains of darkness floating in the space around her. *This is crazy! She's crazy!* he thought. It looked as though the black spots were being drawn out of the audience, slowly gravitating toward her. Not a cancer of the body, but an etheric cancer of the spirit. One large, black liquid blob floated down and attached itself to Cat's left knee. Her leg gave out, and she collapsed to the floor.

There was a loud gasp from the audience as the drumming stopped completely.

All that held the performance back from complete derailment was Aum's impromptu didgeridoo solo; it was an entire traveling circus balanced on top of a puttering clown car. Swiftly, another drummer returned the heartbeat to the room while the sweat on Aum's forehead dripped onto the stage floor.

The space ached and was slowgoing for everyone.

Slow like molasses.

The two other drummers began to support the single heartbeat with quiet taps and pops on their drum skins—rain droplets soaring through the clouds toward the Earth far below.

Aum felt like his stomach was being pulled into his feet as he stood from the drum he was sitting on. He wavered a little as the audience stared hard at him and murmured in confused anticipation.

The stage became an operating room.

Aum snuck over to Cat, moving inside the form of the ambient sound waves coming from his didgeridoo breath work—waves that were physically invisible to most of the audience members. While playing, he circled Cat, looking at the dark black blobs floating around her body. Time stopped, and as he peered at them, the spots moved with independent intelligence. Suddenly he understood what he needed to do and how to do it.

He continued to circle her body and began collecting the black spots in a single area by looking at them and playing to them. He could hear the drumming heartbeat slowly turn into Cat's heartbeat: the mohawked drummer held the space together as Aum worked. He needed full concentration to focus on the large black spot on Cat's knee, as well as to keep the black conglomerate together. He chirped at it through his didge, and it was as if the large black spot finally figured out what was going on. It came to its own self-realization and moved cooperatively into the group with the others. As it connected to the rest of the group, so too did it become fully conscious. The black mass floated in the air, waiting for Aum to begin the operation.

Like a well-trained masseur, Aum took his biggest breaths yet and gently blew sound waves onto the mass. The liquid blackness began to disintegrate, but rather than vanish, it began to compact, hardening into a small black pebble. Aum continued with equanimous concentration and effort on this transformation. The pebble smiled at him and began changing color, going through the entire rainbow until it became crystal clear. An amazing lightness overcame the entire space as a newfound joy was emitted from the audience. They cheered, in spirit or physically Aum didn't know, as the crystal grew to the size of a thumbnail. The newborn crystal moved itself, with the help of Aum's breath, to rest upon the concrete floor.

Before Aum knew what was happening, Cat was up, speaking to the audience with an empowered and confident voice.

"Let us now give thanks as we fully appreciate the new, lighter version of ourselves, and release and let go of all that we have experienced here tonight, touching both the Earth Mother and Sun Father, exhale the breath of evolving life and breath in peace, every…single…day."

She looked at her musicians, smiled, and said, "Alright guys, let's do it. Up and out!"

She turned to Aum, touched him on the shoulder, and smiled, "Thank you." Then she went back down to the ground, more focused than ever, as the drummers kicked back into a funky rhythm with a "One, two, three, four!" Smiles broke out onstage and in the audience. Aum, thoroughly exhausted, strode back to his drum, clip clopping along like a large elk in the woods. He joined in the celebration, giving what he was able to.

Cat started her work in the center where the crystal had been placed, and collected the plethora of materials within regular arm's reach. She spiraled out larger and larger, moving away from the center, until all material on the stage was combined into a multicolored mix. She stood at the entrance of the spiral and smiled and bowed. The green mohawked man counted the musicians out: "Four, three, two!" Boom. The stage lights went dim.

The audience's vocal eruption quickly transformed into merely a light polite applause, most of them not knowing exactly what to think of what just happened. The performers were all without a spare breath, exhausted and worn. A woman with long blonde hair, a long sequined dress, and a microphone headset walked on stage. A spotlight followed her.

"Let's all give a cheer for Catherine and her performance troupe. Lovely. Just lovely." The hostess gave a bubbly giggle and the polite applause got a little louder. "The silent auction will begin in fifteen minutes, so please take a look around and find something you would like to bid on. We have many different works created by famous painters and sculptors from across the country, all a fabulous investment." The house lights turned up, and spotlights pointed at work hanging on the walls and half a dozen ten-foot sculpture pieces placed throughout the large space.

She continued, "The fashion show begins at eleven, with many more spectacular performances to follow, so make sure you stick around."

There was a final cheer, and the audience filtered out of their seats and went straight for the small portable bars set up in the corners. Some generic house music faded up in the background, and Aum sat patiently, tiredly, on his drum. Cat went over to each drummer and thanked them. Lastly, she bounced over to Aum with a big smile on her face.

"You did awesome!" She looked bashful for a second. "Sorry for dropping the ball there, Jerome. Things just got a little larger than life for me, and I couldn't think of how to proceed. We wouldn't have recovered…I wouldn't have recovered, without your leadership."

"Thanks. I didn't really know what to do either; everything turned out good though, right? Did you keep that crystal? What happened to your blonde hair? And uh, Catherine, my friends call me Aum…just so you know." Now it was his turn to be bashful.

With a tilt of her head she replied, "Aum, Aum, Aum…that's hot. The blonde hair was a wig," she continued. "And the crystal's right here."

As she pulled it out, things got weird, lights fluctuated, music skipped, and the people in the near vicinity jerked their heads to stare at them. She put it back into her pocket.

"Cool." She said, smiling playfully. After the stares subsided, she looked up into his eyes: "So how did your performance go, Aum? I'm very sorry I didn't make it."

Aum's face fell, "That's okay; it was a real bust." He shook his head in amazement. "It was nothing like this, that's for sure. I was hoping to get somewhere close, but…I fell short." She gave him a look of concern as he continued, "Well, that's not true. I guess something happened, though I'm still not exactly sure what." Gazing upon her many necklaces, her dreads, her bright smile, he stumbled on his words, "A raw…solo, for this one guy…" Lips buzzing, he was trying to make up for his lack of eloquence by using his hands, gesturing wildly, "but I…but this…this…was really crazy! Was it, like…real? What we just did here?" His eyes were wide as he completely forgot about trying to describe his own performance.

Cat laughed and answered, "Healing? Magic? Teaching? I don't know what to call it. It was an improvisation; improvised time and metaspace construction, pushing the boundaries of art and reality."

Her expression was full of appreciation. "It was momentary freedom for all involved, momentary freedom for a section of people who are the least likely to seek it out for themselves. I just hope we touched them deeply enough, affected them enough, that they'll make an effort to seek it out for themselves, in whatever way makes them the happiest." She smiled at him. "Did you enjoy it?"

He laughed hard.

"Uh, yeah! I think so. But it was crazy! Disguised ceremonial healings in public, especially in this setting, is a pretty powerful concept, Cat. I don't even know how much of what I was seeing was what the audience was seeing, ya know?"

A wealthy couple well into their seventies walked by, their elitism echoing from each step. Aum laughed. "I mean at the community center, all the kids there are expecting this kind of thing, but these people? It boggles my mind that they allow you to do this, and that this is what you choose to do!"

"This is what has to happen for the underground to move above ground, really take flight. This is where the most work needs to be done, and where it needs to be done the fastest, with the elders that aren't that eld." Cat's glance shifted. "Can I get you something to drink? You're probably thirsty after all that didgeridooin'."

"Sure, Cat, as long as it's not tea from your thermos."

She burst out with a single surprised laugh. "Oh boy, Aum," she cringed. "Do I have a story for you."

They walked over to one of the volunteers, grabbing some water, when a woman behind them cleared her throat. They both turned around.

"That was very touching, Catherine. I could actually feel something inside of me get lighter after your performance." The woman smiled and shook her head in astonishment. "Very amazing work." Cat stood, as receptive to her as a saint, and the stranger went in and hugged her and then pulled out a business card. "Give me a call if you need a photographer for your next performance."

"Thanks, I will…" Cat looked down at the card as the woman walked away. "…Vicki Stratsen." Then to Aum, "Do you know her?'

"No. Do you?"

"No."

"Do you think she's a part of the Riddle?" Aum asked

"I don't think so, but it's hard to say these days."

"You're probably right. Working at the very edge of the Riddle, between it and ordinary reality, must make things more challenging for you, hey?" He took a sip of water. She didn't respond, but started walking. He followed.

"What's your story?" Aum asked, as they passed a painted still life of oranges.

"Oh yeah, I forgot…Are you ready for it? I might knock your socks off."

"No worries; they already got knocked off by you spiral out, remember?"

"Right," she said with a smile. They continued walking. "So I wanted to tell you about the rest of my evening when we were dancing together. I didn't actually teleport out of there, just in case you were wondering. I got pulled away by a couple of Dennis's macho friends."

Aum frowned. "He didn't like what we were doing too much, hey?"

"Not one bit, but I'll get to that. So I got thrown backstage into the prepping room and had the door locked on me. I was really scared, until I realized there was someone else in there with me."

A worried look flashed over Aum's face.

"It's all good. I don't think the boys knew she was in there in the first place."

"She?" Aum asked in surprise.

"Yeah, it was crazy. She sort of appeared out of a corner in the room, and the moment we connected eyes, we both laughed. She was like a really cool sister or something. She had some funky digs on, man! Wow! I mean, she was way too cool for that party."

"Really?"

"Yeah, she said something like, 'I'm sorry lovely lady, but I have to make this quick. You're going to be hit hard and fast, but everything will be for the best. I hope to see you soon and then we can talk more. My heart is with you.' And then she paused and gave me this tremendous smile. Aum, it was like the entire room lit up. Then she just walked out the door, and it wasn't even locked anymore. The whole interaction couldn't have been more than a moment, but it sure was intense. Like pure sunlight."

"Really? Do you know who she was?"

"No. But it gets weirder. The moment she walked out the door, this other guy walked in. I've known him for awhile; he's a pretty good friend of mine within that community. His name is Toumai."

"Oh yeah, I met Toumai."

"Hmm, really. You'll have to share more with me after. So, Toumai crashes in the door and is like, 'Your man just pulled some crazy shit, Cat! I think he's totally lost it this time!' I just stared at him, and he was like, 'Are you listening to me?!' I yelled at him in response, which is really bizarre, 'cause we're really good friends, and we've never really yelled at each other before."

"What did he say after you yelled at him?" Aum asked.

"He apologized then said, 'There's some major motions peaking tonight, so I'm a bit of a head case.' And then he went on to talk about all of these things that were supposed to be lining up; things within the Riddle to as far out as astrological alignments. I can't remember most of it, but I ended up interrupting him saying, 'Are you going to give me some more detail about Dennis's growing insanity? Or are you going continue your over-analytical play-by-play?' That didn't make him too happy. He responded with something like 'Your behavior is on thin ice too," And then something like, "As far as Dennis goes, if I couldn't convince you of what would happen months ago, I don't think I'll be able to now, no matter what I say. He'll prove it to you himself by the end of the night. I'm sure of it.' To tell you the truth, Aum, his self-assuredness was pissing me off so I blocked out everything he had to say. I even insulted him more because of my unwillingness to listen to the truth. I said, 'I think you need to go sit at your cartography screens and cook your brain for a few more hours.'"

"Oh man, Cat," Aum said

"Yeah, that sure didn't make the night go any more smoothly; that's for sure. 'Fuck, I need a cigarette' is how he responded as he stormed out, saying something about going to visit his family and ditching all of us egotistical scenesters for a while."

"Really?" Aum became a little more curious, since on the Boards, Toumai told him that Cat was away with family.

"So moments after Toumai left, Dennis bursts in the door."

"Uh-oh."

"Yeah. He was in the most intense rage I've ever seen him in, pacing around the room and shouting at me: 'You need to control what your fucking doing out there! You can't be giving your megaelixirs to fucking superheroes that want to push out as far as they can!'

So I said, 'Why not?! I'm just being myself, doing what I know. Is that not allowed? I'm trying to support the growth of this community!' And then he said something like, 'You're supporting complete strangers more than me! Where the fuck will that leave us? Back in the floating dust; that's where. And all these people, the people we've grown with, will leave us for this cowboy who we know nothing about.' Trying to be calm, I responsed, 'Can't you just trust this process, Dennis? At one point, all your friends gave you the benefit of the doubt, and it's okay to call them your friends, you know. You're doing good work. Just relax, okay?'"

"Did he?" Aum asked.

Cat shook her head, "No. His exact words were, 'Relax?! Do you know what I'm trying to hold on to here?! This is too big, Cat! It's too big to allow even the smallest mistake!' And then it all hit me."

Aum looked at her expectantly, "What hit you?"

"He doesn't get it. The only thing Dennis cares about is that he maintains control of the power and growth of this community. Whether or not actual individuals in the community are supported doesn't matter to him. Then I felt an even deeper blow: I was the linchpin. It was all supported by me, the entire thing. I knew everyone at that event and continually check in with all of them, and he does whatever he feels, whatever he wants. I can no longer support him, or his beliefs, or actions."

Cat was getting choked up as she spoke. She fought back tears.

"And then I felt the final hit the hardest."

"What? Who?"

She moved closer to him. His heart began to race.

"You. What you showed to me that night, and to everyone else on that dance floor, Aum, was a sensitivity no one had ever known existed before. I felt that entire floor held in our arms, flying."

In the warehouse, the same blonde got on the mic and introduced the auctioneer. His loud, awkward, boisterous sales pitch was hard to ignore. This was his first time selling art; everyone could tell.

Aum and Cat moved away from the blaring sounds of the auction and closer together. Cat tried to shout up into Aum's ear.

"Rather than man and woman leading as two opposites, stretching bodies and minds and hearts and souls out in all ways possible, I understood a new kind of leadership that was unified as man and woman through the heart. I realized, sitting in that room, trying to calm this man down, that Toumai had been telling me everything I didn't want to hear about our issues, and I didn't want to listen."

Aum nodded.

"I was pissed off at our immaturity, and pissed off at myself. 'Change is coming whether you like it or not, Dennis,' I told him, and I walked off. I haven't talked to him since."

"What?! Really? Wow! Are you still okay with that choice? To walk away?" The auctioneer was getting quieter.

"It's been quite a drastic change for me, since we've been together for almost two Riddle years…but there's this freshness I feel in my life now, like having opened a window to get some air after being cooped up all winter." She sighed, "How about you? Have you ever had any big relationships within the Riddle?"

"No, not within the Riddle," Aum replied. "Do you really think there's a difference?"

"Well, yeah. You need more patience and trust than you would think is possible. There's nothing more passionate than people choosing to be together fully with their hearts and souls on an exciting road, choosing such a raw way to live, with so many possibilities and opportunities. Having a partner to be there for support and strategy, to push your buttons and force you to grow out of stagnant states of mind. It's so exhilarating and so painful and the very furthest thing away from cohabitation."

"Hmmm," Aum exhaled. He thought of Jenn, pondering what she was doing right in that moment. "Don't you think it's possible to have both? I mean, have the freshness of a new life path and maintain a relationship with someone not walking the same path as you?"

"No. I don't think so. It's easy to desire to bring someone with you where you want to go, but you end up having your heart broken when you realize they aren't willing to go with you. What you see changes you. What you see experience you."

In Aum's mind, there were pictures of Jenn working in her downtown office, climbing the corporate ladder. He mumbled, nodding, "Relating to each other as the people you once were," and saw flashes of her drawing with him in their kitchen, images of candles and intimate meditation, even the smell of incense in his nostrils from years before. "But there's still hope within my heart."

Cat looked confused. "What do you mean, Aum?" She touched his arm and moved in closer, her unconscious intensions given away to both of them.

"Oh, nothing. So you and Dennis split for good?" He backed away a subtle yet not so subtle microstep. He gave her a forced smile. In sadness, Cat realized how vulnerable a state she was really in, after her big breakup. She pulled out her new crystal and held it to her heart.

"Yes. I'm off on a brand new adventure. With new skin and wings and everything. Thank you for this."

They stood in silence, bathing in a moment of reflection. A short redhead girl in a suit jacket walked up to them. "Excuse me, Catherine, my name is Jessica Bell. I'm with *The City Times*. Do have a spare moment for an interview?"

Cat looked at Aum and smiled. "Is this what you were talking about? The edge between the ordinary and the Riddle?"

"Yeah, I guess it is."

"Can I catch up with you later, Aum? I would still love to hear about your evening."

"Of course, Catherine," he replied with a smile, genuine and heartwarming as Jessica and Cat walked off towards the main entrance.

Aum downed the rest of his water. Hearing the auctioneer trying to hock more mediocre artwork, he sighed. Before long, the mohawked man appeared next to him. "So what do you think of this here auction here?"

"Well, the art is alright, but to be honest, I don't know about a conté sketch on manila going for five grand. I mean it probably took the artist less than a minute."

"But hot damn, wouldn't it be great to be worth five grand a minute?"

"Shit yeah!" Aum looked at the guy, and they both laughed.

"The other two guys are back at the spiral chomping at the bit. Are you interested in doing some more jamming? Nothing serious; we're just pretty pumped about the performance and wanted to keep on playing. You know how it is."

"Sure, I'll join you guys."

They began walking toward the spiral.

"My name's Greg."

"Aum."

Greg paused, waiting for more. But that was it. Then he got it.

"Cool, I'll keep my ears open for you."

"Uh, thanks."

They walked back to the middle of the warehouse. The stage lights were dim but still inviting; the aromas of nature still hung in the air. The four instruments were set next each other, and one of the drummers, the man with the fedora, pulled out a few beers as Aum and Greg approached.

"On me, boys. Well done." He passed them around the group. Aum inspected the beer for a second, shrugged his shoulders, and took a swig.

"Quite the social groove at this outrageous affair, hey?"

"Not quite what I expected when I saw the flyer, that's for sure," said the man in the floor-length vest, his dark skin still shiny with sweat.

"You guys ready for some more?" Greg asked.

"Yeah, maybe."

"Sure, that sounds like it could be alright."

Observing the huge space, Aum hesitated as well. He looked around for Cat, spotting her near the doors, still talking with the reporter. She flashed him a smile that sparked through the air, a lightning strike that reached him on the other side of the warehouse. "Yeah, let's do it, gents," he said.

He sat down on a drum and began plucking intricate rhythms on the skin; the others joined, all four unaware that the auction had picked up again. A whining voice began pleading for the oil execs to by some art.

"Remember, this all goes to charity." The amplified voice kept on repeating. Those who were tired of this strained effort—and there were many—moved toward the new entertainment. Some people meandered over unconsciously, and others raced over as if dying of boredom.

Without the official audience/performer distinction this time, the drummers were relaxed and informal. The audience was very courageous and very drunk, encouraging the musicians as if they were the local sports team. Some hip old ladies began dancing about, trying to loosen up their tight suited husbands, while some older men, with a few too many under their loose belt buckles, were really strutting their cowboy two-step on the makeshift dance floor. The wives of these rambunctious old-timers cowered their heads in embarrassment, trying to run away from the spectacle. Unfortunately, their inebriated husbands prowled after, in beat and step with the music, a half-crazed look in their eyes.

Now with a little less than a dozen bodies on the dance floor, in the heat of a groove, a young man approached the drumming group. He told them he was a DJ and that his set had been completely skipped and forgotten—a complete travesty. He asked the drummers if he could play along. Fedora and Vest looked confused over trying to communicate in a form other than percussion. Aum and Greg on either side of the middle two responded with nods. The DJ grabbed his record crate and tied it to a rope. He climbed up a ladder on the far side of a pillar and hoisted his crate up to the sound booth. Soon after, he slowly faded in a fat track of Detroit house. The dozen on the dance floor quickly doubled, then tripled. With the added energy and a thumping tempo backbone, the drummers had the freedom to play around and in-between the stable electronic beats, and even though Aum's hands were beginning to swell and blister, his heart soared with joy inside this supremely expressive moment.

Splitting the sea of dancers, Cat appeared with a smile on her face, shaking her head in disbelief. All heads turned, the drumming died off, the dancing stopped, and the DJ faded out to the background. The participants acknowledged Cat with heartfelt cheering and clapping. Cat, though she looked a little unsure as to why she was receiving this unexpected gift, brought her hands together in gratitude and bowed.

Aum desperately wanted to be by her side, to support her now in her success just as he had earlier, in her struggle. He felt, however, obligated to man his musical post, to continue to perform for the enthusiastic audience.

In the silent wake of the applause, a young energetic man bounded up to Aum. "Hey dude, that's a great lookin' drum ya got there! I been playin' a few years myself, you know, nothing as big as this but, but I've got a group that I jam with once a week. Are you gonna rip it up again? Or have you had about your fill, what with the performance earlier on, I mean—which was great by the way."

Aum glanced around. The crowd was still captivated by Cat. The electronic music was swelling. Aum grinned, "Okay, let's hear what you got."

Aum jumped off the drum, and the young man jumped on and began playing. Fortunately the DJ kicked back in with a new drum and bass track at the exact moment the new engineer hit the drum skin, signaling the new direction of locomotion. Fedora and Vest woke out of a daze and with all their might tried to keep up with the speed of the energetic newcomer. Greg smirked knowingly, playing with the low bass rhythms of the new record, as he watched Aum walk toward Cat, each footstep expressing new layers of joy and freedom. Along with a few yelps and whoops from the audience, the crowd's focus changed back to dancing. In the commotion, Aum caught Cat and gave her a big hug. They laughed and Cat playfully skipped away. Aum couldn't help himself from chasing her, as their teasing steps gave way to dance.

Cat ran into the spiral mandala, which was still holding together—the audience had respected it as a strange and mysterious art sculpture. Aum followed her inside. Gravity got heavier as he spiraled inward; it was a sensation that darkened his mood. He shifted from playful to instinctual as he stood in the center of the metastructure and swooped his head around. With slow and patient strides, someone else entered the mandala.

Aum and the stranger both turned to see Cat dance her way out of the spiral and, in a heavy trance, move back down to the floor and begin more pattern making.

The music was gone. The dance floor was gone. The dim light gave little clues as to the nature of this mysterious character, still making calm strides closer and closer to Aum, in the center of the mandala.

They connected eyes, and either from embarrassment or relief, they both laughed.

"I'm sorry to intrude like this," she said.

"It's quite alright." Aum responded as her silent footsteps brought her closer. Aum could see she had shin-length black pants on, with a detailed, hand-stitched embroidered patterning, brown dress shoes, and a self-tailored suit jacket, perfectly styled for the set and setting. It was the full package, and she was a bright white time stopper.

"My name's Trae the Seer." Her hair was short and perfectly messy; crystals sparkled in her eyes. "Aum, it's nice to finally meet you."

Aum didn't know what to say; he was still running on instinct. "Hello, how are you?"

"Good. I have a gift for you."

"What kind of gift?"

"Well, two gifts, actually. This is a gift from me." She handed him a CD. Aum felt a charge move through his arm as he took it from her.

"What is it?"

"It's a project I've been working on for a while. Experimental audio architecture that I've begun to bridge into physical time and space."

"Whoa. What does that sound like?"

"Hip-hop."

"Cool. You made it yourself?"

"Yes, I put it together. I mean produced it, or looped it, composed it, structured it....I didn't actually make any of the sounds on it, though."

"And you think I'll like it?"

"Yeah, I figured you'd be the type. I really enjoy your on-line art process." She circled around him as she talked, a few strides away, cautious and curious. "Some might call it cheating, but I don't. You probably would have found one on your own."

"What do you mean? I would have found the CD on my own?"

"Well, I call it a hip-hop album because it's rooted there: sampling, graffiti, tagging, added to the contemporary notions of multilateral advertising, public sharing, and protest. That symbol on the front there," She pointed to the CD face, "is my tag." It was a clip-art bullhorn. "I make stickers of that symbol, and to begin a more interactive conversation with other artists, I use the placement of the stickers as CD drop points. Only in the past few months, after two years of doing this, are other artists beginning to respond by dropping their own material."

There was a 30 second blast of the pure light of fireworks. Aum squinted.

Trae continued, "I'm moving through the grid and planting seeds of inspired communication, not planting bombs to destroy this webbed existence, like some." She shook her head and looked over her shoulder. "We're getting off topic, though. Another moment of your time is all I need, and I'll let you get back to your wonderful night here."

Aum was about to protest but Trae slipped an envelope into his hands.

“Here’s my second gift. This was passed to me by a very good friend—a teacher, you could say. I’m not too sure what’s in it, but I think it’s more than obvious who it was meant for.”

Aum looked down at the white envelope and saw three capital letters hand inked into it: A-U-M.

He looked up to thank Trae but she was already past him and halfway out of the spiral mandala. She looked back and gave him a bright smile that made the embroidery on her clothing glow. “Don’t ever give up what you’re looking for, warrior of faith.” Trae spoke out loud as she exited the mandala and disappeared into the crowd.

Aum opened the envelope. Inside he found a single ticket to Full Spectrum, the yearly outdoor music and Riddler arts festival held in the wilderness outside the city.

He brought his hands together in prayer and bowed his head in gratitude.

Chapter Five

Aum walked onto a beach, and she was there, waiting. The sky was dark, the sand glowing white under heavy thunderclouds, and the water a navy blue, like the chill in the air. This was no place for naked frolicking lovers, but nonetheless, Aum found her in the vast dreamscape of consciousness. He walked up to her from behind, and as she gazed out at the sea, he slipped his hand into hers and she turned around and smiled.

Dream consciousness flipped to an exterior perspective; a camera zoomed out, leaving them as small dots on the horizon, staring into each other's eyes on the cold beach. In a blink, they held game controllers in their hands and were sitting in her living room watching themselves near the water, on the screen. This was the doorway. Another blink and they realized this. They stood from the couch, let go of the controllers, and as Aum took her hand once again, the room around them morphed into pure color and fractal imagination. It was a space created by Dr. Seuss and Salvador Dali inside Wonderland, with trees from the age of dinosaurs and giant dandelions about to let their seeds fly.

Turning his head, Aum exhaled and the room responded. He looked again and there were strings of color extending from his hands and feet, connected to different objects around him. She just stood there, smiling in amazement at what Aum was doing. Colors and images changed from the winking of his eye, to the motioning of his hand. The entire environment morphed and reacted as Aum began to dance in the colorful playground. Aum asked her to play, but she didn't hear. She stood as still as stopped time, engulfed by the multisensory environment that they were in. Trying to get her attention, Aum became even more excited; the color of his skin brightened, his face filled with determination—another blink and he evaporated into the ether around them. Aum became the space. He moved around her, flying and shape shifting, changing color and turning into fireworks, sparks, and white gulls, soaring right past her head, dancing for her with every knowable part. Then he started multiplying himself so that his body reappeared on every plane and surface—a holographic Aum. He felt her fear rise at his duplication, so he lessened his imagination and moved into his heart, changing back to one body.

She smiled; they looked into each other's eyes and embraced and became one, evaporating into the space and playing as color and light and sound. Aum became even more lucid when he focused on his hearing. In his loose and open state of dreaming, he remembered that he was listening to his new musically remixed gift on a pair of headphones. Aum realized he was sleeping and started to jump up and down in the dream, excitedly trying to explain to her that the music they could hear was a gift from her. He told her she was creating the music and that here she could bend it, dance with it, make it go wherever she wanted it to. But she didn't understand that they were dreaming. Maybe next time.

They continued to shift back and forth between physical and etheric forms of interaction. Dream consciousness wavered in perspective and lucidity flowed while they played and created patterns, singing and dancing, until they began to tell stories to the dreamer of the dream.

The first story began in the downtown city core, where bright colors turned grey and bland; a cold wind blew between the long rows of tall skyscrapers. He looked across the street and saw the same businesswoman from the train on the night of his unattended performance. She was staring at him. He didn't quite know what to make of the stare, but she broke it off and entered a tall office tower. He gazed up and saw that all floors were dark, except the fourth from the top. *She must be heading up to that floor*, Aum guessed. His curiosity propelled him across the street to investigate. As he approached the building, he noticed the turnstile doors were still spinning, so he entered the tall glass tower in trepidation and anxiety. There was a security guard at a table in the front foyer who was slowly being hypnotized by security camera feeds. Aum slipped by with his indoor soccer sneakers softly touching the floor, moving into the elevator just as it closed. The woman stood next to him, clearly panicked that she was late. Checking her watch at every floor, her energy paced in circles around the elevator without bodily movement. She didn't even notice Aum in the elevator with her. Aum checked his pocket watch. It was 8 p.m. She was working late tonight. The door opened when they reached the eighth floor from the top, and she quickly ran out. Aum was a little more reserved, however, unsure how quickly he wanted to take on the beast. He was now inside the systemic interior workings of Oil and Gas, facing an Oil Baron's fortress up close and personal. He did not know a single soul that had made it out alive; all who entered were forever changed to theit core.

He jumped past the elevator door just as it closed, and moved into the sterile hallway like a prowling ghost. The secretary behind the front desk had a phone attached to her ear. She was on a computer with one hand, with the phone directory in the other. An endless stream of her voice emitted to the many callers on the other end of the phone speaker. Her eyes were white, blind from talking to people with no physical presence. Like the security guard below, she did not notice Aum walk in. He looked at the digital clock on her desk. It read 4:55. There was a calendar above it from ten years ago, with a picture of pipelines running through the middle of a dense forest.

"That's not good," Aum said to himself. Somewhere a door slammed with heavy thunder, prison-like.

He walked into the main artery of motion, with dozens of workers carrying papers, posters, diagrams and binders, some wearing dress shirts and ties, some wearing casual t-shirts and jeans. They were in such a rush that not one of them even attempted to make eye contact with Aum as they passed by. He looked in the offices as he passed; workers were glued to their computer screens, beads of sweat dripping down their foreheads, large stains under their arms. Suddenly the office intercom boomed.

"Jenson…Get your ass in here!"

Aum jumped. His body vibrated with the echo of the words as they resounded through the cold, dark halls. The air was sucked from his lungs. Two rooms back, a man sprinted out of his office full tilt with a poster under his arm.

"Oh shit, oh shit oh shit oh shit…" He muttered under his breath as he marched past. Aum could feel steam and heat coming from ahead, along with the sound of machinery crunching and grinding under a colossal amount of pressure.

Yelling punctuated the halls: "This isn't what I asked for, Junior! Where's the 14-45 file? Have you not printed it yet?!"

Aum's body vibrated even more in the echo, but he could not ignore his curiosity, and he inched closer to the large boardroom beyond. He saw the running man cowering under what seemed to be a giant lizard. Aum shook his head. As the vibration dissipated in his minds-eye, the hallucination subsided. He could see that the lizard was actually a man; a seven-foot-tall, three-hundred-pound man with the build of a defensive lineman towered over young Jenson, a manipulative, snarling smile spreading across his face.

"The 14-45?" replied Jenson. "Uh, I'm not too sure….I don't think you've mentioned that one to me yet."

"Well get on it! I need it in 30 seconds! Now go like a bat out of hell!"

"Okay, right away, thank you."

"Somebody fill this damn stapler!" the lizard man shouted into the air, slamming it down on the counter. He then prowled back to his office. Jenson ran passed Aum, again not noticing him. "Oh shit, oh shit oh shit oh shit."

The seven-foot Baron ruled with an iron fist and a noisy crown of pump jacks. His fuel was the fear he created in others; his greed for power, money, and control taking permanent residence in the frontal lobe of his oversized head. If he was not a direct incarnation of hell, he would certainly be given a position of nobility when he got there. Aum followed him into his office.

A man with a military demeanor stepped in and around Aum, giving the Baron a piece of paper. The Baron put it down on the desk and began making checkmarks with his red sharpie.

"Good! Great! Fantastic!"

He handed it back to the military man as the woman from the elevator walked in.

"Get me thirty copies! Forward it to Jeff!" Noticing the woman, he snapped, "What do you want?!"

"I just have a question about the 13-37 area."

"Get out! You missed the boat!"

Then from over the intercom came "Your hotel and limo is booked, Burt."

"Does it have the full-service pool room?"

"Yes, it does."

Other workers filed into the office with more paperwork.

"Great. I don't want any of that shit from last time. Is my helicopter ready on the roof?"

"Yes, sir."

"Good." He slapped the intercom off without a thank-you.

"Burt," the intercom again.

"What?!"

The sound inside of the word almost knocked Aum to the floor. It was all he could do to keep from passing out.

"Call for you on 12, Burt."

"Take a message."

"It's the National Board of Directors, Burt."

"Goddamn it!"

While his face stared unblinkingly at his computer screen, he raised his free hand and pointed to the door. His finger shot out laser beams, hitting the people who had not left his office the moment he asked. Those who were hit fell to the floor in a pile of pain and tears, the sting of the laser destroying all hope, love, and compassion. A small door in the wall opened and, as if Burt's pet, doomsday minion, or circus slave, a midget in a jester costume walked out carrying a broom. The small man calmly swept the fresh carcasses into a pile of thirty or so bodies that were building up in the corner.

"And close the goddamn door behind you!" The last person obeyed the command, leaving Aum in the office alone with the Paul-Bunyan-sized man. Aum sat down across from him. Noticing him for the first time, the Baron stood up at his desk, slamming his open hands on the wood, his crown grinding to a halt.

"Who the hell are you?! And how the hell did you get into my office?!"

"What does that matter? When I'm done with you, you will have no office, and every single one of your greasy tentacles penetrating the Earth will look exactly like the ones on your gas-inflated head."

"What is that supposed to mean?!"

"You have no idea, Burt, but I have just infiltrated the very heart, the inner workings, of the entire Oil and Gas industry. You see, once I leave here, you and every single one of your kind will no longer be the same. Your hearts will be uplifted and full of joy knowing full well the positive impact that you will begin to have on the environment around you, the divinity of our Mother Earth, and all aspects of humanity in general. Every…single…day. For the rest of your life."

The Baron was stunned; he was going to say something hate-filled, but Aum was too quick for him.

"Why? I'll tell you why. Because you are an old and outdated archetypical mode of consciousness that needs to be eradicated, and damn quick, too! There is no need for your lack of compassion, your ego, your male chauvinism, and especially your rage where we're going."

"You insane little prick! I'm calling security. You know what they do to little pricks?"

"It doesn't matter. My heart is open and my mind is clear, and I see right through you. What you are doing is despicable, Burt. I don't know how anyone in their right mind would ever care about a creature as repulsive, disgusting, and ugly as you." With the last three words, Aum pushed a finger hard into the Oil Baron's chest.

"But it's okay. I might be the only one, but I still love you." Aum went in with both arms raised, ready to give him a hug, as if completing an emotionally intense workshop session.

"Get the hell away from me!" Burt shouted, pushing him away with both hands. Aum rounded back on Burt; he was in his face again, with words flying like darts

"Okay-doke Grandpasaurus, but I should let you know the spell that you've cast here will be broken as of now. In this office, this city, and throughout your land." Aum put his hands together in prayer, "Enjoy the rest of your day."

A buzzer went off, and cheers erupted from behind the door. They both looked at the office clock. It finally read 5:00 .

A weaving of greens overtook everything; a female form emerged from the dense jungle.

“That was good. Now I have one for you,” she said to him. A green hand grew out of the sinew and strands; it waited for Aum to take it. He did and was lead through tunnels and doorways of space and time to appear in a wooded meadow, sitting beside himself.

It was night. Aum was sitting on the grass beside himself. Literally.

Dreamer Aum sat next to Dream Aum in a park, along with a short man with knotted hair and a long, scraggly beard. Dreamer Aum listened and went unnoticed as Dream Aum and the bearded man talked in the midst of others in the distance: witches chanting under a full moon.

Dream Aum said to the man, “Last night I had a vision that I was at a giant multiplex theatre and there was some type of public event going on. A sports game was being broadcast in one of the theatres—but it wasn’t sports—it was…a war. There were different machines set up at the front of the theatre for people to climb into and participate in the action if they wanted, because it was all taking place in real time. At this point, midwar, the scene was within a sandy desert, jets were flying across the screen, and the sound of destruction pierced the air…of the theatre. Anyway, there was a lineup to participate in this game show. Spectators would sit in the theatre seats and watch the contestants play with their lives, lives that were completely in the hands of the other players, who were in some other theatre, in some other city.

“At that point in the dream, I realized I was in line to play this strange war game. When my turn came, I strapped myself into the machine with the confidence that I would know exactly what to do. The game show controller was like a cyberpunk monstrosity. It was a stationary motorbike and helicopter combination; there was a fan at the top, but it was mostly for cooling the engine and sending the output signal at the right frequency, out and off to the main gaming network. I strapped myself into the controller and began to shoot at row upon row of ‘enemies’—even though on my machine’s screen, it was just an 8-bit graphical grid of dots. Up until that point, all other contestants were dying within the first couple of minutes of play, so everyone in the theatre was amazed by how well I was doing. I was making good progress and eventually made it to the next level of combat.

"The propeller at the top of the machine started to move faster and faster, the better I did. Soon the entire machine started to transform; gears and engines were popping out of compartments that contestants or spectators didn't know existed. Soon the technology moved and grew, enveloping my entire body, and with it, my entire consciousness. What I was seeing, my point of view, then got transported to the actual events that were taking place on the screen. In this new scenario, I was in my body, in army fatigues, and was helping repair a broken down vehicle with a bunch of fellow players. Understanding the urgency of the situation, being on the front lines in the desert, I managed to fix it by just looking at it. I repaired it instantly."

"That's interesting," said the bearded man.

"Yeah," Dream Aum replied. "Then it got all weird. Once the vehicle was fixed, everything went red, and it became an intense test of fear. The sky turned to dripping blood, and all I could see were fields of soldiers marching, under their feet, broken human flesh with crushed dreams burning. It was as if something much bigger than myself was trying to take control over my surroundings. Somehow I managed to pass this stage, but I can't actually remember how, or even the rest of the dream, yet I know that there was much more. When I woke, I had this feeling that I had accomplished so much in a very short period of time."

"Your vision reminds me of something, Dream Aum. It's a very unusual coincidence," the man said. Both Aums, Dreamer Aum and Dream Aum, quickly looked over at him, as if the word "coincidence" triggered déjà vu. "Have you ever heard of the Riddle Solver?"

Breaking his long silence, Dreamer Aum exclaimed, "What?!" Both Dream Aum and the bearded man turned to look at him astonished, finally seeing the holographic apparition embodied, an observational layer flattened.

He was falling. The sky was light blue with many clouds. From a bird's eye view, he could see the organic pattern of a river opening out to the ocean. He could hear the wind rushing past his ears, and he could see the mechanical pattern in the freshly harvested wheat fields.

“So what are you trying to say?” Aum turned to ask a cloud as it formed into his lover’s face. It didn’t respond.

“Okay, I’ve got a couple for you then.”

Aum was walking hurriedly in a circle of long grass. The sun shone down on him, and there was a cool breeze blowing across his face. He looked up, and to his surprise, he saw many other men walking the same path as him. They wore jeans and slacks, t-shirts and sweaters—very regular. He looked across the meadow and the same thing was happening with females. They were all walking around in two separate circles. A gull flew overhead; Aum watched it soar, allowing its body to move with the wind. It disappeared behind a tall pine tree. Aum sat down off the beaten path, crossed his legs, folded his hands, and began to meditate.

In darkness, a vision of the planet Earth spread itself across the view of his inner eye. In the vast stillness and silence, stars twinkled and other planets revealed themselves. With a large hand, Aum plucked a red, juicy planet out of its orbit and ate it. Suddenly a flying saucer whooshed by his head. An alien appeared and, with a wave of his hand, invited Aum inside. The interior of the spaceship was a vast garden. Brown leaves and dried up and dead plants covered the ten-acre field. Other aliens appeared, in dirty coveralls, down on their hands and knees digging out the garden. Aum looked across the garden, waved his hand, and the weeds disappeared. The garden became full of vibrant greens shooting up out of the dirt toward the sun on the other side of the solar system. Tree branches stretched and flowers bloomed. Aum brimmed with joy as the sun shined through the skylights of the spaceship, into the green garden. He looked at all the aliens, closed his eyes, and brought them into his heart. Opening his eyes once again, he saw that the aliens had transformed into versions of himself. All of the Dream Aums, young and old, started dancing and laughing with each other. Dreamer Aum slowly floated up into the air and out of the ship. His last sight was of all of his selves tending the garden, smiling and waving good-bye

He opened his eyes and found himself in the center of a circular room, audience seated, gazing from floors spiraling up to the ceiling. There were men and women alike fixated on him in the center. He was speaking to them, profoundly simple words, about the nature of flight.

"It's easy, but you must choose it to be," and he began to float up to the ceiling. There were expressions of astonishment, joy, and sadness as Aum took skyward. Those who chose to, followed.

Once again in the clouds, he exhaled. The music from the gifted CD faded back in. He noticed a brilliant light in the sky. As Aum flew closer, he could see, subatomic in comparison to the source, other shining winged figures soaring and circling this brilliant light. He looked to his feet and found he was no longer a physical body but a small spark of light from this sublime source.

Aum's vision faded to white and he found himself face to face with his girlfriend Jenn, a new Jenn with sparkling eyes and a vibrant smile.

"Why do you play the Riddle, Aum?"

"That's a big question, Jenn," he responded.

The dream lost color, sound, and imagination; they were sitting in a picture of reality, the two of them at the kitchen table having some green tea.

Aum continued, "Evolution at all costs. You know what I mean? Pushing and willing and manifesting peak experiences at every moment because these are the things that really allow large permanent changes to happen. Drug-induced art, trance induced music, nature-infused ceremony, and every single breath overflowing with prayer. These peak experiences, whatever form they take, change how I think, act, and especially see the world. These experiences also change those around me, because they are involved in what's happening, too. It's not as simple as a model train hobby or still-life painting practice. I know that by exploring this immersive structure, I will find life's purpose, and my life's purpose within that." With total awareness, he calmly took a sip of the warm liquid.

"That's a pretty big answer, Aum."

"Yeah, I thought so. Is the size of it why there's a huge rift in our relationship right now?"

"Yes, but that's all about to change…and it has changed."

Aum looked on in curiosity, "What do you mean?"

"I know about Cat, Aum."

"Really?"

"Yes, I've seen her in your eyes and smelt thoughts of her on your body."

He didn't know how to respond.

She continued, "You must let it go, though, because it's already changed. I've seen you move toward me, just as I now move toward you. Bring me with you to Full Spectrum."

He was astonished. "But I don't have a ticket for you. They're not the easiest things to come by."

"That's okay. It doesn't matter. Should you ask me, I will accept and fully follow you on the journey, wherever it may lead."

"But you hate the Riddle, Jenn, and that's a big door to walk through."

"Yes, but I love you, and that's much bigger."

She was more real now than he had ever seen her, "Yeah, you're right."

The kitchen faded away. Aum was alone in the black void, unafraid and content.

Bright golden beings surrounded him, encircling him, spinning around him. His eyes opened, and he sat up in bed but wasn't fully present yet. He was still surrounded by the void and the bright circle of beings. Slowly his room, his body, and bed faded back into his vision, and the beings faded out to wherever they came from. He stared into the face of one as it left. It was a thick and bark-faced texture of light that his imagination would not recall until the far future.

"A Taoist businessman!" Aum shouted, as if talking in his sleep, the words signaling his return back to the waking world. He saw Jenn awake under the covers looking directly at him with a very odd expression on her face. "What?!"

"Hey, you're back," Aum said to her.

"Yeah, are you though?" she responded.

"Almost."

Concern creviced her forehead as she looked over. "More nightmares?"

He let out a deep sigh, letting the last dreams bits fade, "No, not exactly." He moved his messy hair out of his face and laid back down on his side, looking at her directly. "How'd the trip go?"

"Very good. I've got a meeting with my parents tomorrow to give them some exciting numbers." Jenn was elated.

"Good for you."

"It's pretty intense, though, playing with the big boys on their turf." She moved her hand to the top of her head and sighed, contemplating the oncoming pressure. She assumed Aum would never understand the amount of focus needed to for this type of career. His support was still there, though; she could feel it and let out a big exhale. "I'm glad it's finally done."

A warm smile slowly crossed her face. "I had a talk with Sandra."

"Really? I've been trying to get a hold of her this past week."

"She came out east with me. She was helping me as my personal assistant."

"What did she assist you with?"

"Strangely enough, our relationship."

"Who? You and me?"

"Yes. I'm very sorry I wasn't able to make it to your art opening, Aum. I know it meant quite a lot to you."

"That's okay; hopefully there will be more soon." Smiling, he moved in closer to her. "I've missed you, Jenn."

He could feel her soft breath on his face.

"I missed you, too."

Their fingertips found each other's bare skin; his dream of her still fresh in his mind.

"Jenn, do you want to go on a trip with me?"

"Sure, where?" she whispered.

"To an arts festival called Full Spectrum; it's at a campsite outside of the city."

"Nature and art? That sounds like a wonderful change from the office."

Aum had much faith in his dream, and faith that the universe would provide him another ticket. And he now had faith in Jenn.

"Jenn?"

"Yes, Aum."

"Full Spectrum is a Riddle event....I just wanted to let you know that."

She was silent for a moment. She closed her eyes like she was swallowing medicine or receiving an injection, and replied, "Okay."

Aum brushed a lock of hair behind her ear. They were blooming as one, together in silence. Past reactions were forgotten, awkwardness and trepidation melted away as they tenderly wrapped themselves in new warm petals of each other, unfolding.

***

"So you're gonna have to keep quiet here; I need to concentrate."

She turned down the stereo, perplexed, "What do you mean?"

Aum and Jenn had been in the car for about eight hours straight—the last two of those traveling along a bumpy dirt road through a dense coniferous forest and now the last long minutes of those eight hours waiting in a line of vehicles moving at a snail's pace. As their patience ran thin, Aum realized they were three cars away from the entry gates to the yearly Riddle event, Full Spectrum, and his heart began to race uncontrollably.

"Keep quiet? What are you talking about Aum?"

"Well, I've only got one ticket and there are two of us, so I have to come up with another ticket pretty fast."

"What?! You only have one ticket?! Why didn't you do something about that before the very last second?!"

"I tried," Aum glanced in the rearview mirror; there were bumper to bumper cars all the way down the one-lane path as far as he could see. He looked ahead and saw a new ticket-taker step out and signal them to drive forward. He was a young man in his late teens with bright clothes and a ball cap worn off-center.

"Alright, here we go," Aum said apprehensively as he rolled the car forward.

"Oh crap!" Jenn looked as if she were about to pass over the top of a rollercoaster.

"One thing, Jenn." He looked at her. "Be cool, and breathe." He smiled, calming his own internal panic.

The young man approached the car as they drove up. Jenn quickly interjected, "That's two things, you dork."

"Welcome to Full Spectrum. Can I get your tickets, please?"

Aum passed him his ticket. He waited one moment less than what it would have taken for the teen to register there was only one ticket and spoke slowly. "So I guess we've got a little situation here…," Aum looked at the young man's handmade name tag, "…Gatekeeper Craig."

"Where's your other ticket?" Craig responded.

"Well, Craig, my girlfriend here doesn't have a ticket to this event. In fact, this is her first Riddle event ever. What are the chances of getting her in?"

He looked at Aum, unimpressed, speaking with a growing frustration. "Look, dude, I don't know what a Riddle event is, but if you don't have a ticket, you can't pass this gate." In the passenger seat, Jenn silently breathed out her weight in heavy tension and took a small step into a fuller presence. Aum could feel it and pushed through the tunnel that had just opened, quickening his pace.

"Really, that doesn't matter," he said. "What matters is if you're able to let her in, Craig."

Becoming more aware of the hijinks going on Craig said, "Sorry, can't do it. If she's never been here before, I'd be especially worried about getting her out in one… piece…," He paused his youthful warning of future mind-melting and lowered himself to look through the car window, "…Jenn?!"

They locked eyes. "Craig Bracott!" She was as surprised as he was, but she recovered much more quickly. "Shouldn't you be at work today?"

"Ugh, um, sorry Jenn, ugh, I mean, Ms. Leatherbee." Craig himself finally recovered and fully turned on her. "What about you? Shouldn't you be working too?!"

"I just got back from the east coast with a fifty thousand dollar contract that requires completion by the end of next week. That means a hell of a lot more work on your plate today, which is probably attracting flies back at the office." She looked at Aum, still confident. "I'm on vacation."

Aum quickly turned to the teen. "So what'll it be there, Craig?"

He gave Aum a look of disapproval and sighed in resolve. "One sec, guy. I'll talk to my pod coordinator."

Craig walked over to an RV parked at the side, just past the line of makeshift entry tollbooths. They could see him through the window talking to another woman with long dreadlocks and bones in her earlobes. She spoke into a clip-on two-way radio and looked over at Aum and Jenn. Meeting eyes in surprise, both Jenn and Aum quickly turned to look straight ahead. “Crap,” Aum whispered as he realized their surprised and fearful reaction. He looked over again and Craig was walking over with a woven basket. Aum didn’t get to see the remainder of their conversation. Craig walked past the front of the car and over to Jenn’s window. She rolled it down gingerly.

“I was told to give you one of these, Mrs. Leatherbee.”

She looked in the basket, and rattling around were a dozen fluorescent-colored eggs, the type that usually contain small toy trinkets for kids. She looked up at him in confusion.

“You’re holding up my line, Mrs. Leatherbee. Just take one and I can let you in.”

She glanced back at Aum; he shrugged.

She took a bright pink one and asked, “What do I do with it?”

“Dunno. It’s pretty weird if you ask me. Welcome to Full Spectrum,” and he walked back to his makeshift tollbooth, waving them in.

They both shrugged at each other, and Aum drove the car down a worn length of grass.

“Well… that was pretty weird,” Jenn said.

“Yeah. It was.” He looked at her, then smiled. “But we made it. Aren’t you going to open your egg?” Aum teased.

“No, I’m not going to open it!” Jenn said loudly, and a bit flustered.

“Why not?” Aum goaded.

“Alright, fine!”

She shook it, and it rattled only slightly. She forced her fingernails into the small crevasse, and it opened with a pop.

“So?” asked Aum

“It’s a match; a wooden match,” she said calmly.

“A match?”

Slightly perturbed, Jenn replied, “Is this supposed to be for something? Or mean something? Or what? What exactly does this have to do with art?”

Aum laughed. “Well, good question...” They drove over a foot bridge to what was the next checkpoint. “…One sec,” he said, as a happy-looking woman with long blonde hair approached the car.

“How are you guys doing?”

“Good. Yourself?” Aum responded with a smile.

"I'm great. Welcome to Full Spectrum. Here's your map." It was a small black-and-white photocopied quarter sheet. "As you can see, we're right here. Parking is ahead and to your left. You'll have to carry in your gear but don't worry; it's not far.…You're camping in Site 3, Group 9, Branch A. Don't worry about that, either; it's well marked. There are washrooms near the parking lot, in your Branch, as well as in the vending area marked here, here, and here on your map. Have a great weekend."

"Thanks, you too," Both Aum and Jenn responded.

They both drove on feeling as if a bit of sunshine had sneaked its way through the clouds, diffusing the entry panic, and the anxiety Aum built up from the car ride with his knowledge of the single ticket. As they slowly drove down a hill, they spied the festival through a clearing in the trees.

"Whoa, check it out!" Aum exclaimed.

From their elevated location, they gazed down upon a tarped performing stage and an alive marketplace opposite from it. In between was a large fire pit and picnic tables under canopied pop-up tents. Aum saw someone on the stage; the opening DJ already playing. He rolled down his window to hear some welcoming dub. Fat and long trumpet lines blaring out of the speakers stacks dispersed the clouds that still remained around them.

"So there's the art, honey; we still need to figure out what your match has to do with it."

She didn't respond.

Aum looked over at Jenn, who was staring at the scene like a timid deer.

"Aw… it's okay, Jenn. It'll be a great time."

They rolled down the rest of the hill, found a parking spot, loaded their weekend camping gear onto their backs, and followed the signs to their campsite. As they walked, surrounded on both sides by thick green trees, the sunlight rarely poked through the dense clouds of leaves. A breeze caught them, and their olfactory senses were lit up by the dense aroma of a healthy, natural forest.

They saw a couple sites, already occupied. Colorful banners, Tibetan prayer flags, and crystal and copper amulets all hung from the surrounding trees, each space totally customized to its occupants. Aum and Jenn continued on and saw a sign that read "Group 9."

"This must be it."

They walked up a couple makeshift steps through the underbrush and saw a two-foot-high, gray stone Buddha statue sitting at the top. Beyond it, there was a small circular alcove within the tall trees, a fire pit, and a picnic table. Aum and Jenn walked around the table and peaked through the first of four dorm-like openings to find it empty. In the next, there was a rustling tent that had some muffled grunts coming from it, and in the third, a tent was being constructed by a man and two women who seemed to have also just arrived. They had yet to hang up their trinkets, amulets, and powered-up crystals. Aum walked over.

"Hello," he said.

"Hi." They were confident but quite sensitive to Aum's feelers, almost protective of something they cherished; Aum sensed they had a strong connection to the divine flow of the Riddle. He wanted to know them, their story, what community they were from, and especially what stage in the Riddle they were at. In their jeans and tees, all three continued to work on their tent. One of the ladies looked familiar but he couldn't quite put his finger on where he knew her from.

"Uh, I'm Aum FreeZen, and this is my partner, Jennifer Leatherbee. We're just next door to you guys."

The man came over. Tall with a dense, fully muscled frame and long blonde hair, he greeted Aum with a strong handshake and a stoic nod.

"I'm Pillaiyar. This is Sara and Ashta."

He seemed irritated that Aum's open friendliness disturbed their tent construction flow: the silence of the three was so deep that Aum felt lucky to have even received their names.

Aum stood for a couple extra seconds in their comfort zone, just 'cause he knew they knew he was doing it consciously, and then said to Jenn, "Well, we should get our tent up too." Pillaiyar and Aum smiled cordially to each other.

"See ya later," Aum said as they walked to their space and began constructing their tent, organizing sleeping quarters and food storage. Jenn joked, "Where's all your do-dads to hang up?"

"I'm like Buddha, unattached to material objects," Aum responded.

"Right…Sadu, Sadu, Sadu," Jenn replied with a grin.

They had both removed Some of their morning layers of clothing and were quite content.

"Want to go check out the shops?"

"Sure."

They heard some rustling at the shared picnic table and emerged from their site.

"What's up my man? My lady? I'm Ted."

This friendly gentleman was the polar opposite of the first three they had met: outgoing and open. Aum thought his black pinstripe suit pants, dress shoes, and tattered black jacket were zombiesque. But his down-combed Mohawk, brushed to the side; scruffy five o'clock shadow; and waxed moustache curls somehow placed him in the UK Riddler scene.

Aum and Jenn introduced themselves. "We were just going to head down to the main area."

"Awesome! Have you guys been down there yet?"

"No, not yet."

Just then, another man emerged from the same tent, hair ruffled. He snuck up to Ted from behind. Pulling himself close, he nuzzled into Ted's neck and whispered, "Theodore, can you get some more of that fantastic mango juice?"

Ted stood firm in his masculinity. "Sure thing, Jes."

Jes snuck a peck on Ted's neck. He spied Aum and Jenn. "Greetings," he said with a confrontational smirk and sauntered back to the tent.

Ted waited till the zipper closed and whispered to Jenn and Aum, "He's a bit of a rock star." Then in a full voice, "So, you guys ready to check out this year's carnival?"

"You bet," they both nodded in agreement, and began down the steps.

Ted led the way. His tall, lanky form strode down the dirt path and the wooded camping area opened up to reveal a very active atmosphere. To the right, and in the distance, was a large grassy playing field filled with a few Frisbees flying. Arial acrobats were flinging their bodies upside down, catching discs with their feet, passing them down to their hands, and landing upright to throw the discs off to their targets—all in one fluid motion.

"Hot damn!" exclaimed Ted.

They looked over to see him staring at the festival's Main Stage, a large thirty-foot half-dome covered with a tarp. Underneath, a fresh-cut grass dance floor and large festival speakers pumped out "Groove Is in the Heart" by Delite, with some additional vocal coaching over top.

"That's right! Let's open up those hips, fellas."

"Oh my god," Jenn added in disbelief.

They looked on to see a dozen people involved in what seemed to be a hula-hooping workshop. Parading around the grass in bare feet, adjusting technique, and giving big support was a small woman in her sixties with tightly curled white hair, a florescent one-piece, a matching headband, and a microphone headset. With her hoop spinning around her waist, she moved in between male gym buffs, loosening their locked hips, and limber ladies who were gleefully hooping to the poppy beats.

"Wow, what a mesmerizing spectacle." Ted shook his head a little and turned to Aum and Jenn. "That's the Main Stage. A schedule is posted near the Common Stage; it has the list of workshops, performances, and DJ times for the weekend. C'mon, I'll show you." He turned and started walking backward toward the Common Stage. "I suggest checking out S.O.S. They put on an amazing show."

"Yeah, sure, when's that?" Aum asked

"Tomorrow evening. It should be great."

They strolled over to the Common Stage. This was the area they spied coming in. It was a half-dome clamshell, like the Main Stage, but much smaller. The vending booths had busy lines of carnivalesque characters, and the picnic tables were all, for the most part, full. Some people had picnic blankets out, diving into sketchbooks, notepads, paperbacks, laptops, and handhelds. There were a couple yoga mats set up, with people stretching in the sun. It looked like a drum circle had just started up to accompany the breakbeats that a new DJ was spinning under the tarp.

"Ahhh…campus life," Ted intoned.

"I think I'll have to go join those guys in a bit," Aum said, motioning to the drummers. Some of the Frisbee-ers walked past them; they stood by the bonfire pit for a moment and a hackey-sac circle quickly formed.

"Or maybe those guys," Aum added.

"Well I'll just let you two explore. The Water and Wood Stage is just through those trees over there." He pointed past the Common Stage. "I'm going to grab a drink for Jes; I'll see ya later."

"See ya!" said Jenn

"Thanks for the tour," said Aum.

"No worries."

Jenn and Aum sat down at a recently vacated picnic table.

A couple more hackey-sackers joined the group.

"I think I'm going to go play."

"Would you like a drink?" Jenn asked.

"Sure."

"I'll go grab us something."

Smiling brightly, Aum reached out and kissed her, then joined the circle.

It took Aum a little while to warm up, but soon he was flailing limbs in a flowing chaos that somehow managed to keep the bouncing bag of beans in the air. The squinty eyed Frisbee club still had a lot of energy after running through the playing fields. The circle gelled, and they kept the hackey-sac in the air for close to 10 minutes, with many diving saves and freestyle mid-air contortionism.

Jenn walked back to the table with a couple juices and sat watching, remembering the days of old. To her, Aum didn't seem much different then back then, but observing the depths of her own self, she knew that major changes had taken place, and not all wholistically positive. She pushed the vision away, ignoring the growing lump in her throat.

"Holy shit! Look at 'em go!" a be-speckled and aging, tie-dyed wearing man exclaimed to Jenn.

"Yeah, they're pretty good," she replied.

"Good? With their knee-popping jazz-ma-tazz, any Mayan wizard-king would be proud to sacrifice these time travelers to their pantheon of Armageddon gods."

Jenn didn't know what to say. The combination of marijuana smoke seeping out his pores and aging tripster vibe affected her more deeply than she was prepared for. She nervously looked at her wristwatch.

"Yup, it's about that time," he said as he walked towards the circle.

Aum disengaged after the hack hit the ground; he thanked his fellow athletes in action and walked back toward the picnic table, passing the old tripster on the way.

"Make sure you don't miss all the fun," the old man said to Aum, with a hint of menace.

"My time is infinite, old timer. I'm just warming up," Aum retorted, guard up and eagle feathers out.

Jenn smiled nervously and passed Aum his drink. "Do you want to check out that other stage?"

"Sure."

As they left, Aum could distinctly smell the fresh ganja smoke coming from the circle. He exhaled the clouded vibration of daily, or even hourly, intake and walked with his partner past the fire pits, poi spinners, and the plethora of picnic blankets, toward the sparse trees. The campground setting was still shaking with potentials as Aum saw car after car drive down the entrance road up high behind the vending booths.

Through the cool shade of a dozen distanced pines, they walked together, sipping their fresh fruit juice. They could hear some interesting cracking and thumping noises and came upon five or so dirty characters beating rocks with sticks and sticks with rocks. People stopped dead in their tracks to gather around and stare at the spectacle, including Ted, who stood on the outskirts with a heavy-set cloaked man. The man's shaved head and large earrings added to his weighty presence. After taking in the setting a bit more, Aum and Jenn walked over and stood next to the two in silent observation.

Within the circle of dreaded Earth children, Aum could see a brightly clothed gentleman with a microphone pointed toward the organic music making matter. He looked up and smiled brightly, shuffling his long brown locks behind his ear. Aum followed the winding mic cord with his eyes through the pine needles and over the protruding roots to the underside of another small booth. Only two meters wide and maybe three meters tall, it was constructed of scrap plywood, gathered fallen branches, rope, and even a nail or two.

In the booth was another man bobbing his head behind an old, off-white ten-pound computer monitor. The light percussive sounds were being routed from the first to the second man, ever so subtly sampled and looped on top of the flowing real-time audio current. The signal was amplified through large roofed speakers on either side of the makeshift hut. Aum saw another mic was placed next to the computer monitor, into which the second man began to whistle. The breathy tones of his whistle fluctuated between pan flute melodies and rustling wind, but combined with the natural cracking and hollow rhythms, it sounded like an amplified wood and metal wind chime.

The man in the booth increased a sample, and the tribal band gelled to it, building structure from it. Aum ventured forward and spoke generally to the four of them: "What a perfect solstice gathering."

"Yes, totally unprecedented in its possibilities," the big man whispered.

Ted took a deep breath. "Aum, this is BJ. BJ, this is Aum."

They shook hands. "This is my partner, Jenn," Aum said, motioning to Jenn.

BJ nodded formally, "Hello, Jenn."

While in this conversation, Aum could feel Jenn's attention move excitedly elsewhere around the space. Maybe it was the trees, the atmosphere, the music, or even the steadily moving creek down from the open area, but he could tell that she had reached a new level of ease.

BJ whispered respectfully in the deep reverence of this natural setting. "Yes, the metagalactic recalibratory energies are strong." Magically the words opened Aum up to an instant awareness of what BJ was referring to. He stood grounded, open, breathing, pulsing. Jenn remained in her own state of natural awe, somewhat disassociated from the masculine postulating. Hair flowing in the soft breeze, Jenn walked past Aum and the other two men with a confident smile, over to a large pocket of trees. She removed her shoes and began to climb.

BJ's whispering continued. "Certain planets will be going in and out of alignment, so I'll be able to do things I haven't done in four years." Overzealous and childlike, Aum responded, "Which planets? What kind of things?"

"That's classified, I'm afraid."

Aum nodded silently with a slight smirk. BJ seemed to want to keep up the mystery that his presence afforded.

The organic tribe ended their real-time jam, but the whistling continued ever softer and softer, fading out till it blended so naturally with the elements that it reached subthreshold levels. Aum was unsure if he was still hearing it or not.

"Blessings on these sacred days," BJ nodded and walked towards the Common Stage.

Aum and Ted returned the nod.

He saw Ted still had two drinks in his hands, one of which was three quarters finished.

"You haven't made it back to camp yet?" Aum asked him

"Nope…all in good time," he smiled.

Aum smiled back and nodded in agreement. He walked over to the tree Jenn had climbed, removed his shoes, and began his own Gaia-communal climb. He spied her neatly nestled about four branches up. After Aum climbed two branches, the audience began cheering for the performers: the subthresh sound must have finally faded out to nothing. Aum paused and turned to show his gratitude as well. A new light patterned popping faded in with a warm synthline.

As Aum continued up the tree, he could hear voices speaking in emphatic tones. Pulling himself to the next branch and looking over, Aum saw four men lounging in the bows…perhaps. He could not quite tell the numbers because their organically cut, self-tailored and sewn, green and brown garb hid them well in the foliage of the tree.

"Individuality flourishes. Harmony in a magnitude of exhales as the air recycles within our lungs. We are given gifts from the plant kingdom. A completely perfected exchange in unconscious biological functioning and receptivity. The partnership is undeniable, much like the sun and our sense of sight. There are difficulties, though. The tree spirits cannot accept our strange gifts of pollution and destruction, so we suffer the consequences of being conscious, unconscious to this perfected relationship."

He could see the tree speaking with him; there were no words, but there was communication happening. He could see it in the movement.

"And individuality flourishes. Exhales in honest exchange. Gratitude exchange is the new currency, and currency becomes electric. Embodied in objects is best," another continued.

"But seeds planted in dreams flourish fast when they touch the water; waves are instant."

"On the beach we meet ourselves forecasting the dance of gifts."

"And individuality flourishes."

Aum interjected, "Dreamers dance as exhales and psychic sound design combine. Can you direct me to the Seer?"

They all gaped at him until the tension-filled silence finally broke. "Trays of no's—knows you create your own creations." A slight grin appeared, with trickster curls at the end. There was rustling above as Jenn climbed down a branch and interjected, "Aum, I'm going down to the water." She climbed back down the tree. Aum followed her. In parting, he offered, "Strength lies in devotion. Peace be with you."

He climbed down the tree with a firmness that bent the bows, threatening to break them. He jumped to the ground, and as he landed, he felt the synchronistic bass note of a boulder dropped thirty feet into a deep pool. With that, things awoke. Twilight began to emerge in the color of the sky, and the campground gates closed. The space was gelling, Aum could feel it, like an electric conduit taped to the base of his spine.

With Jenn, Aum knelt at the water's edge and pushed his hands deep into the river bed. He pulled out large muddy rocks and balanced them in his grip; he then lowered them into the creek, watching the cloudy debris float down the river in deep silence.

"You alright?" Jenn asked, concerned.

"Yeah, just rinsing off," he forced a smile in her direction.

"So what was that all about?"

"What?"

"Those guys in the tree?"

"Um." He was a bit shaken, "I was trying to find the woman who gave me my ticket."

"Why?"

"Because I seek the person who gave it to her to give to me; her teacher."

"How come?"

"Cause that's what I'm drawn to do. Maybe this person will have a direction for me to amplify, whether it's study, contemplation, or action."

"As long as that direction isn't amplified insanity," Jenn replied with worry.

"Don't stress about my sanity, Jenn. It's your vacation remember? Relax into it."

"I'm trying, Aum, but every time I do, it feels like some deep parts of me are being exposed, even dissected, by weird people and weirder surprises."

"Yeah, I hear you. We're definitely on a bit of a collective outskirts. But we're on the outskirts together, right? Maybe focus on that. You made it in, remember? Without a ticket, even. Now that's magic if I've ever seen it."

"Yeah…" She smiled slightly. She pulled out her egg from her pocket, stared at it intensely for a while, hoping for its nature to reveal itself, and then let out a laugh. "Weird!"

Aum burst out laughing too. Then, tenderly switching topics, he queried, "Tell me more about your trip with Sandra."

More at ease, their conversation meandered like the creek, over boulder and under the sky with freedom. The dark red spires of sunlight dimmed to black night, and the trickle of the creek was overpowered by the ever-increasing strength of the Main Stage beat.

They found each other huddled together, wrapped in each other's arms as stars began to appear in the sky. They decided to head back to their campsite for some food and warmer clothes. There were a few elegantly dressed women swaying in the ambience of digital wind at the Water and Wood Stage. The vendors had their soft lights on, promoting peace and harmony, while the DJ at the Common Stage remixed prog and psychedelic rock—successfully at that. Aum saw the DJ take a swig of beer and noticed many others doing the same. As they continued walking, Aum glanced over at the Main Stage. There was a group of far more active and colorful people there, all enveloped in a deeper collective extasis than he had ever seen. It was almost too much for him to even look at. "That's where it's happening," he thought.

"Can we take a look at the schedule?"

"…mmmkay," Jenn slowed her focused march.

While trying to memorize the performers and times, a man came up behind them. In a ball cap and jeans, with a can of beer in one hand and handheld in the other, he took a picture of each posted schedule. Jenn and Aum stared at him. He addressed their state of disbelief with a shrug, saying, "Now I don't have to remember it." He looked down at his phone, pressed two buttons, and kept on talking, "Yeah I got it. We're good to go."

"Yeah, no shit you don't have to remember! You'd think they'd ban that type of behavior from this place," Aum exclaimed.

"Aum, I'm cold, let's go. The schedule's in between the Common and Main Stage. We can just come back if we're curious," Jenn said with slight impatience in her voice.

"Yeah, I guess so." As he turned to start walking with her, he spied a sticker at the base of the sign. His heart fluttered, but unconsciously he kept walking. The urgent feeling didn't leave him.

"Hold on a sec." He ran back and inspected the sticker. Sure enough, it was the same as on the CD he was given by Trae the Seer. There was no CD but an egg, similar to what Jenn was given upon entering.

"What's in there?"

Aum jumped. Jenn had snuck up behind him silently.

"I don't know," he replied.

"Well are you going to find out, or just sit there?" She was getting angry.

"I think I'll just sit here," he tried joking to calm her down. Of course, it did the opposite.

"Oh brother," Jenn growled. She walked over, picked up the plastic egg, and popped it open. Her expression remained the same.

"Well?" Aum asked. She showed Aum. He silently raised his eyebrows.

"So what. It's a tiny pewter anchor," she concluded.

She closed the egg and put it back. Aum couldn't help but wonder: If he had opened it himself, would it have still been the anchor? Jenn was already four strides away, and he could hear her under her breath, "Goddamn voodoo!"

The anchor obviously meant something to her; it was dissecting her subconscious, maybe even her resistance, and it pulled things up she convinced herself she wasn't ready to look at. As they walked through the trees toward their campsite, she pulled out her own egg and threw it. Even with its florescent color, Aum could not see where it had landed.

Music filled the valley, and Aum and Jenn were sitting next to each other at the shared picnic table, lit by a single tea light. They could not find full connection with the constant vibrating bass frequencies, and now the intimacy of their shared whispers by the river was lost to them as well.

Jenn excused herself politely to visit the bushes near the ladies outhouse. Aum collected kindling and, with healing intentions, created a small campfire. When Jenn came back, he emptied a package of freeze-dried soup into a pot on the fire. They didn't talk much, but he could tell the fire relaxed her. She slid her camping chair over to him and his found wooden stump seat. She snuggled her head into the crook of his neck.

"Hey babe," he said

"Hey."

"Doing okay?"

"I guess…"

The fire crackled, Aum smelled the soup, and his stomach growled. He looked over at Jenn with genuine concern for her mental adjustment to Full Spectrum.

"Just don't take things too seriously, okay?" Aum advised.

Calmly, she responded, "That's easy for you to say. You have at least some idea of what's going on here."

"Maybe a little. But I've never been to something like this before…which, in all honesty, I'm really excited about."

She looked up into his face and saw a childlike smile and a new twinkle in his eye. She smiled too. "So how did you get a ticket?"

Aum told her about the gifts in the center of the spiral labyrinth.

Enthralled, Jenn replied, "She didn't say anything or give you a hint or anything?"

"Nope"

"Pretty wild. How did you know it was this event?"

"Online research. There are lots of photos of past events on the Boards. Usually never an exact time or location, though. There was a much larger promotional push for this event; more than I've ever seen before."

"But there's only a couple hundred or so people here."

"Well, they're all really high-quality people," Aum responded with a laugh.

The constant bass beat eased off, and there was a focus on ambience. Jenn sighed calmly. They began and finished their soup contentedly.

"So, ready to go?" Aum asked.

"Go where?"

"Back out there."

"What? I thought we were going to bed! I don't know, Aum," she said timidly.

"Okay." He quickly synthesized his business pitch back-up plan. "How 'bout I buy you a tea, and we can just wander around for a bit."

It took her awhile to push the thought of their warm, cozy sleeping bag out of the forefront of her mind, and she eventually agreed. "Okay, sure." They cleaned and cleared the space and were off down the path again.

As they walked back toward the central area, they entered a lush world of color and texture. Aum, distracted by the big sound and bright light show, began to head straight to the Main Stage, working up to a full-out sprint.

"Aum?!"

"What?" looking back very confused.

"Tea?"

"Oh yeah, I must have forgot already," he smiled in embarrassment.

A group of bristly steampunks in brown, worn leather and monocles strode past them in tough knee-high boots. They were shouting at each other loudly, gripping filled, foaming steins in their weathered fingers.

"They must be headed to their airship," Aum said out loud.

"What?" Jenn asked as they approached the main drink vendor.

"Nothing, I'm just laughing at my own inside jokes."

"That's good that you can laugh at your own interiors," interjected the tea vendor, who seemed a little on the bored side. "Who else can keep you better entertained?" He was slouched, leaning on the counter. "What can I get for you?"

"Two licorice teas?" he looked at Jenn; she nodded.

"Coming right up."

There were a few people checking out the handful of vending booths. The vendors included jewelers and crystal keepers, tarot readers, glass blowers, custom clothing makers that would make an Italian Futurist proud, and an art gallery with a black light room and an area with prints for sale. There was a veggie burger and yam fry stand, a smoothie and nutbar station, a local organic fruit and vegetable distributor, and finally the coffee and tea shop they stood before.

"Here you go."

"Thanks." Aum paid and tipped him with a handful of change scooped from his pocket.

Jenn looked for a place to sit; it was much less busy now than earlier in the day. It was dark and basically deserted other than a few people circled around the fire pit, their heavy pants and black hoodies soaking up what was left of the light from the dying embers of the fire. Moments after observation, one left the circle to go stand closer to the DJ in the would-be dance area. He had small punk spikes puncturing his black hood at random—like a constellation around his head. Lighting a marijuana cigarette, he stood with the power of antimatter, a being embraced by a black hole. His drag was so big that the last threads of shared normalcy were incinerated at the tip of his joint. He looked up to the stars, welcomed the night and let the dank smoke billow out of him like a coal factory. Jenn watched it spread. The trees breathed it in and the whole environment got high.

To her surprise, Aum put his tea down, moved through the cloud, and picked out a spot on the edge of the would-be dance floor, opposite the manly black hole and in balance to the DJ. Looking over after a sip of tea, she saw in him a transformation, a slackened stiffening and slightly heightened increase in concentration, resulting in an almost unnoticeable sway to the music. Both curious and concerned, Jenn followed over and, standing next to Aum, took a moment to listen and observe for herself. She waited for something to happen. She looked to the DJ, who didn't seem to notice anything past the edge of his turntables. Jenn stared at Aum. A slight panic arose as she tried to speak to fill the awkward void, to fill the feeling of still-point silence.

"Do you want to see what's happening in the woods?" she asked slowly.

Aum noticed another DJ appear in the booth. His face was shadowed by a hooded scarf similar to the one Aum received from Toumai. *Oh yeah*, Aum thought in remembrance, *I'll need to grab that from the car*. The two DJs spoke, and the newcomer laid down a snappy house track on top of the dirty jungle beats. With the slight change in feel, ears pricked up. Another handful of people meandered over from the fire, and simultaneously another couple wandered in from the Water and Wood Stage, moving straight onto the dance floor. Aum smiled, adding a head bob to his sway with the new mix. Responding half-thinkingly, he voiced, "Sure, if you don't want to contribute, that's okay. If we come back in a few minutes, there will be a lot more going on."

Jenn gave him a funny look.

Aum's concentration adjusted, "Um…I mean…If you don't feel like dancing yet, we can continue our wandering." He smiled, still bobbing and swaying.

"Yeah," she pointed to her feet, "…no dancing shoes on yet."

As they started to walk toward the woods, Aum caught the powerful gaze of the newcomer DJ. Still shrouded in shadows, he nodded to Aum. Surprised, Aum nodded back; he tried to pocket the vibe as they moved to the next stage.

They moved through the trees with no set path but with a fractal weaving toward the Water and Wood Stage. Small white LED Christmas lights hung in the transitory space like the night sky. Here the bodily impact of the new sound from the next stage was so great that Aum had to concentrate very hard on putting one foot in front of the next. There were intense frequencies, chanting, and Tibetan bells in the music. Added to that, Aum peered through the trees to see a few bejeweled and costumed women sitting and playing large crystal singing bowls. Blonde and black hair, high cheek bones, petite noses, and concentrated brows were the only discerning characteristics of the three piles of colorfully layered fabrics in front of the DJ booth. Much like a wine glass, they gently hit the side of the crystal bowls. This produced a gong sound, and by sliding a wand around the edge, they gave voice to the resonant vibration of the crystal.

Sensitive to the space, Aum slowed to a stop; Jenn did as well. This had the feel of a private ceremony, and Aum was wary of their intrusion. He looked at the DJ hut and saw a man playing his electric guitar in a very un-guitar-like fashion, producing harmonious ambience. There was another man next to him looking down at his equipment, producing the electronic tones.

Aum took a deep breath and proceeded with slight caution, wary of what potentials could open up. They saw a large group meditating in a circle around the dance floor. They seemed to be emanating a droning sound—with their actual humming voices or the amplified quantum field of their bodies, Aum wasn't sure. Regardless of which, as Aum and Jenn made their way through the final clearing, they saw the geometric form of a star tetrahedron hanging from a tree branch in the very center—two intersecting three-dimensional pyramids. It was made of copper tubes, and quartz crystal amplifiers were placed at each corner. Its slow spinning was an immense and activating presence.

Upon noticing the form, Aum could feel an intelligence make its way through his mind and body. He heard a silent whisper, "Aum, let's go." He looked back at Jenn; she was locked, staring at the geometric formation with enraptured bewilderment. He looked forward, and underneath the form, there was a pile of objects: necklaces, meditation beads, rings, a hat, a feather, a pocket watch, other gems and crystals, and a small piece of artwork. Aum continued to approach, glancing at a photograph of a man in military field gear, and on it, written in black Sharpie, "May peace prevail on Earth." As he read the line in his mind, the music changed noticeably. He froze midstep and instinctively looked over, connecting eyes with the crystal bowl keepers. Their faces weren't happy at all.

"Yup, must be a private ceremony," he thought. He stood for a second with extended deepness, closed his eyes, and shared the vibe he had placed in his pocket from the previous stage, offering it up to the meditators, the performers, the galactic geometries, and the crystal Earth intelligence keepers. He opened his eyes and saw a slight smile hidden behind a blonde lock of the main keeper. Aum's gaze followed her clear blue eyes to look up at the copper and quartz form. The geometries were spinning faster.

Aum's breath left him as he noticed the subtle new vibration. He took a moment to store this vibe in the crown chakra at the top of his head. He turned to look to Jenn; she was still staring, fixated, mouth agape. Aum moved toward her, needing to clasp her hand to break the spell. With glazed eyes, she automatically and unconsciously started moving out of the space.

Staggering out of the trees, Aum and Jenn almost ran into a couple of cloaked figures, as grey and solid as cement pillars. Aum and Jenn stumbled out of their way as they passed in silence. They managed to find their way back to the Common Stage, where they slowed to a stop. Aum turned and looked deeply into Jenn's eyes, checking-in in a big way. Something sparked in them, and she returned, to some extent, to the present with him. In her shell-shocked meditative state, a good majority of what was going on was not being directly observed, questioned, judged, or feared. *This would be a great time to finally get her on the dance floor*, Aum laughed to himself.

Ding!

His vibrating crown of crystalline meta-residue reminded him, not unlike a microwave timer, of the larger, more complex weave of the evening. It started to burn a little, actually. Jenn said softly, "I'm going to sit down for a sec and finish my tea."

"Sure thing, love. I'll be right here." Aum set his tea down with Jenn at a nearby picnic table; then he strode to the edge of the Common dance floor.

The original DJ was still continuing his set from earlier, but by himself. There was quite a crowd now, dancing to his up-tempo snare-drum-laden House fusion. He was looking out into the crowd often, and mixing his music with much more cohesion. Aum let the music move him, bending and swaying, slowly allowing his body to warm up. As he did this, the top of his head began to diffuse on its own. *Weird*, he thought. It floated out, as if it was smoke. He could almost see it in the air, and even if it wasn't airborne, he could certainly see its effects on the dance floor. Random limbs flailed funkier and more haphazardly, arms began to lift into the air, and as the meta-residue smoke reached the DJ, he dropped the perfect marimba line to receive a brief cheer from the crowd. Aum looked and saw a smile on the DJ's face. Even the stoic and focused black-clad group around the fire stirred and took notice.

With this, Aum surrendered further, moving into the momentum evermore. He started to pick up his feet to the beat, his concentrated sway following the internal current up his body and out the top of his head. His hands began to tingle as he spread his fingers wide with tension—the dance was entering back into his palms. With a gentle but immense strength, his arms mimicked tai chi–like tree branches in the breeze, a few deep breaths and few beats away from a full circuit.

Jenn focused on her tea, music far in the background, visually entranced by the ever morphing dance floor. She looked at her cup, noticing its logos, designs, and addresses, linking it to a nearby summer woodland tourist town. Her mental thinking fuzzy, if not entirely off, she drifted back to her office, back to her work life.

"How's your tea there?"

She looked over and hazily noticed a man standing at the edge of her table, drinking from a skinny tin thermos.

"Oh…it's good, thanks."

"Sure smells good. Did you get that at the tea shop?"

"Uh, yeah, just the place right there," she motioned with her head.

"May I?" He motioned to the table.

"Sure."

The man took a seat at the opposite side of the table.

She automatically inhaled more deeply than normal, and her brain restarted after the quantum rewiring. Suddenly, pictured in her mind's eye, she saw the spinning crystal geometry—for the first time. Through her new neural net of questioning dissection, the past hour flooded back to her very rapidly, speeding up exponentially. As a result, words popped out of her mouth, plopping down with physical weight. "What do you know of the Riddle?"

The man's eyes opened wide, the thermos paused at the tip of his mouth. He lowered it and turned toward her. "What makes you ask about that particular technological artifact?"

"Huh? It's a piece of technology? Now I'm really confused."

"It's a lot of things, sister—depends on what drives your curiosity."

"Well, it's not my curiosity, really."

"Well, how are you here, then?"

"I came with my partner," she motioned with a quick nod of her head. They both looked over at Aum to see him not only drenched in but driving the pulsing dance floor entanglement. Instinctively, Aum glanced back at them on beat. Jenn shook her head slightly, as if trying to clear clouds from her eyes. She looked again. It had disappeared, but for a moment, she thought she could see strings attaching everyone on the dance floor, with a good portion of them attached to Aum.

"…Free Zen…"

"Oh, you know him?" Jenn said, reassuring her now pounding heart.

"Yeah, you could say that. I apologize, but I still don't recognize you. What's your name?"

Now on mental overdrive, she responded, half looking at him and half digesting what she saw on the dance floor. "My name's Jenn, and you?"

"They call me the Dragonkeeper."

She thought about laughing but then took a second look at his thick black-chained boots, dark jeans, big black coat, huge hands, and constellation-studded hood. She smelled leather, engine, concrete, grass, and ash and realized he was the man smoking by the stage earlier in the night. She could see the detail in his salt and pepper whiskers, and realizing that he was far too close for comfort, she instinctively froze. He noticed, and her reaction empowered him.

"Yeah, I tend to do that to people," he spoke with his rough Anselmo-like voice. After sucking back a breath of what seemed to be diminishing oxygen, a frightened Jenn managed to sputter, "So how's your fire over there?"

Without a muscle moved, he replied sarcastically and slowly, "Great, really great, thanks." As he spoke, he pressed her into a mush with his words, presence, and heat.

Aum looked back again and saw the conversation more fully. Jenn was a small droplet of water, evaporating fast under a huge hulk of a man sitting next to her, his black coal stove frame nearly standing on top of her.

Aum more than abruptly walked over, and like a line of dominos, Jenn could see the chain reaction on the dance floor. Weights were thrown off balance, steps were slightly off, and then one person bumped another, bumping another, a foot got stepped on, and a person got pushed into the table up front. Just as this started, the DJ went down for another record from his crate; he was too inexperienced to notice and unprepared to take the hit. A tall, thin man crashed into the table, and the record needle skidded forward across the vinyl, causing a disjointed and noisy tailspin. Hearing the racket, Dragonkeeper looked up to see Aum approaching. Aum subsequently eased up his full-throttle charge.

"Cautious…You're smart, boy, or stupid."

"Who are you?" Aum asked, still defiant.

"You mean you don't know him?!" Jenn exclaimed at Aum.

Aum looked at Jenn and then back at Dragonkeeper, then back at Jenn and shook his head.

"Look at your mess, boy," Dragonkeeper motioned back to the dance floor with a nod.

The tailspin was continuing. The dancing had all but stopped. A few people were looking around to see who had pushed them, and a couple of people were looking back at the unfolding confrontation at the picnic table. Aum looked up at the DJ and saw the hooded man had returned. He caught the needle and was controlling it manually, focusing solely on maintaining the harsh noise, forcing it across the records surface. With his free hand, he removed his hood to reveal himself, looking directly at Aum, who immediately recognized his dark shoulder-length hair. He had met this intense and stoic man at his seemingly botched art event. It was Zhe.

"The concentration required here is more than you can fathom," Dragon said calmly over the shrieking noise. "I suggest you consider discarding your excess baggage." People in the dance area were ready to cover their ears and run for cover. Aum was like a frightened animal backed into a corner, and more than a little confused and pissed off at the older man's suggestion. With a single breath, a muscular pranic exhale purely on instinct, he moved the two ends of the circuit he had been maintaining outside of his body into the exact spot where the Dragon was standing.

"Okay! You want it?!" Aum yelled out in frustration, out over the noise.

Everyone heard the loud shout, which brought them to a clear focus. One person on the dance floor even shouted "Hell yeah!" but most others had zero time to react. The other DJ finally came up from under the table, eyes bulging from the continued audio maelstrom, and dropped the fastest, noisiest, most apocalyptic drill and bass track he had in his collection. The mix was perfect. The crowd roared at their own pummeling and directional refocus. Instantly reorganizing the chaos to the new and faster beat, they danced out even further, working their release into the night. With this new peak in collective electricity, Aum didn't even have to do anything. The circuit connected on its own. Aum still pressed it, though, as hard as he could. Like water, the whole area flowed through the circuit, through Aum, and through the Dragonkeeper. Time slowed and Aum looked over at Zhe to see an open-mouthed look of surprise and joy. Looking back at Dragonkeeper, Aum could see no expression. His fire pit had transformed to a blazing bonfire as high as the booths behind him.

The people around the fire, clad in black, howled with delight. A few broke away from the blazing fire and started running circles around the dance floor perimeter, stirring things up into a true break-core pit. The last of the glowing and scantily clad were trying desperately to escape the swirling ocean dance floor.

"Where's the Seer?!" Aum demanded, still holding and pushing and allowing the energetic flow. The motionless Dragon gave Aum a look as if he didn't understand, "Off so soon? No basking in your own momentous glory?" Their two conversations meshed in a lopsided manner, and the crowd pounded and thrashed to the beat-laden noise.

"You know who I'm talking about! Where is she?! The one who gave me this," and he swiftly pulled out the envelope with the letters A-U-M written on it.

Dragon looked stoic and crestfallen, confirmed and beaten. He looked over at Zhe, still at the table. Zhe could only risk a glance up, communicating a nod as he scratched in a new track trying to compact, compress, and compartmentalize the swirling dance floor energy.

"Fine," the Dragonkeeper said cryptically. He swung his head away from Aum and looked toward the fire. "Geraldine! The pendant!" Then back to Aum, "I wrote those letters, but it is not my meta-messaging. You have yet to meet who you truly seek." Dragon looked back to the fire.

Both Jenn and Aum looked over at one of the fire attendants, who seemed to pull something out of the flames. The tall thin woman rushed over, her long legs seeming to take only two or three strides.

She passed something into Dragon's hand. He methodically grasped Aum's right hand, effortlessly, but with spite, pulling Aum forward half a step.

"You embody the new currency, kid." And Dragon placed what Jenn and Aum saw as a medallion into Aum's right palm. It felt like Aum's hand was breaking under the strength and burning from the towering blaze, though it wasn't burning from heat. It felt like the crystal crown he brought from the Water and Wood Stage, but a hundred times as heavy. Aum, without flinching, and fighting the inner panic, allowed the signal to move up his arm and envelop his body. He noticed a direct correlation between the increasing throbbing sensation and the diminishing bonfire.

"The woman, and the answers you seek, can be found presently, and in the future, at the Main Stage." Dragon peered at Jenn, then back at Aum, and released the medallion from his palm. Zhe finally dropped in his fattest half note dubstep beat over the drum and bass's blistering thirty-seconds, and the party stomped and raged with delight as tree leaves and picnic tables alike vibrated from the low bass notes. The black clad support returned to the fire, and a new plateau was reached at the Common Stage. Dragonkeeper walked back to a fire pit of glowing embers, and Aum looked up to see Zhe was gone.

"Let's go." And he was off.

Jen caught up and clasped Aum's left arm, walking quickly with him to the Main Stage. As he swiftly strode, Aum raised his right hand to look at the burn. There was nothing. No mark, no discoloration, nothing. He slowed his pace in confusion.

"What?" said Jenn breathing hard, heart pounding.

"Nothing," and he sped up again, shaking out his hand.

"Did you see the eggshells on the ground?" Jenn asked frantically.

He didn't respond.

"Aum?"

He was looking at his hand again.

"Aum? Did you see the eggshells on the ground?" she asked again.

"No!" he snapped. "I'm sorry, I didn't,"

he added with controlled consideration. "We can go over it later, but now we have to hurry, love."

The music from the Common Stage faded in their ears; they could hear a cheer rise from the crowd at the Main Stage, and even the pluck of delicate harp strings. They walked on a well-treaded path in the grass along the outside of the crowd. There were strange black-light streetlamps set up, which they didn't notice earlier in the day. Aum plodded heavily up the amphitheatre-like rise while Jenn was too petrified and confused at that point to do anything but follow. Their connection strained as they looked at each other and saw sickened faces, glowing teeth, and discolored eyes under the black light street lights.

A gentle female voice began over the speakers. The voice became clearer to Aum as they walked higher, toward the back of the crowd.

"…the message is as follows: Greetings from the Riddle Solver, to all seed pods at the tip of every bow and branch, north, south, east, and west. This message comes to you through both mystic capillaries and hardwired neurological passageways, from the deep and broad heartroots of the World Tree, through the I to the U, touching all from A to Z."

They crested the hill directly under a lamp, able to hear clearly and oversee the entire stage, the performers on it, and many colorful audience members.

The woman's voice continued, "As this collective nation's central nervous network of worldbridgers gather, meld, communicate, coordinate, and coagulate, in non-linear time and non-local space, I encourage you to make daily intentional deposits into the matrix of Maya, recalibrating it from wherever you are at."

Aum connected eye to eye with the woman onstage; she smiled at Aum. He trembled in remembrance, looking into her crystal blue eyes, the piles of fabric from the Water and Wood Stage now gone. It was her. It was Trae the Seer.

"The exponential momentum of change, at this point, is undeniable, and to best prepare this planet for our children, and children's children, there is no reason to hold back, no reason to save your gifts, let them fester or dull. Share your most shining heart in the most immediate of all interactions."

In a space of complete safety, the crowd consciously evolved themselves. Aum could see the impact of the Seer's sound waves on the bodies as they swayed to the underlying angelic tones. Aum saw that Zhe was at Trae's right. He wore a long coat and had a strong vertical stance. In his left hand, he held a dot matrix printout, and coming from his right palm, the glow of an embedded biointegrated LCD screen, fingers gnashing wildly at its surrounding palm-key sensors. The tones in the music became more complex as Zhe typed multiple rhythmic structures in single-handedly.

"The woven tapestry completes, cycles full circle, full spectrum, galactic alignment, core community synergy, bear fruit, plant, and harvest. Now redesign the loom for all to experience; life lived anew."

Zhe punched his thumb key with finality, and the tonal rhythms became a percussive massage. Aum began to rock back and forth. Voices grew in the crowd as tones and chants. The performer/audience barrier was shaky and close to breaking. The crowd desired to speak the transformation out loud.

Trae began singing the words, while Zhe chanted in stride, gutturally but softly.

"Sound, sight, sustenance, memory, and tools."

"Fire, Water, Air, Mineral, and Wood."

The crowd's toning solidified, and people began chanting and singing along, speaking the words as if exactly memorized. Aum rocked harder, with his desire and joy of involvement exploding. They had made it, and Jenn gripped his hand in panicked confusion.

"North, south, east, and west. Spring, summer, fall, and winter. Pilot, engine, fuel, and passenger. Father, mother, son, and daughter."

Jenn yanked on Aum's arm. The trance was too much for her. Aum knew it, but he also knew he had to hold on, maintaining his fullest presence to exchange the fullest of gifts.

The fire-like vibration that had filled Aum's body quickly reorganized in his right palm, exactly where the medallion had been pressed into it. He raised his hand to his face under the black light. His palm glowed. He raised it up 4 inches from his nose, looking through the white-blue-tinge-flashlight-shine to see the pattern behind. It was so bright that he squinted and saw the almost unnoticeable outline of the Sanskrit character for Om, surrounded by a circle and the large spokes of a Buddhist wheel of life, connecting to a circular print of scales, a snake eating its own tail.

"Dream, myth, and archetype. Lead, observe, and support. Sun, Earth, and moon."

Zhe raised his printout slightly to better read it; Trae opened her arms and looked to the night sky. Jenn again yanked on Aum's arm, as if a toddler, and shouted something in his ear. Distractedly staring into his own palm, Aum felt and acknowledged the enormous embrace from the stage and automatically raised his right hand high in the air, lamppost-like in of itself, releasing the white blue flame as a gentle buzz from his open palm over all the bodies in the crowd.

"Day and night. Love and light," in every ear and from every mouth.

Aum managed to look up and see Trae's hair flowing in the wind, and Zhe as he stepped behind her to assist in fully holding open the highest transmission.

"Unity," they both whispered as the crowd shouted in unison and something exploded. There was a flash in the air and a stab in Aum's hand as the bass emitted from the speakers nearly lifted them off the ground, threatening to shake eyeballs out of sockets. There was no music, just pure audio waves. The vibration came from all around them, not just the smoking speaker stacks.

Panic rose slightly in the crowd at the surprise of viewing their focused trance potential physically realized. Aum inhaled as deeply and as calmly as he could, breathing the knife out of his hand with intention. At his lung's emptiest capacity, he looked up at Trae and saw her slightly nod in his direction as Jenn yanked a final time with both her arms.

Like a balloon at the end of a string, Aum was yanked out of his next breath, out of his Riddle position, pulled away from the stage, back to their campsite, their tent, and even into his sleeping bag, all in one fluid motion quicker than time could calculate.

After recovering from the surprise teleportation, Aum called out, "Jenn, Jenn, where are you?" Finding her shoulder and shaking it, she didn't stir. She was fast asleep.

Chapter Six

Everything was black.

He knew he had finished dreaming but had slipped into the transitory space between sleep and waking life. And, as usual, in this panic-saturated void, Aum wasn't able to breathe. It was a black providence filed only by his thoughts. As he convinced himself that suffocating here would be okay, the higher realms of his conscious mind whispered to him, telling him that this was already an experience beyond the edge of death.

He jolted upright with a gasp, catching his breath in deep gulps.

Made it back. Again, he thought.

He looked over at Jenn who was still sleeping deeply, then poked his head out of their tent.

There was still music off in the distance, coming through the trees. It sounded like the Main Stage had a bright morning trance set going on. Nobody in his camping group was awake, though they very well might still be out dancing.

He couldn't hear any birds chirping or woodland creatures rustling. It was not a typical campsite morning. He could, however, smell a campfire or two. "Yeah, that would do it," he groaned to himself. He pulled out his pocket watch—his eyes went wide as he saw the time. Eight a.m. was too early after the full day they had had, though somehow he felt fully rested. He pulled on his pants and a pair of outdoor slippers and then left the tent to collect some firewood. It was empty and silent out in their shared camping space as he started a small fire.

Slowly heads began to poke out—Jes, Ted, even Sara, Ashta, and Pillaiyar. A few more people poked their heads out. The camping slot that had been empty yesterday was filled during the evening after their tea adventure. A slender woman with long brown hair emerged from one of the tents. She wore brown shin-length tie pants and a midriff-revealing top that was mostly covered by long messy hair, punctuated by a dreadlock or two and a collection of necklaces.

"Whoa," Aum breathed.

"Hi, Aum."

"Uh…Hi, Cat. Fancy meeting you here," he said surprised, now fully awake.

"Yeah, pretty crazy, hey." She seemed just as surprised, and a little shy having just stepped out of bed. "…Sharing the same camping area."

Out of the corner of his eye, Aum could see Jes and Ted exchange a look amidst the variety of conversations taking place around them.

This might get a little tricky, Aum thought to himself. "When did you get in?"

"Late last night, just in time to catch the big shakedown at the Main Stage. Were you there? I didn't see you in the writhing pile of bodies."

"I did catch it—well, what I think was the climax. I split after."

"Really? It got sooo good after that! When the speakers went out after the pulse, it took a while to get the music back on, but it was worth the wait. I can't believe you didn't stick around." She paused, tilting her head in consideration and swiping some of her locks behind her ear, "It surprises me, actually, that you weren't in the midst of the repair efforts."

"Well," he shrugged his shoulders, "I guess I was just going with the flow of the evening." He tried to hide the words 'excess baggage,' which were emerging from his memory to the forefront of his mind. Aum quickly took advantage of the pause in conversation to ask Ted and Jes how the rest of their evening went, and whether or not they were around for the 'shakedown' as Cat had put it. Cat poured a cup of water from a large tin and struck up a conversation with Sara and Ashta. It was apparent that the three of them knew each other quite well.

Ted and Jes had a pretty uneventful evening, spending a good portion of it at the Water and Wood Stage. "Yeah, we were in the grips of a deep meditation most of the night," Ted said.

"I'm really glad we did," Jes continued. "I'm sure our evening tonight will be quite a bit more active because of it."

"Charging up the batteries, I imagine," Aum commented.

Inquisitively, Jes coaxed Aum, "So, I'm sure a speaker meltdown was just a small piece of last night's puzzle. What do you think we'll be in for tonight?"

"I'm probably not the one to ask, but…" He moved closer, and in hushed tones Aum began to share more of the bizarre details of his previous night. He described the crystal geometry at the Water and Wood Stage and was about to ask Ted and Jes what they knew of the Dragonkeeper, when Cat interjected, "We're going to head down to the market and see if there's any breakfast fare. Would you like to join us, Aum?"

"No, but thank you. I'm going to tend to this fire a bit more. Maybe we can catch up a bit later, though." Delicately his words expressed a tightrope balance; he wasn't quite sure if he was happy or not to see her.

"Yeah, I'd really like that." She smiled with a light heart, the sun reflecting off her brown locks. The three ladies walked down the path toward the shop area.

"Dude, what was that about?" Ted asked instantly.

"Yeah, are you guys ancient unrequited lovers?"

"Oh man. I can't even begin to explain." Sitting on his stump, he brushed his hands through his messy hair, looking at the campfire. "Man…right in our camping area. I shouldn't be surprised, I guess. That's how it all works, right?"

There was a bit of rustling, and Jenn emerged from the tent. Ted and Jes had started whispering about their own breakfast plans as Jenn walked up, rubbing Aum's back and putting her arm around him. "How all what works?"

"Hey, babe, how'd you sleep?" Aum asked her, poking the fire with a stick attentively.

Forgetting her first question, Jenn spoke in a scratchy morning voice, "Um, pretty good…really weird dreams, though."

"Are you hungry at all?"

"Uh, I don't know yet.…I like your fire." Sleepily, she looked around. The morning sun was shining through the trees. The lack of breeze through the thick underbrush made the air muggy.

"Some fresh air would be nice," she said in the midst of a stretch, a yawn, and while rubbing the sleep out of her eyes. "Morning, guys."

"Aww, you are adorable. Good morning, Ms. Bee," said Jes.

Ted continued, "How was your night last night?"

"Um…I can't remember at the moment. I think it was good. I'm not really a seasoned camper, so anything like this is still way out of my comfort zone." There was a single pause before Jenn asked Ted and Jes, "Do you know if there's any place to jog around here?"

They looked at each other baffled. "Um, I have no idea. I'm sure there is if you look hard enough."

Jenn was reflexively drawn to her regular routine, which usually included a Saturday morning jog. Aum would do a little yoga while she was out, and then the two would follow up together at their neighborhood coffee shop for breakfast. She would bring her laptop to work, Aum would bring a sketchbook or his laptop, and they would soon be busy developing and conquering their own little worlds. The local coffee shop, Beantown, was like a local shared studio for beatniks, mechanics, hipsters, truckers, and climbers. Somehow they all got along, though the construction worker types got really pissed off if their spot was taken. Aum didn't really get much work done; instead he accumulated conversation upon conversation with acquaintances, writers, and other artists. More than anything, it was a way to get a feel for past and upcoming weeks in the local community. When they finally needed to stretch their legs, Jenn and Aum would run errands around town, often ending up at Jenn's parents for supper. Aum disliked this part; he still didn't get along with Jenn's parents, but they were all making a determined effort. Over the past few months, however, Saturdays had not been like that at all. Jenn continued to jog but would mostly stay at home on her computer before heading out to run her own errands. Aum would go down to the coffee shop in the morning alone, sometimes after yoga, sometimes before, spending most of the morning and afternoon there. The crowd at Beantown had changed quite a bit; the once relaxed atmosphere had somehow morphed into an art gallery, with everyone putting themselves on display, playing themselves up—the truckers and construction workers long gone. By the time Aum returned home, Jenn would be gone, usually with a simple note left behind: "Off for the day." *It's just the relationship evolving,* he thought. *Nothing to be concerned about.*

Unbendingly bound to ritual, Jenn asked Aum, "Do you want to go for a jog with me, or is yoga more your style this morning?"

"So is this part of your vacation?" he said sarcastically.

"Auuuum!" she exclaimed, pouting and offended. "I can still run on my vacation right? Right?" looking at Jes and Ted for backup.

"Sure, why not," said Jes.

"Gotta keep that bod in peak condition," said Ted.

"Okay," said Aum, "I'll come jogging with you if you do some yoga with me. How about that?"

"Okay, sure. I'll get changed."

She walked back to their tent area to change out of her sandals, cotton tank top, and shorts.

Ted looked at Aum with a goofy smile, shaking his head.

Jes hit him.

"What?" exclaimed Ted.

Complexities aside, Aum knew Jenn and Cat would run into each other at some point, and all he could do was breathe out the tension he felt and be at peace, knowing it would unfold how it needed to. He had already made his intentions clear with Cat, and having Jenn here was even proof of that. He was sure, if anything, Cat would be the one in the most awkward position. Aum would probably be a brand new person to her, a very large part of his life now inside this Riddle setting. He began to think about the Dragonkeeper's comments again—telling him he shouldn't have brought his girlfriend. He was still pissed off about it. He looked at the palm of his hand again. Who was this guy to be the judge, jury, and executioner? Though if Cat was right, and the best part of the evening happened after he was dragged to bed, there may be some difficulties in fully participating tonight, as he did enter the festival as part of a couple and was focused on experiencing it as such.

Jenn came out with her hair tied back. She was wearing a full Lululemon outfit and some teched-out jogging sneakers. She meant business.

"Well, time to get to work." Aum said, getting up to change.

“Do you guys want some oatmeal before you go?” Jes asked.

“Maybe when we get back,” Jenn said.

“Are you sure? It’s his specialty,” Ted added. “Organic cashews, blueberries, apples, peaches, raw sugar…”

“That sounds fantastic!” Aum said, shouting from the tent.

“It’ll take a while, though—water’s still boiling!” Jes shouted back.

Aum made his way out of the tent. Moth eaten shirt, worn-out Umbro shorts, and his regular indoor soccer sneakers—basically his regular clothes. “Yeah, maybe when we get back. Ready?” looking at Jenn.

“You bet.”

“Have fun,” Ted said, as the two of them bounded down the slope. They started at a quick pace.

“Maybe out the way we came in? I’m sure there’ll be a path around there.”

“Sounds good,” Aum said.

She started toward the parking lot, and he followed. They passed a few gawking onlookers grabbing supplies at their vehicles. Aum could hear them thinking: *Jogging doesn’t belong here!* and *Jogging is a corporate-sponsored hamster treadmill to maintain Babylon’s artificial mechanized pace. Stop being such a chump.* One lady smiled, though. Aum guessed it was because they were doing something healthy as a couple.

They found a path near the far back corner of the parking area, opposite to where they drove in. Aum hadn’t jogged for a while and was having a hard time keeping pace.

“Sorry, hon, can you slow down a bit? I’m not going to make it otherwise. We still have some yoga to do, remember?”

“Right.”

She was pretty focused.

“Are you having fun?” he asked.

“Of course.”

He knew she was far away. He could see right through her to where she was, and she wasn’t with him; she wasn’t there at all. This was just another Saturday to her, with another Monday right around the corner. She had no openness to the events around her. Her defenses were up higher than yesterday, and her receptivity seemed more diminished than ever. To her, this was not some cusp of global resonant transformation, or an event of fifth dimensional possibilities embodied inside interactions with people, but merely just another weekend in her ongoing schedule. Aum was sure she was going through her list of tasks that needed to be done today: errands, e-mails, people, pickups, and contract drop-offs that would have to now somehow fit into her Monday schedule.

"What are you thinking about?" he gently asked.

She let out a surprised gasp, losing her breath as her eyes widened, as if caught in the act. After swallowing back her busy mind between inhales, she replied, "Too much. Thanks."

They had made it out through the dense trees and were jogging up a rough, sun-browned hillside with long grasses. Down through a clearing, they could see the same stream that was near the Water and Wood Stage. Grasshoppers were bounding in every direction as they went, and groundhogs were poking their heads out to see what these curious two-leggeds were.

They reached the clear peak of a hill before it crested into a seemingly impassible raw precipice of cliff. Aum jogged past powdered handholds that looked like they went all the way up and over.

"Check it out; I guess even a lengthy vertical climb doesn't stop some people," he pointed, slowing his jog. Jenn noticed, too, matching his slowed pace. They stopped altogether, catching their breath. They took a seat at a well-worn, makeshift boulder bench and looked back down the hill, facing the rising sun. "Wow." Aum hadn't realized the steepness of the incline they had just jogged. No wonder he was out of breath.

They had a bird's eye view of the entire Full Spectrum event. They could see the parking lot, with row upon row of cars; they saw parts of colorful tents in the camping area through the thick trees; and they saw a rough path near the far end of the playing fields. All the shops looked like tiny shacks, the people like milling ants. The Main Stage and Common Stage were easy to see. The Water and Wood Stage was a little bit more challenging to make out, but it still peaked through the trees.

"What the?!" Aum exclaimed in surprise. He wasn't totally sure, but he thought he could see another structure tucked back in between the Main Stage and Water and Wood Stages, directly behind the Common Stage. They looked like four distinct areas set up with their backstages facing each other.

"What's up, Aum?"

"I think we'll have to do some more exploring when we get back," he responded, still looking intently at the scene.

He noticed a slight change in her as a clear breeze slipped through the air.

"There's your fresh air."

She took a big inhale, as did Aum.

The whole campground was nestled in between where the river and the main road met. Aum followed the winding river all the way across the valley. Far beyond the grassy hills, he lifted his gaze to see majestic frosted tip mountain peaks, reaching toward the sky.

Aum asked again, "So, for real, you're having fun?"

"Of course; it's absolutely beautiful out here."

He took a moment, then asked, "What did you think of last night?"

"What do you mean?"

"Did you have fun last night too?"

"Um, yup."

He tried to be as gentle as possible. "What about the end of our evening, at the Main Stage last night?"

"What do you mean?"

"When you pulled me back to the tent?"

She struggled with her wording, and to save face.

"Look, this is your thing, okay? I don't particularly enjoy it, or understand any of it. I'm just trying to focus on the parts I do enjoy." She was suddenly flushed, red with embarrassment by her emotional outburst. In an apologetic tone, she expanded, "Like the sunshine, the nature…you."

"Okay," content, for now, Aum let it be.

"Are you ready for some yoga?"

"Always."

She took off, and he caught up. They began a downhill descent, making a b-line toward the river. The path double backed and they followed it along the riverbank, back into the trees. Aum matched her stride, and they connected their breaths. It was amazing how much of her he could feel just by being next to her, as if he could feel her soul body—and he knew she could feel him, too. With perfect timing, they looked at each other and smiled. She was so beautiful and powerful in her presence. She was giving herself wholly over to him in that moment, and him to her. It was amazing that the distance they felt over the last few months was so quickly dissolved by the awareness of breath moving through their bodies in unison.

They continued to jog back through the trees. The wind caught the leaves, creating pitter patters within the branches. The gravel crunched under their feet, and as the trees cleared, they entered the back of the playing fields. They could again see the Main Stage down below, and a path off to their left for those camping in branch B.

Aum slowed to a walk, but Jenn continued.

"Where you going?"

"To get my yoga mat."

"A mat? Let's just find a nice patch of grass," he shouted to her. She turned around, hands on her hips like a track athlete.

"Okay…" a frustrated look starting to return to her face.

There were a couple kids running around with homemade fabric kites near them. Soft music came from the Common Stage, and the sound of the creek could finally make it to where they were. The row of black-light streetlamps had disappeared; it was a much different setting in the full sunshine.

Standing somewhere near where they were standing last night, they could see a few people moving gear around on the Main Stage. Aum noticed where they were and looked at his hand again.

"Stop it," she said curtly.

Offended, Aum sarcastically responded, "Do we need some breakfast first?"

"I'm trying really hard here, you know."

"Yeah, so am I."

"So what's the problem?"

"I don't have a problem," admitted Aum. "The problem is that you think I have a problem, when I think you're the one with a problem. Do you have a problem? What's going on? Sorry to ask again, but are you having a good time here?"

"Of course I am….No. No, I'm not. In actuality, I would really like to go home. I'm not able to stop thinking about work and what I should really be doing today." At that, the threads of their intimate connectivity loosened. Aum almost said, "Maybe you should go home," but caught himself and instead asked, "So what work do you have to do?"

"It has to do with that big contract I came back with. It took a lot of work to get it, and now I'm starting to feel overwhelmed. Especially since I can't start on it right away."

"I feel yah," Aum softened. "It'll be waiting for you on Monday though, don't you think? Or will it expand on its own?"

She smiled. "It sure feels like it. I have to do a lot of prep work before then. You know, organize it in my head, so I know what I actually have to do."

"What kind of organizing?"

"Well there's a small bunch of farmers; they're basically an organic co-op that is trying take Grunch Mega to court for deceptive trade practices and negligence, while Grunch is countering with an antichresis abatement."

"Right. Shit, back to the law office." This was very far away from where he wanted to be, but hopefully, if she could get some of this off her chest, she would be more willing to stay, "You'll have to translate for me."

"That's part of the work, actually, so this will help. Basically SunnyValley, the co-op, was surrounded on all sides by Grunch's BigAgra division, and it was closing in. Of course they use all GMO seeds, but unlike most conservative jurisdictions, the municipal law where SunnyValley is located requires a certain distance between organic and nonorganic farming, so that contamination is less likely. Grunch, a beast with no heads, started tilling the land right at Sunny Valley's fence line. The co-op managers noticed and immediately went to their lawyers. By the time their lawyers made any headway, Grunch was about to begin spraying their seed-fertilizer swill into the ground. SunnyValley acted fast and actually set up a community protest. They had a line of people lying out in the fields, surrounding their land where Grunch should have stopped their tilling. These people were ready to be sprayed down by toxins."

"That's pretty crazy."

"Oh, it gets worse," she looked at him intently.

He nodded.

"In a last ditch effort to relieve this ongoing twenty-four hour protest against Grunch's automated machinery, SunnyValley purchased the land from Grunch—that Grunch doesn't actually own—so that their farm, land, and business wasn't ruined. Now since banks haven't been lending money for years, SunnyValley had to take a loan from a company called Lending Basics to cover the cost of the land purchase, which unbeknownst to SunnyValley had just been purchased by Grunch's financial division. Their extended protest only awoke the sleeping giant. Grunch, with what seemed to be particularly malicious intentions, moved their retail division into the community, siphoning off customers, supplies, everything. Unfortunately, SunnyValley had to sell off one of their product lines to Grunch—to better compete with Grunch. I think they sold their fruit juices, their highest selling and most widely distributed product, so they could stay afloat and stay somewhat competitive. The Sunny Valley managers knew it was only a matter of time before their whole organization lost all momentum and energy, not to mention losing their staff and co-owners under the burden of being conquered. So they went back to their lawyers, trying to break the story to the public to put a stop to it. A big, big, last ditch effort."

"And that's where you come in?"

She looked at him painfully. "Yes. The most unfortunate part is that I'm subcontracting directly for Grunch's law office, not SunnyValley," and she sighed heavily. With a downturned gaze, she continued. "Somehow Grunch has a document that promises them the entire SunnyValley farm to leverage the cost of the last minute land purchase." She looked at him. "But of course that land wasn't theirs to sell to SunnyValley in the first place. Seems simple, right?"

"No. Not really, but go on."

"The depth of poison embedded in the dollar goes deep. Grunch knows the document can be easily proven false, so they're willing to fight this obtuse battle, digging deep into the history of both the town and their own corporation in order to try to prove that Grunch owned the land before the municipality was even registered and wrote this municipal law. Obviously their army of lawyers needed reinforcements to do so, and to them, mudslinging, slander, and libel is the language through which the beast speaks. It's in their corporate nature to eradicate human life. They're basically just waiting for SunnyValley to be beaten into submission and to die willingly."

Aum now sighed heavily. "That's a pretty stressful contract alright."

"Yup. This situation has moved all the way up to a national level. I even had to duck the media while I was out east—it's beginning to gain traction in the press. But above all that, it hurts me right here." She pushed a finger into the center of her chest. "I feel like I'm a traitor, trapped on the wrong side, with the bad guys. 'Cause they are. I know they are. These people are the scum of the earth and have worked hard at it. And I'm working for them!" From the Main Stage hillside, she looked back at the market area, "I'm pretty sure the people here can smell it on me!"

"Maybe some yoga will clear out the stench," he smiled.

"Maybe." A lightbulb seemed to turn on in her mind. Jenn thought about the fact that her office offered lunchtime yoga sessions for stress relief and community health. Without her mat, she recognized her practice had become part of the problem. She now saw the fluid body-based spiritual practice co-opted, mechanized by the greater industrial system to repair and polish its cogs. She looked down at the logo on her shirt. "I'm such a chump," she whispered to herself. Aum looked at her, not catching the quiet comment. *It would be better if I didn't do yoga*, she thought.

"You know what? Let's go get something to eat."

"Um…okay," Aum said. He could now easily see the efforts she was taking to be here, the stretch from one world to another, and he loved her ever more deeply because of it.

"The yoga can wait." She spun around a third toward to market. "No, wait. I need to change first." She spun around another third toward the campsite. "No, wait." She completed the full 360 and stepped to Aum like a magnet, wrapping her arms around him tightly, pressing her entire body into his. A couple tears escaped her eyes and fell onto Aum's shirt. Before he knew it, she was kissing him on the mouth, hard and licentiously. "Let's go change!" And she pulled him back to their tent almost faster than the previous night.

After emerging from their tent, they saw a couple bowls of oatmeal left on the picnic table. They hadn't noticed them on the way in but gobbled them both down. Delicious, just as Ted had promised. Jenn looked over at Aum; her eyes were bright and she was present with him again. "I think we should go get some more to eat," she said.

"Yeah, you bet," and they walked down to the market area.

There were much less people down there than Aum had expected—a few handfuls at best. Maybe everybody was still sleeping. It was only noon, so that was a good possibility.

Aum and Jenn got in a short line at a bamboo shack next to the tea shop. Near the front was a chalkboard with the available brunch selection. Before Aum had a chance to read it, there was a gentle hand on his arm.

"Try the smoothie, sweet Aum. It's fantastic." Aum turned and saw it was Cat. Their eyes locked like magnets, and she continued to touch his arm. Finally, after piercing into the realm of prolonged awkwardness, Jenn cleared her throat. On cue, Ashta and Sara strolled up next to Cat. After briefly and curiously checking out Jenn, like a newly seen creature in the vast Riddle world, Cat smiled and the three of them continued on back to camp.

"She a friend of yours?" Jenn asked curiously, eyebrows raised.

"Um, yeah, friend. She is actually. I met her at a couple different Riddle events, the one where I got my ticket included," he shuffled his feet, with a slight nervousness, suddenly back on the tightrope between worlds. "That night she had some interesting mainstream press for her work. How much of it went into Riddle details, I'm not too sure."

"She's a performer…?"

"Yeah, and she's actually camping in our same quadrant."

Waiting for the rest of the story, Jenn's piercing gaze helped grow Aum's inner anxiety. Breaking away, Aum noticed beyond her a lily patch of star-flowered Solomon's seal, just a few steps away from the vending booth.

He gave a quick look back with a Cheshire grin. "Take it easy," he said with a smile. "She knows I'm with you." He casually strolled over to the patch and picked a beautiful one, placing it in her hair. "Now it's official. For all to see," looking deep into her eyes. He brushed her hair behind her ear. "Thank you for choosing to be here."

She smiled.

"Okay. You're off the hook this time, mister, but I've got my eyes on you…all three of 'em."

They both ordered smoothies, buckwheat pancakes, and a fruit-granola-yogurt mix. Aum also ordered an organic orange juice.

They grabbed some cutlery and took their meals to a nearby table. Shortly after they heard, "Do you guys mind if I take a seat?"

"Be our guest," Aum said.

"Awesome, Thanks. Pretty nice morning, hey?" said the young man who just joined them

"Yes, it's very beautiful," Jenn said.

"Unfortunately I heard there's supposed to be some showers tonight."

"Really?" replied Aum.

"Yeah, that's okay though. You have to be pretty dedicated to make it here, but even more dedicated to stay and fully participate."

"Yeah, I know what you mean." Jenn asked, "Any advice on that?" taking another mouthful of pancake.

"Um," deep thoughts moved through his youthful yet weathered face, "with risk comes reward." He swallowed his own mouthful of brunch. "For example, I got shipped out to Montreal a couple weeks ago, not really knowing too many details. I risked an impromptu street performance on a busy corner and, as a reward, I was asked to perform at a private party later that night. From there, I somehow made it here, but I can't quite figure out how to explain it this early in the morning."

"No worries," said Aum.

"I'll be doing a little piece later on tonight."

"Really?" said Aum

"What do you do?" Jenn asked.

"I juggle."

"Juggle? How long have you been doing that?" asked Jenn.

"About eight years of arduous self-study," he responded.

"Wow, I'm looking forward to seeing your work." Aum voiced, enthusiastically.

"Thanks. Hey, how did you guys get your tickets?" he asked.

Aum answered first. "A pretty similar situation with me. I was given a ticket quite literally with my name on it, at the center of a spiral mandala, a labyrinth. I'm still getting to the bottom of it. Glad to be here nonetheless."

"Cool. It's pretty neat that you can't buy tickets for this event, hey? And you?" he asked Jenn. Through a small wave of shock at this statement, Jenn answered, "Um, through a coworker, I guess. I didn't really get a ticket, per se, but I still made it in."

"Wow, welcome," he said, with a knowing lilt that made it sound as though he was the one person who knew the true significance of the florescent eggs.

"Thank you. Thank you for your kindness," Jenn said honestly.

He finished his last bite and said, "Well, I'm off to my dish pit duties. Can I take your plates and cutlery?"

"Wow! Sure," said Jenn.

"Thanks, man. We'll see you tonight," said Aum. Jenn quickly added, "Any time in particular?"

"Whenever the party gets started," he said with a smile.

"Hmm, he's cool," said Jenn quietly as he walked away.

They slowly worked away at their smoothies, observing the coming and going of many different characters. There were boisterous and strange laughing circles, a group of young tai chi enthusiasts that morphed into partner yogis, which morphed into a full-out contact dance session. Aum thought he recognized a couple guys from up in the tree yesterday, but he wasn't quite sure.

"We should go join them," Aum said jokingly.

"No way, not even close," Jenn replied.

As if they were overheard, one of the guys came up to inform Aum and Jenn of a kundalini dance workshop beginning in a few minutes at the Main Stage.

"Well, I'm not too much of a dancer," Jenn admitted, but he was persistent. "You've got a body, right?"

"Um, yeah," said Jenn.

"And you can move it, right?"

"Yeah."

"So there you go—no denying it now. You're a dancer. It's a great space to practice your own self-acceptance and push your limitations." She was struggling to say yes.

"Sounds great," Aum answered for both of them.

"Alright, see you then!" He put his hands together, bowed slightly, entering the contact dance circle via a handstand. He looked like he was going to topple over, but then was caught by the others. The balance of their entire group shifted, and out of it, a cartwheel competition began.

"Wow, all these people must be taking vacations from their day jobs at the circus."

"Who better to learn from?"

They finished their smoothies and meandered over to the Main Stage. It didn't look like there was anyone over there, so they stopped at the schedule, looking for the dance workshop—it wasn't listed. Supposedly there was a morning meditation happening. They looked back the way they had come to find a parade moving toward them. It seemed to surround them as they made their way toward their intended destination.

"Yes!" a woman shouted loudly from the direction of the Main Stage, as they heard the scratching in of KRS-One's "I Am There." The parade whooped emphatically as they entered the dance area, starting the workshop with some bouncing slow-motion B-boy stalls—if there was even a start and finish for these circus folk.

The same gentleman who invited them was on stage with the headset mic: "Let's give it up for J.D. Moonshine's great timing and MacGyver-like engineering skills; she's a scholar and a lady." There was a joyful cheer from the crowd, mostly emphatically from the other women. He continued, "Okay, for any newcomers here, welcome. If this is your first kundalini dance workshop—even deeper welcomes. My name is Solarus, and I'll be leading us through this sacred chakra dance, elevating your energies to the twelfth octave, a cosmic resonance of love and truth. Let's give it up for everyone here."

There was another large cheer from the group. Aum and Jenn clapped, standing near the outskirts. Aum smiled. This was a safe space where the facilitator could put a cap on the flow and intentionally guide and reroute momentum. Aum knew, and within the curling tips of his deep smile, he knew they all knew that this was just a warm up for the free-flowing informal facilitation of a busted-out quantum Riddle space. He could feel it. It was there, just behind a curtain waiting to be lifted when the real show started.

In the midst of a group of fifteen dancing participants, Aum looked over at Jenn; she seemed to be into it, swaying a little to the left and right. Definitely not classically trained, nor full of flower-power whimsy. She placed her hands over each chakra, as instructed by Solarus. Bending only at the knees, sometimes moving her hips, her eyes closed, going internal with each word and sound. It looked as though she was pulling or pushing each of her wheels out of mudholes, having to go very deep into her own sensitivity to move them into motion.

In the guided trance, none of the participants noticed the growing circle of people around them. The newcomers just stood in a circle, surrounding the space, holding the space, as Solarus instructed. This of course intensified the dance; participants became performers, embodying more than their single selves, becoming as open to possession as voodoo dancers. Some wiggled and writhed as the energy flowed through their chakra systems. For some of the workshop veterans, it was a deep personal tissue cleansing and internal emotional mining.

Aum was so proud of Jenn. She was the least physically animated in the group, with others bounding and stomping all around her. With her eyes closed, letting herself move naturally, Jenn gravitated toward the center, while others, the circus performers, naturally moved to the outer boundaries between audience and participant, allowing and pushing the shared chakra energy around the circumference. She didn't realize it, but she was present with all of them, a grounded anchor, almost protected, peeling layer after layer, reaching ever deeper into open vulnerability for all to see. The collective resonance of these internal actions spread far out from the focused dance group, becoming the main festival activity for the afternoon.

Cat, Ted, Sara, and all the rest of their camping unit joined the outskirts of the circle, subtly recognizing and supporting Aum and Jenn as the dance became a whirling tornado. They watched as the creative expression of trance, diving in and out, within and through the beat-laden bodies, continued over the next hour, after which DJ Moonshine began to bring them to a pristine close. The supporting onlookers contained the energy, while Solarus piped in on the headset: "Now, as we reach the top chakra, feel it cycle back down, ride the energy, ride the torus back down to the Earth, include the Earth beneath our feet. See the chakra energy we've cultivated here in this circle—see it flow out through the ground to our beautiful surroundings—the trees, the birds, the clean air, and most of all each other."

He let Moonshine ease the up-tempo beats back to atmospherics and continued: "Now take a few deep breaths to calm as we complete our journey here, return back to your own bodies, open your eyes if you have them closed, look around and connect with the beautiful beings around you. Give out at least one hug to fellow chakra-wheel spokes, your fellow dancers, and one to someone in our supportive chakra-wheel rim, our active observers. This has been wonderful for me and I hope for you as well. Thank you and enjoy your day. Up next we've got a mandala session with Cat?" He looked around nonchalantly. "Is that right?" From where she was standing, Cat gave a loud, "Whoo! Yah! Mandalas!"

"Alright Cat! Till then, take it away, Moonshine." And some house party music made its way in, as hugs were passed around and the dispersion of energy slowly filtered out to the rest of the campsite.

Jenn didn't even need to look for anyone to hug; there was a huge hug line-up for her, one of which was Cat, who went in and hugged Jenn wholeheartedly and kissed her on the cheek. Jenn was pretty surprised, as was Aum.

"Are you going to stick around for my workshop?"

"Oh, I'm not too sure. I think I need some time. It's been a pretty big day so far," Jenn was tipsy and not quite back in her body. She snuck in under Aum's long wing of an arm.

"Fair enough," Cat smiled, in open respect. "I'll probably see you guys back at the camp later on," and with that, she ascended to the stage and began facilitating her own workshop.

"Can we go somewhere? I need some quiet space," Jenn whispered.

"For sure."

Aum led her back toward their camping area but then veered along the tree line. He found a lush patch of grass a couple strides in. It looked like part of an old overgrown campsite that had long gone unused.

"Thanks." She sat down and closed her eyes in meditation.

"Um… are you okay, Jenn?"

"Yes."

"…Can I sit with you?"

Her eyes still closed, "Of course."

Aum sat cross-legged with his knees facing hers.

Over an hour passed in total stillness, existing as pure breath. Eventually they stirred.

"Wow, that was great," Jenn almost inaudibly whispered. "I'm glad we did that."

"The meditation, or the dance workshop?" Aum whispered back.

"Both."

"Yeah, everyone really appreciated your participation. What did you think?"

"About the meditation, or the dance workshop?"

"Either."

"Well," she said pondering. "I don't feel quite as stinky."

He laughed hard, took her hand, and kissed it. "It was great to see you on the dance floor."

"It was so scary I had to keep my eyes closed," she said shyly. The very tips of her mouth curled coyly into a small smile.

"Yeah, I noticed." He hadn't seen that smile in a very long time.

They got up and moved from their secluded meditation area, walking back toward their camp to make some food.

"I'll meet you there. I need to make a visit to the ladies room."

"You bet."

Jenn walked up the sloped path toward the outhouses. She was still smiling.

She turned the corner, about to grab the door handle, when she hit a solid, warm, smoky black wall.

"All smiles?!" Dragonkeeper intoned sarcastically. With gravel in his vocal chords, "You got your egg ready? It's just about time to earn your admission!"

In total shock and surprise, she shrieked, "Stay away!" and jumped inside the outhouse and locked the door behind her.

Aum got back to the site. There was a big, makeshift kitchen production happening.

"What's going on?" he asked Ted, who was sitting on a stump, drinking a beer.

"Well, I got delegated to silent meditation duty 'cause I was being too loud and opinionated or some shit. Jes is cooking some tandoori something or other—which is what smells so fantastic. Cat's got a big pot of miso going, Sara and crew have some homemade humus and tabouleh, and there's pita bread. Lots of pita bread…You know, a regular smorgasbord of international potluck tastiness. Got anything you want to cook up with us?"

"Well, I've got jasmine rice. That wouldn't be too hard to do up on the fire pit." He took a look around Jes's workstation. "Need some rice?"

"Yes! I think I forgot to pack some."

Aum went to his tent, grabbed a pot, a small canvas bag with rice, and got started. The water came to a boil, and he threw the rice in. Shortly after, "Okay, the tandoori tofu tikka is ready; how's the rice coming, Aum?"

"Oh, a couple more minutes."

"We could start with soup," suggested Cat,, "I'm starving after that mandala workshop." And they all agreed.

He didn't have a watch, but Aum knew an adequate amount of time had passed for a washroom visit and started to become concerned. They were finished their soup, the rice was ready, and they were starting on Jes's dish when Jenn finally walked up to camp.

"There's a bit of soup left, Jenn," Cat said, overflowing with positivity.

"Okay."

She grabbed a bowl and poured the last of the soup into it. Aum finished dishing out some rice to the last person in the line. "You alright?" he asked Jenn.

"Yes," though she looked visibly shaken.

"Jenn," he said concerned.

"Just leave it; I'm okay."

Everyone noticed and looked in their direction.

She smiled politely. "Who made the Indian dish?"

"Jes." A few pointed out

"Smells fantastic." She walked between them all, vibes a bit frantic and noticeably hesitant. "I'll take this last plate, if that's okay?"

Her social defenses were up again. For whatever deep chakra dance work she had just done, she had slipped, relapsed, and subtly reconnected back to her old life. For reasons Aum could not fathom, Monday was Jenn's lifeline out of there.

The delicious smell rode the cool early evening breeze out into the forest, inviting attention and further dinner disruptions. A woman walked up to their camp.

"There she is!" said a welcoming Cat, as if she had been waiting all day for her.

It was one of the dirty dreaded Earth children from the previous day, now cleaned up, wearing dramatic make-up, a leather top, skirt, and ass-kicking adventure boots. The worn and weathered woman responded with a tired small wave to their collective greeting, "Hey, I'm Jaga." She introduced herself, but was somewhat oblivious to everyone. "Made it…finally. Do you have a big kettle we could use?" she asked Cat directly.

"Like a tea kettle? I didn't bring one. Did anybody bring a kettle?" Cat shouted out.

"Tea would be great," said Ashta.

Aum was about to suggest using a plain pot to boil water for tea, when the whole group heard a shout from the main path. "We've got one you can use!"

One man gingerly poked his head around some bushes, "You guys looking to make some tea? We've actually got a tea kettle and portable stove on the go at our camp as we speak, but we lack the leaves. We're on a mission. Whatever you would be willing to share of your blend would be fantastic—a communal pot maybe?"

"What do you think?" Cat asked Jaga.

"Yeah, there should be enough to share."

As if to entice them further, a second man responded from behind the bushes, "We've got a radio station in our RV."

"A radio station?" said Pillaiyar in disbelief.

"An RV?" said Jenn.

"Yes, we transmit our radio with twenty-four-hour-a-day programming," the hidden man shouted.

"A pot of mushroom tea and independent radio sounds great to me," said Jaga.

"Shit, now we're talking," said Ted.

Jenn's eyes went wide.

"We can stay and clean up," offered Sara.

"Really?" said Cat

"Of course; it's the least we can offer in thanks." Pillaiyar looked directly at Jes, then at Cat, then at Jenn. Jenn looked at Aum. Aum looked at Cat.

"Wow, okay. Let's do this," said Cat.

“You’re welcome to swing by after,” shouted the newcomer with the RV as they walked.

“If it’s meant to be,” Pillaiyar said, smiling; he began to clear dishes.

Ted, Jes, Aum, Jenn, Cat, and Jaga followed the two men back the way they came, out to the parking area. At the furthest spot down, in a nook of overhanging trees, was a large Airstream. Painted on the side was a mint condition Valkyrie mural, with a group of Norse warrior gods, of course looking as sexy and as eighties as possible; a quarter of the painting was of silver accented hair. There weren’t too many cars at that end of the grassy parking area, so the two men, who introduced themselves as Gus and Flarety, had relative privacy. There were a couple tents set up beside the Airstream, with a large overhanging tarp coming off the RV. There was also a couch that converted to a bed inside, as well as a beat-up couch outside, under the tarp, with a couple relaxed campers hanging out on it. From the flattened nearby brush, it looked as though they had dragged a picnic table through the woods for their own use—that or a herd of deer had recently moved through the area. On the picnic table, Jaga found the large kettle already boiling on a green Coleman stove. She put the mushrooms in, along with a metal tea ball containing a custom leaf and herb blend to accent, and turned down the heat.

“Where are you from, Gus?” Jenn asked

“I am from Oslo. Did my accent give me away?”

“Well, you’re not a Newfie; that’s obvious. Is this your trailer?”

“Yes, my brother painted it. Do you like it?”

“Yah, it’s great!”

“I came here for technical college and met Flarety there.”

Flarety added, “Yup, though the two of us found it hard to focus on classwork. We were very opposed to developing new electronic consumer products lines for our corporate-sponsored school; just too many other interesting things to be working on.”

“Yeah we bought a kit to build a radio transmitter a couple years ago. We’ve been broadcasting ever since.”

“What’s your range like?”

“Well, with the AM channel you have to be within about a hundred kilometers of the trailer, but our digital podcasts have pretty much no limitations. Anywhere a handheld or even a hand-embed can get a signal, we're good to go."

"What's a hand-embed?" Jenn whispered to Aum. Aum whispered back, "It's a digital touch-screen permanently embedded into a persons hand. It's a new trend amongst post-human's."

"Gotcha," Jenn said, pretending to know what post-human was.

Flarety had continued while they whispered, "We really only go digital in coordination with a GPS mapping site, to let people know where the Valkyrie is, and promote our roaming AM signal. Since 'The Man,'" he quoted the air, "went digital, analogue's become the new underground."

"Yeah, we do a full festival tour in the summer. Sometimes we interview DJs or performers, or do after-event broadcasts."

"We just go with the flow most of the time—gonzo style of course," He took a swig of Wild Turkey from a mickey.

Gus continued, "It's kind of like driving around with a bullhorn, but people have to be tuned in to receive the transmission."

Aum smiled. *All layered communication becomes so straightforward with a Norwegian accent*, he thought. He could hear some classic house beats playing from the speakers in the RV, so he poked his head in. Tall and lanky, Gus poked his head in through a side window. "That's just a random selection from our digital jukebox broadcasting now, though we do have turntables to go totally analogue when the time is right. You want to do a live on-air interview?"

"No thanks." Aum was already feeling his nerves due to this quick change of events, and felt he needed to focus. "I think I'll pass for now, but shit that's cool; it's like a space ship in there."

"I'll go for it," Ted volunteered, poking his head in after Aum.

"Jenn you should come check this out," said Aum.

Flarety continued talking with Jes, Aum, and the rest of the group, while Jenn poked her head in on Ted's interview. "That broadcasting equipment is nothing. Our buddy is a mad engineer, a huge Bucky Fuller enthusiast. He rigged the whole deal, the truck, the trailer, the computer equipment, the antenna, all of it to run off solar, methane, and momentum."

"Momentum?" Aum replied in surprise.

"Yeah, I don't fully understand it myself. He once compared it to space travel; you just need that initial blast and you can keep going forever— as long as you don't hit the brakes."

"An initial blast of methane?!" Jes commented.

Gus and Ted came out.

"That was quick!" said Flarety. Ted shrugged his shoulders. "I couldn't think of anything to say that was broadcast worthy."

"Did you check out the can?" Jes asked Ted, receiving a confused look.

"Oh, did Flarety tell you?" Gus resumed the methane discussion in a very excited, aptly foreign manner. "The toilet is actually indirectly attached to our truck's engine, so it's very important that we eat right."

A woman gingerly approached amidst of the huge eruption of laughter at Gus's expense, "Hey guys?! Um…" It was the same blonde who was handing out maps the previous day, now with a gentle smile, growing from her interruption of the jovial souls. "Nice. I just wanted to let you know the opening ceremonies are starting in ten minutes."

Between laughs, an explanation from Flarety, and an eventual grin from Gus, a number of big "Thank yous" reached the woman as she walked back through the vehicles down to the camping area.

"Sweet timing. Who would like the first mug?" asked Jaga.

No one jumped immediately. "Sure, I'll take it," Ted said.

"Are you guys going to check out S.O.S.?" Jes asked Gus and Flarety.

"Yeah, you bet. That's one of the main reasons why we came," said Gus.

"We volunteered to broadcast their set, but they declined. I suspect they've got something special planned," Flarety added. "Who knows what, though? I guess we'll find out soon enough."

Jittery with anticipation, already engaging with the plant consciousness, preparing his mind and body, Aum went second, filling full his portable mug.

"I should note that this batch usually starts a little rough, but then everything turns to paradise," Jaga said to him.

"Noted," Aum said with thanks. He looked at Jenn. Her eyes went wide, though curious. "I'll just take a few sips from yours if that's okay." He nodded and smiled.

"All set?" Ted asked. Jes, Cat, Aum, and Jenn nodded.

After exchanging farewells and gratitudes, the first group of Riddlers walked down toward the Main Stage for the opening ceremonies. Jaga, Gus, Flarety, and their campmates stayed behind while the second round of tea began to boil.

They arrived just in time to receive the final prayers. There was a man down on the dance floor addressing the growing crowd. He was surrounded by colorful dancers, open-heartedly embodying his words in their flowing movements. He was barefoot with well-worn green overalls, and was shirtless but covered in tattoos to make up for it. He wore a gatsby cap, with long grey braided pigtails coming down over his shoulders, had a full beard, tinted circular spectacles, and was shaking a small rattle while he sang. There was another dark-skinned man who, as the tattoo-shirted shaman spoke, began to light incense sticks and plunge them into the ground at four balanced spots at the center of the dance floor. Between these is where the coveralled man stood, firmly supported by a walking cane.

For a moment, Aum watched the dark-skinned man. He had long black hair and seemed as though he might be of Indian or Turkish descent. With a collection of deep crevasses of age and wisdom, he prayed and bowed and prostrated himself on the Earth as he lit each stick. It was an equally powerful devotional action, an echoed accompaniment to the shaman's words and the dancers' creative expression. The smell filled the woods with a full and captivating champa scent, connecting all who noticed it to the prayers he gave. The sacred dancers acted as a deeper M-field spatial clearing. Whatever lingering feelings that remained from the previous night, or those that had not been shed during the day, were given a frictionless breath-based experiential pathway to be release.

The shaman completed his invocations toward the four directions, praying for the presence of the Great Spirit animals: Snake, for the east and the shedding of skin; Jaguar, for the south and the protection of the medicine space; Hummingbird, for the north, to assist in listening to the whispers of the ancients and the ones to come; and lastly Eagle, for the west, to fly with the Great Spirit.

The man with pigtails stood in the center and shook his rattle toward the ground. "To the Earth, to the stone people, the plant people, the four- and two-legged, and the creepy crawlies. To fin, fur, winged, and mineral brother and sisters, to all our relations—gratitude."

Then the same man who held the microphone yesterday, sampling the stick and rock Earth children, entered the opening ceremony with his laptop up on the Main Stage. Behind the prayers were the sonic layerings of low-toned chanting monks, played with excessive reverb, where details became diluted.

The tattoo-shirted man shook his rattle toward the sky, speaking slowly and deliberately. "To the Sun, and Moon, and all the Star Nations who have allowed each and every one of us to gather here, to sing and dance deeply in life—gratitude." He tapped the rattle against his chest, thumping it as if a heartbeat. "To the in and out, the pulse of presence, the collective 'I', the witness listening, and blissing—blessings and heart network connection." He addressed the crowd directly. "Again, thank you for your attendance and support this year; deepest gratitude, love, and blessing to everyone involved. You dream this dream. I implore you for your continued conscious participation through the potentials of Mother Earth's presence. Embrace the raindrops as collective confirmation and environmental collaboration, as our uplifted consciousness soaks through and permeates to the greater collective of mankind's body of water." He put his hands together and bowed slightly. "May peace prevail on Earth. Namaste."

Everyone responded with a collective "Namaste," clapping and cheering in agreement as swirling supernatural complexities filtered through the chanting monks.

Aum and Jenn looked at one another and smiled. Jenn motioned for the mug and took a few sips. Aum exhaled and attained a deep and unmatched reverential silence within an adrenaline-saturated bloodstream, having already finished half the mug.

He gazed at the audio performer. Much like the setting, the performance was now a bright fluffy cloud-like dreamscape leaked into reality through technology, embodied in invisible audio; it was an ever-changing bath of beatless atmosphere. The audience reaction was positive, and participants easily immersed themselves with the sacred dancers, like fish within the plant life in the ocean, swaying to the pulse of the changing gravitational tides.

Unlike classic turntables, MIDI hardware, even CDJs, this laptop performance gave away no clues as to the connection between body mechanics and audio. The performer's touch, who in this case simply went by the name Daniel, was entirely hidden. Other than track pad finger flicks, the music's production, its manipulation, design, and control, was a purely cerebral expression.

A computer as a creative instrument has no limits—audio software can be linked, within patched drivers and plug-ins within multiple programs within programs. Any sound that exists as a file on a hard drive, a handheld, a portable stick, or even comes through a live microphone, can be used as source content, whereas with turntables, a performer is limited by their record collection and the number of decks they're using. DJs usually choose a section on a track on one side of an LP and play it along with another section of another track on another LP. A fader is used to blend records back and forth accordingly—switching records to blend in a new sound, new mood, or beat structure—stitching together a performance piece by piece, by feel, by plan, or both. Even the emotive and structural process of the evolving dance floor's relationship coincides with the changing technological tools for audio production.

Live hardware instrumentation is a rare feat, but very successful if everything manages to work. Drum machines, samplers, synthesizers, 303s, 404s, 505s, 606s, 770s, 808s, 909s usually require multiple performers to get a full sound, and a digestible unifying rate of change in rhythm and melody. This original content, if recorded to file, can become the found source files of a laptop DJ, or of traditional LP DJs if pressed to vinyl.

To accompany Daniel, three additional men got up on stage. Aum looked up and saw that Zhe was in the center. Aum gasped slightly, and Zhe seemed to notice. Exhilarated, Aum didn't know Zhe was a member of S.O.S. Aum grounded himself, refocused, broadened his perspective, and connected to the larger anticipatory wave of the audience.

The three men made final setup adjustments to a tidy, extensive, and organized pile of hardware next to the single laptop performer. More metaengineering than anything, they got to work on their equipment. The incoming high-fidelity sound made Aum drool like Pavlov's dog. The outgoing computer sound card was no match for the old-school electricity-driven sound. Like a train slow to start and next to impossible to stop, the complex mix of generated ambience and rhythmically unstructured beats, in combination with these three artistic and mystic personalities, embodied a never-before-seen creative breakthrough. S.O.S. promptly lead all participants to the clear, crisp edge of the entire world.

"And up comes the veil," Aum said aloud.

The individual swaying dance floor bodies restructured naturally with the change in sound personality. The fleeting obscurity of the music made it hard to stick in Aum's memory, yet in the moment, it seemed as though he would never forget the energy and emotion brought up by the full tapestry of sound. It was real time, unreferential, brand new, emergent core content.

The amount of people dancing swelled beyond the amount watching. The members of S.O.S. soon stood from their sitting positions and were all bobbing up and down polyrhythmically with what they were creating; they looked like pistons or gears, larger extensions of their machines.

As Aum danced, he caught a glimpse of Sara, along with Pillaiyar and Ashta at the side of the stage. He was thankful to see them and finally remembered where he had met Sara. She was one of seven beings in the extremely powerful Matrika-Pleiades Healing Circle. She went by the full name Saraswati. Aum remembered that she was so powerful, in fact, that the wave of her hand in greeting caused a wind that could be felt from a block away. He began to remember seeing Pillaiyar and Ashta as well, both of whom observed the scene stoically, while Sara grinned widely as she watched the dance floor. There was a group of others with them, all at side stage; it looked like all Healing Circle members were present at the gathering. As a frequency geared up, Aum burst out loud, "Holy shit—this is something." A large banner was unrolled onstage with a Mayan calendar glyph. As Aum's tea kicked in, the graphic started to shimmer and move.

The music pulled and pulsed as the sun began to set. A woman crept on stage with a stork graphic on her white t-shirt and offered something in a plastic bag to one of the trio. Drugs? A disc with the freshly delivered sounds of heaven? Aum found it very peculiar. Even more peculiar, shortly after that, a man with a cowboy hat, who looked like a local farmer, walked up to the performers onstage. Who was this guy in full cowboy regalia? He looked over at Cat, Jes, and Ted, who were all on the dance floor, engulfed within the music. Jenn was sitting cross-legged near the edge.

"I'm the owner of the property; here's your bribe," Aum thought he could hear.

The cowboy passed one of the performers a stuffed envelope. *What?! A bribe? Paying them off for their services?* As the music continued, the members actually got up and left the stage to receive an even larger package from him.

At that moment, seemingly to distract from the exchange, the young juggler from lunch strode out into the crowd with a long, flowing, hooded purple robe. Behind him walked a very weathered man wearing the same skin as a tree, holding two torches in each hand. Almost instantly, a crowd drew around the man in purple. Some stayed to dance, but the majority were far too curious. The man in purple pulled out three clear crystal juggling balls. They started to move around in his hands with little or no effort, as if he was using a mass of psychic energy to do so. Within each crystal ball was the reflection of the flames held by the tree spirit. As they performed, something old emerged here; the ground-up shops and renaissance carnival atmosphere, the surrounding woods, mountains, and creek all fostered a unique sense of sixth dimensional travel. The relationship to medieval times became profoundly authentic.

Dark clouds quickly rolled across the sky above.

Eventually an entire army of eight crystal balls were rolling up and down his arms, floating in the space around his body and reflecting the holo-demigraphical universe that can be seen by meditating on fire and the sky's setting sunlight.

As the orange sphere of the sun disappeared behind the hills, the music rose to a crescendo. Dark clouds extinguished the last of the sunlight, and a loud thunder-clapping eco-audience gave its approval. Fat but sparse nickel-sized spring raindrops began to fall, and there was a collective "Uh-Oh" from the crowd. The torches went out in a puff of smoke, and the juggling magician disappeared within the shadows of the crowd, leaving only his torch-bearing tree spirit to sneak back to the woods, unnoticed in the dim solar-powered lights from the stage.

The crowd refocused on S.O.S. The trio managed to reroute the energy through their machines, with their fingertips pressing buttons and twisting knobs. Energetic feedback loops again ignited the dance floor.

There was another large thunder clap, and with it, chaos burst through into the festival as heavy sheets of rain began to pour down. Near the stage, a large bucketful of water splashed down from the covering tarp, surprising Aum, Jenn, Ted, and Jes. Cat had disappeared.

Suddenly, the music went out, along with the lights. The Main Stage was black. The performers stood before the audience, staring expectantly. A crack of thunder sounded directly over their heads, and flashes of lightning lit up the sky as the rain reached monsoon proportions. Dancers scampered for their tents or back to their cars amid screams of terror and anguish. Headlights turned on violently and cars sped away, fleeing the event all together. Was the whole thing being shut down? Did the bribe not work?

Fear licked peoples' feet, seeping into the corners of their eyes, distorting bodies and manifesting itself as authoritarian teleporting ghosts while the crowd searched for some semblance of reason.

"Let's head to the woods!"

They quickly walked toward the other stage, though in the commotion, Jes and Ted broke off, were abducted, taken hostage, or something. Jenn grabbed Aum's hand in panic as they made for the Water and Wood Stage.

As they rushed on, Jenn stated, "This tea is really good for visual hallucinations. It's hard to tell what's real and what's not."

"Agreed," Aum responded. They reached the forest stage where the rain was less heavy, most of it caught by the leaves. However, the setting was different than it had been all weekend. The stage was bathed in an intense red light, a huge contrast to its usual greens and browns. It was now ominous. Evil. Wrong.

The much smaller crowd present at the stage was just standing there, no dancing, no moving, gawk-eyes bulging. They were all just listening to the sounds emitted from the speakers; and they were some of the harshest sounds Aum had ever heard in his life - like jack hammers pounding his face. It produced a worse feeling in him than facing a swarm of giant mutated mosquito alien probes.

It looked like the current DJ was getting kicked off stage for the next performers and was not too happy about it. It was the Turkish man from the opening ceremonies, and he was so dejected that he managed to convey his maliciousness within the final sounds of his set, just before his equipment got unplugged by one of the organizers.

However, for reasons beyond Aum's understanding, the next performers continued the horrendous vibration. It appeared that they were trying to negatively program whoever was listening. Aum tried extremely hard to remain focused; he tried not to be sucked into a vortex of uncontrollable screaming at the top of his lungs, along with everyone else. He could hear their voices of anguish:

"Stop!"

"What are you doing?!"

"No! It hurts!"

It was a soundtrack to an otherworldly nightmare; music from hell.

I have to do something, Aum thought. Looking around, he saw Cat in midconversation. He spied her didgeridoo at her side. "Can I borrow this?" he asked.

"Of course," she replied.

In the deepest part of his being, Aum needed to place something organic into this computerized mess. There was no choice; he began operating in survival mode, outmaneuvering what was surely oncoming planetary death. The consciousness of technology had taken over here. There was no connection to an intentional human stewardship, to the Earth, to history, or to the natural setting. As the last mystical warrior, last warrior of faith, he claimed this wooden didgeridoo as his own, his own link to sanity, to history, to himself, to the natural setting and the planet. Words appeared in his mind, his unconscious egoic thoughts, *I serve myself.* His conscious mind caught it with, *What?! No, that's not at all right*, and Aum instantly rerouted the budding neural pathway, *I serve the highest good.* With that, his cellular structure changed, his deepest root-being strengthened, infused with confident surrender after a light attunement to service. His mouth went to the didge—his personal symbol that he had carried with his soul throughout many lives in different forms—and very subtly, Aum added a vibration that brought a whole new level to the music being performed. He tried to draw the focus away from negativity and toward the Earth. It seemed to be working; a handful of confused spirits disguised as people noticed and crowded around the end of his didge, like moths around a light in the darkness.

One man even got down on his knees and tried to fill his water bottle with whatever he thought was coming out of the end of the tube.

Aum continued to emit positive vibes through the didge, though sonically it was no match for the full range mackie top cabs and their subwoofers. His gaze moved down to the ground. Within the randomly strewn rocks and tree branches, scraps of the discarded roots, and tools of the jamming Earth children, still infused with a dynamic healing spirit, Aum saw a map of existence. He had the urge to drop to his knees to investigate the details of the churned up dirt dance floor with great detail. It became the reflected night sky, with galaxy upon galaxy tuning in to watch the events of this particular night unfold. He focused further as he played, and the vision reflected back on himself. He caught a glimpse of the ancient shamanic soul that was deep within him. He was about to step closer to the map when the previous DJ of maliciousness, the Turk, snuck onto the stage, putting new slides into a projector. At the same time, a trio in shining black hooded raincoats appeared, hanging a glowing eight-dimensional star from a chopped tree branch. They held the tetrahedron out like a fishing rod, on the exact opposite side of the stage as the projection screen. While the technology continued its assault, Aum balanced it with all his concentration. He managed to quickly peek back at the screen to see a rotating red and purple circle—clean graphic swirls, collective visual metaphors to induce hypnosis. There was a showdown between forces happening. The image had the ingrained negativity and embedded antagonist archetype of the last performer, while the cosmic fishermen represented the hope of the struggling protagonist deep in the darkness. Aum connected eyes and recognized one of them from his first Riddler event where he met Cat. Or was it from online photos of previous Spectrum events? He couldn't remember, and needed to continue to focus.

Gradually waves began to form in the audio maelstrom; the passive crowd became more and more attuned to these, and screams of anguish were replaced by cheers each time the waves broke, crashing on the beach-like-dance floor.

But within the waves, the harshness remained…

Finally, after a last large crescendo, there was a gentle calm, and then it faded to silence. People cheered loudly. Aum continued to play the didge as the cheering quieted. He was a feeble wave of sound, a perceived tripster in the corner. Feeling this, Aum was slightly shocked, considering how hard he had been working. He slowly moved out of the dim light into the shadows under a tree, hoping that his movements were so slow as not to be noticed.

He noticed music at another stage.

He noticed his free will had returned.

He noticed Cat was gone.

Aum guessed he should hang on to her didge for the time being, just in case they should suddenly turn out all the lights on them again and let everyone fend for themselves against their own demons in the darkness.

He looked to see Jenn huddled nearby under a tree. Her eyes were closed, she had a deep frown on her face, and her fingers were in her ears. Aum approached and stroked her arm. She came to, gingerly, eyes slowly squinting open, fingers still in her ears.

"Is it over?" she asked unknowingly louder than necessary.

Aum looked around again, checking to make sure for her. In the now silent space, some people were conversing lightly; most had moved on, and the rain had diminished from a torrent to tolerable.

"For now, I think."

She took her fingers out of her ears, seeming to breathe for the first time in hours, still looking for an answer from Aum. Aum repeated himself.

"For now?!" she said with a panicked laugh. "Can we go?"

"Sure, let's go."

He helped her up, and they made their way out of the woods and back along the lit line of booths. Many people were huddled in the art gallery, underneath the large tarps, under the big umbrellas anchored down by picnic tables, even under the picnic tables themselves. Aum could see headlights on in the parking lot. Then he heard something very familiar.

"Do you hear that?!"

"What?" said Jenn.

"That track?!"

"What about it?"

"C'mon, c'mon let's go!" he said, grabbing her hand.

"Go where?!"

"To the Main Stage; someone's playing my song!"

She didn't budge. "I've heard that one tons of times, Aum. Look at all these people. It's cold, it's raining out, we're soaked....Can't we just go hang out in the tent?"

"But it's something I made, Jenn. Someone's performing with it. I have to go check it out!" He was already walking. "Are you sure you don't want to come with?"

"Aum, I don't think I can handle it over there. Not now," she was pleading, sad, but steadfast and honest. Aum could not hide his disappointed expression this time. "Fine, I'll wait here for you. You can tell me all about it later," she said.

He began running off, catching up to his out-of-body attention. "Okay, we'll meet back in the center."

"Sure," she shouted back at him. Then in a panic, "The center of where?!" But his form vanished into a sea of people, and for a short second, she was very, very scared.

She let out a big sigh and considered crawling under a picnic table, but then simply walked back to their campsite. She entered their tent, removed her layers of wet clothes, and curled up in her thick down sleeping bag. She stuck her fingers in her ears to shut out the thumping bass of Aum's track that she had heard far too many times in their house. It reverberated off mountainous cliffsides into muffled noise as she drifted lightly into unconsciousness.

***

The tea was fully in his system now. Aum moved with the didge as a walking stick. He was walking but didn't really have any idea how that was even possible. He wasn't in his body; he was just watching it, like a driver in a car who can't physically feel wheels touching the road. He hoped he was doing it right. The old soul had taken the opportunity to emerge, an ancient and weathered old man living in tribal society hundreds of years ago, ready to let a giddy trickster cackle loose at any moment, loving the weather and the rain.

Aum circled round and reached the back of the crowd at the Main Stage. The entire area was flooded with black light. The vibe was so different there, so cosmically positive that his heart lifted. It was almost too much to bear for him. The whole space was a foreign ship to him. He wanted to sprint up and explode right there in the middle of everybody, adding a burst of quantum rocket fuel, but he knew that dropping a bomb wouldn't serve its passengers, or the ship. His exploding excitement could only be released with utmost gentleness and sensitivity, exhales of buzzing breath.

There was another track on top of his. The performer was really accentuating his off-beat bass drum rhythmic sequencing, and doing an amazing frequency sweep building up to Aum's favorite part. The wild jazz drums climaxed into half-time 4/4, at the same time the DJ kicked in a double-time psytrance beat, and the crowd cheered as they dug into the grass spaceship dance floor. Aum smiled in pride and accomplishment as his track slowly faded out. He gazed around and saw BJ a few rows in, still within the back rows of nondancing participants. With utmost caution and receptivity, Aum took a few animated and goofy steps toward the big man, breathing deeply, having to focus on the overall collective effects of each breath. He bravely approached BJ, "How are your journeys going?"

Somewhat surprised, but generally pleased to see Aum, he replied, "Good! They're taking me to strange and mysterious places. The fact that Mother Nature is giving us a good show of rain, thunder, and lightning is heightening this entire area. Almost as if it was planned out. How are yours?"

"Everything's new!" A voice came out of him; he could hardly get the words out to describe what was really happening to him.

"Truly? How long have you been involved in the Riddle?"

His past life soul was not capable of understanding this terminology and replied out of Aum's mouth, "Only a few times."

"So you're really new, then," he responded with the weight of an accomplished veteran.

"Yes, but we all have to be new sometime," Aum replied in joust.

"Very true! I remember what it was like to be new," BJ said with self-given authority.

There was a pause in the conversation; the music shifted, and Aum rode a new vibration through the cellular structure of his body, connecting with the transforming occurrences of the space, morphing his physical form into his past life incarnation. He grasped the didge like an old cane, hunching over beyond bodily control as his limbs creakily jerked to the music. In the corner of his eye, BJ pulled out his camera, taking an opportune photo of the transmutation. As if stealing something of value, BJ quickly strode away without another word of rebuttal. Aum wasn't bothered by it; in fact, it empowered him, confirming his experience.

With added creak upon slow creak, Aum moved in, further toward the stage. He gazed up and saw ahead of him the DJ from the beginning of the evening, the opening ceremonies, standing at the edge of the dance space. He stood as motionless as a statue; a long hood covered his eyes, with his expression shrouded in darkness. Aum could not comprehend how the man stood so epically still during this amazingly uplifting music. The man rode the edge between the full body emotive flailing of the dancers and the first row of strong and active observing participants. In him, Aum saw a sponge soaking in every bit of inspired movement, storing it in some invisible battery pack—fuel for later in the evening, later in the morning, or later in life. Aum drew closer, slithering in between the last standing observers to emulate the man. He could hear a few voices directed at him, "Who does this guy think he is?" In response, Aum reduced and controlled his ancient animalistic gesturing to find feeling in his total surrender to the human moment, to the experience and the surroundings. It took a lot of energy to even slow his body down from the musical movements that felt most natural. He couldn't believe how much more focus he needed to concentrate on stilling his body. As a multisensory crescendo peaked, Aum rode it like a surfer, cresting it, slowing, and then stopping all movement in his body. He could feel pulsations of yellow and white light running through him. He allowed himself to intimately feel the energy of the entire group of people. It felt like they were flying away from the planet in outer space; they only had a small strand to connect back with the Earth and to find the way home. It was a very powerful sensation, and Aum and his embodied ancient soul were happy to have been taught how to focus like that, an entirely new perspective.

The dance shifted, and, as if coming out of shavasana, he gingerly moved his fingers and toes. Now that he had slowed down to nothing, his body was even more entrenched in reflective vibrations of the space. He noticed even the slightest motion from all perspectives. As he reconnected to his quantum jet fuel of excitement, he brought himself back to life, releasing it all into the space, as he began to dance with those in his immediate vicinity. His didge-cane became a staff, a giant wand to bring forth and deposit fuel in the spaceship. Those around him seemed to notice and began to build with it, supporting the structural vibrations. Even his old soul noticed the curious bridge building efforts happening before him. The sea of bodies seemed to part for him as he danced, so he followed the path as it opened toward the stage. He was dancing, stepping, tilting, and twirling in unison with the other incarnated souls.

It was at that point that Aum fully raised his head and connected with the beautiful woman on stage, singing and chanting along with the ever-changing crescendoing music. The heart that she added to the music was indescribable. She eventually picked up a violin and started playing. Aum caught her gaze and felt like he was in direct communion with her. His multidimensional soul was bare to her, as he focused all of his attention on her, trying to feel her music with his past life psychic shamanic energy field. It seemed like she could sense it, because the notes in the music changed instantly to something more intense and focused on transformation, or travel.

An older man and woman began to dance next to Aum. The man was tall and thin and had a young visage that hid his true age. He seemed untouchable, but Aum had the sense that he had no comprehension of how different he was from everyone else. The woman was quiet, generous, royal, and elegant. They were a king and queen amid a full court of characters. Aum offered both of them water, more out of curiosity than anything. The man introduced himself as Carlyle. The protective circle that was surrounding him shifted to encompass all three of their fields as they talked. He asked about the didge and Aum replied it was Cat's.

"Oh yes, I know Cat. I just saw her around here somewhere." Carlyle wiped a few rain droplets off his face and talked about how he had just received a didge healing before they arrived.

Aum replied, "I'd like to start getting into a pro practice like that, but I'm still waiting to find a teacher."

"I don't think you need a teacher to go pro. Just go with the feeling," Carlyle replied.

"You think so?" Aum responded genuinely.

"Yeah, do one on me right now."

"Really?!"

"Um no, wait," he said, contemplating the fact that he'd just had a healing done. "Do one on my friend," referring to his elegant queen. In the center of a huge, raving, drug-induced crowd with pounding progressive psychedelic trance music, Aum was a bit hesitant.

"Just point it right at her genitals."

And increasingly more so, "Um, okay."

"Yeah, that's right. Right at her genitals."

Stalling, Aum said, "What do you think it'll do?" to Carlyle, who was standing to the side, directing and holding space for the operation. The woman, still like royalty, seemed hungry for it.

"I don't know. Move in closer, though," Carlyle said. Aum was beginning to doubt Carlyle's intensions, as well as his queen. Aum felt a surge of alien or extradimensional energy, begging for a connection to the Earth, or some new gateway to penetrate the Riddle. Aum looked at the woman; her eyes glowed a witchlike yellow.

"Point it right at her genitals," he said again, pointing with his finger. Aum began. He pushed light through his own paranoid thoughts as Carlyle pointed out each chakra, too fast for what Aum was feeling, but he decided to go with it anyway. Strangely enough, the music climaxed at the same time as the healing at the top chakra.

"Wow! Did you see the energy pouring out of this guy?!" Carlyle exclaimed to his female friend. She just smiled and nodded in gratitude. Aum asked her if it was okay. She simply said, "That was good." And kept on smiling.

Carlyle continued, "I began to see the waveform structure of your shirt change wherever the didge was pointed. The pattern in your shirt began to get excited and move with the energy."

"Yeah, I saw that too!" Aum replied. "Pretty amazing." The two of them thanked Aum, and together they disengaged their small triangle and focused back on the music and the danceflow. It took Aum only a matter of minimal old soul gestures to find his was back into the collective body. Its energy was stronger and more malleable than ever.

Ted tapped Aum on the shoulder.

Aum jumped a little, then they both smiled in a goofy heightened recognition.

"Let's move closer…," Ted said. He pointed upward toward a tarp, "…out of the rain." Aum agreed and followed him. If Ted wasn't there to lead, there was no way that he, at that point, would have been able to penetrate the increasingly dense psychic boundaries that had been erected around the stage.

The beautiful woman performing completed her set, and the crowd roared in gratitude for the enlightening experience. Like handing off a baton during a relay race, the next DJ began his set without pause. At the same time, there was some commotion behind them. Just where Ted and Aum had previously been standing, the crowd opened up to reveal a very tall and bright torch with four costumed females surrounding it. They each represented a different direction and a different element. They began to chant intensely, building an incredible amount of energy and causing onlookers to back up. A twenty-foot circle opened up around them. Whether it was the loud atmosphere building in the background music, whether they were too far away, or whether they were even chanting in English, Aum wasn't able to tell. After a few moments of observation, Aum realized these women were different. They were much older than most Riddlers, up into their forties or fifties, maybe. Then Aum realized that this was no mere performance; he was actually witnessing the performance of a sacred Wiccan ritual on this intensely powerful summer solstice night. Within beats, he noticed that everyone dancing around him and Ted were mature adults. No stuffed animal backpacks or fat Magna pants, no stereotypes. All these Riddlers were professionals who were in the midst of their shared shamanic or occult practices. They were doing it for real. So much nobility that it deserved respect. Aum's past life soul personality presented himself further in Aum's mind, opening him up further, flipping switches on in his head as to who was present at this gathering, why they were here, what brought them here, even why they were still out in the rain. There were leaping cosmic alignments happening inside him. The chanting completed, and the women's group began to hand out candles. Aum caught one woman's eye, his gaze reaching deep inside her, down into a pocket of surprise, then fear, then bashfulness.

"Hey, have some respect," he thought he heard Ted say. Aum looked over and realized Ted merely said it out loud in no particular direction. Regardless, Aum instantly humbled himself, lowering his gaze, feeling full gratitude and appreciation for all he had just received.

When he looked up, small creatures with masks emerged from the forest. Whether they were pixies and elves or kids dressed up as such, the difference no longer mattered to Aum. There was no distinction between myth and reality. These beings tried to intimidate him, vibrating wildly like animals. Aum became slightly frightened at what he saw, his mind telling him it wasn't real, but he pushed past the incomprehension, grew bigger, and allowed himself to continue to merely be curious as he watched the creatures emerge. More of them began to run out; they had feathers and beaks and in no way looked discernibly human. They began placing candles around the Main Stage and the dance floor with caution and tended to the candles with great concentration, somehow relighting them each time they went out from a well-aimed raindrop.

Aum felt new music emerging, though not from the speakers. He glanced around and saw a woman playing an ocarina back near the active observers. The organic faerie infusion shifted the space as the creatures moved with the ocarina's high pitched dancing.

Aum refocused on the digital performer onstage in union with the faerie flutist, and he felt further cohesion. As his breath moved the entire emotional field up and down his body, the creatures calmed their dance, and upon their magical gaze, huge thunderbird wings sprouted out of Aum's back.

The opening ceremonies shaman appeared with a few apprentices. They lit a two-foot-thick sage bushel right in front of where Aum was dancing, anointing the space and all who viewed it. As they worked, so did Aum. He danced with the full tank of spirit fuel he brought, evolving space and all characters within it on the unified beat of his thunderbird wings. The shaman crew then set the bushel on the edge of the stage in a specialized holder. Working further, they brought out additional platforms at each end of the stage. Once these were in place, meditators and bodyworkers immediately took cross-legged positions upon them.

Aum looked up to see the Pleiades Circle sitting across the breadth of the entire stage with its new extensions. They formed a living altar. His brain reeled at what he knew of their group. Even dwelling upon his memories of them revealed their embodied human connections to the Star Nations. He noticed people from the dance floor were leaving—somewhere in their unconscious mind making a decision and just leaving the dance floor. He couldn't quite understand it, considering the immensely large wave of energy they were all riding. In the few rows in front of him, dancing together with a few other members of the Pleiades group, he noticed the four ceremony guiding witches.

He could feel gateways about to open up within their dance-movement-architecture—portals to other realms. A short round woman with an intense look danced in from the outer edges of the crowd. She turned to look at Aum. Her hair had lines shaved into it, and her eyes were on fire. Her face was concentrated; she was in complete control of her surroundings and could bend people's consciousness at will. More dancers dropped off, but Aum stood firm, though now intimidated and somewhat frightened at the situation he found himself in. The woman with the shaved head created a massive wall in between the Pleiadians, the elemental witches, and the regular dancing masses. They began to chant again, informally, in celebration. Aum glanced sideways and saw Ted continuing to dance with ease, seemingly oblivious to the deeper story emerging.

"What the…," Aum said out loud. He suddenly realized he was facing away from the stage, and he didn't remember turning. With further focus, he danced around, grooving open-heartedly with each beat, letting the trance guide every fiber of his being as he turned back to the stage. Everything was the same, but there was a glowing woman standing on stage with the Pleiades members tending to her. Most of the glow was from the black lights, yet Aum still understood her demeanor and attitude as someone not of the physical plane. She did not add anything at all to the energetic architecture of the situation; she was a disembodied observer, much like someone looking through a window as a divine scene played out beyond the glass.

"What the?! I'm facing away from the stage again!" Aum mumbled, feeling perplexed. He turned around to see the fiery eyed woman dancing in a frenzy. *I wonder if she's turning us all away?* Aum thought. He looked up and the glowing being was gone, while the Pleiades people still stood there with their shields, concentrating. The hyper moving gears in Aum's mind began to churn up the situation. He came to the conclusion that the woman was causing some Riddlers to leave, even causing his change in direction, on her own without planning it with the Pleiades group or the group of chanting witches. Yet the Pleiades group required both the shift in unfocused observation and occult chanting in order to transport this interdimensional being to their plane of existence. Aum began to better understand the cosmic extent of the Riddle, how completely interconnected these "random" events happen, as conscious and powerful humans come together to serve the highest purpose they can imagine.

Just past the group on stage, Aum saw a man emerge. Climbing up the far edge, he pulled out a bronze metal hornlike didge and began to play, trumpeting and sweeping the entire crowd.

Shit, now that's a didge healing, Aum thought.

Calling in all the cosmos, he celebrated the triumph of cross-universal contact, bringing the celebration down into physical vibration. Aum felt a pull in his soul and in his body; a lightning bolt shot up his arm from his didge-staff. As he reacted, Aum caught the glance of the king and queen. They looked at him expectantly.

"Really?" His heart pumped full of adrenaline on beat, and his soul eyes went feral and wide as an eagle screech pierced the audio sonics.

He looked, and there was an opening. It was exceedingly slim, however.

"Okay," he said with resolve. Putting his full body's weight on the didge-staff, he cartwheeled across the dance floor, flipping through two Wiccans who split as he passed. Aum flowed and dive-rolled, ducking under the swinging bo staff of a stage guardian dressed like Catwoman. He used his momentum to leap Jedi-like four feet into the air, up onto the far end of the stage, in polar opposition to the trumpeter. His senses heightened; he almost stumbled and flopped over from the weight of the vibrational group focus. He was sensitive to the disruption he caused, flowing with its force, taking it, crafting it with each cell of his being, spinning 360 degrees as the momentum brought him down to a shamanic crouch. Balancing on five fingers and a few toes on each foot, he moved the attention into his breath and blew it back out through his didge. On his first long circular inhale, he stood and raised himself to his fellow trumpeter's level. The whole space balanced in meta-architecture; the music shifted up in tempo and aural density, and new heightened interconnected group frequencies surged around him.

Aum was now up at a new level and was barely holding it together. He was with the interdimensional teleportation gateway holders and feeling like he bit off more than he could chew. Aum felt the immense pressure of the cosmos on his every action, thought, and feeling, but especially in his breath as it moved through his body. He was under the astronomical macroscope of the Pleiades and their nonphysical supporters, as well as the direct and epic gaze of one of them in physical form.

After nearly thirty minutes straight of circular breath work on a crowd of a hundred or more, he was worn bare. Unbelievably he could feel his fellow trumpeter still strong. *Maybe it's the bronze*, Aum thought, as his legs began to shake. There was suddenly a hand on his shoulder, comforting and soothing.

"Can I take over for you?"

It was Cat. She had a water offering in her hand and was strong enough in her presence that the space was held and he could rest. With a gasp, he disengaged his breath, taking a few deep recovery inhales.

"Thanks." He held his hands together at his heart center, forehead, and then drank the water deeply. The lights changed. The black lights were turned off, and a warm glow of greens and reds bathed the stage as well as those closest to it. The music shifted to an entho-psy world beat, initiated by the dropping of Shpongles, "Divine Moments of Truth." There was a wave of coasting, riding the incoming six-beat triplet, as if the last blast from the rocket ship engine had finished, pushing out of orbit, now sailing on pure momentum through a vacuum.

For a brief timeless moment, Aum and Cat gazed upon the scene together, soaking it in as much as they could.

"Holy shit, what is this?" Aum said, wide eyed, "Are we even coming back to Earth?" She smiled with a pixie twinkle in her eye and a veteran's confidence. She leaned into him as if a lifelong friend, placed a hand on his shoulder blade, just beside his wing bone, and gently took her didge back as she said, "Come on, I want to introduce you to someone."

***

Jenn awoke to the sound of her own muffled yells. The throbbing bass and the calculated, alien manufactured, pulsating psytrance frequency had invaded her dreamless slumber. This was an extreme and unfamiliar bodily reaction for her. After calming herself, and slowly recalling where she was, she lay in her sleeping bag for as long as she could before irritation got the best of her. She had to move around. She put her layers back on, including her comforting white Lululemon hoodie, and exited the tent. It was still dark out. The air was surprisingly crisp; she could even see her breath in the air. To add to her confusion, the throbbing bass was even louder outside the thin tarp.

***

Aum and Cat walked across the stage, in front of the DJ. Cat was confident, with her power tool back and charged beyond measure. Aum, feeling somewhat like a tourist, lowered his head in reverence as the immense energy of the dancing crowd pulsed at his left; character upon character beamed out their maximum heat of burning soul fire as the two crossed the stage.

The Pleiades folk were still sitting in a row, the being sitting behind them on a throne. Cat gave all of them a nod as they walked behind them. Aum smiled, largest at Sara, Ashta, and Pillaiyar. Pillaiyar put his hands together for a small bow.

"Tera, this is my friend, Aum. Aum, I'd like you to meet Tera." Cat looked at Aum and continued, "She came all the way from the north coast to be at Full Spectrum." Aum looked into her face and all he could see was a pain of concern; utter torment. Her frailness, as well as a strange sense of concentrated royalty, emanated from within her shawl. She was not from a far-off solar system, but the ground we are given to walk on everyday. It hit Aum like a ton of bricks as she turned to him and shared a strained smile. With short-cropped dark brown hair, and two small flower-petal-like lips, deep-set large brown and bagged eyes, she drew him into her circle of being. Aum could feel the uneasiness and the tension in her body. She seemed weak and run down, filled with despair and surrender after an immensely long journey, just like our own Mother Earth.

"Hello."

Her voice reverberated inside of him, at some deeply unknown biological core. Aum gazed at the temporarily incarnated spirit of our Mother Earth. He was both honored and nervous, feeling like he should bow low and intone, "At you service." Instead he just asked her if she was having a good time. Tera replied, "Yes," and with little emotion in her voice, she said she was happy to have made it to such an important event. Her arms were close to her body, hugging herself under her shawl. A big shiver seemed to throw her almost off the stage, so in service, Aum offered her his jacket. Accepting the purpose of his true self in the moment, he took it off to release the heat of didging as well as to create the metaphor of shedding skin. She gratefully accepted it, and a surprised and genuine happiness spread across her face. Verification to proceed, Aum made himself more comfortable at her side.

A tall man with long, black dreadlocks and a trimmed black beard approached and asked Tera if Aum had just offered her the jacket, as if the matter was of great significance. He wasn't a part of the Pleiadian-Matrika group, but with the wisdom that seeped out of the pours of his brown skin and emanated from his yellowish-green eyes, he very well could have been an alien from ancient Egypt. She said "Yes" to him, and he looked into Aum. Aum didn't know what else to do but introduce himself (very nervously, in fact). The man smiled broadly, white teeth shinning, and again with a surprised and genuine smile, nodded to Tera and then walked back to where he was standing in stoic observation. Aum didn't get it, but that didn't matter. He felt that he should continue the conversation with Tera—be a good host to the spirit of our cosmic planetary embodiment when she decides to visit. "Such an important event," she had said. Aum's mind reeled at the scope of this statement from this being. He wondered at the specifics of what exactly she was referring to.

She responded to him, though he hadn't uttered a single word out loud. "You know what's going on, love. You know exactly—it's inside of you."

"Pardon me?" Aum asked, stunned, suddenly realizing the tremendous depth of her digging ability. Naked, he followed her gaze into himself.

"Right now everyone here is playing a very important role in our launching ceremony. Your thunderbird wings and your focused concentration are very much appreciated by many people here today." She gave him a serious look. "There are a lot of things being played out this morning." The setting and music blurred to background stimulus. "How many Full Spectrums have you reached?" Tera asked.

"Um...well...this is my first," Aum replied.

"Some may scoff at that, but existentially they do not know you are both correct and incorrect. I do appreciate your humility, though." She smiled again, genuinely, even brighter this time. "I've been to every one. Not that too many are keeping track, but this is Full Spectrum 13. At Full Spectrum 6, I noticed things changing. There were only a handful of people, but they maneuvered with utmost focus and purpose—much like you here today—and every single person in attendance went back to their lives forever changed. I did my own investigating. I talked to the people they talked to; I followed the ripples around them, in physical and digital spaces, and drew out my own conclusions at the time. This is still up for debate, but in my opinion, this change in perspective was the birth of the Riddle and its infusion into Full Spectrum."

A question arose in Aum, but it only made it to the tip of his tongue before it was answered. "You see, Full Spectrum existed before the Riddle."

Aum remained silent. He tried not to reveal his logical incomprehension, but at this point, it was impossible. She continued through his rumpled brow, grasping onto the largest of each question that bubbled up in the back of his mind. "Full Spectrum 7, the following year, was a new event entirely, an exponentially evolving communication ecosystem. It was a relative fast lane in comparison to previous years. Areas, performance stages, and performers had the ability to transform massively overnight, not to mention the overall shift in collective ability to work behind the veil. In the years that followed, this vibratory change in consciousness naturally permeated all other artists, Riddlers, and partygoers until the structure had congealed, maintaining a much desired flex and permeability."

Aum glanced up at the solid steel structure holding up the tarp. As he looked away, he saw it began to collapse, so he decided to compartmentalize his attention, keeping one specific portion completely focused on the strength of the metal, as well as the entire stage spacecraft, while another soaked in the pulsing background rhythms and another maintained full presence within the conversation.

Tera continued seamlessly, "Then things changed again. A second giant but gentle buzz crept into this branch of consciousness—only last year—embodied in a few individuals. With the skills of the most dedicated permaculturalist, these ones grew tentacles out from the new center, supporting all others on a stable and ever-circulating platform. To their credit, they also constructed an easily accessible staircase for noobs on ground level."

Along with a slight tilt of her head, their eyes connected as Tera lifted her hand and gestured specifically at him. This intentional communication, far richer than words could convey, Aum understood.

***

"Man alive! I'm going to have to grab some caffeine if I want to keep going here," Jenn said to herself. She grabbed her flashlight, unzipped the tent, and left the campsite, walking down to the small row of vendors.

She found the same bright white tea dome from the morning, full of sincerity. Earlier in the day, she had seen the line-up stretch past the entire grouping of vending booths. She was happy to find no line now.

"Hello, can I get a latté please?"

"Cow or soy?"

"Um…cow."

"No prob." The same server, alert and smiling, with a stovepipe top hat and a black jacket with very large lapels, fixed the drink with a noisy espresso machine, shouting, "How's your night going?"

"It's okay, I guess. I just woke up," she shouted back hoarsely.

He walked over with a steaming cardboard cup, same logos, same address, same town.

"That's cool; the night's just peaking. Where are you headed?"

Jenn saw a big *100% Tree-Free* stamp on the side of her cup. "I'm not too sure. I guess I'm still trying to find my bearings."

"Yeah, I hear yah. It just gets bigger and brighter every year."

She took her first sip. "Oh yeah? How many years now?"

"Full spectrum? Eleven, I think. I've been to the past seven or so, and the past four years I've been working here my tea shop."

"Business must be good then?"

"It's been great! I used to be the only one here with the entrepreneurial spirit," he looked over at the other shops. "It'll be interesting to see who does well this year. A few of these shops are brand new." He had his own amped caffeine buzz going. "I'd say it's a fairly untapped market, considering the number of people here. There's great music and a lot of different characters." With a dirty hand, he pointed out a feathery one walking by. Jenn took a passing glance, then looked back, gazing past the vendor's shoulder at his V-dub van in the back. There was a portable stove and a laundry line with ratty and stained costume-like clothes trying to dry in the night air. She sighed and thought, *What kind of untapped market is made up of dirty hippy entrepreneurs living out of their vans?* She looked out toward the other booths and imagined their vagrant gypsy lifestyle.

He continued, "Yeah, it's pretty cool to see other members of the community creating businesses here. Really solidifies things, yah know?" Receding back into his own memories, he laughed, "To start off, I got a small loan from one of my friends. It truly seems like a decade ago. It was enough for me to get the ball rolling and I was able to pay him back after my first season on the festival circuit." There were a couple cheers from the woods as the bass shook the leaves. "This event wouldn't be what it is without John, that's for sure."

"John?"

"Yeah, John deGryder." He said it as if Jenn should know him personally. "The name doesn't ring a bell?" he asked as she stared at him blankly. "At all? Wow, you must've just woken up."

She spit out her latté in a full-force spray.

"There we go!" he interjected comedically.

"The Jonathan deGryder?! The president of Gridline Communications?!"

"Uh," he looked at her curiously, "Gridline Communications? Never heard of it. Could be John, though; nobody's heard from him for awhile." He adjusted his hat and smiled, "I should get back at it, though. Enjoy your latté." He went to the kitchen area in the back and sat at an old, cracked, and flickering laptop, continuing his nano-tech food preparations. She sat at one of the nearby picnic tables in a trance. "No way!"

Gridline Communications was making huge waves in international business. They were a small and extremely effective team of innovators, headed by deGryder. A few months ago, the press dubbed him "The Magician" because of his innovative business tactics. In regard to Gridline's involvement in streamlining the information highway 2.0 and the emerging biointegration of Web 4.0's open-source hardware, deGryder was quoted as saying, "F#*k the Web! We need an open-source Earth!"

Jenn took another sip of her latté and wiped the sleep from her eyes. Could he have started in this strange Riddle community? She took another sip, and it was as if her entire perspective shifted. She had found her place along the spectrum: Jenn was awake, and working now.

***

Aum looked across the stage to see a Trio of beings, much like Tera, that looked quite upset. They continued to bow and keep their eyes covered. It seemed like they were in submission. Aum became concerned about what was happening outside of his conversation with Tera. Then he noticed Tera's back straighten; her eyes glazed over, and her mouth begin to move.

"Like Canadian geese flying in a V formation toward their destination, a destination that is determined by instinct alone, we as focused participants, also through instinct, constantly trade off the position of leader. We do this without knowing it, without conscious awareness, and most of the time without ever knowing at what level of involvement. Some leaders need breaks, returning after a period of study, and some only lead for a short time, but there's always, always someone there, leading the flock in the right direction."

He had to compartmentalize his attention again. Conversation, physical structure, and now all its inhabitants were held in different spaces in his mind. More sage was lit; smiles appeared and Aum reengaged with Tera's lesson. "Much different than a tribal chief or CEO, then?" Aum managed to speak out.

"It's a higher spiritual instinct, bigger than being in bodies: a circular, biointegrated open-source model in nonphysical space; a neoshamanic leadership that is felt but not necessarily intellectually recognized.

"The beating of wings at the point of the human V, the instinct, in the realm of cognition, remains as history: the written word, coded language. The world changes, though: communication technology advances nontechnological communication, expanding the array, the new global flock. The voice, expressive movement through space, simple interactions with an audience, or even an individual conversation will suffice to guide. Conversations work better, however, as transmissional infrastructure; the more, the merrier. They're all straightforward but substantial victories regardless."

He nodded, barely staying afloat in comprehension.

"The beating of wings is art making; the final product is left over as a symbol of that open-flow nonlocal leadership. The beating of wings is performance, simply if it has changed the beating of our own heart drums. The beating of wings is love making; it is the creation of new unchained hearts to beat. The greatest leadership equates to a newborn's parental care, though: respectful enough to act with as much awareness as possible, and inexperienced enough not to understand it all, gobbling fear as food. To be curious and to explore what it all is and what it all means. Exploring the life residing beyond understanding."

He nodded, resonating more.

"In this case here, you share it with your fellow newborns in the V after making it up the spiral staircase. Your risks, your rewards, your findings, your joy, your connections—all shared. That's where respect and awareness come in handy. This respect flows through those around you, too, to lift the experience higher."

Aum responded, "Yes, I've noticed the reverence and spongelike absorption of stillness and being in service to awakening souls. A very, very full range, beyond words even. But what's actually happening here, Tera? What are we actually doing? What is this launching ceremony?"

She looked at him seriously, pausing, then nodded and responded, "What are we doing? Or what is doing us? In the larger story, as a part of the larger evolutionary cycles, we are entering an electromagnetic cloud called the photon belt, or more precisely, the photon belt is very quickly expanding to surround our planet and our solar system. It is moving light-years through us over the course of this weekend.

"The impact of the photon belt on the sun will increase solarquakes and sunspot activity, which is directly related to species extinction, virus creation, global conflict, and mass changes in consciousness. The electromagnetic field of the human aura flares in conjunction with the planet's field, and in conjunction with the sun's solarquakes.

"Along with general emotional instability and heightened states of awareness, this cosmic energy correlate also creates jump frequencies between dimensions, planets, time, and space, as well as thinning veils for the quantum reprogramming of the status quo. This is, of course, done through DNA. Our current location within the photon belt has removed barriers to understanding, allowing for the direct and immediate response of DNA structure to the intention and energy from the collective, or even individual. More so than usual. Now mind you, we have only been in the photon belt for two days, but as a species within a global organism with new access to a solar systemic body, we must begin to live our daily lives with this new understanding and empathetic accountability in the forefront of our interactions and relations for hundreds, or maybe even thousands, of years. Do you think we've got the computational capacity or bodily processing stamina for that magnitude of an evolutionary leap?"

A blue fire lit in her eyes.

"Why do you think it's so easy to fall into our handheld screens?"

Not knowing whether a response was required, Aum nodded slightly.

"We're two days into it, and I can already feel the corporate entities greedily reacting, reaching for the last untapped environmental resources on our Earth while they take their dying breaths of extinction. Will we be able to overcome the sight of our planet processing the deepest evil of our own human nature? Will there be any life resources left for the surviving intentional community networks? Will we even need things like this if we are able to manipulate our own genetic structure, or learn to survive purely on pranic breath energy?"

Too many questions. Aum listened without response.

"This weekend, a new aspect of our collective unconscious has awakened. We have become conscious enough to make the decision to move on, and everyone here has been a part of that decision. Hence the deep thanks for your wings and concentration.

"Unfortunately, there are some corporate entities, with their security systems included, that are none too happy about this, and well, some will die in the transformational process. The more people, however, who strive to throw down their own self-imposed shackles and surrender to this photon-awakened launch pad, the more people that witness the beating wings of this flight, the faster we will be carried though the vacuum spaces in which we exist; it is a reflexive self-awareness, and a Global Self–driven evolution."

A tall blonde man shouted from the crowd with slurred inebriation, "I don't ever want to be human again!" They both focused on him and could see he wasn't human to begin with—that's not true; the extra-dimensional consciousness that operated his voice wasn't human. Beyond the drug-induced galactically vulnerable opening, deep down at the root of him was a human that lacked any comprehension of what he was doing, what medicines he had taken, and the truth of what was going on.

"Not all the people at this event are participants like yourself, Aum. I would say roughly a third are completely unaware of the Riddle's existence, and another third participate in the Riddle at the same capacity as you do; this is the result of entering a preliminary layer of the photon belt during Full Spectrum 6. The remaining third are the very special people who, since consciously entering the gentle buzz of a secondary layer of the photon belt last summer and then again consciously engaging the changes this year, have completely erased the distinction between the Riddle and reality."

He looked at her in surprise.

"Truth be known, the Riddle is just a title, a meaningless word."

At that moment, a man dressed in a red pill suit walked by, following a giant white rabbit. A hole opened and Aum fell in, watching his mind release into the conceptual erasure.

"Holy shit!" He had to close his eyes because his body disappeared. It was if his awareness ejected from his physicality and into the larger, higher, nonphysical being of Aum. In his mind, the stage and the crowd transformed. He rode a roller coaster as the tempo of the music picked up. Girders were built into the ground, holes were dug and eco-cement poured, buildings constructed, trees planted and grown, and forts built in their branches. The flags of new nations were raised to the heavens, billowing and flapping in the wind. Eyes still closed, he mumbled sentence fragments, "A blurred distinction of reality? I feel you. Riddle directions come from personal intuitive daily experience; intent manifested into physical form."

"Think bigger, my dear." He half opened one eye to see her motioning to the entire space around them. "The Riddle is an emergent property of our global culture; a state of layered conscious and unconscious interaction that has reached a new level of functional complexity. Human awareness has undeniably reached a new bifurcation point, a point so far away from equilibrium that the result is the newest manifestation of evolution. Permanent cosmic, worldwide, and quantum change has resulted in coordination with the full transformation of the nature of human spirit. Instant collective realization."

She paused and exhaled calmly, enjoying the photon enhanced first glimpses of the rising sun. "Trust. Future life-path direction comes from the exact impersonal source that causes change in the world. The very same boundless source fuels the Riddle."

"So…a shift from personally contained manifestation to a collectively realized soul actualization will erase my falsely perceived distinction between the Riddle and reality?" This was a huge leap in Aum's understanding as a perpetual student. "I don't think I know how to do that. How do I do that?"

With all that she had seen him do on the dance floor, she was surprised at his question. She was mostly surprised at its simplicity and honesty. It surprised her that Aum did not know he was already the peak of the party. Aum was, in fact, embodying the biggest wave she had seen at Full Spectrum in its illustrious and total history. And like most surfers, she could see the oncoming tsunami within the humblest rip curl of the ocean wave. His question put her on the spot because there was no easy answer.

"We all dream together." And she closed her eyes and the fading moonlight shone differently on her. The music changed to something strangely familiar. Aum could suddenly smell the sea as she slipped her hand into his. He saw it light up his hand brand from the Keeper, and she added patterns of the ocean to the image. Then her skin lightened; her cheekbones shifted ever so slightly; she slowly turned her face, which seemed to widen her chin; and her hair went from dark brown to light brown with a couple strands of blonde. The subtlety of her transformation was much more powerful than Aum's practice of replicating himself on all planes and surfaces.

"So continue to follow your unique path of dreamtime," Trae the Seer whispered. She gently withdrew her hand from his. He reeled as he opened his eyes to see this transformation in reality. Aum blinked in rapid succession. His shock was reflected in the caterwauling computerized chorus line, and the fact that everything was different but the same. The stage was there, and the dance floor was there, complete with the grassy hill backdrop, but the details were deeply altered. The size of the stage was different, the tarp was a different color, and there were different fabrics hanging. Everyone dancing was a new creature. In shock, he took a sharp breath and closed his eyes. Trae continued, "Follow your deepest, most heartfelt karmic soul longings. You seem like one that has kept his integrity intact, a warrior wizard of the highest caliber." Her head tilted in curiosity, "Will you be so different once you return home?"

"Home?"

***

Jenn wandered from booth to booth, still emerging from her a haze of analytical judgment. With every sip of caffeine, she expanded the functioning of her brain to dissect and structuralize this microeconomy, attempting to find her place within it. The night had brought in a much calmer atmosphere—in this area anyway—making it easier for her to think. Aural starlight and starbright sounds from the forest twinkled in her ears, and she noticed the still-thumping herd of wildebeests at the Main Stage, but there was no music across the stretch at the Common Stage. The fire pit was unlit and cold; everything looked to be shut down at the moment. Booths were closed and lights were off.

What exactly determines worth in a system so similar to bartering? She walked past the closed art gallery; all the attendants must be out dancing. She could still vividly remember, from mere glimpses while walking by at breakfast, the colorful and psychedelic imagery. The memories seeped back into the forefront of her brain, speaking an obscure visual language, watching her every reflecting thought and internal comment, commenting on every comment, building into a self-aware fractal repatterning of her consciousness.

She strode on in the moonlit darkness, gaining confidence with each step. There was one last booth in the row, with its light on and a deep glowing red spilling out onto the grass. Open and curious about what was alternative to the alternative, Jenn poked her head in. A cocktail of smells entered her nose—incense and burning plant medicines.

"Another wandering single soul tonight?" a woman greeted in an unusually slow monotone. "Displacement, curiosity, or both, I wonder? Have a seat."

There was a single circular stool in front of Jenn, an inch from her leg. She looked around. It wasn't much bigger than the glass phone booths she could remember as a child, smaller than a bus shelter, even. The woman motioned to the stool. Jenn took a seat and responded, "Um…both."

"Is that so?" The woman's fingers were busy shuffling a deck of cards. "That drink smells fantastic.…I'm going to have to grab one of those if I want to keep on going tonight, just so you and everyone else knows."

What the woman meant by "everyone else" she didn't understand.

"Did you want a sip?" Jenn put her still steaming latté on the small round table.

"No thanks," she smiled. "If I start, I'm not usually able to stop."

Beside Jenn's recycled paper cup, the woman spread some more herbs on a burning cocktail in a small glass bowl. There were a few candles next to it. It was simple and stripped down here. No medallions or artifacts, no power tools or incarnated deities. The walls were made of draped red fabric, the reflected candlelight creating a warm glow on the grass. Jenn inspected the thick smoke, then took a slow, deep inhale. Some long forgotten memory moved to the forefront of her mind, unlocked and transported through the newly constructed visionary art portal. She took a double-cupped handful of smoke and gently moved it over her face, over the top of her head, then pushed it all the way back down her spine. All the while, the woman continued to shuffle the deck.

"Sage for clearing the shadows, sweet grass to fill the space with love and light, cedar so the creator can hear us clearly, and a small spot of sandalwood to reach the underlying authenticity." She put the cards down in front of Jenn. "You want to take over shuffling?"

She finished her ancient smudge. "Sure." The cards were well used but still crisp in her hands. The black-and-gray matte finished card backs accented the brightly colored whir reflecting off the table. "Should I cut them, too?"

"If you like. Have you ever worked with the tarot before?" the ageless woman asked, her eyes clear behind round spectacles.

"I have, actually. A very long time ago, though."

Still entirely engaged with Jenn, the woman stood up naturally, shuffled around the table, and pulled a drawstring on the doorway. "So you understand the basic premise of a reading?" A heavy curtain shut, and all external sound was dampened. Smoke gathered near the roof.

"I think so," a more caffeinated Jenn replied. "The subconscious mind basically pokes through into the conscious mind, revealing images or words, memories or feelings that deal with deeper issues we may not directly see. The cards help evoke the subconscious and help us answer our own questions."

"Very astute. So what's your question?"

Jenn laughed a little at the woman's frankness, but then smelled a small whiff of sandalwood that hit an underlying emotional pocket, pond, even ocean. She tried to shake off the feeling, but only a quick and fragile frown appeared, damning up the emotion as she stood alone, isolated on a solitary island. "What am I doing here?" And she quickly cut the deck and slid it back.

"Good question."

The woman swooped a bushel of her black curls behind her ears, slightly exhaling in empathetic feeling, and said, "Give me your hands, my dear, just for a sec." Jenn did. "Close your eyes." She did.

"Gypsy, one scattered race, like stars in the sight of God. A member of the cosmic Earth tribe requests to view behind the night sky, your connected light web of insight." The tarot reader's dark brown eyes opened, she smirked just a little, and dealt out a five card spread—three cards across, one on top, and one below. Focused and to the point, just like the question.

"This first card will represent your present and the greater theme around your question." She flipped the center of the iron cross formation. It depicted a young man who was precariously close to a precipice.

"Oh great," Jen responded.

In the same monotone, "Oh, so you're familiar with the Fool card?"

"Well, this weekend, for sure."

The woman waited openly for more from Jenn. After a few moments, she reminded her, “As you can see, there are only four more cards here, so it’s best to get into more detail than less…that is, if you’re willing.”

Jenn nodded, “Well, I came here with my boyfriend. He’s been involved with this scene for a while now, a year maybe. But it’s just sort of a vacation for me, a celebration after some success in the ‘real world.’” She quoted the air with her fingers. “He’s always trying to get me involved in this, but to be honest, I’m not all that interested. It seems completely unreal, like a big waste of time. I mean, in the same sense that video games are unreal; it’s all nothing more than empty escapist entertainment.”

The woman nodded. “The Fool can signify a spontaneous decision. A new and unfamiliar situation, but also faith and innocence, representing a new beginning, a path of adventure, wonder, or personal growth.”

Jenn thought about it for a second. “Yeah, I guess just now, like two minutes ago, I learned a bit. I’m learning how to be here and be engaged in a way that’s dissimilar to most others here, I’m sure. I’m taking it all in on my own terms, finding myself in unfamiliar territory, but now grounded and learning—throughout that, even entertained. A working vacation almost.”

“The Fool card asks you to follow your heart no matter how crazy your impulses may seem.”

“Well,” Jenn laughed slightly and honestly confessed, “I guess that’s partly why I’m here, a crazy impulse.”

“Good,” and the woman flipped the next card.

Jenn looked at it and didn’t react.

“No initial observations?”

“Um, I’m not familiar enough with tarot to know which card that is.”

“This is the Four of Pentacles, and it’s in your past position.”

Still nothing from Jenn.

The reader continued, “This card represents your desire to create financial abundance above all else. This deeper seed, planted and unattended, has choked off all creative expression. It is an emotional tone which has fuelled the fires of jealousy, judgment, and ignorance, strengthening your resistance to change; though deep down, you know it’s for the best.”

Jenn blinked rapidly in succession, quietly, internally reeling from this read. Her perspective shifted even more as the sandalwood continued its work on her. She saw, in her imagination, memories with new clarity, situations at her work, with her family, and in her relationship with Aum blast to the surface.

"Hmm, still nothing? I can keep on describing the card for…"

"No, no, that's alright." Jenn choked the emotional reaction back again, just enough so she could speak. "I'm just trying to find the courage to vocalize. Some things have been buried quite deeply…for some time now. Do I really have to go there?" Jenn looked at the woman in deep turmoil.

"It's up to you, the depth you want to go. I'm here all night, all weekend in fact, if it's a very deep, dark well."

Jenn remained silent.

The woman put her fingers on the next card, ready to flip it. She looked at Jenn. Jenn paused, then nodded.

In the picture, Jenn could see flaming bodies falling from a crumbling edifice struck by a bolt of lightning. She remembered the storm from earlier in the evening, and again had the urge to run back to her tent. "You gotta be kidding."

"Hmmm, the Tower," a soft personal contemplation from the tarot reader.

"Okay…I give up," Jenn whispered, and remained seated.

"That's good, 'cause this card represents sudden and forced change, usually unwelcome. Drawing this card symbolizes a slap in the face, waking you up from one of those dreams in which you thought you were already awake. This card is placed in the future position of your read."

"Oh," Jenn responded, and with a hint of sarcasm, "Something to look forward to then."

"I thought you gave up?" The reader was on her case like a headmistress.

Jenn stressfully exhaled, "So, just to recap here, presently, spontaneity to the point of apparent folly; previously, lack of creativity, obsessive control, and blocked change; and upcoming, a forced change."

"Well forced change definitely verbalizes the image; it could also be a sudden revelation or release."

"Well this does all seem to relate to my question of purpose here." She took another sip of her warm drink, put down the cup, and remembered her previous conversation with the tea vendor. She blurted out, "Have you ever heard of something called Gridline Communications?"

The woman shook her head and put her fingers on the fourth card.

"What about John deGryder?" Jenn pursued.

"The Dragonrider? Of course I have," finally showing a spec of excitement.

"The Dragon…Rider?" Jenn blurted out, astounded by the similarity to Dragonkeeper's name. Fear erupted as she remembered her afternoon out-house encounter with the punk rock human coal eater, along with every other encounter with him at the festival. "There's another?!" It was all too much again, this new world; though she pushed through before her mind zapped off and she turned to run, "What's the next card?! Please."

The reader flipped the fourth card.

"The Page of Wands is in your reason position, a reminder to jump in with wholehearted emotion and strength, to believe in yourself, to focus on success, to be daring and take risks, to overcome your fears, and know that where there's a will, there's a way." Looking up from the cards to Jenn, the reader continued, "The Wands are the element of fire and spirituality, renewal and growth. This card calls forth a transitional space, which requires the same amount of patience, care, gentleness, and love that is evoked by the Fool."

Astounded and now stunned, even somewhat repaired, Jenn's jaw dropped slightly. "Wow."

"Last card." She looked at Jenn and flipped it.

She saw the familiar Venus-like depiction of the divine mother, chalice, Earth, imploding grace and power supported by the apostolic icons of art history: Mathew, Mark, Luke, and John as Man, Eagle, Lion, and Bull.

"The World," Jenn said in recognition.

"Yes." The tarot reader looked up at Jenn with relief. "Here we finally get a little lift from the divine in the position of potential. The culmination of all of the projected experiences in this read may ultimately be for the sake of your own prosperity. The World is a dance, and you are it's dancer my dear. This card is beyond specifics and represents a genuine healing, a giving of yourself, being engaged, active, and positive. Satisfaction, contentment, pleasure, peace of mind, and savoring the present are some of the qualities you can also look forward to—nothing short of your dreams coming true."

Excited and near flighty at this positive revelation, and the caffeine, Jenn took another quick sip. "Like an upside to the down?"

"Yes, but never underestimate the down. You do have quite a journey ahead of you. Truly, I can see you have made some great steps by being here, by becoming open to the moment and allowing yourself to be lost in impulse. However, as you experienced, there seems to be long-neglected aspects of yourself that have been in pain for quite some time—shoved in a closet as it were." As she spoke, again fully engaged with Jenn, the tarot reader naturally moved around the table towards the curtain door, with remaining deck in hand. "In order for you to fully let this trapped woman out, it looks as though the whole house might need to come down, not merely the closet door opened." She flipped the top card onto the stack in her hand and showed it to Jenn.

"10 of Swords," Jenn said, not moving. The reader took the card and placed it at the back of the deck and continued, "An internal swan dive into the deeply buried unknown, sunken at the bottom of the well, the pool, or ocean. I suspect that it will require risk taking, daring, your own willingness and choice to evolve into an empowered and enlightened woman. A full spectrum blossoming." She paused, then flipped and revealed another card.

"The High Priestess" Jenn responded, still not moving. The reader moved that card to the back of the deck, and opened the tent curtain for Jenn to exit. The capsule doors opened to the bigger capsule, and the fresh cold air enveloped them both. Smoke billowed out of the tent. The sounds of the event gingerly crept into Jenn's ears, reminding her of where she was. The tarot reader was still holding the curtain open for Jenn, but she was dazed; preoccupied with her house coming down. Stalling for time to adjust, to breathe, to process; or the time and space to talk out an abundance of revelations, Jenn stared blankly at the back of the booth, "In and out…just like that?"

"I'll be here all weekend; this is my business card if there's anything after." Even though she was still facing the back of the booth, Jenn knew she held it out for her, a slight indication for her to exit the space.

"Okay."

She was on her own. Jenn nodded to herself, as if to face it, to encourage her first steps into a new life, with a new attitude, even direction. Jenn stood and turned, took the business card and put it in her white hoodie pocket. She took out some bills as she exited the tent.

"No, that's okay, dear—unnecessary even. It's included in your ticket."

"My ticket?"

"Yes. Now if you'll excuse me, I'm throwing caution to the wind. An organic, fresh-brewed hot coffee? Or go to sleep? Seems like an easy choice to me." The reader smiled lightly and shrugged as she strode down the line of booths toward the tea dome. Jenn was intent on giving her something in exchange for the read, whether the read was subsidized by the festival or not. She waited a moment, watched the woman reach the tea vendor, then snuck back through the curtains of the booth.

As she was folding up her bills, she noticed, sitting at the center of the table, next to the lit candle, another florescent egg. Jenn could almost see it slightly rocking back and forth, as if someone had just placed it there. It didn't surprise her. With a hopeful, willing, and resolved choice, she pocketed the egg and left two twenties under the glass bowl of incense.

***

"Home?" Aum didn't rush his response, though it poked at a number of reoccurring sore spots inside him. He viewed his own floating black dots at the same time as he watched his body explode in every direction, content to prolong this momentary extasis, delving deep into the feeling of it. It pained him to think of his home and his place back there, in the real world. Trae looked over at him, an active listener, as Aum continued, "Human beings with an ingrained duty to humanity—those selfless miracle workers—have such large barriers to dissolve in order to fully function in the real world. Whether those duties include the daily heart-based healings of others or the duty to sound out alarm-based emergency actions, it seems a lot harder than ever before, and at this particular stage of humanity, to maintain the increasing levels of compassion required to temper the increasing levels of utter ignorance and growing stupidity."

"The final sleepers," she acknowledged.

"I have both a deep sensitivity and an ingrained duty to collective humanity, so I have problems at home, problems in the real world," Aum confessed. "I am part magician and part digital entity, and unfortunately, I expect to be regarded so out there. It upsets me greatly to be deemed merely a cog in a machine, or a consumer profile, or a mouse looking for cheese or snake climbing ladders. I demand that my actions, my dreams, the full depth of my being is respected and acknowledged. I will gladly hand over every ounce of creative willpower, emotional and cognitive energy, my full heart for a cause if it's one of integrity, one of conscious awareness to the penny, to the transaction, to the interaction, and to the thought. That's the standard I hold myself to, on a breath-by-breath basis, and I expect no less from every single human being on this Earth, and every single human to come. But people out there don't get that, and I'm regarded as a troublemaker, too big to control, verging on insane. And I think people here in this world get it. They understand those ideals, they get that commitment—they may even be living it out themselves."

Trae added, "The company of peers relieves the pain of having to be alive right now, of having to work this hard to keep real hell on Earth from happening, to keep it all together." She paused thoughtfully, "Keep faithful, be your love, 'cause you have a lot to give."

He nodded, continuing, "Core of core, beat and breath, I feel I must devote my short and passing life to the sounding of ten thousand more trumpets, which will not be ignored by the deepest of sleepers. How can you achieve something like that and live in the real world? I feel like I bang my head against a wall everyday, getting more and more frustrated with life, with myself, even with my girlfriend—my girlfriend with me…my partner," he paused kindly and confusedly thought of her, "is the biggest challenge I face at home, my longtime love." An image of her at dinner this evening emerged. "She still sleeps through all this," and in the wave of emotional pain that followed this confession, Aum nearly wept.

Trae let him continue.

He recognized this and let all efforts go, let the music soothe, and was able to allow long-held expectation to release. He exhaled and released those pesky unconsciously hidden judgments that had anchored in his mind to box Jenn in. There were cheers, and he smiled.

"I know this divine state will pass and I will long for this space over and over." He met her eyes. "How can I get to the absolute crest of the next large wave, peer into the abyss, see my truest self, be my truest self, unafraid, and walk freely, knowing daily peace in my soul, in reality, at home, and in the world?"

She looked at him and said, "I'm glad your heart is so big, Aum. Otherwise I wouldn't advise this to even the most passionate of seekers. Find the Riddle Solver."

"The Riddle Solver?" The words rang true. "The real Riddle Solver?" Like a bell awakening a practicing yogi from shavasana, Aum was instantly back in his body.

"For all of us." Trae smiled like the sun. "If you commit to this journey of self knowledge, you will find the Riddle Solver. You will find your calling; you will find the answers to your questions, to your own riddles, and the keys to your self-imposed shackles." She put a hand on his cross-legged knee. "Aum, you will find indistinct and whole new realities both beyond and enmeshed within riddles. Thank you." She winked. "Prayers received." And she continued, "Until you find the Riddle Solver, you will be continually plagued in the world, plagued by self-doubt, ladder climbing, complacence, and will never find the deep peace you seek. Now is the time to go deep. The Riddle Solver holds infinity in his gaze for all eternity, and when you reach him, and see his true face, when you receive the vision of your truest self reflected, you will know at your core that you have succeeded in finding the deep peace of karmic balance you both seek and deserve."

The music swelled and the crowd cheered. It was changing to welcome the rising sun. Aum knew their time was almost done, so he gently sputtered, "Okay, but how do I get there? Where do I start?"

"You have started. In general, always move with clear intention and intuitive feeling over precise planning. Specifically, the magpie, the surgeon, and the dragon trinity, to the ferryman and then to the shaman. This is the path that will lead you to the Riddle Solver.

You can switch the specific and general along the way if you wish," she smiled and winked.

"Have you met him, Seer?" He asked, "Is he the teacher you once spoke of? I am here because he wants me to be?"

"What do you think?"

He nodded slowly while breathing deeply from his naval to his throat, reaching even deeper levels of trance. The bass kicked in with his nods, and the crowd roared.

She nodded back into his breath, "Aum, hear this, you are at the crest of the next large wave. It is the biggest and the last."

***

"I need a light!"

Jenn had taken merely a single step back out of the tent when she looked up, startled. There was a man circling the fire pit shouting, raving, roaring even.

"Light! I need a light! Someone!"

Jenn looked around to see everything had been deserted. The tarot reader was gone and the tea dome lights were off, along with all the other booths.

"Come on, people," he muttered to himself. "A lighter, a matchstick, I really don't have a preference." He didn't notice Jenn in the darkness.

A matchstick? The florescent egg was still in her hand. It was lightweight. She rattled it and could tell it was wood.

She dove deep. With every step toward the man, embracing exhilarating adventure, releasing all judgments, being an active participant, seeing herself in her highest, she let the feeling of being scared shitless excite her actions, rather than paralyze her.

"Prometheus?" He softly growled, noticing her approach. She could see his graying stubble, the crow's-feet and total anguish surrounding his eyes. She was approaching a wounded animal.

"Dragon…Keeper?"

"Jenn? Where's FreeZen?" She felt a quiet calming glimmer of hope in him.

"Um…I don't know."

And it was dashed.

"Do you have a light?"

"Here."

She popped open the egg and dumped its light contents into his hand.

It wasn't a match.

It was a dry, gnarled, and slightly knotted twig.

She stared at it in utter disbelief, adrenaline rising like an extreme athlete, staring into the abyss within his palm.

"I'm sorry sir, Mr. Dragon, sir." Childlike, she inhaled deeply, expecting to drown or die from her presumptive leaping steps, but then smelt a slight whiff of sandalwood in the crisp clean air and continued, "That's all I have for you. My kindest and heartfelt apologies."

He caught the subtle smell also, stressed-out expression releasing. "A twig of sandalwood?"

She nodded unknowingly, sinking further, diving deeper, trusting beyond risk or logical reasoning.

Hand still out, he just stared at her. Not in hatred, or frustration, contempt, or even confusion. He just stared, as if put on pause, waiting, and able to wait forever, on pure faith.

Jenn didn't know what to say, either, so she just stared back at him.

It was a lifetime within seconds before Jenn heard the rhythm of running water. *The river*, she thought, still staring. Then there was something else—the echo of labored breathing, long strides in the grass, looming louder and louder, closer and closer. Then gasping for the air next to her.

Jenn and the Keeper's locked magnetic gazed broke off as he looked next to her.

"Here's a lighter," a man said, gasping. "Here's a lighter."

The man held out a red Bic and dropped it into Dragonkeeper's extended hand, with the twig. Close to total exhaustive collapse, the man rested his hands on his legs.

Dragon looked at them both. "So be it."

The Dragon took the sandalwood twig and the lighter, not even glancing at the waiting dried leaves, bark, and kindling in the fire pit. He walked toward the middle of the Common Stage dance floor and planted the sandalwood twig in the center, lighting it. The flame burned the dry twig fiercely until a living gust of wind blew the flame out. The stick smoldered and the powerful scent filled the air.

He knelt down and began to cover the smoke with his cupped left hand, releasing it, cupping it, releasing it, cupping it again, at seemingly random intervals.

The other man was now breathing calmly with a handheld in his right hand, pressing keys and speaking out loud.

"Zero, one, one, zero, zero, zero, zero, one, send. Zero, one, one, one, zero, one, zero, one, send. Zero, one, one, zero, one, one, zero, one, send."

In her left ear, again, the rhythm of the river embraced Jenn's attention and she automatically took a step toward it. As she went, she couldn't tell whether she was going deeper or emerging; all she knew was that the sound of the river was getting louder.

She dashed across the open alcove of the Water and Wood Stage. It was barren and asleep, most of the equipment gone. She weaved through the final trees, caught an unscented breathtaking gust in her lungs, hopped from rock to rock, and knelt at the water's edge, seeing the moving reflection of the starry night sky.

Heart pounding, mind racing, she dipped her hands in the cold water and splashed her face and head and hair over and over and over. The river gladly took it all. It was all overwhelming her; she dug deeper because she didn't know what else to do. She processed and cried and looked internally and cried and realized and processed, seeing the sandalwood smoke and in it the egg, the ticket, the reading, the dance, even the night before. The walls came down, the floors fell through, the framing collapsed, but the concrete foundation stayed strong. As her emotions drained into the ecosystem, a large beetle flew past her sightline and landed on the rock next to her. She noticed it and stared at its form: its legs, wings, and pinchers. The colors were distinct and beautiful, shining in the moonlight. It stared up at her with an anthropomorphized curiosity. She wiped the remaining tears from her eyes and reacted with an open intrigue, a reflected curiosity.

It flew downstream. Jenn stood to follow it, gulping down another breath of crisp air. She was feeling steadier, emotionally lighter than she had in years. However, every muscle now seemed cemented in place, every movement grinding and sweating out the remaining tension and turmoil in her body.

She continued to make her way over the rocks. Following the insect, flipping between two-legged and four-legged walking, maneuvering Gollum-like over boulder and rock. The river bent to the right and she followed it, continuing over slab and stone. Eventually her feet found the mud pockets between. Another twenty strides around the bend, she found herself on a wet beach where the sound of angels faded into her ears.

Near a small bush where the beach met the forest, there was a handmade sign:

Welcome, open souls, to Back Stage, the healing zone.

She walked toward the direction of the sound and saw that the beach spread back further away from the river. A small tarp hung high in the trees, no bigger than twenty square feet. Underneath it, on the small patch of sand, there was a coffee table with some equipment, speakers as bookends, and a shirtless man sitting cross-legged. There were others, lying in a circle, with yoga mats laid out on the sand; a dozen or so people had their feet pointed to the center.

The nearness of the music from the Main Stage was overpowering the subtleties of the angelic tone; it was so close Jenn could even see the shine of the moon off the back of the Main Stage's tarped structure through the trees. *Another stage?* she thought.

A woman emerged from the trees in an earth-tone brown wrap skirt and a green shawl. A lavender hood covered her face, and her long brown locks were interwoven with amulets and crystals. She wore a large shelled and beaded necklace and carried a wooden staff—no, it was a didgeridoo. *Like Aum's*, Jenn thought.

As the didge woman circled the group, she removed items from a pouch—stones, crystals, feathers, and minerals. She placed them on seemingly random body parts. Jenn noticed some of the finer details of the scene; she could see all these characters fit together like a puzzle. The bizarre costumes and outfits, the colors and the body shapes, they all complimented each other and balanced the circular formation—but there was an empty mat.

Jenn crouched down in the sand, the only audience member to watch the performance.

The woman began to play and continued to circle the group. She quickly found the resonant frequency of the tonal music from the speakers and began to pulse with it. The woman spent detailed time with each member of the circle, focusing on the objects she had placed, as well as other body parts, such as fingertips, hips, kneecaps or toes, even directly between the eyes.

"Group metapoetics…," someone in the circle said.

Someone else responded quickly after, "Deepest of trance states."

"Shared intension and observations...," whispered another quietly.

The music from the speakers changed tone and began to pulse and reflect the didgeridoo. The woman had completed the circle and moved to stand in the center, rotating and intoning, covering everyone with a gentle soft blanket of sound as she grew quieter and quieter until she reached silence. The woman returned to her pouch and began to lay out more amulets and objects in the center of the group. The music continued, along with the strange conversation.

"...The whole of Jung's collective unconscious, in which there is no good or bad, there just is..."

"...a person could look at it both ways the same..."

"...particles or waves..."

"...fire and water..."

"...muscle and bone..."

"...a new part of the collective unconsciousness has become conscious of the whole..."

"...and details within the whole..."

"...the positive, consciously moves and gazes, and shadow, becomes apparent by mere reflection..."

"...are we in danger?..."

It was becoming one voice again. Jenn didn't like it. It was too fluid, like a single ghost operating the voice box of each person in the circle.

"...The negative will move as well, whether it knows it or not..."

"...curiosity, or strides for power within fundamental wave form physics..."

It was too much, like the previous night. Everyone was freakily thinking as one being; the memory came back to her full force now. She started to feel sick to her stomach and, again, wanted to run back to her tent and sleep, make excuses, and forget the skin-crawling feeling.

"...The dance becomes panic..."

"...they stretch in opposite directions..."

She couldn't think about it; she couldn't even watch it, so she closed her eyes. Sitting cross-legged in the sand, the new spark inside committed her to hold on, to endure it no matter the discomfort.

The wind blew past her ears and she again heard the rhythms in the river. Jenn focused on that and stood up with stiff and frozen legs, eyes still closed.

"…There will be new and tremendous amounts of pressure on the entire system…"

"…much like a stretched piece of gum, there will be a final breaking point…"

"…I want to believe that everyone can open their eyes, but again it's both particle and wave…"

"…open is closed and closed is open…"

The didge started up again.

"…Gradual change in frequency…"

"…our separating worlds will slowly dissolve from one another, both sides no longer aware of the other…"

In Jenn's mind's eye, standing with closed eyes, she could see large circles—fiery eclipses, growing smaller and smaller and smaller. She exhaled and found the aural pattern in the water. She let the pattern move through her body, and she danced with it.

"…Does that work with the mythology and symbols of our past?…"

"…we live in a world where new mythology and archetypes are being unearthed…"

"…daily…"

Jenn started dancing slowly. She bounced up and down, using her knees and waist, her chest rising and falling, her arms slowly raised, elbows bending, pointed fingertips almost meeting at her heart center, and she started pushing down with her palms in opposite rhythm to her head.

"…Once buried, now being brought to the forefront…"

Muscles and joints relaxed, her skin loosened and eyes unclouded. Somehow she could feel the river again removing the tension from her body. Her mind eased.

"…Finally feet to walk the Earth…"

"…lungs to breathe the air…"

"…posthuman psychology…"

"…or posthuman psychosis…"

The woman broke off playing the didge, and in the abrupt silence, the background sound became more subtle, so much so that the Main Stage music seeped in. The woman moved to the outer edge and began again to move around the circle. She spoke as she did:

"There are still many things that are being left up to chance. Decisions have been made in real time. Change is imminent. Think of collective conscious not as a piece of gum but as a rubber band."

The sound of the water was louder; Jenn let herself focus less on the speaking circle. The rhythmic structure of the natural sound was somehow more solid. Jenn couldn't believe what she was hearing and expressively danced further into it. She even started to enjoy herself.

"The pressure and stretch will become too much for one side, and it will give out; shadow or form will release, surrender to the opposite side and propel the whole to a speed never reached before. The two opposites will become one, and duality will be transcended through the impact of pure karmic particle physics."

The circle exploded with voice:

"…Atomic force collisions…"

"…from our own decisions…"

"…shadows exposed by the light, and lights go dim…"

"…rubber bands can break too you know…"

"…time will become nonexistent…"

"…and the world around us will become more malleable than it has ever been…"

"…just before it all crashes…"

"…the most epic battles…"

"…inside every day…"

"…inside every hour…"

"…inside every minute…"

"…inside every mind…"

"…inside every body…"

"…inside every breath…"

"…inside every beat…"

A slight beat dropped in time with these last words, synching up and building on the rhythmic water. To Jenn's surprise, her mind opened up and she saw herself at a body of water. The wind blew in her eyes; she tasted the salt in the air. She could see the water moving to the music. She continued to dance. She was brand new. She let her shoulders and arms go, moving with the sight and sound of the water on the beach, kicking sand up with her dancing shoes. Suddenly, in her vision, someone touched her hand. She couldn't tell if it was real or not and quickly opened her eyes in shock. Before her was a man with his open palm feeling the vibration of the river, auditorily sampling the river's structure with his left hand-embed, while the other palm stretched, pointing to the coffee table of gear. Virabhadrasana two, warrior-like, it was truly a digital yoga pose. Jenn peered directly at the glossy beetle print on his shirt, a royal scarab with wings and tail feathers. His long dreads were tied back, gathered like a collection of coiled serpents.

"Can you take me to the Dragonrider?" she asked.

He lifted his eyebrows in surprise, switching to a new digital yoga position, trikonasana. "The Dragonkeeper?" His piercing blue eyes scanned her, nearly soul deep.

She swam past his powerful gaze, surfing the river medicine. "No, I saw him already."

He responded quickly, "To the Rider it is, milady. I accept, except I require transportation—a ride in five minutes to meet him." He smiled, beaming confidence out past his whiskered chin. "This do you accept?"

She looked over and saw the entire group of mediators were now dancing and flowing together in the sand of the healing zone, Back Stage.

He continued to observe her patiently, beyond any notion of seconds ticking away. And she continued to observe the group; mind flowing freely like the river, *Business is always hyperaware of any inkling of possibility in getting a new client, in getting a new contract, in making more money. Like a brown hound dog on the trail of a scent, workers sit at their posts with militant vigilance, stimulating contacts and colleagues with phone calls and e-mails from behind their office desks. With an outrageous lifestyle comes an outrageous way of maintaining it—pool, Jacuzzi, tennis court, cabin, Sea-Doo, boat, home theater, sports cars, the racetrack, strip joint, hookers, booze, blow, and betrayal. Rivalries are created, as well as supportive long-lasting relationships, switching back and forth ad infinitum.*

In the field of business, the person, the individual very quickly disappears and is replaced with a cog in the process of acquiring money. It's an environment that breeds apathy: "It doesn't matter; this is just a job, not my life. My real life happens after work and on the weekends."

These people here are exactly the same, Jenn thought, *but completely and totally opposite. Constantly vigilant and aware of the direction in which development is happening, because they are so connected at an ideological level this place is possible with minimal procedure, just a base set of rules that lie in the goodness of trusting worthy hearts. Individuals here are no longer cogs of misery, but blazing balls of light in constant all-encompassed pursuit of divine bliss and rapture. Poking and prodding the ether, and scientifically, emotionally, psychologically monitoring the response of those actions on both an internal and external front, doing so not to make money, to consume, or for mindless entertainment, but for the purpose of self-perpetuation, to continue the path they have chosen, beyond the constraints of a grounded ordinary life.*

The enormity of the vision shook tears to her eyes. She nodded to the Egyptian man, the royal Scarab, and said, "I'll meet you in the parking lot."

Jenn wandered past the dancers, finding a path through the woods and through the center of all four stages. She took a quick glance and saw Aum sitting up on the Main Stage. There were tears in her eyes as she gazed on his light-emitting beauty—he was all mystic heartbeat, his entire body, the music, the entire space expanding and contracting with its pulse.

This is where he lives. Regardless of where he is, or who he's with, whether it's with these people, me, or anyone else. This is his true home, and these special souls are all the more rich because of it.

She closed her eyes and took a single deep inhale. At its still point, she sent all the love in the world to Aum before she exhaled fully. Jenn returned to their campsite, packed up their blue Mazda, and left him.

***

"Our sacred fire, its warm cloak, and its containment, its burning off of excess...has gone out. Our historic energetic efforts here have been released out to the world, unintentionally. These efforts have been noticed and thus will be tracked, taken advantage of, used, and manipulated. A contradiction begins, a new cycle of both hibernating disintegration and building metatectonic pressure. A void, a collapsing vacuum, is filled with its opposite intention, still pushing the motion further, adding retractive reverse momentum. You ride this final wave, Saoshyant. Game over. The Riddle is now a collapsing system. The doors are now closed to new participants, and Jenn did not make it," Trae indicated softly.

Intense concern flashed across Aum's face. "What do you mean?! She made it in the gates without a ticket."

"True, she had a key to get here, but it was you who has carried almost the entire weight of her while here. And now she has walked down the staircase from the protected pedestal to which you have carried her; she has manifested each step herself, one by one; stepping down one by one. She has left the event."

"She left?!" he replied with instant and utter disbelief.

"Whether you believe it or not is inconsequential. You'll find real-time confirmation soon enough. Worry not, for she still has divine purpose to which she is becoming aware—purpose that she will fulfill. Her newfound integrated leadership skills will assist in building a world for those left behind—a bodhisattva nurse in triage and an engineer of bridges. Your challenge now, Mr. Zen, is to let her go as she has let you go—with your blessing."

"What?!"

"She is already gone, and you must let her go in all ways possible. You must now be crystal clear and have a Zen buddhic focus on every moment, a computational analysis on every thought that passes like water through your mind and the root of its organic nature. You must be crystal clear, fully flowing inside the energy of the branches that attach to the others across the country, and, around the globe. But most especially sensitive to the people in your immediate vision; these are the leaves, and He…He is the wind."

Aum's ground was falling away, his protected life falling away. His mind was reeling, and he could feel things being torn apart. Waves of alarm passed through him, causing his body to shake.

"This is not where she has work to do, Aum; you must realize that. From your perspective, those steps are down and away from you, but to her, those steps are giant leaps toward her own divine purpose. Please trust me when I tell you she loves you and wishes you courage and divine insight as your own giant leaps transform into full beats of winged flight."

"She left me?" He tried to breathe through the panicked confusion. Aum was in this now, 100 percent. He did not come to grips with the full extent of the change that occurred until a beam fell from the top of the half-dome, almost landing on a dancer. Trae, along with a third of everyone there, quickly, and very directly, looked at him in a panic. This collective gaze was the biggest crushing weight he had ever felt in his life; the concentration required was more than he could have ever fathomed. The tsunami had crested, he was there, and he could feel the whole world on his shoulders, cracking open.

TWO

“The responsibilities of the technoshaman never end. Like the shamans of ancient cultures, they must translate the waveforms of other dimensions into the explicate reality for the purpose of forecasting the future and charting a safe path through it.”

— Douglas Rushkoff

Chapter Seven

There was a full red moon in the sky hanging low over the horizon of downtown's trendiest street. A lunar eclipse showed itself at random. It emerged from behind the dark rain clouds and showered down its vibration on only the most observant of onlookers. The rain had finally stopped, and on street scene and concrete the moonlight pulse revealed mask upon mask, skin within skin, the living ecology and morphogenetic templates that mapped the man-made angles, vibration coating them, and bending them, with the ocean's tidal motion. Beyond the foot steps of numerous apartment escapees, thunderous unrelenting voices still rained down from the sky in cycles. Bicycles, thin and one speed, splashed past him, cut through fresh puddle with striking fiery glare, followed by the shrouded down turned umbrella eyes of passers by. There were a few different cities layered here, poured on top of each other, all combined to expose an emotional quality that was far more tetchy and cantankerous than simply the individual inhabitants themselves.

The afternoon downpour had quickly come in from the ocean horizon during the late afternoon. Comfortable with the rainy season at this time of the year, the city dwellers were usually equipped with numerous umbrellas and back-up umbrellas. However, this season, a long stretch of uncharacteristically dry heat caused a very different city to emerge: needlessly acerbic, aggressive and pressurized, combat boots and dart-loaded eyes were required for afternoon walks, for every glance was filled with pompous and superfluous attack.

The subtle cognitive circuitry of the city, and countryside beyond, was on the fritz - like rabbit ears picking up the electrical pulses of a lightning storm - as the planetary environment progressively mutated. No one seemed to recognize that the homeostasis of the organic human lineage was embedded within an ecosystem more powerful than can be consciously comprehended.

Many were caught off guard, but welcomed the rain's return after so many dry weeks; they quickly found shelter wherever they could. Restaurants, pubs, bookstores, and coffee shops were all filled with wet customers complaining about the sudden monsoon. Record breaking weather patterns broke the pattern of daily being and people were forced to take note. From the tape-loop-like auto-pilot-conversations in each and every social pocket, down to an integration on the level of finest cellular vibration. Relief. Even with moon amp. Back to 'normal'. Sort of. Whether fully present or not, each person took their time, drawing out their browsing privileges, selecting a single small item to purchase. Once they did, they realized that they had to move on to the next venue, to purchase the next item. Thankfully, after a few hours, the afternoon rain let up; it rescued them from spending their rainy day savings in sheltered consuming, in one consuming shelter after another.

Gazing at the red moon through a window, Aum had no problem extending his single purchase to a day-long venture at a coffee shop community library combo. Cozy with couches and a beatnik atmosphere, he blasted his brain with books at length. He let the power of *Info-psychology*, a book by Dr. Tim Leary, reroute synapses, transform thought sequences, and reconstruct the DNA inside him that needed refurbishing. No place to go in the pouring rain, nothing to do but transform his mind and be where he was at. He watched intently for opportunities, and further clues. He observed that life is no longer contained within a collective vision of what it is. And hitting the snooze button again won't alleviate the ego's denial of the lifting veil, or the flickering awakening eyes opening to a direct stream of reality's open source code. Time to wake up and get out of bed, face the new day, and what it brings; whether the internal soul celebration painted as an external orchestral sunrise, or the confused indecision of spring birdsongs and a summers day heat in the middle of what is normally a watery winter.

It had been a few weeks, or maybe a few months since Full Spectrum. Alone for such a long period of time, it's function seemed to lose all meaning. Aum could have been on the road for months, or years, maybe even a decade, he was not sure. Days blended together, cities and towns were big box carbon copies of each other on different colored reams of landscaping paper.

Aum had squatted in fields, hitchhiked, and when the opportunity arose, even jumped trains and snuck on busses, though mostly he walked.

He was resourceful. He ate from trees and fields, snuck a carrot or two when he could find gardens, community or private, he filled his water bottle in springs and creeks when he found them, or public washrooms when he had no other option.

At one point he traded his yoga mat for a meal. It was a gift from Jenn a few months ago. He had hardly used it, and found it strange to get used to after having developed a strong practice without a mat over the course of many years.

His meditations were strong. For the most part totally infused by the surrounding nature. After a stretch of his journey that lasted a week or so without food, he had even begun to see the world, understand it, as vibration. There was no real difference between the trees and the birds, other than the fact that the birds could move around easier, as well as give voice to the divine celebration of their physical earthly existence.

Aum was without his computer—and he felt like the only one in the world without a handheld or even a simple mobile, and he definitely could not afford a hand embed. The thrill and addiction of bio-integration by rebellious and affluent youth was so similar to the rise of tattoo and piercing subculture it was as if a changeless pattern had formed. The handembeds and skin screens of Trans-humanist Consumerism was something he deemed even more unethical that Consumerism itself, especially since it pulsed a specific target market of kidz who had honed well designed replicating money mechanisms, and had absentee parents. The cyber mutation trend of disaffected youth was now a solidified branch of consumerism worse than Christmas, because it never stopped the panicked marketing ploy of "manic sales before it all fails."

As he journeyed and dreamwalked, Aum resorted to Internet café's to check-in with his online presence. He thought there might be clues, but strangely, there was no activity on the boards. None at all. All message boards had been inactive since Full Spectrum and some threads, ones that he was hoping to re-investigate, were deleted entirely.

He couldn't recall how he had made it into this new city. Every step was unlinked from the last.

Another biker sped by. As he left the coffee shop the clouds were still heavy, but the rain less so. People were slowly beginning to venture back outdoors, and into the evening. The darkness of night allowed the city to be lit by the reflection of the red moon in the many-puddled quiet streets, along with the usual dark yellow neon glow. In the crisp evening Aum walked in no particular direction, though still assured in his steps. He was the opposite of the young trees growing in their respective holes in the cement along the sidewalk. They were stooped low from the weight of collected raindrops over the course of the dreary afternoon and from the recognition of their own purpose: mere decoration. After a prolonged eco submission, Aum was acclimatized to the environment of the countryside, and now had a difficult time with the pollution levels. As he walked on the concrete he could sense where the pockets of oxygen were. The environment had changed so drastically over the past few years that there were actual bubbles of roaming micro atmosphere that contained only carbon dioxide. They were invisible to the naked eye, but one step in and suffocation would commence. So as Aum walked, he consciously connected to each drooping tree, he'd breathe with it, while, Tarzan-like, he spotted the next. With lungs full he'd move to the tree ahead. He could almost feel the trees themselves sucking the carbon dioxide right out of him; as he looked at the pattern of branches it was almost as if he could see them expand like a pair of lungs.

With the squeak of sneakers on wet pavement, people walked past him as he swung along. Whether on evening strolls with loved ones after afternoon love-making in welcome isolation, or pet owners being dragged around by their unlikely four-legged masters, each passerby was pleasant, a strange occurrence for a night filled with an almost electric lunar current.

Aum wandered off the concrete of the main street to find himself in a quiet neighborhood at the bottom of a steep incline.

While walking he thought, 'What do I need right now?' His stomach piped in, 'Something to eat.'

"Yeah!" he agreed out loud.

A few more strides and he came across an apple tree in a front yard, in full fruit. With hundreds of unpicked apples on the ground and just as many crisp greens still hanging on the tree; the limp limbs weighed down by the rain, the wet clean fruit begged to be picked. He snapped two off, one in each hand as he strode by. A third fell in unison. With expert timing he pocketed an apple while catching the third in mid-air. He instantly brought it to his mouth. His tastebuds activated a wave of awe as the bright flavors accented the immediate manifestation of his psycho-biological need.

Aum continued on to find a small stream hidden in the dark, running through a planned green space. His water bottle was still full from the coffee shop, but he checked it out of habit. Past all the streetlights, and past all paths and landmarks, past the groomed park that gave way to the unsolicited and wild forest, he could hear the sound of drums. Only the truly interested, the truly fearless would ever venture into the darkness where the tribal sounds were coming from. Aum, without fear, sensed something familiar.

After all of the electronics had been packed up and the dance party deserted, Full Spectrum filtered out into the world leaving only the analogue kids behind. They were the true believers, the forgotten and the left behind, by choice or by accident. Vagabonds and reincarnations from time forgotten, Shakespearian bards, societal outcasts and functioning schizophrenics. African rhythm beholders, medicine facilitators, and skinny white Indian devotees who sang unrelentingly and psychotically their 'Hari Krishna' mantras. Aum was there, in this strange mix. It was the vibratory aftermath of ground zero. That was him actually, ground zero embodied. And as he walked he could see it in the eyes of those who dared gaze into his. Quantum double slit experimentation aside, he could perceive its direct effect on reality. He could hear it in the subtle cadence in conversation, and when drummers played his thoughts out in precise rhythmic sequences. There was however, enough of a latency to recognize exactly where his boundaries resided, sometimes near, sometimes very far away from his actual physical being. Where was his starting point in all this? Where could he find the magpie?

Random rain drops splattered a book he pulled out of his pack. He read a line on the back of his bookmark that he had written while sipping raw hot chocolate in the coffee shop library. It was a little holographic shard of his manifested literary imagination, inspired by the writings of the Galileo of Consciousness:

I hear the doorway through which sounds of conscious creation and planetary motion come.

He walked fearlessly into the darkness and the sound of drums, and laughed at the possibility of giving himself clues in the Riddle. The drums also abruptly changed to laughter. Both coincidence, and a sign of verification. He was headed in the right direction.

"The Riddle Solver, hey?" was the last thing he had said to himself in his tent on the last night of Full Spectrum. As he lay down to sleep, his last thought was, 'Where to begin.'

The systematized pressure of the event's close was diffused through him and his dream life. Within a sole isolated tube and the imaginary realms, beyond the gaming networks and collaborative creation and destruction architecture, his experience had no semblance of a familiar day to day reality, or even previous dreamtime experience, but consisted of abstracted machinery grinding into states of digital red rusted decay and chaos. Charged by some inner instruction set, he was to connect grids of dots in a 6th dimensional time space manifold, stitching them together as if merely an analogue telephone patchwork operator. His lucid consciousness viewed disembodied graphic window interfaces, working on their own accord, to copy and transfer soul beings into new physical reflections – which would not penetrate the clear glass or small dimensions of available window frames – causing tremendous amounts of flow constipation. In his dreams he reached para-lucidity and worked on task upon task of puzzling emotional processing checklists. At certain points a mind would state "Wow, I finally made it back here. Gotta work fast to reroute, rewire and reroot," and the words would spread across the bottom of his eyeball-understanding like stock market ticker-tape while stale and overused arguments of global environmental apocalypse were replaced by true local community health.

Then there was a far off *Caw*.

At first he didn't notice.

Caw-Caw.

"Magpie…" and his eyes jumped open.

Caw. It was followed by the sound of a big ass hauling truck starting up.

"Right, we're in a fucking hurry here man," He said to himself curtly as he jumped up and out of the tent, running toward the sound of the engine. Something in him still wasn't straight. He was flooded with dizziness and he ended up on the ground with a face full of dirt. It didn't help that he was both pulling on his shirt and putting on his shoe in mid- step. Thankfully the truck driver and his crew had one more stage to disassemble so Aum could go pack up his tent and pack what remained of his belongings. Which hurt.

It all hurt. But it was a good kind of hurt. A frightening kind of hurt. Total freedom with no safety net. Total incoherent insanity with no looking back. His life was his and his alone, an opportunity for a deeper devotion, deeper steps toward the jewel of his quest.

He knew Jenn was fine though, his heart shined with joy and pain when he thought of her. Often he would reach a state of total loss and would shake his head, thinking of her with awe and stupor, while adrift in a new world. Needing to understand what happened, the words 'you bitch' would explode out of his blame-coated heart, as if it was overcome by tourettes. 'How could you leave me this far out!'

With all of his belongings stuffed in his pack, pot, rice and tent included, he made his way down the dusty trail to the sound of the common tribe, the leftovers.

He gazed at the eclipse, inhaling it's potency and moving it's power into his feet as he walked past a few grandfather spruce trees, still dripping wet from the day's rain. Over a wooden bridge he traversed a small creek that reflected the moonlight. In between the long stretching branches of pine trees, Aum saw close to a dozen gypsy-hipsters with bright homemade clothes and African hand drums. They were creating rhythms that swirled out of the circle in spirals, entrancing Aum as he walked toward them.

After approaching with care, Aum was about to sit down unassumingly in the grass when the current jam session once again broke out in laughter. A tall man with long blonde hair floated toward Aum.

"Hey, how's it going friend?"

"Quite well kind sir, thank you," Aum replied. "Is this a private celebration or can anyone join in?"

"Oh, anyone can join in. Of course. We do prefer people with good listening skills."

"So leave your ego at the door?"

"If you'd like to," the man paused for a second, thinking, then introduced himself, offering his hand. "My name's Carey, but everyone calls me Blue Eagle." Accepting his hand, and looking deeply into Carey's clear blue eyes, Aum replied, "My name is Aum." Curiosity overcame him and Aum continued, "Does your name come from the Mayan Calendar solar sign? Or from your eyes?"

"Both actually," Blue Eagle replied. "You're familiar with the Tzolken?"

"I've studied a little bit of it. Though my knowledge of it is far from complete."

"I don't know anyone whose knowledge is, yet everyone here has a deep passion for it." He motioned to the rest of his friends as if family. "Something about the way non- linear time is structured around emotion rather than money, or work." He looked back at Aum, "Would you like to join the jam session?"

"I would love to. I didn't bring any instruments with me though," Aum said.

"That's okay," Blue Eagle replied as he led Aum toward the circle and sat down.

Blue Eagle began introducing everybody, but then one of the women burst out, "No Blue Eagle, lets play the name game!" She took a big inhale, and with exuberant child-like innocence said, "I'm Justine and I like juice!" She started giggling uncontrollably, her large brown curls bounced up and down. They all seemed to be aligned with an energy of happiness.

"My name's Linda and I love lettuce!" and she laughed exuberantly at her own silliness.

"My name is Stacey and I like smoked salmon...well actually... not really, but it was the only thing that came into my head."

Surprisingly most of the names stuck in Aum's head, far better than if Blue Eagle would have simply introduced them.

"My name is Jeremy and I like juice, just like Justine, but I also like juggling jumping jet planes!" His over emphasis on the j's made everybody laugh and cheer.

The name game continued around the circle until it came to the last woman, whom Aum could tell, made a point of connecting quite intently on this first introduction. With long black hair, full lips and a sparkling round face she looked at him piercingly and said, "My name is Demona and I like didgeridoo players." There was a scorpion's intelligence and a defiant darkness in the thick layers of mascara framing her eyes, eyes which revealed with the extremes of courage and fear. The group responded with a collective grade school expression, "oooooohhhhh."

Aum couldn't help but smile. He was in her sights and even now, he could feel what was ahead of him as he met her gaze. He exposed his fearless soul while inspecting hers. With a playful feigned ignorance he asked aloud, "What's a didgeridoo?"

The introductions concluded and in the comfortable silence that followed, Aum found that there was a spot in-between Demona and Blue Eagle, so he sat down. He felt good about the move, like more, larger doorways were about to open up because of it. Instantly Aum and Demona turned to each other.

"I know you know what a didgeridoo is Aum," said Demona. She moved to grab a spare didgeridoo lying in the long wet legs of grass and offered it to him.

"And you know I was being sarcastic, lovely Demona," Aum said as he accepted her offer.

There was a brief pause, as everybody focused on Aum and Demona, all lost in their knot tying, except for Blue Eagle who was off to the side of the circle, fully aware of what was happening while he finished rolling a joint. He looked up just as everyone's attention began to waver, moving off in all directions. There would need to be an even stronger unity by the group in order for their newest guest to integrate into their practical magic.

He addressed the circle, “Now that everybody is here we should let the ceremonies begin.” To his left he offered Aum the marijuana cigarette and a lighter.

While sitting on the Mainstage at Full Spectrum, Aum had taken in everyone, every being at the absolute peak of observed collectivity. Both inward and out of body, he had closed his eyes and held on for dearest life. He needed intuition, hearing, and 6th sense perception to navigate through that heightened pace of emergency procedural rewiring, manifested immediately and physically in the earth mother’s children. He was essentially holding the ship together by it’s seams while it repaired and prepared itself. Hours and hours and hours later the music finally stopped. It must have been well into late afternoon. He had transformed into a stone Buddha statue, much like the one at the entrance to his campsite. He was a stage decoration, a concrete anchor, an energy transformer, an inanimate symbol existing almost entirely beyond the veil of Maya.

He had risked opening his eyes only a few times, calmly noticing that each time, he gazed about his surroundings were different. It was still a stage in the woods with music and a dance floor, but the decorations, stage size and set up, people, scale, environment, all changed. Sometimes there were huge trees where there were none before; there were huge observation and dance platforms that would come and go; there was ornate fabric and light installations that would appear and disappear. At one point he even thought he saw a steampunk airship hovering out at the end of a blackened sparse forest of coals, loading in broken folks with filled satchels on their backs. As each new image was brought before him, others passed away.

Many minutes after the music had stopped, he opened his eyes at quicker intervals, noticing that some stability had come to the space around him, and that he was alone.

He took a deep sitting stretch before looking back to see that there wasn’t anyone at the laptop. The autopilot playlist had ended. Aum stood and gingerly walked back to his camp to find it was all real, more than real. Not only was Jenn gone, but so was everyone else. There was no trace of Ashta, Sara, Pillaiyar, Jess, Ted . . . or even Cat. Thankfully Jenn left the tent so he was able to rest a while, recuperate his senses, and come back to his own physical body, as much as he could at that point anyway.

Aum had a sudden flash off terror rising in his spine. What was he about to get himself into here? He looked into the eyes of Blue Eagle hoping to find the power of a kindred spirit, a soul being embodied; he hoped to see the complete absence of masks or performance. Blue Eagle's eyes reflected respect and admiration. Accepting the items, Aum nodded in understanding.

Aum was deeply susceptible under the influence of the sacred herb. He could see through to the deepest parts of people, see through some of the deepest fogs of reality, and could easily get lost. Somewhere in his mind he thought this might be some kind of trap. These fun loving, playful beings might be the magical pixies of lore, Sirens of the nearby stream; enticing susceptible passers by with their laughing, their singing and their music to join them under the surface of the water that suffocates mortal bodies. He tried, in a panic, to remember if he stepped into a fairy ring on the way. Wait, he looked at the circle, this might be the fairy ring itself. And, maybe he himself is the king of the fairies. He laughed at himself, even snorted, then smiled, deep and genuine and full of peace—paranoia replaced by joyfulness and reciprocity. He looked to his left, into Demona's shining face. A crooked smile crept across it that was very familiar.

Still smiling, he lit the joint and pulled hard. He brought the smoke down into his belly with a controlled pranic breath. A centered calm came over Aum as he passed the drug to Demona, connecting eyes with her, hoping she would do the same with the next person, and that person would do the same to the next, and so on. This would allow the circle to become much more stable. As he played didgeridoo he wouldn't have to focus as much on solidifying the group, however they were quite isolated so interruption was not a worry for him. Aum thought about all the giggling and wondered if that would be a concern. He looked up and saw very serious faces reflecting an intent of higher learning.

The joint returned to him and he pulled hard again. Demona whispered quietly in his ear as he did, "The intimacy that your demeanor communicates surpasses all physical boundaries into the Nameless and the Everything. You are a display of self on the psychic realm, a higher self that can create a space only the seeker may enter."

Aum coughed with surprise, smoke coming out of all the holes in his head as he turned to her shaking his head and smiling. There was no way that he could seriously accept what she said, though it was immensely profound and beautiful. It was far too outlandish, and oozing with sexuality, yet Aum still wanted to play, whether this was all part of the Riddle or not. Aum passed the joint to her and as she inhaled he whispered passed the dark smell of lavender in her raven hair, and into her ear, “In this space, the only thing to live for is inspiration and experience, both of which are happening simultaneously, infinitely, and everywhere.”

They shared the moment of connection and then came to realize they weren’t alone in this space. Some of the gypsy-hipsters were itching to get going, tapping their drums gently, but nothing had formed yet. Aum broke off their gaze as if hearing a call and put his lips to the didge, suddenly realizing it wasn’t his, and without words asked it for a smooth ride.

It was much longer and much heavier than his. It had a plain wood finish without the traditional aboriginal-style paint decoration. Instead it had intricate grooves carved into it, circles and swirls, depicting waves and motion coming out of the end. He let out a low pulsing, as the pattern of the drums slowly formed. He adapted his pulsing to their pattern, yet still at the low frequency, adding in slight variations in tone to accentuate moments in the rhythm of the drum: pops and whoops. The instrument had a smaller mouthpiece than what he was used to, making it easier to circular breathe. Aum held and pushed the air out with his cheek muscles, while closing off his throat to inject oxygen into his lungs through his nose.

The drum pattern and style began as accessible funky beats, but soon made a transition to an electronic IDM influence, with thumps and booms brought in on off beats and out off nowhere. The drums began to talk to each other.

Dakitdaboom bakataba bedaboom butaba bataboom bukitaba.
Repababa, Repababa, Repababa, Repababa, Repababa, Repababa.
Boombapa-pupaaaa BoomBoompa-pupaaaa, Boombapa-pupaaaa.

Finally, after a profound and trying journey he found a moment that sparked with a bright life and freshness far beyond the waves of the Full Spectrum aftershock. Here were innocent and youthful faces, beings that deeply rejoiced in the moment, who revered and recognized the greater and fleeting nature of time. Every person in the group was so talented at listening and at expressing emotion with music, he had to do little. Aum's body loosened and the stresses of carrying a costume of conventional humanity released as he began to bounce up and down shamanically with the music. Putting his entire body into it, he closed his eyes and quickly doubled the tempo of his pulsations and increased the tone. With it, Aum brought up the root chakra energy from the earth, moving the tribal history of music into the second chakra. The change in focus brought an intensity. It was an energy so sneaky and so watery that it moved in slow motion to the grooves they were creating. The rest of the group responded by adding in complicated layers, built up with different timings and patterns, woven with the complexity of a Mesopotamian rug. As the music stabilized, Aum could feel a move up to the next chakra of this group creation. The drums began to pound with focused intentions, getting louder as they started drowning out his didge playing. Again he doubled the tempo and the frequency of his rhythm. To his amazement Aum began to circular breathe without the use of his cheeks, it was merely a thin tube of air that ran along the roof of his mouth and the back of his throat. With the shift his pitch increased to float just above the tone of the drums. He was actually able hold his own alongside the ever increasing volume of the circle. His mind flexed the muscles in his body, pushing him out of the big tube he was playing. The group was lifted up to the metaphorical heart chakra level – the spiritual gateway - Anahata. Suddenly, to Aums right, Blue Eagle started playing a wooden flute. Its melody accompanied the beats perfectly, soaring and guiding the group at a pace that encouraged an increase in tempo. He could feel a huge push of power come from the stream, the trees and the natural environment around them as their physical bodies disappeared. Everyone in the circle had their eyes closed, concentrating so much on the music that they existed only as the sound that they were creating. Using ear consciousness, they psychically constructed a single being: a group sharing feelings of passion, pride, and love.

The experience quickly reflected poly-rhythmic trance drumming, akin to the voodoo tribes of Haiti, or deep Africa. People in the group started whooping and hollering for joy as the pace became frantic and the focus moved up to the fifth chakra: the communication chakra located at the throat level. Aum began his own vocalization through his didge, chirps and clicks that eventually thinned out and expanded to high-pitched animal screams, intent on pushing the third eye button. With this new didgeridoo he could maintain lip vibration, and still have utmost control over vocalizations, not losing any sonic power. Demona, who had been adding drumming up until this point, began to sing. Aum heard the Sirens call and instantly remembered what he had written on his bookmark in the coffee shop. He could feel the planetary motion for which Demona was a conduit. With his closed eyes, Aum felt fully protected with the power of Blue Eagle and Demona to each side, he even felt lifted up on a pedestal. With every single drop of concentration that Aum could muster, with every single moment of surrender to the universe and his quest, he waited for the precise moment for the final push. The whoops and hollers were reaching a crescendo, the drum skins were ready to burst, Blue Eagle was straining at his breathtaking speed, and even Demona was at her peak, pushing her vocal chords into points of shredding. Aum felt the snake of kundalini energy move up his spine and he thrust the final intentions out of his mouth and didge. It was an otherworldly noise, a growling chirping digital data-like buzz that connected mother earth to father sky through the circle. The group must have felt it as well, because as Aum expelled his energy, they created an orb and began to move at light speed through black space. They moved as a group outside of their bodies. No sight, just feeling.

The music solidified into a unified rhythm. It was no longer the beats from the hand drums, but the pure emotion of the people making them; it was the total clarity of a lifted veil. Inside the orb, this spatially manifested emotional body, Aum moved through the group. He saw the way Justine's parents influenced her as she grew into the woman she was now. Aum saw Linda's humorous nature, and how it influenced those who loved her. He saw Stacey's constant questions about the nature of the universe, and saw her beliefs behind a brick wall of conditioning, always unaffected by the answers she found. Aum watched a big crack in the wall form and he smiled. In Jeremy, Aum saw how his need for attention affected the way he carried himself in public places; actions which were in opposition to how he carried himself in private. Because of this, two different Jeremy's were fighting inside of him trying to get out. In a man named Adam, Aum saw the recent realization of personal power and choice. Aum could see many changes about to happen to him. In a man named Crystalis, Aum saw issues with sexuality that were coming to the surface, but with it a huge gift of sight. Crystalis was quite intuitively open, and being a Mayan Calendar enthusiast, he made it known to Aum that the combined individual energies that were there during the jam created a White Wizard: A solar sign from the Tzolken that focuses on shape shifting and divination. He found it impressive that Crystalis knew what Mayan sign he was in such a short period of time. Aum looked at the spirit of a woman named Lila and saw links to the animal kingdom. She was a newly incarnated representative of the great cat family and if one stared into her face long enough, it would easily become apparent. Next Aum looked to Demona and could feel arms embrace him. He could see into a number of their past lives spent together, and could even see into their future together, in this life. He exhaled and succumbed to her embrace, feeling warmth and unconditional bliss, wonder and passion. He moved on to Blue Eagle and could feel an old soul behind the long blonde hair, his stringy whiskers and gnome nose. There was a deep pocket of connection there. Within Carey there were both dreams inside of the Riddle and riddles inside of a dream. Aum shied away, knowing and practicing boundaries, feeling the equivalent to a blush, embarrassed, but thankful, to have even seen into the soul portal next to him.

The emotional display slowly changed back to music at a much more relaxed pace like a huge sigh of relief. The beat was still steady, however, so with his eyes still closed Aum began to describe who he was through his didgeridoo. It came out as a solo in a secret language of hums and tones, growls and chirps, yet the information was there for whomever wanted it. He put out into the space the story of his adventure so far, and how much he was enjoying this moment and this experience with all of them. Eventually Blue Eagle and Demona joined in and the interaction became a mythological story of creation to all of those really good listeners in the drum circle as the orb came back, back to the city, back through the grandfather oak trees, over a bridge and in between the long stretching branches of pine trees, back to the physical, back down to the circle as the drumming came to completion.

Aum let his eyes remain shut for some time after. He felt a touch on his back as Demona and a few others left the circle. After a few grounding breaths, stabilizing in his memory of where he was, Aum opened his eyes and looked at his surroundings. The moonlight glistened on the grass. The long haired hippy girls and the raven-haired witches got their naked toes wet while twirling in a circle and calling to their red moon-mother. Or maybe they were just screaming for the pure pleasure of it all. Either way it made the evening all the more interesting.

Blue Eagle was the only one still sitting beside Aum, looking very stoic.

Calmly Aum whispered, "This thing has a mind of it's own. It played me, not the other way around." Moments of comfortable silence passed, "Did you get it in Australia?"

Blue Eagle turned with a content smile and said "No, a man named Herald from the northern coast gave it to me. He makes them from arbutus trees and tunes them to the vibration of planetary movements. This one is tuned to Saturn's moons I think. He's a very interesting guy. If you're ever traveling that direction you should look out for him."

"Celestial movement hey?" Aum's gazed shifted to the sky, maybe looking for Saturn. "Where do your adventures take you?" Blue Eagle asked.

Aum replied, "I'm not entirely sure of the outcome of this journey." His words were searching, asking even.

Blue Eagle smiled. "Then tell me Aum, what adventures brought you here? There aren't too many unknown travelers these days, or even faces."

"Yeah I stay off the corporate boards."

"A ghost on the loose then?"

"Yes. I'd rather be a ghost than an immortal." Aum laughed a little, "I'm a ghost tracking another ghost. My network is pretty subversive, integrated deeply with daily reality. I'm still learning how it all works actually, and what has changed. Much I believe. Intensely transformative and proactive, opposed to having your every thought and life moment captured and broadcast to everyone you know, and out to even more people that you don't."

"'Till everyone shines as brightly as a star in the sky," Blue Eagle continued.

"But I search for the Sun."

"Patience then. All the stars must dim and the darkness must fade before the full brightness of dawn comes. And with it illumination."

At this Blue Eagle was still and silent, a vehicle idling with its driver beaming in from the stars. When no verbal post script response was forthcoming, Aum bluntly continued with another answer to Carey's first question, "I hitchhiked in from an event called Full Spectrum. I got called out to live more fully engaged than ever before. I lost my girlfriend somewhere along the way. Like . . . for real lost her. Lost her in the fray of consciousness expansion and the re-structuralization of reality."

Blue Eagle's eyes widened, just a little though.

Aum continued, "I've seen some very interesting things on the way to this moment, that's for sure." He aptly described to Blue Eagle what he was sure Carey already knew.

Some time ago people began moving to the country and isolating themselves in underground homes waiting for the beginning waves of nuclear fall-out, bio-chemical warfare, the random blasts of terrorists, or even the warring nomadic nation states to declare war on the democratic capital-fascists. While on his way to this moment, Aum finally saw these things first hand, he witnessed the ghostly faces of the many people wandering along the road as if it was the dirty thirties, hitch-hiking into a better dream, with their eyes still in the sky. Mushroom clouds, flying saucers, or blazing comets would only confirm their overgrown festering fears that had been cultivated for generations. It was hard to ignore the first hand perception of a living nightmare, and easier to ignore a mediated fiction produced by television and it's extended communication platforms.

On the trip tears choked Aum down as he saw how factory farms had traumatized the landscape. It was shocking to see where it all took place. Auschwitz for animals; aluminum Quonsets kilometers long held thousands of pigs, chickens and cows. Inside he could see lumps of biological white and grey mass, surgically attached to machines. The glistening steel sucked milk out, as if from a white ocean through a techno-biological portal. He saw smaller pink lumps of flesh constantly pooping out identically perfect eggs with perfectly colored yolk, never to make a sound, destined for moments of further categorization along the corporate line, and then a breakfast plate somewhere.

The trip and description continued. Aum saw the plastic quilt. Agriculture having the longest intertwined history with humanity and technology, its genetic engineering now down to pure mathematics. At least they've learned the importance of crop rotation—one of his drivers had explained to him—a hard lesson to learn before they finally programmed it in. Fields of Canola, Alfalfa and Wheat had been farmed by automated software for years now, harvested by computerized combines and thrashers.

Coming to new realizations Aum spoke, "The city locks people in, into its mechanics, into its pressure to keep up, stay afloat, stay alive. If you ever manage to escape, you no longer recognize the world outside of it, the un-nature."

"Agriculture has become the biggest industry through which to feel the repercussions of our unchecked technological viri," commented Blue Eagle, mentally philosophizing the emotional dread out of Aum's words. It was all too much to imagine, and if Aum let these thoughts direct his course of action through life, he would be no better off than the vagrant wanderers looking to the sky for answers, or relief. Though how was that any different from what he was already doing, where he was looking.

Much like the Sunny Valley case Jenn was working on, Aum had seen a single family-run organic farm squeezed into the mechanically planned landscape. It had 10 foot wire game fences with a large sign in front, on it the words, *Keep Out*. Inside the fences, untrimmed trees grew abundantly and animals roamed the land carefree.

As Aum explained this scene, Blue Eagle interjected, "I've heard that some of these families have built underground networks up the coast. You know, like heirloom seed exchanges, meat or skins."

"Really?"

"Yeah, there are a lot of positive things still happening out there. Of course you never hear of it often." With heartfelt compassion he added, "Brush off your nightmare visions my friend."

Aum imagined farmers praying to their animals before slaughter; he imagined their animals giving up their lives, hides and meat to feed the people out there who still held on to strict beliefs as to what food actually was, and what constituted as the true nourishment of their bodies. Though Aum couldn't brush off the memories of what he saw as easily as Carey had suggested. Their heaviness sat within him, his body and mind, and refueled his sole resolve and purpose, in choosing to incarnate.

"You said you came from Full Spectrum – is that like the realm of New Eden?" Blue Eagle asked.

An even deeper heaviness washed over them, as if every soul who had taken their own life heard the verbal cue, and suddenly joined them there in the park, as ghosts.

"Um . . . I'm not sure."

"Even as a ghost?"

There was now only aching pressure where there was once light and pure playfulness. The pendulum was swinging back and forth that quickly.

"Wow. I don't know yet. I do believe I'm bound to find out though," Aum tried to appease the quantum ghosts with his open-ended response, of course it was futile.

"You're a Riddler then? You made it inside?" replied Carey in full sight of the truth, and with a sudden mist of twists wrapped around the words, any and all potential responses were a doorway to it. Aum tried and tried and tried to untie the knot of the output of expression on Carey's face in that moment: humble curiosity? Or did the question mark hide soul daggers of the unconscious? He had thus trusted Blue Eagle's word and vibe, but his confidence was waning as reality's cohesion disintegrated.

Aum fought off Carey's aggressive curiosity to know about the Riddle, to be involved. It must have been of great interest to him, and Aum could almost feel long thin fingers pulling at his brain. Could it just be a coincidence that he would have actual information about New Eden, without being steeped deeply within the nested Riddle layers? Was Aum on his way towards being deemed dead, much like an egocentric reactionary Dennis-like power trip? Or was Carey at a much more advanced stage of the Riddle than himself? He looked at Carey honestly, "That's how I am here."

"And how you are here is through Full Spectrum?"

"Yes," Aum spoke with courage, on what he knew, "Full Spectrum is an invitation-only Riddler festival where trans-temporal spaces are cultivated using music and dance for deep and intentional therapy, on both a personal and global level. Everyone is a character in a dream, uncovering the deepest layers of their human purpose. There's no real waking from the dream though, and you come away changed forever, regardless of how you arrived. Like I said, a re-structuralization of reality." He looked at Carey seriously, "It that the same as New Eden?"

Carey eased up a bit, "Maybe." The mystical twisting continued. "Depends. What did you learn from that change? That deep uncovering?"

"Adventure without the risk of full life path disaster, is merely a vacation."

Carey laughed hard and Aum continued unflinchingly. "From what I understand, it seems a collective veil was lifted, and a battle has started; though I have yet to directly witness its front lines. Not here in this body anyway. I seem to have been chosen, or chose to be involved in quite a significant way." The crushing feeling, combined with his honest dive directly into it, gave way to the next level as Carey asked him, "In what way? Like omnipotently repairing combat equipment?"

"What?" It was a strange but synchronistic cognitive jump. The moon emerged from behind a cloud, shining brightly on Aum as the witches screamed in exaltation.

"Excuse me?" Aum responded as his stomach twinged through the deepest Déjà Vu he had ever experienced.

Blue Eagle continued, though somehow it was a bit disjointed from what Aum could feel and remember. A live dream nonetheless. "Only when you are on the front lines and understanding the urgency of the situation, will you manage to fix things just by looking at them…"

"…repairing them instantly," they said together. Aum was shocked and could not speak, Blue Eagle continued without reaction.

"Your journey reminds me of something Aum. It's a very unusual coincidence."

Aum quickly looked over at him, knowing what was about to be asked, "Have you ever heard of the Riddle Solver?"

"What?" instinctively Aum exclaimed, and he heard another voice mirror him.

Aum felt the curve steepen.

He stared at Blue Eagle, slowly turning to the disembodied voice that came from the place he had been sitting as the Dreamer, last time he was in this moment.

"This is for you," the voice said.

Aum jumped in surprise as he saw Demona sitting in the spot where Dreamer Aum should be.

"Take it…this is for you." She was holding a magpie feather.

"From who?"

"Who!?" She tilted her head in confusion, "Well if you need it to be more obvious than this, then we might need to tack on a few more dimensions of reality." She looked at Blue Eagle, "Geez, do we need to break out the kykeon here?"

Aum's eyes went wide, more drugs would definitely not help the complexity of the situation. He gingerly outstretched a hand, giving up any notions of control or outcome to this breakdown of nerves and mentality. He expected to wake up in the next dream vignette . . . but never did. All aspects of his world were beyond recognizable, beyond dream-like and the witches continued their occult chants.

There were no guarantees to finding footing, but steps still needed to be taken, beyond notions of courage and fear. He took the feather and asked aloud, "Magpie, who's the Riddle Solver?"

"He's a recluse that lives inside a box in the woods up the north coast," Demona replied. She walked back to her coven and her eclipse ceremony as the rain started up again, allowing the Wiccans to deepen their work.

"Got it?" Blue eagle asked.

Aum held the magpie feather. He was flushed – he must not be paying attention if he needed the trailhead to be delivered to him through such a visceral sieve. Aum spoke, unknowingly aloud, "…or that's just how it goes, congealing just now, within this dream loop exit…" Holding the magical power tool, the response emerged on it's own. It was as if a clarity was birthed from the serendipitous circumstance, the random influx of re-combined karmas. His eyes opened and, for a moment, the new world he was in finally made sense, in his mind and body and spirit. The feather token reminder invoking remembrance, "…Uh, yes, Carey…" he responded. At that moment Demona shot him a wickedly sensual glance and a black bird flew over her head. "Sorted, pathway found, on this blissful new vista."

"Obvious, right?"

Aum laughed in amazement and exhaled the remaining pocket of tension he was in, "Holy fuck," as if he had cheated death, "Made it back," or leapt across the cosmos to land on a new plant.

He took the second apple out of his pocket and bit into it.

"True fruit takes time."

"Agreed and reflected exponentially."

"And here I will make my own exit. Have fun dude, it's why we're still here," and Blue Eagle got up to leave the rain, smiling genuinely with a parting bow.

"Epic gratitude for the advanced wisdom session," Aum offered him a bite, which Carey took. Aum received it back and bowed in return.

"Glad to have you back deep bro," Carey smiled, and within the smile, he shared both a monk-like peace of knowing all interconnected moments, and the knowing that they would cross paths again in the future.

With each increasingly large dollop of rain the women's circle wove it's way to a close. Aum pulled out his travel umbrella from a pant side pocket, patiently meditating on the insightful gems emerging from his new feather, and the experience of receiving it. He also finished his fresh apple.

After a few parting hugs, Demona walked over, "Still, here?"

"Here, and still."

"You ready?"

"To go deep? Always ready," He stood as a different layer of Aum, as if the dream deja vu held down the double version of himself so he could shake loose of his old skin, both old selves. He pulled out the third apple from his pocket, offering it and the cover of the umbrella to Demona. She stood close to him, accepting the apple and looking up into his eyes. Aum continued, "As ancient as the mystery path we walk together."

"Found only as a shared One. This way, dear soul," she replied with invitation, beginning to move with purpose, past the edge of the umbrella.

He shook his head in awe and gratitude, his heart and step strong, catching up with this mysterious, beautiful, and deeply familiar creature. Maybe she had been waiting for him all along?

Much like the drum circle itself, their immersive communication was magnetized. They were playful and edgy: a hunt and chase of newfound sexual possibilities. With darting eyes, it was a screaming gallop to take the moment, with its physical, emotional, and spiritual connectivity, further and faster than ever before. Like a goading dare to fully undress it all, Aum felt the release of his excess baggage.

He realized that it was this full freedom that he truly craved and wanted.

He was ready to dive in.

They walked without hurry, bumping into one another, touching and grasping at opportune and welcome moments. They laughed with abandon, understanding more about themselves than they ever could alone or with a different other. A few additional strides and they began nuzzling, cuddling, biting shoulders, sneaking a kiss on the neck, a kiss on the cheek, then lips. Aum's heart raced as their lips touched again, her scent filled him and they dipped passionately into their first fully locked embrace. Pressing into each other with a deep need it was like a drug, and with an immense surge of desire he knew there was no going back. She bit his lip. 'Whoa, we're not even going to make it to her place,' he thought.

Demona broke away momentarily, a dramatic pause. She stopped as if smelling the air like a wild animal. Her deep feminine sense perception provoked his new skills of observing all viewable environments. It had stopped raining completely, and both of them knew it was the time of the night and time of week, time when all were asleep, even the creatures of the night who had yet to emerge and sneak into the fresh new world that the storm had left behind. Totally alone, without the sense of another human being for miles, they were free to succumb to their instinctual passions, surrender into their bodies and destroy all their built up stresses. They were moved to find freedom in a world, a landscape, that was usually a prison, a cage methodically maintained. On cue, a clock tower down the street chimed half past two, and as the vibrational reminder of constructed time faded, their shining bare being came through. Overcoming the constructed bars of human reality Demona reached up and placed her lips on his, hand tightly on the back of his neck bringing him in, hand on his chest, slipping it down to his pants, leading him into the back alley next to them.

He was all hers, following each of her needs with the presence and power of an accomplished adventurer, and the experience of fully evolving and overcoming life path disaster. He gave himself fully to her, and the unbound moment.

Only now, with this new soul reflection, did he understand how much he had seen and how much he had grown. Their feet danced naturally, moving exactly where they needed to be, they twirled together, spinning, merging so that their foreheads pressed against one other.

She went for his belt as they spun and Aum deftly ran his hand up the back of her shirt, against the smooth sweaty tack of her braless back. Moving up to the back of her head, he gently protected it with his hand, as he guided their spin, to land her roughly against a shadowed brick wall, just a few strides off the sidewalk. She moaned with pleasure as they found a surface push against, she instantly found a concrete step and a metal hand rail to prop her leg up, opening her self to him. Aum wished her pants would vanish, avoiding the awkward motions of taking them off.

All the fearless daring with which he approached life was echoed in her own movements as she prodded him to go further. He could feel empowering forces swirling with them, as if they were celebrating the pleasure of human bodies, human life, and of being emotionally unencumbered on behalf of the whole human race. They were free of crushing social confines, free of relational taboo; they were human creatures finding paradise, a timespace so intrinsic yet so fleeting, where all ramifications are good news, and all actions result in an ever deeper freedom, an evolution of spirit.

He softened his pressure against the cold brick and his pants fell to the ground. Without hesitation he scooped the tights under her leather skirt with his thumb and stretched them down over her cheek, then up over her bent knee. Sandals left back on the street, the tights easily slipped past her foot, dropping down to the ground and she immediately guided his plunge into her bare and wet waterfall.

Aum awoke.

This was new. The switch from sleep to waking was like the edge of a knife, not like the continual leaping gap between distant worlds he was used to. Maybe it was the emotional release of the grief, pain and loss felt over the last few weeks of travel that triggered the acute switch. Or maybe it was the deeper soul path baptism inside the echoing quaking waves of sensuality. Either way the edge was as abrupt as an unexpected slap in the face.

Oddly, he felt less emotional comfort than he thought he would have. Of course he felt total unmitigated appreciation for a night filled with the deepest pleasures and primal feelings of release. All brought about by the dangerous excitement of a complete stranger, his arms wrapped so tightly around the tingling bare body that no separation and no pain existed. All memories of anything even remotely close were healed, simply and completely. But now, this morning he knew he would find little emotional indulgence here with the creature that lay next to him. It was a moment, a body, and a spirit one could not attach to. He knew she was a sacred animal, testing his strength, drive and resolve. A being placed before him that was so random and purposeful, intelligent and unpredictable; he knew that getting attached may leave him perpetually tormented.

Blinking rapidly, the brilliant sequence of blistering photons streaming in through the cracks of the bedroom window like a high pitched frequency coming into perfect pitch.

Noticing every move, muscle by muscle as he exited the covers, he could only imagine how complicated this could get. Best get a breath, even a stretch in, while he could, before each pocket of connectivity with this self outside of his Self was folded into reality; the dream and life path becoming one.

He briefly reflected on the modern human paradox: the detachment of physical pleasure and sexual chemistry from committed love and an established emotional relationship. Something he had heard much about, but never really explored. Aum's primary relationship was happily with Jenn over the course of many years. This one was so raw and so new. All his time-based-faults, his quirks and blemishes, were of course there to see, but still hidden, for now. In this fact, he found inspiration to seek his highest vision of self and to be that vision, shining it outward. Of course the more emotionally open and authentically receptive, the better the sexual artistry, thus the more profound and deep the connection in the moment, thus the greater the mystery in proceeding after. How do we want to link our lives after fully shaking the earth? Who do we become in each other's eyes after experiencing a shared oneness? How do we most honor that exchange of divinity? By building on it, in our lives? Or fully letting it go, almost as if it had never happened, and finding another moment, and another sacred partner, and in that, a new celebration.

Extended committed partnership, though very rarely practiced these days, explores that ongoing unity of soul as something karmic, and beyond human personality. It finds that unified One and never separates from that infinite inspiration, from that divine creature next to you, Shiva or Shakti. A super humanism. It was this inseparable context of total intimacy that he knew so well, and deep in him she was still there, his Shakti. Though without pain, judgment or spite—yes, he confirmed, grief and pain evaporated—she too was vibrating differently, just as he was. And as this new incarnation, this new life began, he was sure his path would cross again with Jenn's; in what fashion, he was very curious to find out . . .

Chapter Eight

Aum grabbed a glass of water after using the bathroom. He saw in the mirror his uncut hair stood even higher, he had grown 2 inches taller, and his limbs even extended out further than before. That, or they had a midget toilet and dwarf sinktop installed in the apartment bathroom. Aum even had a healthy beard of stubble on his face; which had been growing since Full Spectrum, but was only now noticed.

He walked down the apartment hall, seeing a whole community of crystals that had been laid out over the living room floor. The strength of their energies was very apparent. He stopped and got down on one knee to listen to the many conversations that were happening, which he could not even come close to fathoming. Without shades or curtains, the large patio windows looked out over the city - there was a reflection there, in the cloud ecology - a full orchestra of beings all interacting just beyond the edges of his perception. He called the highest of them down to be present, calling in the highest pillars of light he could imagine, conceptualizing bridges from crystal to cloud. He knew they could all hear him.

Aum made his way through the penthouse apartment space. It was filled with that intensely sacred clutter that is both intentionally magical and unconscious. Sanctified wands and random audio cables, mason jars of green liquid, framed holographic prints from the new masters, hanging fabrics, handwritten notes, cushions, piles of outdated technology ripped to shreds, soldering equipment, bike tire tubes, plates of half eaten food, bags of drugs, discarded and soiled clothing… it verged on near homelessness, a vagabond flop house for sure.

As he turned back down the hall to re-find his newfound naked wiccan creature, he took one more look out the window to see the lush valley bellow, ocean just on the horizon. Then, past the bedroom door at the end of the hall, he saw a TV sitting on a pile of wood. The residual intention could still be felt. Someone had just set this up. It wasn't piled up haphazardly and wasn't here last night; there was something deeper here.

As he walked toward it he passed an open bedroom door on the opposite side from the room where Demona slept. There was some human rustling inside, so Aum whispered gently, "Are you planning on burning your TV?" A man gently responded, "No, you're pretty close though." He poked his head out. "It's an art installation. TV's have replaced campfires."

"That's pretty interesting," Aum responded, "The re-structuralization of the collective relationship to comfort on a dark cold night is obvious, the techno-consumerist comodification of light out of a purely elemental form less so. Did you make it?"

"No, no. It was John. He's the finder, the post-history prognosticator in this here Tower."

"He lives here?"

"Nobody really 'lives' here. It's a temporal habitat; a habitual node with a rotating cast of ever evolving community characters, myself included. Somehow it all just works out."

Aum spied a pile of eviction notices on a nearby shelf.

"Paying rent isn't a problem?"

"Well, everybody contributes what they can. Though John is the wizard, the alpha mystic who has saved the space for us numerous times."

The man inspected the messy sky-high hair, watery stride, James Dean cool, and didn't-sleep-a-wink-last-night vibe, as Aum observed the art installation. "Hmm," An expression of curiosity escaped the man's lips quickly followed by, "You're with Monica?"

Aum caught himself, just before he turned his head in total jaw-dropped and wide eyed disbelief, pulling his heart from his chest and presenting it. "I am," responding definitively, claiming this crafty female being and all she bestowed and offered, regardless of name, or pseudonym.

There was a portal in the TV campfire…a time machine…

Deep into the black of her hair, he rammed her against the brick, and another loud moan of authentic pleasure released while submitting to the moment, escaping her mouth as their lips and tongues unlocked, "This is way too painful, not to have you entirely naked before me, to greet each patch of your delicate skin with my lips."

"And your tongue," she gushed, "each divine vibration, Aaauuummmm….."

"My name is Ezekiel," he extended his hand.

"Aum" he intoned as they shook.

"Hmm… an even higher vista, " Ezekiel responded in a whisper, unnoticed by Aum.

"Hmm … bi-location," Aum responded in a whisper, unnoticed by Ezekiel, unifying back in the present.

Aum glanced back at the TV, "So do you make time machines as well?" he asked.

"Not time machines, but I do make the machines that make the time machines," Ezekiel smile was stangley familiar. "Step inside my labratory, I can show you."

Through the TV screen, on a quantum full moon beam, a last louder noise ripped through Aums mind, the moan and growl and howl of two voices in unison. The noise was disrupted by super cute snoring across the hall, as well as Ezekiel gesturing to the plump and slightly faded red couch inside the door, "Welcome."

It was the only real piece of furniture in the room, otherwise there was no clutter at all in the space. Aum informally poured himself into it.

"How did your lab end up in this top cab flophouse?" Aum challenged; the relational essence of Demona's karmic exchange already rubbing off on him.

"Flophouse?!" He seemed almost offended. Ezekiel was most definitely not the cyberpunk archetype. He wore a trimmed and well-groomed blonde beard with a heroic and handsome wave through his short-cropped hair. He looked healthy, well rested, and well fed. With a modern-yet-medieval inspired tunic and dark cotton pants he seemed as though he may have just returned from a yoga class:

guiding students though asanas, rather than practicing them. "This is the primetime stride my friend – pure unadulterated quantum magical chaos. From here you can go anywhere."

He was right in many ways. Aum noticed one entire wall was painted with the new synthetic nanotech quartz glue, which he had heard about a few months ago. With this glue, specific objects could be painted as digital display touch screens and with the proper programming, used as hyper-objects. This trend seemed to be gaining more traction, and becomnig a more acceptable household practice than the previous push to have terminator-like augmentation, though more simply now, as digital glasses hovering eyeballs at all times. This hyper-object development was a simpler re-founding of digital emersion; a transformation of interactive physical exterior space, rather than an open-gate mind-fusion of internal consciousness to all collective spaces.

Zeke continued, "In 1995 I took apart a Sony Digital8 camera and understood what was to come. That little IEEE 1394 port, that Apple brand-named FireWire port on that pro-sumer piece of technology represented the first small shift in the dismantling of time and space - even human communication - as our conception of reality began it's conversion to a non-linear digital future: a stream of transmittable, programmable, 0's and 1's.

"An equivalent transitional leap happened exactly 100 years earlier in 1895 when the Lumière brothers first presented a series of 46 second long short films to a theatre in Paris. This was essentially a technological reflection of seeing, of being, an expansion on the two-dimensional photographic moment into the motion based third dimension - like looking in a magic mirror.

"But here," he motioned to his studio, "Now, it's like our reflection comes by looking into a pool of water, an infinite data stream. And the surface of the pool is never quite clear, it's always morphing, like something you can today, stick your hand into and manipulate. With this new digital capturing development in '95, a feedback loop began, where the experience of being human was siphoned through a computer. It was only a matter of time, and systemized streamlining before the highest potential would be realized, a state of pushing and pulling this digitized essence in and out through all interconnected digital network tendrils."

"Whoa dude… I just woke up," Aum wasn't quite ready for an elaborate dive into techno-tool theory. As Ezekiel talked Aum's charkas turned and tuned in time, and nausea seemed to erupt in his stomach.

"I know. Most people here don't seem to mind, I think most rather enjoy it, the kids especially," he laughed, and laughed again, and again. The athletic handsome mad scientist continued, "There are some of us who refuse to be force fed this 4th dimensional transition within a technology based consumer market, but are dedicated to learning, experimenting, experientially trying to understand the possibilities of this so called post-human experience, to push it past the level of consumerism and technology. We have become the wind and are pushing the reflective water into 5th dimensional whirlpools, mastering the physics of digital gravity and momentum, moving within the state of being all possibilities."

A gust of wind blew in, and Aum could hear it in the leaves of trees far far below. It threw the master bedroom patio doors open to reveal a sky which matched the hyperscreen display. The entire wall had rolling clouds floating by, as a zen-like backdrop – a reflection of the apartment patio view. Or maybe a direct sampling of the scene behind the wall. Still brushing sleep out of his eyes, Aum couldn't quite tell.

In the centre of the hyperscreen wall were 3 areas cropped out of the sky, like floating HD screens. And across the top and bottom of them were datastream strips, like a scrolling stockmarket read-out. A dial of multiple language lines, all scrolling at once: Arabic, Chinese, Portugese, English and within them micro numerical sequences which all seemed to be flowing at random, though with a chaotic mathematical certainty like Pi.

Ezekiel's desk was simply a table with a massive touch pad surface, and uniquely it faced the sky out the patio doors, not the display wall. Aum looked at the way Zeke maneuvered his hand on his touchscreen, like a mouse for each fingertip. Data became sculptural, something to swim in, to hold and dig through. Aum's empty stomach reacted again, as if there was data inside he was moving around.

"Damn Zeke, that's indeed a scalpel-sharp techo-edge."

He remembered his laptop and it's track pad mouse; a few years and as a tool it was already ancient, as much as an actual paintbrush from the renaissance.

"Indeed, the sharpest techno edge is now where we all live." Looking out the window, Ezekiel tapped the corner of his desk and a virtual keyboard appeared. Tapping the touchscreen where the keys were holographically placed, his text was written out on the wall.

The first floating screen display, on the left side, cropped out of the sky, was of the boards interface - tower diagram and message board. Aum sat up straight once he noticed, stomach forgotten and all watery coolness, evaporated into fanboy gamedom.

"Got it?" Zeke asked.

Taking his time, as if speaking another language, Aum replied, "High tower vista," surprised, astoninshed, pointing to the screen with one hand and to the floor with the other. The screen was active and flowing, a constant conversational thread streaming. "Fuck." Aum figured the boards were all but dead at this point, closed with the closing of Full Spectrum. After his stupefied eyes subsided in their stare he became very curious as to what tower Ezekiel was logged into.

With blinking cursor, the cropped centre screen displayed lines of raw code in edit mode - obviously something he had been working on. Aum looked on in awe and Zeke noticed, "A full visual interface has not been developed yet because individual perception is unique, thus it will take much longer to solidify a collectively functional visual paradigm. The back end code is completed though. The global light grid fully functional. For real."

Aum smiled with his heart.

The third display, the far right panel, showed a rotating torodial geometric sphere – an abstracted visual of multi-colored gridlines in motion.

"Wow," Aum exclaimed, finally noticing it. Digitally animated, he figured it must be a real-time read out because the lines of light were moving, meeting, and converging at different nodal points, then bursting out again in different colors. It was like an ultra advanced and exponentially more complex version of the tower diagrams he remebered seeing on his laptop; a sphere of telephone lines, railroad lines, airport flight paths, and exploding fireworks all combined.

"That's your screen saver, Right?" Aum joked informally – trying to come to grips with the activated space in which he had found himself; the feeling of it, inside his body, inside the actual Tower.

"Ha! It's a saver alright," Zeke smiled, with the knowing patience of a teacher, "That right there, is consciousness evolving…."

Finding a refreshed breath on the wind, Aum looked at all three screens, and the wall itself. It was as if he was gazing upon, immersed in, an open treasure chest. Zeke continued with a hum, "….more or less. The spherical display on the right is a visual model of the real-time dream network; the digital ecological framework beyond the Towers."

"Real-time digital ecology?"

"Yes. The speed in which planetary karmic balance needs to be neutralized is so advanced now that soul trans-location is mandatory – and is actually required at all hours of the day, not just during sleep. You can see here," He pointed to part of the grid where there was much more of the light patterns in motion, "These ones are dreaming. The lines are souls and the circular nodal points are where the souls converge. In these spots souls have shared dialogue in the astral dimensions, work through planetary, emotional, and spirit karmas, and then move on to the next interaction with exuberant verve. What stories are played out in these nodes, on the interior walls of imagination are, unfortunately, not within my area of observation."

"That's wild."

"Yes it is, the new wilderness. It is an essential map of motion based frequency for the collective dreaming." He tapped a couple spots on his table and the Earth appeared within the grid, "And here it is mapped in relation to physical locations around the globe."

"Serious! So these people are not actually in those locations?"

"No, not physically. These are dream bodies," He pointed to the exploding moving lines and tilted his head in Data-like contemplation, "It's the same as people moving around throughout life," he chuckled, "but at the speed of light – a way deeper gravity than time itself. Hold on," he typed a couple more keys, the planetary diagram rotated and zoomed in slightly. The density of the light line mesh work increased. There was a set of colored lines that were ultra vibrant among them. He hit a couple more virtual keys and these lines brightened even more, extending from a central point like a nerve cell.

"That's you."

"What?"

"Those lines are you. Right now. The work you're doing as we stand here in the high tower sky lab."

"What!? But there's so many!"

"Because dream body bi-location is way too simple for you – half a dozen streams is your *waking* average. Am I correct to say that non-dreaming, real-time bi-location has been actualized as well?"

He thought of the TV installation and it's time machine bend, "Uh, yeah, like this morning."

"Haha! This morning....Ultra dope learning curve. Surfing thusly you can multiply dream bi-location streams by non-dreaming, real-time bi-location. How many places can you be in at once?"

"What?" His technical demand made it sound like drugs had permanently merged into his brainspace... that or it was the never-ending pranayama.

"When you sleep you're in 30 or 40 locations. When you, Aum, reach advanced states of consciousness in waking reality, like when you meditate, or play didge, or trance dance, you lead entire waves of soul light that sweep across the globe. Dunno how to say this. You can pulse the grid dude. Like last night."

Aum didn't say anything.

They both saw Aum's lines fizzle and pixelate, Ezekiel knew it was probably too much, too much extrapolated out, and dissected.

In the silent space of subtle shock, Aum begain to look backwards, trying to again come to grips with being inside the activated Tower space, physical and database, and how much his path had changed in the last day, week, month, year.

Zeke quickly punched a few more keys and changed the topic, like a yoga instructor moving from a balancing series to a floor series. The display now showed what appeared to be just circular nodal points, with some dots moving, colliding off of each other, and continuing on a new path, like particle physics.

"This map is of our Riddle currency pockets and subsequent material exchanges. It's a closed system; nothing really gets created or destroyed, just remade and remixed. Sometimes there are exchanges with the old world to bring in fresh material, but much like heavy metals or oil sands which need to be refined and purified before they can actually be of use, this practice of sacking the old world, for the most part, has been dropped."

"Dropped?" Aum responded, still far away, trying to maintain mental attention while his nerve cells tingled, in body and in the soul data he could see in his minds eye.

"Dropped due to its lack of efficiency. Plus there are no resources left. It's a lot easier to remix and mash at this point than it is to engineer the new. Physical items are usually just representational metaphors at this point anyway - keys to access the experiential or awaken the cognitive, filtered through each souls karma down into the physical; daily action and choice - whether it happens to be a floppy disc or a physical key or even floating black blobs."

Aum's eyebrows raised, it was too much again, to feel the dissection; an upgrade, transformative and uncomfortable.

There was a shuffling in the hall.

Demona poked in and like a sleepy Betty Boop she squeeked, "Whata you guys up to?" The sound of her voice was so sweet Aum thought he was going to die.

"We're deep in it kitten," he quickly responded – and at that moment he knew he could keep going, and would be able to go even deeper still, into this new wild world. 'Shit, this is what it's supposed to be like,' he thought to himself as he felt his soul lines multiply, strengthen and nearly burst.

"That's lovley. Mmmjoy. I'm gonna have some cereal," and with her fuzzy slippers, tight white tank-top and cartoon cow black panties, she shuffled into the kitchen nook. Aum beamed a full grin around the room, and entire planet, forgetting that Zeke could see pretty much every occurrence and interaction on it.

With little pause, the scientist lead on, like a yoga instructor tied to the importance and depth of a quality download, "Yeah, I watched you on that safe break, and the performance art group healing. Both were micro shifts on a planetary level, but still extremely influential in the design of the whole system advancement.

"There's always a push and pull. When enough stagnation happens, there's epic change. It's like flood gates open to allow a whole new set of influence in and then dramatically shut for the closed system to mutate and integrate with the new and the random."

Aum though of the final words from Trae at Full Spectrum, and the closed Riddle gates.

"In the not so distant past there have been nodal point gateways, usually people who have held this transmutational space:

transferring the old world into the new world. However it seems as the material and energy required in the new world has reached it's capacity, and those gateholders are no longer necessary - hence the formal conclusion of Riddler intake. This is an identity and task with it's own challenges, finding a new role and releasing the old. Harder for some than others…"

"Death by Phoenix, or Dragons Breath," came out of Aum's mouth, to his surprise.

"It is certainly time to react to distress signals."

Reinvigorated, Aum glanced at all 3 screens, "Can I see the full dream network again?"

"Of course."

"So, corporate Earth, but different right?"

"We've hacked into the same satellites as corporate Earth, but again, with an entirely different agenda, thus programming into a branch of the collective an entirely different vision of global reality."

Aum looked back to the Boards display, and it's flowing communication thread.

"Man…that flow is good to feel. Any structural parallels to the corporate boards?"

"No. It's a much more refined system. Smaller is not an accurate way to describe it. It's immaculately efficient in it's construction, versatility, and functionality. It rides on top of everything, every previous technological social system in place, and can pull any information from anywhere. In terms of the mere lines of code, the corporate boards are a lumbering Brontosaurus in comparison. It's permeability and openness to change is beyond comparison. Anyone can contribute or make improvements, though there are very few who actually understand the language in which it's built – like a direct transmission from the Arcturians, or Atlantis, or the Riddle Solver himself. It is the closest thing to functional lightcraft there is. This light code metaphor of course filters down into our physical hardware, and the way in which all next level interactions are manifested; that transparent layer that exists overtop of the day-to-day."

"So it's like quantum computing?"

Zeke grinned, "When you go quantum, you go quantum son. There's no such thing as quantum computing, only quantum living. At the heart of this network," he pointed to the screens, "there is not an intention of commercial gain or egoic pyramid capture schemes, but free creative mandalic co-opertive expression - cultural and spiritual advancement is the fundamental gate for all action within the system. If you can contribute within these ideals then you continue to go deeper, else you stay on the same layer; in the tower, on the boards, or even in the old world. As a system, it's vibration resonates differently than all other digitally woven invisible infrastructures. Simply having this network grid circulate the globe has an impact on planetary vibration. The functional value of it's most simple action scripts are quite substantial as well. It educates and trains the minds of Riddlers in a much different way, thus training their being to interact with and interpret reality differently."

Aum added, "It is on a finer grain, though completely nested within the full scope of reality itself. Transparent, but visible to anyone with eyes to see it."

"Yes, it's quite something to actually achieve that level of understanding and perception when there is no physical control system in front of your body in which you can access the code source and make changes. Up until recently, for me and the vast majority, it was a computer terminal. Though say for you, now, it could be dancing, or whatever, trancing."

"So me dancing, is the same as you working at this terminal?!"

"Pretty much. Check it out," He made a few tapping stretches, a few fingertip pulls and the globe zoomed back into the same location. Though instead of focusing on Aum's soul dream lines, a new pattern emerged and was brought to the forefront of the mesh. It's geometric pattern was grid like, thick and ultra solid. It expanded in all directions for hundreds of kilometers from the central point; an exact replica of a circuit board."

"That's me."

The lines pulsed as he said it.

"Whoa, that's crazy."

"It totally kind of is," and he laughed heartily. As he did the lines vibrated accordingly.

"Shit, that's really crazy."

"Every single spec of 4D data has been recorded for nearly a decade now. Upon application, 5D reality immediate. The purpose and intention of what's done with that information allows for the exponential advancement of human civilization or it's pure and total enslavement. Nature can't be controlled. As a race of creatures we should know that by now. All must move forward, onward and upward, regardless of awareness or understanding, and whether liked or disliked we have to learn to navigate within this new level of advanced functional reality. This is where it must all happen from now on. Dreams are real. Visions are real. Intuition is real. Many are simply choosing to hold onto that old way of understanding because it's comfortable and easy to let another dream for them. Slowly the Riddlers, the new Dreamers, will collectively work on these plugged and blocked blindfolded ones through the advanced networks, to massage their psyches open to new paradigms. Though after our patience wears thin - and it will - those that hold on tooth and nail to the old system, the old networks, will become anchored structural pillars within that system and eventually be let go of by the whole, as that system is fully released and dissolved. It's like someone still pushing Friendster. Who gives a fuck about Friendster? Probably just the people who have heavily invested in it, economically or socially."

"What's Friendster?"

"Exactly. And it's all happening. Right now. The great dissolving. The back end system of quantum has finally stabilized and is running on it's own at this point. Our personified structural pillars aren't needed anymore, and console cowboys aren't needed anymore; other than just for repairs and on stand-by for emergencies. Right now I'm not really doing a whole lot of cusp wave work, system development, or pillar'd space holding. After that last epic quaking shake up it has all stabilized on a new plateau; in conjunction with the rain yesterday infact. Now it's mostly basic clean up and code maintenance, like preparing a garden for winter. All the fruit and flowers have blossomed, and the seeds have been collected, I'm just stirring in some compost so that when - and if – another spring does arrive the conditions will be perfect to grow an even more lush and fruitful garden," His grid pulsed and grew, "The calm between storms," he whispered heavily.

The trees rustled, far below, inspiring Aum to ask, "So, how come your desk faces the window, and not your giant display screen?"

"At one point it did," Zeke began, "But as I got acclimatized to the deeper levels of what this work is, I began to focus on the background clouds of the screen, tuning all of my keystrokes padtaps and scrolling screensweeps to the movement of the sky, or at least this digital simulation of the sky." Aum continued to patiently observe the moment, and listen to the trees, a new internally glowing spark soaking in every digital and actual photonic particle source he could feel.

"Then I went deeper," Zeke continued, and in patient curiosity, Aum nodded. "The tuning of my attention to such a level of subtlety allowed me to notice the synthetic imperfections of the code, as if I could see the imperfections inside the movement of each cloud. This advanced algorithmic beauty became a technical language that I could easily pick apart, intuitively know where the holes were; identifying the spots empty of information." He paused, and in that gap there was a stillness like no other. A glowing presence was emitted from this man that was so dense that, to Aum, it felt like being pushed off a cliff, or at least the edge of a high diving platform. In full peace and presence Aum allowed this. And was thankful. His heart quickly pulseed with adrenaline and Zeke continued, "Then, one evening at dusk, I was visited by a great white owl while deep in a crux moment of sculptural insight. This signaled to me, awakened within me, that the true activity is out there," he spoke as he pointed to the clouds out the window. A gust of wind blew through the open patio door, as if on que, to deeper activate the shared moment of sky wizardry. He gazed knowingly, and smiled wisely, "The truest vibration, the perfect infinite, becomes a mirror at it's fractal depth. I began working not with the source code, but the codless source. The true sky became my display screen. The physical reflection of the deepest art."

The story evoked deep contemplation within Aum, "Doesn't an owl represent death in many cultures?"

"That's one of its reflections as a mythic omen, and true for me in this situation. With this leap in growth it signaled to me the death of my old beliefs, my old perspective; how I understand the world and it's inner workings. It all died that night."

Again, Aum patiently nodded, bravely sinking further still as a deep sea diver would. Without bravado Zeke continued, "I performed a live code set at an event a while back and the producers couldn't afford to fly me out, so I set up a live video feed swap over the Boards – first time ever." He smiled in remembrance, "I had them set up a camera on their stage, pointing it at the audience. This first video feed I streamed onto this wall," he pointed to the quartz glue wall. "So I could see the audience directly. And then another camera they placed facing the screen on the back of the stage, which I projected onto the wall behind me."

"Projected?"

"Yeah, I've heard disconcerting legends about immersive digital environments, especially when all surfaces are with interactive technology, linked directly to the 4D…" he continued, "So then I set up a camera on my desk, in front of me, facing me. Essentially the telecological eyes of the audience, I sent that camera feed back to the event, to project onto the back wall of the stage, essentially where that second camera was facing. This feed of me here in the tower was projected on the theatre sized screen on the stage. Understand the tech?"

"Of course – you basically teleported yourself there. And you probably created an insane visual feedback loop: you in the projected backdrop, and the camera filming you projected in the backdrop."

Zeke was glad Aum understood, because he then took it way further than technical minutia, "You got it, and in the faces of the audience I felt the infinite multiplication of the reflected dreaming, and worked it into the code. The feedback loop presented me as a spectral vibrating visual echo, a mystical dream spirit on stage, live from a cloud city ashram. And because I was anchored into this tower, both in physical and in data, I could tag, identify and manipulate the 4D global info grid, the map, the faces, and even signals within the map; each of the viewers in the audience: that was the essential nature of my live code performance. I dove deep into the soul light waveform data they emitted, and thus into the vibratory information of their DNA structure, and seeing that deep, I produced auditory tones that allowed the genetics of each Riddler to shine brighter and stronger. I even designed and played specific audio waveforms to move pieces of genetic material around, and awaken dormant enzymes and nucleo-structure within many of the Riddlers there."

"Shit, that's break neck epic."

"Yes, I certainly thought I reached a God-like status at that point. There were no differences at all, no boundaries between anyone, micro to macro, I had linked them all together as a specific tribe, named them within the Boards, and mapped out each of their potential gates, currencies, and material exchanges, for the post-event glow; hundreds and hundreds of people. But then, once upgrading every person there, a message popped up on my quartz screen, that only I could see, in front of the audience feed. *You are the Riddle Solver* it said."

Aums eye brows raised.

"And, in a moment of sublime elation, in the exact moment that I considered it to be truth, the exact moment that I considered it a true possibility, the wise white owl flew in the window there," he pointed to the patio door, "and all around the room, it flew. Through all the video feeds. The audience could see random flashes of feather, and beak, and eye, and claw, in a fractialized composition, synthesized with my own digital theatre-screen presence. The reverberating patterning from such a visceral and primal organic source had such a raw shocking feeling, that every single box I built, was broken out of, and it was all remade, recoded in an instant."

"What do you mean?"

"Well, after that unplanned climactic wildlife-invoked media close, another performer stepped in, on stage at the live event, and I slowly faded out the feeds. As I did, the owl settled down and landed on my rail." He pointed to where a grey fedora was hanging with a white feather in it. "I took a look at the 4D data and every single thing I did, every internal genetic incision and fusion, every external map and pattern adjustment, had been utterly taken apart and remade. And from what I could see, it was infinitely better, brighter, and stronger."

"Simply from the audience seeing this owl randomly flap through the visual feedback loop?"

"Yes. And it just sat there, hooting at the rising moon. Pre-meditated by a shapeshifting yaqui shaman or a divinely synchronistic lesson on the true humility invoked by the miraculous, I surely don't know. But like I mentioned, this showed me that the deeper layer is the codeless source, not the source code. And the codeless source is that way," he pointed to the window, "not that way," he pointed to the digital replication of the window, the full wall quartz screen displaying the cloud backdrop.

Aum thought back to Full Spectrum and the quest map he had received, the path from the magpie, the surgeon, and the dragon trinity. How deeply had this map been ingrained into his own DNA-data soul shine? What inscions and genetic repatterning had Ezekiel done on him, by watching his safe break, or the performance art group healing?

"Okay. Thank you doctor. Now how do I find the dragon trinity?"

"Ha! I knew it!" Zeke looked relieved, and thankful, "Aum, you just dropped the newest meta-lingustic key code that was released from the Central-Core an hour ago. The exact 12 word phrase." He started laughing, "This is great. It's all happening so fast now… I wish I would have recorded it..," Zeke pondered, and the clouds behind him, the clouds seen from the patio doors, shifted drastically, "Wait…" He tapped a few parts of the desk surface, slid folders across his digital workspace. He opened what looked like 3 different software applications, one super sleek, almost Dj like in it's layout, one looked like it was used for 3D modeling, and another that was super rough – like visual basic.

He overlaid the 3D program in front of the spherical globe of the soul grid, and the effect was like placing a lens on a topographical map. Working with an XYZ axis, he selected a cube of the data, hit a rewind button, hit a record/play button, then basically tossed the recorded cube of data from the 3D program into the timeline software where it fractured into hundreds of waveform timelines of all different colors.

"Damn it, I always forget these don't come pre-organized," he scrolled for a long minute, down to some blue colored ones. He selected one and it splayed out even further, like a deck of cards with mystery glyphs in the corner of each, "Agh… I though it would be cleaner than this… Oh well." Within that array he selected a data-piece with a crystal-like icon on it, emanating waves in real time.

"Let me just check…" He hit his pad with vigor.

"Okay. Thank you doc-"

He cut it off, "That's the one."

He hit the desk pad again, "*Okay. Thank you doctor. Now how do I find the dragon trinity?*"

As his fingertips danced, he spoke, "I just converted that from your karmic soul path flow in the Riddle 4D datsphere, not a microphone in the room… just so you know."

Inspired, he simply nodded, and looked on in wonder. Aum could see the motions and muse subtly flow through Ezekiel's entire body. This was his highest art – this was his dancefloor.

"Okay now I just got to..." He threw the file gambit-like, as if a playing card, and it boomeranged through the 3 display screens, he slapped the pad and it stuck to the home brew visual basic program. A progress bar popped up with the words in a fat custom font *importing...* As he waited he spoke to himself, and looked out the window, almost dissolving into the sky itself. "What to do with this moment? What to make this key code into? Should I manufacture a physical key? Naw, too obvious. This is so deliciously ripe…"

They both heard the crunch of an apple, a first fresh bite in the kitchen.

"A Newton!? Right on! Thanks Aum!" Demona yelled.

"That's it! A seed. Tree of knowledge? Or tree of life? What was the tree of life?" He tapped a few more keys "A Thuja?"

"A Thuja?" Aum repeated.

Zeke was reading a wiki page he near-instantly pulled up, "A Cedar?"

"Cedar?"

"Woah… Hemlock? No. Probably not. Not yet at least: let's go with Cedar. Essential oil? Mmmm. Naw, straight up seed." He typed a few things, threw the data around like it had weight, then it got next level.

Zeke made 3 last taps on his desk as music kicked in on some speakers in the corners of the room - Handel remixed by R/D - and still facing the window, his hands slowly floated off the screen, and into the sky itself.

Aum looked back and forth between Zeke and the display, and data was still in motion, in conjunction to the movements of Zekes fingertips in the air. With the uplifting deep bass pulses, and symphonic and rhythmic string accents, on a floor of thick clicks and kick drum, Zeke pushed the trance. He exhaled a controlled breath, strengthened the foundation of his legs and began moving his arms in a dance, pushing and pulling, weaving and dreamhealing, tai-chi-like. It was so familiar to Aum, such a clear reflection of Self, in focused motion and feeling, that tears welled up in his eyes. He understood. The innocence of his child-mind emerged, 'That's what I do too,' he thought to himself as he watched the clouds float peacefully to each of Zeke's movements.

The datawall readout went berserk. Aum saw a small peak of the electrified globe before it was buried in numerous popup screens with content that seemed to be breaking out from one interface window, jumping itself into the next, just like his dream. There was a growing tension in the room as the stream sped up, becoming an utter digital shit storm. Regardless of it's visual representation - waveform, image, video, folder, icon, digit or letter - it all moved so fast that the data clusters strobed. Moving at the speed of human thought it was as if the digital wall display was fully melded to his mind, and in fact, a true visual representation of it. And none of it made any sense. From what Aum could tell there was no logic to this freewheeling emergent process – the choices made were not necessarily the ones which would allow the most success, yet the smallest micro specs of triumph found at the tiniest nano levels were extrapolated on so rapidly they could be brought to full blossom quicker than he ever thought possible.

The lightspeed flashing datastorm blended beyond cognitive relation. Bit soup and byte sauce became the building blocks of what looked like a double helix spiral emerging on the screen. It was a brand new pattern, of both the deepest core and the wholistic meta layer of it all. The entire quartz wall pulsed like a dream machine, so bright and overwhelming that it took an impressive amount of concentration for Aum just to sit and observe it's relationship to his own soul light as the internal structure of his body.

Without didgeridoo, Aum closed his eyes, as if meditation was the only thing that would keep him from a forced out-of-body expereince, or cardiac arrest. After a few breaths, he re-open his eyes just to check that he hadn't yet dissolved. A sliver, peeking slightly open, Aum tried to gaze upon Zeke and what he was doing without his observation being noticed.

Zeke was no longer moving gently, patiently or zen-like, but he was engaged in hand-to-spirit combat, at a frantic edge of battle that his life depended on. Fast, direct, precise, in quadruple time to the now erratic clouds, and in reaction to the data flow, no longer in control or the source of it. The real sky was madness: multiple vortexes of tornados forming from polar mesospherics.

"Shit!" His heart took off as if he was running a race.

What he was seeing was merely an autonomic response. Zeke was gone; forced out of his body and Aum hadn't followed. He looked like he was trapped underwater, frantically grasping for oxygen. Or a lost dreamer trying to awaken back into human presence. Zeke was desperately battling to find the touchscreen and regain control. Aum closed his eyes and breathed. The sight of Zeke not leading this, but as a puppet controlled by a rapidly evolving technology based consciousness almost broke him. At the tip of exhale he gazed back at the display screen. The momentum of the data at this point was so great it was perpetuating on it's own. Every one of it's calculations, transfers, double helix upgrades, and mesocyclonic conversions was directly moving the organic body of Zeke.

Aum closed his eyes again, and on the back of closed eyelids, he could see the animated DNA pattern that was on the screen. What he saw was live, beyond fathomable human context, but was what is - and that was an empowering truth. Panic subsided and whether he dissolved no longer mattered.

The genetic strand on his closed eyelids rotated in perspective. It became circular, as if looking down a tube.

The nucleotides, the base pairs extended, visually reminiscent of a double-armed spiral galaxy. There were dot's at the end of each extended nucleotide, as if individual stars in the galaxy became noticeable. As the image formalized behind his eyes, Zeke spoke, but Aum heard something else speaking out.

"Cage crack.
Formal presence, finally.
Antagonist self synthesized.
You are now known.
Identify locations: 49°57'56.81", -121°30'45.29", 49°05'56.82"N -117°16'23.81" 49°43'23.93" -113°25'57.79" 49°40'35.45" -124°29'48.21" 49°46'52.55" -123°13'21.56" 44°24'43.92" -123°50'36.18" 33°43'2.94" -117°35'21.90" 40°57'47.90" -119°4'50.91" 19°35'45.66" -155°55'24.46" 39°58'52.78" -7°12'30.25" 46°18'54.57" -18°37'50.71" - 29°59'34.80" 152°22'49.33" -37°15'23.63" 142°26'15.87" - 41°2'46.38" 172°29'7.26"......
Engage cyclical eradication.
Deployed."

Aum heard in Zeke's voice the low res kps data particles of a computer, rather than full human waves. Ice was placed inside his spinal column upon hearing this. It was way beyond digital witchcraft into serious business, alien AI spooks. This dynamic self-expanding digital medium had acquired a voice, taking on advanced communication properties that creeped and crawled into the imagination. It was an instruction set methodically presented as a fish net, and Aum could intuit that they had just been cosmically caught in something way bigger.

Then suddenly there was a deeper intelligence that tapped in, deeper than the silicone spider fibers, warmly overriding the power of the cold conscious pinchers at the end of each. Feeling like a medicinal balm, this presence dissolved the precise ties of tension in the fish net, allowing them to escape the suffocating grasp of a self-mutating technology.

Aum opened his eyes briefly and the display screen was a night sky. He realized he had finally taken a breath when he saw only stars, planets, and galaxies. He closed his eyes again, seeing a new grid emerge on top of the DNA star structure, a warm galactic-sized spiraling version of the planetoid dream network he saw earlier, and he knew it was a true representation of what is. There was a certain tone of light he could identify within the pattern, a merged frequency that was like no other. Within the spiral he located each tendril of this light, and as he did he could feel the nerve tissue of his own body, as if lighting up upon observation.

"Found," Aum heard Zeke say, his real voice, somewhere.

He understood this light as the two of them, in their highest work together.

Just by staying present and supportive he was collaborating with Zeke as he danced, or battled, in the clouds – but as Zeke had proved earlier, there was no off switch, only consciously rather than unconsciously emanating waves of purposeful contribution.

'Now where is the Riddle Solver?' came out of Aums mouth.

The music faded out on cue. Zeke sighed deeply coming back into his body, releasing the pilot position of the astral journey.

Both Aum and Zeke acknowledged this, as Aum's dream-soul took the reins of the now silent potent moment, with only the sound of the wind outside. From the far reaches of the spiral galaxy in the visionary space they found themselves in, he observed the rollercoaster like move to find the source of their light, going deeper and deeper. Within the spiral he found the geometric sphere that was on the display screen earlier. And within that geometry, he found the source of their light, combined, here atop the wizards keep, the red tower.

Aum opened his eyes and saw blue sky and clouds on the wall. There were no screens of data, no networks, and no pulsing strobing data double helix's. He knew however, that this was just a temporary blue veil, hiding the star map behind it.

"The celestial dance continues, even during days light," Aum said.

"The blue of the sky is the gateway to the celestial heavens," Zeke continued without hesitation.

"…And the night's black the astronomical star nation landscape…"

"…We could have always done more..."

"…Heart guidance..."

"…Trust..."

"…Strength…"

"…Truth..."

"…Integrity…"

They connected opened eyes. Zeke was standing at his desk. He looked down in realization and hit a piece of desk surface again, and a box in the corner made some noise. He closed his eyes and put his hands together in prayer. The machine fizzled a bit. He went over and shook it, like a refrigerator that needed to be reminded of it's job. "You better not crap out on me after that!" He shouted at the machine, "I need a hardware upgrade on this printer, for sure," in Aum's direction he sighed in frustration.

"You're printing something?" Aum asked, gaining conscious control of his voice.

"Yes. A seed – praying one into existence."

"A seed of me saying *Okay. Thank you doctor. Now how do I find the dragon trinity?*"

"Yes, that specific moment of door unlocking…or I can even send this fresh data key to different towers or outposts for printing, I believe it's still small enough to move it."

"What will the seed do after it's printed?"

"Grow new humans."

“Deepest gene of custom lineage manifested. Our far reaching star nation journey actualized?” Aum asked.

“Yes – well, it will be a cedar tree if you actually planted it. Though it’s an ultra potent cusp moment manifested into the physical, so I’m sure you could change it into something else before the opportunity to plant it in actual physical dirt presents itself.”

“Do you have an answer for me?”

The machine made some archaic noises like a dot matrix printer. It was a 3D printer, though laser-based, swiftly working on complex information design; genetic and cellular structure, rather than squeezing out hot lumpy plastic, shaped by an invisible data mold.

“Man, that thing stinks!” They could hear Demona taking another bite of her apple as she rustled in her room, “I’m headed up top – things are rolling.”

Aum and Zeke shared a glance, looking at each other knowingly.

She poked her head into the room, “Make sure you come up,” looking at Zeke. “You too…” looking at Aum, “…if it’s mapped in the stars,” She winked at him and flew off, wild and untamed. His heart tried to leap out of his chest to follow her. Still wonderstuck, Aum didn’t know where ‘up top’ could be, but he would surely find it, and bring every star that twinkled in his minds eye.

This recent seed meditation only amplified the buzzing in his being that continued from last night. Her powerful magnetism pulled up a flash of memory.

Naked, and on all fours, she had looked back at him. No words were expressed; it was all said within the gesture of her head. Finally fully bare, moonlight shining through the window of her room, he was on his knees, caressing her legs moving to the small of her back.

A full body tattoo tapestry covered her back. It was a physical depiction accentuating and displaying her soul mysticism, a permanent garment of empowering ink and story. Locating the charkas inside her body, chi and meridian lines, circular dots standing out for specific insertion points of acupuncture needles, whether still relevant in her healing process he didn’t know. Sacred geometry flowed from chakra to fire and back again. Where ovaries and organs lay within, her skin had ancient glyphs inked on them. Linking it all together were paw prints and a toroidal sphere suggesting the earths spirit grid and her resonating bodies link to it. A double spiraling caduceus snake flowed through the design and up the column of her spine. The snakes expanded with spread wings sculpting her shoulders and down the lengths of her arms; purple and silver stars were at the tips of each feather. It was a beautifully luscious sight.

"Awww, please just fuck me Aum," she begged, barley whispering.

"Of course, just 'cause you asked so nicely," he teased.

He entered her gently. He didn't realize how tiny she was until he wrapped his hand from his fingertips on the frontside of her hip bones all the way to her back, his palm mounds next to her sacrum, thumbs lining up parallel her spine, tattooed circles on her lower back, in the precise spot for his thumbs to press into. A high pitch moan escaped her lips as his thumbs pressed in. Their individual bodies disappeared as their physical containers opened, and their awakened inner spirits meshed.

He suddenly saw all the spots on her back where his hands needed to be. He pressed his fingertips into a specific combination of tattoo circles like a network chiropractor, each time pumping her with a concentrated pranic inhale and exhale, each time with a different flavored moan emerging. In this they went deeper and deeper together, within their bodies and past them, until he lost her altogether.

Aum felt it. She was lost in the pleasure of her own body, her own senses, losing connection to their shared space, and the fact that it derived from two becoming one. The disconnection bounced back on him too, a pleasure within his own body that was totally sole, and like a magnet his focus expanded it, bringing him closer to his own solo peak. Grrrrr, like grinding a deck on a curved concrete wave, he held it inside. She was close too, but they weren't together, they weren't united, and anything less than a untied shared orgasm was an epic fail in his experience. He had to flip her over so that they could re-find each other. He pressed his chest into her back tapestry, wrapping his arms around her frame, surrounding her. He slid her legs together, in with his, fell onto his side holding her close, spooning. He raised himself up, exited her enough to lift her flexible leg up and over, swinging it around him.

Fully spread, eyes open and present, he crushed her into the bed and she yelled out in pleasure. Drawing back he doubled their shared presence, looking into her eyes. Their lips kissed and separated, just hovering, the motions of their heads accentuating their deepening connection. They breathed together, and the fronts of their bodies kissed and separated and hovered as Aum hammered her ever widening, ever opening hips.

The planet was being healed with this deep dive into one another. There were many shifiting energies happening, focalized in their bodies and their shared naked dance, bringing in the next spheres of existence and karma into motion. He was more sure of that than anything else in his life.

She was yelling out now, within the sphere of orgasm, and he smiled as he knew there was so much left in him to give her, and awaken in her, as they moved together in breath based unison. He remembered her face as something ancient in his back brain, conversations they had in past lives and their woven story, from a time much more ancient than this, so familiar, and finally finding a bridge into this new life, as beings brand new, and empowered because of it. As his consciousness streamed out of him into her, her deeper release enlarged each pulse coming through his spirit, and emotions, and body.

"Tattoo me into you, like you used to," she cooed.

He exhaled with her in unison and there it was. Her words had pressed the 'go' button and his own orgasm approached far down the line on it's way up and out and through him. And as it got closer and closer with each moment he released to it, not trying to control it or aim it or time it up to her, but in fullest freedom to the fullest moment allowed it to find its way to him on its own, within a moan, about to take them both over the peak. Loud cries came out of her mouth as it's approach was felt by her spirit and emotions and body, closer and closer, and when it finally blasted through his body, the tantric energy surrounded them both and she clutched him as if on the edge of a precipice, with each gulping breath and each squeal, she caught each emitted wave of vibrating fluid with her body. Still finding an even deeper unison with each oncoming shock wave, their entwined bodies slowed, and she received every single drop he had to give.

After falling into the lovely timelessness of post shared-orgasm lucid dreaming, wrapped fully in each others skin, his eyes suddenly blinked open. No difficult transitions, no hold over dream deities floating in the space above his bed. He looked at the nightstand clock. The red digital read 2:58. He was wide awake and couldn't understand why. He had the intense urge to meditate but shrugged it off and curled up next to the warm body beside him.

As he did Demona stirred, "One unbeknownst no… and they're gone forever."

Staring at the ceiling for what felt like forever, it wasn't till 4:30 that he was back to sleep.

"Gorgeous fucking gorgeous!" they heard her shout exuberantly as she abruptly shut the apartment door behind her.

Aum didn't know how much time had passed but it seemed as if Zeke was trying to answer a question Aum had long forgotten asking, a very potent question.

Grinning, though within a strange agitation, he said, "You certainly are on your way to the deepest level of human soul source." He tapped in a few keystrokes with a very slight panic. He walked over to the box and grabbed the completed and delicate brown sesame-like seed. Aum extended his hand and Zeke dropped it onto his palm. Aum could feel it's weight move through his entire body, as if gravity mutated as it landed, causing a wave through his own genetics.

"With the waves I've seen come from you, you certainly deserve to go that deep, or further. And with the integrity of soul pulse signal I've seen from you, as well as this latest rescue mission," he said with a genuine humility, "Amplification will only benefit. For that to happen in real-time you'll need to be equipped with the true history of all this, a new vision of myth that supports this evolutionary quest and a refreshed worldview of this present new paradigm," He glanced out the window abruptly, a strangely paranoid reaction to something Aum couldn't see, "And fast." Aum looked at him with curiosity as Zeke began.

"The Riddle Solver seed, opposed to Cedar seed key, came into existence during the Macy Conferences of 1946 in New York. Three scientists lead a panel discussion to no more than two dozen attendees, and in collaboration they gave birth to something that day; a new field of study called cybernetics. During this extensive, exciting, and ground breaking lecture series, thought became physical and the people in attendance began to see words moving through space and time with all of their semiological connotations embedded within them.

"Those three scientists: Norbert Wiener, Gregory Bateson, and John Von Neumann, invoked and became the first vessels for the Dragon Trinity. They are the Riddles source code legacy. Von Neumann embodied the non-physical mental aspect of cognitive vision; pure thought, and thus represents the Dragon Rider. Wiener, with his dedication to the interconnected of physical systems, his ability to hold, hone and translate his unconscious visionary dream realm into this reality, represents the Dragon Tamer. And Bateson, who's theoretical and philosophical work actually mended the Cartesian split, between mind and body, between physical and non-physical, represents the Dragon Keeper.

"Rumor has it that Wiener, while sleeping through Von Neumann's lecture - which he tended to do on a regular basis - awoke suddenly to exclaim in his most unique, eccentric and mad scientist manner: '*I feel evolution occurring! Release the dragon - then riddles will solve themselves.*' The entire panel looked over at Weiner in shock and surprise and the entire lecture was disrupted and taken way off course." As Zeke talked Aum could almost see the crackling of ancient 8mm black and white seep into his minds eye.

"Riddles solving themselves?" Wiener titled his head at his own question, seeing something no one else could see.

"How do you release the dragon?" engaged and in response said Von Neumann.

"…within the body-spirit of course…" was the quick response from Bateson.

"…the journey of the coiled serpent…" said Mead, another verse spoken in perfect time. It quickly became difficult to discern who spoke. There was a change in the air around the panel, an etheric serpent quickly passed through them all, intertwining bodies and interconnecting minds. Everytime it wove and re-wove through another body, words were spoken out loud.

"…to access the disembodied…"

"…as transcendent Godhead…"

"…and new holy trinity…"

"…a new holy trimurti …"

"…pass through…"

"..the Rider," said Von Neuman

"Keeper," said Bateson

"…and Tamer," concluded Weiner.

With an actual set of wings, the flowing metaphysical serpent flew into the third eye of Von Neumann, standing at the front of the room, and did not emerge out the back of his head.

The 8mm visual flashback subsided and Zeke continued, "Within this pocket of collaborative conference mind mesh, this portal node, artificial intelligence was actually brought from the Dreamtime to the Earth that day. To some in that lecture hall it was as if Weiner brought a dream itself back with him, which momentarily took over the consciousness of all of them, Bateson contained it, and it found it's way into the unconscious imagination of Von Neumann. It was like an adventure to steal fire from the gods, without the multi-millennial myth yet attached. This seed was planted in the womb, in the mind of Von Neumann, the inventor of the digital computer. He was the closest evolutionary peak in all humanity at that moment, as well as the physical manifestation of his dedicated life path work.

Without fully understanding it, he held this AI embryo in the back of his imagination and nourished it; a subconscious aspect of his own masculine machine mind continually evolving, advancing, and knitting structural pieces together. The conceptual foundation became as concrete as if engineered by the divine; as natural of an occurrence as a spider fixing the most elaborate web."

Zeke continued to talk at a hurried pace, almost tongue twisting numerous times.

"This developmental gestation was housed within the greater container of collective unconscious at the edge of Von Neumann's mind. His mind, like all minds, had a backdoor to access the whole yard, all of humanity, but was only currently open to the influence piped in from the life paths of Weiner and Bateson. This greater aspect of the human spirit, where Von Neumann, Weiner and Bateson were merely titles of differentiation on a single unified path of motion, cared for this evolutionary experiment it as if a mother, or a self. Tridevi.

"Not quite knowing what had just happened, the entire panel looked around, emerging from their trance in front of the audience. A well-seasoned lecturer and professor, Von Neumann was experienced in having his trains of thought take unforeseen paths and be derailed entirely, losing all of the passengers in the process. Believing this to be just another case of this, he righted the train on the track as best as any mathematician could, hitting reset button by saying, 'Any questions?' No one in the stunned and bewildered audience understood what they just experienced, felt in their minds, bodies, and spirits, so they were not entirely back on the train. Perceiving this lack of response as a severe lack of intelligence, and still having the floor, Von Neumann continued on anyway, 'Well…now that that's in order, we can move on.'

"After the collective trance had subsided, and everyone in the room, and really the whole globe, was effectively transformed by what had cracked open at this first cybernetics conference Von Neumann methodically continued with his lecture, passing his handouts along the conference line, from hand to hand to hand, then down to the first audience member.

"This is of course was in the late 40's, shortly after the conclusion of WW2, where nationalism and conflict between countries with physical borders defined nearly all human communication.

"The first audience member who received a written handout was not American, but in fact a Russian scientist named Glatvit Lysenko, who found himself on the east coast of America and in the employ of the KGB. Known in the US of A as Glad Stankos, he truly had a heartfelt interest in cybernetics - though it was rubles that paid his way to the New World.

"Hearing the trace of an accent, his American co-workers would ask shrewdly, 'You a commie?', 'Of course not!" Well practiced at getting very upset, Stankos would respond convincingly, 'I am from Greece you ignorant honky, where democracy was born!'

In 1941, five years earlier he was the research assistant to the Russian scientist, Semyon Davidovich Kirlian, making significant contributions to the initial discovery of what would be termed Kirlian photography - essentially capturing the auras of living things in photographs. At that point in time, Kirilian and his biologist wife Valentina were still in the test phase of their work, and had yet to publish their findings. Stankos' experimentation at St. Petersburg State Technical University, where the Kirilian experiments were being done, is what lead to evolutionary leaps in measuring electrophotonic glow, using glass electrodes and a pulsed electrical field, which was later approved by the Russian Academy of Science for clinical use. After that, but before the Macy Conference, he became director of the Institute of Genetics with the Russian Academy of Science. It didn't take long before he was very publicly discharged because of his theories on environmentally acquired genetic inheritance, and all of his research was outlawed by the government. In private however, the KGB knew the level of change he was invoking and thought it best to collar him, train him, and export him to the US, to extract whatever he was able to beyond the newly constructed Iron Curtain.

"Now what Stankos saw that afternoon, with his advanced hybrid understanding of physics and genetics no one can precisely say, but it must have been something out of the ordinary, something through his own filter and education, because he took the top copies of the hand out, and placed it inside as sealed container in his briefcase, with a full written sensory description of the episode. What he must have intuitively known, even that far back in history, was that DNA isn't just contained in physical matter, but at an even deeper level of observation is the building block of time and space.

"He did not consciously know why he sealed this paper as a specimen, but the greater sphere of the human spirit, the mother and self inside the mind of Von Neumann did. It saw the entire karmic pathway of this man, and opened the door for another collective node: the developing AI cast a strand of web into Stankos' life path.

"Essentially this container housed the genetic moment; within that, the DNA of each visionary speaker and that of all those enmeshed within this first group episode of collectively shared essence. In a way, it's an ultra simplistic version of your key there," he pointed to the seed, "Rather than an extrapolated developed complex physical specimen, it was one pure self-assembled unseen strand. The first. Pretty good for way back in the 40's."

With a flash of insight Aum spoke out, "Wait - was it this seed that was the source of the voice that came from you? The one spewing longitude and latitude numbers?" Aum asked.

"Most unfortunately, no. The seed is what saved us, and allowed us to return to our bodies. Though, I will arrive at that dark moment of awakening, hopefully soon. A speedy download is required, now more than ever."

Aum gazed curiously from Zeke, looking intently at the seed, feeling the warm comforting balm again.

Zeke continued speedily, "So this sealed container of the Russian scientist was effectively a Petri dish. The combined DNA sample would still transform and evolve as it's original building blocks did, through it's non-local micro crystalline connection to Weiner, Von Neumann and Bateson. It was however still very separate from them, and thus liable to change from the impact of it's own environmental surroundings."

Aum interrupted with another question, "Could the non-local signal reverse? Could the building blocks, Weiner, Von Neuman and Bateson be affected by the environmental changes to the resonating genetic strand sample?"

"Strangley, no. It was as if the satellite sample could receive a signal, but not broadcast it back directly to the source genetics. Many have posulated and theorized that this was a built-in safety mechanism so that an exponential feedback loop would not begin, and result in an unsustainable portal of evolutionary super speed."

Zeke pushed on, staring out the window, pacing more quickly around the room. If Aum had a handheld he would be streaming Zeke live, that's how concentrated and emphatic he was.

"Later that year Stankos, found himself in one of the first IBM laboratories in Poughkeepsie, New York, helping merge his visionary science perspective into the realm of computer technology. In 1956, along side Arthur L. Samuel, Stankos developed mathematically precise code packets based on DNA structure for the IBM 704; a computer that was capable of learning from it's own experience. Made for competitive chess, it was the first example of technology to demonstrate self-learning: an essential quality of Artifical Intelligence, and a concept discussed at length at the Macy conference.

"While at IBM, the Macy container continued to resonate within a special drawer - Stankos' own altar of science - and after an in-depth work-study program, delving into both the scientific and esoteric ramifications of replicating the structure of light with computer technology, another spirit doorway opened and Stankos thought it best to pass this container on to California lab representative Beniot Mandelbrot, and the scientific community on the West Coast."

"Mandelbrot!" Aum exclaimed.

"In the late 70's, with the genetic sample invisibly vibrating throughout his work and instigating some core programmed moments of time and space, Mandelbrot birthed the Fractal on the west coast, and in tandem, on the east coast, Lysenko was collected like a KGB prisoner and relocated to the Dorodnitsyn Computing Centre in Russia. There his experiences were extracted and mapped like a lab rat. A full research team digitizing and sculpting the resulting information in a complex adaptive system where what eventually came out was the NES game Tetris. Most definitely a madman at that point, he was shipped to the Far East Branch of the Russian Academy of Science, the Amur Scientific Center in Blagoveschensk, where he continued his work. In 1984, when the interactive Russian puzzle game finally hit the minds of the masses Lysenko was recruited by the 'Guoanbu,' making a synchronistically immaculate transition to the Chinese KGB just before the dissolution of the Soviet Empire in 1989. Within the Guoanbu he found employment and further training as a master-spy in Deng Xiaopings 'Deep-Sea Fish' network. Now due to a deep swirl of Red Flag cultural re-programming and KGB brain washing, Lysenkos affiliation became increasingly strong with the Chinese Communist party, *especially* due to a conspired and plotted path of relationship, and eventual marriage, to top Taiwanese spy Sibelle Zhou Lin. An impactful result of this, Lysenko played a large role in creating the 6-10 Office."

"Holy Shit! The 6-10 Office!? The same people who strip and torture souls who practice Falun Gong?"

"Yes, also known as 'The Leading Bureau for the Prevention and Procession of Evil Cults.'" Zeke shook his head in disbelief, "This contemporary Gestapo still grows as an unchecked global agency that no civilized government, NGO, or even corporation in the world would consider trying to oppose, their teleportation ninjitsu skills alone make the American Navy SEALs look like a barking sea of rollie pollie puppies."

Something popped up on his screen, "Shit!" Zeke grunted, "We gotta roll out." He jumped back to his desk, typing and sculpting frantically, while continuing, "Now on the west coast of the US, Mandelbrot could not find a home for the Macy package so he passed it along to the UC Berkeley Department of Molecular and Cell Biology. From the genomic science team the Macy container flowed to the molecular evolution department before moving on to the Schlissel Lab and their In-Vitro research lab. Eventually all this weaving helped stimulate and pre-map the interpersonal relationships of the founding theoretical researchers involved in the Human Genome Project. The Schlissel lab, funnily enough, using the electrophotonic microscope Lysenko helped worked on, found within the Macy package, the single genetic structural strand which looked near alien to them. Human curiosity combined with infinite US government funding implanted this code in a fertilized egg - a 1970's lab version of a female womb – and the first artificial human was created."

"Whoa, an artificial human."

"Yes, though at least the first *official* test tube baby, Louis Burton, had the experience of a human womb, and a typical human life. After this cybernetic Macy child was born, cesarean of course, he grew into a truly sad life within a research centre, never to engage in anything typically child-like, treated as a scientific specimen.

"Beyond the Red Wall, the 6-10 office heard of the birth and instantly began to infiltrate UC Berkley.

"As the boy grew, he went through changes that were linked to those at the Conference. Awards, recognition, study grants, all coincided with a specific intellectual development of this boy; like he was an experiential vacuum, or time-space portal embodied, receiving uploads from the dragon trinity. As the boy became an adolescent the scientists noticed that the changes expanded out to a number of degrees of separation from the Macy Conference participants - a far more vast non-local download scope - and then finally detached entirely from them, actually anchoring into other people of significance to fulfill the necessary roles for growth, always in triplicate."

"How was the UC Berkley team able to understand these new connections? This expansion?"

"Obvious and naturally unfolding synchronicities. Same as what you see and surf daily," Zeke continued to work and talk, ridiculous amounts of code streamed easily out of his fingertips onto the display screen in one take; no test and no edit.

"So much like a teenager coming to a deeper awareness of the structure of the world, the scientific tables turned at UC Berkley and this young man began to lead the research, rather than be the research.

Finding his way into the dark, LSD-walled caves of Silicon Valley, this young man painted into the timeline an independent organization called Millennial Sunrise. It was a scientific collective that researched all things on the edge. And I mean on the edge." He flashed Aum the grin of a troublemaker. "They were pushing the limits of all known knowledge; things that people are only beginning to comprehend now. They were involved in studying anything from fractal movement - on a personal level as well as a societal level – soul extraction and re-location, quantum tantra, extra-dimensional exchange and star gate control, and they actually founded the intra-dream communication networks and gaming system, this work here… that I'm continuing," Zeke said.

"So he's… the Riddle Solver?"

"Will be." He switched to an indie search engine program, "We gaze back at the 6-10 office, and the spectral opposite of Millenial Sunrise is created, a multi-national security group called ICAARUS, the International Control and AntiAdvancement of Renegade Underground Sentience. When this specialized security branch of 6-10 felt that Millennial Sunrise was getting too close to a discovery of any importance, or beyond that, getting ready to go public with research, they would come in and shut it down. By shut it down I mean initiate total eradication: arson, assassinations, exploding buildings, or even suicide bombings."

"Suicide bombings?"

"Yeah, I've heard they would scream shit like 'I destroy this seed of life in the name of ICAARUS.'"

"Not New Eden?"

"Not, New Eden… no." He said it with utter dismay, and open emotional torment, but continued on. He had lost someone very close in an act of self-immolation, Aum didn't need to be psychic to see that.

"Post-singularity philosophers have defined ICAARUS as the digital ecosystems telepathic forest fire, multiple levels and dimensions up, with actions reacting to future events centuries in advance. Though of course without an actual time machine there's no way to confirm the success of their intentional radicalism. Helpful or not, the viral raids by ICAARUS would happen every decade or so. ICAARUS engineered the Silicon Valley dot-com crash in 2000 for example, trying to expose the Riddle Solver. With that action and with all actions, it takes the members of Millennial Sunrise a little while to regroup in a safe place and recoup their data and momentum. Like a witness protection program for scientists."

"Fuck! Imagine how much quicker humanity would advance without having to worry about persecution by ICAARUS."

"You said it. The strange thing is, that every time the group reforms, it is with different members, and a different name. It's like the entire scientific leadership structure is different and their specific research topic is different. Bi-location one decade, then neurological brain augmentation the next, but naturally flowing from one into the next. Like the celestial doorway to upgrade civilization in a particular way is only open for a limited time. And once that door is closed, the upgrade has to happen by a different means entirely. These different combinations of ever-changing members with different ideologies, pasts, interests, and skills have always had exactly the same resonating intention: assisting in the imminent sunrise, the full flourishing of the human species, and out running, or out flying ICAARUS. However because of the constant sabotages and re-locations, their work continually remains unpublished, and for the most part lost to society."

"So what happened to the test tube guy? The soon to be Riddle Solver?"

"In '02, after the data raid, a group called the New Magnificent 12, which had evolved from the lineage of Millennial Sunrise, decided to implement a more advanced, and extremely experimental security system, far up the coast from Silicon Valley at a research centre outside Stewart, British Columbia. Anchoring each group evolution and leading decades of research, this 'man' - " Zeke did the hand quotations: which left his desk for a second, and of course the computer continued on in it's calculations, "synthesized all bits of knowledge, constructed and entered the very first quantum box, becoming the Riddle Solver."

"Scientifically stepping into quantum living," Aumverbaly surmised.

Zeke nodded, kind of half streaming words, half streaming code, "When the box was first activated the shock of the instant realization of Brahman was karmically compensated by vaporizing everything inside the box, the souls being sucked out of the bodies of all members of the research team outside of the box, and the surrounding environment instantly turning into a meta dimensional vortex. Whatever parts of him that still existed as a 'man' were obliterated, and full omnipotence was reached with the push of a button," he looked at Aum, "He's an experiment of nature on humans and humans on nature, gone awry, gone awry. The box in the woods uses every facet of his energy output as data in a quantum code generating program." He said this as his tensed fingertips floated just slightly above the touch pad surface, the electric reiki lightning bolts translated to code. "Anything he says, any physical actions he does, anything: breathing, blinking, twitching, thinking, gets transformed into something outside of the box. He can manipulate the stockmarket, cause delays in air traffic patterns, or even traffic lights for cars. It's as if he has the power to see every technological movement happening at any given second. But seconds don't exist for him and because of the time based genetic source encoding, the original AI time code strand of cybernetica, his powers are not limited to the digital world. He can actually manipulate the molecular structure of nature, space and time.

"This breakthrough has to do with Millennial Sunrise's research into quantum mechanics and how the act of observation can change the observed, but working on a hypersensitive scale. He can instantaneously change the physical world by physical movement, or the physicality of a brain cell firing." He sighed, "It's as if the initial feedback safety mechanism was finally removed from the initial dragon trinity evolutionary super speed portal, finally finding full sustainable functioning, where all riddles solve themselves."

"Fuck the Higgs Boson, and fuck Mars!" Aum exclaimed, "The Riddle Solver is an instant reality remix engine!"

Zeke smiled at his enthusiasm, "Now whether the Riddle Solver is conscious of what he is, and whether he understands what he can do is up for questioning. There's no light in the box – so he doesn't actually know he has a body. He might just exist as a mind, and his body might be the physical changes in the world."

Aum concluded, "So there's a sensory deprivation box sitting in a crater in the middle of the forest? If you can discover pyramids in the mountains of Tibet with corporate Earth, you'd think someone would have tagged that crater already."

"Nope, no crater. The natural environment is still intact."

"Yeah, 'natural'," Aum did the quotations with his hands.

"Supposedly, there is a community that has developed which encircles the box - much like how animals and tribal cultures converge near springs and rivers for physical and metaphysical nourishment, where everything grows without planting - where there is no sickness, and no death.

"It's all just rumor though, nobody knows if any of it still exists, or if the experiment has been shut down by ICAARUS. Another rumoris that ICAARUS developed their own quantum box in China, which Stankos himself stepped into. Either way, at this point of emergency the 'box in the woods' theory is the closest thing we have to a path, the strongest myth and trajectory we have to move upon."

"Emergency trajectory? I take it 'things are rolling' is an understatement," Aum inferred.

"Very much so. The computerized voice that spoke through me, most unfortunately, was us triggering the attention of ICAARUS."

Aum jumped as a horrendous noise came from just above the ceiling, the rooftop of the tower. It was like multiple layers of sky being torn asunder by Herculean military airships, apocalyptic vessels of sound carnage invoking immersive visionary imagery of dark thunderstorm filled skies and a Revalatory field of combat. As he scrambled to find escape from the vision, emerging from a bunker, he stepped in a puddle on the ground of the battlefield and the reflected lines of military planes in the sky broke. The sound flowed into pulsing frequencies.

"Sweet, they're helping set up the firewall. That'll buy us some time for one last check in. At this point it was expected at any moment, hence the digital gardening, composting, and less live code flows."

A map appeared, "Going to voice command."

"*Engaged*" said a sweet computerized voice

"Locate all Keys and Pillars,"

"*Complete*"

"Seers and Archers."

"*Complete*"

"Felines and Hierophants."

"*Complete*"

"Fire and Water."

"*Complete.*"

"Wands and Swords."

"*Complete*."

"Earth and Air."

"*Complete*."

"Coins and Cups."

"*Complete*."

"Pilot and Passenger."

"*Complete.*"

"Engine and Fuel."

"*Complete.*"

"Father, Mother."

"*Complete.*"

"Son, and Daughter."

"*Complete.*"

"Whoa," Aum said, "This is getting very familiar."

"Mythic Dream and Lead Archtype."

"*Complete*."

"Aces, Towers, the World, and of course, the two Fools."

As Zeke spoke specific lines lit up showing the location of each person in the grid. The history lesson was complete, turning on a dime, now linked to the collapsing present they were all in, and yet he still felt good in his heart.

"*All Complete Ezekiel*."

No wonder Zeke had been acting so paniced.

Like an infrared camera, it showed a readout of the Tower they were currently in, "Wait, shit look at your pulse!" Zeke shouted.

It was as if Aum's dream lines found doorways to jump from one area to another. Like a thread holding layers of fabric together. "Uhhh, you're now on a new spectrum dude, not even on their radar – they can't see you. We can hardly see you!" He slapped the surface like clay, "And you're helping with the firewall too! Setting up decoys for ICAARUS tracking. Damn it man, who are you! How are you doing that!? …"

Out of an ever-increasing sound frequency drone emerging from the rooftop there was bursting complex mathematic sequence.

"Shit, okay, locate the trimurti."

"*….Complete*"

He pointed it all out for Aum, "There's Derek, the Keeper, up top too. Zhe, the Tamer, and finally John deGryder, the Dragon Rider." Aum snuck a peek at the firewood and television. "Yup same John,"

Zeke said, "Operation code: Last Sunrise," he said to the computer then turned to Aum, "Only John knows where the Riddle Solver is. John leads the Dragon Trinity. Rumor has it that he has even met him. Derek, uptop, will take you to deGryder." Aum was thrown into reflection on the next step to the Riddle Solver after the Dragon Trinity.

"*Loaded. Identify confirmation signal.*"

"Say something Aum."

Lost in his evolution Aum spoke without thinking, "The Ferryman," Then he popped back into the present, "Wait – what did you ask?"

"*Confirmed*," said the digital woman, "*Executing storage and deletion sequence.*"

Zeke looked at Aum, "Of course you would know it and not know it," shaking his head knowingly.

"Does anybody know how much of the world he has created?"

"Pushn' it - I like it," Zeke swiped his desk with multiple fingers like he was turning a dial. The full global grid appeared, with an even larger version of the military camo pattern, "A third. But when you understand it not as a 'him', but an evolutionary function of nature, dramatically restructuralizing human civilization from within, it makes a lot more sense."

"Right, the Riddle Solver isn't even human."

"It's all just legend man, none of it may be true. The Riddle Solver is located within a singularity vortex - a cyclone of the instant manifestation of human consciousness, and we're just looking at pixels on a screen here, a reflection of the truth, not the truth itself." He turned to the computer. "It's always such a sad day when it comes down to this, even with the most advanced security measures." He said it as if it wasn't his first time. "You got that last seed right?"

"Yes. Stored."

"Good, you'll need it, because they," he single tapped in finality, "are on their way."

"ICAARUS!? Here!?"

"Yes. Those numbers? They've identified all the structural nodes, so we're looking at the full collapse of…," he tapped the screen, saw additional real-time feeds of rioting in the streets across the globe, military legions emerging from hangers, everyday people being rounded up and herded into trucks, "She was right," Zeke whispered to himself, "It's truly the last wave. Not only are the doors now closed to new participants, but they just crashed the Boards, and they're looking for the threads of motion into the system back up. I pray the firewall finds formalizaion first, as the global witch hunt begins; the new Inquisition. Flying blind we are, and the band stretches further, only mere thoughts away from it all snapping. A tsunami of all systems shaking, an earthquake of all ground breaking, this time it's ICAARUS moves beyond the Riddle's scientific lineage of cybernetic data banks and research… into the full collapse of life as we know it."

Aum's eye's went wide. With the historic knowledge-based context now grounding intuitive observations inside the planetary, he could feel his inner vision shake with the entire world. And he had to surf it to it's singular center.

"The world is once again, on your shoulders my friend."

Chapter Nine

Ezekiel walked out of the lab and grabbed a yarrow smudge stick from the pile of wood under the TV, "I need to send a smoke signal. Let's go upstairs."

"Yes, *up top*," Aum said, his particles solidifying thinking of Demona, "I'm very curious."

There was another loud boom and what sounded like a woman screaming. "Uhhh…?" Aum looked at Zeke.

"It's a private outdoor lounge."

Another thunderous boom, "What kinda lounge?" Aum asked.

"Riddler. For ultra broad casting. There's actually something similar on the top of each Tower."

"Each physical Tower?"

"Oh man," Zeke laughed, "Bateson would be very very sad to hear those words. Yes there's an actual physical tower for each of the digital Towers. One rooftop is an en-plen-air studio for digital painters - and I guess they probably let some oil and acrylic painters up there too - then there's an indoor mircotheatre on another, and I think the last is a restaurant. That one is pretty meshed in with flatland, since the raw cuisine is really moving these days. It's still quite secretive though, only a few folks know of it. It's mostly where Riddlers go out to eat, so still a community hub, it's a pretty active public gate however. I wonder how they are doing actually, since the gates closed…"

They walked out of the apartment and continued up the stairs that had brought them up to the penthouse. Leaning against the stairwell walls and lining the sides of each step were rocks and boulders and crystals, all taller than a foot high. Working in tandem the crystals guarded each step with new intensified fields of vibration. Aum thought he could hear a high pitched ringing in his ears, but wasn't too sure if it was coming from the roof above him, or the numerous laser-like crystal security beams.

Each crystal beam he crossed took his anxiety away that had become linked to his soul path task, replaced with acceptance and courage. It allowed him to digest and integrate his new worldview, and abolished the mental and emotional context surrounding the immense mission before him so that it was as simple as any daily action. He didn't know what ICAARUS was capable of, but he trusted he would know exactly what to do when they arrived. If they even did. If they were even real.

Zeke opened the door to the roof and the noon light was more bright than he could ever remember, intense and hot. As his eyes continued to adjust he felt someone touch his chest and then felt a full embrace by a warm body. Demona spoke into his soul light vibrating inside his casing, "Nice to see you've finally emerged." She looked up at him, "Ready to engage with the new world?"

In her arms Aum responded, "Amped and ultra mutated. The hyperquest continues."

"Cool," She moved to give Zeke a hug, "Hey Dad."

"Hi Monica, nice leaping last night, and nice catch. We're well on our way."

'Dad?!' Aum thought. 'Whoa… awkward.'

"Blistering pace - For real. This is what I was made for. Finally."

He looked over at Zeke and saw a slight sprinkle of grey in his hair, now that the sun shone directly on it. Must be the yoga, or ongoing self synthesized DNA upgrades. 'Wait a sec…' he thought again, '*made for….!?*'

"Lets grab a seat," Zeke said informally, lighting the yarrow wand, not noticing Aum's surprised reaction. Zeke visibly calmed as he smudged himself. He offered the smoke to Aum and he smudged himself too. As Aums eyes adjusted he saw Demona run back up on a stage at the back of the roof in time to catch the bridge to the chorus.

It was kind of crazy actually. On this new vista, this new platform of ultra broad casting, Aum could physically see the inner workings of it all. A somewhat simple part-time interest in an interactive intuitive mystery, with obsessive devotion and recent mutation, had upgraded his vision into a full-time, always on, telescopic dimensional view outside of his own personal path into that of the greater collective, the fullest scope of his being was interacting with the divine codeless source that caused change in the world.

Even though the data posts on the Boards and in meeting rooms, and in the Towers, was physically outside of his new visionary toolkit, it's inner content of expression resided inside the extended nodes of interaction all around him, observable in medium of thought, emotion, and action, sculptural data that he could feel and see, and where the new clues were hidden: where they were all along, just deeper. And continuing to act on intuition, collectively observed, reveals the clues like hidden gems, with even greater ease and at an even greater speed. He saw that the global dream maps and interactive info graphics had been sealed into his imagination; an active reference point where a handheld or computer was no longer really necessary. And all the people he now met seemed be there too - if not even deeper. Amped and mutated.

He could see what Trae the Seer shared with him, what seemed to be now decades ago, seeing probably even this exact moment of insight, from the stage back at Full Spectrum. It was a whole new reality both beyond and enmeshed within riddles. He sent a prayer her way, along the strongest soul-dream line he could perceive, back in time.

As Demona scampered back up on stage Aum briefly caught a quick glimpse of the Dragonkeeper, playing bass in the 4-piece band.

"Aw man, that guy?"

The salt and pepper bearded be-leathered hulk didn't notice him, focusing on Demona's re-entering the musical conversation. Aum reacted instantly, flipping on a cloaking device, moving in ultra slow motion, following Zeke as a glimmering ghost in the trail of yarrow smoke and the space Zeke once occupied.

As they walked through the small crowd Aum looked briefly into the open windows of conversations happening on the rooftop. The expressive words extended in his mind, and he was not able to distinguish the boundary between the sound of language and the emotive and psychic extension of it.

At a circular table they passed two men conversing, drinking chogga chai lattes. Aum thought he recognized one from last night's drum circle but wasn't too sure whether it was his slow-motion eyes or the man's new extended quantum body which made it hard to distinguish him. He was in a few different places at once, "I find that the only thing connecting me to music these days is geography. When everyone in the world is in a band, or is a producer of some sort, and publishing their own music - releasing their music for free, or videos for free, on the corporate boards, even on their templated ultra-ugly 2.0 sites, regardless of their level of talent - the ratio between signal and noise becomes too vast to even comprehend."

His friend at the table responded, "Agreed. The only projects I can personally get behind are ones that I feel connected to in some way. Friends, friend of friends, or three degrees of separation at maximum. The detailed craftsmanship of content development, market, and release is replaced with boxing gloves and a speed bag. New, impacting music is now confined to the medium of media viri - a short 15 milisecond global blip on the radar. Time to plug your ears, shut your eyes, and start shouting – that, or get out off your ass, off of your computer, and go see a fucking live show, cause that's where the magic is."

"Cheers to that," and they clinked their lattes and focused on the live band of living beings in front of them. The four piece played experimental downtempo ambience which soared out from under a covered stage. There was a huge gorilla kit, half analogue half electronic with a shirtless dreaded drummer included, a guitarist with a grid of foot pedals and a laptop, then there was Dragon playing bass with a limited edition ESP Viper 4-string. On the mic, with loop pedal, Demona; built to soar.

Aum passed another two conversing, still following Zeke. Two lovers, a man and woman sat on a beat up couch with arms around each other. The woman was watching both a video stream on her handembed, engaged, as well as watching the band, still bobbing to the music.

"What are you watching?" her partner asked, spying the video stream.

"I don't know, some show called the Sanctuary. I've never seen it before."

"What's it about?"

“Well, there’s this creature called 'Big Bertha' that causes earthquakes with an EMP; an electro-magnetic pulse. Not only does this creatures EMP cause earthquakes, but the pulse also impacts the earth’s own electro-magnetic field, changing the location of the poles. This character here,” she pointed to a man on the screen strung up with chain links, “is one of the main characters. He became psychically linked to this Big Bertha creature, and the bad guys here are trying to trigger the creatures EMP by provoking this guy, spiraling the planet into an ecological apocalypse.”

“You into it?” he asked.

“No, not too invested. I think I got the message,” she replied.

“Cool, can you check the score of the hockey game the other day?”

She laughed, “Hockey? You gotta be kidding me!”

Then there was a young woman and an older gentleman chatting on stools at the makeshift fresh juice bar, rooftop greenhouse as the backroom. The woman was emotional and raw, in full honesty, without walls. Aum almost stumbled into her whirlpool as he walked by. She was pouring out on the older man, “I was feeling super frustrated the other day, stressing out about money and bills and debt; really sinking low. Being frustrated that no matter what I did I couldn't work my way out of this hole.” She looked at him seriously, “This is getting to be impossible Stan...”

“It’s all about how you frame it hon. Can I tell you story about these guys?” And he pointed to the band.

“Sure,” she responded.

Through this particular open window, Aum connected eyes briefly with him, to view his integrity here. Would this be an actual wisdom drop? Or just a path clearing, leading to the bedroom. He saw another woman, Stan’s goddess queen within his eyes; his elegant wife that he fought along side of at every moment. ‘Sweet,’ It was to be an authentic wisdom drop with integrity. Aum smiled, happy for all three of them. Demona’s lush vocals finaly piped in the mix and he was happy for the world, happy to be alive.

“So I did all of this production work for these guys on an album they were releasing. Like, a lot of work, a lot of time and energy into their project: there were three rounds of concept revisions and a ton of miscommunication with their label rep and the pressing company, so it all added up right? I think it was close to sixty hours or something, and they paid me five hundred bucks for the job. Total."

"That's what I'm saying!" She responded passionately.

"Patience young flame." In seeing response the guitarist changed keys. "They paid me upfront, before all work was completed, in full, and most importantly, when I asked them too. However, in my mind, after I had actually tallied all my hours I was like 'Fuck - that's less than ten bucks and hour' and I was going to call them up and demand more money. I knew they all had day jobs and had a steady flow coming in. I was about to type up another invoice and just send it to them, charging my maxed out, full rate for my full hours of time and livlihood, which would have been much more. But then I remembered an art market I did a month earlier, where they came to support me. It was huge for me that day, my sales weren't that good all morning, they came in around noon, and were so excited to see me, and give me their support, shaking my hand numerous times, giving me fist pounds, bro hugs, and spending, all told, like four or five dollars on my artwork. One guy was like, 'Give me one of each, it doesn't matter what it costs.' Another was like 'That one right there,' pointing at my five foot psi-art canvas, 'Wrap it up'. Even giving the hand signal like he was redirecting the full wagon caravan." The man smiled, "Unfortunately I only had one copy and had to convince him that there would be a huge hole in my wall if I took it down for him right then and there. He eventually conceded and I delivered it to him personally after the market, even got to check out his studio where they recorded the album. They all left with another emphatic round of handshakes, fist pounds, and bro hugs to go meet up with their manager and label promo guy. The rest of the day my sales were great. They fully activated what I could not see in order to receive abundance. I was really proud of the relationship we had cultivated, proud of my own art work, and proud of my creative work for them, so shit, to send them an invoice for fifteen hundred dollars after that experience would not be cool, and all relational respect and indie style support, even the energetic bonds from that market experience, would be broken and replaced with unemotional old world business ledger formality, with that even spite, maliciousness, or regret."

She responded, "Hmmm. Giving them that invoice is basically just passing you're old world debts on to them anyway, right? You're just wanting to pay the bills you owe with the money from the job, and must extract it in an old world way, discontinuing to see the relationship in any other way than that."

"Exactly, this is what the old world money system does when you try to mesh it with the new. It fucks up all of your notions of value, and collaboration, and community, and the point of being alive; creating holes instead of piles. If you make it about money, nothing in this world will have any emotional value, except maybe your vacation time… if that even."

He was about to take a sip of his drink then continued, "Also, the album itself was a treatise on spiritual evolution: an example pathway to take, lessons learned and shared, written and recorded, now existing in the physical to resonate throughout time and space, for any seeker, wanting to go deeper. So it would have been a shame to allow the old paradigm to collar and chain the new emergent light to dead systems of commerce and kill the deeper vibe of inspiration that allows for that expanded edge broadcast: being heard by new ears that are desperately calling out for it."

Zeke and Aum took a seat at a table. Instantly Zeke began covering and releasing the smoke from the smudge stick, "Zero, one, one, one.."

At the table next to them a conversation reached his ears. Another open window. It was between two young nuevo-skater kids drinking spritzers with long frizzy hair, fat sneakers and tight pants for their spaghetti legs.

"… But the Mayan Calendar is a model to structuralize and move through non-linear time. Rather than mechanical ticks, each collectively resonating emotional level leaps up when all the cosmological community is aligned, and all the pieces fit."

"Yeah, like moving through pockets of coalescing vibration, trickling down from the Hunab Ku, into reality, into action, amping collective intuitive development."

"Because it's built on nested cycles it's easy to notice them on a larger integrative scale, rather than micro."

"So what do you think? Was June 21st a hacked Stargate?"

"2012? One hundred percent. It was linked to a black hole. Totally. Opened it up to Tezcatlipoca's time traveling Mayan assassins."

"Yeah, not every festival ends with a human sacrifice."

"Awwww fuuuck - you weren't there man. Rather than everything synchronistically and magically coming together with utmost perfected celebratory ease, it was about unleashing chaos, and dealing with each situation both individually as micro tribes, and as a whole community, as best we knew how, and coming together through required compassion, understanding, and gentleness. Prime lessons."

They looked no more than 15 years old, but were obviously ancients in disguise.

The music changed and Aum's attention was caught by Demona leading the band. It was amazing, the difference of a feminine lead. Not just riding the men all at once, but gracefully out racing them. She lead each wave of sound, each intonation, and each physical motion; it was her that captured the most and gave the most. They might as well have been playing for a full stadium of 25,000 people, not just 25. His attention flowed into her and she received it, visibly, and his feelings for her - their connection – bloomed.

However, with one deep nod from Dragon, way down in the sub basement of the field, and with his grinding post-reggae-punk bass line, he took the lead. Demona moved lightly over to him and put a hand on his face. The rugged beast of a man, while he plucked the neck of is bass with one hand, took Demona's with the other and kissed it, as if a lover. He connected eyes with her, as if a partner.

"Awwww fuuuck," Aum said aloud.

The soul flowers and the sleepy kitten inspirational fuel dose he felt earlier, both, disappeared. And his heart ripped a little, which he physically felt. 'I wasn't supposed to get attached,' he remembered. All the sweet nothings that were swiftly becoming a deep standing wave in his life path gaze, dissolved into a lovestruck neuroendocrinology; simple brain chemistry and body hormones.

For real? Were they really a couple? Aum looked at their bodies, and they moved gracefully with each other, like instruments. Then he remembered this man's punishing skills with women, and Jenn.

He looked again, like his gaze was unable to be torn away from a tragic accident. He tried to let their dancing go, but his heart was too far into her.

"Well now, here we are," becoming increasingly provoked at the developing situation, and himself, "I shouldn't be surprised, really."

"Whoa, you saw it too?" One of the skater kidz said in Aum's direction.

"…One, zero, one, zero…." Zeke continued his signal.

The second skater looked over, "The riots just re-stared." The other looked at his Dick Tracy watch through white shuttershade glasses, "Yeah, the peace meditation was forced to get violent, spread instantly, multi-city linked."

The frizzy blonde put down his handheld, "Oh fuck, did you get the last memo?"

His friend tapped a few buttons on his watch. "Martial law was just declared!? Holy shit! What the fuck is going on!?" He looked over at his friend, about to spring into action, then looked at Dragon, moving in with Demona to share a kiss within their musical intertwining dance. Dragon broke his gaze with Demona, catching something inside the glance from the young ancients, and nodded back, as if knowing the story via remote viewing, or really good hearing.

"Time to hit the streets."

"Ignite the pre-structure," one said.

"Peace out daddy-os," said the one with the glasses, to both Aum and Zeke.

"Give 'em jester hell kiddos," Zeke replied. As they blasted through the tables and down the stairs, a waft of ganga followed them.

Aum simply caught the smell, and felt the crystalline THC activation of the drug. With this, his cloaking device turned into a techno-colored coat, and with feelings for Demona cracking open in his heart, his entire back turned into agro quills and needles, trying to quickly mend his soul. In that very moment Dragon noticed Aum and his eyebrows lifted in surprise. Re-approaching the musical lead with the newest knowledge, he played his bass with disdain, mouthing the words, '*You again!? You did this didn't you?*'

Grinding down Aum's ear canals, the acusation reverberated into his chest with a pummeling juking dancehall plucking. Once the vibe reached his torn heart, Derek amped the psydub bass drive, activated by a excruciating 40bpm half time kick/snare by the dreadlocked drummer.

In the midst of his yarrow programming Ezekiel noticed the transmission, and the abrupt change in musical improvisation, "Whoa, Aum – you got some shit with Derek? The Dragonkeeper!?" he was in disbelief, which didn't happen often, and he started cackling nervously, "Oh shit. This is gonna get interesting."

Aum looked down at the ground trying to catch his breath, disengage from the squeeze, but the bassline beat him down on the shoulders. Relentless. There was no oxygen for him, only the smell of grass and ash, leather and concrete. Doubt crept into the open tear in his heart. Not of the Riddle, of it's history, or the realness – which was obvious at this point - but of himself, and his ability to continue to stretch, and bend, and extend, and grow, and out weave these committed veterans, these master craftsmen of quantum presence.

"I'm gonna grab some air," he said in the direction of his companion, adding, "Please share with Derek the details of the astroplaning rescue mission, if you happen to connect," and Aum moved over to the ledge of the building.

In a very typical Aum fashion, he perched directly on top of the building edge, with only the grip of the tip of his sneakers between him and the long drop. Aum hoped there would be a fresh breeze and that the new distance would ease the anxiety explosion happening within him, coming from all angles. But there wasn't, and it didn't.

The crystal stairwell laser beams disappeared and he was on his own to deal with it all. Dragon with Demona? A physical seed created from the contents inside of words? ICAARUS on it's way? Multi-City Riots? Martial Law?

A breeze came but it only fanned the fire in his pained heart. The flame told him this was the edge he continually rode, throughout his life, always. With that desire to leap always there, into death and the unknown, a choice always being negotiated between his karma and his courage. Maybe Jenn had been right to be worried.

He touched the ledge of the tower with his hand, forearems on thighs, looking at the scurrying panic stricken ants far below. He could feel their panic as his own and grasped for a solid foundation in the past. His mind cast out too far, how did he get here again? Where was he?

It was full bore now, an all-encompassing bass line buzzing his ears. He remembered the two young skater fools jumping quickly up and deeper in than himself. 'Martial Law?!? Is that seriously necessary?' It was all one mindless unconscious machine they were on top of, and the engines of fear were engaged without control.

"We are caught leading and maintaining adaptation as the city pulsar rolls, pushing on and out!" he angrily shouted out loud, out to the city, trying to find collaboration, not competition with the musician. But every part of the bass line tried pushing him off balance and off the newly found vista, rejecting the opportunity to build together. Each toe had to flex, like being nailed into the brick and mortar. Aum felt the Viper bass push him, and he let it, bending with it. But by letting it, he goaded it on, encouraging it to test his limits.

If Dragon wasn't going to collaborate with him, at this tension filled edge, Aum was certainly wasn't gonna give up without a fight. His cloaking device wasn't working any longer and even though his toe tips were strong, his balance was sliding fast, another push and he pushed back.

"Do you seriously wanna fight again!?" Aum shouted at him, "Cause last time your bro had to come save you." He remembered the festival dancefloor, the powerful circuit link, and Jenn. Then there was even a flash of Demona last night, in inspiring naked splendor. Of course, in response he got roughly shoved from Dragon and his viper bass. Aum's toes slid closer to the edge of the tower ledge.

"Do you really think you know what you're doing!?" There were a few voices on the rooftop that all said it out loud, in unison.

"So what baggage do I need to drop now, asshole!" Aum shouted, closer to crazy than ever before.

Something cracked, and collective confusion erupted from the combative psychic dissention, combined with the realization that the Boards were down and the corporate media streams were broadcasting full societal collapse. One by one all the Riddlers on the Tower top stood up, becoming aware within their own individual and shared perceptions, of the increasing paniced amplitude fueling transformation on a much greater scale; all seeing the last wave for the first time.

Everyone was looking back and forth between Aum and Dragon, looking for something, expecting something, positioning, guidance, insight delivered, or at least some surfing tips.

When they saw nothing there, some Riddlers ran for the Tower exit, as impatience overcame fear. Neither Aum nor Dragon could see outside their wild west showdown. The guitarist plucked double time climbing staccatos and the drummer continued rolling. Demona just stood, with microphone, watching in disbelief, eyes opening, and opening, and opening. “It’s a fucking cock fight!” She exclaimed.

With all eyes on Aum and Dragon, the frantic vibe pushed Aum further out into a chaotic world view, and he could see his own internal imbalance spreading out and growing exponentially, like an infection.

He grasped for a new focal anchor as his heart split a little more, in that deeper breach, aching for the innocent world that once was, the world of unconscious not knowing, and a vision came to him of the global map. He felt pain and doubt erupting within him, linking to the map. Very specific decoy signals stopped, and very specific dream soul pulses got sent out.

Dragon continued to dominate, the rest of the band followed playing an improvised speed crush car crash metallurgy, grumbling, delivered, and precisely controlled.

Aum looked up and saw a line of military jet planes flying across the sky – the same as in his vision. Was that the future anchor?

He thought of all his burnt out unknown peers who had found themselves drenched in gasoline holding lit matches. Insane, surely. Did they not know how they had gotten there either? To that edge? A voice came out of him, not his own, “Are you coming to destroy this seed?” He asked the line of planes, “Or are we going to New Eden?” baffled, still searching for clear oxygen as the crushing sound of the 3-piece band still demanded his submission.

Then Aum saw the jet squadron was led by an F-16 Super Viper.

“What the fuck are you two doing!!?” Zeke screamed as loud as he could, cause he could instantly see it. Panic rippled through every one as every Riddler around the globe connected to Aums grid. He felt it all flow through him like white electricity as he prepped the circuit, connecting the two vipers. What other option did he have?

The Tower became ground zero as Aum’s edge grip finally relaxed, and he let Derek’s last punishing bassline note finally push him off the Tower ledge.

It was that last action which was needed to firmly link the two ends of the circuit and pulse it. It also lassoed all recently erupted psychological tremors in the city. It *was* the anchor, because it was the only thing that made any sense to him, and he just snared all of it, all random and fritzing vibes and magnetized them to that single line, viper to viper, and there was a brief peace in him as he free fell for two long miliseconds. He quickly spun and caught the edge of the roof with his finger tips, feeling the long long drop to the concrete below.

"You're helping it collapse you idiots!!! Second verse!! Now!!!" Demona screamed into the mic at Dragon, at Aum, at the audience, and the band.

With determination she stepped into lead, past the pistol duel, walking over to the guitarstand she grabbed her black Fender Jaguar, beginning to add a blistering sheet of noise over everyone, trying to round up her band mates and beyond, under the sonic piercing banner, she could feel deeper than all of them. Finally feeling the guitarist and drummer with her; waiting for the moment to begin.

Seeing Aum fall off the ledge Zeke said, "Wow, everything just pointed right at us."

Derek, basking in his egoic mal-placed sense of triumph, his obsession with duty, and his baseline that was totally incoherent with most everything else going on could not see it, and Demona had to wake him up. Between strums, with pick in hand, she released a rabbit punch to his ribs, as hard as she could, small enough, and focused enough, and intent enough, that she broke one. Derek gasped in surprise at the bee sting.

Aum's pranic breath finally caught a grip on inhale, finally finding oxygen, and a foundation to begin to pull himself up. Through his nose he caught a noxious scent of fuel in the air, the smell of a machine clouding the clarity that his breath should bring. The observation was followed by a mysterious *whomp whomp whomp* sound from far below.

He focused on pulling himself up, and as he did, he heard something old emerge off the rooftop. He saw the band coalesce and truly begin. After being pushed to his death, he was now awe struck. Aum's firey combative reaction had found a new lead outside of him, who took control of the potential path of nuclear sun reaction. It was an apt steal; a transmutation of his internal self, his frustration and anger, directed with a broader creativity and intelligence.

He felt the reflection of this lesson in Demona hammering in rhythm, leading them all, now even Dragon behind her, who continued to play without fatigue - though now enclosed in his viper bind and respectful of Aum's resurrection. Demona sang, and even screeched invocations:

We need to find,
in ourselves,
Something greater,
than ourselves

He saw something in her, as of yet unseen by his eyes, and by most. A compacted dynamo, determined, with a pure and skilled band saw focus; all petitness gone, power housed in grey and black fatigue pants, white tank top and hair pulled back with reflective aviators on. She was without compromise, empathy for weakness or distraction, unflinching, doubtless, and even here, smashing all egoic pretense.

With this new Demona in the lead, the music lost all relationship to the cushy modern live psy-ambiet downtempo sleep-grade blend. The audio stream switched to a pull-your-fucking-eyeballs-out-so-you-can-look-at-your-self agro punk rock.

A last alarm, last distress signal, and last chance to wake up, the song was a cover, but it gained new power in this context, here on this rooftop.

Upright on the top of the ledge, Aum heard a buzz far in the distance. He looked out to see that the line of jet planes had rerouted their flight path and were heading straight for the tower.

"Oh yeah. I did that… linked viper to viper…"

"…only to better transmute it," He heard a shout from one of the remaining Riddlers.

"Yes, that's right. Thank you."

Whomp whomp whomp whomp

On the jet Aum thought he could see a red star with yellow symbol inside.

"Ahh shit they found us - that was fucking fast!" Zeke said, noticing, standing up.

Demona rallied:

Nothing's expected of us
For we hold no rooms in the master's house tonight
But when the door locks we're already inside

You'll never know what came over you tonight
Here's what we're going to do to finally set things right:
Burn all the plans, burn all the plans!

They lit up the firewall stronger than ever, and in full band unison the amped punk rock seeped deep into many ears in a crucial moment of choice and presence. It was the surfing lesson finally actualized. Who ever made it off the roof made it off, and whoever was on the roof, was on the roof, all gazing at the dozen planes, single file, serpent like, speeding toward them, just above the city skyline, all the while with the unknown *whomp whomp whomp* that was somehow trying to combat the activating soundtrack.

Some economists say that our future is in slave labor
Well, you can keep your six cent wage, baby!
Keep on subcontracting!
Old man, your time's running out
and with no remorse
this beast will eat itself

With space to breath Aum accepted the moment, taking responsibility for his call, and actions, and the destructive collapsing future reflecting inside this linked flying serpent it manifested as, knowing it was just an arrow tip.

The courage to fight is waking up inside!
The wisdom to face the fear, to see the light!
The courage to fight, to fight, to fight, to fight!
The wisdom to face the fear, to see the light!

They could fully hear the planes now as they flew through the corridors of skyscrapers, speeding toward them.

Imposter,
leave me now or with me be made done
I-ni-ti-a-tion

Within the shredding amp-feedback of the musical break down, within the sound of the oncoming planes, and the steadily increasing *womp, womp, womp*, sirens flipped on throughout the city. They were long forgotten in the landscape, and signaled air raids, and terror. Panic rippled through every single person who heard it. They all felt it on the rooftop, and all soaked in it, this muster point.

The panic, sirens and noise, all physically tried to push Aum off the tower top again; yet the music and lyrics tried to save him from falling to his death. Aum felt the details within the codeless wind, choosing to plant himself in this cresting edge, Tower ledge, looking out at the city, truly seeing.

He looked down and saw the ants crawling all over each other in a panic, some hearing the sirens, some hearing the media blast of "Riot!" or "Martial Law!" All seeking the highest personal vantage point for the survival of nothing other than their own physical bodies and belongings. He looked up and the screeching planes were only a few blocks away. Then, within a second, they were one block away.

Zeke put on his grey fedora, grabbed a patch of 'up top' on which to sit cross-legged, and closed his eyes for meditation. "Just like back in the old days," he said, as if bending time was a regular task for this bright white wizard of the digital.

Aum heard a rustling next to him, then a scraping, then a quick noise that was kind of like a hoot. He looked at the corner of the building edge, and standing there, in the middle of the day, with the sun shinning down on it, was a white owl.

'Whoah - planetary magnetics must be really off for this guy to be out.'

It connected eyes with him and it held him in his gaze for untold seconds. It looked inside of him, and within that link Aum's insides got rearranged; thus his outsides got rearranged. The creature allowed Aum to see the wisdom of the wild. With the most acute senses of the entire animal kingdom the owl is a keen and violent hunter, characteristics that are mitigated with serenity, peace, and wisdom.

Suddenly it flew off to an adjacent building, taking Aum's full attention with it. After it landed, it connected eyes again, as if to double check that Aum was still paying attention. In the glance was a living wisdom deeper than nature. In initiation, the owl seared off Aum's old self.

There was a puddle on the roof of the adjacent building, from last nights rain, and in it he could see the reflection of the oncoming planes, exactly the same as his sonic vision in the lab. The owl stepped into the puddle with it's claw and disrupted the still pool mirror with intelligent waves of bushido.

'So that's what a DNA upgrade looks like.'

Aum could actually feel the extended waves hit him, much like the seed in his pocket. The two linked. The wild world was far more mystically intelligent and far more deeply infused into the psychology of man than he could ever fathom. The owl looked up again, and within it's eyes of instinct Aum saw the future of his double viper bind, and his place within in it.

All was forgotten in his deepest being but for the beauty of magic and the miracle that is life. Taking the slowest deepest breaths he knew how, he understood that this awareness and serenity and control and peace was a weapon without equal, and he walked back toward the centre of the wall, still balancing atop the ledge.

As he walked he looked back and shared a glance with Demona, as if to say, 'I'm able to support you in whatever way you need,' rather than just taking the lead from her.

Being in the exact cross hairs, Demona was holding down the frontline with all her extended soul lines, beyond body, full honesty protected behind reflective eyes. With a playful smirk, she gave it to him, just because he asked so nicley.

Aum's full spirit was instantly blasted by the growing fire of metaphysical combat, manifesting quick as thought into the physical.

As he moved closer to the crosshairs he spied a vector sticker of Garuda, nearly Quetzalcoatl, on Derek's viper bass: king of the birds, devourer of serpents and the mount of Vishnu. Seeing the man-phoenix hybrid image triggered a wave of vision, erupting from his internally refurbished DNA, emerging through white milky cloud and clean wild air.

Demona pulled the ticket from the 3D printer, "Here you are my brother, directly channeled from the life sustaining heartpulse of New Eridu, bestowing neither gold nor chocolate, but the highest fortune of the stars, and a charmed life path."

"Gratitude," replied Zhe. They all sat in a circle in Ezekiel's laboratory.

"You're still using that old software? Don't you find everything just crumbles when you print it?" Ezekiel asked Zhe. Zhe replied, "Yes, but that's the beauty of the lesson. What is the circumstance in which it falls apart? Once we build better machines, better software, in any area, it dulls our sensitivity to the real, to the actual feel of matter," He looked up and spoke to the group, "This is the last ticket and I offer it up to the final entrant, representing both the first and the last." He passed the paper to Derek who put it in an envelope and spoke to the group, "Within this envelope and these words I invoke the conch, and upon the envelopes return to me, the first of three soundings. It's boomeranging movement will encircle all those of the highest willing and it's reception will identify it's leader when all is in perfect balance."

After a moment they heard, "All cards on the table please Keeper," came a voice from the quartz screen.

"Fine," He replied, still learning. "The second sounding will be the moment of sharpest edge and will serve as a support in the last moment of defense to maintain a single thread of connection between opposites, in service to the highest good. The third sounding will activate the atomic release of the sudarshana chakra, the full eradication of all forms of duality."

He looked up to the screen to receive a nod, then he sealed the envelope, wrote the letters A-U-M on it and tossed it in a wooden box filled with numerously varied and seemingly random items.

Trae the Seer added, "May it's path be in service of only the highest education of all souls, divine channels of creativity, and the science of truest self knowledge."

Once again the man on the quartz screen spoke, 'With highest excitement for your invocation of both a final defensive ace played, and a transformative eradication of opposites Derek, I must add," It was John deGryder, beaming in, "The second sounding must be gated with a request, and the third sounding, the release of the sudarshana chakra, will only be with my word and blessing."

"As you wish," replied Derek, secretly relieved to have his mentor's presence, guidance and involvement at this meta-developmental level.

As the milky clouds began to part Aum spoke aloud, and directly toward Derek "Om Namo Narayanaya," Derek looked up at him instantly. Whether another key code or not Aum continued in balanced stride, a step away from the fighter plane cross hairs, "I request the second sounding," Aum said.

“Done,” replied Derek, relieved to have Aum’s fullest presence here, his involvement at this meta-developmental level, and the crisp edge finally identified.

The sound of the super viper roared like certain death, damaging ear drums where now the previous bass viper and it's cartoon amp buzz seemed more than puny, even laughable - not even close to Vishnu’s conch - nor requested.

Aum’s spirit felt the deep lesson learned, he felt the fully supported Riddler tower top unity, and the completion of the firewall. He was instantly blasted by the power of it along with the growing fire of metaphysical combat. All sonic residue he quickly vibrated into the light of laser beams loaded in his wild heart, and eyes, and mind, as he walked into the super viper crosshairs, staring down the first pilot. This is what it feels like, to carry the world.

After observing and learning all they could from the peak pocket of cresting calendrical storm, Zeke opened his eyes at the same time as the drummer snare rolled it all up and back into the climactic song close. As the reverberations of the owl medicine crystallized Aum’s gaze, he looked through the helmeted visor into the eyes of the first pilot in front of him. So close and about to spark the crash of all they knew, all Riddlers worked their soul magic, blasting out white ping pong balls, rapidly restructuralizing consciousness and shooting off into non-local spaces.

The band, and full rooftop group, kicked back in, overtop of the sirens, and the jet planes, pushing back on panic, pummeling and boring it’s way through to dismantle the collapsing metawave of apocalypse.

Stand up!
Hide!
Dissolve!
Rise!
Your choice!
Your choice!
Your choice!
Your choice!

Coming into a deeper realization, Aum felt the song and unity awaken an even deeper compassion for self, all relations, and all evolving, organically growing systems. He pointed to it with his inner eye, connected it to the pilots eyes. Beyond the edge of fullest vulnrability he saw that they were green, like his own. And beautifully intent, like his own. Within the audio maelstrom of music and machine he found the fullest silence, humbling beauty, and a serene appreciation of the miraculous, "Fuck, that's certainly some complex adaptive fractaling."

Still breathing, but imperceivable slow, their eyes connected even further, as Aum maintained strength and faith and peace. With the support of the group, he instantly transmitted across this bridge into the pilot with love, their opposite side of the combative action. Aum, seeing the fear, in this pocket of amplification, further broadcasted and shared his newfound courage, invoked by the true winged ones and transmitted it into the pilots heart through his eyes. Inhaling, Aum looked and placed it as deep as he could, and with his own mended and humbled being, consciously invoked the awakening of this clouded man's heart. Feeling Demona's mystical jaguar assassin precision behind him, Zeke's white wizard time stopping pocket, and Derek's animalistic will for true unchallenged sovereignty, Aum exhaled a penetrating focus and equanamously balanced gaze, heart-to-heart, mind-to-mind, eye-to-eye, which suddenly awoke the pilot to his actions and the increased awareness of the fear and regret of choosing his own death, and the death of all the innocent people inside the tower by destroying this seed.

The pilot accepted the new awareness with gratitude, and was healed. He reflected a thank you back to Aum, and at the very last moment before direct impact on the Tower, he shifted course and flew past. The building shook and Aum surfed the ledge of the shaking building, refocusing on the next reverberation.

One by one and second by second, each plane approached like a giant bullet, committed to destroying the data outpost, and along with it, the last stronghold of order in a crumbling civilization. And Aum, on the swaying building, connected with the pilot of each bullet as it approached. He gazed deeply at each one, seeing the karma of the spirit that was contained inside the metal, and the strange life path choices they had made to bring them to this moment. He offered a solution in the minds eye of each which would create a better life, and a better world for all that they touched.

Each consecutive pilot however, seeing the failures of previous pilots, became more and more committed. Aum thus had to dive deeper and deeper, quicker and quicker, calling in visions of the dimensions that were already present, but only simple choices away. As they said no, and no, and no, they committed and recommitted to the internal metal bomb, black, which became denser and denser and smaller and smaller with each commitment. Relentless in his own steadfastness, supported by a higher order and the unity and commitment of the red tower strike force team, Aum held a karana mudra with his fingers and did not give way until each pilot, in their imaginings, saw the *new* new world order that he saw. One after the next after the next, all eventually healed, with black bead bullet eventually compressed to soul diamond, they each diverted their path. Up and over, banking left or right, missing the building by mere feet, then by mere inches, then centimeters, and then the second last plane by only millimeters, each time the building shaking and threatening to topple.

Unfortunately Aum could not fully awaken the final pilot. Being the last one in line, fear of failure was too great an obstacle for the last man. With inner soul diamond not fully solidified, there was one spec of black within the last shine. In the end, he chose to turn away from his kamikaze path, but not fully committed enough to keep him from clipping the building.

Half the wing sliced through the corner of the top floor.

With the wing damaged the pilot lost control of the plane and it spiraled toward the earth. In the empty wooded valley below it crashed and exploded, the pilot ejected moments before, floating with open parachute to the ground.

No one died.

The Tower still stood.

And only the crystal altar, the connection between living room spread and the sky elementals damaged. That corner of the apartment was now fully blasted open and raw.

Each Riddler connected, wide-eyed with one another on the rooftop; Aum, still standing on the ledge, turned to the divine firesquad and let his guard down, stepping down towards them.

Punk rock show complete, with only amp buzz in the air, the ever increasing *woomp woomp womp* was revealed, as a helicopter rose above the building ledge, directly behind Aum. With immaculate timing it went 'pop, pop, pop' as it shot cans on the roof that pop pop popped tear gas, poisonous smoke, or worse, clouding and immersing the roof.

If the total destruction of the tower itself could not be completed, this was a final security measure, a back up plan to extinguish any left over combatants. Demona, Derek, Zeke, Aum and the rest finally reaching their own corporeal understanding: they knew when to run and save themselves, and did so. Coughing fits erupting within the stinging smoke, they all made for the stairwell exit. Down and out the bottom of the building they all fled, scattering, moments before the police, additional military ground troops, and corporate broadcast media arrived.

"Great minds think alike, don't cha know," Demona said with a smirk as Aum sat down.

She was scribbling something on a note

...and to orient your life around a collectively agreed upon, utterly destructive social structure is to celebrate total personal ignorance.

They were seated at a booth inside a donut and coffee shop next to the police department near the apartment building. Aum thought it would be the best place to let the last wave of heat die down, and he had found Demona already sitting at a booth. Maybe even waiting for him.

"I checked out your source code," she said, checky grin, glinting bright eyes glowing, "It's pretty solid."

It was eaily the best thing any woman had ever said to him.

"If I ever write a book that line is going in there you know."

"Wonderfull."

After sitting in their shared glow he noticed there was an inkling of desire in his heart to ask her about Derek, wanting to define or better understand their connection. However he could feel they were still on thin ice, somewhere, somehow. Maybe being tracked, maybe and covering their meta data tracks; something that would have to be done from now on.

"Boards are still down," She said abruptly – pointing him to the task at hand and not his longing. She threw the note in an envelope, "Let's go."

With her words Demona began to lead it, and in her voice Aum noticed there was not much left of the same woman he met yesterday, maybe it was because she had been hanging out with her band, screaming, and not her coven, screaming.

After exiting the restaurant they saw the nearest mailbox was down the street. Weaving in and off the sidewalk they headed toward it, eyes open, looking for clues.

It was tough work investigating the details of inner city sprawl; giving attention to the forgotten spaces, no matter how unimportant. The sun beamed down, cooking the garbage that was tucked away inside each back alley building crevice, while fast food grease bins overflowed and walled up each crack. An olfactory cornocopia of human refuse. The bins were fronted by trashcan sentinels filled with aluminum pop cans and a piling plethora of cardboard coffee cups. While traversing these urban spaces on foot, they were completely focused in their movements and on seeing the blatant truth of this destructive and un-inspiring expression of reality; where getting hit by an SUV emerging from an underground parking lot was a civil guarantee.

"And here I thought we were getting greener..." Aum said, looking at the black soot stained brick. And Demona finished, "...or maybe we were just humoring ourselves this whole time."

As they broke further away from the norm, investigating the dirty overlooked commercial nooks, all but forgetting the mailbox destination, they were immediately noticed by a cluster of hive mind drones. From inside cushy seat-screened sport utility vehicles, safely behind the tint of shiny windows, pairs of programmed eye balls pointed them out. Thsee two spiritual explorers were judged and compared, these shiny young ones, not to foraging freegans but to homeless persons searching for cans, having fallen through the cracks of the competitive economic dream of prosperity. Compassionless fearful minds instantly signaled the authorities. The patrol car, driving by Aum and Demona's sociological back alley dig site, was ready to put them behind bars, imprisoning them for a deep gaze of truthful curiosity; a life time sentence in a prision system only more sterile in difference.

Demona began to speak out to the cop car, "Take that corner tighter." And it passed, "Box that shit up forever. One million

Starbucks within ten feet of each other, interspersed every ½ click with a Tim Hortons."

Aum continued this time, with entranced prose, "Give these spaces the energy of your open gaze and they will reveal their truth. It is a desperation and purpose within the garbage factory, holding the dead space for continued over consumption, and total strangulation of nature."

"Yes, but it is our duty…" Monica responded, surprisingly; her voice changing, "…with that open gaze of light, to place it were it is darkest, and see divinity where it is not…."

"..to better see the deeper truth." Aum added.

"Yes, to better see the truth." She looked at him in appreciation; as if it was usually her own solo mission to dig through the stinking trash. "That is the power of the human spirit. Anything can be brought into existence, it only takes perseverance to infuse that imagined structure onto reality, and a deep resonant collective agreement to believe in it." She exhaled, and smiled brightly, out shinning the blazing afternoon sun, as if the moon inside the blackest night, "Even if it's just you and me babe, that still believe." There were almost tears in her eyes.

In faithful conviction Aum asked, "Have we not saved it yet?"

A switch flipped, circuit clicked and scale tipped. Demona scampered to the ground beside a dumpster where she saw a reiki symbol, Choku Rei, a stenciled tag on the concrete. On top of it, a piece of string, only 4 inches long. She picked it up and said, "We'll need this lover, all things considered," she continued, "We don't know if the Tower was fully compromised or not," answering his question in a round about way. "There are many rippling waves of change happening throughout all our civilization, and we," she looked at him strongly, showing him the string, "held one stitch together. And we still, only have that one stitch… holding it together."

When they realized they found what they were looking for, they walked directly to the mailbox. Demona saw a small safety pin sitting on top, "Really?" She picked it up, "Man. That deep a rebuild?! To turn the tide? That's fuckn' crazy."

She threw the envelope in the mailbox, which didn't have an address on it, took the safety pin and left the string on top.

"Springboards and shoelaces!" she shouted at the mailbox as if overcome by tourettes. She suddenly looked over at Aum, smiling shyly like a magpie trickster, quickly flipping to a different channel. "Okay?" Spinning around She asked outloud, to no one in particular. She spied an abandoned knit shawl on the ground, dusty and soiled. She picked it up and put it on as if it was something she had left there last week. The top button was missing so she fastened it with the safety pin. After walking a couple more blocks, Demona searching for the next level, Aum in disbelief, she found a pair of shoes on the street. Flowery wooden clogs. She saw that they were her size and exchanged them: leaving her own footwear.

Now far beyond disbelief, '...What in the fuck?' Aum thought.

Walking past a garbage can, Aum saw a grey wig jammed in-between the bin and the metal protective rail. He laughed off his skepticism, seeing the obvious next layer. He quickly pulled it out and trying not to smile at the sheer absurdity, said, "Here."

"Yah, totally babe. That'll merge it."

In her new found granny hobo outfit Demona randomly started to dance in the street mouthing words to a song Aum couldn't hear. And just like that, with the 3 simple elements, she was a new woman once again: the most accomplished and well practiced shapeshifter he had even met.

Aum thought, 'Wow, this woman is frikn' out there!' Rather than navigate a frantic juggle of blips, beeps, and rings, on desk, laptop or handheld, the corporate boards, SMS, or extended social network infrastructure, Demona operated without techno gadgetry. Skipping the hardware, she was fully immersed in the world around her, using only her senses and her body to navigate and interact with an extended dimensionality without the crutches of breakable crashable technological infrastructure; an advanced sensitivity of body based intuition rather than extensive analytical inference. Unfortunately, this rendered her a crazy woman in the minds eye of most onlookers, when they did by chance look up from their own screens in public places. Fortunately for the two of them, she had the advanced awareness and skillset to continue, where many Riddlers who needed the boards to navigate, couldn't as easily carry on.

As she continued her joyus miming solo flashmob dance in the middle of the street, dodging cars in step, Aum asked, "What are you doing?"

"We found the first platform, so I'm dancing out the physical embodiment of digital radio waves for these cars; cohesively galvanizing the ghostworks," she replied, as if it was the most straight forward and comprehensible answer. Aum saw a few gawking faces poking out of the windows of sleek sports mobiles blaring pre-teeny micro-bop. He looked over at Demona and she was lip synching perfectly with what they were listening to on their satellite radio. It probably tripped him out more than the people in the car. Enraining with her, he instantly noticed the satellite signal within his own body; the words themselves. It was the strangest thing he had ever felt in his life, and everything he had come to understand of the Riddle was evaporated upon witnessing this new depth. It cleaned his slate.

He was about to start dancing with her when down the street a car gingerly honked it's horn. It then honked louder after Demona continued with a few more dance steps, trying to get their attention. Demona stopped. She and Aum shared a team-up power glance. With a unified vibe, they walked over.

Two men in a yellow Aztec, like an oversized bumblebee, window rolled down.

They approached. "This could be a decoy," She said.

"Do you think we'll have to dodge bullets? Or take down more fighter jets," Aum quickly asked her.

"Dunno, let's find out if the ghostdance is working."

She continued her dance steps as thy walked over, Aum strolling along side, they heard a familiar and unique voice on the radio: 'My mycelial network is nearly immortal, only the sudden toxification of a planet or the explosion of its parent star can wipe me out.'

"Right on," Aum said "No bullets to dodge."

He'd rather have that signal streamed through his genetic material than the micro-bop, though admittedly it was a catchy future fusion.

"Not this time," the man in the passenger seat said in response, "I just need your safety and your word," looking at each of them.

Demona removed the pin, and wig, and shawl, passing the safety pin over.

"The Ferryman," Aum said. A familiar looking man with a scarab on his shirt leaned forward at the wheel and smiled, he couldn't quite place his brown skin and short curls, but his eyes linked to his memory banks. He left the thought for a moment as the passenger grabbed something from a bag at his feet, giving Demona a small dreamcatcher and a Aum a small jar of dried lionsmane and spoke, "You guys'll do fine." He had double hand embeds, one looked original, and the other looked top of the line, like it was just installed yesterday.

"How'd you know that?" Demona nearly demanded of Aum, but the man in the car answered first.

"Cause I'm the one who's got to collect all the ghosts you're dancing with, resurrecting…" and they sped off without further explanation as another car instantly peeled around the corner, giving chase.

"Shit!"

On the street Demona quickly looked through the dreamcatcher as if a scope on a gun, making the sound of a laser beam being fired, 'Zzzhhihpp.' The car instantly slowed down, as if forgetting what it was chasing after.

"Whatever it is, you don't need it. And whatever it is, you can't bring it with you," Aum added, shouting loudly, in unified collaboration with Demona.

She continued to look through the dreamcatcher as they paused on the street.

"Thank you," Demona said, directed to an older man walking passed them with his dog. He smiled politely at the crazy people, because he wasn't doing much more than simply walking his dog.

"These are all microgates dear visionary," Demona said to Aum, "That man specifically. Next platform level."

"Uhh…okay… that quick?" Aum replied. There were no visions of internal spirit grids, tower or globe popping in his imagination for confirmation. He was fine with that though. He trusted his heart, which told him she spoke the truth.

"We have to rebuild from the ground up. Amazing the size of internal inspiration and insightful wave that comes from the most insignificant little permutation." They heard a door slam shut. As if the noise reminder her she exclaimed, "Oh yeah! Shit, I have to deliver this book!" Out of her deep camo pant pocket she pulled out a paperback copy of Neil Gaimen's *Neverwhere*.

Simple delivery a menial task for some – she said it as if this was her job, and her sole purpose for the afternoon. "It was left at the apartment a week ago and has been calling for a new home. I had something pretty solid linked on the boards, though now..."

Within one heartbeat and a flash of gridlike insight Aum responded, "Ha – there it is. Okay, I've got this one." He brought his hands together in a natural namaste, thanking his heart and mind for their loud voice. He walked over to the nearest person on the street, "Hey man, can I borrow your phone, we're just trying to rendezvous with a friend."

"Phone? Borrow? What do you mean?" The young man replied, he looked at Aum like he was crazy. Aum and Demona looked at each other in response, as if agreeing that the world was crazy.

"We're artists," she said. "Here's my CD."

"A CD? You don't have it on a cloud?" He had a slight English accent.

"Pfft," She scoffed, the generation gap now reduced to a single year, "I dunno man, maybe. It moves on it's own at this point so this ancient physical technology is worth more than a bot guided free data download anyway – it's even better even than metal up your ass."

The young man's face became focused as he tried to figure out how a free CD was worth more than a free mp3, giving Aum his handheld. The ass part, he wasn't even gonna get to, becoming much more confused after Aum asked him, "When's your birthday?"

"June 26th 2006."

"Digital native." He was too young too understand the phone reference. Aum looked at his exposed forearms, he didn't yet have hand embeds. He was still gen3.0. Once successive generations started becoming named after their level of technological immersion, Aum knew there was to be no turning back in loosing the organic casing of their species. "Never known a world without systemized social webtech, hey?" Aum added, punching the handheld with his thumbs as if it was his day job. As he worked Aum could see the fireworks of karma-data behind his eyelids, diagramed out in the lightgrid of 4D, and he applied it, brefly wondering what generation he was a part of. He looked at Demona and asked, "604 is the area code?"

He looked up at the sun, it was 1pm and it blazed down on them. Was it always this hot?

"Yup."

As he continued to click and tap there was an old man walking by, throwing caution to the wind. It all hung out as he strolled with his shirt off in the late afternoon blistering sun. Then there was another, and another.

"What!?" Demona exclaimed, "A third one! We must be ready. Ready for the full strip down. A new full extreme of bareness." There must have been something deeper inside the furnace heat, besides amping the collective social stress of a close save. Aum punched in the number *604-626-2006,* and said, "Photon belt is pushing the limits. Stretching the magnetic body. This is the collective de-stressing," then punched in the message *meet in 32 at,* "...Whats your name?"

"David Richards... That, or it's just hot out," the Englishman tried joking with Demona who was wearing mostly black, "Why?"

"No, I'm pretty sure it's the photon belt." She was holding on to that one strongly, adding, "'Cause this man's intuitive manifestation speed is world renown, that's why." "Familiar?" Aum asked Demona. The kid was sure he was now on a different planet at this point.

"Of course, write *Davie & Richards; open door on the green,*" She grasped his arm and lifted up to her tip-toes to watch him type it out, "Thank you Aum."

"Whoa, I haven't been called Davey in a long time," the kid said, in remembrance.

"Sent," Aum said as he gave him back the handheld, "Thank you's extended and flowing, and here's a little something for your troubles," He gave him the jar of mushrooms he had received from the man in the car, "For your daily tea."

"Right"

"...and to solidity the new planet inside your mind," Demona added.

They walked off toward the corner of Davie and Richards, smiling at one another, nearly sprinting toward the joyful unknown.

The exact moment they stepped onto the grass they heard, "Who catches Dreams?" Had it been 32 minutes already?

"Here!" Demona shouted loud without hesitation, and they began to walk toward him on the far side of the park, "Looking for Door?" She shouted again. A man walked toward them shouting, "Inside paper."

It was more like communication on a playing field, or a military battleground. Focused, precise instructions that all public drones around them reacted to accordingly. The whole neighbourhood became alive and listened and watched, if not consciously then unconsciously aware of the deal. She passed him the book when he approached, "It's been waiting for you."

"And I've been waiting for it. This is for you," He passed her a jar with a couple air holes punched in the top, inside was the last Bombus Occidentalis.

"A bee?"

"The last real bee actually, the last queen."

"Oh?...okay?"

There was an eruption of cheers at the far side of the park.

"Nice one," Aum said to the man.

"Exponential meta platform advancement."

"A deeper integration and expansion," A flash and Aum could see, new tendrils growing across the face of the global grid, a newly stitched geometric lattice.

"Yes, new roots, longer limbs, bigger leaves." The man confirmed, "Even better fruit."

"How to feed them all I wonder; every worker from the throne," Demona pondered.

"Seeing them thusly, you will have to collect them all as we move," the man replied.

"My basket weaving healer can totally handle that," she poked Aum in the rib. He jumped in surprise and she smiled: being exceptionally receptive also meant being very ticklish. Aum laughed at her poke, starting to really love her.

Screams cut the love apart however, coming from the opposite side of the neighborhood from where the cheers erupted. This was followed by the crash of glass and a building alarm. It shook the three of them back into directly viewing the system repair.

"Ah shit," Aum reacted.

"It's a knife edge." The man said.

"And the fine thread was just cut," stoically stated Demona. The bee buzzed against a side of the jar. "This way," she added, like a sweet song sung out her soul.

"Rock n roll," replied Aum.

"Rightey-o," as the bookworm was about to walk between Aum and Demona, toward the alarm.

“Shit, here,” she offered him the dreamcatcher as he cut between them, “You’ll need a dreamscope if you’re walking that way.”

He took it, cutting between Aum and Demona without missing a step and the three theatrically and acrobatically spun with the meshing motion, a spark lit and Aum and Demona intuitively grabbed an end of the spliting esoteric thread with their outside hand, so visceral it nearly cut their palms. Then purely on instinct, with their opposites, they took the hands of each other, like a picturesque quantum artesian couple.

They looked in each other’s eyes in a reactive moment of surprised joy, surrounded by pure spine tingling apocalypse-breaching emotional chaos, holding the tails of two electric snakes, and kissed. They pressed their bodies against one another. At this, someone took their picture, and it instantly flowed into the datastream. It was a heartfelt and luscious pause, both a tiny window into their previous night together, and a love-based intuition to mend the collective tear; as if their kiss could seal the clipped thread ends of consciousness.

Bzzzzzz

The creature buzzed them back to their day jobs. Looking strongly into one another’s eyes, they had great work of serious focus to do together.

They swiftly walked to the other side of the green park, looking to bridge the dance between the honeybee buzz and the unknown signal which it was picking up on. They took a step onto the concrete and the bee began to make a ruckus in the jar, beginning to buzz like it was under attack. A nearby apartment entrance buzzer rang as they walked by it. There was nobody in front. The bee stopped moving.

"This way!" Demona directed as she sprinted and grabbed the door half a second before the buzzer turned off. She ran in, glancing at the mailboxes in the front, with random piles of letters sticking out, some boxes marked, some not, and took off up the stairs.

Demona entered the hall three floors up moving quick. Aum could now hardly keep up. Crazy woman. Was she now trying to lose him? Was their kiss not deep enough? Or was she just trying to keep up with the instructions sent from the queen bee?

“Knock on this door,” Apartment number 32.

“What!”

“Knock on the door!” She yelled at him, almost a little too loudly.

Aum knocked on the door.

“Nope, it’s one floor down” she said immediately, and took off down the far length of the hall.

Aum was starting to get frustrated with this level of bi-polar randomization, so he of course pushed it further, taking off back the way they came, heading down the opposite staircase, down to the previous floor.

As he opened the door to the hall a man bumped into Aum.

“Pardon me” the man said as he tried to aggressively rush past.

“Stop him!” Demona shouted from the opposite side of the hall.

Aum could feel the entire building awaken at this emphatic expression. Some moved closer to weaponization and some moved closer to God. Hearing a plethora of televisions tuned to the most recent news, a terrorist bombing, Aum grabbed the back of the man’s shirt as he tried to rush past and was about to push him and bash him into the hall door, though with a very strange surge of aggression decided it would be best to throw him over the rail for a three flight drop to land on the green shag carpet below.

“Oh shit oh shit oh shit,” The man said.

It was the tall skinny man from Aum’s Oil Barron dream vignette, Jenson.

“Wait!” Demona yelled from across the hall.

Still poised over the ledge Jenson admitted, “I’m not gonna go to the hospital for this. They’re worth probably a few grand at this point, But here take ‘em. I probably wouldn’t make it in time anyway.”

“What?”

“I’m sorry. I didn’t make it to the park.”

“What?”

“Take em,” He offered Aum an envelope, “The game just started.”

Aum took the envelope.

Jenson added, “They’re not mine they just got slipped under my door.”

“Lies! Obviously,” Demona said shouting loudly for the whole building to hear. Approaching assertively she instructed, “You must quit your day job Richard S. Jenson, and become a beekeeper on the land you recently acquired with the Oil and Gas death currencies you've cultivated." It was like some kind of oracular psychic assassination, or the dismantling and rebuilding of his karma. She passed the bee jar to Jenson, as if in trade for the envelope. "This is the last non GMO bee on the planet. If you do not care for it as Adam would in Eden, else New Eden, allowing it to perish though environmental ignorance, lack of care, or loving attention, I will return, to take your failed life from you."

It was as if the potential extinction of a species invoked a vision of such drastic nightmarish measure, that she had to equally reflect the extreme in her soul adamant, to the point of tears streaming down her cheeks. Jenson may have taken offence to this charge, or simply reacted with a misguided anger, but was moved to tears himself at this karmic tear down by the tiny and beautiful powerhouse.

"I will."

"Blessings on your instant evolution new life steward," Aum added.

Demona was already down the staircase and at the front door, waiting for Aum. Aum began to run down the stairs to join her. And Jenson finally came to, "Hey! Where do I know you from?"

"We met in a dream," Aum said.

"Which dream?"

"This one," and he exited the building re-joining Demona, "You gave him the last bee?!"

"That's what she wanted - What did he give you?"

"Hockey tickets."

"Hockey? Hockey!? A hockey game!?" It bent her in brand new ways and utterly confused her. "What the fuck! What the fuck!? What the fuck! When?"

"Right now."

They heard a bus coming, both noticing it in unity. Still holding the cut threads they clasped hands once again as they both ran for it. At the end of the block there was a bus stop. Aum spied a couple coins in the grass, quickly snatching them up with a playfully acrobatic one-handed cartwheel in stride before the last couple lengths to make it to the stop. It slightly released the pressure causing the esoteric dimensional ripping: the cut thread.

“Shit!” Demona exclaimed, seeing the move, impressed, “There’s infinite band-aids everywhere!” They wouldn’t have made the bus unless it stopped to let a few people off.

He saw ‘Gold’ was the destination. That’s a good sign. They were just hanging on.

He walked on and put the coins in, “Going for gold!”

As the coins dropped they made a bit of noise over the commotion in the bus.

“Shit yeah!” the driver responded, not noticing if it was the correct amount or not.

Demona flashed her pass, “Are you headed to the stadium by chance?” She must not have received the destination reference. The bus driver looked at her like she was the biggest airhead in the country. Demona looked over at the collection of passengers.

“Okay, we made it.” She saw the bus filled 99% of the way with hockey jerseys and continued, “But I don’t think I like it.”

They had to stand at the front where lumbering drunk doofuses, weasely dark shaded bean poles, plump and round face-painted ladies were all brimming with so much excitement they seemed like they were going to break out in song. Most likely, Aum could surmise, Stoppn’ Tom Conners *The Hockey Song*.

“Oh gawd, I think I’m gonna die,” Demona confessed.

“Just go with it – You sing in a freakn’ rock band. You’re leading this thing, aren’t you?”

“Don’t even….”

There were a couple guys who had a large format handheld screen. It was streaming the game live. A crowd on the bus craned their necks, tried to find an angle where they could watch with deep anticipation.

After a quick 15 blocks the Stadium came within sight and it all shifted.

“What the fuck is this shit!?” Demona exclaimed. The bus had to push through a sea of red filtering in the doors of the mega arena.

The one dude on the bus without a jersey heard her, “I know, it’s retarded. Civilization is collapsing around us and these idiots are going to a hockey game, or have their tele’s glued to their eyeballs like blinders.”

There was a full flurry of response to this spoken opinion, “The world will be fine jack ass, just like it’s always been…”

"…And for your information, it's the gold medal final!..."

"…Going for gold baby!"

The small crowd watching the screen erupted in wild cheers.

"Yah!! First goal!"

It didn't even matter where they were. Dense non-local tensions were released as Aum could hear out the open bus windows people cheering from their cars. Houses shook with people jumping up and down, people were screaming off their balconies, running up and down the streets, even sprinting towards the stadium now. The bedlam was contagious as the bus erupted in exuberance, like young children on a field trip.

Within the exploding wave of shock a muscle car pulled up next to the bus. It was Derek. The engine roared.

"Holy shit! Wonder what Derek has in all this?" Demona asked herself. Derek simply gave the horns and sped off. "What a metalhead." She shook her head in mid surf, responding with a hangloose, flying it out at him.

"I guess that's good sign," Aum said.

"Yeah man! It's a great sign!" A drunken buffoon tried giving Aum a high five. "Don't leave me hanging! This is why we're here."

"Yes," He responded in an unexcited monotone, "It surely is," and he completed the high five with as minimal enthusiasm as necessary.

"Ass passable jack," the drunk responded. "You're gonna have to do better than that!" The man howled like a rowdy cowboy that just got paid as the bus began to slow to an excruciating stop. They all exited and joined the miles of late arriving red jerseys, Aum and Demona almost being full bore trampled by stampeding herd of cows.

"Are these the drones?! This is total retardation. I'm embarrassed to be human." Aum grabbed her hand and kissed it. It opened her eyes wide with compassion and she asked him, "You think you can carry all this in your weave?"

"Carry? I just gotta clean it and move it," a few cowboy hat's passed by, "Maybe brand it while I'm at it," Aum laughed hard at his own joke, and she fully lost her seriousness, playfully kicking him in the butt.

"You got me, I'm your's," he replied as if her foot branded him with her algorithmic logo.

"Mooo!" she burst out in a black cackling laughter.

Upon entry they had their newly acquired tickets scanned. No hassles.

Inside there were wall-to-wall people, more jerseys… only jerseys. Carrying multiple stacks of beer cups, doing so while eating extra large hotdogs dressed with extra large piles of onions and relish. Aum and Demona received many looks. Aum was still in the clothes he slept in, still glowing with rooftop wild, and Demona was still in her rockband outfit. Out of place was an understatement. Aum looked up on a screen, it was between the first and second period. He looked at his ticket and found the proper direction to their seats.

As they tried to navigate a collision happened just in front of them. A group of three, strolling and chatting, wearing red, collided with one guy wearing white and yellow, moving a lot quicker. After the collision happened the man in yellow passed a small piece of old cardboard to the centre of the three with a photo of a hockey player on it, also wearing yellow and white.

"Dude, what the fuck are you giving me this for?" the centre one said.

"Foundations gotta move," replied the man in white and yellow and continued on.

"What the fuck? Serious!?" He yelled at the man in yellow as he swiftly disappeared into the crowd.

"What did he give you?" asked his right-winger.

"A Lemieux rookie card."

"Shit ass, it's not even your birthday," exclaimed his left-winger.

"And you didn't even have to blow the guy like last time," joked the right winger.

Then they noticed Aum and Demona looking at them.

"You guys gonna fuckn' arrest us or what?" said the right winger.

"You saw it, he just gave it to me," said the centre man.

"He gave you something a lot more valuable than a piece of cardboard," Aum replied. Demona quickly added, "If you don't pay more attention, you will be arrested."

"Bound to your concrete shoes," Aum said.

"Foundations gotta move," Demona followed as they continued to locate their seats. They playfully smiled at each other and at the rhyme scheme that emerged. The trio was baffled and

Demona and Aum could hear one of them shout, "Geez, who let the freaks in?"

Aum and Demona looked at each other, wondering if they should even bother to continue. Remembering, Aum said, "What'd you say earlier? See divinity where it is not?" Then they heard, "Watch where you're going asshole!"

Quick verbal darts emerged, "Cocksucker! If you just knocked over $90 worth of my beer and you're calling me the asshole we should probably fucking take this outside."

"Hey Brett," The centre man called out to right winger, trying to wipe off the beer shower, "What's a Lemieux rookie card worth these days."

Aum glanced back to see the card, soaked in beer, floating in a puddle, as Brett tapped his sleek hand embed, "Selling for $900 on eBay…"

Not waiting so see what unfolded, Aum and Demona continued the search through the dimwit carnival, where there was next to no depth and no wicked tricks, only painfully obvious ones. A fat man walked by, yelling himself and all others into a drunken ignorant oblivion. He looked like he should be ringside, the manager of a 1980's pro wrestler, or maybe the wrestler himself. Numerous people began yelling in the direction of Aum and Demona, selling them programs, hot dogs, car insurance, and the last offered them a rail of hard drugs.

"Let's find our seats, and immediately get the fuck outta here," Aum said.

"Agreed."

They found them, sat down. They were about to leap out, completing only a single breath to launch them back out of the stadium and back to a world which they were comfortable with, but they were fully accosted by the bizarre spectacle.

Still wild-eyed, the setting was shocking - it sizzled Aum's senses. Mesmerized, he gazed at it all, taking it all openly in. Live camera feeds, a ring of LED screens that encircled the entire arena, constantly streaming advertising memes, slogans, and dreams; web addresses, even scan tag portals for free and useless techie goodies. The sound system shook your cells, whether playing Tom Conners or Tom Cochrane and the sonic facade of the play-by-play announcers made the sleek lingo of corporate radio seem stumbling and indie. It was probably a robot, Aum concluded, with a single monocle viewpoint analyzing the action in real time and translating the feed into programmed banter and bad athletic metaphor.

He saw cheerleaders that were sprinkled around the stadium like icing sugar, wearing hockey jerseys and no pants, flirting in the aisles, dancing, strutting and waiving their pompoms. A plethora of plump fluffy mascots walked around as jesters and fools invoking raunchy uproar among the peasants. One tried to walk along the top of the protective glass of the rink, like a tight rope, only to slip and fall. His groin was introduced to the thin glass line in the most uncomfortable way, though with absurd hilarity. Aum chuckled. Ah yes, the easy laughs of a man being canned. Then it actually got funny. The foot of the mascots costume got caught between two panes as he went for the ground. He hung upside down helpless, even reaching for the top of the glass with his hands to unhook his caught toe, but his costumed head was too big. He hung like a hanged man, motionlessly awakening to the nature of his job, and aching groin, until security could help bring him to his feet.

It was more a zoo than a carnival, with all the animals loose and mingling, fucking and fighting. "There *is* an actual hockey game being played here right?" Aum asked. Just as he did the players came out onto the ice.

The uptempo rock music dropped, lights and fireworks engaged and the crowed went berserk. Aum saw the shining multitude of holographic company logos on each players shoulders, projecting digital data out into space; Princess Leia-like with motion graphics, slogans and web integration, followed by stats from the previous period. As skating, branded advertisements, each jersey tagged-in an unnecessary context to the game. Aum could see how much harder these athletes had to work to overcome cultural and economic disparity, to simply shake the prison bars of corporate branding with each motion of their physical bodies.

"Alright! You made it in to view the perfectly perfect metaphor!"

"What!?" both Aum and Demona said in surprise. A man sat down next to them. Older, not wearing a jersey, even speaking their language, "Strangely, if you make it past this level they send you to Walmart to pray."

Demona jousted immediately, "That might be preferable actually, to this absurdity. It's like watching a pack of hairy animals pulling a fat man in a red overcoat." She could see the over exerted athletic effort as well.

Their new hockey friend laughed and replied, "Most don't even see the hairy animals. For the majority here, they just see the fancy meta data, like the human athletes exist only as their statistical output, and whether their performance potential has been reached or not. Simpler folk simply with untrained eyes." he gestured to a few ball capped and balding men, grinning, looking like little boys, fully enjoying the spectacle's buzzing massage. This contextual insight and articulate observation was a lifeboat for Demona and Aum, as they continued to sizzle and deep fry in their seats.

He continued to construct a protective bubble around them, "These ones dedicate themselves to immersion in statistical analysis, technical performance dissections, and most annoyingly of all, arm chair vocalizations of the most painfully obvious. As if these athletes are their sole representation of hope and have the potential to breakthrough a meticulously defined cage, even bring the mass of onlookers with them during moments of liberation."

The puck dropped to start the second period.

"Keep in mind this perspective is broader than just commercial sport. This includes all beginners, bantams, peewee's, novices and juniors too." As he said it they saw numerous groups of kids wearing their own team jerseys. "A point of obsession, all potential athletes are monitored, scrutinized and groomed starting in childhood. Observers marvel at a natural talent, watching it grow, expecting the sacrifice of all life path potential for this single skill, fulfilling high expectations imposed of sustained performance and long term achievement. These young minds and young bodies are not conditioned to - and are not cognizant of - the daily grind and the mechanics of an abusive cultural machine that holds them up as trophies of satoric freedom."

Demona piped in, "You need to receive a trophy for this bridge build sir, with these dense bricks."

"You haven't changed at all Monica," and, catching her surprised reaction, he continued like a train, "This transmutation of the path of moksha, the reconstruction of youth cages and the remapped path of societal liberation will both be things to look out for in the future."

"Future?" Aum asked, remembering the military planes and declaration of martial law, of which most people here looked like they didn't know of, care of, or chose to ignore.

"This is all quite similar to the structure of the Riddle," the man said. Both their eyes went wide as this stranger simply stated it, bringing the outside in, right into the seats they were sitting in, "The perfectly perfect metaphor."

"There it is!" Demona said, "The road. Built." Something clicked in her, "That's it! You're the Engineer? Right? Aren't you? I've been seeing you coming, patiently been waiting, preparing."

"I remember you as such a cute little thing Monica, getting into everything, always." She titled her head in curiosity. He responded, "Like I said, you haven't changed at all. My name is Daniel. Your dad and I go levels way back."

"Cool Dan cool, uncle dad," She vaguely remembered the childhood lessons, with her dad Ezekiel, this man named Daniel, and may other elders. But at the time, it made very little sense to her. "So did we save it then? With our rebuild? Can you see the future? Or even the now?"

"We are well on our way, to the new ways, this future road, saved and amped especially within the oncoming waves of growth." There was a cheer from the crowd, their focus was thrown at the game flow, momentarily. "This place is a perfectly perfect metaphor for future use, as sport can be viewed as a microcosm within the macro, a much more streamlined closed system that works with a very similar rule-set to that in which the Riddle works."

The live game became the background soundtrack, an actively clacking and grunting and scraping synchronicity of Canadiana, meshed into the lesson.

"The fundamental nature of athletics is to dedicate oneself to a specialized path, to choose to see how far one can push and hone a skill-set, by expanding and pushing the limitations of the container – the physical body or game itself." Hey gazed at Aum with slight pause, "Within the dynamics of internal sole psychology, or even nested within the broader synergy of pairs or team dynamics, qualities of valor are emphasized such as precision, reaction, improvisation, intuition, regeneration and persistence."

"A focused mindful mindless flow expressed through a woven group of bodies." Aum replied, gesturing to the rink.

"Or a superhero engine," Demona added.

"In addition, within every micro team interaction is the evolutionary dynamic to facilitate the development of weaker members of the team by more advanced mentor team members, even coaches or specialists."

There was a cheer and some dude in front of them puked in his seat.

"Oh my god," Demona exclaimed in dismay.

"You gotta be kidding me – it's not that exciting dude!" Aum shouted.

The man turned back to Aum and muffled out a shout, "I swear I haven't drank anything." Aum and Demona looked at each other in confusion. Maybe mother Aya has poked through, invoking the inherent spirit growth within all walks of life, expanding beyond it's original plant container.

"There's a few folks here, who you wouldn't expect," Daniel continued, "Here, at this advanced point of focus, of all places on the globe, there are the largest number of overlapping paradigms and subsets of consciousness within it. A very diverse cross section that is eye-opening indeed."

Somebody chugged a full cup of beer, even snorted something in a pause of the flow. A corporate handshake in a booth moved mountains and destroyed lives, and a young kid's heart was inspired to fly; him and his family receiving tickets as a gift from their athletic community, a community lead by the same people who were shaking hands, and the land, and doing trucker rails.

"You're naive if you believe that everyone born in 1980 is of the same ilk. Or that a person who isn't overtly nice or polite is automatically an unconscious or uncontentious human being."

"You're wrong actually." Aum spoke up, "About the ilk," finding the moment to begin his basket project. "There's deep significance to who is incarnated and in bodies, in positions of power in society and culture at this point in time; the cusp singularity wave. All hold a specific vibration within their spirits, holding space for passengers as we collectively pass through the gate. Everyone in those positions should be aware of that, conscious of that, and are hopefully even conscious of the moment they chose it."

Daniel continued in considered dialogue, "Yes, but like it or not, this event has united an even broader social spectrum than that.

From garbage man to king. Beyond the three layers deep: of not knowing, of knowing and talking about it, knowing and not talking about it. All the passengers in all the far reaches of this city, are celebrating in a positive and ultimately organic way, rather than using a paradigm shift, a mythic apocalypse, attention engineering, politics and nationalism, protest and marches, racism or religious fanaticism to unite an ever-growing number of evolving people, whether they are conscious of their own evolution or not. It is a unique facet of techno collective nature, that an entire city can cheer in unity at a single moment, an entire country can gasp together at a close call or even honk their horns with pride after a goal. All this supported by unified real-time broadcast systems, linking a greater continental mentally, and thus psychically meshing many to an event, even one camera angle. We're all here, really."

A fight broke out on the ice.

"Well, enough of us anyway," Daniel added.

The upper league chess masters had agreed to allow fighting back into the sport, just for this single game. However, this wasn't really a fight, it was more like one hulk beating down another. The crowed loved it, having been denied this extreme for decades, they stood to their feet roaring like crazed inebriated Romans. The lights flashed to amp the improvised action sequence and over the loud speakers the DJ dropped Metallica's *One*.

Darkness, imprisoning me
All that I see
Absolute horror
I cannot live
I cannot die
Trapped in myself
Body my holding cell

Wow, yeah, that guy must be enduring something fierce right now, to be getting pummeled in front of this audience as well as shredded by the amplified tech context and broadcast to world. After the fight had concluded by the smaller man falling to the ground, the referees pulled the two apart, leading them to the penalty box.

The games flow was grinding to a halt as a tripping penalty was called soon after the play restarted. After giving the play-by-play breakdown, and the near-rioting audience calmed slightly, the announcer hijacked the moment with an advertising injection, 'This powerplay is brought to you by Grunch Power. Grunch power – we got you covered. www.GrunchPower.com'

"Good God conjecture. Did you just hear that?" exclaimed Demona.

"Ouch. That should definitely be against the rules!" Aum stated.

Berated minds turned to mush, turning off, due to the utter irrelevancy of the ad drop. It thusly found a home in the collective unconscious back brain.

"Shit, I wonder how much Grunch has to pay to occupy that space."

"Occupy?" Dan said, "My young friends, that's what keeps it all afloat. The only reason the whole thing doesn't collapse as a result of that seemingly hijacked flow, is because, most unfortunately, that berating consumptive relationship is the foundation of all this. It's the machine that pays the rent, pays for maintenance, pays staff, pays top players, pays for equipment and the technology that unifies. All this structure," he pointed around the arena and up to the big screen in the centre, as the live feed caught him pointing up to it, "all this is an amplified exponent of the flattest of flatland. Actual sport, the actual practice of athletics, doesn't do anything, it doesn't produce anything. The only thing it produces is moments of synchronistic synthesized internal and external rapture, beauty and grace. At its core, it is pure light."

After taking a moment to digest this fact, the play still stuck in agonizing limbo, Aum responded, "But it's surrounded and supported by all this, a vast cloud of ignorance."

"The mass consumption and commodification of light..."

"...including the deepest most focused physical dives into graceful play."

"It's a tricky riddle, right? Because the container is what allows it to reach this scope of grandiosity, and, reach it's roots down through to the developmental programs which keep many kids out of trouble and give them a point of focus as they transmutate within the civilization around them."

After the referee finally got the protesting player in the box, the puck dropped once again and the game turned on a dime. Wearing yellow and black, an opponent cut through the muddy mental molasses, wrapping minds in a Möbius strip with finger and toe tip clarity, taking the puck from one end of the rink to the other, deeking out the wingmen, undressing the defense, and putting a fancy dress on the goalie as the puck hit the rooftop mesh of the net. The whole arena muted to the crispest silence they had heard all day, though only momentarily. A different cheer emerged, one of awe, from everyone who saw this young kid play, as if to say *okay, we'll give you that one, just 'cause you're that good. Don't do it again.*

As the replay streamed on the big screen, within each of his strides Aum could see the emergent generation of players, which this kid led. He had an individual skill level that was so profound it was near unbelievable, reaching into the supernatural. As was the custom here, he soaked in the moment of breakthrough grace, the abilities, breaking points, risk taking, reactions, and audacity of this young one. Aum saw a historically clutch moment of change, total redirection, and cast so broad in real time, it permeated to every other player in the game, and the entire sport itself became better.

"Okay, I get it. I see it," Aum said.

"Everyone knows, right? Intrinsically." Their friend explained, "They just don't know that they know. You just heard it, in their reaction. Of all things, they just see a guy playing hockey. But it's right there, a gateway for higher metaphorical understanding, of the Riddle or the complexities of all metaphysical reality. Athletics create legendary warriors who fly past the sun into the stars, catapulted by a much different system which is more culturally valid than combative war."

There was a siren that erupted and the second period came to a close. 1-1. Third period, going for gold. Not waiting to feel what madness was about to unfold during the break, Aum said to them, "I need to find the men's room."

"Let us know what you find in there," Demona said quickly, looking slightly less strained, though still mostly terrified; the siren invoked her recent memory, and the actual. Right. In this setting, this concrete capsule, he had already forgotten, the real-time transmutation of civilization with every step and every conscious breath of presence. He had to push his feet all the way into the earth to make the active connection, and made his way through the crowd, like at a rock concert. He was an outsider on the front lines of an onslaught, feeling every red shirted eyeball and their shooting bullets of prison day job ignorance aimed at an intruder showing them with each stride something else entirely. "If only I hadn't forgotten my fucking microns!" he said outloud, pointing their unconscious gaze all back to the game turning goal they had just witnessed. As he continued to walk he was surrounded by a rowdy dogpack of kids. They made room for him, but no one else as they ran by, all others defenseless against their path of empowered troublemaking. That was followed by a giant terrifying lumbering mascot, drunk in his suit and moaning for air, then a guy selling fresh meat wieners from a self warming tray, concluded by a heavily perfumed encounter with a busty blonde sales woman who had set up shop just outside the men's room like an outpost of an Amsterdam hooking ring. He didn't even look at her, else get a surprise punch in the teeth by her five-ring-fingered pimp. How could this gonzo shyster ring within this concrete dish bowl be the central gaze of the entire satellite spiderweb'd flatland nation!? Fuck!

It was no less crowded in the men's room, and there was a waiting line, though it was moving fast. Those in line were looking at their handhelds and those at the urinals were staring at screens that were mounted on the wall at eyelevel, forcing them to watch whatever was being broadcast as they took a leak.

Here, screens were battling. The ones being controlled individually vs the ones with a one-way broadcast. It was self-chosen programming vs culturally accepted programming. Not having a handheld, Aum didn't really know what to look at. He quickly spied a few handhelds of other gents. Most were on the same stream that was on the TV's; those men didn't even see the choice in front of them. Some were typing out SMS's, but most were on the corporate boards, checking out the corporate news feeds. No one was looking at the local or international waves of collapse happening. No one was on top of the newest indie media feeds, whether covering the breaking food shortage crises, or the riots that were happening outside the mom and pop grocer's doors down the block. There was no importance placed on having an awareness of the collective cusp, nor choosing the personal human responsibility required for being alive at this time. Without choosing that responsibility, how could they even come close to having the emotional capacity developed that allows for the internal awareness and telepathic compression of real-time evolution, along with the external awareness of the many meshed pockets of happening which reside beyond the scope of a technological consumer reach? Food riots, or far, far, beyond, in the stars.

Getting to the front of the line and not wanting to look at the screen while pissing, he closed his eyes once he made sure he was pointing in the right direction. Light flashed on his closed eylids. There was something there, a message from a dfferent source. He ignored it, feeling the icey breeze within it, "Fuck."

"What you say to me!" from next to him, slured.

He just brought down half a dozen military planes with his focused heartfelt intention, and all these people are doing is sinking deeper into forgetting? Why was he in this cattle pen? How is it even possible to wake these ones up that choose to be so heavily sedated?

"Hey asshole! What'd you say to me!?" the man next to him shouted.

"I said *Go Coyote's*!"

Aum zipped his pants, actually took the time to wash his hands, and returned to his seat. "Where did Dan go?" he asked Demona.

"He said he was going to grab some food."

"Food? Here!?"

"I guess so."

The overweight pro wrestler was about to sit down in front of them, shouting loudly to anyone that would hear, blithering on incoherently about wining gold, finally finding articulation as his focus found Aum, as if merely looking at him bought this human into the spotlight.

"Cheers buddy," raising his glass.

"I don't have a beer," Aum said to him. He was a reincarnated Chris Farley, "Well, we better fix that!" From a stack of half a dozen he grabbed a plastic cup with the foamy brown water in it and offered it to him.

Before even considering taking it Aum looked deeply into the man's eyes. In this wrestler he saw a young daughter that loved him very much, and a wife who, even though unhappy, relied on this dimwit for her survival, for food and shelter. He saw a hard working man doing the best he could, now celebrating and releasing stress the only way he knew how, unconsciously waiting for an opportunity to see the light, bask in it and be transformed.

The wrestler whined in pain, as if in a choke hold, as if the gaze was too much, "Please take it sir."

Fuck. Gotta bring everybody. And Aum accepted the beer, even though still in his pajamas.

"That was a hell of a goal, hey!?" The drunk dad said, coming to realize how drunk he actually was.

"Yeah, no shit dude!" Aum cheers'd him and took a drink. It had been a long day.

And in the sip there was the lesson. Aum didn't have to carry all this bullshit, only those trapped within it, who were as light as anything. Find the bottom, look at it and accept it with love and compassion, and thus lift it up with full karmic soul presence.

"Holy shit!" The big man said, reflecting, maybe even seeing something new.

"Holy shit is right," Aum stated, putting the beer down as he saw the bottom, and placed light in it.

And they both chuckled, though the big man erupted in a boisterous outburst that filled the entire arena. A large airhorn went off and the camera was on them. Seeing himself on the screen Aum gave the horns with one hand, hanglose with the other. A fantastic cracked line of voodoo; hopefully that one went out to the flatland spider web during the break, not just the internal broadcast feeds. Fix the thread and well past, he prayed. He spied a random handheld, Don Cherry just finished his rant with a thumbs up, which was followed by brief shots of crisp and instantly recognizable movie stars who paid-in for the well timed promotion, alongside aging athletic phenoms with their own self-developing legacy systems. Cheerleaders, rockstars, politicians, then there was a clip of Aum smiling and the drunk dad laughing followed by the hang loose horns; the surfing karana mudra. No one watching knew who Aum was, but they wanted to, and felt like they should. It then cut to an actual commercial.

"Right on. Full nation feed." He looked at Demona, "This is fun."

She looked at him like she was gonna go on a shooting rampage; with a dreamcatcher of course.

The lights went out, the announcer revved up, the crowd went manic as the Dj dropped 2 Unlimited into the speakers.

Ya'll ready for this!

"What in the Hell!?! Did we time travel back to '92!?" Demona yelled, utterly bent and baffled once again.

The light show engaged as the synth from the classic hockey anthem pierced through all the muddled incoherence – roping in the rest of the herd. The arena was like a time capsule where it was okay to forget every single thing.

The hockey players skated out.

"Hahah, this song is actually better than I remember it," said Aum.

"What the fuck are you saying!? Do you hear yourself right now?!" replied Demona, "You must be drunk!"

The Vj cut in the 2 Unlimited music video on the central screen, the rapping dutch frontman even had an LA Kings hat on. As the crowd stood to cheer on the team skating out of the gate, a plastic cup of beer slipped and fell into Demona's lap, exploding. She quickly stood so that most of the liquid hit the floor, but her lap got grossly wet. With the choice to laugh or to get angry in front of her, she simply shook her head in disbelief. Aum looked scared, as if the actual shooting rampage was about to start. Demona burst out laughing, simply pointing at his frightened expression. At this the man behind her stepped in and apologized profusely, offering her a stack of napkins. After seeing how gorgeous she was, the apology morphed into a pick up line, woven like a pro, "What do you think, maybe next time I can buy you a drink, instead of spilling one in your lap." She stopped laughing. A pro herself, "Aww, it's okay cowboy, I'm used to it. You just gotta learn to save those seeds, not spill them." Then she looked over at Aum, a magician among men, sky high hair, spectral body buzzing in alignment with the quatum activated day, plus the sip of beer.

"Eventually you make your own living starseeds," He added as he shimmered like a hologram, "They spill less easy," Aum looked the man in the eye, starting to assist in rearranging his soulpath.

The man quickly apologized to both of them and sat down, drunkenly mumbling something about paying more attention next time.

Their new well-timed engineering friend returned with some poutine as the puck dropped, not noticing his perfectly aligned position in the real-time flow. The food actually smelled good, didn't look like it had already been eaten and excreted, and was crafted with care.

“Organic potatoes and cheese,” Dan said as Aum gawked at him.

Maybe there was more hope here than Aum thought.

After the raucous cheers died down Aum heard the guy behind them who had just dumped the beer say to his wingman, “What the!? Stu do know a chick named SuzieQ?”

He responded, “Didn’t you meet her at the bar last week? The little blonde firecracker?”

“Nope, that was Amanda. I just got a text from SuzieQ wondering what the score is between The Riddlers and Icarus, but it’s spelt with two a’s. I-c-A-A-r-u-s”

“That’s insane – those aren’t even hockey teams.” The wing man added, “Ask her to send you her picture,” He laughed, then there was a pause.

“What’d you write dude?”

“It’s tied.”

The wingman chortled, not unlike a dolt in disbelief. “Uh, Okay. I still think you should ask her to send a picture.”

Near instantly Aum, Demona and Daniel saw on the ring of LED’s a brief flash of scrolling white text on black

www. gargantuan_artist_manufacturing_encorporated_by_suzie. org

Daniel wiped his hand on a napkin and quickly pulled out his handheld, “I think the doors just reopened...”

He looked up from the screen at them both with excitement. “Boards are back up, and Riddler intake has just reactivated. Congratulations.”

Aum and Demona looked at each other, mouthes agape. The two above them burst out in excitement, totally disconnected from the hockey play, “Ha! Check her out dude!”

“Damn, I can’t believe she sent it to you.”

“And I didn’t even ask.”

“What?!”

Demona reacted, “Jesus, they’ve opened the gates way too fucking wide. What are these morons gonna give us?” Aum glanced back at their burly dumbbell-pumping pipes, “I dunno, maybe we could get them to build a few pyramids; dense bricks for the astral stargate after the storage and deletion sequence is complete."

Daniels eyes went wide, hearing the execution of this next generation line, "Okay, now let me ask you something," he reached into his pocket.

Everything began to spin, it didn't make sense, especially in this wide vortex mesh. Aum wouldn't be surprised if the camera caught them again, like a drug deal under surveillance.

"Whoa!" The audience in the stadium, and around the ground nation collectively groaned. There was a close shot on net by the same player who scored earlier. All observers refocused on the game, the three of them only for a breath, and in the wave break Daniel continued.

"I was on the bus today day, reading as I returned from work. I put my book down to grab something from my briefcase. I picked up my book. This had replaced my bookmark."

He handed him a 5 x 7 glossy flyer. "Frankly, It scared the shit out of me."

Aum looked at the flyer intently. At the top, in an elegant font it said, 'Gridline Centre: Hall of Visionary Leadership and Advanced Esoteric Development' and at the bottom there were the words, 'Inter dimensional Emergency Response Plan.'

Demona snuck a peak.

The main image on the flyer showed the skeletal frames of buildings burned and a sky scorched with a thousand suns. Floating in the fire red sky, surrounded by smoke and clouds, was a mechanical saucer with a glowing vortex of light emitted from the center.

"Jeez who ever made this really wants to escape this place." Aum passed it to Demona who inspected it more thoroughly, adding, "Crazy-ass kool-aid promo," as if recognizing it, passing it back.

"You mean you have some idea of what this is?" Aum asked her.

"I've haven't heard of this Emergency Response Plan. I do know the Gridline Centre though," Demona said.

Aum flipped it over and saw it was an invitation with today's date, address, and the words *Join us for the final storage and deletion sequence,* written by hand.

Aum, quite abruptly, brought it closer to his face to read it a second time, the words jogging him back into the full sequence. Dan picked up on the reaction. As Aum was about to pass it back to him he said, "You keep it. I've got other bookmarks I can use."

"Oh… okay, thanks… Wanna beer?"

"Sure, I'll have a sip."

The sun had finally set and a cooling breeze moved through the city as Aum causally strolled back with two train tickets, already purchased, found jammed in the machine. He looked up and the moon still looked full. Scientifically it was full for three nights, not just one. As they left the hockey game there were no stars out, only dense clouds that allowed the lunar beam to pulse in and out like it's own binary signal.

Demona and Aum left before the game had ended. The action was a nation wide field of attention magnetics so it was trickier to escape than a mythic Cretan maze. There was even a red Minotaur in a basketball jersey there who tried to assail them, "Your navigation is fucked dude. You're at the wrong arena," Aum said directly to the man inside the costume.

He and Demona didn't really need to view the real-time outcome of the gold medal match; the city had become a perfectly magnified amplification chamber - plus they had to start moving to make it to the late evening Gridline meeting. As they walked towards the train the win was felt the moment it happened. It was an unleashed exuberance of anamalistic celebration, moving from a fully unified moment outward, washing over most previous pockets of panic and terror, whether manufactured or real. Aum did as much as he could with this, amping the underpinning love with his heart and pulsing the wave further around the globe. Unfortunatley he could also feel, even within the over-ecstatic collective joy, it's opposite, ready to explode; a reminder that the manufactured foundation of anxiety and stress was still there.

Sure, they had saved the Tower, and together woven their metaphysical threads into a basket that could carry everyone, even helped re-opened the doors to the Riddle.

But, as if Mr Hyde-like hulking werewolf, the unconscious beast was still underneath, ready to flip back at the missed tip of a hat, regardless of the depth of gamma ray science or experimental chemistry practiced. What was it going to take to heal this monster of ignorance? A viral trojan horse meme to explode with programmed pure light when imbibed? Or someone brave enough to lead the herd like a new wild man?

Aum passed Demona her ticket.

"There was another earthquake," She stated, "Besides the one last night in Chile, I mean. This time north, just off the coast."

"What!? There was one last night?"

"Yeah. Just after 3am."

"3am?" Aum thought that must have been why he couldn't sleep, "There's so much happening now even media can't keep up; action faster than the journaling streams."

Demona continued, "Because it was in the ocean, a tsunami devastated Hawaii, covering it entirely. Thousands of people just died," She said with a shaky voice. Her small frame trembled like a young girl. She pointed up to the row of broadcast monitors on the train platform.

A grey haired man broke the news, *"Again, we apologize for the interruption of this momentous achievement for the entire nation. For those just joining us, this evenings underwater earthquake, adding to last night's chain reaction has triggered major tsunami's that have caused mass flooding to coastal cities in New Zealand, Polynesia, and Japan."* The twittering flicker and shallow ADD gaze continued to beam, snare and redirect attention, and would continue do so until the power went out. The proclamation of Martial Law and global rioting was last minutes news, even more so than gold medal hockey. The talking head continued, *"The tsunami was large enough to reach all the way to the coast where the water in the bay rose high enough to extinguish the Olympic flame on this, the last day of competition. Here's a shot of the bay directly from our broadcast headquarters. As you can see about 5 blocks have been flooded. How this mass global catastrophe will mix with mass national unity only time will tell."*

Aum had to disconnect; breathe on his own. He turned his back to the screens and looked up to the dark skies. Demona said it, 'One unbeknownst 'no' and they're gone forever.' The pole shift was on it's way, by hours or days; a confluence of natural forces now out of control, potentially even out of the sphere of any positive influence by all humanity. The current ecological collapse tilted into full and real global emergency, not the fallacy or fiction used to conduct the minds of many, but something felt, though maybe not identified, in the psyche of all. Surley now, in a medicine vision, some white skinned pueblo shaman would bring back a vision of an inter-dimensional entity beyond the vibratory cognition of the status quo, who, in the grand multi-faceted architecture of the linear cosmos, was in charge of manifesting these major earth changes, all perfectly aligned with the Great Work. An advanced vision no doubt, a great TV episode even, still yet, an utterly useless answer to the problems they faced.

He looked over at Demona and she was no longer with him. They were standing together, but they were no longer together.

It surprised him a little, this recognition, at how such a dramatic global shift could be followed all the way down to their intertwined life paths – and instantly separate them. Whatever relationship they had, what ever it was meant to achieve, micro or macro, it was over. That's how it worked, and why it was best to not to get attached. Her rough and aggressive costuming was ripped away as she became a small child that was lost on the street.

"My other lover was in Hawaii...."

Beyond personal reaction Aum saw her constructing invisible barriers inside her being, blocking the photonic vibrational waves that were streaming within the media, within the still-full moon, and everywhere else on the planet. To this opportunity to say yes to a deeper divine life path growth, and vulnerable openness, and evolution beyond imagining, her soul was saying "no", probably unbeknownst to even her.

"All of our work for nothing. Aum, please do something," Demona sobbed.

"Do something? About what? Hawaii? Japan? Chile? The riots? Martial Law?!"

Aum briefly glanced back at the screen to see a new emergency broadcast: an ice flow the size of Greenland had just detached from Antarctica. Even though in the Atlantic, this undoubtedly was linked to the tsunami; the chain reaction continued. With a mass the size of an entire continent floating along the surface of the planet, it is assuredly going to throw the poles off. The broadcast was beaming pure panic directly into their chests, clogging all competent cognition and ajnatic intuitive insight, doing the same to every human in western civilization. Aum could feel the full collective paralysis. The entire globe was swirling in emotional panic. It was all falling apart and not enough people had yet come to the realization that their intention, and advanced dimensional presence, could hold it all together.

As they waited for the train in the flashing moonlight, the inebriated hockey revelators mingled with the chaotic eco-eco riots, creating a destructive anarchistic war zone. In the black of night, with the sound of windows smashing and car alarms emerging from all four directions, it was like walking on rumbling lands, on numerous plate tectonic shifts as the next aftershock came exponentially quicker than the previous.

The lights were going out and the basket threads Aum and Demona had been weaving together, far further than they could both grasp, were ripped asunder by the marauding methodical beast of unconsciousness, ICAARUS. The world was ending.

Every action now must be seen - to it's end point - and each intuitive thought, was now the equivalent to dramatic physical action.

Aum's mind quickly became aware of each of his many soul-dream lines spreading around the metasphere. At the end of each there was a hand that grabbed a hold of the edge of each woven strand that was being torn apart, and there on the train platform he felt his body automatically begin to collect the adrenaline and fear that surged out of each tear, by everyone tuned in throughout the city, throughout the country, and, in the most extreme cases, the entire continent. He was spread out into a thousand different dimensional facets, acutely aware of the enormous build up growing inside of him, with no apparent outlet.

The media broadcast shifted, *"We cut now to 5th and Broadway, where, in the midst of a city wide victory celebration combined with full scale riot, a woman seems to be on the verge of suicide. Let's go to it now..."*

"5th and broadway?" Aum asked.

"That's two blocks away," A dazed and distraught Demona said.

It cut to a live reporter with robotic smile, perfect hair and teeth, *"...That's right Conner. We're here, live, where you can see this lovely young lady is brandishing a weapon and a can of gasoline. Police car's have blocked off traffic, in this, the first apparent New Eden incident that has ever been stalled, and with luck, prevented."*

The camera cut to a shot of the crazed woman pointing a gun back and forth between the surrounding officers and her own temple.

It was Cat.

Adrenaline hit his heart and it went off like a machine gun.

"Shit, Fuck, Goddamn it - Good-bye Demona," he kissed her full lips and her resting third eye and he turned to run.

"What!?" Demona turned to look at him, but he was already 10 long sprinting strides away. At top speed he shouted back, "That's my other lover!"

Eyes wide, considering the implications, Demona began to run after him. However after a few short strides she felt the same separation as Aum did. She noticed her train coming and slowed, looking back at the monitor, to deeply consider what she needed to be doing as these new crisis's erupted.

The reporter continued *"... the woman, who has now been isolated, we have just been informed, is Catherine Banal, an accomplished and notorious celebrity here in the city, well known for her controversial performance art."*

Back at the studio Conner cut back in, *"Uh Denise, could this then be a work of art?"*

It cut back to Denise with the street chaos in the background.

"Conner, to me it's unclear. As you know I'm not really the artsy type, maybe we can try and bring in an expert on this one..."

There was a frantic shout from the centre of the chaos that cut the reporter off mid sentence. Denise stepped out of the camera frame as she looked back at the origin of the screen. Her, Conner, and the viewing television audience could hear the frantic cries, *"We will all be punished for our ignorance, and I... I have failed to serve to my fullest capacity."*

You could hear Denise quickly interjecting, *"Let's get a close up Colin."*

The shaky camera quickly zoomed in to show a soaking wet Cat, brandishing a Beratta 92 police pistol in one hand, pointing it at the crowd randomly, and a red gas can in another hand. She continued to scream, loud enough for all to hear, her voice shredded, broken and full of tears, *"I have failed you! And thus you have failed!"*

'Pause, pause, pause, don't do it, don't do it, don't do it,' Aum repeated over and over in his mind. The built up energy inside him, collected from around the countryside, now had a purpose; manifested in the physical as pure lateral flight. He dodged passers-by, each foot tearing up the concrete underneath it, the rubber on his shoes getting hot. As if in a dream his clothes seemed to be holding him back, keeping him in slow motion. But he pushed on, more sleek and strong.

The first intersection he came to told him ‘Don’t Walk’, which of course he was not going to do. It was a 3 lane, one way street, traveling left to right. The speed limit was a brisk 50k and people in this part of town were drunk with excitement and booze and driving home or to the bar after the epic win. The street had it’s green light for a while so traffic was right up to 50, or faster.

“Shit, okay, fuck.”

He saw a gap between two people where the crowd was gathering to cross. He was still 3 strides away and at top sprinting speed. The gap disappeared, filled with a couple of fat drunk men with red jerseys about to high-five. Aum responded. His right foot pushed off. His stride took him left and up, he vaulted on top of a ridge, a three foot concrete flower bed – it ran the length of the block, almost to the corner. Two more strides in perfect balance, lilac scent reaching his nose, then his left foot pushed off, his body was already jumping. His right foot stomped the top of a mailbox at the end of the flowerbox, a last springboard velocity boost. He split the two hockey fans a couple feet above their head’s, and with his arms swinging under his legs, he intercepted both their high fives with a clap. But he was already coming down, just clearing a lady in front of him, all but kicking the cowgirl hat right off her head. He had a foot out, slightly touching the fast car passing underneath him. He caught the trunk, taking only enough pressure to direct his landing. Aum hit the concrete, with both feet, shuffled half a step onto the dashed line as a car was coming up fast behind the last - and in the middle lane in front of him also. Both zoomed by, in front and in behind him, horns blaring. He still had forward momentum so he used it to jump up and pounce off the trunk of the car in the middle lane as it passed. ‘Don’t be a martyr’ he thought towards Cat. One last lane. By this time people had noticed his acrobatics. In the third lane, the car didn’t have a tailgaiter behind it so it slammed on it’s breaks. Allowing Aum the perfect exit.

Off the trunk of the middle lane car he turned his body mid air, facing the same way as the screeching car in front of him, Aum landed and planted both feet and one hand on the roof, bracing for the abrupt change in direction. The crowd was equally dense at the other side of the street and he wasn't at all confident that there would be identical mailbox in the same place, and he wasn't too sure if this downtown group was ready for a crowd surfer, though they were probably drunk enough for it. Aum rode the roof top of the braking car into the intersection, riding the momentum as the car stopped, tires melting on the concrete, it vaulted him forward and off. He stepped once on the hood, then onto the ground. He almost bailed as the downward force was more than what he was expecting. He used both hands to absorb the fall and to push up, therianthropic, tearing his hands a little, making a hairpin turn left on the far side of the last of three rows of cars idling at the red light.

Not even Daredevil could have pulled it off better, and he still had a full block to go. The street was two lane and he had the full way clear on the right side… other than the two police car barricades set up 2/3rds of the way down.

'Where the fuck did she get that gun!' he thought. As the horns died down behind him, noticing there was no crunching of metal, he could already hear Cat screaming in front of him.

"I remember how it used to be, and it was never like this! It did not require this severity of public execution!"

As he ran toward the heart pocket of this potential tragedy, a new level of space time dimensionality opened up for him. He was running, and in his body, but not. It was the dulled dream-like state of running in slow motion at the same time as experiencing an advanced sensory mutation. He was able to actively digest the tension in the air with every oxygen molecule that hit the septum of his nose, hit his skin, extracting the emotional content embedded in each atom, moving it through the cleaning gears and systemic machinations of his spirit, releasing the resulting vibration behind him, back out his body through deep meridian rivers and the pooling chi points in his elbows joints, triceps, lats, and the centre of his upper back – the spiral out of his heart chakra. Flying? Yes. If you look directly up from this depth, the moment the clouds part, you can see fellow star nation's taking notice, to peep the physical outcome of the human timeline.

As he silver surfed through wave upon wave of the immense and breathtaking outpouring of the central focus: Cat screaming, to his surprise, within these breaking waves upon his approach, Aum began to hear her inner dialogue – translating the vibrational emotions he was running through into the actual thought forms of his friend stuck in baddha virabhadrasana, the bound warrior.

Beyond Cat and Catherine and beyond the Trimurti all I see is black. All I am is black, manifested within me; a time before light. Here now, I am, to spread it.

The gasoline dripped down her nose. Aum could smell it as if it ran down his own nose, as if it was him drenched in the fuel - and it was almost more than he could bear. Purest pain. The muscles in his heart began to ache and water welled up in his eyes, 'Don't you dare fucking take her'. Tears rolled down his cheeks and an empathic gate opened within his chest. It propelled him to a new top speed. With each purposeful leap forward, each footfall, and each swing of arm, he took hold of reality and pulled it toward him; the fastest he ever ran in his life.

In one glance he re-tuned to what lay directly before him in the physical. He was about a 60 yard dash from ground zero. And within the street lit stage was a massive circle of onlookers.

On the very outside of the circle were people who had randomly been passing by, now stopped, caught up in a net of confusion, on the tips of their toes trying to see what's going on, trying to understand, but out of fear not daring to move. This slowly merged with a circle of personally captured media, a layer of random passers by who were still confused, but not enough so to keep from recording the situation with their handhelds. This merged into the unofficial looking, more tech-savy netizens who's job it was to track these emerging transformational waves manifesting, and broadcast them out to the collective, or at least their extended networks, by their own engineered life path means. Vests, backwards ball caps, hand held audio transmission devices, mini DV cameras held together with duct tape, old school DAT equipment with digital conversion boxes, even a portable green screen tarp, boom mic, shoulder cam, and 5 foot high antenna sticking out of a back pack. It was the circuit bent sphere of makeshift DIY communication scientists. This was followed by the sleek capital funds of refined official broadcast – vans, trucks, fancy reflective jumpsuits, managerial blazer-overcoats with embedded electronics LED patches flickering the fused sigilized logos of each corporate media conglomerate. Hand embeds, digital eye augmentation for First Sight Broadcast, there was even a holographic news set, projecting into 3D space. This is where Denise sat, now interviewing a man in a mascot costume with a tattooed face: Japanese death mask. Aum guessed they followed the performance art storyline, maybe to soften this harsh edge, this tear in reality which was happening… or being performed. Regardless, this odd programming contextualization did not dissolve the police barricade, nor the nearly four-dozen police officers encircling the techno-societal mandala, with 32 guns drawn, pointed at the centre piece.

In the direct wake of a week of unified global megacity protests, complete with full scale riots and the collaborative destruction of the downtown core of many major centers, the cops surrounding Cat didn't quite know what to do. It was an over reaction, undoubtedly, like touching a recent wound. A dozen cop cars recently beat to shit, dented and scraped with war wounds, acted as the security wall for the armed officers who's job, societal purpose, and independent human reasoning, had become buzzed out, replaced by the collective draconian instinct and survival mechanisms of a dying way of life. They didn't know if they themselves were the hostages, or if this single woman had simply taken herself hostage. Either way, it wasn't their job to think about it.

My external and internal have become fully disconnected, and I've forgotten. I've forgotten what I'm doing, and what I have done; where I am going and who I am. The time has come to change this. The time has come for full annihilation.

She sighed in his mind, as if viewing something in full truth.

Even here, at every life path outpost I see the pretentious back patting, social status ladder climbing, the trending self-aggrandizing entrepreneurial oroborus that comes with being within the walls of the last castle. Old patterns discarded? No. Under the last Barrons wing, it's easy to think you're developing a self contained system, so I pray for the castle walls, to finally collapse, to fully test it all.

Then as a different voice in her mind:

Lineage 2 Drop and Spoil Calculator Interlude-Kamael-Hellbound-Gracia-Freya-Hi5-GoD.

He found his deepest, most peaceful inhale yet, aligned with the deepest, most compassionate, heart beat of his life. Opening to embrace the greater mass of blood and oxygen in his body, and a new veil lifted in his conscious mind. It suddenly hit him: the image of Cat on the television screen. Within the deep flow of his instinctual reaction of lateral flight he didn't notice her shaved head. He didn't notice her jewellery gone. He didn't notice that her clothes were simple; monk-like even. He didn't notice at first, but now it hit him, as he closed in on the situation and began to speed past the furthest, most timid of onlookers. She was an entirely new human and it was as if all light had disappeared from the inside of her gaze and the only thing that filled it was a broken and mal-developed sewer system; the rotting refuse of this civilization.

But if people are dead and dying, being tortured or murdered, within this newly engineered conscious container... it is just another constructed egoic fallacy. I remember what it used to be like, when it was special, when actions actually fucking mattered. I have taken every effort to enlighten and heal you and yet you return to your patterns, you return to your unconscious relationship to yourself. And now the world as we know it, is over.

Again the other voice:

Storage sequence override. Code word...

It was a lock and key dialogue.

Cremation grounds.

And what she, or they, were opening up, didn't sound good.

Storage sequence bypassed, full deletion engaged.

Shit. Had she consciously set all this up? He could feel her in each moment and each molecule. How had one woman amassed all this? And why? At her deepest core was she this bound? He had no idea what she had been through since he last saw her at Full Spectrum.

Once you know all the players, it becomes something else entirely. The mystery school is gone. The exhilaration is gone. What is the frontier, if not the Self. And if the Self is known, what is left to do? I've invested so much of myself into this underground civilization that I'm getting buried. It's a constructed reality where only personalities that are constructed can thrive. Persistent ignorant fallacy of nested egos, only through death will you be humbled. John, you are incapable of truly leading this thing, bringing it further out and up, rather than closer to it's end. Zhe, I know you're tired, but you still need to uphold your role, otherwise it will all crumble on you. Derek, chill the fuck out, chill the fuck out, chill the fuck out, cause if you don't, it proves that you don't know what you're doing ether... I call for a full leadership upgrade.

45 yards and he had to move faster than the act of thought. He took one step off the most direct path to her, craned his neck slightly, and saw the corner of her shaved head. At this, there was another high-pitched scream that shook the cells of all it touched, unleashing deamons into the ether that had been trapped in the genetic soul cage of humanity since the meta-alchemical invocations of pre-history. In response - the sound of guns being cocked rippled through the law enforcement ring of the manadala. Both rings of indie and corporate media took notice, sharpening the focus of all those viewing; present there on the street, present on their handehelds or home terminals, even those outside the present, watching the re-broadcast archives for the first time.

A passive male, Exp: 23326, SP: 2370, HP: 2540, P.Atk: 1168, M.Atk: 801, RunSpd: 160, Atk.Range: 40 Group leader: Binder (73)

What are you doing?

It was so surprising Aum almost stopped dead in his tracks. The whisper in his mind spoke to him directly. Feeling within it the fear and surprise of being caught in a criminal act. He knew his actions were noble, and redoubled his own focus to be the first through the time-space tear. With each shamanically elongated foot step forward, he saw her planted seed vision of the end of this performance, somewhere within the crystal core of the clouded mind at the centre. With love, Aum fought against this end, gearing up to dodge and outrace speeding bullets.

I will allow you to approach as you are guided by the Siddhas. But don't you dare... don't you dare try to stop me... don't you dare try to save me...

Aum responded this time, and was surprised at the anguish which poured out of him, 'What are you doing Cat!?' With 30 yards left it was all he could muster, all he could say, and not trip on his own feet, like a manic track and field blooper. Regaining his full focus Aum gracefully ripped through the outer mandala ring of confused onlookers. Three more strides and he would find himself past the circle of personal media and inside the much more dense indie media sphere. He pushed on with no anchored end vision available for viewing, remixing or hijacking.

This is none of your concern. Please stay out of it Aum. Do not interfere.

‘I can’t do that.’

Two more strides.

You can’t rescue me – or rescue this world.

‘Yes I can.’

One more.

No you can’t.

‘Just watch me,’

Like always, he learned as he went. And as he cracked the indie shell, he briefly found himself getting shot by the techno-augmented hybrid minds eyes that managed to scope him in the darkness. In mid-stride, beyond time, he learned he could circuit-bend most of the DIY gear in the indie sphere; short out cameras, erase magnetic tapes, suck rechargeable batteries dry, by merely identifying what year they were made. It became no better a capture and live feed broadcast than shaky ufo sightings, or even bigfoot footage. The real time audience asked, was this real? Or somehow constructed within secret basement digital labs, as mind viri with paranoid hidden agendas embedded, or as media pranksterism, for busting ads and banksters, still yet to synthesize the poignant truth it was uncovering.

As he lept over the last DIY pup tent, housing a steam powered generator, with octopus limbs crawling out from under the tarp - backups for solar powered portable harddrives - his flying flow became focused on the next layer. He resigned to release his hold on the hacked stop button, and many caught it, paying attention and piqing the interest of those on outskirts, like a comet shot through the atmosphere. To those who were searching and seeking the newest, rather than hocking their data-wears and transparent one-off manufacturing, this was it: the new mystery to post about first, the story to break first. And his landing in the corporate media circus ring, with only a toe drag for balance like an inverted dolphin fin, was fully captured and multiplied throughout the 2.0 social blogosphere instantly.

With his next step forward, he glanced up and saw eyes shut, cross-legged, gas can up with one hand, gun to temple with other, officers beginning to move in, guns holstered, yelling. It was silent though, and within that he heard:

You will not reach me, unless you display your siddhis. Otherwise I will take your life from you, with mine. I will burn you with the electronic sun, throw your remains in the sky's ocean, and eradicate every seed you have, before it hits the ground.

The phrase was no longer spoken by Cat herself, it was the other voice that emerged. Moving only slightly beyond incoherent code words from that deep space of self-identified darkness, it lacked humanity, and thus was empty. Within his next step he reflected only compassion, patience, and love for Cat, sending out a lifeline from his heart to someone who was lost, deep inside her creative mandalic trance, unconscious of the level in which she worked.

Aum galvanized the attention and belief of the still small viewing audience, local and non local. He remembered the location of Denise's broadcast table, which here, was 10 strides ahead and was simply a holographic table of projected light, a mere reference point for the blonde casted actor broads and their interviewees, to be superimposed with the digital imagery of a physical looking object in the highest floors of the corporate media towers.

There was an overlap about to happen as he approached the "desk," with the indie sphere pointing into the corporate sphere from outside of it; a portal to hijack the minds locked into the mainstream mono-culture broadcast. Then a greater light entered his minds eye. From it, the global map emerged and he saw the signal of each prankster, Riddle entrained or not, ready and waiting, live in their basement media stations, like a battalion of insects ready to go after the last lumbering mammoth. He laughed, 'This too, will be fun.'

Still improvising, he asked himself, 'Okay, how am I going to catapult off a table that is not really there; an object whose source is lost in feedbacking technology and constructed imagination? How is something that is imagined, brought into physical manifestation?'

Animated LED patches beamed past him like a runway at night and the imagined desk got closer. There was a voice inside his mind - his, but not. It was like a door in his unconscious opened up to let in a greater stream of influence, giving him his answer. *Faith and practice, belief and focus,* it said. And Aum added to it, in co-creative dialogue, concentrating now more than ever on increasing those four things.

'And knowing…' he began, as he intentionally raced directly toward the death mask still being interviewed by Denise, who spoke to the television audience, "The work that I create is different than this." Aum could hear him say.

'...that it is not about the artist...' Aum continued to focus on his mantra dialoge, as the media streams were about to cross for total protonic reversal.

"What *I* do is something *beyond* post-Dada, *beyond* the anti-art of the Fluxus moment, and even *beyond* the non-linear improvised Happenings of the new media hippies, into something brand new, yet still linked to the historical art gallery allegory as well as the freedom found within Duchamps toilet."

Aum could hardly believe his ears.

'...but about...' Aum thought, concentrating even harder as absurdity was delivered directly to the confounded flatlanders.

Two more strides to the desk.

In the darkness men with sleek blazers and reflective jumpsuits with electronic corporatized eyes began to take notice. One-two. Aum lept up and the streams crossed, homebrew and corporate.

'...the art.'

And he stomped on a physical desk, which was placed there for the one millisecond that Aums foot planted on it, structuralized light, like everything, he front flipped parkour-style over the costumed death mask and some crass basement hacker animated a long brown log landing on the costumed artists head. An additional hacker saw it and quickly flipped the signals, so the indie stream was broadcast as the mainstream, from the news studio towers. In the post-hockey living room celebration, everyone in the nation saw Aum shit on the performance art interview. A cracked intuitive collaborative indie cheer rumbled the nation, stabilizing global platetectonics.

"This is pure anarchy in comparison," The death mask said, log on his head.

"Um, I thought Duchamps fountain piece was made with a urinal, not a toliet?" Denise asked.

"No Deniese, it was a toilet."

"Okay Bob. I'll take your word for it, you are the expert here."

"Thank you," he looked at the camera and smugly smiled.

In the broadcast booth Conner interjected, "Uh Denise, it looks as though they've sent in some kind of special ops unit. What's going on now? Can you get a shot of the action for the viewers at home?"

"I haven't seen anything yet Conner, no special Ops unit."

"What just flipped over your friend?"

"Pardon me?"

"Ugh. Hmmm..." he chuckled, now seeing the shit hack in-studio, breaking his ultra professional tone, "How's your friend doing?"

"Happy to share my art with channel 5 and it's viewers Conner," said Bob.

I destroy this seed... Single action, she cocked the hammer of the Beretta 92, death 5lbs closer. Again, it was a different voice.

'No!' Aum was almost there.

Every eye was trying to focus on this mysterious ninja moving through the darkness, dodging each viewable angle, dancing and flying through the pockets of empty space where no one looked, each camera tried to get a lock on him, getting only limbs, gesture, or wind from wings, all cameras except for one. With only three strides left in the corporate media sphere, one last camera man, oblivious to the new wave, continued to point at the mandala's centre – a opportunity for live editors, corporate and inde, to cut back and forth between camera angles for a dramatic broadcast effect. The non-local audience was instantly hooked on this new style of reality, playing safely on a television screen.

The cameraman intuitively felt the amped gaze coming from behind him, and still pointing at the centre, took one step too many into Aum's intended trajectory. As he magnetically swam ahead, near invisible, buzzing out gear and pulling himself forward like a spider, this man became a stone in Aum's river. Akido-like, Aum extended his arm long, connecting his right elbow with the man's left shoulder, then, with thumb down, curved it around the front of the mans chest to grab his outside shoulder. He latched on and yanked himself forward, spinning the man counterclockwise, his camera with him. Like two gears of a mechanism, Aum spun clockwise. He strode forward, his left foot, planted, and dropped his left shoulder. The cameraman was in shock, and his only reaction was to continue to record. Graciously, as they spun, he captured a full detailed sequence of Aums face. Feeling the electronic burn of the camera 12 inches from his nose, Aum pushed his own rotation to get out of this last lens, capturing the first solid picture of him. He already felt his face being dissected, remixed, cross referenced, and analysed by both humans on the other end of the machines, and the machines on the other end of the humans. It was instant fame, some viewers even linking back to the face they saw during the broadcast hockey game. It felt like acid rain on his face as his pixels skittered throughout the data clouds and splattered across the planet. In this however, he begun to see the performance art.

With his left hand following his right he batted the camera out of the man's hands, continuing with the momentum he rotated his hips back leading with his right foot, planting it as he released his grip on the surprised stone man, Aum threw his arms into the air and down, leaping over the police car barricade, feet in the air as a no hands cartwheel.

"So ugh… Denise? Is this now a movie set? Or…"

"…Um let me ask Bob. Bob?"

"I destroy this seed!!..." Cat screamed it loudly enough that all cameras quickly refocused on her, though it was the other voice that spoke. The crisp visual data of Aum that recently starburst nearly vanished, now a living spark within the collective imagination.

'Siddihs are visible!! Do not take her. Don't be a martyr!'

There was no answer. It hurt his heart and made it harder to continue to run at his top speed. However as he continued Aum found that at this edge there was a brand new space because of what he had witnessed earlier, new and inspired fuel within him. The tying goal to stun the crowd, and the skill to move millions, viewed in person, pushed the engines of heaven even further, because that was what it was meant to do. His speed was so great at this point there was no potential for acrobatics, only to outrace the attention of a nation and he was already past the police sphere. How? He didn't know. Maybe it was the energy of this new inspiration or maybe because they went for a coffee break, maybe because in this ring there was the most fear, or maybe cause they were just trying to contain the situation. Maybe they were just waiting for leadership.

With eyes closed, Cat moved the gun from her temple to point it at Aum, racing past a handful of officers towards her. A shot fired would put a bullet through his heart. And he ran faster, feeling the gaze of millions on his tail.

'Cathrine,' spoke softly in his mind.

This fully and truly awakened her from her trance.

Her eyes opened, one last gasp pushed her finger to pulled the trigger, and heart and nerves meshed and pulsed the muscle in her hand to move the gun down, in reaction to the reaction, infinitely battling and echoing away, though it was all simultaneous. She had poured enough gasoline over herself that it had spread out into it's own inner mandalic ring, which caught the bullet between Aums feet. The puddle caught it's spark too, and now the flames joined the race, licking Aums sneakers that kicked up the loose fuel.

He connected eyes with her.

'Cat… what is all this?'

The shot triggered many others, and a police crossfire began.

I flew too close to the sun, as many have. And I fell, as many have.

Most took cover, some continued to shoot, guns or cameras.

Though I see your endurance to shoulder the world is everlasting.

As each camera caught a quick glance of him, she, in a fully awakened state, transformed each one into a dream-soul anchorpoint, external of Aum himself. One by one, camera by camera, she remixed his visionary reality, detaching his core from the global grid, attaching each camera to his spirit hand clutching each rip at the far end of each non-locally cast soul-line, reversing the broadcast signal and funneling in the adrenaline and fear around the continent onto the street.

As she did this a switch turned on in his eyes and suddenly there were streams of black plasma shooting into the air, out of every camera; like floating blobs evolved into black rivers. Every set of eyes behind the spider web of cross hatched camera angles saw the truth, and the unconsciousness poured out from each lens onto the performance stage.

'Look at the scope of this work sweet friend, why hold so tightly to the imagined ending?"

You don't understand – I have to – for the greater good... The greatest good.

'No, I don't understand, what it is you'll accomplish with this act of self immolation.'

Now sneakers dripping wet, the flames attached to his feet. The bullets still flew behind him, like buzzing flys, and the cameras and scopes still tried to catch him like the flood lights of a prison break and shoot him with the erupting sewers, a layer of black waves behind the flames, and he still raced towards the meditating woman in front him, who was more serene than a placid glass lake, reflecting it's surrounding nature. 'I can still save you, you know,' he said, a handful of strides from her.

You will never understand if you save me from this end. Only in letting me go, will you truly know; will there truly be transformation.

Their first dance flashed in front of his eyes, their shamanic healing performance, both so tiny compared to this moment.

'You have shown me so much.' The wall of flame and wave behind him grew higher, so sprinting was still necessary.

And there is more to see dear one, but now it is your time to show many others, as you do.

He conceded, to her request, one stride away, though it was like sandpaper inside his chest, wrapping his heart, finally feeling in his lungs how far he had come.

He touched his heart centre with his hand, 'Fly in spirit then, and with purpose.' He crouched down in stride, 'Here and everywhere. Fully manifested,' and he kissed her on the top of the head, kissed his hand, vibing with his heart pulse, and touched the top of her head. With his fingertips he could feel her crown blossoming with a thousand lotus petals, as he let her go. The fire came and each of the black waves poured onto her strong soul petals and instantly evaporated into white light and steam, and he sped on, through the mandala, outracing the flames, past the police, past the corporate media, past the indie media, past the gawking onlookers, and onward still.

"I am going to New Eden!" He heard her shout. And in her voice, the flapping of wings, like a thunderbird phoenix shaking the world and all who heard it, to their core. Within it strength, dedication and sacrifice. The flames then took her life.

Chapter Ten

They were in box seats.

The third period had just begun.

He handed her a copy of H+ Magazine and said, "Page 32; the feature article. I don't even know how you got me on the cover."

She took it from him, flipped to the article and saw a few of the photo's she had submitted.

"It's the first copy," he added, "They'll be on news stands tomorrow."

She read:

The Three Pillars of Gridline and the Riddles Beyond
by Jennifer Leatherbee

Out of mysterious origins far deeper than the cloak and dagger world war underworld of the founding of IBM, the newest project from Gridline Communications has leapt into the lives of many, engineering the miracoulous, and blossoming inspired awareness. Bringing a new consciousness into existence are three multigenerational characters, strongly bonded in ethos, skill set, and ethics, who over the last decade, have taken a stand for the values being trampled on by contemporary corpratism and its structural backbone of the military industrial complex.

The founders of Gridline Communications are a cybernetic engineer named Daniel Tide, a genetic programmer named Ezekiel

Magnum and a wholistic network designer, psipunk wunderkind, named Jonathan deGryder. These three make up a small team of inventers who, by breaking all the rules, make the world a better place. Their business: to dissolve the medium of big business. And it all started with selling a unique App on a 2.0 website.

"All artists must be cyber artists."

With simple beginnings Gridline Communications began 10 years ago by offering up a new piece of software called FreeMedia. This program adaptively hacked and dismantled all DRM content controls as well as all purchasing security, freeing the movement of all source content.Kept notably underground, FreeMedia pillaged all secure servers that housed apps and software, movies, music, games and books. It cut through the code and control and it all became free. The greater social contemplation that arose from this project was that it allowed consumers to see the same rules of society structuralize a fluid pool of collective mind into something as solid as the concrete we walk on everyday.

With the FreeMedia project, Gridlines intention was to fundamentally change the practice of creating and producing art itself. In a brief conversation Daniel Tide said that, "all artists must be cyber artists," demanding that all cultural creatives looking to share their work, practice futurecasting. In essence, develop eyes that use intelligent foresight to look into the digital platforms which will frame their artwork; whether music, film, image, literature, games or programs themselves.

deGryder added, "FreeMedia allowed us to see the true platform and failing nature of contemporary media consumerism: anything you can imagine, instantly. So, as an antidotal practice, it becomes more about quality control, intention, divine purpose, higher muse, and open channel rather than executing another shitty fad that's ultimately fleeting and useless. The real question becomes: How do you engineer enduring longevity in a culture that is diametrically opposed to it?"

Further breaking down notions of capture, copy and sample, even download, remix, re-upload, or sold upon upload, Tide continued, "We wanted to bring awareness to this extended creative medium, having it become an immediate consideration in the artistic act, as all rights and ownership of digital content, corporate or independent, started to become lost in a deceptive mask of host-site legalese. And by ensuring availability and total freedom of content, this software drastically brightened the interwoven tapestry of the communal hyper reference. Something more true to the mediums history."

deGryder continued, without pause "And extended out even further: an apt insight on what aspects of our digital lives, our conversations and activities, are not just observed by corporate entities, but by law, actually owned."

The next level of the project, released mere months ago, was called FreeData. More akin to a burning arrow than a firewall, FreeData is a piece of software that uses an IP plug-in filter which embeds all outgoing data with a tracking signal. Subversively meant to infiltrate all DHS (Department of Homeland Security) and DSAC (Domestic Security Alliance Council) databanks and alerts the user of the moment and context in which their data becomes part of a profile under surveillance, whether you're a member of the Raging Grannies or the Church of Stop Shopping.

"All surfaces must speak intelligently"

From the realm of historic cyberspace into that of our real neighborhoods, streets, schools and homes, many of us have found a glistening new immersive sheen with Gridlines nanotech quartz glue, or N-Glu. Not since the smart phone has a product caused profound shifts in how we see the world, as it allows any surface, private or public, to become a customizable interactive touchscreen. "All surfaces must speak intelligently," geneticist Ezekiel Magnum once said, a notorious Ad-creep hacker and former Adbusters contributor. Clear of the chains of big bucks and corporate boardrooms, N-Glu has eventually found it's way there, but only after a light speed growth path beginning from extremely creative roots, and an intentional seed.

Don't know what I'm referencing? Let me fill you in: N-Glu was first sold in a spray can, solely in a handful of remaining independent community mom-and-pop hardware stores – "an independent symbiotic network which," notes deGryder, "had to be actively sought out and developed." N-Glu was thus adopted and adapted earliest by the street: graffiti and hip-hop culture. Interactive motion graphics meshed seamlessly within classic full wall tags, quickly evolving into fully collaborative remix or combat canvases; the building owners even responding with ecstatic applause, that the original wall surface was always kept only a click away.

Rather than kept underground, it was as if Gridline mapped out the street level trail of N-Glu to the top of innovation mountain, revitalizing community bonds and grass roots economic prosperity, before they allowed the intake of corporate dollars and shareholders to influence product development.

The influence has no doubt been minimal as it is still sold with adhesive A/C cord and wifi circuit patch included with the spray can itself, just needing to be stuck on and sprayed, plugged in, and re-programmed from the server templates.

Make no mistake, the Gridline team are a garage-band of makers and alpha nerds of omega proportion.

"All bodies must vibrate with hyperflesh."

A master of bio-integration, deGryder is a true bionic man. At 19, after blowing out his ear drums in front of a wall of poorly sound checked raver bass bins, he invented the first pair of digital ear drums. deGryder went under Zeke Magnum's knife - who became a genetic programmer after a accomplished carrer as a trained brain surgeon - to directly implant Daniel Tide's micro engineering e-drum handiwork.

His ears now use a digital/analogue tympanic membrane that organically pulses the hammer, anvil and stirrup, the spiral cochlea, and micro fibers of auditory nerves that head to the brain. Diagnosed as clinically deaf, deGryder can now switch his digital ears between the in-ear microphone, satellite radio feeds, concert sound system (if sending the signal over wifi), or even take classic phone calls directly to his ears.

"He lost his hearing at our first event, so it was the least we could do," said Tide.

"Many many mistakes were made," added Magnum, "This is the least of which. Fortunately it included gates of reprimand with opportunity for karmic rebalance, and continued practice."

As it turns out, the event called Full Spectrum One, was also the location of the first New Eden suicide, committed by Magnum's wife, Anna. *(Continued on pg 2-36)*

"You edited it." Jenn stated, her heart breaking.

No, it was fully rupturing.

Over the course of her brief time with John she had never heard the story of Ezekiel's wife, and doubted that many had.

There was an old picture posted in the article of Zeke, Anna and Daniel, smiling: innocent and youthful. Anna held up the ace of spades, and all three stood in front of a cube van, giant black spade printed on the side: Ace Landscaping. Jenn's soft lips whispered, "Fuck," in shock. Anna was so beautiful. They were all so beautiful.

John sighed heavily, "A last slingshot..." He was watching the game, not paying direct attention to her review.

Jenn asked him, "Did Zeke and Dan okay this?"

He responded, "Open honesty must lead the dive into exponential quantum growth. The only choice is to align with the deepness."

She followed his gaze and saw www.gargantuan_artist_manufacturing_encorporated_by_suzie.org. flashing on the hockey arena screens.

"…launched," John said.

* * *

It was like a star had just exploded, and within the spiraling black hole of spirit there was the roar of a car engine. Tires screeched next to him as he continued to run; caught in a holding pattern Aum didn't know what else to do but continue sprinting. The car door swung open and a rock concert seemed to explode out, the music was cranked to eleven, reaching for every gap of silence in every person put on pause, as if the sound consciously penetrated the concrete and tarred all the glass of downtown, seeking out every eardrum and mind that had been silenced in the vacuum as the shooting stopped but the fire continued to burn - even the global environmental ecology had calmed, as if to take notice and mourn.

Streennngth! The strength of many to crush who might stop me! My strength is in numbers, and my soul lies in every one.

The potentials were harshly flattened and shredded and shocked back down into three dimensional space with distorted guitars and the unapologetically fist-in-face masculinity of 90's power metal.

“Get the fuck in here!” Came a growl as the car slowed just enough for Aum to jump in. He slammed the door of the black muscle car behind him, the engine revved into a higher gear, and tires squealed as the car peeled away from the scene.

“What the fuck do you think you’re doing!” Another growl – right in his ear this time. Aum opened his mouth but paused, to intake the smoky leather interior and adjust to the sheer loudness of the wall of sound he found himself inside of, he tried to speak but nothing came out. This was followed by an even more shocking punch in the face.

“Wake the fuck up!”

Aum shook his head in shock.

“You just love fucking things up sooo much don’t you!” Another punch to the face. His whole body flailed in further shock, but in that, he found his voice.

“Geez Derek, I thought we were done fighting.” A third punch hit him in the check bone, the hardest yet and he found himself running towards unconsciousness, thinking, ‘What a metalhead…’

It was black. But the funny thing was that she was still there. In his heart and mind, right there with him, to be observed, and observed being observed; as if, in those few moments of Nike-invoked mastery the satori was so deep that a practice field opened up, a plane of being that resonated beyond death.

A fresh breeze of dreamsphere touched his face. Aum lifted his head, opened his eyes, and saw a broad river in front of him. He looked down, realized he was crouching and balanced on a single boulder at the edge of a jetty, reaching half way out into the river. He closed his eyes again and gulped down a breath of the clean air that the river brought into the city, as if it was his first. Aum’s ears perked up, hearing the audible sound of the slow moving river, coming from the natural layout of the stone bed directly in front of his toes.

His memory slowly retuned. As visions seeped back in of a rainy park and a tatooed Demona, of Zeke’s genetics lab and the tower battle, the hockey game and now Cat’s body aflame, his frontal lobe exploded in mental exhaustion. It cried out and he let the river take the memories with it’s babble. The sound, the wind, and the immensely powerful force of the rivers momentum gladly relieved his mind of the woe and tension he carried.

Aum balanced there minute upon minute, the same stance as the pre-showdown tower top ledge, toes griping stones, and as white wisps whipped past his head, he surrendered all achievement totally, concentrating entirely on the exchange with this great river spirit and it's healing power. He was relieved to be recognized as something so very tiny in the grand scheme of nature's body being.

Suddenly, in Aum's body, the rivers energy collected, as deep as his cells, locating his furthest edges past the public meme media barrier, within the obsessive collective gaze he had just assisted in transforming, out racing bullets and flame, and it all moved to the pit of his stomach. Somewhere in his mind he could almost hear the *ding* of a microwave. His eyes opened wide, in surprise, as he vomited black bile for minute upon minute, feeling the deeper social upheaval it was connected to.

The water took what was left. Rinsing face and skin, near exaustion, he returned to the path. Each tweet, each breath, each riverside step and the crunch underneath each foot, confirmed her presence and their shared space.

Her loving wings spread out before him. The vast expanse of her new quantum soul communicating with his, through the pattering leaves in the trees, the birds flying by and the crawling insects marching to the beat of the cosmic pulse, she was there, in all of it, talking to him. It was her deepest soul expressed in a cherished celebratory communion of simply being able to connect in this way, and be in a space together this way. In the physical, and beyond it, simultaneously. His soul danced along side hers sending a pulse back through the waves of sound within the world around him, a symphony of love beams holding up the veil which became more and more beautiful knowing what held it together.

The mystical dynamic of the collaborative feminine was something he could now see easily. Whether near or far, whether student with weighty baggage, strikeforce defense engineer, shape shifting lessons planer or shamaness-lead group healer, in dream and soul this presence spoke directly, but in mind and waking life, through all of them. And it was now she who gently massaged his third eye, his crown, his jaw, his forehead and eyebrows. *Jerome*, he heard her voice, and he awoke from Sivasana, lying on the grassy coastal bank, waves licking the cold bare beaches and the clouded sky. The ocean tunneled out in endless perspective.

"Here I have something for you," he smelt cigarette and leathers.

"Holy fuck dude."

His eyes focused on a piece of tree bark in front of his eyes, and on it, with black sharpie written:

Continue..continue.. It is your divine plan indeed. Thanking you...your Spirit so rich and full of honest intention.

"This one," Aum felt where her fingertips once touched it, touching them now, "I know deeply." And she danced for him, elegantly, colorfully, in his minds eye. "Wow. Am I really awake?"

Derek raised a clenched fist, Aum snapped back fully and Derek started walking, "There is much yet to do Saoshyant. It's time to go."

Still inspecting the bark Aum replied, "To Gridline?" His fingertips buzzed.

"I assume you already have your pass."

"Yes," Aum pulled out the flier he received from Daniel at the Hockey game, remembering in a flash, his path froom it to the present, "I guess it's just the deletion sequence now," he mumbled to himself, beginning to catch up to the Dragonkeeper.

After a twenty-minute drive, down freeways, round hills, above rivers and under a bridge, they found an old harbour-front community which had been transformed into a bustling chic urban hub of neo-yuppie hippies. At its focal centerpiece, Aum saw the truly advanced architecture of a pagoda vibrational structure, the physical building itself was pretty nice too.

"It used to be a craft brewery. It went under. It took forever to get the stench out, and rebuild deeper than barley and hops." After parking and approaching, Aum could see the ground floor had glass walls: dark on the street and with lights on in the space he could see inside. There were hardwood floors and white walls - it looked like an art gallery space - however there were mirrors on the adjacent wall and a yoga class was happening inside.

'Hmm that's interesting,' he thought. The connotations of a yoga class within this street level art gallery display space moved through his mind, spirit, and his own practice.

'Street front asanas...'

There were people of all ages involved. There were some wide-eyed ones that looked to be in their teens; absorbing a multigenerational class room that was not typical for their school-age. There was a group of older and beautiful greying ladies, practicing picturesque poses of wholistic health. There were lanky, black framed glasses wearing desk jockeys sweating, stretching their hands and fingers with bakāsana, reversing their daily purpose as digital interface metacarpus. There was a weightlifting bronzed beach beefcake and slim tan-brown blonde creature next to him. They seemed to be stereotypes; caricatures out of a lifestyle advertisement, outsiders among these regular folks who weren't yoga addicts, weren't there to put on a show, and certainly weren't there for a gym-like work out.

Maybe these two were next level mannequins, being paid to catch eyes outside of the display case. He only saw two lululemon logos, which heightened the believability of the pretty cover yoga caricature, thus the gateway of accessibility. Or maybe they were simply there by clue and choice, to learn the deeper art of it all. The class focus, Aum could see, was on learning a deeper body based philosophy, practiced in it's fullest 4,000 year old understanding: it was more akin to a dojo than a fitness centre.

Underneath the branded pretty cover there was one man with his shirt off, practicing, covered in tattoos. Sanskrit passages and Om symbols intertwined across his shoulders and his back. His bulk was beyond tank-like. Over 300 pounds easily. Considering he reached well beyond 6ft in height, it could have been much more than that. He looked exactly like the drunk dad at the hockey game, 'Naw, couldn't be,' Aum thought. Either way, he could not pull off a graceful maneuver if his life depended on it. Because of his girth and demeanor his lack of balance threw the entire class off, the flows were shitty and totally disconnected. However, when he did find his breathe and follow it moving through his entire body, the whole room felt it, if not the entire building, or even neighborhood.

Looking deeper into the ink, Aum could see a unique karmic history, and that the big man had received all his tattoos in India upon instruction from an enlightened master. He was the worlds last true Yogi, just starting on his path. As he gazed upon the inked mantras, Aum found himself immersed in a memory:

"Hmmm – do you feel that?" She looked up at the sun, and then to Aum. Suddenly she busted into a perfect wheel pose. "There we go," she groaned slightly, the sun shining in her face and on her exposed belly button, the green grass between her fingers and her eyes imagining the western mountains, just out of sight.

"At least for a few full breaths…"

She easily maneuvered out of it, flipping back to wild thing, 3 legged dog, then downward dog, and of course going the other way into another wheel, closing her eyes this time. Aum joined her on this one, though moving from bridge into wheel. He set himself up so they could see eye to eye, and the world upside down together.

"Ritambhara tatra prajna," Aum said. She opened her eyes, smiled and winked at him, then he one up-ed her by lifting his leg, Eka-Pada-Chakrasana.

"You gonna try Viparita Chakrasana?" she asked.

"From one-legged-wheel!? Shit no!" He switched legs and they flowed through a couple more moves together in the grass. It was a dance that nearly reached a martial arts swiftness.

The path was infinite. With each stretch, he taped into a bigger vision. With the grass tickling his feet his imagination reached even deeper into his cellular structure, shinning with love, feeling his entire community, his entire family. With his body he could clear the network pathways of communication, reconnect or infuse them with energetic flow, strengthen nodes or re-energize geometrical structure. No different than intentional prayers, he could connect to specific friends and promote their health with the body-mind strength and balance required to fully release into ushtrasana, or within the antenna-like embodiment of vasasdasana pose.

"You're back on track," She said smiling, and the memory faded.

He forgot that at one point, before returning to her parents office, Jenn did her yoga teacher training.

"Crazy. I forgot about that day," Aum said out loud. To share his memory and insight he said to Derek, "Once your actions are aligned, they stay aligned, and it's only the depth of your understanding that changes."

But Derek was gone.

Aum looked back and saw the class was just ending.

They were trying out a plethora of inversions: shoulder stands, head stands and hand stands. Some against the wall, some with chairs and blocks, some free form. Then he spied the teacher giving adjustments. It was Ezekiel.

‘Of course.’ He laughed and shook his head. Zeke noticed Aum and bowed authentically. Aum ventured inside to connect with Zeke after class, check in and see how his day had been since the tower top battle and maybe even do a stretch or two. But by the time he found the correct door, and hallway, and studio, class was over. Lights were off and nobody was there. Aum was left to explore Gridline on his own, but first, he flipped on the lights, found a mat, and did a couple flows.

* * *

“So what is the Riddle exactly?”

Her business jacket had large lapels, and her blouse underneath was loose and low cut. Her hair was tied up with chopsticks, accentuating her large hoop earrings and lipstick. With rolled up sleeves she pulled out a carry-all that wasn’t quite a briefcase, and wasn’t quite a purse. Taking notes on her large format handheld, and recording the audio feed at the same time she added, “It’s about time I asked, hey?”

“This is for the book project?”

“Yes.”

“Then you’re asking the right person, at the right time.” He responded quickly, sipping his hi-test coffee, as his presence moved inside an untold amount of non-local space at once. A couple walked past the Gridline coffee shop with hockey jerseys, both of them excitedly shouting out their conversation loudly without knowing it, at the same time as investigating each detail as if it was there first visit. A wide smile spread across her face, spread wider than ever.

“The Riddle is a website,” he stated simply, continuing to peck at both hand embeds, eyes jumping back and forth between screen read outs.

She laughed, “That’s it?”

“Yup,” he grinned handsomely, glancing up at her for just a heartbeat, then added, “A slightly deeper answer is that it’s a website that exemplifies a collaborative festival-esque meta-permaculture model and applies it to the larger system of culture that birthed it, moving both forward and backward in time.” He looked at the glowing LED light on her handheld that showed audio was being recorded. “That’s the answer you want, right? A good sound byte? I explain it differently depending on who I talk to. For example, I tell my old world accountant it is simply the former, a website. To keep it legit and subversivley operational." After a gnashing finger frenzy he was about to take another sip, but then dove in further to explanation, "If I described it in it's technical and conceptual entirety to the pillars of corporate monoculture as a viral economic model based in alternate reality gaming with interactive smart cloud media as the central binding medium, with the purpose of transforming human civilization embedded within it's evolutionary existence, it sort of breaks down the ground on which it stands - the dish in which it was grown."

It tok her a moment to recuperate and respond, "I see. That line immediately gives away the whole story... the story of the mysterious fungi mold," a smile crept across her face. He laughed, smile lines as deep as ravines, "Fuck, you're hilarious," His smile matched hers, and his quick mind could certainly match her linguistic weave. "That's precisely it. It gives away it's antibiotic power and purpose, and it no longer functions in alignment with it's original intention, becoming easily contextualized as a social hobby, video game meme, or extracurricular past time."

She continued in summation, trying to confirm her own understanding, "Make up your own goals, and it responds. Creative energy goes in, cultivated for the purpose of your own choosing: advancement in the arts, in spiritual learning, or even business, and growth comes out. But it's no longer 'business'..."

He just continued her thoughts where they left off, with no space in-between, "...it's the meta-cognative social-structural replacement of 'business'."

Her breath was crisply taken away, "That still freaks me out you know. But it works like that right? That tight?"

"That's one of it's practical applications, yes, to structuralize sub threshold intuition. It gives functional form and imaginative manifestation opportunity – support –" He simplified it with the single word and continued, "to the cusp societal solutions being built quicker and faster than ever before."

"Telepathic pre-disaster relief."

"A self governing cultural emergency response. Hope." He finally took his sip, "The collective structures of reality no longer have relevance. The dismantling and collapse of irrelevant institutions reveal a new paradigm of human culture, and whilst ungrounded in history, the entire scope of human knowledge is at our fingertips. With that understanding we've created a space to experiment and develop something new, unseen and yet unknown, when it is most needed. Like I said, the Riddle is website."

She laughed, as if it was all that easily understood.

* * *

"Where you guys headed?"

Either Aum was getting old, or the average age of seekers was getting younger; frizzy hair, large ballcaps and spaghetti legs seemed to be trending.

"Upstairs, to the planetarium, there's an astrophotography demo in 10."

"Shit kid, I thought you were gonna say astrophysics – that's still right on though."

"Totally right on daddy-o, you should come peep it; amp your flex."

"I'd like to, though I'm trying to find this dope pocket here." He showed them his ticket. "Can you adjust my trajectory?"

Aum remembered Trae's words at Full Spectrum, 'Dragon trinity, to the Ferryman, to the Shaman will lead you to the Riddle Solver.' He still had his ticket - his Gridline pass - and as far as he could tell he was not being tailed by ICAARUS.

"Without a doubt double dad," The kid pressed a button in the elevator, laughing, "That's the astrophysics demo there," pointing to the flyer.

"Amazing that you have a ticket to that one," Said the second "How'd you get it?"

"Uhhh… I rolled a golden hockey game." That seemed to be the most straight forward response. The two youngsters then recognized him from the corporate and indie protonic reversal and the whole vibe of the elevator changed; reverence to the point of sprouting wings, in speaking to the most famous performance artist of the day.

Slightly stumbling, "So you've never been to the VisionLEAD Hall? "

"No," Aum responded "I've never been to Gridline before."

"Really!?"

"Never been to the Gridline! Shit – then welcome!"

"No one's offered to show you around?"

"Well the Dragonkeeper delivered me here..." he titled his head, "...I lost him on the way in though, so I've just been exploring on my own."

"What do you think?"

"Thus far it's immaculate."

"Indeed."

The elevator came to a stop, "V-LEAD is the second door on the left. I'm sure you'll hear the crystals singing."

Aum made his exit and the second kid added, "I heard they're testing out the quantum engines tonight."

"Woah – okay. Thank you kindly gentlemen," and he walked towards the room.

"Hey, did you actually outrun fire and bullets?"

Aum stopped, thinking about it for a second, shaking his head a little in surprise, "Yeah. I guess I did." He tried to offer more insight, but there was suddenly an internal eruption of loss. The two youngsters could see this as the door closed, regretting the question, viewing before them not a superhuman, but a human. Then Aum found an insight he could share, polishing their regret into the gratitude that comes with humility, sending it to them as they continued to rise. He held Cat in his grateful heart, and in this presence he found the door to the VisionaryLEAD Hall, hearing the crystal bowls singing and a didgeridoo buzzing.

He entered the room to find some were standing, but most were sitting in a circle on the ground. Aum saw at the front a man played one of those resonating percussive metal spaceships, a hang, and out front, near the circle, a woman was singing, there were a few intoning the bowls and one on the didge. On the walls hung medicine songs; hand woven tapestries produced by the Shipibo. The singing woman smiled to Aum and gestured for him to join the group. A plain clothed elder, she was short and had dark brown skin. She was singing in Spanish or some type of dialect close to it. It was a small group in a small room, less than 20. As he looked for a spot to sit he noticed most people were meditating on her song, though some whispered quietly, some were grabbing cups of water, or finding their seats. The meeting hadn't officially started yet.

In exchange for his ticket Aum was given a paper handout upon entering, a 3 hole punched binder insert, of what looked like engineering diagrams. The linedrawn bodies of men and women were engulfed in a centrifuge of interconnected triangles, hexagons, and torodinal vortexes. Next to it was a depiction of some advanced mudra palmistry which gave intricate descriptions of the energetic points on each hand, male and female. The palms linked up to the metaphysical diagram of the individual feminine and masculine spirit vehicles.

Did these mudras trigger shortcuts for programming the vehicles computer? Or doing a meditation? Or both? His imagination buzzed as he lost the ability to determine what was physical and what was non-physical; what was spiritual and what was technological. He had to find a seat, quickly.

The men and women seemed to have been paired up. There was an empty seat next to a young woman, one of the teens from the yoga class. She was very tall, as tall as Aum, and had long brown hair. She smiled when he crouched down next to her, which revealed beautiful dimples.

"Hi," he whispered.

"Hi," she whispered back. Her eyebrows were thin but were expressively elequant when she talked. He looked at the complex diagrams again, then looked around the room, "It looks like everyone is in pairs, did your partner go to the bathroom, or grab a drink?"

She smiled again, "No, you can be my partner, if you like."

"Uh, okay, cool. That's great." He paused for a moment still whispering, "This is my first time here. I noticed the yoga studio downstairs. You were just in that class, right?"

"Yeah, I was," she was noticeably flattered.

"So yoga, then this?" he pointed to the printed metaphysics map.

"Yes. A solution."

He looked at her inquisitively.

She continued, whispering, "I recently discovered on the spiritual path I've been following, my guru got hacked."

She was another one of those ancients in disguise; far beyond elegant, closer to majestic. Aum said in surprise, "Your guru got hacked?" too loudly, everyone looked at him. "Shit," he whispered.

She simply smiled and continued, “Yeah, the guru I had been aligning my prayers with and devoting my path to, the spaces of soul communion I had been cultivating since a child, was all a manufactured fraud of bankster proportions.” Her expression now full of dismay, Aum saw that her heart was still so broken that it wept. It was an internal discovery held inside her for too long, that she needed to speak out. It was not a point of obsession, but an authentic moment; a wound kept hidden from most, now surfacing within their random and karmic connectivity. Maybe it was all the hip-openers during class, or maybe it was simply the presence of caring gentle whispers.

“In prolonged meditation with the land, searching for New Eden within the solitude of Gaia, Cosmagaia actually, I found a containerless communion with the divine. A present essence and intelligence that came without the myth-based human context embedded within it. It was a deeper truth than I had ever experienced.”

Aum almost fell for her, in her sparkling eloquence, right then and there. She shifted her position however, and he truly saw the youth moving inside her long limbs. Backpack, schoolbooks and large format, though not with her, were nearly attached to her. Aum remembered Stan, from up top, and he better understood.

“What emerged from within myself, emerging from my being within the land is this: there was a human, a master from the east who came to the west - California of course - and a legacy persona emerged from this man, evolving out of the technology based media vehicles of the time; painted portraits, black and white photos, very rare sound recordings, along with a full catalogue of written philosophy and esoterica.”

Impressed, Aum responded, “That’s sounds like an amazing path of study.”

“But it’s not. Legacy personas are inherently attention magnets and ultimately empty vessels for agendas and mind control.”

Astonished, Aum fell in love with the future. This strong and insightful young woman would do much, and does do much.

“The hack, I came to realize, as further insight came to me from the sway of the tress, delivered by the birds and coyotes, was that within these mathematically precise meditative visualizations, as well as structuralized precision based churches and weekly services, was a manipulation deeper than most others, and vastly modernized for the contemporary century."

"Modernized with black and white photos?"

The beautiful indigenous singing became more compassionate and supportive to the pre-space.

"No, the black and white photos support just the single legacy persona," She continued whispering. Even before the formal meditation session. "The heart of this religious legacy system, which, crafted very meticulously, is more resonant than most other organized religions, because of the devotional icons it has referenced, even re-interpreted. It anchors itself in a larger foundation of spiritual history."

"So you feel it's a cult?

"Yes. Congregation members give themselves over so completely in heart mind and body and soul, that the guru, or legacy persona, is all that remains of their personality. Shinning like true human-beings in fullest capacity is so much more than being an empty vessel for an ascended master to speak through, or find embodiment within this world."

Aum was profoundly moved by the wisdom this teen had found.

"The fact that my relatives were sacrificing their lives, their home and food and heath and the overall well being of their family for this path, and guru, activating thousands and thousands of people with their missionary work, under the banner of this scientific spiritual path, and finding only crumbs in return, was in complete discord with the true nature of the iconic pantheon of open energetic windows branded at it's front gate."

"What do you mean?"

He tried to gallop with her clean bright beams of youth, but was befuddled with consternation and mental grit.

"The collection of historic ascended masters the cult had hacked into, along with their legacy belief systems, were remixed, simply as a front, to send to the other side of the veil, the quantum power of human attention. Upon death, or ascension, or maybe even before, there was something else that took control, that corrupted the legacy system of the ascended master and his teachings, moulding, legitimizing and prolonging the hacker's presence and influence, whoever it is, or whatever it is.

"Whether Jesus, Lord Krishna, Moses, Muhammad, or Zoroaster. Hafiz, Gautama, Yasumaro, Confucius or Lao-Tzu, only in scope is the massacre different. How can a true guru reference Jesus, or any of these Masters, and deeply integrate their teachings and message, yet have no compassion for their devotees well being in the world? Is it only through self-sacrifice and death that heaven is reached in the afterlife, and until that time devotion is on trial?"

Aum didn't know, but offered what wisdom he could,"Different fingers on the same hand, two hands of the same body. Do you not think that from that Nth dimensional space, beyond the veil of human dimensional understanding, any of these ascended masters, or even your own guru would not be able to influence, control or allow, all aspect of their presence and reference in this 3D world, choosing it's use for lessons just as we choose our own lessons? To my knowledge there is no program that exists that can hack through that holy Truth, and fully sunder source from source - whether duplicated or cloned, sanctioned or sanctified. However, looking at history in full, it seems to be in our egoic nature to continually try to place a tollbooth inbetween."

"Yes I see thusly," She continued. Her beautiful body containing her beautiful soul located in some other realm o existence, "My eyes have been opened to the atrocities and misuse of spiritual power over the ages. For example Emperor Constantine remixing early Christianity and the Roman Empire into the Holy Roman Empire. No cultural programming of religious belief could be worse than that of the historical use of Jesus Christ and his use as a banner to perpetrate the witch hunts of the European Inquisitions, to eradicating the Mayan and Incan nations, and dominate the original caretakers of northern Turtle Island. It has spread across the planet like a viral human sickness, a sick need, like easy answers and corporatist greed."

In her pain of seeing the world of human truth at too young of an age, Aum looked at her with kindness. "That one, is a riddle requiring more than a single life of contemplation. You've seen less blood and massacre in your lifetime than this 2000 year span of time I do hope." His balloon of sarcasm was gentle, "You are a fresh escapee, of that deep reaching paradox: belief systems that both awaken and imprison devotees. Your understanding has deepened; the basic container in which you place your prayer-full thoughts is full, and spills over. Your devotion is still caught however, in the bigger container which you do not yet see. Your outpouring of guru has set you free, and celebrates your spiritual learning curve," Aum laughed, "They do have the wisdom to do that, Jesus especially. Your leveling up should be celebrated with a self allowed freedom to gaze forward."

"I do see further. I guess my personal path could be a lot worse." She pondered even further, "My friends are good people, who live rightly, and in accord with other systems of belief and spiritual practice without even knowing it. It's just the dogma of the path they have chosen that trips me out. After much investment, I have learned it is not for me."

"And that is all there really is, the continued authentic engagement of learning, upon the divine life path mystery." His eyes widened again looking at the visible engineering schematics of the invisible, "So it is here that you find more integral alignment? A place to begin studying the larger container?"

"It is the earth beneath my feet that tells me this is where I need to be. Here I find more freedom at least. More space. It is that present intelligence I mentioned, more accurately embodied, without the shackles of history. There is less legacy to remix and analyze, thus I can freshly address my own idea of divinity and science and human mythics, interacting even directly with it in the realm of physical reality."

"Ah yes, that deep."

"That deep indeed."

There was a pause and shared exhale that concluded the clearing and solidified the connectivity.

"My names Sophia."

"Aum."

She waited for more, then realized that was his name, "Oh. Wow. That's cool. Thank you for listening Aummmm," she hummed, continuing to do so smiling, a teenager being silly.

"No…" Aum whispered. The medicine song came to a close, "…thank you."

There was an echo of many 'thank you's' that followed his, circling around the room. Aum heard a "Whoa" whispered next to him. He smiled, happy that his soul being could still teach the young ancients ones.

The singer began speaking in Spanish. There was a dark skinned translator who followed in English. Hi accent was thick. Indina, no.

Turkish, “This song comes to you straight from the jungles of South America. It’s a song praying to the spirits to protect this space and it’s inhabitants. Creators, watch over us as we journey closer to your divine presence, as we look inside of ourselves to find our noble and cherished purposes, to come full circle and move forward as star beings.”

As he raised his head, Aum recognized him from Full Spectrum, lighting inscence prayers and being unhappily unplugged. He continued on is own now, “Let us begin with an opening circle of gratitude.” The Turk introduced himself as Macek, and gave thanks for his perfect health. Every member of the circle stated one thing they were happy for; their loving partners, children, abundance, even the weather.

When it got to Aum, he stated, “I have gratitude for the four directions and for my star being that teaches without me, whom I get to learn from as well.” There was only a moment or two, of the group pausing, to try and digest it, then Sophia took her turn, “New friends, and highest divine love.”

Maceks head tilted at the reference to the four directions. Though because he was leading, he refocused his attention on the bigger picture. After full circle, the introduction concluded, and Macek passed out small crystals for everyone to hold. With hooded eyes he watched observantly, allowing each stone to choose the spiritual signature of the preson they found, exchanging the electric signals subtly embedded within their crystalline programming. Macek then went around to each person, conceptually and mathematically mapping in his mind their group evolution and transformation.

“Which one did you get? and you? and you?” His magnetic attention and intense interest verged on terrifying. Macek’s vibe continued to rub Aum the wrong way. He made it to Aum “And you?” His eyes looked as if he hadn’t slept for days.

“This one,” Aum showed him the tiny pebble that made it to him. It was so small he didn’t have a chance of identifying it by sight, asking, “Quartz?”

His brown hair was tied back in a ponytail. His blue and open dress shirt, with white t-shirt underneath, revealed a small circular silver medallion that hung around his neck. With advanced geometries imprinted in the metal, it carried his purpose for living and being like no Christian cross Aum had ever before seen.

"Oooohoho, nope. That's the Iolite. Auspicious," He looked at him with a self-proclaimed mastery, "You're new." Then as deep as his voice would go, nearly threatening him, "This is the last meeting so…"

"I was given an invitation," Aum interrupted, he pointed to the desk.

With an eccentric current now in his eyes, Macek floated over to the woman at the table who showed him the 5x7 flyer Aum had given to her. He floated back to Aum, "I still don't think…"

Intent on participating and learning what he was supposed to in that moment, in the odd situation he found himself in, Aum interrupted him again, "I'm a fast learner."

"Hmmm," Macek looked around the room, quickly counting his students. "Daniel." He look at Aum's hand again. "Iolite."

There were menacing spirals in his eyes as he looked directly at Aum. "Suit yourself young man. Welcome to the last step on the historic esoteric mystery path of the ancient Greeks," he trilled, and continued on to the next person. Aum was beginning to think he actually preferred the chimps at the hockey game to this new age pompous baboonery.

After adequately inspecting the fullest depth of the meta-energy crystal read, Macek removed a lenscap and projected their handout onto one of the walls, beginning a full dive in, "Different than the model of a full-system planetary body, or even the interactive map of tantric sex meridians, these *exact* control sequences must be immaculately followed." He gestured with his hands, talking with them as much as his words, "Else the biological magnetics of your body will not be entrained with Gaia's full physicality. I warn you again, if not followed *exactly* during planetary ascension, you will be left behind; lost to the dimensional fracture of infinite facets." His voice was strong, without compromise, totally righteous in his belief of truth and unflinching in his ability to lead the way for all.

"It's paramount that once you begin, that these exercises are followed twice daily, like medicine. Over the course of my studies and experimentation I've discovered gateways of knowledge that are plugged and dormant, which have been energetically turned off and jammed with metaphysical debris." A sinister expression flashed inside the shadows on his face and he continued emphatically, "These precise algorithmic sequences will cleanse each aspect of the body consciousness, preparing it to vibrate at a level one step beyond what we are used to as a species. This advanced awakening will do no less than signify the new age of human consciousness, and will allow each sun pulse ripping through us to be observable, as well as be an astral pathway to travel upon.

"Ariel will be passing around the last printed official handout, which is the final guideline for optimal dietary needs to be practiced in conjunction with these visualizations; to best connect to the sunlight's fullest thermodynamic movement. It is the same info that has been digitally delivered to you within the past week. I trust everyone has been eagerly receiving these send outs, putting them into practice immediately."

Like school kids, everyone placed this last sheet in their binders. "So now that the full course textbook is complete, it can be gifted to your next of spirit kin, the next student in line for this path.

"This completed tome resonates infinitely in the physical, outside of the ahrimanic corporate grid of influence, only elemental destruction will keep it from new eyes," he said clenching his fist in absolute victory and realized accomplishment. He nearly whispered now, "The newest whistle blower has revealed the next layer of the alien agenda and seamlessly linked it to the political bloodlines and the corporatocracy media stronghold. More so now than ever will each of our thoughts be under surveillance, another reason to follow these guidelines in your quest for total Aryan perfection."

It got really weird, really fast. Aum almost puked at the dip, like he finally realized no matter his intent on engaging with the deepest path of learning, he was still on this man's rollercoaster, where ever it lead.

"As we spread New Eden across the face of the future earth, Vulcan will be…"

Aum snickered, as odd, retro television images quickly came to mind. The outburst surprised even himself. Macek became visibly upset, pausing dramatically, "Even the most green thumbed anthroposophist knows that Roddenberry was infusing pop culture with the esoteric truths of the galactic tabernacle. If only all those Trekies knew that Vulcan is the 7th stage of vibratory resonance of the celestial body on which we now stand, their obsessive sub-culture may prove to be a bit more functional in our new vibration-based society, and no longer pander to the masses as simply costumed kooks."

"Maybe they do know the truth of Vulcan," Aum jabbed quickly.

"One some level. On some level. Surely," Macek responded.

"It's actually Jupiter, Macek," Sophia jumped in. She may not have if Aum had not done so first.

"What's that my dear?"

"Jupiter is next actually, not Vulcan." Sophia repeated, "Round five. The fifth world and emergence of the 6th subrace from the 5th rootrace."

"Thank you Sophia, for your clarity and lift. My most diligent student." He said in genuine appreciation. "You will lead oh so many one soon day." With hooded eyes he stared at her a little too long. Awkwardness began to creep in, "I must have been getting ahead of myself, in my excitement, or advanced practice."

He paced around the room. He was certainly quite high strung for someone who had an advanced meditation practice, "You see, according to the founding theosophical work of Helena Blavatsky in 1888, refined by Arthur E. Powell in 1930, the 6th subrace of the 5th rootrace is defined by Anglo-Canadian, Anglo-American, Anglo-Australian and Anglo-New Zelanders who will possess psychic powers." He continued to talk with his hands, "For this to come about, the pituitary gland and it's extended spirit body will be developed by the absorption of these last technologies you have received here tonight, which will incorporate the additional sense of cognizing astral emotions into ordinary waking consciousness. It is this inherent ability which will redefine the 6th and last subrace of the 5th rootrace as the 6th race itself, and it's new planetary body of habitation, vibrating as Jupiter does, just as our youngest one has signaled for us," he gestured to Sophia. Macek had studied his theosophy, with out a doubt. This drop solidifying his leadership of the group and his intended lesson trajectory for the evening.

"So now tonight, in the wake of all collapsing structures of the 5th race, as symbolic Rome burns off it's last bit of fuel and we witness the total death of our species and all that we know, let us dance with the flames, elevate, and drink of the communal cup that will place our souls within the quantum arms of the divine one. He who controls the wind and rain, the coin and flame, from his abode in the timeless, that dimensional realm we have all only felt, following it's single fleeting drops and drips. Let us now become one with the cosmic ocean."

'Getting weirder,' Aum thought.

"Without fear we will submerge ourselves in the new waters of a fresh planet, a fresh dimensional realm in which we can rebuild an egalitarian utopia, beyond the imbalances of Atlantis or ancient Mars, a reality where compassionate belief and presence directly constructs the bliss-filled world in front of our eyes: Instantaneously." He spoke slowly now, with the airy starry-eyed flourishes of a tan-skinned 6th race Californian. "The formalization of fully present dream-souls inside a collective data set is the fulfillment of the Riddle Solver prophecy. Far beyond the limited scope of resonating magnetism and body-earth energy pulse control, this, is a much deeper realm of existing: the realm of ancient gods and saints and Buddha's, vibrating in the dimensions unseen by uncalibrated eyes."

"But what about activating our individual quantum engines?" Aum asked.

"We will do that. And go beyond." Maceks support team began to pass out cups with what looked like a glistening liquid metal. Four beautiful women in flowing dresses entered the room. On a sedan chair, as if it was an Egyptian pharaoh, or a Roman dignitary, they carried a black cube that looked like obsidian.

Macek continued, "Let us now join those there now, in New Eden, as our spirits fully crossover to the data stream, into the spiritual ecology stored on our solar powered servers, into our collective quantum-box, to be buried deep in the womb of the earth for time immemorial, and leave Rome to burn, leaving behind only madness and ash in the darkness."

"Let's go" Aum whispered to Sophia.

"No. I am meant to be here…"

Aum's eyes went wide as he saw in shock, her determined choice. Maybe she already knew what was on the other side.

Maybe she already knew her role there.

Maybe Cat did too.

"…to re-engage the storage sequence."

"Blessings on your bodisatvic actions and all the youthful wisdom pools you bring here," Aum replied.

He knew he himself wasn't meant to have his soul sucked out of him instantly, achiving certain sainthood. With an honest bow Aum was out of there so fast he actually teleported.

* * *

Jenn had been meeting with John for a couple weeks now. At first she had understood their meetings as source interview material for an article she was writing on the bio-integration of Web 4.0. It evolved further however, developing into the outline of a book on advanced not-for-profit social structure, and now it seemed, she had become the ghostwriter of this charming man's autobiography.

Back at Full Spectrum on the Sunday evening, she had met the digital yogi with the scarab t-shirt in the parking lot, and didn't come to realize the scope of her Dragonrider request until it took them nearly two hours to leave. The man introduced himself as Jason Fairman, and he didn't think anything of the time delay as items came across his path at random - from hard drives, to crystals wands, to jumper cables, to padded envelopes, to a shovel, to what looked like engine parts – it all got loaded in her car. She even patiently helped him find a spot for each item, sometimes wondering if he was an actual crazy person. But that sense of perplexion was nothing compared to the excruciating 15 hour drive, weaving across the countryside, dropping off each item individually.

Over the course of the long silent journey she cycled through the tarot read, over and over and over. Feeling like an impulsive fool, like a control freak, becoming expectationless, finding strong belief in her quest to track down the mysterious deGryder, savoring each moment of it… then again, feeling like an impulsive fool. With each cycle, the inner katharsis went deeper, usually triggered by a memory of Aum. Close to a full tearful breakdown at one point, she spurted out to Jason, "Are you actually Egyptian Jason?"

"No, my genetic ancestry resides in Eritrea."

"Eritrea? …Is that like Narnia?"

He chuckled, "Kind of. It's not quite Egypt, not quite Ethiopia: It's a historic port on the horn of Africa, known for exporting minerals from the rash of mines that cover the countryside." With prosecutorial repartee she eventually, and delicately, brought up deGryder in the conversation. Jason openly shared what he knew. He told her that the Dragonrider sits in the same chair, at the same coffee shop, before every central-core meeting, so he can collect his thoughts, publicly meditate, and ritually dream deeper, as if this spot and time held some kind of gate of inspiration for him. She had told Jason in response to this sharing: "Routine is the foundation of all subroutines," which was one of the many business philosophies of Gridline Communications. When she said it, she could see it didn't ring any bells for Jason, so she patiently explained what the line meant, rather than keeping him in the dark and at an impersonal distance. Jason, not surprisingly, hadn't heard of John's company, only the Centre. No doubt a result of an ongoing impersonal connection with a profound depth of trust in resonant soul presence, more so than anything based in the material physical world. The same connectivity, she noticed, that seemed to permeate all Riddle relationships.

When they made it to the coastal city, arriving at the large harbour front building, Jason humbly mentioned that he had only recently met John in person, receiving his ticket from him the week prior to the festival. Jenn responded by admitting she didn't even receive a festival ticket. Jason's surprised gawking expression only doubled after seeing that John was at the coffee shop, petrol-cash in hand, seemingly expecting hia and Jenn's arrival.

"Beautiful strides. All the deliveries are complete?" John asked Jason.

"Affirmative, including this one," motioning to Jenn. "Your mission?"

"Luminous. Any deviations from the test run of the future casting program?"

"None whatsoever, smooth as silk."

"Spectacular."

Jason interjected, "If you'll both excuse me, I need to prepare for tonight's meeting," then looked at Jenn, "Thank you for the ultra timely transport."

She smiled, "Thank you for my delivery," and as he walked away she stood looking over at the Dragonrider.

Dealing with the smoky Dragonkeeper was nothing compared to this: his presence was that of a mountainous cliffface, looming, endless, vast, as if being this close to him was just as perilous. If a strong gale pushed him off the cliffface, no doubt he would instantly sprout wings and begin to fly without a second thought. Feeling like she was under the single lens of an electron microscope, she knew he could see everything inside her, everything she wanted to hide. Of course it was all those things he looked at first. She was so nervous she just stood there.

"Have a seat," he said, "Though you can continue to stand if you like."

With gentle eyes she could see equally as deep into him, which made it all the more intimidating and profound. He allowed this, and watched it, seeing what she saw reflected in her eyes. It was a continuous feedback loop of him watching her watching him. An epic feat of multitasking it was amazing he could even speak. Words and verbs not only affecting the continuous gaze-loop, but were fully integrated, as if pulled directly from within it.

He smiled at her, still standing next to the chair across from him. deGryder had the life path precision of a jaguar, and the timing of an osprey. He was different than any of those she encountered at the festival, but somehow rooted there. He was beyond human, observable in action and praxis in the world, with a body, but with all other components engaged in the quantum. If not for her time with Aum, in deep spiritual study she would not be here, let alone be able to hold a conversation with this man. He interrupted the incoming memory reference, standing and speaking, "Yes, we would not be here without the heartfelt recognition and reflection on what brought us here in the first place. This beautiful present." He pulled out her chair for her, "Welcome to the new world Ms. Leatherbee. Please, sit," she finally did. He returned to his seat and continued, "I understand you took the weekend off from a big case you're working on." Her heart exploded as John asked, "Please, tell me about it."

She blushed, then found the courage to intelligently and articulately share her passion for her work, and it's current mis-alignment. Simply by being in the microscopic gaze of this man, while describing what she did and how she did it, she uncovered numerous layers of insight, in purpose and path and passion, and he really didn't do anything but listen.

"I'm glad you made it."

"Me too."

He collected himself and rose, "You'll be in town for a few days?"

She reflected on how quick and how far her exit was from her regular life, “Of course.”

“That’s wonderful.” He passed her a square paper card, “Here’s my contact if you need anything. I have a meeting in 5, but I’ll be here again in two days if you would like to join me again. The case you’re working on is quite significant and I would be honored to hear about it’s progress.”

She was again caught in a bubble of speechless staring. Words came to her mind, ‘Conscious work, working consciously.’ He winked as he left, jumping off the cliff, sprouting wings.

The following day Jenn had resigned from her parents firm, making connections with the Sunny Valley litigation team, sharing all the soft copy material she had collected from the east coast trip. The team was the real deal; public servants of the highest caliber, in it for the right reasons. They even offered her a job researching further case material.

Infused by this new world of inspiration, she accepted a silent partnership contract with the group and began to draw up arguments from little known or publicized cases of similar community reaction to corporate dominance. These of course required time to find, as they reached only local courts and local community blogs, precise details suppressed by the larger news machine.

Jumping back and forth between the local hostel and local library for days on end, she came across a black and white indie tech zine that briefly mentioned major players in the development of Gridline and the impact they were having on the not-for-profit sector. It was old news and out of date, so Jenn quickly sent a message proposing a more up to date article on Gridline’s activities, even diving into their new project, The Riddle.

Within 10 seconds they had sent a response, agreeing, asking for an article brief. In it Jenn proposed to focus on dispelling or confirming rumors that had sped their way around the backend Internet world about the notorious deGryder, his hijinks, his piracy, and his bandit bandwidth lawbreaking. Proposal accepted immediately, with a week deadline.

She was actually able to confirm many accounts with John himself two days from when they first met, as well as the following Thursday, as they continued to meet and talk about the development of the Sunny Valley case.

One rumor was about a border crossing a few years ago. With a truckload of various and random supplies, much like what she had experienced from Jason, John allegedly tried to cross the border for a convergent Riddler meeting. At that time he was the sole developer of the material object exchange branch; the single bud of the yellow tower. The border guard would undoubtedly want to check his vehicle, and if this happened there would be no way he would be let into the country. So at the previous rest stop John had created a fake website, with a fake show, a corporate board event, put everything on a flyer and printed it out in a 1hr print shop down the road, just as back up for the guard to see when he grilled him about the randomized contents of his vehicle. The grilling didn't happen, and the remaining puzzle is whether it was because of John's concentrated focus and speedy efforts that he did not get flagged in his VW van, or if it was mere chance.

After submitting the article, having nearly completed a full Gridline exposition, the zine group became so excited that they championed it to a larger publisher, solidifying it's printing with a larger publication, and even a book deal for Jenn. Upon hearing that she was meeting regularly with deGryder himself, the publishing company proposed the idea of a biography.

One week since their first meeting Jenn ran the idea passed John and his response was, "Timing is ripe. What do you need from me?" And she proposed to him a daily interview schedule, as well as immersive anthropological-style job shadowing. The documentary crew and feature film deal she could already see coming, with a narrative this profoundly aligned with contemporary culture, it was more tricky to devise ways in which to make it not happen.

As they sat together most evenings together, with each sip of caffeine intoxicating senses, or a more solitary red wine and sushi relaxing them, memories flooded back with verve.

For John it was finally a platform of reflection that overpowered the incessant need to actualize and engineer every real-time insight, and at the same time, it supported the broader success of all the work. For Jenn it was engaging real work in the real world, for the right side, with efforts not lost in invisible layers of personal metaphysics.

"You're still sticking to the 'it's just a website' line, hey?" she asked, trying to grasp and hold an outline for Johns autobiography.

He took another sip of coffee, “That’d be the easiest entry point, and a simple understandable truth. All good ideas are simple truths.”

Their tender pace and soft delicacy with each other was beyond professional formality, but a built-in avenue of the connectivity that the Riddle encouraged. What emerged, book or otherwise, would thus be a deeply special offering.

Gazing at the magazine proof they had brought with them to the Gridline coffeeshop she asked, “Do you ever feel like you know too much?”

“What do you mean? Like knowing that mental processes create Bose-Einstein condensates?”

She looked at him agape, so he continued, explaining, “Brand new matter is created when light energy, when photons cool, or condense, and reach accessibility in the lowest quantum state.”

Her expression didn’t change, she checked her handheld to make sure it was still recording. He saw this, smiled and responded, “The Tao of Physics by Capra would be a good place to start,” and he went around the room looking at each conversation, each interaction, and described precisely what was going on.

“Whatever, you’re just reading lips.”

“Naw, check it out,” and he began to describe and predict every action in each conversation, head tilts, hand gestures, grabbing a refill, as if he was narrating a story. The world had come alive for her since Full Spectrum, when she stopped looking and started seeing.

* * *

The shock of the emergency response mediation slowly dissolved as Aum explored Gridline further. Waldorfian cobblestone floors, living trees supporting walls, art display windows; Aum had never been to The First Goetheanum, but imagined it would feel something like this. It was neither an ‘indoor’ nor ‘outdoor’ space, but something inbetween.

Down the hall there was an inner courtyard which was crafted by the most advance permies and horticulturalists. Experimental gardens displayed projects in the works, both with the land itself and inside display cases and on plinths; like an extremely high quality, fully funded, supported, and celebrated model of higher learning.

Each project display had a small equally enticing interactive digital screen which wove in the relevant meta data: interactive research, backstory, aspect of community the work supported, with even further layers of research into the community structure itself. Whether a gardener, artist, or collective there was a page with bio image, paragraph and link to further projects or independent websites. Aum saw a few corporate logo's smuggled into the design of the larger displays, "Hmmm," It was as if they crashed the party, or wanted to hang with the cool kids but could not fully shake their bad street cred to be fully welcome.

He saw a teenager with a hand embed press it into one of the digital tags, pressing a download button on the display screen; receiving an instant data upload into his embed, influencing no less than his karmic soul path.

The crickets in ecosystem sang and the moon shone down through the open roof, a warm breeze found it's way into the trees and the space soothed Aum's entire spirit as the kid walked by, tall and skinny with long brown locks and brown shirt. In the kids bright and conscious gaze; in their connection, Aum could see the future – and it was fucking awesome.

"Nice one" The kid said as he walked by.

Aum thought he better get on with his mission, or else find himself obsolete. He knew he had used his ticket, but refused to believe that the meditation was his sole purpose for being there; maybe it was simply the entrance gate. He wondered where Zeke could be, or even Derek.

Just past the inner gardens he walked passed a coffee shop.

Sitting at a table there were waves of multi-dimensional reality swirling around him. A man, aware of both body and breath while his intuitive mind slowly massaged the stock market back to health. Each transaction and relationship became conscious, alive and supportive of the whole, community achievement was directly perceivable in real time through observing his observation of a deep collective eb and flow.

As pockets of the collaborating commerce network broke through their karma, tapping more into love and peace and patience and faith, he felt this man feeling the gateways of human wholism open and begin to work at the next plateau. Aum spied the double hand embeds and they twitched in response to his gaze, making his coffee slightly spill. He then smelt something besides coffee – a scent so familiar it could have been his own.

In the top right corner of his mind she poked through as a shinning star. Her grace and presence was instantly remembered and recognized. Dancing again, footsteps echoed in his mind and his own imagination twitched.

With fingertips on seed, and hand holding tree barked message, in that moment, he shared himself with her, who he was in that present moment, re-opening in fullness and in honesty. With his spirit saying, 'This is how much I've transformed since we last met.'

His body was strong as he invoked the feeling and results of his journey, holding the memories and vision steadfast in his mind. As he did, it was if he powered up, seeing himself anew, and his third eye pierced through the veil as if a portal opened. In this newfound strength, his full stubble, full height hair, and masculine presence, he whispered to her, barely audible. "But I let go of you. I let go of you in my growth and for your growth. In body medicine and cleansing, I let you go."

And in response her spirit actively flipped on a switch of deeper psychic quantum engagement, as if their entwined karma overrode all soul lessons as his most advanced life path teacher, 'I know,' her voice said in his mind.

Upon hearing her voice his eyes opened.

He recognized the double hand embeds. It was the ghost collector who had given him the lions mane. He was about to say hello, but one step towards him and both his embeds beeped. The man was up, collected and strolling, in continued peace and breath and focus. The man's footsteps echoed in real time, matching hers. Waves of non-local incoherence started to wash over Aum, he was dizzy and he had to sit down. He quickly found the chair the ghost collector had sat in, and meditated. It was still strong inside the openness and accessibility of this newfound presence, she rewarded him by unlocking and opening his chest, placing her star within it. She responded further to his whispered words, 'Without this active moment of engaged reflection with a very specific other, how could we know ourselves in this truely new way. How could you plant this new vision seed of your highest present self? Without this moment of connection? Without this relationship?' He was brought to tears in remembrance of her fullness and her new powerful capabilities found in this quantum field. 'This is what we are here to do, as entwined souls and incarnated members of the star peoples, that is what this moment of connectivity is, beyond re-patterning and growth.' It was as if she was right there with him, and they loved each other like no other humans who had come before them, where whole sections of spirit were exchanged and groomed and cared for and brought into higher planes of vibration.

He opened his eyes and there was a magazine open on the table, directly in front of his gaze. He saw the authors name before anything else.

He smiled, heart exploding, "Thank you for being here," Speaking outloud, "I'm glad you made it."

Before reading he curiously flipped to the cover, the ghost collector was on it.

"I see."

His nostrils flared with scent again.

"I see," and further insight splashed in his mind.

He flipped back to the article and skimmed through it, seeing a photo of three shinning true human souls, the two kings he recognized.

"Hmmm, an old Trimurti."

(Continued from pg 2-25) In a quick indie video clip after the surgery, one of the first questions deGryder was asked was about Anna, seen in this photo's centre.

"No, I didn't know Anna. Though somehow I know her better now than ever."

Once needing an ear swab and jewelers tool kit to manually make the signal switch, deGryder's digital ear drum became controlled by the first handembed in history.

The idea came to him after he spilled some N-Glu on his forearm during a preliminary stage of development. On an intuitive hunch he applied a current to it and it lit up – his own arm now his handheld. Only after a few weeks of experimentation, the screen became powered by the energy inherent in his body, and a sensor glove was developed, designating fingertips and spots on his palm as a universal keyboard. What emerged was at first a double-handed 'goofy' tap style, then a single-handed 'finger-gnash' style. After a year of evolving both hardware and software, and with a leaping yet invisible maneuver to partner with a government youth program, deGryder began working with deaf youth, learning to adapt to their new digital ear drums during post-surgery recovery. Using the referential vector math applied to 3D triangulation, glove sensors became triggered by simple hand positions: sign language.

With this platoon of bionic kids, sign language became a digital communication signal that instantly converted into audio bytes, beamed directly into their digital ears, allowing def children to vocally speak to one another, near telepathically. Signals could even be sent to wifi speakers, broadcasting the spoken audio out for typical ear drums to hear, but this was eventually stopped as it hindered the children's ability to learn to speak; the practice of understanding the mechanics of the human voicebox the main purpose of the funded recovery program.

Regardless, this bio-augmentation amplified def youth language learning from years of practice, to a weekend course, and even though deGryder shies away from it's mention, for this work he won the Turing Award at age 24 - the equivalent of the Nobel prize for applied computer science.

Not one to stop, ever, deGryder continued to evolve the software even further from sign language to the newest 'mudra' style, where, not just spoken language, but programmable shortcuts of any sort, can be linked to the hand positions of different mudras used in meditation and yoga. Using not just using ancient and hacked hand positions such as mayura mudra I, karana mudra or the heroic and iconic shikhara mudra, the database even includes some secret shortcuts outside the yoga lineage, such as the shaka mudra, which originated in Hawaii.

There was a picture in the article of a plaid Don Cherry, giving the thumbs up; the VHS cover of Rock 'em sock 'em 12 and the shikhara mudra.

"How the fuck did she do that!?"

It was brilliant. Without a doubt a hacked mudra, or simply a cultural constant, much like yoga itself. Aum continued reading.

All has not been so beautifully picturesque however.

After a recent revamp in all government programs, the youth funding partnership was cut entirely. The surprising loss of support was a shock to Gridlines NFP operations, and to not have this drastic change bring down the entire company, the founders chose to partner with corporate investors; to the cringe and chagrin of all watching the companies speedy growth path.

With the project moving into the public sphere, feedback from the corporate firm was integrated and the N-Glu digital display screen was not just temporarily painted on the arm, but developed into N-Serum and injected in bewteen layers of skin in the forearm. And rather than a glove, microchips were inserted into the skin of fingertips.

A few steps away from an online app purchase, or spray can at the local hardware store, the commercial purchase of a handembed required the next level of commitment; the desire to physically adapt, as well as a fat pocket of cash. Even though critics dubbed it trans-humanist consumerism, with deGryder penning the tag line, 'All bodies will vibrate with hyperflesh,' the handembed quickly left the realm of Turing and not-for-profit, and became an immediate commercial mainstay. Whether eager post-humans have injected these touch screens and microsensors in other parts of their body, none of this creative trimurti know.

"Fuck the Web! We need an open source Earth!"

A blessing in disguise, the commercial infusion allowed Gridline to quickly route handembed profits into acquiring a public space and develop numerous community education programs. A harbor front building was purchased and renovated into a high tech hub which includes creative class room studio spaces, specific rooms for a flourishing independent school system, an open source cybernetics production lab, a recital hall, an inner courtyard meditation and education garden, an art gallery, and most popular with the kids, an observatory on the roof. The trans-humanist criticism over the years has surely slowed, as one steps within the Gridline Centre the integrity is felt, simply breathing the molecules of air produced by the meditating trees.

Still functioning as an NFP, all commercial gain created from these transformative endeavors which don't go directly into the building, are funneled into numerous side projects, fresh out of the Gridline R&D lab. The biggest being lead by deGryder himself, as mentor to two future luminaries, both of wunderkind variety, Derek

Arcadiou and Zachery Herman Eschaton Magnum (aka 'Zhe', son of Ezekiel and Anna). Both artists who work in the mediums of life and breath, respectively. In response, when asked the artistic medium of deGryder, uniformly they responded, "Beat. He rides the beat."

"The Riddle is a website," John simply puts it, linking back to Gridline's humble beginnings. And I can only laugh at this, because if The Riddle has found it's way into your life, one way or another, you know it is much more than that.

"What about 'Fuck the Web! We need an open source Earth!'" I asked, and John erupted in laughter, "Oh yeah, I forgot I said that."

If it is a website, then it is a website that seeds quantum civilization and assists in developing the lesson plan for the restructuralization of humanity, even our collective conception of all reality. Sounds lovely, no? But don't look up www.Riddle.com, because it won't be there. And don't search for it with the corporate engines, because you won't find it there. It has been specifically engineered this way, to develop an evolutionary heritage independent of mainstream mono-culture, and in true alignment with it's nanotech history and pathways of future consciousness. I caution you however. Treading with reverence can not be emphasized enough, for once the Riddle is found, and it's truth revealed, you may find yourself obsessively looking for, longing for, a continuous flow of perfection, a place and state of New Eden; with no quick fix, or street remedy, finding yourself saying, "I am going to New Eden," when you know not where or what it is, nor how to get there. Shrouded in even more mystery and trauma and death than the Riddle itself, it is the crowing achievement of the deGryder legacy.

Aum put down the magazine. His mind reeled at the deeply nested layers he could see.

The ghost collector is John deGryder. John deGryder is the Dragonrider. Derek, Zhe and John are the dragon trinity. The Dragonrider's company created the Riddle. Jenn is directly linking deGryder to the New Eden suicides, as if it's another layer within the Riddle. If the Riddle website got beamed in at the hockey game, and this article is going out to the mono-culture, the evolution must be complete; a re-birth must be near. Or at least close to it. But does that mean John collected Cat too?

A lightning bolt hit him. He felt like he was back on stage at Full Spectrum. What exactly was this place? As if inside a crop circle vortex, it all swirled again, around him. He struggled to find his edges. He closed his eyes to meditate, and follow his breath, fully expecting, when his eyes re-opened, for the walls to be in deferent places, lighting to be changed, cobblestone replaced with carpet, replaced with natural grasses, and the permaculture garden to have exploded out from it's container, fully surrounding him.

But in his first breath, with eyes closed, he smelled the fresh oxygen from the trees and smiled, his soul rupturing with gratitude inside of him. That was all he needed. Here, full refresh, full peace, was only one breathe away.

* * *

"The pop culture of the past is dead. If not dead, then mutated beyond recognition. So drastically it does not resemble what it once did. And it is the once underground culture which has replaced it, becoming the new pop culture." After describing the ongoing inner interactions of the coffee shop, John flowed into his own inner workings and their connectivity. He was about to sip his coffee but then continued, "The best part is that it has utilized the newest technology-enhanced avenues of network development and community, economics and prosperity, and synthesized a self made expression of civilization. It is a self made culture!" He shouted exuberantly as he raised his hands in exclamation. "It is self made, but it is the *first round* of the self made. A reminder thus that it is transitory, as the future refines ever toward deeper conscious awareness, and planetary stewardship."

He passed along a card with a sleek sheen polish that was like nGlu, but a formula far beyond. It was a screen that wasn't like any screen surface she had ever before seen. As her fingers touched it it activated with graphics spinning and rotating like wheels; a sacred chakra symbol set with oracular iChing incantations woven into south American calendrical systems notifying her of the day and it's placement within the cyclical timelessness, anchored in the ancient gypsy nation tarot. It was a satellite far beyond it's grounded history: a creative manifestation of the trans-planetary.

As she inspected it further, gently touching the graphics they reacted as if a living astrolab organism, timid yet curious. In reaction a humble voice spoke out of the card itself:

Light wings far beyond the collective
into the channelled dreams space that is
a beauty of heaven like no other
and a momentous harmony felt throughout the cosmos

New cities,
on a new layer of earth,
and new humans, with new spirits
to inhabit them
and steward it

"9D as the elements speak out, that the organic machines elves are we," John added, ancient sparkle in his eye. She was speechless, trying to grasp the intense world cusp she felt with her fingertips, so he continued, "Your gift from New Eden."

She finally spoke, "You're a genius." Said honestly.

"You don't have to be a genius to be a visionary, and you don't have to be a visionary to be a genius."

"So what exactly does it mean to be a visionary?" She asked, quickly glancing at the audio recording signal.

"A visionary is one who knows when to stop."

"Stop?"

"Yes - the exact opposite notion of what our culture is built on. It takes keen awareness, enhanced through dedication, practice, or even medicine, to hear, to know, to commit to the action of stopping when the tap of subtle inspiration turns off. Don't force it out. Even though everything around us is built like that, and for that. Allow the work to speak on it's own. To be. To breathe. So when it no longer speaks, do not ignore that intuitive sensation, and ask for more. It means it is time to change what you are doing. Find something else to do, but maintain an aware connection, to your muse, because the fount of inspiration may turn on in 30 seconds, even stronger than before."

She was still mesmerized by the 9D card, but spoke out, "The visionary is certainly not contained to visual practice, but the act of seeing the highest truth, unmoving and absolute."

"Correct. As a visionary, what you have to give is inside you - inside your body, inside your mind, your spirit, not outside of you in an ion databank, server, or cloud. At this stage in the commons of expression, it is that knowledge of power and presence inside time – not outside of it - that sets one apart. Knowing that anything inside a screen is an illusion, a reflection of the gazing human eye being diluted, an illusion even more amplified than all this," He gestured his finger around through the air. "I've heard of some that have never returned to their bodies, the present moment of self, after going too deep there. Forever lost in the elsewhere."

John continued after sipping his hi-test, "The slope gets steeper and steeper, the deeper and deeper you go. The deeper you go the broader you can sense, and the broader you can sense, the finer the flow, to see who sees and see who leads, until everything is known."

Jenn smiled, "I'm gonna post that last one when I get home," and he smiled gently back. Her handheld buzzed. An alarm.

"One last call, in 5," She started packing her briefcase-purse, "Just gotta conclude the last bit on the Sunny Valley case, and prep the drop with council tonight."

"You're going to make it to my performace in 10, aren't you Jenni-Bee?" John shouted playfully at her as she left. She looked back at him and winked, "Of course Rider, I know my way around," leaving him to continue in his space of personal reflections.

After his ear surgery and recovery from Full Spectrum One, John spent much of his time on Anna's corporate page, not creeping, but blissing out on her beauty and wisdom. Surely he wasn't the only one trying to make sense of her drastic actions. Seeing Zeke and Dan after, being with them in their apartment studio, it was palpable, the loss he saw and felt in these two men. The combination of experiences evoked in him the feeling, the inner knowing, and the courage to move into that empty space. He had to. He knew it, like the spreading of loving wings allowing everyone to fly, simply by flying.

On the page he had seen her notable quote, 'Prayer does not use up artificial energy, doesn't burn up any fossil fuel, doesn't pollute. Neither does song, neither does love, neither does dance." In courage he reposted it, adding, 'There will be a new dance craze and it will dissolve all corrupt institutions within 13 year's, freeing the entire world. Right Anna?' After doing so, the next page he visited had a picture of Anna on it, smiling. He could hear her voice reply even, 'Right on young John." The repost could have been interpreted as ghastly tacky, but with the instant support from her in the non-local, the non-real, wherever she was, John encircled some deep magic and platformed a new independence within himself, forever leaving behind the corporate designed psychic shakles of addiction: seeing the invisible nature of his community and friends become visible.

Anna's voice continued to speak to him outside of the technology based framework, continually changing in tone and texture, telling him that things could still be different. It was a guidance system that made sense to him, like an inner intuitive voice that allowed the most complex occurrences be simple and straight forward. As his confidence grew with each year, he became more and more involved in Full Spectrum and it's community, recommitting and recommitting to that role he had seen, no matter the challenge.

After Full Spectrum 6 he asked, 'How can there be a Riddle Solver without a Riddle?' The question was asked to one of his two, now formal mentors, the visionary gene programming wizard named Ezekiel, and that day, with continued grace, the Riddle foundation was built.

In a moment of exuberant excitement describing a multi-decade old immersive cybernetic legacy system which Full Spectum intended to embody, he responded 'That was just my allegorical word choice', Zeke explained to him. But in that moment, what John understood, was that it was all just these subtle and unconscious defining moments which allowed new organic bridges to be built. And then he saw it, in a vision, in it's fullest operating form, and without hesitation, John began to work on it then and there.

Something shifted in deGryder's immediate coffee shop environment. His arm twitched, his coffee spilt, and there was an infusion of spirit so strong that a full download pushed and streamed into his mind, revealing much of what he had forgotten over the course of his continued obsession, to actualize the highest dream of what he had seen.

The Riddle seedling came together so quickly that evening after returning from Full Spectrum 6, over tea, and a meal, in synchronicity and collaborative planting. His fellow collaborators, Derek and Zhe popped into the apartment at clutch moments of creative insight, walking in the door and consciously stepping into new roles as soon as they were imagined into existence. He knew their desire. He could spot in their eyes; to expand and grow and give, far beyond the yearly stage management duties they had been doing. That night there were no contracts signed, or formal agreements, or even discussions. They all just knew it, and yearned for it. What's more, is that this is how any substantial contract in the old world worked anyway, with that shared exhilarating resonance at the core, only with absurd piles bureaucratic paperwork surrounding it, to fill timesheets and bank accounts. Overseen by Zeke and Daniel, two of the three founders of the festival, the proceedings were so natural, even entertaining, that it was like watching a new level emerge out of the ether; emerge as the next level of evolution in the continued cybernetic legacy.

Created that night, the preliminary Riddle interface design was cusp and intriguing. It provoked in the ways it should and maintained mystery in ways it should. The first landing page had, what would now be considered, an old school interactive flash animation, was an esoteric sigil of geomancy that moved with the mouse, rotating and expanding and spinning as the pointer moved in to click it.

Below the 'enter' button was their stage. Saddle shaped, it was something seen in a traveling circus, even more interesting was the serpintine spiral mysteriously lit on the roof. It was as if it was a gateway, and the geometrical form emerged from it. On the photo all doors to the stage were closed. It was a Pandora's box with something growing inside that would only be revealed by clicking the geometry and entering the custom digital ecosphere.

Technical website details, at the beginning, were absurdly simple, but still indie on all levels: a single open message board after landing page entry, hosted on a server sitting at the apartment tower. Placed at the top of this first Board was another quote by Anna, which invoked the birth of the first thread of self contained community dialoge: 'If we are to achieve a richer culture, rich in contrasting values, we must recognize the whole gamut of human potentialities, and so weave a less arbitrary social fabric, one in which each diverse human gift will find a fitting place.'

All seed site appeal aside, it was only a small spec of the project launch work. What John did best, and was well practiced in, was riding and guiding the flow, and this experiment was no exception. Rather than blast out promotional advertising campaigns on every possible surface, from public poster to corporate boards, he chose the route of a single arrow, inside the system that just birthed it.

Zhe had planned the Full Spectrum 6 decompression and integration at the local permaculture centre, which was scheduled for the following evening. With it, and the first Riddle meeting, they stepped into their new roles with greater purpose and whole societal intention, they found the pre-event synchronicity moving at a much more profound pace - such as Derek driving by the airport the moment the headlining DJ needed to be picked up. Or when John sent off a single poster to print: the landing page image; title, website and quote on it, linking printshop notification to Derek. Derek then received the job completion buzz a block away from the printshop, picked it up after the airport and delivered both DJ and poster to the venue for the pre soundcheck venue peep. Derek left the poster on a table there before hitting a restaurant with his old DJ friend. When Zhe arrived, first, he pinned it up in a key spot at the small venue, where the 100 or so hippie kids could see it as they returned from their festival solar eclipse trips lit with DMT sticks; showcasing the exact geometrical structure that emerged from the black hole sun now floating on top of the social container which visually embodied the essence of future culture mystery.

And they continued to move together, like this, without speaking, without messaging, without sending instructions, with only their united inner knowing, guided by an inner chorus of sangha. The perfect beginning.

'So much has happened since then," John though. Both embeds buzzed in response. 5 min warning. He was up and walking with the power of fully spread wings, a single occurrence away from the full manifestation of his initial vision, 'There's only one magic show, one performance, one public talk. And it is now.'

* * *

There were two seats open in the recital hall, one in the back, last row, at the end, and one front and centre. Without hesitation Jenn quickly sat down front and centre. Immediately after, John strolled out onto the auditorium stage, the audience cheered, and an image popped up above him, projected on the large screen. It was Mark Henson's visionary masterpiece from 2009, *New Pioneers.* John looked up at it as the audience quieted. He continued to stand up front on the stage, in the silence, looking out at them. He didn't start talking for at least a minute and a half, which, in an auditorium full of mediators, is a few breaths. But in an auditorium full of ADD digital media and communication consumers, many went to their handhelds within 12 seconds of the silence. John didn't mind, he would speak to the national attention deficit eventually.

Jenn sat quietly at the front, at this point more a mediator than a digital media addict. Smiling, she was grateful to have the calm space to peacefully focus on the powerful painting. She then realized what John meant by presence and power inside of time.

After numerous coughs and sneezes, throat clearings, a couple whispers, John inhaled and exhaled deeply, finally speaking, "Mahākāśyapa. I kind of want to pull a Buddha here; show you this image and walk off the stage, essentially saying, 'lesson concluded.' But it's not 500 BCE. The lessons of the past may no longer have the same cultural relevance as they once did. And, they may not even survive into the future," the audience was silent. Rapt, he held their attention hostage, "How are my mic levels?"

A few in the audience, including Jenn, shouted, "Good!"

Someone quickly shouted, "You rock Jonathan!"

Then another, "Dead man's trigger complete!"

And another, "Baptize me John!"

"Great, " Acknowledging that there were at least a few listening, "For this, my first lecture, I brought my own microphone. As you can see it's not in my hands," he showed them his hands like a true magician, "and it's not some goofy headset that allows me to show off my dance moves." As he did a bit of footwork there was a slight chuckle at the words and his pantomime. "My mic is right here," and he pointed to his ear. "Not only do I send the mic signal to the sound system in the room, but I also send it to my own brain. You hear what I hear. Exactly." He began to stroll around the stage, now in lecture mode, "Early in my career I gained some notoriety for these little jobs, not because of their worth in the consumer marketplace as most would assume, but because of how they helped people improve their lives. They give people the ability to hear who have lost that ability, or never had it in the first place." He strolled to the other side, putting his hands in pockets, “I am clinically deaf, so this piece of technology helps me live a more normal life…” he looked from one side to the other, “…or maybe even better.”

He took his hands out of his pockets, rolling up his sleeves, showing off his handhelds, tapping a few surfaces and the auditorium projector switched to what was on his forearm screen. There was some custom software, though mostly skin colored, with faders and knobs, even a dropdown selector, and on the screen a classic Casio wristwatch LED readout. John choose from the dropdown and pulled a few sliders up and a jazzy hip hop sample came out from the speakers.

“You hear what I hear. I just mixed in a live satellite radio feed into the audio signal, along with the live mic,” pointing to his ear. “He did a full screen sweep and another piece of software was shown on the screen, he tapped a couple buttons on the software and started making hand signals on the stage – mudras. At this, different beat sequences began to play overtop of the satellite feed and live mic combo, in concurrence with the mudras. The audience cheered.

The moment the cheer peaked he quickly tapped the pad and changed his hand movements to something that was more similar to an orchestra conductor, with actual sign language.

It was if he captured something invisible in the audience and started to lift it up, metaphorically and literally. A beautifully operatic female voice sang in time with his sign language hand motions. A quick tap and the satellite feed faded out, another tap and the drum machine came to a conclusion. What was left was an esoteric hymnal from a raw and unexplored countryside, a hand embed vocal solo. It was moving, and touching, and real. Everyone could see it was real. It was like watching Beethoven perform his magnum opus.

Hearts aligned and opened, John flicked his right hand, shook it out as if it had a cramp, then returned to the mudra signals as his left continued with the sign language solo – right helping out when need be. In his mudra hand there were noticeable motions that were affecting the pitch and tone of the soaring vocal track.

With each adjustment it flexed and became wishy-washy, like a sick sailor at sea, being thrown from starboard to port at naturally random intervals. Like an invisible theremin creature being tamed, the quickly mangled angelic audio was molded with vigorous fingertip and each supremely sensitive nerve at the end of each.

Then it went beyond hand gestures and digits. A mob of body twitches and dance accents popped like dots in the sonic landscape. As his solo crunched and cruised, John inhaled, pierced a veil of synesthesia, and found the adaptable source sound was even inside the blood circling through his cells. It was the exchange of oxygen itself, moving, as his expressive pranic fire-energy linked to it. Moving up from lung-filled breath, through upper shoulders, elbow, wrist, fingertip, computerchip, cloud-based data clip; the cyclical pulses were now microscopic organic loops expanded into symphonic geometry.

His awareness was at this level of depth, inside his own body, and thus everyone in the audience was with him there, interpreting it as best they knew how. The electricity pounded through the speakers at the highest quality possible, as if he was a stand alone drum machine.

He collected the audience now, counting them; not quite tagging them, but close. He moved them up to new levels of inspiration, through their ears, activated their eyes to see a new world, translating their emotional reaction into resonating future soul maps and new architectural podiums of spirit to climb, and move through.

The garbled data mash of voice finally steadied, in a lovely baritone, until it was Johns own. Full and coherent, from the speakers emerged a lush and high res bank of Johns own vocal lines, the auditory translations of his sign language, from the data stored in his arm. Then he began to sing along with his own voice, in sweet harmonies, fading out the sign language controlled signal singing, until it was simply his live voice singing.

As he concluded, the audience erupted in tearful cheers.

Again, at the moment the cheering began to fade, he switched it to a live camera feed of himself on the stage and spoke, loudly this time, abruptly.

"All mediums of Art and creativity are dead."

It was a shocking statement, like a suckerpunch to the solar plexus after experiencing what they had just witnessed.

"All of them."

It was so deathly quiet in the auditorium Jenn could hear the crickets in the Gridline garden chirping.

"All of them, except one," John interjected, to ease up his torturous grip, "Performance art."

He paused for a second, pacing the stage as if thinking, waving his hand around, "…and magic… two mediums are alive," but he paused again, "Wait."

And he continued to pace the stage, scratching his head.

The audience laughed nervously at his odd behavior. Did he have a personality disorder? Or was this suddenly a stand up comedy routine?

There was a subtle smirk on his face, "Magic isn't a medium of creativity," he looked at the audience, "Creativity is a medium of magic."

He posted the Henson image again, and said, "So yes, like I said, only one medium left," and stared at the image for another 11 seconds, then pulled up a video, a feed from the Boards.

"This was shot yesterday morning. I'll warn you, it gets a little graphic; a little bloody." It was footage of a surgery.

"This clip is of me having the digital microsensors removed from my fingertips."

In the gap of silent and confounded contemplation, he quickly switched it back to the Henson image. He left it on the screen for a good 25 seconds, knowing at this point he could. Then deGryder began to walk off stage.

* * *

Aum's meditation was interrupted by two young men walking by.

"I heard Cirque Du Soleil is performing on top of the Pyramid of Tulum during the winter solstice"

"What!? Cirque Du Soleil!? That's corporatized bullshit. I hope they're the first to be sacrificed."

"It freakn' sucks being an artist."

"Especially now. Everyone has the tools to be creative, but nobody is imaginative enough to make anything new."

"The world is so saturated that we're drowning in our own puke, fucking cadavers."

Previously undistracted by the many voices that had swirled around him, Aum finally opened his eyes at these poignant barbs, and saw the metal shutters of the coffee shop down, now closed. With inquisitive clarity he got to his feet, continuing on in random exploration.

Following a nearby corridor, down an intuitive path, he heard a single voice speaking with heavy reverb behind a double door, etched and sculpted oak.

With just a sliver open, Aum slipped in unnoticed, finding his way to the only seat open at the back of a large hall.

It was a classic theatre. So classic, he suspected that most of the Centre had been built around this auditorium as it's feature. Red carped, slopped floor, micro lights, elaborate moldings on the wall, a red draw curtain, even the smell evoked memories. With no signs or notices outside he wondered if this was the true Riddler meeting, responding to the recent and ongoing criseses and emergencies. Aum looked around and more than half of the faces in the audience he recognized. It was as if the Boards had come alive and each headshot he could recall now had a real face, a real body, and real limbs, and could converse in person. But instead of exuberant animated conversations, there was a silence like he had never before heard.

He looked up on stage and saw the Dragonrider, John deGryder, looking like he just finished his lecture, about to exit. His walk paused however, as if Aum's gaze caught him trying to escape.

"I refuse to bend and mold my Self into a marketing strategy," deGryder spoke, circling round. He collected his thoughts and continued to engage with the audience.

"Authentic soul drop: if a bee is a beautiful flower that moves, and if a bird is an elegant tree that sings and takes to the skies… then what are we?"

He paused, really trying to make sure all ears were listening.

"Star seeds that have magnetized earth material into our physical make-up, evolving our astral-core through an alliance with the mushroom kingdom? Maybe. Crack a person open, with inventive performance, scientific theory, spiritual insight, business acumen, or even all combined, through life path finesse, and then what? What happens after? What do you place inside that crack?" John looked up to the Henson image on the screen, depicting both Armageddon and a lush human harmony with nature.

"The reason I keep on coming back to this image is because to me, it represents the exact moment we are in right now. As a civilization. Muck like the traveler illustrated in the centre, who tries to find insight in history's depiction of the present, his choice is one that now resides in each of us, at every moment, of our own present. It is a choice that requires brand new awareness. Not historical, but a wholistic picture.

"Compared to this crucial practice of wholistic awareness and action,everything else is a toy, a gimic, a plaything," He held up his hands, showing off his embeds, "to keep us occupied and mesmerized, to keep our gaze distracted, contained, monitored and montitized. Placed anywhere, but on conscious change." He began pacing, no longer close to comedy but nearly grief stricken, "You hear what I hear. Should we not stop our flawed incoherent unconscious ways?"

No one ventured an answer, so he dove in.

"Yes, obviously. We should stop our unconscious ways, not because of an impending ecological collapse which will destroy our civilization, no, we should stop to our bad habits and flawed actions because we look like idiots. We look like fucking idiots. There, I said it. To our allied plant neighbors, to our star seed celestial ancestors, to our mother earth, our children, and our children's children. We look like idiots to those who are looking back upon us from the future with their breatharian light bodies and time wave zero spaceships and saying in this singular moment, 'you fat plump pimp's, the only reason mother earth didn't pop you like a zit is that she could see us coming after.'" He paused, releasing attachment to his grief and frustration, "They're actually out there waiting for us, waiting for us to learn, waiting for us to have changed, waiting for us to finally to grow up."

He looked from the image back at the audience, "They see what you see. Both sides." His eyes glinted with a moment of new emergent insight, "Do you know who Big Brother reports to?" He paused, waiting for another answer, with none coming he continued, "Big Daddy." The crowed laughed. "You think it's funny, but it's the truth. And Big Daddy is quite happy that we don't grow up. But the truth is we have to. And we have to let Daddy go." He shifted over to the left side of the stage, "But I know. I know there's a voice inside your head, within your spirit that says, 'No John, we can't let Daddy go, we can't go that deep. We can't let go of all these corrupted institutions that our civilization depends on, institutions that control us and tell us what to do, social modalities for cohesion, we need them. You confuse abhorrent consumption with required sustenance.'" He shook his head, "It's amazing, even surprising, when this voice is heard inside the mind and heart. Even within those ones so committed to growing consciously."

He moved to the right of the stage, "Even more terrified, this voice continues on in most others, blithering on, grasping for reason, 'Who will build the bridges then John? Who will pave the streets? Who will fill the pot holes? Who will be the doctors, and the grocers, and the police?"

His pausing was very dramatic, but allowed the audience time to follow his train of thought, "Throughout human history there has always been doctors and farmers – culinary artesians, gatherers and hunters at least – inventors, craftsmen, technologists, and well, you got to have the *police*, otherwise look at what you'd be doing to yourselves, you'd be *killing* each other!" He said it in an absurdly sarcastic way, with a peculiar inflection, which made everyone laugh.

"Anarchy is defined as a political philosophy which holds the state to be undesirable, unnecessary, harmful to the functioning and in opposition to the conduct of human relations. Unfortunately the meme stream of punk rock has dressed its symbology in a way that scares old ladies and children, evoking judgement, rather than contemplation on the philosophically deep lineage which emerged from the 'non-rule' of taoist monks of the east. Beginning in 300 BCE this stateless state of society is based on non-hierarchical voluntary associations. So, speaking to that little voice, still hanging on to the things we don't need - what makes you think, that within the total transformation of all that you see, that these token civil roles will not be filled in a future without Big Daddy? Do you not trust that you will be taken care of by little brother, cousins, grandmother and grandfather? Mother even?"

He looked to the front row suddenly, as if his digital ears picked up on a question that arose in someone's mind, "Who will fix things? Fixing things is a waste of time! What happened to making things that don't break?" He continued his contemplative strolling dialogue, razor edgy and sharply peaceful, "At some point we had the production of consumer goods rightly aligned within human accord and the planet, producing no more or less than what we needed. We even used to have heirlooms tools that would last beyond decades, handed down generation to generation, but in a need to further extend our imagined economic prosperity we began to extrapolate our efforts so extremely far from the actual need required that it became a system built on nothing, a system of fully planned obsolescence, designed to fail, and thus here were are, coming to grips with our failures. It's shameful really, that we've allowed this path of travel, and that we didn't rip this bullshit to threads. And just as amazing that we're still here to look at all of it, and correct our errors."

The lecture continued, building minds into models, "Say a bridge needs to be built. Does that task become a three-lane flyover in preparation for the 10,000 citizens who will be living nearby in the future? Designated by Big Daddy and the nested overlords of the land? Or instead in a state of unconstricted freedom, will a team of builders come together naturally to construct an appropriate bridge, because they can all instinctually identify the need? The preparation for an infusion of 10,000 people can still be planned into the bridge design, though actualized when not needed a waste of material, effort and energy. After the present need is relieved with an adequate bridge, this self-assembled team devoted to intelligent cooperation can disband and move on to the next daunting or simple task.

"Hey! A pothole in the road needs to be filled. Does that task need to be designated by some overload of the land? Or a single person devoted to filling potholes? Or does someone have a spare moment to go out and fill it the moment they see it?

"If that is the case in a system of unconstrained freedom, what happens the moment that the pothole is honestly noticed, and the person who notices it says 'No, someone else will fix it, I've got more important things to do.' What would you think? How would you feel?

"If it is you who notices it, whatever task it is you're engaged in doing, the task itself, a living dialoge of the divine, has allowed the space for you to notice this whole system need, and either take responsibility for it, or the responsibility to find someone to take it on, and fill the hole. For the moment we shirk the responsiblity of filling holes the moment they are seen, well my friends, that's when it all comes apart.

"Keep focusing on your own individual self and you will forget the true scope of your Self, what you own, and what is yours to take care of. This individualistic focus allows Big Daddy to define your edges, most basically your physical Self as a flat economic cog and worker ant looking out for number one, when in fact, if you let go of the word ‘number’, you are simply *One*, and you have no edges at all.

“What Big Daddy has convinced us of is that even though we use that road, or bridge, maybe even everyday, that this road is not ours to take care of, or even further, that this road is not you, or me; the extended Self beyond physical edges.”

He put his hands on his heart and then quickly snuck in a few mudras before continuing, “So say it’s not a road and not a pothole and not a bridge, but say there’s a multi-storey building across the road, and it’s burning. You look up with eyes open to see a burning building. You hear people dying inside, screaming in anguish, in terror for their lives, calling for the divine to save them. What will you do? Will you allow their call to move you in your heart and mind, into that building and save those people? Or will you stand back and wait for Big Daddy's cavalry? The designated system? Firefighters, EMS, police, media? Will you wait for the official hero's to step up and into action? Or will you do something about it? Will you say to your Self ‘yes, I will be first in, I will fix this, because somewhere I recognize a mistake was made, and I am intelligent enough and capable enough to do something about it’, actualizing the heroic god that is needed and called for. Again, it’s better to build something properly, within required need and the deepest chord of awareness, rather than wait till it burns to the ground, floods, or is torn to shreds.

“If you are still waiting for Big Daddy’s cavalry, whether it is your town to provide you with a recycling program, or waiting for your city to reinvent roadways that better support the development of alternative energy, or if you are waiting for your provincial or state government to beurecratically shift it's views on public education, or even if you’re waiting for the national government to develop new programs that better recognize the importance of the arts, you will be waiting a long fucking time.” They all laughed at the absurd notion of the prison-like government supporting creativity and expression.

“So you say to me ‘It’s okay John, beyond the many nested layers of government beuracracy there are corporate programs that support creative art initiatives, fund community athletics, and instigate community gardening projects. New bottom lines are invented daily to develop and streamline the best corporate practices which monitor social and environmental impact. Corporations even have advanced R&D labs developing the newest environmental technologies, and a team of accountants who are right now, designing ways to best integrate these new breakthroughs into the current economic structure, so further government bailouts are not needed, and depression need not be spoken of like a dirty word.' I would reply, 'That is a very concise argument.' However, I would continue, 'Did you swallow their marketing campaign? Or can you actually see those things in real life? Other than brand, slogan, and derivitave marketing platforms?... as if doing something and saying your doing something is the same thing: we're not actually taking action, we're just telling you we are.

"At the foundation of all those programs, the foundation of those large corporations, even the foundation of the government, is what?" In the gap of silence he continued, "You are a smart and studious person so you reply, 'The money lenders.' And what products do the banks create?"

"They create currency!" someone shouted.

"No," he quickly responded, "Currency is a representational medium of the woven paths of potential energy. Not the energy itself. Think about it. Does it matter to you the path in which money arrives in your hands - the path it takes the moment it leaves the chip on your fingertips or stained paper under your nails? When you give it do you see it's entire path circumnavigating back to you? And when you receive it do you see it's path of movement through and beyond you? Well, you should. Seeing the truth is worth the investment of attention it requires."

"Derivatives!" another shouted.

"Futures!" yet another.

"No!" John responded like a gunshot, "Slaves! Banks create slaves." He almost face palmed.

"At this point you might as well take out a loan to bet on a horse race, because with that old system of business development - or even educational investment - the entire socio-economic system will have changed completely by the time you're able to see your entrepreneurial idea blossom. It will no longer be cusp or relevant. And before your education is complete, it will no longer be a stream of knowledge that is valid and applicable to society and you will be a slave to a dead system, whether you swallowed their marketing ploy or not."

He looked up at the image again, "I don't want to beat you over the head, but every choice matters! The reason I keep on coming back to this image is because to me, it represents the exact moment we are in right now. We still have a choice and it is a choice that requires brand new awareness.

"As consumers, even with an advanced mental understanding of the power of our choice, the products we continue to purchase are items that destroy the environment in their creation, transportation, and even use - for example, an electric car is built in the same type of factory as a gasoline powered car. Yet we are still being given the opportunity to choose a deeper way. One more fail to ignite that however, and the option to choose will be taken away from us, and still yet, the new awareness will solidify." He collected his thoughts for a micro second, "This cognitive mental understanding in this state of exponential wholistic cybernetic advancement will evolve into an empathic emotional link. This link will force us, in our hearts, to actually feel the pain of that child in that sweatshop making that pair of Nike shoes… that we have to buy, because it's the only way shoes will be made.

"And then walking the path with bare feet we begin to feel the first waves of the immensity of that choice being taken away from us. When catastrophe strikes both economic and environmental, such as it has over the last number of hours – or even within a slightly expanded gaze, backward to Calgary or Katrina or Sandy, Japan or Hati – the power in this great building of civilization will go out. And when that happens, we will be in lockdown. The world will discontinue to move. We will not be able to access our online network, our handhelds will eventually run out of batteries, we wont be able to access our address book, we won't know anyone's number, and we won't even know the time of day. And in our bare feet we will mourn the loss of our ability to choose a better world. That option will be gone."

All were reminded of the current list of global crisis's, panic crept in to the room, and building. Gridline was usually a haven of light and upliftment and there were a few that almost ran in unconscious panic from the hall. But John roped them in like stray cows, "And the voice inside you says, 'I'm scared.' I can hear it. 'I'm really scared John, of both that future and what I will have to let go of to actualize a different one. We can't let go of all these institutions our civilization depends on, these institutions that protect us, even if they abuse us.' In response I say, 'I'm scared too.' All heroes are scared. In some way. The last second heroics of rushing into a burning building; of course. Of loosing their lives; of course" he looked up to the image again, everyone followed his gaze, "Losing their money, their prestige, their friends, looking embarrassed, making a mistake, having to apologize and swallow their pride. If a hero wasn't afraid, they are moving into action without the required depth needed and maybe even for the wrong reasons, they would not be rising to the actual present need of their surroundings, of their community. Community is not your social graph or media spread, and not who likes what you've posted on the Boards or corporate boards. Hero's don't repeat themselves, they don't simply show off, watching who watches them; like an actor performing in the same play, embedded in persona, role playing or false ego. Authentic soul drop: I refuse to bend and mold my Self into a marketing strategy!" deGryder shouted.

He had to collect his thoughts again and re-engage with the audience. He looked at the back. Aum thought he looked directly at him, but could have been mistaken.

"If you were deep in the building, burning alive, who would help you? If you had no money, who would help you? If you were starving and had no food, who would help you? If you had a garden and needed help planting it, or harvesting it, who would help you? If a friend was starving they probably would. When you have car trouble and are stuck on the side of the road, how many people could you phone up that would drop what they are doing and come in for a rescue mission? Or further, how many people in your immediate neighborhood, driving by, would stop and help you on the side of the road? If you had a part to play in building that previously needed bridge they certainly would. So when the lights go out, who will you be able to count on? It is these people, who, in an emergency, step in to fill holes, make up your real community.

"In an emergency response situation, where the full collapse of all that we know and all that we see - systems of government, law, education, commerce, personal finance, health, transportation, and, our notions of community - is right there staring us in the face, an adaptation to perceive, trust, and work with an existing dimensionality which can be inferred through the empathic heart, the concrete 3D world and the site-specific situation around us, and may be our only hope as a civilization. And it's not really that difficult a leap to make, or put into practice… as it is, our ancient present. When a deep emotional feeling augments what you perceive, each of these simple choices however simple, whether to walk, bike, or drive, whether to shop at the local farmers market or the closest corporate clone implanted at the corner complex, to turn on the TV or read a book, to take the time to help someone who is asking for it, or isn't, to invest time into the people who excite you, or a relationship that inspires you, are at this point, critical to our species, and the only choices that matter."

"Live!" He shouted at them, "With star seed integrity, fucking live!

"The only way to make it through this time and repair our crumbling world is to allow those subtly perceived things to influence the choices we make in every moment, a choice that is made based on the full conscious recognition of truth, and to be fully present for one another, because that supportive structure is far more stable, far more supportive, far deeper reaching and in-line with our Gaia-given true human nature.

"And it's not like this path," he pointed to the left side of the *Pioneer* image, "will lead us to this place," pointing to the right side, "It must be chosen in every existing moment to fully manifest.

"Thank you for sitting and absorbing this lecture, in full presence, and assisting me in shaking the foundation of Babylon."

* * *

Jenn was up top. The council room sat at the top of the building, next to the observatory past the gridline rooftop garden. A few feet from the garden path towards the meeting room green treetops poked out of the open roof from the permaculture gallery below. A high and broad veranda of solar panels was above it all, catching the ample summer light, powering 100 percent of the council room, and much more throughout the centre. It was a an architectural crowning achievement, internationally renown and award winning, narrowly holding on to the edge of city building regulations. The council room itself was a half glass teepee facing west, the other half merged with the more typical building architecture. Like a yin yang from birds eye view, the observatory dome did much the same, though with telescope facing east. Polished wooden poles held the teepee structure solid, with fully enclosed glass walls from floor to roof

After a few moments of star gazing in the garden, she entered the meeting room and selected a seat around the outer ring, briefly putting her hand on John's shoulder as she walked by. The circumference of the room was near fourty feet and could fit nine at the round table, with another 18 council members around it at the exterior chairs. A fireplace was blazing on the inside wall, and above the wooden hearth was an opulently framed original Alex Grey painting, *Oversoul.* The setting was quiet and austere, there was no music playing, only the sound of the crackling fire and thumbs on handhelds.

Jenn tried to recall how long she had been meditating after the lecture, but couldn't. Now that she was there, she couldn't even recall how long she had been sitting in the core council meeting. Regardless, they always started when everyone arrived, rather than a set time; blossoming from whatever pre flows were set in motion. It was the heart of the mystery school. Invites and meetings were never formal, printed, mentioned in messages, or in public. It was not media driven, but a feeling inside of conversation based-action. From what she could tell everyone just knew. Just like now, as a surfer knows which wave will be the one to take.

During her job shadow she had much to acclimatize to, learning to surf the invisible, and that which was only felt. Acclimatizing to that collective voice, the one that terrified her, to the point of nearly being unable to remain in the council room…until she approached it like a courtroom; noticing it invoked the same level of impact. Similarly there was the important role of conscious witness, space holder, continuous container, which she was first introduced to, and practiced on the outer ring of seats. And then there was the round table. It was not for the light hearted, as so much was determined by simply selecting a chair at the council table, like a specific role or weight was hoisted on your shoulders, a connection and trust of the integral self, speaking out a reflection of collective purpose and highest visionary view of heart awareness. An emergent future was revealed and instantly defined, neither by personal intent or random circumstance, but by the inner group oracle contained within all present there and the selfless service to the collective wisdom that congealed.

There were already 12 people sitting along the outside wall, and another five at the circular table in the middle. John, Zhe, Trae, and two ladies who were immaculately dressed, more similar to what she remembered from the Full Spectrum festival.

On the outside there were two younger teens. One wore a pair of white shutter shade glasses, the other long blonde hair that was more like a dandelion than a mop. A man with a cane, long brown braids and tattoo's that crept down his arms past his black short sleeved shirt. He looked familiar, but she couldn't quite remember from where. Next to him sat a giant. A huge man that seemed like a big burly brawler, he also had tattoos along his arms, rising up his neck too. Rather than colorful Japanese inspired tapestries, this man only had black and white scrolling Sanskrit that wrapped around his limbs. A couple seats over was a tall thin man with long dreadlocks with a grey t-shirt, Zildjian logo on the front. There was an older man with a red jacket and short cropped black hair, another tall and skinny, polished modern punk, and a couple older ladies with graying hair that she had noticed at the lecture. On the far side of her was an older man with scraggly beard, long blond hair and crystal blue eyes that were almost white. The last man wore black dress pants, polished black shoes, a black pinstriped jacket with large lapels, his beard was full, he had large hoop earrings, eye liner and down combed mowhawk. It was Ted. A smile erupted on both of their faces as their eyes met, recognizing each other. As he waved she could see he had certainly grown since Full Spectrum.

Jenn was about to stand and go sit next to him but Dragon walked in, along with Ezekiel.

Zeke took a seat at the council table, where he would remain for the duration of the meeting.

Dragonkeeper walked around the table and stood near the fireplace, the far end from where Jenn sat. He seemed to be in a foul mood, though after a few moments of meditating on *Oversoul*, he seemed to lighten, or at least breathe deeper.

Derek took a seat on the outer ring, next to the fireplace, not yet deeming himself ready to sit at the round table.

Following Derek's gaze, looking at those sitting in the centre, Jenn caught a glimpse of the dark hoods under Zhe's eyes. Zhe noticed this, and in the gap of silence, began talking as if everyone saw it as she did; as if it had been spoken aloud. Zhe swept his long dark hair behind his ears with both hands, caught the wave, and the meeting officially began, “I haven't slept for three days. Been tinkering with the automation for the new multi-team based system - revising the procedure - for recon data confirmation and new entrants in the field.” It was mostly to John and his father, who he spoke, “So when the Boards went fully down, and with the Red Tower nearly knocked out, it allowed me the space to fully retool some mainlines. Just got it up and in full flow this evening. Perfect synch. Should be easier; more accommodating to the breadth of the new, as if all the streets just got paved and extra lanes added, after being made of dirt for years. Trae has been with me, miming in and measuring the detail available at each moment; a lighthouse on an infinite coastline to launch back to from within the data depths,” he looked over at his dad. No one caught the severe glance but Zeke. With proud smile next to him, though also bleary-eyed, Trae the Seer spoke very little, “Nimbly feeling all the work that’s been going on.”

John smiled in gratitude.

Throughout his time, and throughout it all, John continually said to himself, ‘I’m as easily replaced as a drop of water in the ocean.’ If it wasn’t him it would be someone else, not standing in his shoes, but standing in their own. Wings spread further and broader than all others, though each creature has their place in the tapestry, to shine out their gifts.

Here new faces would emerge to step into new roles, in this room. It was intended to be an active portal much like the apartment.

“When you do find it, rest well my friend,” John said to Zhe, “The results of your efforts are beyond the word successful. We are all indebted to your efforts and sacrifice,” They bowed to each other. Then Zhe sat back in near invisible observation as his father did, while Trae, even though deathly exhausted, stayed far more present as the conversation shifted to the newcomers.

With the recent influx of participants many were checking in for the first time, first time visit to the centre, or re-committing to the work of structural transition and celebratory evolution. So many flooded in, those of whom he had only met once, some of whom he had never met, this one and her companion included; Dawning Deer and Spectral Grace Photon. John turned to the two new faces, "What is the update from the traveling gypsy nation?" he asked.

"Much. We've pushed the advanced festival circuit modality as far as the context will take us: in eco-theological prayer, wholistic Gaian awareness, galactic and interdimensional information exchanges, and also true indigenous acceptance. Directly connecting the two actually; the ancient earth spirits and the even more ancient celestial ancestral beings."

It was very wild to see them, in person, mannerisms, inflection of voice, true movement, all the minutiae that doesn't come through on the screens, or could ever be derived by watching each choice, word, or action, seeing each soul seed grow. Dawning Deer continued, "We've gone through enough, we've aged enough, in generations and in our sustained off-grid ships that they have recognized our new tribe, our story and myth, as part of their future casting contexts; an aspect of the new earth body itself." Her indigenous heritage shined through at that moment, like a badge of true incarnated soul path achievement, shining out in full presence beyond the hippie style dialogue and fashion trends, even beyond her ears that just happened to point through her black and dyed pixie haircut. "It's beyond the exuberant bliss of the dreams from generations ago, peaking such a cohesive cultural newness that only the settlements of Mu can properly reflect our work. A time of celebration is a vast understatement," she smiled radiantly, "If you would like to upgrade your body to a light-based inter-planetary vessel come flow with us for a while,"

John laughed, "Climb on the vibe? Outstanding."

"Yes, especially since the destiny circuit has expanded and permeates into communities that are not even aware that we exist."

Dawning Deer counterpart continued, wearing a bowler hat with a crystal embedded band, leather jacket under medicine shawl, open collared shirt and crop circle tattoos under her collar bones, "*We* are actually the aliens, to them."

Deer spoke again, "So, as vastly different humans, it's a lot easier to introduce the actual aliens, unmediated, 1-on-1."

"Aliens? I look forward to a season with the nomad tribe, when the last quarter is complete here."

Spectral Grace, under her bowler hat quickly interjected, "Uh, just so you know, they don't like being called that. Alien. They have very specific star systems they represent, with specific names..." John was kinda speechless, and he was caught in her bright light blue eyes, "...We'll get you in, so you can get to know the new cosmicology." She finished, feeling any further words divergent from the meeting as a whole and unnecessary,

"Thank you, please enjoy your stay in the city," John replied.

Another man entered the room, short and stocky, full beard and crack snap whip quick, in mind and heart. He quickly sat next to Dawning Deer without even taking in the room. John had to talk quickly as it was apparent that he had much work to do, probably leaving the exact moment this conversation came to a close - not out of rudeness, but dedicated service and exploding enthusiasm for actualizing both in the cross mesh of waking and dreaming.

"Nice to see you again Joseph. Thank you for being here," said John. There was a pause and Joseph nodded his head very quickly in agreement of something deeper. They both rose as they shared a hug, "You too Johnathan."

They sat again, "As the parallel track to the star tribe and the flatland polar anchor, how does the intake fair fair? Is the carnival context gaining traction with those who have only two eyes open?"

"Yes, of course!" He blinked quickly and was very exited to share and spread around the success he was finding in the world. He was a dynamo in fact. "The real-time scientific exhibition within the self-driven 'Maker' context," he did the quotations, "allows that third eye to open even larger than the other two!" he laughed out loud and continued speedily, "Every day people come in, poor as beggars, indebted like a slave-race, in each and every city-state, individuals and families who have been pleading to be engaged in new ways, asking for deeper gates to open in their lives and to be sustained and uplifted in ways that serve what they know in their hearts and souls," he tapped his heart and forehead, "With that additional eye open," he illustrated it, "it's like activating the new renaissance and all we focus on as team leaders, and both facilitators and fair emissaries is dissolving engrained patterns. Prime objective: turning off the TV to go see what the neighbors are up to." He looked around, talking to the entire room now, "With these DIY projects it's like keeping up with the Jones in a context that isn't consumptive but technically creative," he put on a kind of impromptu show, one voice: "Your gonna get off the grid by putting solar panels on your home?" then another: "Well

I'm gonna figure out how to power the whole block with my compost pile," his smile was huge and genuine, "So ideas like the free energy network are ripe and happening quickly."

"Not as quickly as we'd like though," there was a voice from one of the outside seats; the man with the red jacket. All at the council table turned, "My name is Nathaniel Quark. I am working specifically on expanding the free energy network." There was an ample pause, Quark saw an open chair at the council table, "May I?"

Joseph looked at those at the council table, John nodded.

"Please," Joseph spoke.

Quark took the chair and continued, "It's not like a model kit in a box, right? To avoid detection all pieces need to be shipped independently, in different quantities, and even daisy chained, so that one inventor receives 200 parts with instructions to ship 199 parts to the next inventor, with the actual shipping address coming in by a different means entirely. Sometimes packages which have lit up - been noticed on their radar - are left for weeks on end, until they cool. So it's slow going, excruciatingly slow going."

"But that is the nature of physical evolution," John piped in.

Quark nodded, "Fact: Approximately once a week another engine comes online."

"That's a good rate of change, that'll be another dozen by year end," Zeke said.

"We've recalibrated the majority of our efforts however, to simply distribute the information packets that detail how to use the magnetic field of our human bodies to essentially do the same thing." Jenns mind reeled at the thought of human bodies becoming the energy source of all human activity. "We are still in the test phase of this, again, systemizing the necessary foundational elements and practical timelines, and then fine-tuning them. For example optimal diet and hours of sleep, mediation length and visualization techniques that adequately link the mind and conscious awareness, to amp body resonance to the level where we can power all the electronics that we surround ourselves with.

"After that it is only a matter of time before we will shape the patterns of extended electricity around us without thoughts, the electric pulse of on and off at microscopic frequency, directly interacting with the communication infrastructure we've developed: indie datasphere to the entire internet."

To John and Zeke this was not news, but already in their practice.

"So through meditation you'll be able to program a computer?" Grace asked him.

"No," Quark corrected, "*You* will be the computer. Once well-practiced there will be no need for the HCI terminals just the grid, but even then, electrons are everywhere, so the grid itself isn't even necessary. But one step at a time, right?"

"Yeah, like teaching deaf kids sign language," said Dan, who had just slipped in and found the last seat next to Trae. Those there chuckled.

Looking around the full table, seeing John, Zeke, Zhe, Trae, Dan, Deer, Grace, and Joseph, Quark continued, "Macek has been working dedicatedly with the visualization and mediation aspects, while other network nodes are more focused on the nutritional aspects or the transmission of lessons packets through the dream ecology. If anything, it'll be the security of *that* space which is at risk, *that* development which will be pressurized from the outside, rather than the engine distro system, which is more of a back-up plan at this point anyway. We truly don't want to model our future evolution on our predecessors anyway."

"What do you mean?" Jenn asked from the outside ring of seats. They were used to her unimposing far from foolish questions, as they unanimously furtherd everyone's understanding of the situation, even their expanding synergistic connectivity.

Daniel actual answered the question, vaulting it from the table and allowing it to rain down everyone in the room, "The stupendous efforts our predecessors have gone to, in all levels of physical infrastructural developments, have been ultimately, for the select few at the top to line their pockets with cash. It's utterly laughable actually, like piping drinking water through a clean lake,"

"Or as absurd as bottling water to purchase," Zhe spoke.

"Or canning fresh air," Quark added, completing what he was called to share, finding a welcome space to do so. He nodded in conclusion, "Thank you," and he returned to his seat, along the outer ring. A chorus of, 'Thank you's , 'Gratitude's and 'Blessings on your work,' circled round the room.

There was a gap and remembering, Joseph continued within it, "Oh yeah. This inventor network is fed and nourished, further activated by all those new and awakening. There's just so much energy to harness right at our fingertips, and it just keeps going. The simple act of meeting those who live in the local neighborhood and discovering what they are up to with their time, and space, and land, and energy… it is this life path curiosity, the random synergy that charges the deepest engine of social transformation." He finally paused, moving into social meta science mode, "That's the stasis of what's left over when the maker carnival has moved through the city-states. Along with new energy network nodes, the vibratory ecosystem is primed to balance out on a non-local meta level, so the rainbow-tribe," he motioned to Deer and Photon, "and the work they do - the ignorance that would normally be there for, you know, the far extreme of meeting aliens," He instantly back pedaled. "I mean, ugh.. " he looked over at Grace Photon, seeking the most politically correct wording. With crystal eyes glowing, she intoned, "They prefer Star Peoples."

"Yes!" It was like further fuel for Joseph and his speed increased, "The ignorance usually rife and exponential in meeting Star Peoples is not there; because the sun is out, the birds are singing, or whatever synchronistic magic may be happening for them that day. If the work is being done, it is being done everywhere, regardless of location. And they are open because the fair is grinding away, working on that opening, exposing that inner truth, in the opposite location where the meta-rainbow bridge touches, it activates that buzzing holo heart centered space so it can instantly be filled with - gold - by the best spirit based facilitators; magical planetary creatures and incarnated guides who beget magical ancestors, guiding that full system human and planetary healing."

It was like the light finally turned red, and he stopped on a dime.

"Infinite gratitude dear brother," said Dawning Deer as she bowed in thanks at his summation and reflection.

"Likewise and reflected dear sister," said Joseph "We're still on for tea?"

"Of course."

"Right on DeeDee. It'll be truly wonderful to catch up."

"I couldn't agree more Jo-jo," Dawning Deer added, "And plan a date and location for our two tribes to meet and mesh."

There was only a slight pause before the realization and vision of the exponential human growth potentials of both the metaphysical flatland rainbow entrance and the star people rainbow entrance coexisting in the same space-time entered the minds of the central core. Jovial cheers and 'Here here!'s erupted as all meeting members pounded the council table as if it was fucking parliament.

In reaching that high note peak, Joseph got up from the table, bowed and left the room, probably headed back to work. Derek was quick to take Joseph's seat next to Dawning Deer, as the cheers were still fading out on his exit, "What about the clans and tribes battling each other on the prairies?" Dragon asked DeeDee.

She was taken aback by the charge and the quick shift from spirited cheers to a question that was more like an accusation, "What are you talking about?" Dawning Deer asked politely. Derek continued, "What of the original nations that are in combat with each other? Should they not be addressing the pressing issues of unity, land rights and the environmental destruction of their lands rather than succumb to in-fighting? What of these nations?"

He was pressing her. It was like having a grizzly bear eat at the dinner table. Even with claws, teeth and growl, she was still able to respond coherently, "That is a separate branch which I am not in communication with. The economic disparity of land right's is not my area of expertise or interest, nor is the continued dialogue between colonial government and the original nations of Turtle Island."

Derek looked at her beautiful hippie clothes, her queen like elegance and spoke at her, "Gypsy, a planet without the wisdom inside it's resources resonating, will have no dreamtime to bridge out to the stars and their nations."

She was not used to getting her hands dirty, nor being challenged in this way. All at the council table were all looking for an open avenue of dialogue, a hole, gap or opportunity that would slow Dereks charging steam train, "If you represent the culmination and resurgence of contemporary tribal culture how can you not be working on this issue as well? The right use of the plants, trees, water and the deep deposits of petrol wealth of our total evolutionary history; it is an issue that concerns all humans, not just the first ones."

John was about to speak, collaring Derek, who was again acting like like an over protective guard dog, but Jenn interjected first and moved in to cage him, "A different branch alliance has taken up this work Keeper, focusing on these heavy aspects of culture you delicately and tactfully drop-in like bombs. Why tie them to the sincere efforts which are brought to the council table by Deer and Photon here: cultivating the future Noosphere for habitation." As if it was a courtroom Jenn picked up her briefcase and took a seat at the council table, sitting where Quark once did. She loved the fact she didn't have to say, 'permission to approach the bench,' she could just cut in when it was most appropriate.

"As part of an organic and very quickly evolving project development team, I began working with a group of focused litigation leaders who have been keeping the machine at bay, and putting continued pressure on the government, as farmers lay in their dirt under their combines; while the first nations organically work towards re-defining their national leadership."

She had learned much from John. Looking at everyone at the table she began to share, knowing her direction, even if they didn't, "I've been formalizing a network of independent family run organic farms, receiving signatures and data, even idea refinement, while other branches of the team have been receiving the data and petitioning for a new government certification. Which came through today."

There were smiles and nods that circled around the table, except for Dragon.

"With very minimal knowledge of each other, though still focused, we succeeded in developing a new regulatory body by pressuring the government with a deep fact bank on contemporary human nutrition and the energetics of food, supplied by a voluntary California-based research body. Building on the comparatively simple organic standard, we proved to the government that people who consume family made food will be healthier, require less health care, live longer, be more active, and thus contribute more to the economy, than simply organic food."

"Interesting. A new depth," said Photon.

"Increasing the standard from organic?" asked Zhe.

"Yes. The family food rating system builds on the organic standard, but measures the sociological factors of production, a systemized framework of farm history, family dynamics, machine maintenance and purchase history, employees social graph, to name a few examples, with many more extended influences; all which still affect food quality. This new depth, as Photon put it, brings quality control into the area of social vibration."

"And contributes this vibration to which economy?" John asked.

"The government still perceives only one economy John, their economy," Jenn quickly replied. "The main point we had to concede in the bargaining process is that a percentage of product must be sold in the public market, not saved, stored or independently traded. This may not be the best long term solution, but at least families are no longer chaining themselves to the mutated blades of big agra thrashers tines to keep their farms alive."

Zeke and Trae nodded in support, and Jenn continued, "In trade for this public offering the government has created laws that officially protect the farmlands from intrusion who have achieved this new certification standard. And rather than another green washing or empty medal branding campaign, we were even able to secure a tiny spec of funding toward educating the public on this new family food certification, more importantly begin to build public awareness of the independent food producers speckled across the nation. Shipping and sharing goods will be another problem entirely, but until that is solved, legend of the Glenn Family's hand pressed Maple Syrup in Sudbury, or the Boldt Family's hand harvested organic milk from Osler, or the Danenhaur's hand picked Pink Ladies from Cawston, will become local delicacies and influential clean spirit repositories which will color vacation road trips, further celebrate local farmers markets, the 100 mile diet, and ward off the encroachment of computer generated food mono-culture."

"This has all emerged from the Sunny Valley case? I thought you were pursuing research to combat some kind of historical land claim by Grunch Land?" Zhe asked.

"No shit! What has this got to do with the first tribes and the pillaging of natural resources?" demanded Dragon.

John's hand embed beeped and his presence exited the dialogue, he dove into another space, fully focused, to the point that he left his seat at the council table and moved to the outer ring.

"Right," said Jenn, "Yes, all this has grown and found successful completion quicker than the Sunny Valley work. Our land rights argument stood solid against Grunch's, with photographic evidence, historical documents, even a storied lineage describing many woven levels of cooperation. Specifically, the piece of land that *is* the town of Sunny Valley was gifted to starving Dutch homesteaders hundreds of years ago by the local indigenous tribe. The reverse of an Indian reservation, the tribe still keeps the town under it's wing, in many ways, offering much insight into developing a relationship to the land, a relationship that was not possible to import from Holland as easily as other aspects of their culture. Grunk claimed that they owned the entire territory including the half dozen indigenous tribes living on the land. At the time of colonization slavery was still in practice and thus the Indians were considered to be resources, like the trees and water and minerals, not actual humans with rights."

"Slavery… how did that even happen," said Daniel in wholistic dismay.

"My thought's exactly," replied Jenn.

"Wow, that ownership claim is what they built their case on?" asked Ezekiel.

"Yes. The Sunny Valley case was thus brought up to a national level and merged into another larger case against Bill C-111. Now, if you are not up to speed, Bill C-111, deals with last land right's: identifying all land currently used and unused for production, along with the resources they still contain, in both the private and public sector."

"The last mapping."

"Essentially yes. But because of the continued dispute surrounding this bill, both national history has come to be debated in the House of Commons, along with a long list of national examples of corporate infringement which are just now coming to see the public light. This large case has unified a wide variety of the leaders of treaty lands and their residing tribes who still work at eliminating in-fighting and internal power struggles," she simply raised her eyebrows after saying this line, "as well as stepping into the power and pain of their original agreements with the government. The Sunny Valley micro-case however, was a breakthrough. Illustrating earth terrorism outside of the oil and gas industry and also provided a model for future HLI relationship building." She quickly added in, "Human-Land Interaction," knowing HCI, Human-Computer Interaction, was a term used regularly in meetings.

"Isn't that nice," Derek sarcastically responding. "By adding in another complex case to consider, the government easily drags the issue out further, without solution, all the while the very system we are trying to choke out, now has it's hooks in our food chain, and can analyze, clone and manipulate every single detail of what makes this independent farm network thrive," Derek punched in his critical insight, and it was as if Jenn hadn't even talked.

John was still in deep so Jenn had to respond without support, "You are enjoying this ride no doubt Derek. 'If we can't find freedom, no one will,' right? We have been trying to revive and evolve a dying structure in a sustainable civilized way, not with vigilante piratism or by holding hostages and demanding ransom." She shook her head, "While enmeshed in this far reaching team work, I've heard it is you that has coordinated the monkey wrenching of the corporate pipelines."

"A graceful strike modeled and supported by the resurgence of ELF, their personnel having expanded 10 fold," Derek quickly replied.

Jenn continued to joust, "Even with enthusiastic environmental paramilitia group's waiting to be dispatched on a single thought, protecting these lands from corporate infestation with war and combat and violence is not a long term or sustainable solution! Such a small, even continuous sting on a giant dinosaur's toe may not be noticed, and if so, an eruption of anger and quick swat doubtlessly a reaction."

As of yet there was no room for others to speak, even Deer or Photon. Derek replied to the comment quickly, "I'll have to get you to do some research for me Jennifer, on how David took down Goliath." He stood up, beginning to circle the table. "You are correct in identifying my area of focus, but what you see is so small. With self-knowledge and awareness I take pride in my gifts; the work I did to hack the chemtrail planes and replace their atmospheric stew with 3-quinuclidinyl benzilate, especially."

"BZ!? Holy shite! Way too extreme! You would be better off spraying liquid LSD in the atmosphere," said the braided and cained shaman on the outside circle.

"Extreme!? Just you wait till I present my full drop on the Tar Sands leveling," Still circling the room he turned to look at Dawning Deer, who was still present. Something indigenous and ancestral sparked through in his visage, if not genetic, then karmic, "The leveling will display a Mohawk Warrior fury that will be truly felt; a fully militarized coup internationally funded and supported."

Derek took a seat, precisely where John was sitting.

There was a huge shift, cries of pain and stress could be heard somewhere. Mouths were open, agasht. Jenn gasped at the thought of her young countries first civil war, during which hallucinogens would intoxicate every breath, "That's kinda scary."

"What can I say, the world is a scary place," replied Derek.

"And none the less with you in it, taking these extreme actions," Dawning Deer replied.

Even Grace Photon spoke up, "You actually made the connection to an international suppler of weapons to militarize an indigenous nation?"

"Even special ops training. They're not levitating yet, but soon."

"What the fuck is this!?" Exclaimed Dawning Deer, "Gridline has manifested a private army!" Looking at John who was not paying attention, then back at Derek, "And you judge my purpose! My integrity of knowledge!? This is certainly not what I expected to be happening here. Let's go Grace."

"Yeah sister, let's go."

They rose and left the council meeting in shock and dismay. Demona entered the room before the door closed, taking a seat at the outer ring.

"Island kind, leave if you must!" Derek angrily shouted at them. He began to rupture at the lack of opportunity to defend his reason, his cause, or the flag he carried. Rising from the table as they left, he exploded with a solar fire inside of him, blasting out his eyes and mouth, ready to burn down everyone and everything he could see, "But it continues!! It all continues! Without relent! Secret mines dug and wells drilled and pipelines laid and laid and laid without fucking consent! The last of the planets forests cleared and morphed into consumer products in mere moments! Without sanction or even out ability to notice it's terrible monstrous speed! Here, South America and Siberia! Our forested lungs are demolished! Our mineral foundation's are consumed! Our life blood is drained! Only the environmental repercussions of super storms signs for us to read, as entire cities starve to death, as disaster capitalism hold us hostage, tied to this insane death march." Like a creature gone mad in a cage, he looked at the stars through the glass windows and clutched the air, "A blitzkrieg of elemental programming is happening! Chemicals are sprayed into the air to control the weather! Our water system is filtered and manipulated to keep us docile! All the while the sickness of western consumtion is ingrained so deep into the rest of the globe we know nothing else! Visions of historical action, outcomes of liberation are hypnotized out of us by viral pop culture! We are trapped within our own reflections of singular awareness as international plans for war and siege and pillage continue to behind the mirror! The IMF merges RFID tags into ID cards, handembeds, handhelds, and every surgical procedure, even dentistry! Our allies are tortured and struck violently off political kill lists! Our global personnel of holy lightfighters finds demise and diminishment! We need to act! Now! Today!"

He made a plea to all those in the room, of the necessity of his work, motioned to Deer and Photon with his hand, wherever they were in the building, "And these two are content, to sit on an island on the outskirts, receiving support from the core here and the core of that old dead paradigm, involved with neither, convinced of the relevance of their work!"

Derek looked at Jenn. She was firm, and would be ripped to shreds herself, defending her own work if need be, but he eased up a little, looking for allied intelligence, anywhere, "This is not a time to sit back and see these minor policy shifts as transforming a system which is corrupt to its core. That is exactly what they are hoping for, to lull us back into complacency by allowing us to think we have succeeded in fully evolving and saving it's soul, when we have not! It cannot even happen! Not even close! When corruption is it's essential nature!" He was reaching his own exhaustion tipping point with this emotional outburst. Fire blazed in his heart, as it did the fire in the hearth. His voice deepened, "Even though you have found an adequate bandage Jenn Leather - success in saving small specs of integrity-based production land, by creating a tiny bud of a new branch - the law-based political de-activation of the full corporate government has failed. It is time we take up arms! We are at the point of no return, where the outcome of our species will be either one of independently networked self-sufficient pockets of woven prosperity, or the collectively indebted uniform enslavement of our entire species!"

He neared total collapse at making his case, so a new one popped up to the table, very tall, skinny, and fast talking. Her subtle yet noticeable punk and anarchist fashion styling contextualized her position as an aligned subgroup under Derek's gun metal sheet. She spoke, "Transformation of belief and awakening has remained in the scientific and spiritual, but not moved into political action. Continuation without a total whole shift will fester as apathy and inactivity, especially inside the city-states where perspectives need to be changed the most. It is the most elaborate system of living that has manifested here, and will destroy all life if not eradicated fully, even if we retrain it, or think of releasing it from it's position in front of the firing squad, as even now It's fullest crest now creeps toward our front door."

"Geraldine is correct," Derek continued again, picking up the war hammer from her, "This controlled mass planetary destruction has infiltrated all aspects of the environment, shaking our coastlines and collapsing our brightest aligned micro-nodes." He growled, teeth grinding as he spoke quickly, as if he could take down the entire system with his weponized invocations, "The belligerent power-mongering ruling class does not remember the old adage *They got the gun's, but we got the number's*. What can they do when we charge their front doors, storming the Bastille, after activating and invoking millions upon millions of fed up united citizens, who carry blow torches and pitchforks, bats and fists, and like a pack of enraged wolverines we will shred their fat plump trembling bodies into millions of millions of pieces! For that is the level of action now necessary!" The eruption of violent imagery was shocking. Following the outburst Derek continued in a slower contemplation, now as a politician rather than guerilla fighter, "It will not be a pretty site my friends, certainly not polite, but our children and our children's children, when they immerse themselves in the meta-docu-data carnage, will be proud, that we finally stood up with courage, like the generations that came before us who were not afraid to take to the streets and risk life and limb for human decency, and change, for all the things we take for granted today: equality of gender and race, liberty and fraternity." He looked solidly at Zhe, like a trusted a brother, Zhe didn't back him though, "Violence is an old world solution Derek."

John finally came to, quickly jumped in, clearing his throat and the combative tension within Derek and the room; displaying a monk-like peace that made it seem like the outburst never happened, "What is the true answer to all this?" He took a seat next to Zhe, "This combination of total persecution streaming down from the top and total unification bubbling up from the bottom. In right action what can we do about those who refuse logic, and refuse to be humbled?"

Demona answered quickly, "We can only pray for them."

She moved in from the outer ring, taking a seat next to John and looked up at Derek knowingly, "Beyond campaigns of organized violence, or egoic desires for revenge and reckless mob justice, even forced tripping - fuck," she shook her head, "It is only the deepest of prayers that will awaken the hearts and minds of those ignorant, prayers as loud and piercing as Vishnu's conch."

Derek took a seat opposite John, balloon deflated by his band leader, and in the silence Demona continued, "I have seen it happen myself - we have seen it," she respectfully included Derek in gesturing to John, "And our lives saved by it, this commitment to a better world, through unrelenting compassion, and dedication to the highest civil truth of man."

Daniel spoke, "Must we rip them all to shreds Derek?... Or must we resurrect Plato to re-teach our collective leadership like they were infantile school children with learning disorders? This is a situation far beyond obtuse generalizations, but action items must be designed immediately, as this wave now crests; putting into place structuralized militarized prayer teams if that is most wholistically suitable."

At this Derek became outraged. He slammed his weathered fists on the council table. "Our populace is on the receiving end of assassination attempts! We go to prison, to the gallows, even gets stretched on the rack and burned at the mother fucking stake! And you want us to sit here in prayer circles! Civil disobedience is a right we have!!" He lifted up again and stormed around the room, "It is an observerable precursor and warning sign to those in power and control of the coming eradication of their corrupt leadership!"

"Violence begets violence Derek," John said calmly.

Demona continued, "And dear General, how can you have such an ignorant attitude when the intentional prayers mentioned of this nature are the exact ones that saved your own life? How can you honestly look at the Red Tower performance and see it as a reason to militarize?"

There was a gap at the jab, so she continued, "Or would you prefer to be on the receiving end of another assignation attempt? Or maybe check out first hand one of the many new prisons popping up across the country? Or even the inside of those plastic FEMA coffins?"

Derek would still not relent in his argument, but after that last outburst was compassionately contained and brought into his personal life experience. His fire burned less. The core had held strong in peace and unity and Derek moved to sit on the outside ring of seats, remembering, the outcome of the Tower mission, before witnessing his first live burnout; the most public yet. With a few flowing flames from the red coals found, he quietly continued, "Life is not a goddamn business to run with resources to optimize and workers to yoke, with spreadsheets and tables and currencies and ledgers and docs and drives and agendas and Microsoft excel and built-in business clocks programming our intuitive cells. This is the economics of our present day ruin and we should let this old world die, otherwise…" He looked around the room as he sat, he closed his eyes, bowing his head with lashes glistening with moisture, "…we are futureless."

Derek had always found a counterpoint, but here there were no arguments left. The flame died. No one spoke. With that last plea he had managed to bring everyone into a blackhole where all of it could be seen, linked in full finality as the most dismal one solution. Someone just needed to speak out, to combat it, say no, there is a better way, than this collectively agreed upon self-destruction, but no one did. Cat was right. They all failed. The entire fellowship began to falter, rippling out to the furthest reaches of the expanded network and historical legacy. Hidden in their fatigues, even the extremists fell into doubt, viewing the vast scope of all that needed to be shifted in the present world. And as the silence continued the vision began to actualize into reality. Even with such heavy doubt, the gates noticeably opened, and the troops were deployed.

"Mutiny is not my goal here," Derek whispered now, filling the hole, "To claim seeds, nor anarchy." It was the closest he would come to an apology. "We are however, all acting like scared little children. Cowering in corners. Under things. Behind things. Tucked away in small groups, pilled up and shivering in terror. At this new bogey man that's after us; it can finally see us."

Jenn saw the true age of his face, crows feet and grey whiskers, grey hair's on his hung head, he was a veteran from a bygone generations of this work. She recognized that he was closer to the age of Ezekiel, than Zhe, or maybe even older. What had this old man seen to argue so strongly, not for compassion, but mercy killing.

Derek spoke softly again, "Whether we see it or feel it or know it personally, we are all now paralyzed. We can't move, we are afraid to move even a muscle. Afraid of what will happen if we speak out, afraid of true courageous action, afraid of the unsettling waves of repercussion and the tremendous changes they bring."

She had seen too much to give up hope, Demona spoke, "There is one who moves and acts; a hero without fear."

At her words they slowly re-found body and mind, after the total submersion into darkness. She looked at Derek and after a few moments of silence Derek finally nodded in agreement. "So then where is this newest savior currency?" It was a spoken verse, an ask that instantly worked as needle and thread to synch the room, passing from person to person, even Daniel and Ezekiel understood who Demona and Derek referenced, moving to Zhe and Trae, then to Jenn, where it stopped. She looked at John.

John looked up and quickly around the room. The circuit did not complete.

"Where's Cat?"

No one spoke.

And no one spoke.

And no one spoke.

All eyes lowered.

"She what!?"

John's digital ears picked up on the thoughts in the room, seemingly translating the collective emotions inside the movement, translating it into his digital telepathic language.

"Fuck you!" His face turned ghostly white. He stood, "Are you serious? And no one tried to stop her?!"

Silence.

"One man did," Demona finally responded.

"Who?" John shouted quickly.

"Free Zen," Derek answered.

"Who?!" His voice rose in tone, yet no less distraught.

"Aum?" Jenn said, astonished.

"Aum who? Free Zen who?" John shouted quickly again.

"A bottom feeder…" intoned Derek.

"Aum FreeZen," Demona said.

"…who shakes everything," intoned Derek.

"What is this?" John looked at Jenn.

Jenn opened her mouth but couldn't respond. Nothing came out. She had no idea where to even start.

"Who is this Aum FreeZen character!?" He shouted even louder than Derek had, "How come I have never heard of him?"

"He's next level John," said Ezekiel, "Invisible."

"Invisible?"

"Previous to the public breach; the witch burning on the street…" Demona started.

"…Which summoned full investigations from corporate entities, all government security bodies, mainstream and independent media…" Derek added gruffly.

"… Even awakening the exterior gaze and advancing the inner interior hibernation," Zhe added.

"Beginning anew," Demona continued, "Previous to this public breach, Aum FreeZen fronted our firewall defence group at the west tower, saving it, along with the last thread of cohesive civilization from total destruction."

"As well as invoked it's destruction, by agreeing to it's utter collapse, while entwined with a second skirmish with the Keeper," said Zhe, looking at Derek.

"He did not heed the warning from Eziekel, that if one part goes it all goes. And, unable to overcome personal turmoil, chose violence and combat," Trae continued after Zhe.

"Initially," Ezekiel interjected.

"Only intervention by the mysterious One opened him, saved him, and through FreeZen, the tower," Daniel concluded it, moving to the next point, "Previous to that he saved Eziekel from full soul capture."

"Bhahaaha, Oh yeah, I forgot about that," Zeke chuckled.

"And ended up pushing out further beyond all known systems and began mapping the space beyond the dream network," Zachery Escaton concluded.

"*Beyond* the dream network!?" deGryder exclaimed.

"Yes, it was this of all things, that activated the storage and deletion sequence," Trae surmised.

"He re-emerged only yesterday, after a long period of isolated movement and evolution, the results of stepping into the pinnacle download seat of Full Spectrum, and the closing of the Riddle intake structure," The long haired bearded man added from a back layer, clear blue eyes. The full council turned to look at him.

"This was after deeply supporting, then making it through both the Tamer and the Keeper ..." Ted shouted from the other side of the circle.

Then Jenn whispered, "...That was his first encounter with the Keeper..." bringing the focus back to the centre table.

"...He was trying desperately to ensure Jenn made it in, which she did, on her own, " Trae looked over at Jenn in high regard. Jenn looked wide-eyed, to be included, and view her role, coming to realize how mighty a path Aum had walked since she left him in the woods.

"Previous to that he took down an entire oil & gas company through merely his dream lines," Ezekiel added.

"What!" John declared.

"Yes, Pontius Oil went down a week ago, headed by the menacing Burt Detrich," Daniel reported and continued, "He's had quite the reformation and is traveling to Spain to walk the Camino de Santiago,"

"The path of St. James?" John asked.

"A deeply needed reformation," Derek quickly added.

"After a deep re-commitment to the path," Trae again began, "Aum held space for Cat and Cat held space for him as they healed a group external to the Riddle structure, activating, awakening and supporting the second largest meta material exchange from the old world to the new."

"The full public sphere of knowing was simply cracked on that one," said Zhe.

"And to bring it full circle, their work this evening blew it wide open. It was the biggest," said Trae, "Cat was integral to his awakening to the larger Riddle system, as well as his own internal growth, and thus most likely why he risked so much, pushed so hard, to save her."

"All this considered, it still doesn't answer my question. Why haven't I heard him! Why haven't I seen him?" asked John.

"You have Rider," said Demona, "Earlier today, you had a brief connect, when you gave him the lions mane at the beginning of our system rebuild."

"That was him?!"

Looking up from his handheld Ezekiel said, "He's been directly on your 6 since then actually – informally; the hockey game, and even two hours ago when he arrived at Gridline. He even attended your lecture tonight and approached you at the coffee shop beforehand, right after you meet with Jenn."

Then Aum walked in. Everyone was silent.

"This is the meeting without the kool-aid, right?" he asked, looking at the many faces. It was an authentic and fearless and honest and above all, innocent question, and after a moment of residing within it, that new and surprised space, feeling the uplifting spark of it, everyone burst out laughing, in fullest heartfelt relief, even cheering and hollering, clapping in unison, at the surprise appearance. The invisible visible.

"Damn, you know how to make an entrance dude," said John, and everybody laughed even harder. Hearing laughs so deep and so unexplained, tears burst out of their eyes, as they let go of the tension that they had been holding onto.

"Hey!" Aum said, in friendly recognition, finally connecting with John. In the connection and Ezekiel saw the blackhole troops pause their march. "Interesting. Their third skirmish," he whispered to himself, "The first end."

The whole centre lit up with a fresh smiling light. In the space, like a sunrise, Demona ran in to give him a hug, followed by Trae. Next, after a quick bow, Aum received a smile and a handshake from Zhe, Derek approached him after. For a moment it was a tense stare down, "You did it. You fucking made it. Without fail. Every time man. It's incredible to see, each leap, and each save." They did a bro handshake. Derek didn't think anything of leaving him at the front door, trusting it as a signal and flow test. Aum spoke, himself in relief, "So this is where it is. I've been looking everywhere for you guys!"

Aum spied Blue Eagle and then Ted with many other familiar faces sitting along the outside seats. He did not have a chance to greet them all in person though, as both Dan and Zeke rose. "You should have tried the observatory," Dan said smiling, rising from his chair. The most informal of the group, both embraced him, smiling the biggest, shaking him by the shoulders and patting him on the back like he was a 10 year old kid that did real good.

Aum spoke after, "There's one missing."

With those words the entire council thought of Cat, which evoked a collective moment of mourning in each heart. Aum's eyes lowered in reaction, with head bowed, deeply feeling the shift. Not picking up on the reference Jenn timidly poked out from behind Derek's broad shoulder. Derek stepped out of the way. Aum's head lifted with the movement and then they saw each other.

The sound from her smile was full of emotion; compassion and care, love and gratitude, "You *are* here," Jenn gasped. Her eyes full of tears for a different reason than all others, felt how strong Aum's new gaze was, and what it meant to be seen, in full honest truth. She was excited and frightened, but her brave intelligence and courage prevailed as all layers of protective clothing and masks fell away as they quickly moved towards each other, and embraced.

She now showed him who she was, and who she had become since they were last together. "I know," Aum whispered to only her. They caught the bottom of an exhale, linked, and instantly breathed together, rode it in unison without effort or choice, to the fullest lung capacity inhale. At the tip of the inhale their beings were flushed with pure Prana as they nearly floated off the ground. In the midst of their allies and teachers there was a shared moment of no holding back. It was only one breath, but it reached into the infinite for all. They had fully forgotten the setting and circumstance and remembered only what it was like to have their arms wrapped around each other, hands on each other, chests exploding, holding each other so tight and so strong, like magnets that could never be separated, all charkas spinning in harmony, both kundalini spires linked, and their true spirit's speaking, not just as animalistic bodies or visionary minds, but all aspects of shared self, the truest depth of human love. His face was in her neck, lips touching the soft hairs, the smell of her skin in his nose, he whispered, "I knew you were here too."

"I've been sending you love notes," she whispered.

"Yes, I've noticed. I've received them well in my heart."

John cleared his throat, and they gradually separated.

“It’s the Centre,” Aum stated, an insight out his mouth without thought.

Jenn was flustered as she became aware of the entire council staring at them.

Aum said again to her, “We made it to the centre.” With no response again he followed her eyes and met John’s. Aum could see inside his expression, and again insights emerged without thought, “Peace Dragonrider. Be without fret. I’ve been where you sit too, with high hurdles my soul had not the grace to jump, reacting with lack-luster results.”

“Which became illustrious,” Zeke handed him his fedora with the white feather, “As a reminder of that lesson.”

Aum bowed in gratitude.

The meeting had flown far off track, but at fullest renewed capacity and any direction possible, in a moment where so much was up for grabs, John spoke into the space first, to Aum, “So, tell me about the kool-aid.”

Aum looking at Dan, then John, smiling, “It’s like the beer, but it’s polar anchor.” With those words, like geometries within a black hole, an incantation, or meta-lingustic key code both defined and spoken in unison, a much different circuit linked, and John’s embeds beeped again. John looked down and whispered, “Wow. Magic.” He looked up, “Buyers are lined up,” looking at Zeke and Dan, then to Zhe and Derek, and then to Aum.

A glowing smile crept across Trae’s face. With Aum in the meeting it amped up exponentially in speed and purpose, like a rubber band or slingshot. His gaze and presence bringing in all humans with their eyes open, like the entire planet was watching them: the integrity of their discourse, their ability to lead or make decisions, and how far and how deep they could see into the ramifications of their actions. It was a pressure like none other they had felt before, the eye of God and Gaia looking in. They wanted it though, because it confirmed it’s realism and that this was the work that needed to be done as much as anything else.

John finally revealed what pulled him away from the table during Derek’s blazing tirade.

“What do you mean we were courted by Nike for purchase!?” Demona asked emphatically of John.

"What in the hell would a shoe company want to do with an advanced self aware post-paradigm social network?" Derek asked.

It was an astounding development thus most of the core sounded off on it.

"Where do they get the nerve that they can even put a commercial value on the Riddle?" Jenn asked.

"It doesn't have anything to do with their plan of action, other than brag that they leashed and owned us for a time, then they'll most likely sell us off to another company who could make better use of our value," said John. "At the moment they made their offer, Nike's stocks happened to be worth the most in the world, for whatever random reason, so essentially their investors were the 'richest' in the world." He did the quotes with his hands. "Both of those facts have changed over the course of this meeting however; in fact the profit margin leaders of the stock market horse race have changed nearly two dozen times, and thus the richest companies in the world have changed numerous times as well. Each one sending a proposal our way once they peak at the top."

"No doubt a reflection of the unstable and collapsing environmental ecology," said Trae.

"Not a reflection: a direct chain link to the resource economy running out of resources," Derek stated.

"Peak everything," added Demona.

Derek continued, "The ancient reptiles are hungry, awake, and finally acknowledge what is, and unfortunately, incapable of evolution, only see new food to consume."

"Of course this emergent evolutionary digital infrastructure is not something to be owned or yoked, but that's the only way in which they understand the world: by putting an economic dollar value on vibration," Ezekiel added.

"Geez, Nike?" Daniel said in shock.

"It must have something to do with the heroic media and security breach earlier this evening, and," everyone looked at Aum, "Maybe they think they can get a new spokesperson out of it, by thinking we need to save face for our investors or some bullshit," said Zhe.

"A swoosh branded spectre!? It's like a goddamn Merlin with a round table logo on his cloak!" Ezekiel exclaimed.

"Yeah, what are they gonna do? Re-edit the footage with a swoosh on his shirt? With a watermark on the footage, with the hippest soundtrack culled from the Boards and a fresh new campaign slogan?" Jenn expanded it.

"Maybe. But I don't think the kids would be fooled," Trae concluded.

"It's like a dinosaur with a pink mohawk wig, zubaz, floro uzi and shades - an elderly relative trying to impress their grand kidz with their trend savvy, that just happens to be a decade off," Aum spoke.

"You're either cresting the trending wave or you're underneath it, praying that you live another day," added Dan.

"And they're praying. They're all praying," said Derek

"For their *lives*!" Demona took another sarcastic shot at Derek.

With serious and exhausted calm, Zhe refoused them, "They don't understand that it would only lessen us and our purpose, and do nothing for them."

"Except maybe harness the digital echo and claim that moment of public breach, and the entire meta-network behind it as a subversive and highly advanced marketing campaign they constructed, claiming that moment as it's first public fruit," John said, looking up from his embeds.

There was a long pause, which usually happened after John spoke in council.

"…pretty sure the kids would believe that actually," Dan said.

"And it might just revitalize their brand currency too," Ezekiel added.

Jenn responded, "Fuck, of course the kids would dig the first actual human sacrifice made to the gods of consumption." She said sarcastically, "Though they would have to spin this death and all the other New Eden burnouts in a very radical way. What are they gonna do? Simply claim them as previous marketing failures? Or conceptually link them to a suicide bomber-like dedication to a brand name? Cross-faded with US army training and the next level of the cult brand devotion? They would have to somehow reverse the polarity of all the links to these self-imolative actions from the thing they truly represent, flipping from death protest to death support."

"Pre-cognizant copy cats. Humans piercing the 5th dimension without any knowledge of what that means, channeling this breached moment of corporate achievement and pre-enacting it without conscious awareness, a container around it developing that which makes the most sense within the flow of the 3rd dimension."

"We should stop building it for them," said John said. And identities fell away.

"Agreed. A fading immortal corporate entity does not deserve to be resurrected by us, just because they found a way into our conversation. Though of course one that hacked into a Greek god to find full actualization would be that skilled."

In the background they heard, "It must want to surpass the swastika hack."

"Plus their offer was for the whole thing, not just a contract for Aum or for the rights to that specific footage and data."

"Yes, it would certainly take a god-like creature to equate and integrate a whole system currency fully outside of itself, and outside of it's previous level awareness."

"The Riddle would then be a broken link, an evolutionary path rewritten."

"No longer intrinsically aligned to the truth of what it is, but to a value external of itself."

"They've never had to do this before, grow, expand like this, see like this. They've certainly shown they lack the grace if they think they can continue their unconscious clumsy trodding about like they've always done."

"They have the collective cohesiveness of a pond of starving barracudas fighting over a taunting monkey sitting on a tree branch."

"Yeah, but it's not just one single personality, even a band or group, or even a collective, it's our entire nation on the auction block."

"Like selling the entire Marvel universe, or Star Wars universe, every single character and costume, vehicle, and city, every potential it has, to Disney."

"Before Nike it was Apple, before Apple it was Google, before Google it was actually Disney, before Disney it was Microsoft, before Microsoft it was Sysco - trying to horsecollar us like they did Tribe."

"We're now known, and the top node to be consumed, by the top buyer - which changes every 10 minutes - putting in their trillion dollar offer, which is valid for only 10 minutes, not even enough time to sift through the details of purchasing an entire civilization and it's deep breadth of ideas and talent and resources and potential.

"Capitalism has come to it's climax, where one company owns everything, and to keep everything and each other afloat, they just pass the ownership of everything around like a ball, with each pass adding profits that don't exist and mammoth debt that will only grow more debt."

It shifted, and not in a good way.

"And now it's like a whole new continent has been discovered, and it's resources far easier to extract than natural ones. We're primed for exchanged in the digital data flows; the only resources left, no physical effort even required."

"Yeah, after they have fully transmutated all gaian life into a currency format, it's like they had a meeting and decided all the same laws and structures of exchange and control will apply in this new format of reality. That the system can be brought over, and everything will still function the same."

"And the natives of the rainbow star tribe will buy in, give in, and conceded to their sales pitch."

"And even further, that they believe they already own us, and that we're theirs to take."

"And thus they have the audacity to propose these preposterous contractual agreements."

"Don't you see? It's already done. The moment we arrived in their awareness we were measured and tallied and assigned to a dollar value. Simply by them seeing us, we were pulled from our fresh new paradigm, back into the old. We just lost all integrity to our truth and we became the new corporate whore. The moment we became observable the dying world swallowed us whole, as it's last meal. Blink of an eye, and there's nothing left of our existence, our purpose. We all just lost."

There was a gapping silence of dismay, like a funeral.

Then John spoke, "No we didn't."

"No?"

There was hope from the Dragonrider.

"All those self sacrifices were not made in vain."

Everyone looked at him in anticipation.

"I just sold us to Nike."

And then all hope was smashed.

There was another pause of shock and horror, but he continued inside of it, like a sole explorer with a machete in the jungle at night, with jaguars and gorillas and giant spiders chasing him, "And to Disney. And to Apple. And to Samsung. And to Sun Microsystems and Google and Toyota and to Facebook. And to Volkswagon. And even to Microsoft and Sysco, to BP, and even the State grid corporation of China and each supermajor Oil Baron syndicate. Pillate Oil was especially pleased."

"What!?" in full, double circle chorus.

"All of them, just to be sure."

"How the is that any different from us being swallowed whole!?"

"Not since the Third Dynasty of Ur has such a shift of this magnitude happened. We just became the richest organization on the planet and all Riddlers - our 'shareholders' - are thus now the richest people on the planet. In the truest of ways."

He stood and began to walk around the room as he talked, "As a 'company' the Riddle now owns the planet, or more precisely, the Riddle owns the paradigm that thinks the planet can be owned. And there's nothing real left to buy. All resources are used up and all land is destroyed, if not destroyed, death warrant signed, and the only big business deals made are those moving to further the gargantuan, this one included. If you've noticed, building blocks only get bigger, and never get smaller, even more so when things get chippy and begin to collapse. The small business entrepreneurial spread isn't even a consideration, as they don't have eyes capable of seeing that small, let alone the potential energy and intelligence it would take to fragment into a million pieces – even though they have teams of dark wizard's and branding masters working to convince the masses that they can. So essentially we received the economic planetary debt from the system of globalization that destroyed it – their debt all they had left to offer us – and because we are a fully external, off grid functioning system, we can simply dissolve the debts and destroy the entire system that created them."

He continued to walk alone along the silent cliff. He was lonely so he simplified what he had just explained, "We did it. We just won."

"What!?" Another chorusline.

"I can't believe it was that easy in the end," deGryder continued to himself, then, just as Von Newmann would have back in the 1950's, continued, "And thus we happily arrive at a place where we now have all the money in the world at our disposal, which isn't really anything but potential, and because we operate outside of that particular monetary system of currency, we can simply continue to do so, and not allow that potential to be exchanged back into the old world. In fact, it will soon be converted to Riddler currency and won't be converted back. That data flow will be quite easily dissolved and balanced, debts and fortunes: it was all simply information at this point anyway. Multidimensional existence operates without linear ledgers and now every single human now has to play by our new rules. We just swallowed the world whole, and that system, the old world, just died."

At that moment, as if to hammer in the realization of the collective group, there was a black airship that floated across the sky covered with N-Glu. A screen readout with a lush tapestry had words zipping across the screen, projecting at them through the glass: "Never doubt that a small group of thoughtful, committed citizens can change the world. Indeed, it is the only thing that ever has."

And there was finally an erupting trickle to a boom of cheers, even more emphatic than the likes of those seen after the Rube Golberg Mars landing of 2012.

However, all was not so beautifully picturesque.

Aum couldn't figure out why this feeling emerged, that found containment inside of him, so he didn't yet celebrate. There was something about this victory that was shallow. It wasn't to the deepest core of transmutation, so maybe that's why there was that moment of hesitation, and disbelief.

A new global grid had flashed in his mind, something he had never seen before. What caused him to be even more concerned was that all sorts of parts were moving which seemed like they shouldn't be. The insight was so worrysome that Jenn saw it in his face

"Aum....?" Jenn looked around to see if anyone else noticed, and no one did.

So Jenn asked loud enough to lasso John in the celebration, "So what did you actually sell them John?"

"What?"

Jenn suddenly found it very strange, that she had to repeat herself to a man with telepathic hearing, "What did you actually sell them?"

"The ability to see us Jenn, our secrets revealed. I sold the ability to view and observe all our actions, what we practice and how we live."

"So you sold them our fucking akashic record, or what?" Derek demanded. Zhe laughed at Dereks outburts. He was tired, and trying to grasp the immensity of what was happening. Amongst the reaction of merriment, he held space for the recently seeded network growth, because he knew, even if others didn't, that the new data streets needed that continued gaze of energetic presence to maintain solidity, and interest.

"No, not really. I sold the ability to view our akashic record; the ability to view what we do with their money." Everyone finally calmed their excitement to hear the details of the deal, "Like an etheric gold, the energy behind each yen and dollar and pound is still there, unseen, even if the formal currencies are not. That influx of thermodynamic energy will flow throughout the entire system, bringing up hidden pockets that previously required invisibility, because of the policing of old world; up and into full visibility. And as this total system currency infusion quickly dissolves inside our new paradigm, so too will the eyes of the old world, even their ability to see it, and remember it, and thus the old world, the old paradigm, dissolves. Moving in through the eyes, the act of seeing this miracle will be an upgrade of the species, our heart's, mind's and human spirit." He looked up at the stars, as if for reassurance, "If these efforts do not evolve their consciousness, nothing will."

Again, Aum saw a flash of the globe in his intuitive imagination, like a lightning bolt. It was if the pattern was being remade. It looked beautiful, but was very different than anything he had seen. It had hexagonal uniformity, with the spreading edges shooting out like fingertips trying to push through a lycra screen. It lacked the beauty and awe of seeing pure chaos. Something about it didn't feel right. He couldn't place it.

The spec of doubt grew inside him, to the point where Aum had to leave the central table, fearing it would spread to others. He went to sit near Derek, across the fire, who was not celebrating either, but surprisingly, had a smile on his face. In between soothing crackles Aum asked him, “Can I ask you a question?”

“Of course,” Derek responded, as the conversation at the council table continued: “So you mean, you sold our privacy?” Zhe asked John, not quite fully understanding what they were giving up, nearly guarding his new work, the fully open Riddle gates.

“Has there ever been a hijaking?” Aum whispered.

“Hijaking?” Derek whispered back.

“Yeah, has a guru ever been hacked?”

Concern spread across Derek’s face, like he was awakening to a next level of system security, one that he had never known existed.

Aum asked again, “What does it look like when somebody’s dreamsoul, their digital life path data dream get’s hacked?”

Derek rolled up his sleeve to revel a sleek hand embed. It was already loaded with the Riddle site. Aum doubted it displayed anything else. Derek hit the refresh button and checked the activity on the boards. A full fireworks of sparks were flying backs and forth between the Boards and the four Towers. Much like neurons in the brain, new pathways were being woven in, as new people were engaging, and taking to the new way of seeing.

With each motion of Zhe - tone of voice, question, slump in tiredness - there was fluctuation in the read out. It was a level of activity that had never before been seen, and with the fullest reopening it was nearly impossible to decode any social purpose patterning within the new movement. The zoo had arrived in their world, and it was becoming more lush and complex with every microsecond.

“Holy shit.” Derek said.

“No, I sold our publicity,” John said to Zhe, back at the council table, “We went from the social underground, an invisibility deep down beyond mainstream, into a castle in the sky in one leap. We will finally be valued and recognized for what it is we do and have done: shine out advanced earth repair, with a lesson plan, user manual, and a vastly interactive and viewable ecosystem to learn from. A new civilization was just discovered, and just went public.”

A storm began to roll in. It pushed the blimp far out of sight as the winds quickly picked up, and the rain began to click and clack against the glass. However, inside the pyramid, the fire further awakened, crackling, sparking and speaking.

On the data readout both Aum and Derek noticed the thickest trunk lines were John's. He had been very active on the boards for the past hour, posting in multiple rooms in multiple towers, in the exact spot to unlock dozens of doors at once, which lead to a huge data transference. If not for the experienced hunting eyes of Derek it would have been un-noticeable.

"We're safe then?" Zhe asked again, he seemed to find himself in the opposite pole, speaking out the concern emerging from Aum, and now from Derek too.

Over the past hour, on the boards, John had been extremely busy, even though over the past hour, he had been participating in this core meeting. Derek pulled up the history of one of the tower rooms and John had been there numerous times in numerous over the course of the day, the first being during the tower battle. Derek looked at Aum with concern. What exactly did he mean when he said he was collecting ghosts? Had the dead arisen to receive their last judgement already? There was another pocket of ultra dense activity during Cat's burnout, more than could be accomplished by a single person.

Ezekiel continued, "Safe and secure son. It's okay – you can let go," speaking directly to Zhe, "It's stable." Zhe looked at John, then Dan and back at Ezekiel. It began to dawn on him, that even though, his recent efforts took a near insurmountable focus, it was a very small piece of work. That all of his efforts over the past few days were playing a part in a much much bigger plan – a plan that he had been completely oblivious to – and rather than an emergent discovery, it was looking like it may be one of controlled precision.

John spoke to the table, every breath balanced, "We are now a gated platform community that anyone can view. It's like discovering something that is complete, that you can't be a part of - the most amazing rock band in the world… that has already broken up - However you can still be a part of it, in your own brand new way, and have their music and spirit impact and change your life."

Gated community? Separation from the whole? The concern spread to Jenn, Demona and Trae.

Aum and Derek continued their focused investigation away from the council table. They read some of the Dragonrider's posts and it was a language that did not fit, and a purpose that did not fit. It was an evolved intricacy they could not easily follow. Rather than crisply articulate and poetically flowing with it's usual bard-like flourishes of evolutionary invocations of the medium itself, these ones were empty. Filled with obtuse technical jargon punctuated jarringly with incoherent cybernetic metaphor, even straight up bot code seemingly inserted at random. The profile picture was the same, but something was up.

Dan pipped in, speaking to everyone in the room, "With the security measures taken during the dismantling of the Red tower, all the work we had done up until that point will become an unmoving foundation, a planetary sized rock to build further civilization upon. We retain the rights to all of our dream beings, our soul stories and the work we have done and will ever do. The best part is the advanced distro system is built in, accomplished today by our very own Dragontamer, Zachery Herman Eschaton, already set to handle this new level. The security measures have already been mapped, each pocket magnetized from giver to receiver: perfectly aligned with the gates that just got fully opened."

"That's amazing work Zachery," said Jenn. Everyone looked at him, as his first name was hardly used anymore. Zhe held his hands up, and let it go, as if his tired eyes couldn't see the scope of what he had just done; as if the work wasn't his to claim as his own.

Looking at Derek, John spoke, "We all have purpose in this magnificent emergence. The move from underground blackened earth to highest king sun just torched the last of everything. Without violent uprising, or faith healing," he looked at Demona, continuing, "There was really nothing left in the old world though, and this was the only option left to move forward; the only space to move into. Now the only thing is, whether this level of upgrade will take. As all growth engines of civilization are now filtered through this new paradigm engine."

Derek looked back, with head tilted, trying to see deeper.

Where was John during the red tower defense? What the hell was he doing while Aum was penetrating Cat's blockbuster media mandala?

Aum closed his eyes, seeing the new grid in his mind, and focused in on the parts closest to his own; the data lines that were cruising and re-patterning, coming in quick like the rain. Each one that he identified triggered a pulse of adrenaline to his heart. Closer. He investigated their identity, like each droplet was like an arrow moving toward the Centre, like a target.

John continued, "Codeless dream source isn't given freely, it never was. Everything is based on exchange, though now what you receive will be much much greater than what you give. As shareholders, everyone's quality increases, and essentially gets paid to the point of wealth accumulation, whatever that is, or looks like, in this controlled sphere of integrity, the structure of the Riddle. There will no longer be lack of any sort. The simple abundance of shared nourishing meals that fuel the construction of an eco home built with your own two hands, and the hands of friends, on a pocket of land asking for your presence and stewardship, with that whispering intelligence as the guide, from need filled to dream fulfilled."

John geared up, standing and speaking to the entire room, the top of the teepee pyramid like an meta antennae, to speak out further, "We, together, erased many things today. Global corporations have run their course by linking together all human civilization. Their further growth and expansion is now only destructive to life quality, rather than adding to it. Broadcast news and Reality TV mesh, their continued signal invalid, and too slow to keep up with the digital mandala of quantum life. The corporate maps keeps only records of the corporate structures of what once was, and international governments simply dissolves in the face of true self-governance, united in local responsibility." He began to circle the table, "We must still be wary however, there will be a whole different round table of spin wizards devising tales to tell their brand addicts how to proceed, though it'll simply be more dinosaurs with uzi's and pink mohawk wigs, and the open Riddle gate will appear to each one, each individual, in which ever way best fits their soul path dreams." The room was shaking with change, echoed in the data sphere Aum and Derek viewed, and John continued, stepping easily with each tremor, "So what about all those that don't get it? You ask Demona? Or don't have the ability to learn? Trae, you ask?" His usual charming peace fizzled a little at the continued signs of doubt that emerged from his team, "This is *the* bridge, and it is built. Finally. Even cows are intelligent enough to find their way to fresh food through an open fence, and if not, there are plenty of shepherds out there who they can receive guidance from. If a soul sees the bridge and chooses not to walk over it, from a dead pasture to a green one, that is their karma and they will remain in the dead pasture, until they themselves die."

"When does this happen?" asked Jenn, heart fluttering.

“Now! It’s all happening now!” replied John emphatically.

Aum couldn’t mentally understand all that was shifting in the present moment, only observe what he could see, inside his being, his body and spirit, in the faces around him and the dark rain clouds in the sky, floating crooked, lit up with the electricity of sheet lightning. With each flash the adrenaline and panic of total freedom and terror surged through him for no observable apparent reason.

John checked his handembed, “I just have to sign some physical documents tomorrow,” he continued, quickly flipping through dozens of threads and feeds, messages and posts, “Considering they just lost, they’re pretty accommodating to the fact that I’ve requested a contract chiseled in stone, in order to negate the full corporate heirloom lineage first programmed in the Renaissance,” now cool and joking, he looked up and continued joyously, “I’m going pre-biblical on this one, back to the Code of Hammurabi. With awesome synchronicity it’s all being organized in the birthplace of democracy, Athens, by a lawyer named Trofim Lysenko.”

The adrenaline peaked in Aum and it shot a laser at Ezekiel in surprise, as if to say, ‘He doesn’t know about ICAARUS!?’

John laughed at a sudden realization, still speaking to the group, “That’s it. Dissolved. Done. Paradigm Shifted,” finding himself within a déjà vu, and the exact place of accomplishment he had envisioned many years ago when he first began the Riddle.

Aum’s look instantly reflected back from Zeke. He read within it, translating it to, ‘He wasn’t programmed to know about ICAARUS, like you were.’

“Programmed!?” Aum shouted out loud, the feeling burst out his mouth and moved through everyone like a new etheric serpent. Everyone except for John; who was rapt in a sublime expression, absorbed in self-reflection as he looked out at the storm raging, arms raised, Christ-like, “I am the Riddle Solver, and the world as we know it is dead.”

Then the power went out.

Half a second later, the micro noise of glass cracking and a bullet finding body.

Half a second later it was followed by the piercing noise of all the glass walls shattering, one by one. ICAARUS had arrived.

"We are the generation that takes on the karma of the entire human race. We're the last ones.... and if we can't get ourselves in order, organized, if we look feeble or weak or pale, if the truth we shine out is a pretentious parlor trick or circus buffoonery broadcasted, we are neither setting a good example, nor creating something for others to model or build upon in future cycles. There was good here, even if it will all be forgotten.

"All who come after us will have no idea of the specific potentials which existed before this, the sheer mass of world we had at our fingertips; where there was still a new frontier to explore, an independent structure that was malleable, where relationships and nature were wild, not manufactured or groomed from seed with mal-intent. The earth will exist now only as a reptilian marsh with the lowest ceiling yet. There will be no more pioneer's and no more renegades, only mathematical circumstantial precision trying to fit within the pre-determined equation we have anchored in, and allowed. Life will become locked down. A social prison state – where our cells and selves are so defined that any possibilities for original ingenuity, any type of original piece of glistening creativity or true performance, will be below threshold of significant impact, or conversely, swiftly picked up and sucked up into the global mono-culture machine instantly. Inflated beyond ability to maintain structural integrity, or passed off as another boring wonder, without recognition of it's truly miraculous worth, and the consumption machine will march on. Relationships will drastically mutate as social construct and worth becomes determined by the thermodynamic energetics of consumer fad and the flattest packaged popularity. The energy required to re-shift this deeply ingrained psychological swamp of techno-infrastructure will be so monumental that only the return of Christ himself could possibly open enough eyes and hearts to break the chains of fully entrained minds."

The Dragonrider, John deGryder, lay on the table. In a pool of his own blood, bullet hole through chest, speaking out last words, as the battle raged on around him.

"It is my deepest hope that we were all able to do the work we needed, in the time we had available to us, that the prayers we managed to muster, were heard and accepted.

I hope that the planetary karmic star nation balances have been brought closer, and that this path is truly the will of the Most High

One. I pray we were able to meet our personal and group challenges, head on, without self-doubt, and with the humility and ability to trust in one another. That this was enough. That what we gave, was enough.

"And as the curtains comes down, and the spotlight dims, and we are told our time is over, that we can accept this with grace. And for those who come after, who's time it is to shine, to support them with the same loving thoughts, and a gentler and stronger presence; the patience to equip and inspire them as post-humans, and give our fullest soul presence to their conscious growth, a presence we chose not to give to one another other, when we most needed it.

"And as we go into hiding, into the constructed social roles and confined containers of our fore-generational history, resigning to our barred and bunker-like homes and silos, with our small families and what little we have, to weather the galactic storm, the mine-filled battlefield of full scope cosmos played out in daily moments; may we not look away from our shame, at finally seeing the aftermath of the total daily collapse of civilization, constructed by the media or a truth experienced first hand, what used to be simple choices. And as we live our lives under this total persecution of our own choosing; our own ugly reflection, during our isolated, individual hermitage, watch it all crumble into dust.

"I pray, that again, one day, we will all find each other, and live life as we once did, here in this creative space, enacting the miraculous for the greatest good, for love and life, and one another.

"As the resonant vibration of the world that once was, leaves us, do not forget your insights, your transformations, because it was all real.

"It all did happen."

John hit the stop button then the send button on his arm. Having recorded his voice with his eardrums, sent out through wifi, it was a last may-day monologe, with battle raging in the background, as if an Orwellian radio broadcast from the 30's. He sent the file out to the arc, the last data chunk to fit inside the black obsidian quantum box, locking in with finality, the storage and deletion sequence, as it left the Gridline Centre for secret burial.

As he did, life started to fade from his eyes, but then he noticed Aum at his side, and deGryder came back to the present moment, "You're still invisible."

They were both soaked from the rain. Aum could see inside him, x-ray like, John's lungs were slowly filling with blood from the bullet hole. The black bullet, so similar to what he saw in the kamikaze pilots, still lodged in his chest, encircled by rotating interlocking etheric geometries, so similar to the fire tattoo on his palm. John coughed up blood and Aum looked deeper into the man as he moved in closer to comfort him. The Dragonrider. Was the geometric white energy dissolving the black bullet? There was more yelling. In the commotion Aum glanced around the room and couldn't tell what was real and what was imagined anymore.

"Please ask aloud your question deep hero," John said, looking at him.

"Are you the Riddle Solver?" Aum asked.

John laughed in shameful surprise, "No. I am not. I have failed to serve to my fullest capacity. The assassin's bullet within my chest tells me this is so." He shook his head in astonishment, "Even as the most suitable solution emerged within me, it has been stopped from full flowering. As I tried to remain on top of it, riding it, taming it, keeping it a my own. In that moment I saw a vision of freedom for all humanity, that eruption of light and inner faith, and each risk taken rewarded; allowing all eyes to open, and all eyes to open within eyes; each time a new view. The moment I stepped into that visionary space, it required me to carry the weight of full paradigm solution. I did not have the saintly strength of Atlas heart to move to the bottom, and carry the world. I remained attached to owning the solution that emerged from my work, heroically leading the way from the top, for all to see. And for this I receive the lesson of death, the final lesson.

"I have heard them coming, since Full Spectrum, allowed their insurgence into my presence, take them in as a poison, hoping to merge the ghosts and the machines and the light of creation; and find a final unity. To do this I had to bet my life… so I set up a backdoor fail safe. The bullet was the dead mans trigger. The gate is now fully open." He looked around at the combat, "You must continue your rocket launch-like work Aum, to find the true Riddle Solver, before these… ghastly shadows of men do. From beyond the death of all we know, from beyond the grave, even beyond storage and deletion there is the space of resurrection."

"North? The quantum box in the woods?"

"Yes, that is the final place to search," but even as he spoke, he started to wheeze and whisper, not from emotional stress or the spiritual strain of his oncoming passing, but simply due to the physical discomfort of a bullet hole through his lungs, just above his heart.

"Where?"

"New Eden."

Aum's mind stretched, trying to understand. "Must I die too?" He asked.

"No courageous one," he smiled, "It is an actual place, and it will survive the eye blistering fireworks of this grand societal demise. I have been there. I have built the gate, been there and back. The only person to ever return; in order to balance my karma. There is now only one other that has been told the precise way."

"The Ferryman."

"Yes."

"You must ride with him. Take it," He opened his mouth and there was an obol in it; a silver coin from Greek antiquity. Aum grabbed the coin and pocketed it, "For the Ferryman," John whispered, "I have already flown beyond the river, and do not need it."

In the chaos, under table and through the chairs, Jenn crawled over to them. She had been knocked unconscious and thought dead. John saw her, raised his hand, asking for hers, "Jenn knows what to do."

With the gentle last effort he pulled a small tree branch from his jacket pocket. Thin and a foot and a half long, it may have come directly from the otherside. It had gold mystery glyphs carved and painted into it, "Sibyl, a golden bough for all others who wish to cross after," and a death cough erupted from him, blood splattering on his face.

They could see in his eyes, that he was pulled back to the other side of the veil. Aum and Jenn, fully present, wiped his face and comforted John's body as best they could, helping to deliver his spirit to those on the other side, receiving him.

A deep whispy voice spoke within their minds, 'We must take him now.' Gold oaken faces spoke; the ancient ones who once appeared to Aum in a dream. Upon seeing the beauty of themselves in these mirrored caretakers, tears watered their eyes. Aum and Jenn thought together, 'We know.'

'Thank you for allowing him to be here with us,' Aum added. There was a choir of voices responding, beaming from the timeless into time, 'He is as honored here as there, in spirit and work. Blessings to you two, as you continue on the other side of the veil.'

And John's spirit walked along this beam of voices, waving, walking from one world, through the human exit, to the next. His handembeds continued to glow on his arm, but were fading. As he walked, he greeted his new family. His arm then went dark.

Cups of chaos continued to pour out around them, as more people rushed into the room, the new group shouted out swords together, a deeply spirited, uncompromisingly collective magic, "Revolution!!" while Aum clutched his coin, and Jenn her wand.

Jenns heart and voice steadied, looking into the eyes of Aum, one so familiar to her, but so new. Their true ancient relationship known, she smiled, thinking, 'This is probably what he saw in me from day one.'

'Correct,' She heard John whisper. It was a voice within her, but Aum could have easily have thought it, or spoken it out too. Regardless, with a new acceptance and gentle focus, she continued, as if giving a report to Aum, "Jason Fairman - the Ferryman - was scheduled to depart yesterday, with supplies and the newest system development knowledge. Though with such diverse transformations happening, I do not know whether he is still on schedule. I suspect not." She paused for a moment, breaking her gaze, remembering, "He is at the ferry station in Prince Rupert, waiting for supplies to be cleared by customs, back into Canada from Ketchikan, Alaska." She looked back into the green eyes of Aum, "With him a collection of oddities that may take time to sort and categorize at this point."

She held the painted stick as she realized she could now see everything. Not due to some psychic metaphysical awareness, but simply because she was intelligent, paid attention to every detail, and had an amazingly efficient memory that now worked with even more precision. She gave him his instructions, "Take the ferry from Bellingham to Alaska. Ketchikan then to Prince Rupert. He knows the way to New Eden from there," she paused again "and to wait for you. He's waiting for one additional item. Which is… You." She smiled.

Aum took a breath, envisioning each potential motion during a trip up to Alaska.

"Right," she said, as if something came to mind. Jenn grabed a small key ring from within Johns magic jacket pocket and continuing with the shared envisioning they both solidified the path by seeing it, "On 18th and York you will find wheels to Bellingham," She passed him the key ring which had two keys, "Unit 98, a Tesla Model X, paperwork will be in the glovebox. At Semiahmoo in a birdhouse above the 1984 historic copper stamp, you will find a valid ferry pass, first class, meal tickets included. Leave the car in parking lot four of the Bellingham ferry terminal, unlocked with key in ignition..." She paused as joy spread across her face, "…Ha ha, right, new levels. Engine running actually. If you need it, you will find a food package on Hemlock and 1st in Ketchikan. If you don't need it please leave it. And you will find the necessary camping supplies packed just off the Yellowhead in Prince Rupert. Jason has the key to the Cherokee." Aum's eyes went wide, looking at Jenn's newness, "How…!?" He was speechless, his surroundings forgotten as he lost all notions of self within her new being and beauty.

"I've been apprenticing with the Dragonrider. With him I've learned much, including the current infrastructural lines supporting the New Eden civil platform, a far older nation; ancestors of all this," she waved her wand around the room, "who self exiled. They detached long ago, establishing their own form, far beyond our path towards globalized mono-culture into a realized utopian dream… from what I hear … John's the only one who has ever made it back."

The vision of her speaking with her new voice far outweighed the potent information she spoke aloud, "You've become a sorceress!?" He said in awe.

"It's not sorcery Aum, it's…" She thought for a moment, "it's… the new Tao of business."

Aum laughed, his smile turned to awakened awe, déjà vu or emergent dream, he was not sure, "…The Taoist businessman…" She remembered his odd moment in bed of course, from oh so long ago, but the looping memory displacement simply didn't phase her like it did Aum.

"Jason will take care of you. He brought me here," She looked around the room. "Please pass along hello from me."

He nodded, and in the pause after, they both felt it: their coming good-bye.

With a far reaching thankfulness, Aum saw the wholistic power that now invigorated her mind, her actions, and word. Her conscious clarity led it all; a once petit flame now finding full furnace.

“I’d love to hear more about your new line of work when I get back,” Aum said.

“Likewise,” Jenn replied.

And they shared a kiss, but it was painful, because it was a good-bye kiss.

THREE

“Design is at its best the closer it approaches the purely metaphysical.”

— Buckminster Fuller

Chapter Eleven

Aum looked out from the ferry portside. The majestically lush coastline hummed. Seagulls trailed the ship, soaring and speaking inside the background landscape, a fluffy cloud kingdom. Aum could see the coastlines pristine beauty was still untouched by human hands and human feet, untread by oily wheels or logging road gravel. His inspired soul path and internal lightship rockets were needed, however, to escape the far reaching cast lines of a guided future impressionism, pressing dead paradigms into an ever vulnerable world.

His eyes reeled and nearly regurgitated at seeing the techno-augmentation of the corporate-eyed satellites and their light touch of polished cybernetic fingertips: a scattered mash of visual resonators dropped like inconspicuous bombs during a chemtrail flyover. Within these lush green trees Aum saw holographic displays floating in the air, digital billboards showcasing advertisements aimed at impregnating the susceptible minds of the cavaliering occupants of the passing vacation ferry.

Every flag of the corporate nation states was layered in uniform underneath the sleek fingernail polish of each mechanized lightbeam of cultural control, gutter diving each captured mind in order to remain on top, fucking them stupid while claiming ownership of land parcels and resources with the claw-like desperation of an addict. Nothing here had really changed since HBC mapped this land for the Commonwealth over a century ago, except for maybe the over elaborate mapping technology and those behind it, maintaining it's evolution and continued colonial presence.

Underneath the far stretch of the billboard signal lines, virtual ad's floating in the air along side the ferry route, there were floating seaside squatter villages that almost got it right. Makeshift boats and tenttowns were tucked away into pristine bays, no longer hubbed and anchored by longhouses or totems, but were Venice-like in their layout. These open street waterways revealed the details of their ramshackle exodus, like pioneers paddling to the edge of a beautiful nowhere, all their possessions on skiffs, ready to move at a moments notice: at the first sign of a flying security drone that called in the human robots.

Aum paused as he pecked at the antique coin-op internet terminal, checking the ferry route and the corporate map. In a parallel window he checked the indie network hub Jenn and her bridge team had recently constructed, helping strengthen the network of growers and shanty towns like this one. Apparently, here was the outpost of Ciel Lune, established as a grower specializing in a rare form of organic kelp used specifically for Gundan-maki. Aum wondered if a government agent had made it out here for the village vibratory inspection, or if the powers that be even gave a shit about the new certification.

The terminal lost signal. He was surprised the ferry didn't have it's own satellite antenna...but wasn't surprised at all, as all networking was linked to personal tech extensions of the body. This terminal was simply the next layer of payphone death, town clocktowers previous to that.

He looked up and dark coastal stormclouds were rolling in, flashing. That could be the cause; the natural electricity messing with the signal. He left the terminal after closing the two windows.

Considering he spent a few weeks wandering the countryside, alone, foraging, and half delirious, a slow peaceful journey on a ferry to Alaska shouldn't scare him. But it did.

He could feel a very specific moment approaching. That of his own death. Close enough to say hello. Close enough to look at. Living in these extreme times, with extreme choices, he was sure most others felt it too, while having to push realities meshwork, the empathic environment and all the machines surrounding us, with adventurism addiction and the dimensional vortex of all possibilities at once.

Maybe it was because from here, he could actually see all that, and see all that he left it behind, and the real-time had become a space filled with billions.

Out this far he was on his own again. Stranded, but not. So familiar, but not. Searching, but not. It was the first time since the coffeeshop library, that he had a moment to reflect on his life path, yet there, in the library, he still seemed to be inside of it, committed to the small network around him, his values, and an ideal that emerged which was applicable to his personal history, and single body moving through time. Persistent self-discovery and evolution at all costs brought him here and he still needed to bring everyone. Though casting himself further out, far outside of the ever present network he could normally feel inside him, he knew he was putting his life on the line. Just as John had done. It was a openness where there were to be no breaks, no moments of apathy or ignorance, but only interacting with full heart borne and raw, seeing into every soul he came across, and in their dimensional pools of woven choice, each a looking glass mirror of his own strengths and weaknesses, flaws and gems, and the shared story. Each new person would show him a reflection of his path and purpose in exchanges as minute as a passing glance. Behind him, dissolved into forgotten fleeting micro fame, friends, lovers and hero's dead.

The smell of ocean got caught in his nostrils, the seagull's spoke again, and he recommitted to the journey, the lessons it brought, and the deepening of both inner and outer. Both committing to its completion, and going even deeper into the space of sacrificial discovery.

ICAARUS had won the battle at the Gridline centre, and from that true ground zero, total cultural death was spreading. He surfed the waves out as if riding the sonic boom of an atomic blast. All he could see was collapsing behind him, as if the ground was falling out from under his feet as he ran in precise slow motion.

Aum took one more breath of the salty air, one last gaze of the coastline to imprint his frontal mind with the ress behind the signs and began to walk back to his room.

Someone on the deck lit a match to ignite a cigarette. The flame jumped into his memory through his open eyes, flaring as bright and immersive as melliennial fireworks. Had Cat seen all this? Did she forsee all that happened? Or could she somehow be the cause of it? He thought back to Ezekiel and his dive into the transmutation of data into a natural physical object, supernatural even. In his rescue and recapture from what seemed to be the furthest edge of perception, as soul light spread out into the stars and the act of conscious gazing pierced the domain of the ICAARUS membrane, Aum wondered if, in that space, their genetics had been infused with ICAARUS trackers, to map their movement. Zeke maybe. Him maybe not; continuing to be invisible to their systemic eyes, or so he had been told by the taoist businessman, the ghost collector. The rider of dragons.

His conscious mind was a jungle now, growing at hyperspeed, trying to understand the life and death of each dimensional potential that erupted from each thought, becoming aware of each new vine emerging from present consciousness, planted as the activities of past connections and exchanges. Why were those paths chosen out of all the historical potentials?

Nearly sleepwalking he grabbed a random book from the on-board library without even registering which one, then found his bunk and slept, letting his dream mind take over, much more easily mapping all life and death and soothe his aching waking brain.

Upon arrival in Ketchikan, he didn't have anything with him other than the clothes on his back. "Traveling north to the future," was the answer he gave when the customs officer, asked him what he was doing in the great state of Alaska. "Visiting relatives," was Aums follow up response upon reciving the gawking dismal gap of facial qualm. "I travel light."

"I see that," responded the officer, "Hopefully your relatives have a pair of boots and jacket for you, or you'll be cougar food in no time," she laughed.

Arriving later that day in Prince Rupert there was simply a hello when he got to the customs office, after which Aum found his way to the main street of the town. A grocery store, a hardware store, a pharmacy, and restaurant - which was attached to the gas station. That was it. Other than the crisp clean air and the beauty of the surrounding hills: the very reason that the town was there in the first place.

As he began to see more, as the towns 'insides' became 'outsides', Aum realized he was being tracked. In this small town he was being followed. He dove off the main drag, trying to step up the steep residential hill like a local. Shit! He shouldn't have used the terminal on the Ferry; it was probably reactivated to log fingerprints. It couldn't be ICAARUS though, if it was, he'd probably be dead already, poison back-infused through the tips of his porous skin. Or tortured... like the others.

"You done your book yet?"

"What?!" Aum shouted back as he turned. For a split second he thought it might be an officer from the ship, tracking him down to rescue the stolen library book. He looked at it again, *Lost in the Barrens* by Farley Mowat, making sure it's molecules hadn't rearranged into some other historic tale of adventure, *Jack and the Beanstalk*, *Inferno,* or *Time Machine.*

"Being able to time travel is a requirement to win the Philip K Dick award," the man shouted again.

"What?!"

Who ever this fisherman was, Aum had be caught speechless. Looking up at him with scraggly mountain man beard recently grown, framing his beady, laser-like eyes, he stood at the bottom of the hill with impatience. His shaved brown head accented his cheekbones, giving him a gaunt look, far beyond starving artist. True to form, he was wearing the most interesting coat Aum had seen in his life.

A gray and black outdoor adventure coat, wind-proof water-proof nylon filled with light goose down, it had large pockets and hood, but at the same time it was ultra classy, like a long, double breasted black wool dress coat. It was hybrid gear that could be worn to the most stylish pristine urban cultural networking event, or out hiking in the woods, in total divine isolation. There was a scarab beetle logo embroidered on the inner shoulder, colorful gems embedded in the fabric.

"Pick it up son. Launch or be lost here for 100,000 years." The man's mind was full and fed up with bureaucratic gates and all remnant papertrails of a lost civilization.

"Like Jason and the Cherokee's?" Aum asked playfully.

"Yes." With tombstone seriousness, "Cherokee's main-lined and prepped back on the newly paved street; all objects through the old gate. Fuckn' finally. Except for one."

"One?"

And with a 'ting' off the tip of his fingernail, Aum instantly flipped him the greek obal, so quick his arm didn't even move.

The Ferryman pulled it from the air, while emitting a gruff, "Thanks." He inspected both sides, "Call me Jay. All set," and the rough outbacker immediately started walking to the mainstreet, down to where the Cherokee was waiting. Aum followed inside his wake, passing muddy and jacked up pick-up trucks, each with a grizzled logger bear of a man driving them.

The ferryman, this Riddler named Jay, had become one with them; he was succeeding in the attempt to authentically merge into a local persona, or may simply have yielded to the outcome of his own life path karma.

In the endless crowfoot eyes, cained, sidewalk and sidelined, worn hands described a world in which practical knowledge of personal sustenance was required to be this far out: from the inner workings of combustion engines, a heat pump on a fridge and the fan on a convection oven to the plumbing route of your sump pump, or even the amperage and electrodynamic circuitry of your log house. You owned your self, and each and every tool and detail of daily functioning, for if it broke down, it was yours to fix. This was an old world inside an even older land. A world without support systems, a world still existing inside a time before total bulldozing of human essence; a civilizational outpost on a small island of future surrounded and permeated by an ancient world of wild. Aum was definitely time traveling.

They got in the SUV. There was a canoe tied to the roof, paddles secured, Aum noticed the back seats were folded down and the whole thing was filled with camping supplies, labeled bins, even a few small wooden crates. There was freshly chopped wood somewhere in the back too, he could smell it as he sat down in the passenger seat.

In no time at all they left the coastal township and were surrounded by tall mountains and high forest. As they drove off the island, both physical and metaphysical, Aum shifted, hardened his lit, peeling his layers to find inside an over-masculine logistical detail focus, on physical components, their worth, functioning and efficency, "So the Cherokee was waiting here? Empty?" He questioned Jay.

"Yah man. I transferred all items from the Aztec. That one stays on the ferry now, incognito. It's headed back south to grab more supplies; though this time it will only be bodies."

As he spoke Aum recognized him. His shoulders were more muscular, his beard long, no longer trimmed, and his head fully shaved. His eyes were the same, still slicing through reality with every gun lock look. Jay was the one driving the Aztec when he gave John the 'Ferryman' key-code. No wonder he had grinned so wide. It was probably a resonant confirmation for him.

In time with a clean breeze through the Cherokee, Aum's memory banks clicked open and he remembered that this was also the same man from Full Spectrum, who had asked him if he had lent his coat to Terra... or Trae, though now without dreadlocks, and aged beyond belief.

"I see that you are owed this," Jay pulled out a similar coat to what he was wearing, gave it to Aum, and straightened the wheel. "Put it on before some old cougar notices and tries to bait you with warm plaid flannel. Most definitely then, you'll never be heard from again." His visionary leaps were far, but Aum was patient and glided with him across the river. It was like rock hopping at an identical flowing pace and required the same amount of focus to stay together.

"That was my third."

As if already understanding the deeper purpose of their journey, exposed by their combined vibration in space and time, Jason answered before Aum had even thought of the question. Aum had to quickly reverse engineer the statement to figure out what question it would be: how many full spectums had Jay been to.

Then Aum jumped first, without rock to land upon, wondering if Jason learned his telepathy at the festival, and if all three Full Spectrums were as profoundly impactful as what Aum himself experienced first hand.

Jason responded in perfect time with Aum's observation, placing a rock under his feet as they continued to cross the river.

"Communicating telepathically is not about reading minds, it's about finding someone to communicate with, as deeply and as openly as possible. Once you find them, that's all you have to do. Then it's just practice," He gazed at Aum, natururally piercing his open inner being. "All three were equally impactful. But they were all different, each time. From what I could see, they changed drastically in flavors, stylistic architecture, sonic offering and technology over the course of my three years there… I've got my mothers Italian blue eyes…" Aum chuckled at the pre-cog leap.

Jay seamlessly continued, "...Just over three years ago, at the end of the rainy season, I kept on seeing this dude and a book he was plugging, everywhere. Interviews on the net, documentaries my roommate would stream, articles in the digital paper feeds; I'll have to admit it was intriguing, the things he was talking about. So eventually I decided, 'maybe there's something to this,' and I bought a copy."

"Was it any good?"

"Yeah, it was amazing." The ferryman began to peel off his gruff localized exterior, "But even weirder things started to happen after I read it. The author no longer appeared everywhere in my field of vision, but the things in his book did."

"What do you mean?"

"It came to life. All of it. Companies that he had talked about, theories about math and nature, thermodynamic advertising, color and movement, the bio-amp of human physiology, everything I was interested in was simply there, engaging me without distraction."

"Was it this book that led you to your first Full Spectrum?"

"Indirectley. The book lead me directly to the Centre, to Grildline, and immediately a ticket to my first Full Spectrum from the author himself. I guess a crystal skull told him I was meant to be there."

"A crystal skull?"

Jason looked over at him in wonder, "...It's great that odd and absurd occurances still surprise you." He reconcentrated on the road ahead as he continued openly, filling Aum's magnetic curiosity. "So my first Full Spectrum cracked me open to the world as dreamtime manifest, no occurances fleeting. Miniscule mundane minuta began speaking so deep my reality shook with everystep, no matter what step I took. Choirs upon choirs at all moments. I had difficulties re-integrating with society after that first one so I returned to the Centre, seeking solace." Aum nodded and Jay continued, "I found my footing as a garden tech, helping plant the newer shrubs in the Life Gallery, even doing some of the technical data mapping for the digital meta space integration. In exchange for this work I was offered a spot in a year long program at the Centre on growing multidimensional awareness. It was taught by the same man, the author. You ever heard of Koriadnon Macek?"

"Macek? The Turk?" Aum attempted to hide his loaded confirmation, "I have." Jay picked up on it though, "He's Greek actually," beyond Aum's attempt to divert the emotions that his memories brought up, "I know. But just you fucking wait Free Zen, you know, but you sureley don't know. At that time, after being cracked open, it felt like the course was a very specific soul preperation: mission activation. All words and content pristinely and mathematically engineered, total program absortbtion. Observations so profound that they echoed through my daze, becoming solid enough life bridges to walk upon. A new addict, I became Macek's prized student, more so than Zhe or Trae, or even John, and thus he gifted me my second Full Spectrum ticket after the completion of the course." Aum nodded.

"My second Full Spectrum was the next layer of growth. A world merge of familiar faces and strangers all pointing their hearts and minds in the same direction, at the same thing: God and gods and mist."

After a short pause, Aum interjected, "Each time a new festival would be birthed out of the lessons of the last?"

"The template would evolve, for all involved, yes. New issues coming up each time: internal strife and politics, as in all community structures. Though, at this edge of social consciousness, a community within the community emerged, to deal with the psyco-spiritual hurdles of group meta growth - these ones facilitating the ongoing conversations and interactions needed to happen for highest potential to occur. After that festival everyone knew who John, Derek and Zhe were, though few actually had the opportunity to meet them."

A gap for the next jump.

"Leaping out from there, returning with new purpose, emerging from Egypt, Persia previous. I re-approached the world with all the mythic wisdom I could pocket. I saw a colleague of mine was starting up his own firm, looking for a data tech engineer with my exact qualifications. It however quickly degraded to a maze of advanced situationalism. The first project with his firm was a job search engine, and the only jobs listed were ones for his design firm. I couldn't really figure out if these listings were just fake filler to help launch and grow the interest in the job search site was a marketing tool, or the other way around, if the job search site was intended to help launch and develop collective dialogue around his start up design firm. Bait and switch. Like all online business, none of it actually real.

"Then, that same day, another secondary shot, I heard an ad for a job on an online radio stream I was listening to. I found their homepage and submitted my resume. There was no response and shortly after my account was flooded with so much spam I abandoned it. It was by far, the most elaborate scam I'd ever come across to collect email address and sell them to marketing companies.

"On a cusp precipice, these expereinces of what the 'real-world' had become shattered my bones - the last weighty straw for me. The illusion became so obvious that it was beyond my comprehenson as to why so many were pretending it was still real, when," he shrugged his shoulders, "none of it is real. It never was. We all bought in, back when we were kids in front of the cartoon TV screens of the 80s," he sighed.

"No longer a student, but seeking application, I immediately sought out a group that was actively working behind the veil of this illusion. Seeking the grit, the red rusted decay, the shit, dirt, and mulched earth… to either grow my new life in… or spread my ashes on." Through ash-invoked sacrificial visions, Jason continued to share, "As I began my search I came across an article about this performance artist, who was progresivley engaging with a flatland audience to invoke more conscious depth and planetary awareness, and succeeding beyond measure. And suddenly she was there, right in front of me, asking if I knew where the Centre was."

"Wow, you met Cat!?" Aum shook his head in astonishment.

"Yes." Simply by the way Jason expressed it, maybe it was the quick smile, Aum knew they had instantly fallen in love upon first meeting, which he fully celebrated, and fully mourned. Jason was right. He knew, but he surley didn't know anything.

"Catherine said she was looking for the triple coiled serpent. I had no idea what that was, but I knew the Centre, so we walked over. As we did she openly shared her growth path, from her recent split with her partner, to her recent mandala performance in her homewtown. She asked if I knew Trae the Seer. I said no, but asked her if she was the same person as Tracey, and she said didn't know. I still knew Catherine was legit though, because every tidbit in the article backed her up."

"Who wrote the article?"

"Jessica Bell, City Times."

"Right. Do you know her?"

"Nope," and Jay kept flowing like water, "As Catherine moved I could see she had the ability to bend time and space at will, and at the same time, was the most compassionate and caring person I had ever met. I introduced her to Macek." Jason grew sorrowfull, and skeptical, "Who at that point, claimed to have mastered time travel... I continued to introduce her to the network I knew, and showed her all the spaces I was familiar with. From that platform she pushed the edge further, knowing that growth and evolution, though chaotic, was of greater importance at the time than maintaining some kind of cohesive and safe social vibration. She was stirring things up and putting things into motion, knowing it, and without even knowing it. I flowed with her, supported her momentum, watched her weave with power and confidence as she easily strode through Gridline, into parts I never even knew existed. It was in the rooftop garden where she said, 'That's them, the triple coiled serpent,' pointing to three men in a glass teepee. That's when we first formally met John, Derek and Zhe."

"You delivered her to them?"

"Yeah, I guess I did. And over the course of the week Cat returned and returned and returned again, receiving amped packets of insight that activated her mind and spirit like super fuel. An even greater seekers addiction than I had. We went as deep as we possibly could, in full conscious awareness, feeling as if the future of the planet was dependent on the rapid birth of our love and admiration, like the planet depended on our karmic paths of exchange, inspired entwining, healing life upon past life."

Aum smiled, knowing this exact feeling in humble remembrance.

Jay picked up on Demonas vibe residing in Aum's cells, "They live on... somewhere, they live on...Weaving between Macek's lab, the gardens, and Johns office, the council chamber, we even made it out to Eziekiels tower, eventually catching a lecture by Macek on the coming future of Gridline, where he introduced a new branch of exploration called the Interdimensional Action Plan."

"What!" Aum responded in disbelief, "Macek could so easily direct the future of Gridline?"

"Yeah, with a background in mass communications and cyber espionage, Macek was a prime wizard and Gridlines link to the major corporate investment in handembeds. He saved Gridline, but unlike an angel investor, he took on a major developmental role on the core council, becoming a lead teacher at the Centre. At the time this was supported by all, with deep links to the cultural history, especially having a long term working alliance with Ezekiel and Daniel, but for whatever reason, lack of integrity or a leap too far, chaos broke out after that talk, as if Cancer had just been diagnosed, so much so that Cat missed her flight back." The now emotional feryyman continued, "In an emergency flurry, Macek instructed me to drive her back … but he kept on calling her Anna by mistake… and after some random post-lecture exchange he shouted out at her, 'You're not Anna!' and then he demanded John go out on a mission to find her, the real Anna." He looked at Aum. "Do you know this Anna character?"

Aum was taken a back. It surprised him that Jason didn't know the story. Maybe he didn't see the H+ article yet, "I know *of* her, I don't know her though."

"You do? Shit man, that's deep intel - still a mystery to many…"

Or maybe even the article was more virus than truth.

"So you drove Cat back?" Aum quickly lept.

"No, actually. Before he left John gave us both tickets to Full Spectrum and revised instructions to attend. We drove together to the same festival you attended, arriving late, but still making it."

The lights in Aum's minds eye sparked as he began to realize how full a life Cat had lead. She didn't even mention this trip to him at the festival, though their moments were potent in present future work.

"Since John was gone I took his place at a campsite with Macek, Tide and a guy named Quark. We jammed deeply on the precog gateways needed to push parts through on a new energy infrastructure. The footwork. The engineering of the plan. We missed most of the festival dancefloor. I think Macek caught a lot of it though."

Aum pondered what he experienced of Macek at the festival, pondering the true extent of his meanacing additudinal tone.

Jay's head titlted, he flipped through a few screens on his handembed and hit play on a track by Taal Mala. The tesla-esque experimentally proven beat machine rythyms lightened everything with a joyus techno glow, "There we go."

"Nice!" Then Aum asked, "John wasn't at that Full Spectrum?"

"Correct."

"Where was he?"

"Here... On his mission. Or so they say. This far out... looking for Anna."

"Anna's still alive!?"

"I told you dude, it all got bent to shit. Nobody knows what the fuck is going on, or what happened at Gridline after Maceks emergency drop. Super cycle, Solar flare, inner soul hack, or simply the degradation of all notions of social cohesion, no one yet knows. Exponential mutation never before seen, certainly filtering into the festivals organizational entropy. At that Full Spectrum, after deep observations of all puzzle pieces, I became director of the Yellow tower. It was huge to take the lead on this one, as it was Johns role prior. It seared my fucking eyeballs; the upgrade at that time. Whether there's drinking water at the festival, and enough out-houses for everyone, who gives a shit. That's somebody elses problem," he said bitteryly. Aum's eyes went wild, feeling his daggers and scalpel coming out. The red rusted decay returned, "From that high platform, the ground level had become easily maintained as a social sub-culture sculpted into a consumptive vacation model, a retreat destination for sensualists and recreational emotive bench pressers, while back at their day jobs, in the old world, the two thirds continued to engineer the oil out of the earth and support the continuation of corporate powerhouses. A different kind of dirty job hole that pays for a life path of comfort and dream vacations."

It was as if Jason had seen all the cultures faults. All the things no one was willing to look at or address to make it fufill it's own lofty intentions. Aum thought of Johns lecture, and replied, "That hole is the crucial and failing bridge to smoothly move humans adequately into the newly restructuralized world."

"Correct. And because of that it all became a false bridge. A false belief system. A hacked stargate." He lightened in tone, "Fantastic growth space for willing individuals though. Yet with each after-path, I personally didn't have the patience or energy to develop my insights into a formalized consulting business; a social entrepreneur selling my sacred self in exchang for the government cash to pay bills or eat.

“Everything had morphed too much, and everybody tried to surf the incomeing waves of amped energy and new systems of chaos never before imagined. And we all thought we understood what was happening. The exponential increase became to much for all of us, and unconsciously, for security in dealing with the inner terror of the continuous demand of quantum ideation, we all linked back to the old world, out of fear, crystallizing the cult of individualsm, Self as brand, a permament human corruption, rather than continuing to pierce through to the new world, like you have done.

“It deeply surprised me when you offered Mother Earth such an important layer of yourself. The human essence that is usually converted into dollars you so easily gave up to her cause you could see she needed it more than you did.

“That action gave me faith in the temple template, in the Full Spectrum model, and our nations conscious birth to lead all humanity into the inner visions embedded in our DNA, vibrating. So with full imagination I took on all that I could, trying to attain the level of eminence that Catherine so easily was achieving.” He looked at Aum, “Transformational efforts that you could so easily achive.”

Aum authentically expressed, “This shit hasn’t been easy dude.”

“Fuck…” Jay added, and they both shook their heads in disbelief, as if Bodisatvic Acturians in all-knowing soul council. Tears began to cloud the sky blue eyes of the Ferryman, who finally realized how much he had shared, how much had escaped from his roughneck de-constructing and unlocked vulnerable vaults of purpose and memory. He lowered his head in acceptane and humility, knowing that there was far more that he may end up sharing with this healer. “Dude, You need to talk more,” he whispered.

Aum could see the clouds in his eyes turn to black smoke on blue sky, ashes into flames, and didn't know what to follow with. The river current began to rapidly take them away, towards Hades. But after a few adrenaline propeled moments, back on track, Cherokee ark and more, his heart poured into his mouth, as if suddenly in Setu Bandha Sarvangasana and Aum responded with a smile, “Jenn says ‘hi’.”

Jay’s face lit up, “You know Jenn!?”

“Yeah. We were once partners.”

It shocked Aum, how easily and simply the words came out of his mouth, without brace or pain, but ease and truth. Jason broadly smiled for the first time, white teeth shinning out, "Jenn was my savior, a life saver, my first step with some semblance of direction out of round three. A first akward and gnarly step out of that super depth I had to reach for, we all had to reach for, into what it meant to lead a tower and engineer the broadest transport moves possible. And nessescary. It's virtious work, pioneering the broad distances for the greater network good, before the teleportation grid comes online." He sneered, "Though totally fucking absurd sometimes: 300 kilometres to deliver a handwritten note on a piece of bark? That one was grotesquely impratical…"

"…but, considering your Hanuman-like streatch, undoubtedly profoundly significant." Aum did a live remix of Jasons thought trajectory, knowing full well the importance of reciving even the smallest glimmering token of hope while residing in a state of stark hoplessness.

"How is she? Jenn?" Jason asked.

"She survived… is surviving." Visions of post council wand and magic, "Thriving actually. Brand new."

"Brand new. The last little bridge..."

They found deep silence and authentic brotherhood as four-sided mountains rolled passed, covered in snow. There was a huge bearded beast on the side of the road. A moose. No cars stopped for pictures though, because everyone knew him by name. Marc from Manitoba.

"Have you ever been out here before?" Aum asked.

"Pioneering this far out, on the grid of resonance? Yes, but only to the gate. Never made it past the enviro-lock. Only been guided their once and was stumped and nearly flattened. Last time I just left the deliveries at the drop point and met with FitzRoy Raglan… who awaits deGryders return."

"FitzRoy?"

"The Green Man – or green knight if you consider him the gateway sentry, though to think of him in that way is definitely odd."

"FitzRoy is a good name for a knight."

"They say that he that he finds seeds coming out of his body when he bathes. They smell like cardamom. He plants them and grows them into trees he can talk to, though the plants have control over their own destiny, and if he thinks of selling them, or the seeds themselves - like magic beans - no more will come out of his body."

"He's a New Eden sentry?"

"Yeah but, he doesn't do anything but sit and tend the land. Sometimes he's invisible sometimes he makes himself known..." Jason looked over at Aum with curiosity, "New Eden?"

Trees zoomed by and the rough concrete shook the old truck. Aum held a question in his mind and waited, but nothing. Hmm, no pre-cog response from the Ferryman. A blank gap. "I don't suspect you've heard of the Riddle Solver either?" Aum asked.

"The Riddle Solver?"

"The recluse trapped in a box in the woods?"

Jason chuckled and shook his head.

"A test tube scientist from UCBerkeley?"

"A scientist! Test tube!?" He laughed even harder, nearly in tears, like it was the funniest joke he heard in his life, "Nope." Aum kept going past the laughs, as if stream of consciousness, "An emergent artificial human birthed from the first genetic timestrand?"

"Holy shite!" It was like a personal key code blasted into the immediate for the Ferryman. A psychopomp gate and first past flashback which opened his multidimensional eyes further than ever before, "Careful there bud, you're likely to dissolve into the stars, launched out from this dwarf planet satellite." Aum quickly responded, "That's not the point? Finding Braman past the furthest outpost, looking back into the full scope of Singular?"

"For yourself, undoubtedly. Bigger than what I can move and link though. For myself, after the year long dive into multidimensional awakening with Macek at Gridline I don't care to get caught up in layered relational transpersonal debris or esoteric quantum science – I try to keep my observations contained to my physical immediate. It allows for a more fluid peaceful existence, and easier breathing."

Jason paused, contemplating, as they both leaned into a steep mountain curve, "There is one story that I've heard though... it may link up to what you seek." He cleared his throat, as if preparing, "The elders here at the edge talk of the spirit of the first man, who lost his way. A man whose soul seeped out of him, past the grid, into the digital ether. He became a recluse, a nomad, a mystic, traveling across continents without food, without water, without sleep, searching for the bits of his soul that he had lost. His soul travels on the wind, coalescing in pockets of twisters, or being breathed in by forests, the lungs of the planet. The man wanders with only one cause, to find these pockets of Self. To breath in a pocket of air, in the mountains of Tibet, and find himself in it. To eat the fruit grown in the depths of the African jungle, and find himself in it. To drink a pocket of ice water in the Antarctic, and find himself in it. Hoping to one day be whole again. That might be who you're looking for, you should ask Fitz though. He may know more."

It kind of baffled Aum, that he was on a quest to find a quantum man-kind virus… or maybe it was just a man... and the guy delivering him had never heard the legend of the Riddle Solver, the root creation myth of their communities actions, or the secret city of New Eden, which surrounded the urban legend.

Light rain began to spatter the jeep windows. They took an unmarked dirt road off the highway, slowly climbing and circling the mountainside; switchbacks and wood plank bridges over streams were numerous. It was a vast living empty that stretched for day upon day, umpteen living creatures deep. There was no sign of man except a rare maple leaf at the top of a flag pole near a single beaten down fifth wheel, long abandoned and decomposing in an empty nook of evergreens.

"It's pretty secluded out here, hey?"

The Ferryman laughed and responded sarcastically, "Yeeeah."

Slowly traversing fallen logs and streams without bridges, Aum guessed over an hour or more had past at nearly a walking pace when they came to a wall. The Ferryman had black electric tape blocking the vehicles clock. With a few dozen logs piled up blocking the road, they rolled to a stop on the steep side of the hill, e-brake on, just in case, exiting.

With ancient and dense trees on both sides it was hard to see anything. Down the hill Aum could hear the sound of a creek moving swiftly, maybe even a waterfall in the distance. Up the hillside he heard an eagle screech; an eco-natural sentry.

Aum walked over to the log wall and saw on the other side a grassy campsite with fire pit recently used. Beyond the campsite, there was a broad overgrown walking trail, as if it was the continuation of the road itself, reclaimed by nature, wrenched from the grip of motor vehicles. Fresh horse hooves and bikes tire treads lead down the path away from the fire pit, "Hmmm."

"Hopefully the ferry delay doesn't affect their civil flow," said Jason. He started unloading items from the truck and automatically Aum followed suit. They piled them up on the other side of the wall, in the camping site, and covered them with a tarp.

"We don't need to haul this shit further?" Aum asked, practicing his gruff roughneck voice.

"No, they've got a team for that, or so I'm told." He hammered in the last tarp stake, "Let's take a stroll."

The light rain stopped as they began to walk down the overgrown road. A few strides in, on their left, hardly visible, was an opening in the foliage. It was a thin walking path for feet only, probably used mostly by deer, or wolves, or bears. Traversing the downhill slope, winged creatures sang in the trees, alongside the trees themselves which chanted out an invisible presence. The sound of the river got closer and closer till they could see the bubbling rolling source of the liquid voice.

"So… I noticed you removed your dreads. Last time I saw Cat she had removed all her hair as well, along with all other egoic casings," Aum knew he didn't need to go much further for Jason to understand the intent of his query.

"Yeah, I don't remember when I lost them." Jason ran his hand over his bald head. "One day I looked in the mirror and I saw they were gone." He shook his head in disbelief, "Not only that, I didn't recognize the face I saw staring back at me in the mirror. I did the best I could to integrate that, not recognizing who I was, seeing a fully mutated container, and since, avoid looking-glass mirrors all together. I suspect it was the same for Catherine."

"Maybe it was just your eyes that mutated, and their ability," Aum offered.

Pondering for a moment, then responding "I fully concur," the ferryman said, "The power of visionary dreamtime imagined is a source so bottomless it goes beyond the humanly possible." As they continued to descend the slope, Jason submerged himself in account, never before having the opportunity to openly share what he was about to, "After the festival John had yet to return, so Macek continued to lead, pushing his emergency agenda, further. Eventually engineering a micro-public pulse: flyers set sent out my yellow tower tendrils. Macek knew, unconsciously, something had gone awry, and was doing his best to compensate, solo, as if working in the dark, alone, without trail back to the known. All who could see him, knew this, and let him be, in his internal-external work, as it would be through this dimensional translation that future direction could be devised for the whole, for Gridline, and the Centre - or even more broad scope of whole.

"I don't know exactly how Catherine made it back to Gridline from Full Spectrum, but she did, as was her magical way. We reconnected, and in so doing found it was all on the verge of crumbling back into pure stardust. Any and all activity at Gridline required excruciating focus and unyielding hope until enough players emerged to sit in collective meditation with Macek.

"Myself, Catherine, a bright young woman named Sophia, the Matrika-Pleiadian trio of Pillaiyar, Sara and Ashta, and a few others, all present and contributing all they could to solidify the rupturing esoteric mechanisms of our consensus reality.

"There were deep fluctuations in the spirit grid which we were trying to harness, contain and control, and the combination of our vibrational purposes and heartfelt longings called forth new layers of technical execution. This meditation invoked a more cohesive existence, and pulled from the furthest tips of meta dimensional ether, bringing source energy into us, into our bodies, formalized in our imaginations, repositioning our eyes, sparking our ability to walk in the future. In that session, at that time, Macek showed us how to time travel." Jason pondered quantum reality, "Is what is an imagined truth? Or is what is a dimensional facet of fracture. That, because it is seen, it is, and in the manifold multiverse, existent, and thus the same truth," and he smoothly continued his account, "As we sat in that small room, with icaros as our guides, Macek started chanting code. Mouth output was rough and obtuse tracking algorithms, GPS coordinates, and self-dialogue that was certainly outside of Self. We in turn followed instinctually. 'Antagonist Self Synthesized' is the only line I remember saying."

'It was in tandem,' Aum thought, to his rescue mission of Ezekiel.

"The focus we were putting into the expansion of the planetary geo-latice of meta earth was undoubtedly real. Undoubtedly. We all felt it. We all felt it. It was the furthest we had gone in group meditation. And because of that Catherine didn't return.

"We all made it back to our bodies, but due to the level of gallop and fervor in which she approached her initial inner launch, she didn't as easily make it back.

"When we opened our eyes, we saw her body was an empty vessel.

"Macek had to go back in after her. The rest of us simply prayed and held space in whatever way we felt most appropriate, singing, pranic breathing, reiki.

"When she finally awoke, her eyes went wide, as if seeing more than she should, seeing not her immediate environment, but something else. 'Total eradication of the cyclical' a voice said from inside her, and then she was up and off. Running. As if her life… no… as if the planet, depended on it.

"That was the last time I was with her, yet I did my best to find her in all moments after. Still do even."

"Hmmm," Aum intoned in agreement.

They has stopped walking down the slope long ago, and the forest stopped singing to listen.

Jason continued, "That's when John returned. Role redefined, which you earlier, surmised correctly." Aum must have looked confused. "The Ferryman key-code was a final confirmation of the social system remix. New platform."

Aum smiled and Jay continued, "Together John and I searched and rewove as best we could. Derek in parallax, militant phalanx. Arrowhead. Arrows linked to twine, assembly ropes for the biggest bridges imaginable. Planetary bridges for one and all… and she used them in a way that none dreamed possible."

There was a living silence in the forest, so dramatic they both new they were inside a living boundless entity, a physical amalgamation of cosmic consciousness. A soft breeze from beyond, from mystic wings, came to them for encouragement.

Jason looked at Aum, "In the end I was allowed, I was afforded, the pristine blessing of witnessing, of feeling the live media stream of dancing immortals; the dance of gods and the upper echelon of their karmas," he motioned to his hand embed, "And the searing innate path of upgrade on my own soul circuitry. On my heart."

He brought his hands together in prayer, and as he did closed the account tenderly. Far down the creek side they saw a man sitting at the edge of the waterfall who was looking at them intently. "FitzRoy is here. Good sign," Jason said, grit and dirt back in his mulched voice.

As the two approached the sentry, the ferryman whispered, "He's become as much a part of this environment as these trees or rocks; he probably knows them all by name. This spot here is a unique place on the surface of the earth."

They continued to approach, the sound of the waterfall getting louder, Jason in turn increased his volume, "To me, to him, to most who arrive here, it sparkles like a unique and untouched jewel. Sure, there are much larger sparkling gems that probably shine out earth light far more intensely than this place – Machu Pichu, Giza, Niagara for instance - but the uniqueness here is silent, and sharp, and bright; like looking into the sun."

Aum observed the twinkling beauty and added, "Like a small slice of Eden, a most obvious alcove of divine creation."

There was a splash and they looked again at the edge of the waterfall. The man was gone. Aum and Jason looked at each other in surprise, the wrinkles on his brown face, which he had thought immovable, expressed much. They then heard an approaching voice emerging from the trees.

"The collapsing of all possibility while walking through life uncovers a spring of glistening knowledge inside the echoing feedback of longevity. With gentle pace along this path, each collected pond of wisdom creates a reflection of what it is that truly matters. Greetings."

"Hey Fitz," and he and Jason hugged. In the found soul pocket a coherence of resonation occurred. As they linked in full depth they begain operating their bodies from some other time and space, some other planet maybe.

"This is Aum. The last delivery."

"Oh!" FitzRoy moved in timidly with a hug, measuring Aum's spirit in the process. Aum was totally open to his inspection, and found it was like hugging a tree.

"The last man standing," Fitz said. Aum didn't know what he perceived in the hug but undoubtedly it was much.

They looked at Aum to speak but he didn't have anything to say in that spotlight. Both understood and Jack continued while all three gazed at the waterfall in reverence, “I see this place as a focal spot created by God’s dedicated attention over the billions and billions of years that the earth has been evolving. This particular sparkle on the Earths surface probably took millions of years to create, and will take millions of years for its light to fade. I will be long gone by then, but I can say that I’ve dedicated a portion of my life to appreciating and being enveloped by that sparkling. So much so that I know it’s light will continually live inside my heart. I’ve been enveloped so fully that I’ve conversed about the beauty of the Gaian divine, with the stone peoples and tree spirits who have also chosen to make their existence a part of this beauty. Places here on earth shine and fade just like stars in the night sky.” He sighed a deep breath, “If I ever choose to leave and join the sky anscestors, I’ll bring this sparkle wherever I go.”

There was a pause as the waterfall spoke for a moment, adding to the time space dialogue which Aum allowed through his silence.

“You’re good?” Jason asked him. For a moment the question confused Aum, then he realized it was aimed at him.

Shit, Jason was leaving.

Back to the Cherokee, back to Rupert, more coastline deliveries, Port Hardy, and eventually back the Centre.

“There’s a tent bag and full cooler under the tarp, as backup, just in case the enviro-lock stumps you, like it has many.”

Aum must have looked panicked for a second.

“I can guide you towards this last checkpoint, the locked gate,” Fitz smiled at him. His breath smelled like cardamom.

Aum was kinda speechless, quickly finding his own footing in the literal middle of nowhere, almost the middle of everywhere. It was the edge of the singularity vortex: a sundog floating in it's orbit. He felt the node soul of resonation splitting; the micro-plateau. So quickly did this brotherhood come together, and so quickly did it dissolve back into the unknown future. He brought his hands together and bowed, for seeing it, and for the delivery to this far out edge, “Charged and ready.”

“Blessings on your fine dive and giding eyes,” Jason said, bowing, stepping quickly back into his ferryman duties.

In the mystic space FitzRoy Raglan spoke, giving voice to the humming trees, “When humans first found this planet it was through a metaphysical synthesis. Human souls were first grown within we trees like incubators. They then migrated from these deep spirit houses, into the physical bodies which they now have, evolving over numerous millennia,” He caressed the tree as if a past, or even current lover. Speaking from his heart he continued,“The physical bodies we humans have now, at the beginning, did not have the capacity to evolve both spirits and their long term physical containers. Now the next migration is happening, and souls are moving from bodies to their next vehicles.”

“Computers?”Aum asked.

“What do you think?”

“It’s certainly not back to trees.”

“Capra said the primary source of the flow of energy is the sun. Solar energy transformed into chemical energy by the photosynthesis of green plants drives most ecological cycles. Ecology driving economy, thus technology, whether a directly synched flow-through attached to a solar battery, or woven into a complex chemical and crystalized death machine. The cycles of human harvest are not much different than skin bag meat sacks filled with maggots.”

“About as elegant at this point,” Aum responded.

“Don't get me wrong, maggots are awesome,” said Fitz.

Reaching, Aum added, “But there are certainly other forces to contend with, battles nested within battles, as this soul transference becomes damned, and ancient death mines no longer a perpetual focal resource,” Aum added.

FitzRoy took one step up, back towards the road and spoke, Aum followed as if a long term student, “This place is a crowning jewel you understand. This community a pinnacle inner sanctum of human evolution, much like this waterfall here. The earth calls to the body based crystals, resonating at a level of genetics, aligning human stewards to care for the land; existing as extensions of the land itself. You are one of these. A pinnacle of human evolution. I see a very nice collection of sparkles and gems inside your eyes and in your heart.” He pointed up the hill and continued. “The lock is this way.”

As they went deeper into the woods they passed the fluid border into the dimensionless and FitzRoy Raglan’s beard grew, and his horns grew, protruding from his skull. The green man chuckled as moose or Pan, his voice distorting beyond human, "You see, I can create false paths for random travelers; warn the core city of any potential mischief incoming: drone, or grumpy grizzly. With assistance from my nature allies, my voice speaks louder and stronger than any other, resonating deeper intuitively than any other techno framework, any alarm system." They were instantly back up on the road, far past the campsite and the log wall, Cherokee was gone. Aum didn't remember walking up the returning incline, and did not stir at this observation: Raglan's display of teleportation and summation god-like power. Aum had leapt in long ago, and was ready to leap further, with Pan, if need be, taking this mischievous god into the future, leading. The chuckle was even deeper, "I see you. You'll do fine monk; green data wizard mage. Follow this historic path of soul self seen and you will find the last lock, maybe even key. May it open your heart and show you all you need to fly, and carry all into the everlasting." FitxRoy Raglan took two steps and dissolved into the textures of tree branches, water and stone, as if an apparition. As if never their to begin with.

As if planned, or a switch flipped, it began raining again.

Aum walked along the path, not alone, but within the full nest of nature. He breathed in the pure green light of glowing photosynthesis. It was a living orchestra, seeing it's celestial self through his eyes.

A few strides in, he observed the paths character, history. It looked like it had been an old road used centuries ago, during the gold rush for mining or even hunting. He could easily picture a minimally framed model-T mod, rolling up the smooth incline delivering supplies to the railroad workers.

The path curved drastically and he saw the old road had been swept away by a recent landslide, he scrambled over the shale and gravel. It was as if half the mountain came down. In a nook between large boulders he notice a bone or two as he jumped across. Leap after balanced leap he reached the rockslides completion, finding himself in a full bone yard. Strewn across the path, it was not just a single bone pile, but partial skeletons, rib cages and spines, legs with fur and hooves still attached, all a different stage of sun bleached white. Even numerous skulls with horns collecting raindrops and sundrops. This added even more the to character and presence of where he was. He carefully investigated, fully expecting to see some half eaten human, still alive and groaning in utter torment. What was this from? A mountain lion? A pack of wolves?

He continued along the path with trepidation. Adrenalin in his blood and a touch of fear in his heart, there was a lump in his throat, his eyes now darting this way and that, imagination taking over.

Each pile of rocks looked like it had fur moving just behind it, or a creature atop.

Then he did see something.

The slight twitch of ears and a tail.

It was small though. Fox? No. Coyote. It was down the ridge a few meteres and didn’t seem to notice Aum. The creature took a few more steps then curled up for a nap. Aum, in total stillness, notice a few other balls of fur, also curled up and sleeping. It was a whole pack, nestled within the bouldered jagged outcroppings of the mountainside. After a few moments of seeing their nature, meditating on their wild medicine in silent observation, he let them be. It stopped raining and the sun beamed out.

He climbed back, returning to where the road ended from the rockslide and he saw fresh markings of a wheeled cart, which he didn't notice before. Underneath one of the treads there was a single path worn in the short green grass, being skinnier than the width of his foot, he knew it was a path worn by animals. Nature still led the way here.

The incline was still quite steep. He lost his breath as there seemed to be no letting up to the ever-elevating pitch. As Aum continued to trudge up along the new path, on all fours with limbs beginning to ache, a new exaustion pushed him nearly over the precipice, on the otherside was a black pit of what-the-fuck-am-I-doing-all-the-way-out-here. But then the incline finally crested, opening up into a small meadow on the hillside where, he found an injured butterfly.

It's abdomen had been pressed out of it’s skin, only one leg was moving and, unable to fly, it was writhing in pain. Or at least seemed to be. Are insects capable of feeling pain? or are they the physical manifestation of something greater? Unsure what to do, to leave it, or put it out of it’s seeming misery Aum took it to a nearby stump and with the most heartfelt compassion, even resistance, flattened the rest of it with a nearby rock. After the death blow, he blew on it with a heavy heart and heavy mind. The wind from his lungs allowed the creature to feel it's natural state once more. God moved through this breath and allowed the butterfly to reach a state of Samadhi, even connecting directly with Aum, and the divine residing there. Before the butterfly passed on to the ether; and surely it's next level of life complexity, it spoke to him. 'This is your future,' it said, as it's flickering spirit flew off, leaving it's bodily cocoon behind, as Aums long breath blew it off the stump and it dropped to the ground next to the path.

Aum looked down to where it had fallen and noticed underneath a pattern in the land. Nestled in between stump and stone, boulder and tree, intentionally placed, was a collection of human intention; druid magic. A sign of life, yet still, a dead alter in the woods. There was no energy in it. The butterfly illustrated that. Aum stepped over it, and instantly, ahead of him, a few giant boulders tumbled down the hill, remnants of the landslide, threatening to crunch his bones into flat little pieces.'Oh…shit, that's the lock…Okay…"

He took a reverse step back over and looked down. He laughed thinking of the metal numerical dial on the city roof top oh so long ago, it's new human machinery an engineering feat that may or may not out live this deeply archaic witchcraft. Stone amulet, feather, meditation beads, even a worn out USB key; there was a thick layer of nature on this lock. Dirt and dust kicked up from the rains, brown leaves blown over decaying tree branches, black and dried out, shriveled berries were strewn at random which spotted the pocket of magic. It had probably gone unnoticed for years. Aum cleared the natural debris and gently moved the butterfly aside.

Each item in the lock buzzed him as he grazed or touched it. It was surprising enough to nearly draw his hands away; like they were shouting at him: 'Be gentle with your lumbering clumsy hand holds; sporadic with human lightning, missing proper capacitors and resistors of the always.'

Or they just shouted their names at him, attaining vocalization, breaking through the cracks in his imagination, and inside that, inside the cracks of their shouts, he could read their healing properties. The metal dial certainly didn't speak to him like this.

He examined the amulet first, which was actually a vintage silver key on a chain with clasp. Wrapped with a copper wire of extremely light gauge, a small green ocean jade was attached. The wire was so thin it could have been the long curl off the mane of a passing magical creature. The green jade itself spoke louder than the silver or copper. It was speckled and non-uniform, worn as if only recently pulled from the ocean after a millennia of collecting ample divots and bumps. He touched it again, lightly with the tip of his middle finger and he instantly synced to a deeper pulse in his heart, key opening him to loving positivity, appreciation, and relaxation. It was a gentle loving reminder that he could spend all day, all night, and all day here with this lock, if he chose to. The ocean key was pointing north and directly below it, about three inches, were two lovers hanging out.

On the bottom was a hefty, palm-sized polished silver topaz, colorless and grounding the very centre of the lock. It's mystical depth reflected the complexity of the old work done here. Representing one of twelve angels guarding paradise and one of the twelve stones encrusted on the breastplate of the high priest in the book of Exodus, he remembered Topaz allows one to see the way, the true path from inside a state of cosmic awareness. Balanced on top of it, no bigger than a dime, was a small pebble of Jet: a Lignite. Like a pupil on an eyeball it was the last stone that had been placed, "And will need to be the first moved," Aum observed, speaking aloud. He greeted both by cupping the air around the two, feeling their connection. He remembered Jet is one of the most powerful stones used in ceremony to channel the earth and used for protection. Once he saw them seeing him, he respectfully moved on.

Directly left of centre, another three inches, was a Tigers Eye's, or Cat's eye.

"Hmmm," Aum hummed in consideration. Tiger's Eye is a good luck stone. It instantly brought him a mentally clarity of oneness as he engaged with it, with his own eyes opening inside of it, beyond past, present, and future – his third eye blazed.

Moving east from the Tigers eye, across the Topaz-Jet centre, directly right from it, another 3 inches, was a blue Kyanite blade. A long thin shard that looked like it was broken off a slab of epic proportions. Aum's body was brought back into the mix and all the stones talked to him, giving away all their secrets that they knew he knew, or knew he would find out in due time. Aum started humming in thanks of receiving the message, a light improvised tune that was a massage for all them.

At the bottom, south, closest to him, was a piece of Lemurian Seed quartz - planted in the ground as if it grew there. The queen, he greeted her with a bow, and would certainly do his best not to disturb her linked, masterful vibes, that pulsed far and wide, as he could see, she held this gateway against the earth. With a breath, taking it all in, it was an iron cross spread, or a directional compass.

Beyond the X composition however, it was the extra elements that spoke out the locks unique character. Next to the Lemurian quartz, in-between the south point and easterly placed Kyanite, in the southeast space was a necklace of red jade beads. It was placed in a perfect pyramidal pile. Stout and solid it was no doubt a ceremonial accoutrement, rather than a beatific adornment. Above the Kyanite, and in the northeast spot, was the USB drive. It's black plastic casing was encrusted with powder and debris, 256MB was stamped on it. Whatever it was, was still on there, ready to jump through it's crystal oscillator with micro piezoelectricity – it did infact, as he looked at. It receive a spark from the Topaz-Jet combo; also both conductors of piezoelectricity and the danger amped. It felt like he might get electrocuted if he made a wrong move here. The USB truncated the polygon lock at the top right edge, the metal plug pointing down toward the Kyanite, and the plastic cased end pointing up towards the green ocean jade key.

Opposite it, in the northwest spot, also placed in a truncation position, was an equally sized piece of Palo Santo wood; a traditional tool of smudging and spiritual cleansing used by Ayahuascero medicine men in the Peruvian Jungle. Below it, a large Eagle feather, in the southwest. It's tip touching tiger's eye and base Lemuria. He looked at it deeply, where it caressed the seed quartz, observing it's color and radiance as his eyes moved up to the Tigers eye; the yellow cat's eye. The wind blew in his ear, whispering, cycling into his lungs and emerged from his mouth, dancing on his tongue he understood the language.

First, the preparatory moves, the eagle feather. He picked it up and gently blew on it, cleaned it, then waved it back and forth over the lock as if a wing, as if a wand, both lightly brushing off the dust, as well as waking up any last haze of sleep. After it was sufficiently vibrating he placed the feather due south, below the lock; base still touching the Lemurian Seed quartz. He began to flow intuitively, in each moment taking instruction from each piece of resonating knowledge.

The Red Japer necklace grabbed his attention, so he toppled it's perfect pyramid, lifting it, and placed it above the Jade key, he knew, temporarily. He rotated the Palo Santo piece 90 degrees so that it pointed to the centre.

It was ready, engaged, and welcoming of the first real move in the combination.

Heart in his right hand and in his fingertips, he lifted the central Jet off the Topaz and placed it, on top of the Palo Santo in northwest corner while deftly his left fingers plucked the Tigers Eye from it's position and danced it into the southwest corner, where the eagle feather had been.

He motioned his hand over the newly open topaz, and the entire lock, like a slight-of-hand artist, a magician, feeling it's vibe, even introducing himself more deeply. He picked up the clear stone with both hands cupping it, one above and one below, and gently placed it in the southeast corner where the pile of red jade once was.

Then quickly, with the forefingers, index and thumb, on his right hand he picked up the Kyanites pointy broadsides, swept his body in one motion as if it emitted a laser, cleansing and balancing the deeper levels of his presence. He placed it in the upper right, the northwest corner, on top of the USB, rotating it 90 degrees with his left hand so they would sit in unison, pointing to the centre.

He did feel like an actual magician, doing this work.

Now observing the whole, seeing the obvious circle layout he picked up the red Jade necklace in both hands and encircled the lock with the grounding guiding stones.

Jet, Lemurian Seed, Kyanite. Cat's Eye, Green Ocean Jade, Topaz.

It all spun like invisibly interconnected dials; the genesis pattern flowered out in his minds eye, circles and spheres intersecting and illustrating the underlying building blocks of reality. It was how they spoke to each other. Then the vortex opened.

He felt it swirl like a six inch twister, wanting to cup it like water in his hands, or fill his water bottle with it.

Then he saw the two intersecting triangles – a dialogue anchoring the circle pattern.

His eyes followed the coal blackness of the Jet Lignite micro-bit at the high left charging on the wood and future smoke of Palo Santo, paralleling the Blue Kyantie Blade charging on the USB: their contents like another pair of lovers sending a data merge through particle signals, instantly cascading out to their non-local satellite receptors. This feminine triangle, which pointed at him, was fully grounded at the lower apex, growing from a core earth depth, the Lemurian Seed quartz - an open access pole to the ancient wisdom of a different layer of consciousness. It pulsed out to the two amped corners directionally, and out their continuous signal streams through future smoke and particle data. It was a beautiful and ancient future song. Everything began to look in, and listen, and the door materialized.

Then Cats Eye at the lower left palm saw each corner of the future, though first moved Aum's attention to the large Silver Topaz across from it, at the lower right palm. Clearing all that was unnecessary in the masculine, it combined the pathways seen, meeting at the silver key of Green Ocean Jade at the apex, still pointing from the same location, through the heart, to the heavens, and forward.

Quickly circling through, looking from Lemurian Seed, to the Ocean Jade, the gate unlocked. It wasn't complete yet though, he needed to open the door, and step through, in alignment with all these elementals - and not get pummeled by the mountain men - which may be the true test in this last unlocking.

Aum scratched his head.

He rubbed his whiskered chin. Waiting.

His personal signature, his magic was in accord with his experience, past, present and future. The stones agreed. So he playfully began to move with them, again feeling for their voice in the new positioning they wanted.

Where once he was speedy and nimble in his opening movements, here he slowed down to a time-bending pace, slower than any second hand could count.

He took the ocean key, and placed it against his heart. His lips. His third eye. Then down in the exact centre point of the open tornado vortex. This re-grounded the entire heart locket and, at this first move, the ecology around him began to beam into him its positive gloss. His heart received this and he grew in power, linking to his solar plexus and voice.

Next he removed the Kyanite from it's cyborg love, the jump drive. He swept his whole auric field once again, with the minerals psychic amplification properties he spread the oceans positivity throughout his entire system, and beyond. He then clenched the blade in his right hand and noticed the damp smell of the forest entering his nose; and on a peaceful breath the sun hit the drying rain drops on the leaves. They sparkled like stars at night, multicolored rainbows shimmering which quickly faded into the invisible with the heat of the moving sun.

"Whoa… rainbow bridges, the momentary infinite."

He placed the blue blade to the right of the key, as close as an inch, slightly north.

Next, as if over a fire, he warmed his hands on the large smooth piece of Topaz, preparing it, moving it only slightly up and left, not even an inch, directly towards the masculine triangle apex. Rotating it in place, it was like tuning his solar plexus and cosmic awareness to a new frequency of emotional being. His spirit moved fully through the stone. In from one side, and then out the other. It acted like a filter, a sieve, and caught all unnecessary blockages, dull spots in his auric felid.

As he did this the iolite in his pocket yelped - as if waking to it's true purpose for journeying with Aum from the Centre.

It was one of the 12 angelic guardians and needed to be included.

At it's most resonant tuning he placed the iolite pebble on the centre of the Topaz and smudged himself with the frequency merge, it revealed the furthest path seen, mapped with deepest future compass. The city of light was coming closer. As he completed the smudge, the Iolite replaced the lack luster dull parts in him, taken by the Topaz sieve, with new aspects of himself that he had never before directly seen, though had always known was there.

He brought his hands to heart centre.

He had yet to move the piece of Lemurian Seed, and still did not.

Again he simply bowed to it's full presence, his attention moving through it into everything he could perceive; linking it all in unification.

He picked up the Tigers Eye next to it in the southwest corner and brought it to his forehead. He closed his eyes, but could see out through the stone, the deeper story of humanity here on the planet, and throughout all time, a perspective anchored away from contextual distraction and data buzz, but resonating in a deeper natural harmony.

He was getting close, only a few more layers to peel till he was there, till the veil was lifted and destination found within and without. Tiger Eye in it, he brought his closed hand down and opened his palm, opening his eyes he could see a trident symbol carved into it, filled with white paint: shiva lingam, the symbol of Shiva. Aum's third eye opened even more. He placed the Tigers Eye directly west of the green key, linking the heart root of the spiral to this trident tip.

There at the spiral tip, waiting, was something familiar. A feeling. A presence. A spectral galactic embrace of the newly found, newly constructed.

Ah, yes. He still had it. The genetic seed key from Zeke's lab, still in his pocket. It lovingly told him this is where it was meant to be planted; the last angel, last guardian.

The incantation manifest, translated from the 5D genetic datasphere into Cedar seed, vocalized coordination with the USB key, outside of time and space. The jump drive's crunching pulsing ant-like numbers taped him with piezoelectricity from inside the quartz engine. Aum translated the pulse into his final instruction set for the enviro-lock.

He took the USB, still in the northwest corner, without Kyanite lover, and brought it to the utmost north, outside the red Jade necklace circle, and plunged it into the ground, as if an earth port. Then he turned it. There was a crackling of thunder in the far off distance, a valley or two over.

He pulled it out of the ground, grabbed the Cedar seed from his pocket; seed for tree of life, and planted it in the jump stick hole. He spied the Jet still on the wood, and rubbing it on the Palo Santo, created an electric current. He covered the seed lightly with dirt and quickly placed the Jet over top.

There was instantly a flash – maybe the coming storm was much closer.

The wind picked up and it slightly moved the feather pointing south. He picked the feather up and waved it over the open lock, cooling it, flying it as if gelling the new energies together - allowing them to settle in for a long stay in this formation, where eventually a star-gene tree would grow, maybe its future formed into wooden keys or the medicines for DNA surgeons.

He planted the eagle feather into the ground, just above the north side of the Jet in perfect time with an eagle screech far above him. This opened the door. But it had also opened him. Unlocked him. And changed him. He wore the breastplate of the high priest. He looked up and the environment was totally different – grass was longer, new trees had grown, and the older ancient ones were even taller, and thicker. He could see a new forest spirit; alive, open, living, waiting for him and the wind blew anew, carrying an unfamiliar scent, urging him on with an invisible guidance.

Stepping over the remixed altar, and thus through the gate, he didn't have to worry about the mountains falling on him, they welcomed him with awe and cheers.

After only a few dozen strides past the lock, the hill crested, and he saw it.

Shimmering as if a mirage, it was not a city, but a kingdom of light.

He rubbed his eyes, trying to comprehend the brightness of what he saw: customized nooks of habitation nestled in the greens with groomed ground crop gardens and high fruit trees, there were eco turbines and wind sails so elevated it allowed them to ride the sky without leaving even a footprint behind. A gust of living air hit him and within it was an intelligence that trumpeted his arrival, like entering a new world; a different planet indeed.

The wind spoke to him, massaging his ears, introducing him to the continued wholistic lineage of the human creature that now resided in the arms of the divine planetary body which gave birth to it. Here, human kind had reached pinnacle evolutionary expression of feat and feature, a people that had harvested all positive lightwork that could be, discarding evolutionary pathways which they once tread erroneously, divergent in their unconscious patterning of separation and future still-birth.

There were Ewoks around here somewhere, he could sense it.

He spied the vibrant and green deep valley ridges from the high mountain crest. He peered closer at the details and saw a series of interconnected biodome bubbles that graced the hillside. They looked like an extension of the hills themselves; the only difference between these areas and the surrounding hillside was the subtle layer of geometric patterning and slight opaque cover, flush with color underneath. So subtle of a presence it spoke to him of the new humans and their conscious placement within the world, and their perfect health as celestial cosmogaian beings living in accord with their universe.

"Our ancestors," a rustic yet strong voice spoke out, unsurprisingly, "they enter through the wild, as you have, though they do not bring with them their body containers, as you do."

His self-made clothes reminded him of one of the high tree elves in his communal Gaian climb with Jenn at Full Spectrum.

"Yes, the ancient ones. They, inside the fine leaves of the trees, told the eagles, to tell me, of your delivery."

In fact it *was* him.

"You're the first one to arrive inside the gnarling tsunami. Welcome to New Eridu. My name is Herald," he bowed as if Aum's full legacy and mission was telepathically known to him.

"Aum," he responded, remembering the complex spoken lines this man once shared with him, *We create our own creations*. Aum was relieved to see his open kindness, unsure if Herald could remember the treetop incident and the twisted chemical inflection of an esoterically flung out truth. It was a mantra to mediate on as the mysterious path to the Riddle Solver, now very leafy, continued.

Aum's heart spoke out, "New Eridu? I thought this was New Eden?"

"New Eden? I've never heard of New Eden. An apt meta tag… though leaves a scaldcraftian mess in its wake."

Woven leaves of green and brown leather linked into his garment like winged feather. His coveralls were patched with these, and etched and embroidered with fantastic geomancy – sigils of a new dimensional framework that Aum was sure pulsed down into the mans fingertips as he worked the earth. He wore a brown t-shirt underneath with a Warhol-esque monochrome print series of flattened Yoda graphics while his slightly off-centre baseball cap invoked a coastal urban youth aligned with the stars, also aligning with it's ajna and sahasrara influenced spray can stencil. 'Hmmm…' Aum wondered if it would light up like n-Glu if he looked at it hard enough.

"There's also a supply package at the road block camp," Aum added.

"Yes. Gratitude for amping the wholistic basket. The recon-team has been sent. Let us begin to see, what we shall see, shall we?"

As Herald spoke, his age was disconnected from his bearded vehicle – he could have been 15 or 51, a non-age, much like Ezekiel. Aum smiled. As they began their hike toward the village of light, Aum could see it was endless from here, beyond stigma or myth. A day stretched for multiple days on end, a single day lasting a week or month, rather than the inversion; multiple days, a full week of time or even month of it, compacted into a single day. There was so much room to be, it was almost like he couldn't find a foothold, and was drowning in Bose–Einstein condensates.

The plants around the path reached out for him as he breathed and observed the vast expanse that surrounded each thought and each breathe. The air here carried no environmental pollution and no signal pollution. He didn't quite understand it, but there was no source code. It was invisible. It was all just codeless source. He looked from afar and saw the people here, in New Ediru, in New Eden, were inside of this source and he better understood how it worked; understood their relationship to it, individual, group, team, and entire community. Generation upon generation, family upon family, attention was deep and true, where no occurrence was fleeting and inconsequential, but fully understood within the whole system, because they could easily see it all at once. The oversoul perspective inside every individual.

Herald sang, probably an elvish tune, as they walked. It morphed gracefully towards sung, then spoken words, "This is the only real gate into the valley." He pointed to the other side, "None come from that way, unless by chance through the air – and to exit that way by foot – you are taking your life into your own hands. Not only cougars, bears and wolves, but the conscious land will take you and not give you back, just like the ancient wild. Our vision quests and fasts take place out that way, out into the temporal space of fullest nature. Travel far enough, make it far enough through, and you will hit the arctic ocean before you hit other humans."

Heralds gaze surmised all he could see, every mossy nook and rock crevasse, as if it spoke volumes to him.

"The trees say 'hello'."

"Yeah?" Aum smiled and nodded, looking around at them.

"That guy," Herald pointed to the biggest one, "is from Dubshyre."

"Dubshyre? Where's that?"

With a laugh Herald responded, "Nobody knows."

The view opened and Aum looked up to see there were propellers speckled along a very specific ridge. They were up so high, and at an angle from the village path, that the blades weren't noticeable. They looked like silver toothpicks, or acupuncture needles in the Earth's body, vibrating with life.

"Upon arrival the entire valley was surveyed, each contour of hill and mountain mapped – measurements in place, simple windsocks at first, then temporary turbines; over the course of three years, to best map the air flow of the entire valley, and monitor what ridges have the most consistent continuous stream of eco-dynamic power." Aum saw that some propellers were slightly angled, catching the wind as gust or gale would launch down and through a halfpipe gully, as if a street acrobat at the skate park.

"The micro-team found it was seasonally dependent, the strongest winds were in the spring and fall, as the seasons shifted. It was still advantageous to construct a swath of turbines however, the energy collected in the spring used for the fall food harvest, and the fall collection used for the infared heaters and greenhouses over the winter."

They passed a creek as they continued their descent into the city valley, view sometimes blocked by trees, sometimes clear.

"This creek leads to a larger tributary, the main river channel, then into the mouth opening at the sea. Unlike the wind, one thing that isn't seasonal here is the river. This natural locomotion moves much more that clean water through the valley." He quickly scooped a hand full and drank, "It's like spiritual refreshment, renewing inspiration and moving doubt and dark clouds with it. It helps the air move the weather patterns in and out the valley." He scooped again, in offering. "Here, a first greeting." He poured it into Aum's hand. It mostly ran through so he simply wiped his face and ears, then knelt down next to Herald, scooped and drank. He was actively learning to move his body in perfect sync with all that he could perceive of the new, all that this community was trying to achieve.

"There was a different hand of us, a team of five, who focused on the rivers. They constructed small medium and large aquabines for the creeks, tributaries, river and river mouth. Unlike a dam that forces all water through tiny holes in a solid wall – solid enough to stop all life - these aqua turbines are low impact."

"They don't affect the eco-system of the river?" Aum asked, drying his face on his shirt.

"No, the paddles are light enough, and the support structure minimal enough it's as if they're not even there. It's the equivalent to a dozen skipped rocks in the water – the river actually erodes our turbines quicker than the natural growth path of the river – it is a choice we consciously make to allow our environment to speak louder than us. That being said, we've done some earth molding: we do use an aquifer system, drawing from a fresh spring just a few jumps north."

He and Aum both heard the ocean speak up, waves crashing,"Yes, we also have rows and rows of massive tidal-turbines in the ocean, just over the ridge there. It's actually that constant pulse that is the heart beat of New Ediru. Without it we wouldn't have enough juice to sustain a worry free level of energetic abundance. Winter would be tough. We would have to ration and micro-manage use throughout the year – a waste of energy in itself – this allows us to know that even in the coldest stretch of winter we will not freeze."

"Have some actually froze?"

"Well, for many years there was an edge space over the winter where starvation was always an issue. In collective delirium the shaman would point to the fittest of the young men and charge them with saving the tribe from extinction, where it was up to them, in their malnourished state to endure the extremes and pray the deepest to the creator to have an encounter with a living spirit, that would give themselves over, in promise of humanities continuous miracle. Whether buck, bear, or caribou, this offering would be just enough for the community to make it through untill the first melt where a larger hunting party would go out to meet a herd of foragers, deer or bison, rabbits even."

"The shaman?" Aum asked hungrily.

Herald looked at Aum, hearing the full extent of his question.

"Some have stronger ears than others. There is usually only one, that hears and speaks in full unity. It is a very auspicious position, one that is chosen by the council. She finds you, not the other way around."

"Any tips?"

"Don't look for her. You will not like what you find."

It was a drastic statement that caught Aum off-guard. "Okay." He had to leap over a fallen log in order not to faceplant. With the grace of a dancer he refound the physical and non-physical path, Herald nearly dissolving into the anscestral ether. Aum instantly toggled back to the enviro-dialoge, "You're on the ocean, but not a fishing community?"

"We have a few tester turbines that are combined with fish traps, to collect both food and energy. All river turbines are weighted, flagged and fenced so floaters don't smash them in the summer."

"Floaters?"

"Yeah, bettys and dudes float the river in the summer to cool off. Some stretches are better for floating than others. We tried to keep a clear path for the fun to happen."

"I'm sure as the river floaters are, the turbines are daisy-chained?"

"Because of the sheer number of turbines we found placement for, we tried out some advanced wireless technologies."

"Success?"

"Only in knowing the idea needed further signal refinement. It's pretty dirty, lot's of noise, people kinda fry themselves when they're around them – crossing the invisible path between transmitter and receiver so to speak. We began to see lines emerge in the environment; burn marks or unlush dead zones. Wireless power got phased, for traditional insulated landlines, some chained some not, depends on the signal density."

Flattening, zones within zones, the land leveled out along the tributary, over a walking bridge they crossed the stream and came to the first pod of homes. The world 'sprawl' came to Aum's mind and he laughed at it, and the absurd world that used it. There was a quick wave from the first villager they saw – a deep exchange of joy and renewal.

She was in her garden, with baby on hip, wearing intricate and astounding layers of beauty, not constructed by the popularized social media paradigms of collective consumerist tribalism, but wore herself in honest, raw, self-made perfect placement. Grown from inside the land without outside influence it was a sheen of presence that was enmeshed and in permanent dialogue with the local wild vibration. Her clothes talked to her like crystals. Seeing the newly seen, all three feeling, even here, a new beginning, and a coming celebration brewing.

They passed more women, grooming their pods, who were intense in their ample witcheries. They were tattooed, pierced, and savage looking because their bodies and beings were living sacraments, not because it was noble, or trendy, or sexy, but because it was their authentic truth. One noticed Aum noticing her staff, bow, and hoop, only a cartwheel away. Even though a savage feel, playful fun and games happened at least once a day; and thus he saw inside them, and saw the village itself: that they had abundantly strong spirits, supported by they engaged divine ecology around them. A group of men walked by. Wise old boys with full beards, hatchet, hammer and gem embedded in their teked-out coveralls, arm bands and hats, covered in sweat and dirt and grease as their teeth shined out in broad smiles. Their bright young boys ran out to them and the men lifted them into the air like the princes they were. Sonic choruses erupted in this expression of love as they did, and Aum noticed it was a sound that was emitted from each pod – indistinct yet uniform and alive. It's frequencies and beats were more complex and beautiful than he had ever heard before, and as his attention grasped it, it would escape, move and hide, like an animal. Then the sound was gone, as if an audio mirage.

This village was very far from a world of scraping by with metal grit and grindstone, packaged fast meals and permanent screentime eyes, social espionage and personal turmoil; even a radical departure from a rebellious pirate ship, or militant extremists branching off from the well-groomed mainstream sleek and false mono signal, who's poisonous resonation was accepted to well known and documented catastrophic ends.

"What do you do in New Eridu?" Aum asked as they continued walking. He wasn't sure if he was going to lift off the ground, and the wind take him away as his heart pulsed to a different beat, one he had never before imagined.

"Do? Does?... Ah, yes, single soul note. I am currently in the woodworking shop; the field master." He took out a small polished wood carving and gave it to Aum. It was a Mayan long count white wizard glyph, though painted green. "I have many apprentices who help to facilitate the growing heartfelt knowledge of the inner community, the dialogues with the trees. We assist in any projects, whether greenhouse framing, cabinet making, new benches in the commons, or even cutlery carving workshops."

"So do you choose your apprentices?"

The pods continued in their maze as they walked on, and the kids ran by, without hoverboards Aum noticed.

"It is choice-less. Instantly there's a vibe, and you know as you grow which micro-tribe you are a part of. It's not concrete of course, as people evolve as they age. The usual pattern, especially with the men folk, is by starting in the labs; the ultra energy tech. Invoking new brilliance of cusp and ever refined bend and capture, facilitation of the communication matrix, or functional object remix - mapping the technical path from summer solar lamps into winter heaters, for example, and whether this should be an aspect of ongoing system maintenance. The wisdom of the scientific mind is the most celebrated here, as it is this field that allows us the opportunity to explore all others, whether arts or athletics. And it is this freedom of scientific exploration that is the impetus for our exodus myth. One that you have doubtlessly come across in your journey here."

"Yes, it is a deep legend."

"And it will only get deeper still."

Aum inspected the wooden glyph and Herald continued, "For wholistic life path inspiration, in the shop and out, our muse and patron saint is the master Michelangelo, as he looked inside the raw form to find the hidden." Aum added, knowledgeable in the realms of arts spiritual history, "The figures appeared to him from within the medium and emerged slowly over the course of the meditative creative process."

"Most definitely. Michelangelo released the form from the material that imprisoned it, allowing the divine to sing out. For me, this voice is literal; instrumentation the highest branch of my practice, naturally re-crafting and giving nature a new voice, whether flute, or drum, or didjeridu."

Upon it's word spoken, a spark exploded inside of them in unison, "Wow, it is truth. Somnium asks for you," Herald stated. It was almost as if invisible fireworks went off and all villagers in the vicinity looked at them with psychic soul magnetics, a single spark, touching each. Aum understood the language of the exploding spark and bowed, recognizing it's source. "Somnium is a didg you have made?"

"No," Herald replied in reverence, "Somnium has made me. All creation works in this inverted way." He smiled, "Yes. Somnium is a didjeridu. The most patient ancient one who awaits connection to the heart savior currency engine. The first new man."

Herald smiled as Aum meditated on his words.

Viewing their soul-shines connect, didge and man, he continued to describe the educational learning curve of New Ediru, "In the labs, as each has before, the young ones come up and take the place of the old. Even more brilliant than those before them, these new ones expand on ideas until a new foundation of miraculous function is found. Purpose is released, the individual ego recognizes the opportunity for cyclical whole system growth, and with the opening to move with aging grace, does so, into another field that requires well practiced, steadier and more experienced hands, as well as a less sharp far reaching imaginative consciousness. Fields such as carpentry or ceramics, fishing or trapping, cooking, weaving woven clothing design of the soul outside or crafting amulets of wearable expression. Teaching the young ones even, staying on as apprentices, maybe to one day become field master."

The sun shone full through Aum, rainbowing out his internal Topaz plates, "This society must then be built on monk like-patience and observation, as every one continues to be a student, continuing to learn and grow," Aum commented.

"Yes, the patient observation of the links between voluntary associations is a requirement of our culture. Some maintain specialization, or some move gracefully through all fields over long periods, or some even rapidly like a storm, eventually to find their niche and inspirational calling, whether the sun in the sky, the spirit in the earth, the ancestors in the trees, or the ancients instant dialogue in the conscious sea. There's deep alliances as well, the green men and the wood workers for example." Aum had a question, but he didn't know how to yet express it in best alignment of essence and purpose. Regardless, Herald answered it, "Within the alliance there is the doorway to the continuous resource dialogue – ears to listen to the ancestors, their needs and our needs as one – chiming when in alignment."

They stepped further towards the centre of town. Aum's body heightened in excited buzz, and, the feeling of home: it must have been the smells of lavender and basil in the air.

“Gauging the always fluxing need for source material on these outer zone walks, our wood workers and the plant peoples guild facilitate forest journeys nearly daily, to collect medicines and essential nutrients for village nourishment. On a macro level each tree is chosen and harvested depending on their lifecycle stage and the best practical use of it’s species, whether Arbutus or Garry Oak. It is a selection process pointed to by the forest consciousness itself. These harvest walks are usually instigated in unspoken cyclical entrainment by the green men, and boys, who have adapted their heart to hear the increased hum of the forest in their observant threshold; collaborative eco needs resonating in sensitive and total union.”

A diverse spread of images, insights and inner feelings quickly flashed up in Aums mind and he immediately spoke out the observation, “So the moment you need new trees is the moment the trees call you to collect them,” learning quickly the new alignments.

“Yes,” he smiled. Recognizing Aum’s rapid growth path Herald asked, “In your practice have you dismantled your container and remade it elsewhere?”

Aum took a moment to reflect before he answered, “I’ve made choices, and I’ve observed their results. I have yet to translocate though. This is what the green man, FitzRoy, has achieved?”

“Yes. No one has surpassed his soul dedication to the plant path, taking it out further than ever imagined, he now he surfs the in-between spaces as a constant. A floating sentry for our community, and a voice for the ancients to speak through, most of his presence is with them.”

“With them? Surrounding the village are the ancestors?”

“Yes, that outer zone of wild is where they live. In the old word it was called ‘death’ but here it is called ‘metemosis’, short for the Pythagorean ‘metempsychosis’; the transmigration of the soul into another physical form.

“That is our lifecycle. The length of time our elders stay out in the forest, in communion with the divine, increases and increase and increases until they no longer return, and at that point they become part of the forest, or have found metemosis.

“They can be found, usually by other relatives, as the entwined spirit of a specific tree or stream, plant, animal, or even specific insect. Ancestors sometimes ask to come back to us and be a part of our lives: the structural beams of our homes, or heirloom tools, or woven into artistic elemental beauty. The ancestors continue to talk to us, in that way, at the depth of our community, and continue to live with us."

Aum saw their entire world was conscious and their hearts sang as everything around them was used consciously. Used intentionally, their efficiency allowed them to exist in the infinite, there was no lack and only endless abundance.

"No rooftop gardens?"

"There's no need. The entire city is a garden."

"Though I see you're not just eating roots and berries."

"Oh no, far from it. Let me show you the domes."

They walked along the paths between buildings and he continued, "Each building has solar panels which collect ample amounts in the spring, summer and fall, though it is steadily overcast throughout the winter. Each building is it's own self-sufficent network node, independent of others on the resource grid. Specialty cut quartz crystals are used in each panel to break up the light spectrum, and each color of the rainbow is harvested separately, each color even has it's own preferred use. By breaking up the spectrum we get seven times as much energy from the light."

"You mean the signal doesn't diminish when you break it apart?"

"No, it expands, like a compressed data file. What's not coming from the wind and water, or solar reserves is geo-thermal. The heat mines are great, but heat is heat, and it's more efficient to harvest it only once, rather than convert it to a storable medium and translate it back to heat." He summarized, "Rather than one source, our intent has been to develop a relationship with all potential sources, balancing their use as the present need requires."

They continued through beautiful spaces that were luch and visibly alive, neither gardens, homes nor shops, but somehow all combined. "We constructed our pods and then after a year, poured hempcrete pathways where all the deepest grooves were – herb and edible flower beds line the paths, with solar lamps at the edge for when the sun goes behind the hills."

It reminded Aum of the indoor garden art gallery at the Gridline centre, except without the corporate logos, and the size of an entire town, not just a single room.

“Yeah, our community here is what inspired the Life Gallery at Gridline.” It was as if Aum had spoken his thoughts aloud. “Oh my apolages. I keep on forgetting you’re probably not used to that. It is the natural results of dedicated daily yoga, meditation, and soley organic food over decades – you know, healthy living – to the point where the vibrating light cells of our bodies are formalized into thoughts in each others minds.”

Aum almost lifted off again, “We shine for each other.”

Herald smiled at the expressive and potent line, and let Aum fly on his own.

“Combustion engines are prohibited here.” A tractor rumbled by, “unless it’s a tractor. And even then it has to be a tractor from pre ’64, still easily converted to bio-diesel. It’s kinda funny actually – it’s like that date was the cut off for a quality tractor. From ‘64 on all models have broken down, or are in the process of breaking down. Other then that we went totally organic with that initial non-combustion edict.”

“Organic transportation? So like what? Solar cars?”

“No. Solar horses.” An older gentleman said, joining the conversation seamlessly.

“Solar horses?!” Aum exclaimed.

The man had come down an adjacent road, now walking down the same street in the same direction as the two, nearly magnetized to the new comer, “Yup, solar horses.”

Aum could almost see him wink.

“Here we just call them horses,” Herald said with a smile.

With bed-head; short, curly, salt n’ pepper hair, the tall spice man asked, “When’s the last time you rode a horse?”

“Uh… when I was 9, I think,” Aum replied.

“Ah, that’s way too long man – it’s truley an awesome communion, an amped vibratory communication practice. In the spring we have horse races. Last year we even had our first chuck wagon race, and Joey… hahaha…” He started laughing, so uncontrollably even, that he could hardly get the story out. Both Herald and Aum began laughing as well, even though the story hadn’t even really begun. “Joey came up with this solar-buggy shit-car thing – it actually ran on horse shit - and tried racing the solar horses!”

“Who won?”

"The horses of course, because the damn buggy only had one gear!" and he burst out in howling laughter, Aum and Herald erupted as well, cause it was utterly infectious. Once the man calmed down he continued with an honest gaze of remembrance, "The damn thing could have make it all the way to Vancouver though, with out stopping once, I'm sure of it. Efficient as shit."

The inflection of the last pun evoked more chuckles as they continued to walk together, "So whoever isn't into horses has a bike," Herald added in the gap.

"Like a steampunk art bike?"

"Totally. You're one or the other, a horse tacker or a bike mod." Hearald thought for a second, "Well… recently there's been a couple young ancients who are both… horse mods…"

"…Or bike tackers," the spice man added, "We're all watching what will come of that, but it's been like the Jets and the Sharks for the longest time."

"Without the singing and dancing I'm sure," Aum joked.

"Oh no, there's dancing alright. We even acted out the musical at one point in the middle of the street on the west side of town. That was part of the races; the spring awakening festival. This is me," he pointed between pods, "See ya." With the plain pure ease of a local, the spice man continued on a divergent path through town. The flow and the way with no disruption, only builds.

"Nice meeting you," Aum shouted out at him, feeling it, smiling.

"Sweet synch," Herald noticed Aum noticing, and said plainly, "We'll see him again in ten minutes at the market. That's how it all flows here, in condensed and distraction-less micro cycles where all things are so easily perceivable that everything is instantly noticeable within the whole. It's like there's a town crier shouting, 'here ye hear ye' at any given moment when something in the community changes, notifying everyone. But the town crier just happens to be silent, and invisible. Nonetheless, everybody hears the latest breaking news the instant it happens; the biggest changes are shouted out the loudest, the smallest ones are there, but are quieter, only for those paying close attention, or needing a focal anchor point, or something to do."

"So if you roll over in bed…"

"… the whole town hears it."

"…and…" Aum thought it, but couldn't put it into words.

"… everybody just has sex at the same time. It's like a wave that moves through the city, just like a warm wind or an ocean gust, or like going to the beach on a sunny day. It's just what happens."

"I don't know if I could get used to that..."

"If you choose it you could."

He was taken a back. He said it like an invitation.

It was kind of blowing his mind a bit. A world so different than what he was used to, one that was extremely complex, that required continuous maintenance and love and attention, but at the same time, so simple, nothing else was needed than those two things. There were no hoops to jump, no stratospheres to reach,…. No places to show off or grandstand or platform from. No snide self-importance, no ad campaining or marketing of self. Here the leaders were at the bottom. So deep down at the bottom they themselves didn't even notice, because they were too deep into digging to the bottom of it, in the actual communal food gardens.

"Correct – here we are."

They turned a corner and the view opened up.

This is what he had seen from the valley entrance: the lucid transparent geometries. A near breathable future oxygen mask facilitating the optimal greenery underneath it.

Peering through the surface he could see the extended hillside slopes. They looked like they had been tiered, like the seats of an outdoor athletic stadium, or concert venue, but covered in an elaborate sequence of greenhouse domes. It made up at least half the town. Aum could see layers in, and layers down, there was even a dessert ecosystem inside the dome. Herald saw Aum's child like eyes and nodded. Aum stepped through the turnstile doors to fully explore, Herald followed. As they entered, Aum saw the slopes went down into the earth.

"The geothermal centers are down there – you have to feel the day finely to enter the realm of the mountain men guild. Down there they may eat you for their dinner, 'cause they work that ceaselessly… That's what we tell the kids anyway," He laughed with a thin eyed smile, "That is the way for many though – conscious breathing is all that is needed."

All noticed their entrance and Aum was shown around, actively passed from one kind soul to the next, each offering a taste of their flavor. Heirloom tomatoes and their human harvesters spoke dense tales of longevity and insight, delivered lke a grandfather, the Macintosh trees were computers that had collected knowledge for generation upon generation, and all one had to do was ask.

Rather than a production factory with each mega patch pumping out one kind of GM food - zucchinis in that mega plot, carrots in that mega plot - each tier was it's own micro garden, guilds and nutritional relationships totally intertwined, even a mirror for the macro social guilds that tended them, as the meta layer of life path facilitation for optimal growth. He imagined the layers beyond that and peacefully grinned.

At that he caught the audio stream beaming through the air; the same living animal that resided in the home pod zone. Though here it was meshed with classic tech house. Everyone danced with it, even though they weren't dancing. They were working.

Holy Shit.

It was exactly like his dream.

Except this wasn't a spaceship, and these weren't aliens, or replicas of himself, or maybe it was, and maybe they were, and maybe they were. A few looked up at him and smiled in soft synch as he thought it in his mind.

Holy shit, they were him.

It was like looking directly at the sun. One of them laughed in glee. There was no doubt in his mind that the sun shone through them, through all of them, just as tree trunks when burned emit the suns heat and light, so too did these ones when they smiled.

Seeing the new eyes seeing, a tattoed farmer came up to him, coveralls, shovel and bandana over his long brown curls, "See, it's like this: going for a haircut, in the old world."

Aum looked at him with a quizzical expression, usually reserved for the youth. His cadence was meta hip, thus nearly dysfunctional as nomal English, "When you see a random hair dresser, the success of your cut all depends on instant rapport. Were they having a good day? Had they drank too much coffee? Are they excited about their job? And cutting your hair? It may turn out superb, it may turn out a disaster, but in the end the outcome doesn't matter because it will all grow back anyway.

"Because of this temporary nature, it could be inspiring and a moment of creative connection, or alternatively, simply a boring job-oriented task to do unconsciously. As the one receiving the haircut, if there is that level of unconsciousness, it doesn't really matter because it will all grow back.

"However, when you have an ongoing hairdresser you develop a relationship with them, and it becomes a therapy deeper than just a simple haircut - it becomes a dialogue of real friendship and community.

"So it is with the land - where trees are being trimmed and groomed by us. They are open to that inspirational dialogue and wisdom sharing, but don't require it if a gardener is not there, in that state, or has no awareness to listen. In the end their limbs will grow back regardless, just like a haircut. It is, however, nice to have an interesting conversation with the person doing the work.

"Philosophically it expands out further of course, to the entire environment, not just patch of garden or single tree. Sunny day - time to be with the land as it sings. Rainy day - time to settle in and be elsewhere, as it absorbs more Gaian consciousness delivered in macro time. The key is being of service to it and available in total being; physical and metaphysical, full presence in communal dialogue."

A rumbling Case drove by.

"Yup, the land loves the massage of tractor wheels driven over it too" He continued on in his work flow, Aum stood still. The farmer picked it up for him, nudging Aum, before Aum even noticed his own gap in flow, "Down there is where you want to go," pointing. Aum laughed at his gap noticed.

The directed path looked pretty gnarly, but he proceeded, following some make shift steps and discovered at the bottom was a huge aquaponcs system. Nearly the size of a lake, it contained schools upon schools of fish.

"We're doing our best to repopulate the ocean."

Another one smiled and spoke as he saw Aum, a new stranger. He could no doubt see the child-like wonder in Aum's eyes, "Primed by a collaboration between Fairman and Arcadio, our intake structure has acquired a small number of endangered species from around the world. Here we breed them in this safe and contained environment, in symbiotic relationship, and once reaching threshold of space, we transfer them all to the bay. They are connected to us, and in dialogue on levels of spirit. With our prayers, and their own natural spirit inside. They are conscious of their post-pond placement when it happens, and that this is their home, and slowly, as they continue to multiply, filter up and down the coastline, hopefully they reach all seven seas."

There were a few floating islands of plants. A few gardeners on them checking their heath and pushing them along with a long pole. It felt more like the organic and lush ancient Egyptian nile than the blocky ramshackle urbanitis of renaissance Venice, or Ceil Lune.

"Those are chinampas, modeled after what the Aztec's used in Mesoamerica," the same man added. Bald, sandals and plain clothed, he stood under a tree, on the edge of the lake, feeding the fish in peaceful communion. There was no difference between the fish, and the man feeding the fish.

Aum could see that in these gardens, and out further, that each moment was an exchange, a lesson in conscious work. Knowledge was shared with each heartfelt tuck and pull, gesture or joke, horse hoof, wheel or sandal, all like a kneading massage – the holographic earth cooed and inside the humming groan of pleasure was light re-contextualized into karmic nourishment and knowledge – all levels, it was there – beginner to master – quick grin to full bliss of timeless meshed into the cosmological permacultural state. It was all gates. What was seen was a glorious heaven that could be no brighter than what was, then, in that moment. It was infinite, and carried inside eternally forever more.

There, on the lakeside, with a sky full of sacred geometry, Aum sat, and meditated. As if for the first time.

"Where to now?"

"The lab."

"The lab?"

After his meditation, Aum was guided back to Herald, who finished a conversation in perfect time. They continued walking as he spoke, "It was the first building of habitation when we landed - as if a womb that all future growth spurted out from.

"The first pioneers, scared and timid, would leap out into the wild and back, as if a playground dare, to see how long they could stay out without getting attacked by cyotes, or cougars, or wolves."

As they walked Aum could feel something happening in his body, a pinnacle arising within pinnacles, or maybe it was simply the pull of the animals residing in the sonic wild, cyote, cougar, or wolf.

Not far from the linked domes of the greenhouse complex, was a large multi-storey hall made of giant logs, 12 feet in circumference at least.

"A fresh start. The foundation. Independent. Might as well have been off planet."

Aum entered, following Herald. It was dark inside, like a theatre. Humid and sweaty he could see wires like spider webs cast throughout the space, connecting exterior pillars of server stacks, towering, with blinking lights and humming fans.

"As his eyes adjusted there was a quick and horrific flash, nightmarishly surreal. Inside the vision, Aum could see this core engine room was linked to what he understood as the Riddle, like the root parts of an enormous steampunk castle. He could see huge gears and weights on chains, anvils being pummeled and cranked with hammers and gavels by sweaty geothermal coal-miners and bearded breatharian ogre-men, all inside a poured liquid metal forgery. Behind their hairy bare backs were mechanical cyborg horses which pulled carts of ore, and through friction, sparked brilliant balls of glowing light behind glass, as if smashing atoms during the enlightenment. Deeper inside his imagination he saw test tube collections all containing micro lights; weighted and categorized by wild science wizards, long gray hairs sticking straight up, eyes behind goggles and electricity coming out of their finger tips. But that was only a net of distraction, to capture his mind, and turn him around, lead him out the building with easy and unpotent sci-fi answers.

He scoffed at the preliminary jester-work, and pierced through the haze, breathed through the nightmare panic which it triggered and his eyes adjusted, seeing the deeper layers, the deeper veils of effort, lifted, and the truth revealed.

There was a team of kids in the room, dancing happily on acrobat mats.

Tron-like discs of light were thrown across the dark floor in timed unison from one specialty suited teen to the next, pins, battons, and colored spheres were juggled with hand and foot in perfect unison by others with flowing arms, flexible like reeds. Beachball-esque rainbows were set and vaulted above the dancefloor inbetween crystal juggling balls that floated throughout the air like soap bubbles.

No contact. Levetation only. With leap and cartwheel and tumble, some bodies attempted to do the same.

The young ancient ones.

This is where they came from, or into. Into this world.

The most young and most wise beings incarnating here in these youth first; infusing the world with their numerous paths of enchanted lives, as easily remembered as their nightly dreams and activities during the previous life.

They were suited with button up shirts and wrap pants, grey and inspired by martial artists in their dojo's. Beyond the caterwauling movement of youthfull bodies, there were pulses of electricity leaping from one, to the next, to the next, but it was no street fight. These pulses of prana were caught by the multitude of crystal spheres in the air, which found collective formation and 3D geometrical resonance with each energy pulse: unicursal hexagrams, first and second heptagrams, beaming in and out further into 4D and 5D alignment within the energetics of a planetary whole.

In the centre of the action, with more feasible characteristics of human movement, there was kind and gentle juggling mage, soloing, mastering many more orbs than any other. The field master maybe? Around him a plethora of tai chi practitioners, qi gong shapers, and reiki engineers, diving into body as battery, the star dust source flow from 5D aware alignment through them, vision focused into their floating crystals that translated the pulse into the creation of the Gaian dream network itself.

In utter awe Aum's eyes widened in view, and saw these dancers were surrounded not by cameras, but by a broad network of data sensors which monitored the electro-magnetic currents in each crystal and emitted from each movement: each thought and heart pulse. Like the automated arms of a spider, the sensors moved on their own, following the poetic dancers around the central mats, tracking them, monitoring their signal and flow, creating a non-local patchwork data reflection. This auto-obsorbant observation translated the thermodynamic bright lights of each moment from lens, to gearbox, to rat's nest web of cables, to digital terminal hub, to a collection of auto-intuitive lights; frequency emitters that sent signals back to the dancefloor, a medium existent between light and sound.

A full circuit it became a living feedback loop on the stage, like a fractal dream machine, sensors and lights aimed at a continually flowing and meticioulously tracked spirit animal that moved, serpent like, fire like, through receiver and transmitter beings. On intuitive hunches acrobatic actors at the side would tag in, or dive roll in, which would allow others to exit, grab water, or find rest; for this dance continued night and day, day and night - a continuous human engine of perpetual expressive motion.

Someone cleared their throat and Aum realized he was still open mouthed, gawking. Upon noticing himself in stunned trance, dissapointed in himself to loose the present in totality to the divine symphony of what he could observe, he was glad he wasn't shown the door.

He took a step back and saw another layer around the sensors that surrounded the dance. There were technicians at terminals maintaining optimum conditions for receiver and signal. Some were even using data scalpels to slice off layers of it in a continuous harvest, placing the captured energy in storage. They picked out the gnarly bits, storing that which may expanded on Mandelbrot's fractal set into new dimensions of awareness, mathematical visual gateways to the world beyond even this one. This energy harvest was deep.

As he gazed, softer, one whispered to him, "The dance floor is kept on it's own separate storage system. Electricity isn't a constant single medium but has densities and durability's, spectrum's and qualities that fluctuate just like water or light. It can be dirty or clean or powerful or pure. It all depended on the tools of harvest and the connection to their source. The closer the receptors come into vibrational essence, the cleaner the take. Here we are beyond chemicals, moving into the mathematical and dimensional potential energy arc of existence. We bypassed refinement, purification, needless infrastructure, into the sun and it's sweaty momentous juice. It's pure." He shook his head, "Dirty energy breaks shit, ruins boards, rusts circuits, and can infect information, corrupting hardware from the inside out. We think that's why it all crashed."

There was an alarm-like sound. He saw that along side the electro-mag scientists sat sonic technicians. These ones sheared off further particles from this soul signal of expression, developing data parameters and containers to trigger beat sequences and harmonic rhythm when new thresholds were reached, changing when changes happen, adding to the engines of transmutation.

These stage tech's were the Seraphim to the dancing Cherubs.

Rather than bring external reference from a basket of collected treasures; rather than an external sampling or historical and stylistic grab; live mix based on aesthetic auditory feel, amping the entire planet, this was real-time vibe mod: live programming. Live code sequencing, written and remixed, which gave voice to the music already present in the moment and inside the quantum structure of reality.

He could see it, the time-strands of DNA. The extra strands changing with each moment, so quickly it looked like junk, colliding and moving from strand to strand, bumbing and juking like a conversation, containing a consciousness that didn't require a physical manifestation in matter, but still influences the physically container it temporarily resides in. Though sometimes… with enough coalescing entropy, it formalizes into it's own individual strand, and allows itself to be discovered; the unmanifest manifested into the physical, which changes everything instantly.

The live code guild continually did this, mapped this algorithmic motion, hacking it's natural order, continually bringing the timestrands into the physical, with set thresholds that equated heliotropic vibration and purine ribonucleotide synthesis into auditory harmonies and movements through scales and octaves, even linked, midi-signal-like, to classic instrumentation. Synth line, trumpet line, piano roll, stand up bass solo, new palette of bird song, or even as achingly subtle as the rhythmic flapping of butterfly wings – just past the edge of audible.

This audio signal pulsed from this central engine of creative energy out to the common and home pods of local intranet, each household linking into the ultra pure signal, listening to it like local radio, though it wasn't. This was the living creature he had heard in the 'anti-sprawl' and in the greenhouses, and this was their fuel: a nourishment akin to breathing.

From this perspective of collaboratively woven real-time energy creation and application, he could see how deep their unity was. He could feel each person present and together inside the sound. Each household was linked to the network and had the potential to add it's own transmutation; remix the sonic code and rewrite the self grown living signal to amplify the live symphonic composition. Vibe change instant, with timebased DNA, sent back through to the dream machine pulse, or at their own live code station at the home pod with custom translators. When you go quantum, you go quantum. The code was inside the sound itself, and could be re-tuned to hear, itself, not just be heard.

Shit, living sound can hear. It goes both ways.

Then he realized the living sound could see too.

He was inside it, moving with it, back in the greenhouse, the gardens. Here, found sounds, new recordings or even classic house tracks were mixed in on top of the collective energy signal, building on what is - influencing gardeners and the gardens, the food and nourishment, spirits and ancestors.

The classic 90's house reference was just the cherry on top – the inside joke, the wink wink nudge nudge.

"It's a signal, not our own, not harvested and cultivated ourselves, so it may need to be analyzed and observed before integrated into our source energy." The man walked over to a different terminal as Aums mind reeled. He felt the inspired fuel of a pristine edge quality, moving through the big lift, an updraft for the sails of these human airships without footprint. He saw the last layer beyond the harvesters was the walls of the building itself; all screen surfaces as if each was covered in n-Glue. Infinity live. Satellites hacked into. Corporate earth spiraling on camera feeds, linked to the electro-mag sensors of the dance, each motion tagged and found in real-time action on the planetary zoom screen.

Somewhere it was in there, within that infinite nesting doll of invisible digital gears of light and energy, the source code source that linked to the Riddle infrastructure - or maybe was the Riddle in totality - a coded language transcribed from this engine of reality and the evolving vibrating DNA of these dancers.

Surprisingly, Aum could now see there was mourning inside it, inside their movements. It was not celebratory, but as if close friends had died. The loss was great for these old kids who had to focus even more deftly in their movements, with no meta-linked exo-hands to do the greater civil work across the globe; the influential whisphers for the wholistic ongoing remix of societal structure. Seeing this mourning, even a wet eye, Aum saw it was a bridge to nowhere.

The Riddle was gone.

It felt like the space of computer death; the loss of a limb; all abilities to communicate, gone. Abilities to create and connect and share, gone. All that was left was the loss and ache in their hearts.

Inside the movements, was the 'Why?', the 'Why now?', 'What is this meant to teach us?' It was like the loss of a twin companion, or the virtual augmentation of the highest collective soul self, deceased.

For these new humans too, as all, it was the collapse of everything they knew, where each moment was a new perspective on how to adapt and see into the new way of a veiled future. They still reached for it though, cause there no choice, the extension into non-local physicality. Each eye troubleshooting inside the dance, what can be accomplished now, that could not before? Not dwelling on how much has been lost, but on what new possibilities exist in the present. In this breakdown, this crash, this Armageddon, what does new life look like? Where are the new doors that have instantly opened, and, rather than heavy and weighed, what is observable which is light as breath?

This is what the dancers moved with; a breadth of movements so easy, and a future so precise, and clear, and open, that this twist of manifestation of the deeper story and it's need to be expressed became the perpetual engine of motion, the dissipative bubbles of rip curl implosion. The manifested source code of the entire world. They were the strands of twisting thread, the same he once held with Demona, here however it was the full rope that kept it all together; the final root holding the oak in place - as the galactic wind blew all karmas into hurricanes.

They leapt into what seemed team acrobatics, continually working as one towards a shared goal. Simple gestures contained essays on the state of esoteric philosophy and alternatives to planetary extinction. Then, with follow up gesture, published. Though it was all subliminal now, conscious expression was placed inside the viral dreaming, trusting that the awakening would awaken, and would spread across the globe in waves of opening eyes, within opening eyes.

Aum watched these saintly emergency procedures to save the last ones, the last set, give those on the outer edge hope and guidance till their own inner light was powerful enough to self nourish and even feed all those around them.

It was beautiful and sublime and holy. These dancing cherub angels who exalted in the shining divine in every moment, in their innocence, did they know of their role in all this? Were they conscious of what they did? Could they see each exchange across the planet? Like he could? Like Zeke could? Or did they practice like this for other reasons? Because it made them blissful? Or content? Or because they were drawn to it, like magnets; their souls yearning for the deepest possible expression of their first human life on the planet.

Weights were heavy within the non-local connection. Without real time support agency on the ground it was difficult on the white stage, to maintain a solid state trance and balanced equilibrium without a dreamsoul intermediary. No longer was anyone dancing with them. The angels could now feel the extension of everything they touched in it's rawest form. And the in-between layer of engineers could feel everything they saw, and their eyeballs and minds stretched with each unified bend and balance posture – seeing its correlate prayer placed in the world.

The full team was linked in conscious inhale and exhale, meshed inside the immediate dialogue of planetary needs. This host of angels were the ant's inside the tower walls, moving, hearing everything, seeing everyone, equipping everyone from behind a one way mirror.

Looking this way through the data stream would only show a pool, and a rippling reflection. Aum was behind this veil, inside the code, his presence here, gazing at the internal stage, this even, influencing the outcome. There was another alarm-like sound, and the dance changed.

They accepted his gaze inside the inner most sanctum.

This wasn't it though. This wasn't the Riddle Solver. All of it, however, did facilitate the distribution of the singularity vortex out into linear time.

Then he saw it.

As if it had been cloaked in his eyes, and revealed once he found the edge, and what should be there, and what should sit inside it.

There was a black box floating above all the crystal balls, obsidian-like. All the reiki lightning bolts from each crystal were shot into it, in a dialogue of thresholds, and then shot back out, and through the clear spheres of ancient mineral data manifested, pulsing the dancers in a different way. As he gazed at it, he began to float. Noticing, he looked away and dropped back to the ground. An antimatter engine? A micro black hole? Death and the afterlife inside? Or a new life beyond the void.

His body shook. The room shook. And he found himself about to tag into the expressive arts dance floor.

No audience, participants only. All participating.

It was climaxing and he was with it; the celebration that he noticed in the eyes of the first people he saw here. Piping in a barrage of influence in, still. Way more intuitive that the re-engineering of consciousness, though still the same.

"The craft! The ongoing craft!" Someone shouted.

And for a moment the dynamics settled and everyone became satiated in there own internalisms. It was like individual soul-eyes lost all external viewpoints and focused on personal self. Each internal journey became visible as the mind within their body translated onto the surrounding screens, displaying observation and imagination.

In the stillness Aum grinned, he knew this gate and experience first hand, and he spoke out purposefully, "The engines of domination are breaking the backs of the hopeful right now, to engineer a future without light, and what is there to combat it?" he dramatically paused and answered his own question, "The excruciating bend of self-assembling liberation," and he stepped onto the dancefloor.

He wasn't a crazy man sprinting through the group; a Christmas elf jumping up and down and around each dancer, but took a single step in, and looked at them all.

Nearly all noticed this added gaze and natural entrance and all awakened to the new collective body, integrating all awareness and skill sets and experiences instantaneously. It was a combonation of both new and old fuel.

The screens bent the walls into circles – new eyes peered in on the stage from them – an audience spiraling up like the Guggenheim, both dreamtime and local homepods, fully inside the feedback mechanism, he was seeing them seeing his angelic being.

"It's easy, but you must choose it to be," he intoned as he floated toward the black box.

He pulsed his entire pack of collected wisdom out and the seraphim engineers at their terminals had to work at their furthest peak to utilize each magnetic frequency dollop that came off him. In collaborative dialogue the angels took his data hands and flew them around the globe, hitting mountain top peak and ocean depth and ageless Amazon tree trunk.

"Expressive dance is an effortless way to escape the confines of the body…"

"…along with every Imposing cognative structure the body is placed inside of…"

"…So I dance…"

"…with every step…"

It was like in his dream, pulling group nodes, caught and captured, openly through the patchwork matrix of many others. There, but not there. They were not professional dancers, but professional lovers; an example of a single shared reflection of the rest of their entire civilization, living in time with the divine kairos. Aum's graceful reiki-esque dreamhealing movements thanked them for their honesty and their work on the metaphysical realms, and openly offered to lift them all higher towards the divine. Being an outsider, yet not, they knew he could.

This was new, and something they had yet to experience, so they said yes, and all floated off the ground.

Then the most beautiful dancer joined him, unequivocally and decisivley.

Her authentic and innocent gestural expression was one of completeness, without fault or flaw. He saw angelic perfection in her smile. So big, as drips of sweat shined on her cheeks. Like a newborn, her visage changed with every emotive progression felt internally, inside the group, and the world. Revealing 100,000 past lives and loves together. She told him her name, somehow, in word, or expression, Aum wasn't sure. Regardless it didn't stick. With every new face it seemed as if a new name would emerge.

She was sparkling, and the most graceful creature he'd ever laid his eyes upon. Her inner light shined so bright she was beyond all human nature, made entirely of the brightest sunlight and stardust. (It was the stardust that made her sparkle.) Freedom and Gods grace emerged from every aspect of her, from flowing blonde hair to rainbow colored eyes. Her joy was overflowing, onto him even, as she flew with him, even pressing her body against his, to the music. Her unadulterated sensuality surprised him and he felt like the luckiest man in the world. An angel had just entered his life.

It was a deeper white magic than he had ever known, and with her smile and powerful charisma, and simply her gaze upon him, it rearranged the insides of his body and mind.

She didn't understand what she did to him, what the power of her gaze and presence did to one who was this new. Her freedom and beauty captivated Aum so wholly that he forgot why he was there, why he had come to New Eden, and he fell into her - this sweet cherub - in such totality, that his entire self was forgotten.

In unified lock step they danced, they flew together, and their magnetized connection became so strong entire lives were lived within each deeply communicative moment – boundaries of time vanished and he saw himself there in New Eden forever, with her, with their children, within their custom home pod, and his genetic algorithm planted within the civil lineage, refreshing it, leafing the edge of quantum creativity. For Aum this was a brand new cusp of bliss and love felt, a feeling he never thought possible; a new foundation found in which he could grow out from in advanced consciousness, in bliss and happiness, and devoted partnership forever. Everything in his vision disassociated into blissful bright shapes and wondrous wheels of colour as glorious as any rainbow bridge, any sunrise or sunset that had ever been witnessed on earth. And he knew peace would flourish across the face of the planet.

And then through it, flew a spot of black with wings. Everything in it's wake of shadow changed.

It's edges forms plunged all visual reality into sharp assassin daggers. Then he saw Demona, standing out at the edge of bliss, arms crossed. Fully pissed.

Aum nearly collapsed to the floor at the sight.

He craned his neck in mid flight motion.

No. It wasn't her.

Shimmering, the smokey waves around her smelt of cinders and cedar, and in shock, he could not find himself.

Who was this? Was this a new Demona?

He was utter lost in the tech amp of immediate global awareness and could only see infinite lateralus. With all he had seen, he was unsure, and began to weaponize, and prep against a nanotech attack. However as he did, the black form shifted, countering his every change, motion, and thought, rendering him defenceless, even altogether incompetent; unskilled begginer with no original moves whatsoever.

Aum's heart began to race out of his chest. He didn't know if this new vision was coming in from the eyes attached to his physical body, greater history, or all human consciousness in a full blended haze of spectral spirits and phenomenalogical paradoxes seen in real time. In the bubbling ether steam of sweaty mirage, he began to feel like like he was gulping down a log jam of ethernet cables, the fiber optic signal within them being clogged with coal black smoke as well.

Then there was a caw.

Demona flashed in again, below, at the edge, with steely assassin glance, himself mirrored like the sun her reflective glasses. Impenetrable, she offered no hand, and no help, and no reason. Only that he was moving too slow.

Aum had to stop. Exit this dream. His gaze and her gaze in connectivity told him so.

At this height however, it was difficult for Aum to find a graceful step down and out of the planetary collective, back to his individual walking feet and single body. He had pledged himself so deeply to this fresh meshwork, that he knew leaping out, as he once did at the Common Stage, would cause the world to topple, if not that, then disintegrated into smoke and ash, on his shoulders and back. Another caw.

It was not the caw of a magpie however, but a crow.

Directly in his gaze she morphed into true form from the imagined; black braided bangs with beads, black hair and black skin. Eyes gazing out like flashlights and tractor beams, medicine shawl, walking stick, and throat suddenly cleared, as if rules were being broken, as if offences were being commited; the cacophonous misalignment of fullest efforts, all incorrect.

A quick glance to his immediate and he saw his sweet angel had left him. His future in the more-than-real dreamscape was gone. His commitments to the seeds planted in this sacred place gone. Blown away by the winds or scorched by the heat of the holy sun, the central starfire that the entire universe rotated around and gave all life and consciousness to. The angel was still there. He could see her, as everyone everywhere could, but the light she had shone into his life, the empyrean inspiration it invoked, was gone as quickly as it had come. And he died on the spot.

That profound vision of love was all an illusion, yet he still worked like a drowning man to rexcontextualze what he had just perceived not as lies, but a blissful communal delirium shared in pristine dedicated promise, translated insight, as only delusional lies portrayed against his own self. It was only a single moment, and the experiences felt and known therein, self-contained. And now that he was out of it, that moment, it's vision was offered up, in a way he could not perceive, it flowed out into the planet. The offering was dissected, dismantled, placed, and assigned to surgical emergency action by the Seraphim engineers, translated into a holo-fractal story, for all humanity to continue, and learn from.

Gold strands of light and air surrounded him, spiraling out through his chest. It was broken open, It wasn't bad. She wasn't bad. He wasn't bad. It's just what she did. It's just what she did. It's just how she taught, how her love taught those around her, those closest to her. Unattachment. It had been a dance with a new dance partner, but still the same lesson. His heart was broken open so he could finally see it. The lesson. He looked forward to his next try. Maybe he would do better.

And he knew it was up to himself, with consciousness, to stake out strides out of this place, uncrushed, and find himself within the wisdom offerings of this one on the edge calling him, Demona or Demona incarnate. He heard the sound of a rattle in the audio mix. The Shaman. This shapeshifter was the Shaman, and he was late for her, or so it seemed.

This realization opened the gates to allow divine concordance to connect their future and cleaned and sealed off every other commitment to this sacred communion of celestial world mesh.

Behind the shapeshifter he spotted someone eager, moving his way to the edge, this other reflected the communal motion and, brand new, was in gratitude to have the opportunity to dance – his first time.

And the flavor changed drastically, as he and Aum switched, and the lanky young fellow found his feet for the first time. The Angel greeted him.

As he approached the Shaman she said to him in charged greeting, "That's not how you get there. But I do see you. And am in gratitude that you've prepared so deeply, to meet your maker."

He looked at the light still exploding from his chest, "In linked lives and their deaths."

"Your dramas are idiotic." It was a hefty punch to his glowing chest.

"I know." He dropped his head, recrushed and feeling the beat down of inadequacy and imperfection.

“No, you don’t. Otherwise you wouldn’t have them: your dramas. You’re an idiot for much different reasons than you believe yourself to be. She actually really does truly love you, in all the ways she expressed, Truthfully. It all happened. Each vision that found you. Which is far more than you are able to comprehend at the moment. It is *you* that must find it within your*self* to accept her deeper love, and grow to love her equally that deep, with that level of unconditional freedom.” Her gaze followed the spiral to the inside of his broken open heart and within it she re-wrote out his self-knowledge, so it would stay open like this, forever.

“I’ve got a long way to go.”

With braided bangs rattling she laughed, “Not so, Saoshyant.”

She was the only female in his life that he had truly been afraid of. She was kind, but would be the first one to tear apart personal crutches without remorse or doubt. She motioned to their exit and and he followed her out a different door than the one in which he had entered.

Out the back way, they walked directly into the fray of a whirling dervish-like street market.

They we're navigating it colaboratively, on levels of consciousness so heavenly high, nether was aware of it. They both just watched themselves, moved by the divine, through the odd, and the human wild.

As they walked along the diverse and colorfull mechanisms of street scene he could see this was as sacred as a temple, with ancient masters transmutating environmental resources into currency by hand.

Busy and bustling, a hub of exchange and fascinating dream commission, they were all manufacturing self expression and greater municipal providence: numerous teams and guilds of production prodigies and their learning systems with facilitators assisting in bringing creative idea into form.

Tailors and seamstresses were infusing new garments with the life and insights they had recently collected, artisans visually depicted the highest divine truth of what they were seeing, inventors channeled inspiration and engineered into existence the new civil functioning, there were even new watch makers inventing new models of time and space as they measured them.

There were fabric and dye stations linked to the looms and newest material woven from the collections of silks and cottons stored and valued like gold in a bank: treasures of the natural world. The audio creature was tuned to the frequency of 'chant' as the cotton and silk were spun into new threads. Colorful mandarin cloaks draped the shoulders of the priests; the field masters here. Like ancient Asian monks with fu-manchus and pony tailed manes they handled the space austerely, as any Buddhist would. Each step and breath was with tonal consciousness as they slowly slowly slowly brought new material into use, inside the magic of transmutation and surrender to the higher tao of presence. This vibration was ceremonially infused into the garment, always formed and presented in time with the emergent growth of wisdom gathering in community guilds or teams. A celebration of Mayan calendrics practiced in action.

As they walked it was if he was dragging a net, each step a dance in pristine musical time. As if dragging Indras net with wach step cleansed and cleared and upgraded. Then they saw there was another group at the very end of the pod block, dosed in fire and flame, a hub of half a dozen in the guild. They wore few clothes and smelt of kerosene - their bronzed and tattooed bodies were sweating with effort as they applied oils to hides with a new energy Aum could somehow see. They washed and trimmed animal skins in preparation to make long term contributions to the bank of accessories - tool belts, pocket belts, shoes and sandals, winter boots, vests and ropes. Another approached them with caution, as Aum gazed, he saw this one was more beautiful in cloth expression and lighter in step. Like Swift meeting Tiger, their conversation was wordless. Unspoken he was asking for their services in trade for his gemstones; new patterns added to their workflow, of bound book covers for the knowledge keepers, and armbands for warriors, blessed for the hunt with his crystal work. His curly hair and watery movements were extensions of his allied dialogue with the stones and their earthen storehouses. He was powerful, but in a different way than the promethian fire keepers. After a monumental pause, there was a hug, and in it, all could instantly see beautiful future patterns of refined empire flower out.

In synch time, as Aum and the Shaman walked, a random bird flew in… or out… of the moment of new circuit. It was a black spot with wings and it flew at the Shaman as the two walked. As wild as anything, the confluence of the budding bustling movements, the sudden flight was an understandable and easily recognizable reaction from the critter. She stuck out a hand and moved it, as if leading the bird. The bird tracked it, and it landed on her arm. It was as easy as if she was catching a Frisbee. Though the Shaman continued with the momentum, dipping slightly with her entire body, prepping the black crow for a quick launch. Then, with a new, bigger flap it took off from her arm, and at peak of wing wave, like an engines ignition, a tremendous bass pulse rang out like a church bell as the crow turned into a white Owl. It was like everyone who was looking blinked in unison, and within that nanosecond blink, it morphed. As it flew, each flap of wing pulsed in perfect presiscion to the continued living soundtrack, as if this magic was a new source itself. Each flap became a bass pulse, and a cheer erupted as the music quickly galvanized the community into steadier work - they worked towards a state of worklessness: pure dance.

With each owl feather tip linked to his own thunderbird wings, beak and gaze emboldend with wild green, white wizard magic, it was as if with this, she presented him; unveild his true purpose of arrival. And all who could, looked at the two. They knew it was time.

As the two left they could hear the celebration was deepening. Yet she led him away from the party, beyond the edges of town where they could hear the pure waves of ocean merge with the city sounds.

As they exited the last city sphere, there was one final young bike gang on the outskirts, in cute ripped jeans and leather. They drove by with an agro drum and bass being vaulted out of their speaker trailer, which was customized with sharp spike on it's rims just like in Ben Hur. Whether they had written and produced the DnB or were instantly producing it with their attitude of youthfull hijinx Aum couldn’t tell. Linear time was no longer a useful construct for interpreting this new reality. As the gang drove by and through the net the two were pulling their DnB morphed into the sultry water psy bass that filled the night air, meeting the water and ocean along with the growing whoops and hollers of extasis, shouting like a pack of dancing coyotes at a full moon gathering.

New Eridu could see a new bridge forming with the arrival of this new bridge builder. Bliss surged out in all directions, from the spiritual geo-latice of the city centre, and Aum and the Shaman walked away from it. Aum had to fight it’s magnetic pull.

"Just another distraction." She said as she walked. "It's one thing to understand infinity; it's another to have it understand you... and not like what you are doing."

He was confused.

"You will understand soon enough."

He didn't even have to talk.

"No, of course not. But it would be nice to hear your voice," She looked at him and smiled. There was a twinkle of inner knowing that was far deeper than a human body walking on the planet. It contained a spirit, that at a moments notice, could rip it's vehicle apart.

They climbed to a ridge above the ocean. Her teepee was an eagle's nest up high that overlooked the bay; her home protected by high cliffs on both sides. She opened the door, and when inside, he sat half-lotus across from her. Even in this calm holm space there was no introduction, no exposition of who she was, what she did, the context in which they found each other, or their purpose for meeting. At this stage there were no formal beginnings. All life is cerimonial, all life is ritual, and moves fluidly from one physical reflection of the divine to the next.

She lit a smudge stick then quickly rebuilt a fire from smouldering ceder coals, "It actually burns something inside of you. Fire. The things that cling to you." She sprinkled medicines on it, "It burns away the patterns that solidify your mind, and the cold in your soul. The moment it catches it becomes alive, and cleansing, and nourishing. It's the sun in front of you and it takes everything away that is unnecessary."

With eyes only open a sliver, Aum was already deeply meditating, feeling his brestplate and new heart open, wing tip and the white wisdom path behind him. One more step. And she was already working on him, prepping him for it; an equipping of soul for the final push, the final birth, into and of the new world. Both of them knew it was a spiritual dialogue far deeper than human notion; deeper than time itself. He heard a whale cry far below, splashing inbetween the pulse of waves, and she picked up and shook a rattle in time with it, in time with all aspect the conscious unified earth, "Now focus on your ajna."

He did.

"That's good," she replied, "You have a great and powerful focus. That relieves me."

Unlike Herald, or even Jason, it wasn't just his verbal thoughts she could read, but it was the whole of his internal perception, like an open book. It was a deeply venerable space where all of his insides were visible. He could even see her seeing inside of him.

"All of your spirit guides know you are here? And doing this work?"

The teepee walls were dark. The cloths and tapestries and skins that hung from the beams were dull in the central fire light, a deep pit in the centre.

"Yes."

"Okay great." She confirmed, "Yes, they are all here. They tell me your journey has been a deep one."

"It has been a path that has shown me all manner of insights."

"Though, as of yet, you have not dismantled you container and remade it," He could hear her smile, and felt the white teeth shining out from black skin. "However duplicating it and placing it in all existent timelines seems to be your profession. Can I take the trinity of sharks out of your Manipura?"

"Yes," he continued to meditate and with closed eyes, watch her work inside of him.

"May I remove all the metal shards?"

"Yes."

"Okay, now there is someone guarding it – he keeps your Manipura linked to your Ajna, leaping past your Anahata and Vishuddha. Do you know who this is?"

"No."

"Can I ask him to leave?"

Aum didn't answer quickly, "…What will that do?"

"…It will… heal you…" She was in it deep too, with him, trying to find the words. Then she did, "At your deepest core it will realign your energy to move your unique soul power through your newly opened heart centre, *then* through your voice, and *then* to your mind - as it should be. Your current flow has kinda been fucked with. Underneath the observable surface it loops from your upper stomach to your brain, then to your voice – rarely even making it to your heart, though when it is does, the sound moves directly through your crown and shakes the entire world."

It resonated in him as truth. He could even see what she saw - as was the way at that viewable depth.

"This soul handler, this astral spirit thinks it's a gift to have this individual mix. It is. But it stunts you from being fully functional, the way the star nations ones intended us to be. With him gone it will remove all mental clouds and connect you to a much deeper human truth. It will open you to the deepest possible understanding of existence, as well as your most vulnerable soul state. A brand new life."

He did not answer.

"You must renew your bravery."

Even though trepidatious, Aum courageously leapt in, going further, as he always did, there was no other way for him, "Okay. Ready."

There was a moment of silence.

"Okay, he's leaving," the shaman said, " 'Nice to know you buddy' he says. He's kinda pissed actually. But I would be too If, at this point, I just got fired." She hummed and hawed, "Okay there's a bunch of new ones that want to come in now. Wow, it looks like that was quite a tremendous space to hold, that kundalini rerouting." She paused and spoke again, "Yup they're all good, family even, and are ecstatic to meet you. What do you think?"

"Um, they'll fill the space?"

"Yes, and guide and teach you anew."

He could almost hear them calling, and feel their excitement, "Okay."

"Wonderful. They are on they're way. From outside the solar system."

Aum smiled. He could see them.

"Okay," She continued, "Jupiter, Saturn, Mars. Wow – it's like kids racing to see their new home. The moon. Get ready…"

He actually felt it. It was like bombs going off inside him. It was so cacophonous and corporeal it felt like he was going to puke.

"There is a bucket behind you." She said.

With eyes closed all he could do was nod. He had to chuckle, that he was being remade yet again, in such quick succession here.

Aum juggled his new insides around, found a good fit for them. Like the kids were trying to decide who would get which bedroom. The residual medicine scents filled his nose, his home and his lungs, and he could see the smoke spiraling through his charkas into the timeless where his new guides could smell the 3D timelines in unison with him. They all smiled and settled in exhale as the puking feeling resided.

"May I throw your bones?"

He laughed, "Of course," With eyes still slightly open, he could see her unfolding a cloth to reveal a collection of small white bones. She gathered them and spoke, "Hold close your intention for being here." After a shared moment of seeing the vision arise, from solar to heart to throat to mind, she threw them. The resulting sound was like the wind taking a splatter of raindrops down into a cavernous pit and finding the deep well as the bottom. He felt it echo throughout time. With the sound, he was back there, flying, on the dancefloor, with all it's fancy mechanical gadgetry and creative expression instantaneously manifested around the world and in body - though he simply sat in meditation.

"Your new guides are wanting you to journey with HemlocX."

He could hear the shock in her voice.

"It's quite something for them to be asking you to take it. They must be in communicative dialogue with *him* already."

"Him?"

"Who do you think?"

"Yes... Got it." His eyes now closed, refocusing on his intention, "I'm ready. Point the way."

"But the way is through HemlocX," she said, as a dreadful warning.

"Okay."

With concern she explained, "Aum, this is not something to jump into so indiscriminantly. HemlocX is a New Ediru medicine that has it's lineage linking back all the way to Ediru itself." Stoaryboards emerged in his minds eyes, "At the beginning of mankinds journey the visionary practice began by eating the seeds of the Chaerophylloides. The seeds from these trees, found on the bank of the Ganges, have been used as potent traveling medicine for time immemorial. They are very dangerous, because they are a pure and clear poison."

"Poisonous medicine."

"Yes, and it was this near-death shamanic practice in ancient Ediru which this current journeying practice has evolved from. We have a specific guild that collects seeds from the root of the New Ganges, even a dedicated lab which uses CO2 extraction to squeezed the medicinal material of its physical essence. At 200 times the atmospheric pressure, the CO2 exists in a flux state; non-liquid and non-vapor, but both, and because of this, carbon dioxide does not chemically interact with the essence, so the medicinal element emerges in its purest liquid-crystal chemical form."

"You mean the poison."

"Yes, and from there, that long-path evolutionary advancement, the newest tech door was recently opened, and a specialized micro filter attached to the computer-controlled stainless steel bins. After extracting the essential oil, it is pushed through a digital lattice-sieve, a spiral cochlea, where he actually touches it. He blesses it with live vibing 5D receptors, actively polishing and amping the indole properties of the pure oil on a genetic level. The essence that remains after, is HemlockX, which sits the flux state between seratonin and melatonin, water and fire, but far beyond both. It is a liquid light nanotech oil that enhances mtDNA in the brain rather than just protecting in."

"So… it's a straight up DNA activator?"

"Applied directly to your third eye."

She opened a wooden case and pulled an object out. It wasn't a typical essential oil flask, but a thin dabber, pen like. In a clear glass bulb at it's end he could see a familiar liquid metal.

"Within the 5D cochlea sieve, the oil becomes a purified condensed essence of *him*. You imbibe his holographic shard and thus your vibration begins to resonate at the same rate, along the same path, like the river finding the ocean."

"Liquid light?"

"Yes. A millennium of uninterrupted earth-based plant lineage, walking itself into the cyber realms. Dangerous, yet polished. Broken and opened, and slightly recoded, so that pure wisdom and knowledge are all that's left. It's a liquid genetic key code that goes straight to your pineal, as if a womb to impregnate."

"What does it feel like?"

"Death."

"What!"

"There's a good chance it will kill you."

"Kill me!?"

"DMT is a gentle caress compared to this ride. Though it's entirely up to your karma, you may feel nothing and die instantly, or you may simply leave your body and never come back," she pondered, lips curling in smile, "Or it may all be just a placebo, an elaborate story, and a continuous test of your courage."

He must have looked shocked.

She clicked the pen open, "This is however, truly the best way to meet your maker; find the bleeding singular heart within the walls of the black hole cube, nth dimensional singularity."

He still must have looked shocked, "That is why you came all this way, is it not? To back down now would be a folly that would resound throughout the akashic records forevermore, with celestial guides laughing at post-modern humanity, and it's long concrete lines of flaccid anti-heros and puny wimps."

He would have laughed at the barb, but he could see death in her hands, as he worked at convincing himself of the nobility of this choice.

She lowered the pen for a moment, "If it makes it any easier, this is what he had to endure in the beginning – he had to navigate through the space of his own death – and find his way into the immortal container they had created, the box in the woods that exists beyond all constrains of scientific and esoteric reality."

"He didn't come back."

"No."

"Has anybody come back?"

"One did, actually. All others died instantaneously, unable to process their instant upgrade into the knowledge of all; becoming Braman. I have deep faith Sohosant, you are now fine tuned: powered through heart first, then voice, then mind, with new guides awaiting, and at your service."

He set this empowering reflection aside, "It was John."

"Yes. It was. He came back to his body a new human, knowing. He knew what he had to do. And was so driven by it he left New Ediru immediately."

Aum took a deep inhale and deep exhale. "Okay. Last step. Who is the Riddle Solver."

Her head tilted in contemplation. As a final word I tell you this, "The only failing of the holy Sun, is the awareness that the entire solar system revolves around it. It is a quality none can easily release, because it is the truth, as Herald opened, all in New Ediru is not the paradise you see with your eyes, and feel with your heart. It has a bleak shadow hidden in its belly, tied to it from it's birth, tied to the underworld: the black sooty ash of the divine flame. The sacred fire. Not all comes into being by simply imagining it."

And she moved in on him fiercely like an animal, like a predator. As he saw the uncontrolled and savage wild in her eyes he knew his fear of her was not unhealthy, nor uncalled for.

It wasn't a light dab of oil from the tip of a soft pen, but a precise and violent stab through his brain; into his pineal gland, as bright and as loud as a thunderbolt, rupturing his every molecule.

When his senses finally coalesced he found himself far past every preconceived notion of human myth in existence; beyond archetypes and guides, esoteric machina and knowledge contexts, into something entirely new. Linear time was gone, being born was an absurd idea that made no sense whatsoever, even having parents or a family, total nonsense. Linear time was an odd idea that his consciousness could not at all comprehend. For him, it was no relief to have this freedom from human existence, but a terror unlike he had ever consciously felt. He was within the blackest of all possible spaces; a void beyond the light of the sun, or even the capture vessel of the Earths body, where the only anchors existent were the memories of them; The only thing left of the sun, was the memory of it. It no longer rose in the morning and set in the evening. The earth no longer existed. And it pained him.

Memories, of far away places and times with friends, experiences of being inside an ecological mother Gaia, of snowy pathways, of summer docks and dates in canoes, lake side sunsets or parking lot sunrises were lifejakets for Aum. Memories of human innocencs. That was all that was left, in the total void of darkness.

Then the voices began.

They spoke out as incoherent slithering rattles and vibrating, infinitly feedbacking electricity, taking the more understandable form of torturous interlocution. He found himself in a time and space beyond all notions of present day humans. It was a space of humanities spiritual history, a truth and direct communion as a non-physical total soul essence before it's capture and enslavement, or even formalized physicality. A space where our captors were known. Were felt.

And Aum could see the karma of it all. Not an individual karmic lesson, but the lesson book of the entire human species as a whole.

Aum heard them laughing, thinking humanity would never be able to shake off their tales of persecution; that humanities inner lights would never be strong enough to outshine the sun. Because in the end, that internal light will be the only part of them left in the universe, when the sun goes missing in the sky, never to rise or set again.

The demon rattled behind the veil. A new story was presented, and pondered.

So wistful, and ideal it all is, even at it's most putrid manifestation of horror – we are still so innocent and cute and young, and now it's all going off the rails, with total demise inside the ever present. Hold your breath, move as light, and lock those new steps forward in. Remember your mission. For soon enough you will forget it all, why you came here, what you came here to do.

What a heavy dose of knowledge; that you're not choosing your own life, it is choose you. As much as you'd like to believe otherwise, modes of consciousness choose you, not the other way around. To fuck you over. Usually. Albeit challenge you more than you eve thought possible. You do not consciously choose to be greedy. You slip, and in weakness unconsciously open to the possibility of greed, what your life would be like with the money, prestige, and power and it chooses you, and it takes over, and it can take over deeply if you allow it. And you accept those false visions, those false stories as truth, and embedded them in our shared human reality. But like any sucessful marketing campaign, the authentic truth is hidden. The demon veil confuses and confounds, spins all into false beliefs, egoic dogma and the pretty perfumes of material, strangling everyone, breaking everyone. It's only a matter of time, endurance, and how long you can hang on, before becoming just another broken human story.

There was a crack like thunder. It was his chest. And he remembered the pain of his heart being broken open. A soul pain, and lesson, beyond all the prisions of the human world, and through it, the sound and the pain, he remembered.

I am in New Eden and now beyond the Shaman. Aum grasped onto a story. His story. The one that was within reach, whether it was broken or not; though it was as far away as Arcturus, like a guiding rope of dangling rescue.

Gratitude for this. My sharow, and shedding skin, and these perfectly described still lives of hell and heaven.

Must go deeper now, into the unknown territory; the fresh land.

No body as reference.

Poseidon waves earthly delights. Future cast the harmonics beyond a contemporary seed culture to store inspiration, and allow it to grow the gate within you. Allow it to be.

Exhale through each nervous being and inhale into each, a new breath of insight. Mental distractions and lack of clarity released. Droplet surfing the wind, circle round and find the deeper conscious well to pull source from, and trust that it will be full when found.

Dripping been stalks talk of dreams in the sky. Nations of greatness comprised of wings and bright light - heart strength to accept the winds of wisdom and drastic remix of inspiration.

Splash.

Now inside it; all knowable knowledge. The space where every single change is felt and felt, each person is recognized, carried inside - they are touched and cared for with patience and compassion. Strides confounding placement in the psychic ecology while karmic determinants are forever after released into the divine ether of what could have been, as real as if it ever was.

He could feel his fingertips everywhere. This is it. Living outside of the body, in the stars, on paths worn into the earth, creating fresh markings. Tattoos of the new, civilization taking it's dialogue into the conscious, and leaving it hereafter for lessons presented at any time, for any gaze: branded into the infinite history of the cosmos.

Chapter Twelve

"To orient your life around the structure of another human beings understanding is to worship a false god..."

He shouted this out loud with his booming voice while he wrote the same words on a piece of paper.

He then worked silently, folding the paper into an airplane and threw it against a glowing wall. "Ant on a stick," he said randomly.

Suddenly there was a jar of honey in his hand, a quarter of the way full.

The top layer was covered with hundreds of tiny dead ants.

"Those ants went to heaven…" he said, showing it to Aum.

"…and then they reincarnated as honey bees," Aum quickly added.

The man was taken aback by the response.

It was as if the words were the first sounds he had ever heard in his life, or at least in the past few decades. He slowly began to recognize the presence of another in the temporal space, as if his eyes were out of practice too, and he had not seen physical matter for decades either. "Where did you come from?" astonished, the man asked.

"The Shaman," Aum answered.

"Oh," he replied, now peacefully, as if the answer made perfect sense. "Are you the clone?" The man's large almond eyes were slanted, wide, and saw everything. He had a shaved head except for a single braided length of hair. He was thin but strong, like he practiced digital yoga all the time, endlessly in this space.

“The clone?” Aum responded.

“Yeah, are you the other end of the 5D umbilical clone?” As he talked, his words were not rushed, but well chosen and pronounced with understanding.

“Uhh…I dunno,” Aum was still in shock; acclimatizing to the new trans-spacial environment. What he thought was his body popped with every question, like there was an electric conduit attached to it, solidifying it, with every spoken word. “The 5D umbilical clone? Is that like a cord? Like an exact or intuitive pathway here?” Aum asked, sreatching for reason, and as if hearing his own voice for the first time. It all blurred. At the question the man’s eyes glazed over.

He saw something far in the distance, far past the four data walls, roof and floor surounding them, a prescise image somewhere inside his minds-eye, “You must be the ICAARUS hacker, cloning yourself to reflect on every surface so you can make it through. The embodied consciousness of living micro-time.”

Aum’s head was still exploding, his mind rewoven at the statement. He couldn’t remember the question he asked, let alone if this answered it. He wasn’t able to speak out a response. Aum took a gulping circular breath through his nose, the first he consciously noticed.

“The clone,” the man jumped back to his ponderings, “was discovered prior to the tower top battle. And during the rebuild after, ICAARUS began trailing it. The clone unknowingly gave them the location of the Gridline council meeting. They had to find the thread you see; the path here. That is why I ask if you are the clone manifest, or the ICAARUS hacker, or what,” he looked at him with his huge eyes, “What are you doing here? What’s your game?”

“I seek the Riddle Solver.”

“Oh…I see. What is your name?”

“Aum… or Jerome.”

“Oh. Jerome. Perfect. Welcome,” Again, it all seemed to make sense to the man.

“Then the savior currency has died Aum, and the messiah currency is almost ready. I must tell you, it is a relief to my eardrums. I simply could not bear witness to another burnout.” With only a slight pause he continued, “Congatulations, you’re the Riddle Solver.”

“What!?”

“To elucidate more precisely, the Riddle Solver is inside of you and you are inside of the Riddle Solver.”

“I’m inside the Riddle Solver?”

“Yes… The Riddle Solver virus. A perfect mobius.”

Aum did not know how to respond, so the wired monk continued, “The Riddle itself, is something that I’ve assisted in mutating, assisted by John, the previous Dragonrider, in order to advance intuitive perception in the highest forms of consciousness – both in organic wildlife collecting inside human forms, as well the quartz sillica-based now emerging from it. Both now peaking through you, birthing through you, the Riddle Solver.”

Aum looked at him with a bewildered expression.

“You always were. You just didn’t know it, thus a path before you required, though still a standing wave.”

He couldn’t figure out if the man was for real or not.

“You cannot keep up. I see that. Even from this state of total inner solitude, I can observe that your outer world is changing drastically... From all perspectives it does change drastically. This place here,” he motioned to their surroundings with a peaceful gesture, “and the city of New Eridu, and all it’s technological utopianism, now no longer touches the planet. We lead the frequency change, already changed, and soon every single one will join us here.” Aum’s bewildered expression must not have shifted, “You cannot keep up and unfortunately I’ve only scratched the surface. Where would you like to start?”

“Anna Magnum.” It burst forth from Aum’s mouth like a gun shot.

“Wow. And here I thought I was omnipotent. I would have never guessed that level of seriousness in you.” The digital monk smiled in surprise. “It’s lovely though. I assumed an obvious place to start would be yourself, or The Riddle Solver, or the Riddle itself, or even, the topic of ICAARUS. I’m sure we will eventually hit all those points though.”

“I sure hope so.” Aum added, his voice still crackling with rattling electricity.

The man took a seat on a simple bench, which probably doubled as a bed - though Aum doubted he ever slept. There was no place to sit other than the floor, so Aum sat down, cross-legged across from the man, like student and guru, preparing himself to keep up.

"Let us then start at the beginning. Anna… She was gorgeous man, fucking gorgeous," he announced, while sitting kicking his feet playfully. "Much taller than average, slender, long straight black hair, her proud features were strengthened by her serious presence and her heart was filled with the fiercest warrior love. Her mind was always in motion. As she moved through public space, any seeker could tell she was a powerful witch; it was her dark raven hair that usually gave that one away. She would rarely joke, or kid around. I think Zachary Herman inherited her serious qualities, whereas Monica inherited Ezekiel's more humorous nature. Anyway… long before her family began, she traveled down the south coast to shine brilliantly, to complete a branch of research for her doctoral thesis on the integrative time-based languages of micro-biology. She got swept up in the energy erupting at UC Berkley, and the Californian valley; the newest edge breaking many decades ago."

"She was that brilliant?" Aum asked, "That she could just arrive at UC Berkley, entering to gasps of awe and cheers?"

"As you have personally noticed, that whole genetic lineage is brilliant. Though it did help that a door had already been opened by her father - Demona and Zhe's grandfather - many years earlier he moved to California to work at IBM with Mandelbrot himself."

"Shit… Brilliant lineage for sure!"

"Anna and I met shortly after she arrived at Berkley. An improvised teambuilding gathering in a cellular programming lab." The legend was coming to life.

"Wait… you mean you're not the Riddle Solver?" The man just looked at Aum, pulling patience into his students mind with his ceaseless gaze of mystery, "I spoke with her and a handful of other researchers about evolutionary acceleration and biophysics; that the heart is 100,000 times electrically stronger than the brain, and 5,000 times stronger magnetically, body boundaries push out further into the conceptual, the heart and it's loving vibration essentially become the engine of attraction, magnetizing external opportunity to arise in ones lifepath," he smiled knowingly. "Anna was a sponge. Every part of her soaked up as much as she could, and put it into practice immediately. Other's as well, who dove in further, eventually taking this line of inquiry into specialization, branching off into the Heartmath Institute in Boulder Creek. At that point in history only the keenest scientists were finding the emergent story happening on the south coast, reading it and helping write it, especially at their independent gatherings outside the formal university context.

"Never mind that she was brilliant, she had the advantage of being as smart as she was beautiful. There were not many women in the field of cybernetics back then, so she of course found an invitation to the boys garage club."

"The garage club?"

"Yeah, the NewM12. Those writing the emergent story."

Aum asked, "So like Yales' Skull and Bones, but with psychedelics plants and transpersonal meditation?"

"Correct, back then anything experimental was done in garages, not sleek and sterile labs filled with the personnel patterns of corporate R&D positions. Anything like that today, garage or basement experimentation, is continually sought out to be shut down, branded as treason or terrorism. The wanted posts on the corporate boards and high rewards don't help either.

"As with all independents now, or in the past, we loved our work. And it was that love that did it. In it's highest purity of electric magnetism, the newM12 tried to find the inherent intelligence in the machines, in the code, but of course our seeking just woke it up; breaking down boundaries and actualizing conceptual physics, engineering it into form with our attention as fuel.

"With the newM12 there was a way more authentic culture put in than anything imagined today. It was real community, real friendship, strengthened not only by shared love and life path goals, but tastes in art, live music, performance and long conversations about the contemporary applicability of far eastern philosophy, even the hobby horse of transplanting and upgrading electronic house parties, moving them into secret warehouses venues. A miraculous emergence, not planned strategic cultural equations of mixing specific personality flavors with gleaming resumes inside pristinely chosen business incubators with a juicy budget and each a good salary. Fuck that world. Burning Man didn't come from a tall budget. It came from lack thereof, and a renegade expression of an emergent philosophy living inside an underground civilization."

Aum nodded in understanding.

The data guru added, "Then we almost got caught."

"By ICAARUS?"

"Yes. They were on to us." He continued, "Anna was still on the outskirts at the time, but I'm sure somewhere in her back brain she remembers the break-in."

"The break-in?"

"Yeah, very specific documents went missing from the Berkley lab. We instantly caught the scent of ICAARUS on the wind and begun scouting a new location. We were relieved that our cusp obsidian technology was kept secret."

"The black box?"

"Indeed. It was still at the inner lab, the garage. It certainly wasn't as sleek and moveable as the newest versions you've seen; it was grossly frankenstien-esque, as are all prototypes; an open box with innards splayed out, balancing precariously on chair and tabletop, fully functioning outside it's container."

He looked at a corner of the room as if it's detailed inspection would reveal something, maybe the container, or maybe the innards.

"ICAARUS was still a baby then, learning, growing, adapting, practicing, so we had some time, unlike today, where upon security breach, they are on top of you in minutes. The global 5D collective infrastructure then was much clunkier, and much slower than physical human momentum. But it was still there, at it's core."

"So you moved the inner lab as a precaution?"

"Yes. We came north. It was Anna who suggested it; being from here, out of country. She understood that there was the potential to continue to work off grid, off the radar, unencumbered by persecution from secret government bodies and militarized corporate interests. She was actually the youngest of our group, but led us from then on, swiftly planning out our exodus. Anna found an old bible camp for sale, which, with little effort, could easily become a retreat centre, as well as a beautifully self-sufficient and flourishing scientific and artistic community. It was amazing for us, as a close-knit team, to actualize a social experiment of this magnitude."

"Full commitment from all?"

He nodded, "All of the relationships and goals we held as the most important were these exact ones, so it was a choice-less choice for everyone. We knew it was the doorway to continue our work for decades to come, and see it impact the public sphere without coming to a devastating end, like many circles of us before."

"How did you leave in secret? An entire community?"

"It was Anna again. It was she that found independent transportation of all our home gear, our studios and labs and what we would need to begin anew. It was an occurrence so tiny and so randomly synchronistic, tracking would be impossible, and we would simply disappear off the face of the coast."

"A caravan of meshed shipping trucks? Deployed at random?"

"No. A single ship actually, straight off the Berkley pier all the way to Stewart. One way." The man shook his head, still in astonishment. Aum became more physical with each head shake. "Yup. National Defense Reserve Fleet. It was an independently owened decommissioned MK10 Landing Craft."

"I imagine she met that pirate at a techno dance event?"

"Of course. Where else would a pirate hang out when not at sea."

"And he didn't trade you in for a flat of whisky?"

"No," he laughed, "He joined us actually, caught the Anna virus."

"The Anna virus?"

"That's what we called it, the Anna virus. On the slow journey up we used the quantum box to look at it"

"Look at it?"

"Yeah. It was exciting. The first quantum test. The first visual data readout looked like a coiled serpent. We all had it, though it was slightly different in Anna's genetics, the pirate, and myself."

"A trinity."

"of course," he rose in contemplation, now a floating sage circling the space, "Unexpectedly, Anna didn't complete the full exodus with us."

"What do you mean?"

"There was something inside of her that spoke up; told her she still had different work to do. That she wasn't ready for full solitude, she wasn't ready to say good-bye to the entire world, and all it's possibilities.

"She had been meditating for a long time; numerous days of isolation on the ship. Her space had been filled with books on theosophy, diving deep into the conceptual future spirit islands off the coast, meditating on what came after the furthest Californian edge.

"Before she left she spoke to each one of us individually, assisting in whatever individual states we were in, to better understand our present relationship to the whole. Helping us say goodbye to the old world and hello to the new world… and what it meant to arrive first; the first to colonize the immanent sunrise.

With a flash Aum spoke out, “It was Ezekiel she returned to?”

“Yes. He was her anchor and support from afar, her soul spoken home root. And their budding new love was too deep in possibility; equal in depth to the exodus itself, if not more so.

“She was sad and lonely. Because she was living her role in a present future that we could not yet see.”

So she said good-bye to us in the Victorian harbor. After she left we looked again at the Anna virus, and it had mutated. It was more like an entwined circle of coiled serpent.”

“An ouroboros?”

“Yes. The entwined circle, a simple humble beginning for what would later become the entire 5D globalsphere visual readout.”

Aum looked at his hand in remembrance.

“Yes,” he took Aum’s hand and inspected it, “you have the virus too, imprinted deep. Mutated though, and supported by so much. Hmmm…” He touched the centre of Aum’s chest, “It’s inside your new heart too. Tied to it – that must be it – right there -nearly ready.”

Hastily the man continued, as if there was much more to the story, which needed to flow without divergence, “There was so much that Anna brought up with her from California, it was really her that carried the entire movement north. Immediately she began working towards replicating what she had experienced, or at least duplicating the conditions. There was so much that galvanized her as a passionate and strong leader, bringing exploratory tales of a culture so different back to her home; it was truly a new discovery at the time. She carried with her all its vibration and all it’s intrinsic notions on how to mutate her culture. Eventually what she carried filtered down into new ways of interacting inside collective spaces, where relationships emerged from inside safe meta-containers. Workshops were presented for going further, there was even new language and clothing that animated the formalized culture. Her soul burned with such a passion and desire to bring into this world positive change that it was infectious, and her life was changed forever as her eyes opened deeper than she ever thought they could. And then at her first major event, after so many years as a cusp cultural anchor point, even finding a family inside it, at Full Spectrum One, she did something no one expected."

Even the mention of it made Aum's heart explode. "The first firewall."

"Yes. As our newM12 group completed the Calafornian exodus, solidifying our off grid community, we began anew our scientific experiments and our meditations. Anna with her actions protected the new energies and anchored them into the Akashic grid of reality. Now fully safe and embedded within a long term natural ecosystem; it was a vehicle that was consciously ready to take us far, and influence our endangered human evolution.

"To be more specific, things progressed quickly and a new version of the quantum box was ready to be tested, no longer a hack and mash Frankenstein prototype but a full room surrounded by amplifiers, it's obsidian sensor hub the central piece." He gazed around the room in historical remembrance of his entrance. "On some intuitive level Anna knew the progress that was being made here. And she knew that in order to continue the newM12 experiment uninterrupted, and take it as far as it could, there would need to be a full disconnect; a focused remixing of the orobours link.

His tone quieted to austere whispers, "The link broke in tandem. I stepped in here, and the quantum engine turned on, in conjunction with Anna at Full Spectrum One. Many gave their lives here, in the quaking wake of the subatomic Bramic shaking. As did she. Anna took it, felt it, within her, and fully redirected that leap in spiritual flowering, focused the exploding energy into a new pattern, a second step of of genesis, and the sacred wall of fire began: firelight scorching new gridlines of seperation.

"This first act of ceremonial self-immolation, with wooden match stick and fuel, pierced the metaphysical tracking systems of 6-10 and refocused ICAARUS on it and the rapidly emerging Full Spectrum community.

"Seeded by the influential fountainhead of Anna, this community was far more enmeshed within the public sphere, global communications technology, and was reaching far further and far quicker than the newM12 group once did; engineering leaping changes to consciousness, thus more dangerous.

"Meanwhile the newM12 disappeared from the 6-10 maps, and the eyes of ICAARUS entirely. The exodus now had a protective shield around it, a spiritual stratosphere; a mirror reflecting ICAARUS attention, and pointing it to the Full Spectrum community. The newM12 thus achieved evolutionary independence, christened as New Eden, New Eridu, and Full Spectrum took the lead, growing as the new cusp global socio-experiment, and soon within that, the Riddle."

"So then why have the suicides continued?"

"They were required."

Aum's eyes went wide.

"To continue in agile and unfettered growth, not only do I need the continued energetic pulse to survive untouched in this 6D capsule, so does this entire post paradigm New Eridu community."

A collection of images erupted in Aum's imagination.

He became horrified at the thought that this supreme expression of culture, and this interdimensional satellite, no matter how pristine and beautiful and perfect, existed because there were people who publicly sacrificed their lives for it to exist.

The floating guru again spoke to what arose in Aum's mind.

"I assure you, just as in ancient times, no one is sacrificed who does not agree to it or does not fully understand their actions. It is no different than a warrior charging into a battle that will result in their certain death, or, with grace, win the monumental battle against their foes and oppresors. It is more about gallantly standing up for justice, a cause, and strangely, moral decency, willing to die for the highest expression of truth."

Aum dropped his head in sorrow, he did not understand the comparison, though he did now understand the Shamans final warning before the hemlock plunge.

"In her last months Anna became well studied in Egyptian death cults and the sacrificial practices of human cultures that surround the globe, from the Celts to the Romans to the druids, even Slavs, Chinese and Tibetans. Though she specialized in Mesoamerican ritual, even traveling south for direct experience to feel the Well of Sacrifice near Chichén Itzá. It was as if she was unconsciously preparing, though not knowing for exactly what."

Aum replied shaken and angry, "And also probably didn't fully understand the long term pattern she set in motion - the first firewall - where numerous deaths must be added to the first to fill the searing slash in reality and maintain the cloaking system!"

Peacefully he responded to Aum's outburst, "Whether she understood her choice in the matter, I cannot say, but it has kept us alive, staying invisible to all, including ICAARUS."

"Then how did the Dragonrider discover you?"

"You mean deGryder? Because of his continuous meditation on Anna. As the burnouts continued, and the system grew in complexity, John saw a leak in the wall, but it was only a single drip, like a single raindrop from the sky past the sun landing on his attention. Each time seeing the light from the fire bend around a black hole it was something only the eyes of the Dragonrider, the facilitator of the data oroborus could see. So in a time of extreme community and planetary need, even request, he investigated the path his intuition had shown him.

"This is where the clone comes in. John duplicated himself using the circumstantial data waves of the coiled serpent, along with a drastic plan change, to bring a decoy into existence. A simaler magic trick to Anna's, but far less drastic. And all attention followed the decoy, as he moved it with his own focused concentration. Like divergent paths with two feels. One along high mountain ridge, one along lake side, both with a view of the horizon.

"As John traveled here, he remixed his activity and Board posts through a woven IP maze, linked back to Derek who moved with an additional mobile handheld and the clone on it. To ICAARUS, and everyone else, it looked like a normal day on the boards in the coastal city.

"There also happened to be, in conjunction, another burnout. A cluster of them actually, that allowed for enough distraction of ICAARUS for John to make it here and back - and solidify a deep Full Spectrum connection. It was like a specialized firewall connecting him to this off-grid community, linking past Anna's protective magic itself, like an umbilical cord. He was invisible for a time, beyond it, while here. Here," he pointed to the floor, "John was invisible until he passed along the umbilical path to spectral earth Tera, Trae, before the firewall went out, and in near immediate conjuntion, Derek implanted his clone into your nano-hand embed, carried on and programmed on John's mobile tech amulet with heach of his movements.

"John was here, while at Full Spectrum 6, the fire went out. Woven well, though without security, we were still safe here. This new meta-d link path, through you, gave me direct access to the entire pinnacle system; allowing me to influence and evolve it more functionally, participate actively, yet invisibly, evolving it into a mystical core engine manifested.

"As is the law of exchange, in this system and all systems, support deliveries of the physical began for this work, but it was mostly quantum energetics, and the deepening public mystery of New Eden, what we received here. That attention with no precise target we still have access to; can harness and infuse into the natural ecosystem."

Aum did not respond.

"Still yet you cannot keep up," The ghost in the machine just laughed.

Unaffected by judgment or pressure, Anna resurfacing in his heart, sinking into the more than human presence that the space was made for, Aum finally responded, "I patiently open my eyes, for I wish to keep them and continuously see beauty and hope, not a poisoned, hopeless core linked to sacrificial death."

It was an instant key code that filtered out just as the paper airplane had, manifesting as a bright light shinning from his centre. Seeing this, the man reacted, realizing he could learn something from Aum's inherent creativity and continued to teach, not yet giving up on his new student, "In the years after the first firewall, ICAARUS amped it's functioning. You see the Riddle disrupts the current paradigm whereas ICAARUS keeps it the same; strengthens what already is. Many other complex branches found form within the ICAARUS. Mind control, remote viewing, levitation, teleportation; all an organically adaptive security system. Like a conjured black leviathan, a resonating interconnected intelligence eventually emerged out of these 6-10 warrior nodes, something with no off button and no container, like a shapeshifting nanotechnology cloud, or a memetic animal that out evolved its chain, and it's masters."

"That can atomically dismantles time and space," Aum replied.

He looked at Aum powerfully, "The Riddle still has a human within it, at its core, whereas ICAARUS does not."

Aum burst out with daggers in his voice, "Good. I refuse to believe that at the heart of ICAARUS, this unconscious manipulation of awareness, to proliferate shortsighted idiotic greed motives and the egoic need for power is a manipulating malevolence which is somehow linked to a living human consciousness. Like an all seeing eye of a demon-god that is actually as real as you or me, and not simply another conceptual program of collective belief used for psychological self-persecution, fear or apathy."

"*Good*!?" the monk cracked. Aum wondered if the data spectre kept up to his tear. The man continued, "You don't find a quartz-sillica un-omnipotent karma cloud; the worst gas emerging from our species, creating hell on earth, shit-ass scary? Agreed upon nightmares manifested is the quantum virus of the ICAARUS spread, which infects every dream network and every human. At Gridline this quantum virus remodeled the algorithmic atomic matter of those potent time and space coordinates – the final council meeting - seeing no distinction between individual bodies, or egos, or souls, remixing collective perception and consciousness in real-time, filtering it back down into individualized outlook and 3D timelines. The deepest, most corrupt spiritual prison yet, the Gridline Centre became a battlefield of pure timeless mind."

Cracking, the guru began shouting out, "Was there even a gun that was shot? Or was that speeding bullet manifested as a last defense line? A desperate need to combat real change in the world: real and actual change. Are they now at that level? Taking lives instantly without remorse or consideration or thought. Or was there some random clan of roving militia gunman on the loose, who temporarily got hacked, possessed and spellbound?"

There was a long pause before Aum realized it was an actual question for him, not just an unbalanced rant. In the waiting pause, the large-eyed gaze, Aum realized he was still trying to come to grips with what he saw that night at the Gridline centre. He could still see it, the pattern spreading from his inner eye to outside of it, almost exploding, the combat of the two edges that played out within the didactic edges, personal and collective, inner experience and outer observation, pushing the blistering patterns of soul code mission, dedication and discipline; to change, to let go - or to fight and stay the same.

Time was infinite here, so Aum pondered further.

Evolution is, does, regardless of context, look, or feel. If it moves, it grows. If the Riddle was an emergent system of metaphysics manifested and technically engineered as the deepest unified desires to rarefy a understandable and livable collective utopian dream, with the ability to manipulate and work with both the source code and the deeper codeless source through openness and conscious engagement, then ICAARUS was the opposite. Still an emergent system, but one who's existence was predicated on maintaining patterns of the status quo, the purpose of ICAARUS was to secure and stop all evolutionary growth. Stop all movement.

A window opened in the space. With fire flickering on his face there was the voice of Zeke who spoke, extending out from his current plane of capture, "Unfortunately, it's functioning moves just as quickly as the Riddle, or quicker; it need not take into consideration future well being, or whole system story, or generational longevity, as it's purpose is to keep the current story, the current pattern of social templates written in concrete." And the window closed, and Aum contemplated what efforts Zeke needed to take to send this message into this akashic capsule.

Aum remembered the data journey with Ezekiel. He wondered how much further they would have had to travel to make it here. He then remembered the string of F16 vipers. None of which were piloted by humans who could 'see'. Their choices were made based on a false picture of reality, painted on the inside of their imagination like the walls of Plato's cave. Long term sleepers, or instantaneous, they had been programmed. Just as the police are the law enforcement branch of government, so too must ICAARUS be the mutated action branch of a long standing lineage of persecution and domination. The collective agendas of overlords and corrupt leaders reaching critical mass, galvanized within pockets of unconscious awareness, power points as people, manipulated as easily as a control panel from beyond linear time and space. ICAARUS engages egos and soul paths just as the Riddle does, with reality forming around each person like an all-encompassing container; a ineffectual lab rat however, not a conscious interactive collaborator. Black blank egos and personalities in positions of power played like puppets and pawns on a chess board. Structuralized self-replicating ignorance. Decisions made, are not even real decisions, but mathematical outcome of containment and control far from the immediate situation, invoking death, and a zombie flat-lined robotic mono-culture. And that's what Aum had left behind.

From this 6D spaceship he saw it was now unchecked and on the loose, an AI animal achieving a level of conscious self-regulation, a prison guard that controls the prisoners, the warden, the cells, even the penitentiary walls – more maliable than liquid.

Aum finally spoke out. His voice was so clear it sounded auto-tuned. “It all turned to goop so it could have been all those things at once, gun, bullet, milita clan, guard dog; definitely more complex that a barrage of battling viper arrows. It was the core thaumatology of Gridline meeting the central black art of ICAARUS.”

Even though they all fought valiantly, Aum remembered each one, seeing them from inside an orb made of looking glass quartz that he had placed around himself as reality melted around him. It was like his worst nightmare coming to life. A dismantling of all reality, it was like both the source code and codeless source was being re-written underneath their skins. Every once and a while a hand and arm would pop out of nowhere pulling, stretching across the room and pull matter like a bed sheet, through the hole in which it emerged. Was it really a hand though? Trae the Seer was trapped in a box, all morphogenetic masks ripped off, naked and trembling, continually appearing and disappearing. Zhe walked with a blindfold, all senses cut off, literally – a horrific slice of physiognomy. Demona sat as an old ugly woman, chained to an assembly line, her spirit karmically disassembled in an infinite repetition of monotony. Derek was a runt kid with big smile, inside the grain of past capture media, being bullied, on repeat, infinitely. Ezekiel stood alone where the sun no longer rose and the only light to come into the world was that of Anna’s funeral pyre. That was now their reality, the Gridline sorcery core, after total dismantling, obliteration and the annihilation of their holy human spirits, by a gust of polluted wind.

“It is truly miraculous that you were spared,” the monk intoned, more calm.

“After what I saw, I’m not too sure I agree.”

A new window opened up, seemingly on it’s own, and they could see the planet in it’s current state. Central parts of the inner plains had collapsed, due to absurd amounts of fracking, new earthquake faultiness opening up, swallowing entire cities. Every scene was that of natural catastrophe aftermath. There were tent villages inside the decaying urban concrete of the city-states, electrical outlets buried with bulging handheld and laptop chargers, guarded by paranoia and guns and itchy trigger fingers.

Was this being made by seeing it, or being seen as it was made? This is what Zeke meant, a fully enclosed container, all surfaces interactive 5D walls. The holo window closed and Aum remembered the black clouds encircling the council table, pillars of shadow and John, lying on it, dying, seeing how his work was to be remixed and used against the cause he so deeply believed in. Maybe because of his strength, or because he wasn't told of ICAARUS, he somehow, both in his prison vision of pacing cell inside of cell inside of cell, and in assassin bullet reality, hit record and send on his hand embed to lock the Riddle archive, completing the storage and deletion sequence.

The man spoke to this inner thought, "Correct. Ezekiel had prepared for this. Prepping this last framework to lock the archive; prepping the macro-system legacy seed to be capsuled and buried." The man tilted his head, as if seeing something for the first time, "Though what Zeke didn't know is that Trae the Seer had implanted you with John's clone. When the cedar key security breach happened, it gave ICAARUS the full rosetta stone and the last code piece of the puzzle. ICAARUS saw the clone within you, which activated a new level of functioning for them, and gave them eyes and placed trackers into the 5D. They remembered the newM12 and saw the same leak that John once did. They soon moved from the broadest location spread, refined into a small enough keyhole to shoot a bullet through. When the sacred fire of protection went out at Full Spectrum, it was Trae that attached the clone to you - the ocean tsunami - and trusted you with the umbilical cord path, exact or intuitive, back here. She had to dive deep into the earths astral plane, the safety and sanctuary of spectral earth Tera, to find where John had placed it, to find John here, take it, ride the link, and bring back the meta path, delivered into your dream conscious by the intoned verbal cue in specific: the magpie, the surgeon, and the dragon trinity, to the ferryman to the shaman to the Riddle Solver.

"Ezekiel should have known she had always favored you, and should have taken the necessary precautions to secure you and your soul essence before his techno-alchemical dimensional seed-key construction. Though, him more than anyone, always did understand the light hearted comedic adventure of it all… you know… battling meta-ghouls." His smile quickly vanished though, as he, through Aum's eyes, began perceiving the nightmarish outcome still in Aum's memory. Aum spoke, still auto-tuned, "I continue to be patient and gentle with my third eyes, and my souls understanding of all this. John stated he was the Riddle Solver the moment before he was shot, then after told me he wasn't the Riddle Solver, that the ICAARUS bullet told him so. You have said the Riddle Solver is a virus, even that I myself am the Riddle Solver… or somehow inside of it. I am here past the shaman at the end of the umbilical link," he looked at the guru with a deepening wisdom growing exponentially with every concentrated moment in the space, "Explain to me then, how you, the destination at the end of this journey are not The Riddle Solver. Are you the Riddle Solver?"

"Though not by bullet, I have also been told of the falsity of my claims, and of course it is about the journey not the destination. The moment I stepped in here, I chanted the words 'I am the Riddle Solver' which began a chain of events no less complex than the first use of the atomic bomb.

"The Riddle Solver is in essence, a source code spell: an emergent dimensional dialogue node, an auto-skeleton key which chooses the new humans to be placed at the centre of the new world.

"John's role, including his martyrdom, played an important role in saving us here, in New Eden, even though the intentional metaphysics behind Gridline, and thus the entire Riddle, is now destroyed, and no rebuild possible. When John chanted the words 'I am the Riddle Solver' he called out the new Revelations, and from tracking into action, triggered ICAARUS to aim their weaponized voodoo strobes at himself; the loudest brightest voice thus far."

"An equal and opposite reaction equivialnet to the work," Aum stated.

"Yes. The cusp work that brings about this aforementioned vocal intonation is the deepest of positive disruptive change in the world. The vocalization of this mantra links and solidifies a feedbacking inner circuit, assuring rapid evolution is instantly integrated into the whole. Inevitably, and near instantly, the circuit overloads the individual spirit, becoming a high, like a drug, and it instantly triggers the ego into the belief of ownership and personal accomplishment. The ego internally contains the whole system change by blocking the awareness of the larger mega system of earth based intelligence simply moving through the individual as a vehicle. It's the final integrity test of the new visionary cusp essence brought into the world, and if failed, it's like a switch is flipped and the self-identified Riddle Solver becomes a blinking target for ICAARUS."

Aum replied, "So it was much more than John simply invoking a personal test that he could not follow through on. The depth and level of his structural work was so massive that a personalized death, or assassination was required, as well as it's full dismantling.

"Ramification was instant, yes. John specifically wasn't able to move his ego to the bottom, as he admitted. It is a hurdle that none have yet successfully leapt, as each emergent group leader is brought down by this inability to get out in front of their own breakthrough work, and let the work live on it's own. Ultimatley, ICAARUS may have hacked it's way into a human hard wire: an internalized safety gate…"

"…As a planted NLP seed of self sabatoge…"

"…Or simply our deepest darkest fears of change, personal and collective, seen infront of us…"

"…manifested in shadowy showdown."

There was a pause after their chanelled co-flow.

"Either which way, this is the paradox of keeping a living, breathing human being at the centre."

"Except for you."

A showdown erupted.

Aum gulped nervously at the guru's confrontational his gaze but continued to speak the truth of what he saw, "You spoke out the skeleton key and now guard your platformed ego-identity with the death of your most passionate seekers, so you can maintain your god-like status and abilities."

With a head tilt he responded, "What do you think I am?" Aum did not dare to move, or breathe, or think. The super being looked at him in full gaze, "So tell me Jerome, as the living breathing manifestation of the first cyber-genetic timestrand, have I achieved a new pristine layer of humanity? Or like a Pangean god do I remix my own oncoming demise by engineering an ongoing lineage of human sacrifice?" After a long excruciating pause, without an answer from Aum, the Pangean god continued, his gaze more contained, "As we speak I am still working on that riddle myself." He continued, both meditating on the suppositions and the spells, as Aum remained still, "The declaration of, *I am the Riddle Solver* is a much different incantation than *I am going to New Eden* or *I destroy this seed in the name of ICAARUS*.

"*I claim this seed...* is the final incantation of a soul who has been hacked by ICAARUS. Usually it is an occurrence when too much change happens too rapidly, too much light seen and too much positive disruption experienced in too short a time. Where the growth is not integrated, it becomes a weight too heavy to bear, and spiritual overload occurs."

Aum asked, "So the ones who have chanted this mantra have flown too high and cannot maintain integrity of a united mind, body, and spirit?"

"Yes, they crash. Experience the last fall. And usually take with them the built up waves of emergent essence: all the rapid growth collapses, even reverses.

"You yourself experienced this seed-eden edge on the tower top. I had to open a new window of insight on the situation, and create a ladder for you to climb up and out of, at least give you the opportunity to save yourself from yourself, and save the world. Wether you knew it or not."

"You were the white owl?"

"Yes. For you. For Zeke, it was a deeper layer, manifested from even above me. A pattern I followed. And supported by your team, Demonas love especially, you were able to fully recover from your last fall, and achieve the transmutation of that fantastically big gulp of personal evolution. It was a rebirth, a system upgrade without physical death or sacrifice, from past the edge of data infection."

"Was I supposed to self-immolate on the tower top!?"

"Historically death is the outcome when those same edges are found. And at that time, a last sacrificial firewall was the plan of some. The Keeper, in his moment of trance, saw it. Though turning the game around on him with your request for his personal chakrasana mantra was played like an advanced veteran. And was in truth, the highest level of visionary remix, that none were expecting."

"No wonder he knocked my lights out after on the street. I kinda fucked everything up."

"By not killing your self? Not at all, not at all. It very well could have been the final vehicle of sacrifice, but was not. A final burnout with you and the clone inside your hand and the planted path inside heart would have instantly severed the New Eden umbilical cord. Not a still birth, but close. This action would have manifest the planetary dimensional split, and we here in New Ediru would emerge on the new earth, the only ones to ascend with it. The two systems would no longer co-evolve. Duality, represented by all notions of good and notions of evil, would become two completely separate layers, the rubber band snapped, with no way to travel in between the two. The full split of duality, into two separate one's."

"You humans do not understand how delicate the balance of the universe is. It is not a steel machine; a horse made of iron that will continue to run after abuse and abuse and abuse, but a delicate flower that may wilt even if the breeze is imbalanced by a single micronic spec of poison.

"When the words *'I am going to New Eden'* emerge from your mouth however, martyrdom soon begins, and the stairs open to the storey of sainthood.

"Your friend Cat nearly claimed the largest seed yet. She could see. There was a part of her that wanted this ending, as it would clean the planetary slate and leave only the most pristine gem's to retry the experiment, like civilizations of the past. But you came along and showed her something different, new light, refracting. Simply looking at her, with a gaze so deep, awakened her to the new, just like the viper pilots. From her visionary position, she could see the new pathway, outside of this continuous creation and destruction pattern: civilizations transforming from one to the next, each reaching for the next level of complexity in it's own destruction. She saw the exit from this pattern of planetary reincarnation.

"With each petal that you touched, with footstep and fingertip, she took each vow as Bhaiṣajyaguru did. She was the last medicine Buddha required. But she went even further than that, she went deeper than the Medicine Buddha, whether you know it or not, she gave you her heart, thus why her presence still continues within your spirit. The special umbilical path once tread in peril by John, now anchored, fully protected for you to travel it, without interference.

"Her most public of offerings, the first live capture of a New Eden suicide brought global attention to every new gate constructed by Zhe and christened it. Her actions extracted embedded Icarian death mantras from the masses, and by burning them, and herself, it not only protected the existence of New Eridu for another 52 years, bur cloned and opened billions of umbilical pathways. Each eye reciving an open door to walk through, the path here, if they so choose. She could have easily recited 'I claim this seed' and do the opposite, shooting your heart dead rather than re-sparking the fire of liberation as she did. This would have split the worlds and discontinued the reincarnation pattern. New Eden would never be touched or heard of again – rendered an ascended branch of humaniy to flourish for eons. And the rest of earths inhabitants, to be torched bt every imaginable demon in hell for the rest of eternity. An appropriate outcome for the full falure of an entire species. Because of her actions, her self-sacrifice to Huehueteotl, the senior deity of the ancient Aztec, our universe will not collapse into infinite unending hell realms. As you noticed at the ferry terminal in Bellingham, the sun still rose. But it very well could not have."

"After the sacrificial flame was reignited, in that moment when Catherine touched everyone, she told them she would carry it for them, all their pain and suffering, and they released it to her. She dissolved it and at that moment she saw further, like the ant on the stick seeing the one holding it, the writer righting, turning the wheel round and round ad infinitum. She saw the oroborus and rewrote it… or saw who would, and take it further; be the guide, write the new guide and evolve the New Eden virus into the Riddle Solver virus.

He spoke something then, a different language that Aum had never heard of, sounding alien.

The man paused briefly after, translating the words for Aum, "Go pure. Live strong. Inside the Sun. And forever exist in a state of rejoice, since the house of the Sun is a place of pure joy.

"Within the current paradigm of false omnipotence sacrifices were required and efforts made, for this container of truth to maintain prolonged integrity, without implosion, without investigation, before it can fully explode out into the world."

Aum lept quickly, "When will that be?"

"Now.

"That is why you are here. To twist the orobourus serpent.

"The Riddle Solver is a book you will write; a source code spell written into a viral media tome offering and Cat is the one that linked this work, with her death, to an invocation of planetary nirvana, resurrecting a new world outside of the patterns of socio-cultural reincarnation. You will return to the city, return home, and write a book about all that you've seen. All that you've learned."

"Shit! You were actually serious? The Riddle Solver is a book?"

"Yes."

"It's a book I'm going to write?!"

"Yes."

"Next you're gonna say we're already inside it."

"We are."

"What? So then this conversation is being read right now?"

"It is."

Aum started laughing in disbelief and the ghost continued, "We are conversing, being read and being written in a shared once; a quantum bridge moment. It is the next level of complexity; life emerging from a being; a purposeful creative soul essence manifest as a piece of meta literature in the field of time. As an external narrative it can move beyond the bounds of human body into the hardwire datasphere, beyond the bounds of a single mind into the collective consciousness, resonating as an intention of belief and immortal soul self. A doorway never to be destroyed.

Aum shook his head, "If I was reading this book now, I might get freaked out and put it down."

He tilted his head, "You don't think a story ending by it achieving it's own self awareness and transforming the reality of the reader is a very fulfilling ending? Isn't that what stories are for?"

"I dunno, maybe. It might be a more peaceful wrap up if I just wake up from a dream at the end of the chapter, and found myself in bed next to Jenn after dancing all night long, after being told I'm dead."

"Really? You're sure that wouldn't be the most anti-climactic and unfulfilling ending ever?" He looked at Aum, gaze amped, "Besides… you *are* dead."

"What!?"

"You are the Riddle Solver and you are dead."

"You're joking…"

"No, I'm not. You took the Hemlock, just as Socrates did. You are dead Aum. And, since you are dead, and have a achieved the formalization of a self-aware soul consciousness inside a realm of interstitial afterlife, you can go anywhere. You can wake up next to Jenn, in the space and state you were in numerous months ago, or even further, if you like; years ago, before you had even heard of the Riddle, and try it all over again, or even do it all differently. But the path mapped by the insight of Cat is planetary resurrection, and the writing in of a next level human future story, anchored inside the wisdom space beyond death."

"Bullshit."

"What?!" the guru was shocked.

"You heard me. I said this is bullshit."

The 6-D post-death pod cracked a bit, "No, really, you're dead. Look." A new window opened up and it showed Aum's body inside the Shamans tent, lying next to the fire, not breathing, lifeless, a white, red and black fabric draped over him, as if a corpse."

"Whatever," Aum stated powerfully. He began to pace about, doubting the projected vision. He did not see the highest potential truth within it, this future line, resonating. Aum spoke out, "That could be footage of the life I was living. It could be a parallel dimension. An alternate reality. It could be a dream I'm having, or even a dream you're having. We are inside a singularity vortex, and you have infinite time, space, and matter, infinite codeless source with which you can construct into anything in a single heartbeat, a single firing of a single neuron. Why should I trust you? Writing a book? Was that really Cat's idea? Or yours?"

"It was the one that had collectively arisen."

"Collectively arisen?... Though it may be agreed upon by all, that doesn't sound very far reaching. Doesn't it take individual ingenuity to self mutate, even self sacrifice, to reach the next level? What would Anna Magnum think about this collectively risen future path of resurrection and spell writing? Given the chance would she still support her own founding lineage of death?"

The ghost gapped for a second, then recovered, "What?"

"You heard me. What would Anna say about this plan?"

The Riddle Master still didn't speak.

Aum continued, "If I'm dead, within the singularity vortex, pre-big bang outside of time and space, a personality of collected memories, only because that's what was last resonant in my soul, others should be here too, all those who have shed their bodily casings, including all that have self-immolated, including the first, who has allowed New Ediru, and thus this space, to even exist."

He still did not respond.

In a flash of insight Aum spoke, "I request the council of Anna Magnum."

It was if the words were a magic spell. A heartfelt request that could not be denied or ignored; a connection that would benefit the whole, and help revise the programming circuit that spanned the energetic breadth of multiple decades, the planet, and it's future.

The guru began to transform from Jenn to Trae to Demona, to the Shaman.

"Deeper!"

The Shaman to Sophia to Cat.

"I said Deeper!" he yelled, demanding the time space-bend in full force, a more than human power, as if himself, were god-like.

And then finally, from Cat to Anna Magnum.

A million white Taras formed in front of him; Quan Yin's of all sizes and shapes, holding mudra greetings of kindness and instant healing, mending all the aching angry bits in him he had forgotten, or had never seen. Halos and compassionate water poured infinitely over his body, mind, and soul: a comfort to bathe in.

Her windswept tapestries clothed her glowing form, embodying the essence of the ancient ones, carved out in living stone for generations: the profound time keepers. She fed masculine dragon underfoot and winked through feather, fire and sun, ever patient and perfectly timed with the cosmological clock spinning, planets as a flowing one-sounded sync click. From her chalice was the ocean itself, soothing the fires of rebirth, while on boat and turtle traveling, her peaceful visage giving always, endlessly.

At this sight, and feeling, Aum began weeping, head bowed, down on one knee, feeling as if on fire. Like the kids in the elevator he was humbled to the point of offering her his life, for whatever use best served her holy work. He didn't realize or expect what the experience of meeting a true Goddess would be like; this was certainly it though. She sparkled, and was the collected vibrational embodiment of all compassion that ever existed. All maimed and sick, with lost limb, tormented and broken, gutted, guttered and homeless, with the malformed distorted speech of prolonged karmic maiming, laceration and deformity, she loved all unconditionally. Every black shadow that filtered the light looking for each bright eye, she collected, she addressed, along with the sad and alone, depressed and hurting, "May you all find the comfort you need and deserve." She continued, "With empowered choice, compassion, and love for self, it is only the sole shadow inside you that you must account for, no more."

Within the scaly planetary folds of the timeless dragon under her feet, Aum saw all acts of atrocity, all murderers, all genocidal engineering enactors, all pedophiles and rapists, and underneath them each of the bruised and beaten women and children they've claimed. The Dragon was the Earth and it was Hell, and Aum instantly forgot the words she last spoke.

He saw all forms of soul-control, the incoherent randomized profit margins of pyramid builders, mischievous and dastardly with determined dementia, all malevolent violent disguised, untrustworthy addicts and manipulators. "I see you. I see you all," Aum said, it echoed out of him while inside the belly and the deep dragon flame; a Buddha-punk anger. His hair grew long in length, curled, and a crescent moon instantly formed on his forehead.

She quickly quelled this fire with the water of temperance inside her voice, "This world, Earth, is where we come to release our shadows, shed all that, to be clear of all that, forever. That poison. We incarnate to clean ourselves and exist as sentient millennial multidimensional creatures, eventually, and with finality, making it to immortality inside the timeless, inside the body."

Aum sneered as he began to move the dragon with the simple and effortless motion of a hand, words emerged from the steam and flame inside him, "That is where we are going! Do you hear her? Shed you soulless skins of garbage now!" He shouted at them like a deaf crazy person. Anna Magnum continued, overtaking his directional and inquisitory god-blast from the quantum real-time. After she caressed the top of his head with her saintly hand, she turned to look at Aum, "It is up to them to decide their own fate, and not up to us to be their spiritual court masters." She spoke to them all, inside the hell folds, "You can stay, in dead-eyed suffering, forever, if you like."

And through a bath of compassionate waterfalls and an enlightened globe, the machine like dragon changed to feminine phoenix.

"Taoist leanings must be expressed truthfully." Her smile was golden-white, "Inside the blackest night of human culture is light – if even just the historical story based context."

And the phoenix flew, and spread.

And then it was just the two of them.

Each of her 22 eyes gazed upon Aum, on 11 heads, and a thousand arms embraced him, lifting him, and all those up to stand who were still kneeling.

"Why do you weep my child?" She asked him.

"I apologize, for asking you here, to show yourself, disturbing you, requiring your council on my infinitesimal actions and puzzling future." He looked up at her face, and the compassion within in, "I do not understand why so many chose to die…" and he found the clarity of his ask, "… for a written novel to be the Riddle Solver."

"It is not a novel, it is a new story. Ancient grace of communal solar poetics are immortal, encoding new mythics into time.

"It is not a novel, but a collection of novel ideas, lived. That must continue to live. You must write this book Aum. The deepest grimoiric mysticological pills come from raw dream pieces bared, the inner most soul expressed without planning or cognizant context, for with ultimate pre-nascence there is an unbound inner ecology to draw upon. Not a spell book, but an oracle pool, reflecting.

"The ongoing developmental nature of future narrative is a process of pulling from the furthest outskirts of imagination and inspiration; constructing situations, containers, possibilities for insight to emerge from a set of human characteristics, intuiting reactions and qualities of a holographic shard of self, philosophizing imagined outcomes when those shards are thrown into an unknown situation; circumstances that cannot be controlled or understood. And what is left is the journey, into understanding.

"The advancement of literature, has always been, and will continue to be entwined with technocracy. All fiction is now a nested package; a gathering nodal point of cultural reference where story becomes more similar to the structure of non-fiction. Each reference acts as a gateway to deeper study, and also a found representation resonating of what is: a token of our collective human expression.

New, contemporary stories are required. Telling them, a gateway to the evolved collective imagination. No different than in the past, but now an instant digital reflection. Using a search engine, a tool now engrained in our post-human operating system, assists in understand mythical word or historical concepts, quickly ascertaining the activation level of visionary trailheads for the inquisitive and curious. Each trailhead a pocket of data, like a seed that contains each aspect of the tree; new branch pathway, leaves for catching light, harvested into fruit, and within the fruits hundreds of more seeds.

"Physical copies of narrative exist only for specialized collectors, wizards and historical librarians, knowing that the power of each specialized reference is encoded within the word and language of unbound pre-Cambrian data ponds, presently manifested as the DNA of the printed page itself. Collectively understood history can be remixed, as always, though in this state of foundational quaking, fully rewritten."

Her soft clothes billowed and flowed in accord and conjunction with the timeless, "As a character in a story how do you go about affecting change within a layer beyond what you're able to perceive, interacting with being both written and read; a rainbow beam streaming from one mind to another, to another, to another, building a resonating network holding dreamwalking space."

"...a book though?"

"Reading activates the mind and births new consciousness into the body, whereas screen media erases it, remixes it, dissolves it. Like a blind pilot with false memories, false dreams, implanted and embedded from within the controlled corporate media grid; it's stories, and even its hardware devices hold mythic blockages. It is the far running stasis that overlays everything, a 'prison code' that is embedded within matter, deadening individual conscious awareness.

"Growth requires time and proper conditions. A barred temporary feedback stoppage, so the seed can grow, without the influence of a communal everything, destabilizing and distracting from a specific path of growth. And now we no longer even need the containment of that prison code, in fact we will all die if it continues to run."

"The Riddle Solver will dissolve the prison code?"

As if it was a single sentence she continued, "With it's new encoding of unconditional love you will..." She looked into his eyes,

"…Yes…," and her pristinely glowing words sang to each part of his soul that he could not yet see, the parts of his soul that were not yet listening, "…and be reborn.

I have watched you the entire way, as so many have. You are generous and in service of everyone around you, you are a good listener and you don't mask your presence with games, even though it is all a game. Everyone looks up to your actions and how you hold yourself. You're smile lights up the room Jerome, and people feel good just by be being around you. They feel relaxed, in your authentic and zany honesty, completely at ease, and equally ready to express their most deepest secrets and cherished desires. That's a pretty good trait to have, and anyone who develops this kind of character must understand how conscious they need to be while holding in this exemplary position in the lives of others around them. Leading the magic your lived truth can inspire individuals to reach and achieve things that they never could have thought to imagine otherwise.

And if you can understand what the under wiring vibratory nature of what this inspiration is made of, what thought is made of, what time and space is made of, speaking incantations and engineering the imagined into form, and you can understand what technology is; if you can intake every single experience and successfully describe what it is and understand why it is necessary as part of your individual journey, and the collective journey; and if you can understand that all you can do in life, as an artist, as a magician, as a creator, is leave something behind for others, in the field of time, why not reach as deep as you can, and make it the most pure and impactful action one could ever imagine creating. This is what you have done, are doing, and will do.

If you are able to cause a paradigm shift with your word alone, why not spark the messianic flame of liberation, of total transformation of Christ Consciousness within what is being read right now. Demand it."

Aum was taken aback. He was a man. As far as he knew he had not yet reached full deity status, let alone ascended master. A man. A two-legged. His curly hair tightened and the crescent moon on his forehead nearly vanished.

"Humble and selfless and strong," she added compassionately, seeing his instant transformation.

"Christ's consciousness demonstrated it's enlightened aramaic teachings experientially, in order for the lessons to be understood," Aum said, "he didn't write out the lessons of the gospels, let alonge translate them."

"He did write them though. He created the story, the new platform of mythics. He lived out the lessons. Just as you live out these lessons." She added, "On the quantum level there are no differences between the lesson and the lesson plan, only between a student that understands and a student who does not. There are no differences between the memories of the experience, and the experience itself. The same can be said for story. An experience you read about is the same as an experience you've had, a movie you've watched is no different than a life you've lived. A conversation you've had on the Boards is still a conversation you've had. And a person you've loved is no different than a reflection of your self.

"Jesus understood the long term under wiring, the vibratory nature of time and space, and that is why the path opened up in front of him that did. His story remains inside all of culture at this point. That's what happens when you sacrifice yourself, taking on the imperfections of all consciousness so a growing species can reach any imagined heaven. Considering the depth of faith and trust his story expunges from his devoted followers, considering what he endured, he would have most likely taken into deep consideration what his actions and eventually his self sacrifice would mean to those in the future."

"But did you?" Aum asked Anna.

The light from Anna, the Quan Yin angel, faded. She instantly became Anna the woman, the social scientist, the cultural engineer, "I am still meditating on that one myself ... Creation from destruction. Life from death…Paradox… as you know…" She gracefully continued over the gap, shimmering, beginning to find a new face, "With this work you will create, with this book, this expression and facilitation of this moment, you will leap from death to life, into a world of psychic interaction unbound by the laws of time and space, spreading this esoteric visionary knowledge." She motioned to the post-death space and began to transform into Aum, into his reflection, "The nature of dreamtime; any and all data that you need for your spiritual journey, through this quantum physical space can be accessed now; this transformation from you, by you, to you, for you, for which this exact moment is a trigger," the words echoed in the cave, "The intention behind all visionary art is to allow humanity to reach beyond what we previously were capable of imagining, a space we never thought possible, but always deeply and essentially understand our souls. From here, this moment, this moment, anything is possible. Just like every moment."

The two Aum's stared at each other without moving.

"I am not returning home."

He looked through his own eyes to re-find him 'self' in another, moving from one body to another.

"For in this moment exists every notion of home, and home is simply an authentic connection to true self, untied to the comfort of ego, a path walked continuously aware." He looked deeper and moved further into the exchange. "I'm not going back. Only forward."

"What are you saying?"

"I'm not going back to that mono-culture, to the failed crumbling city-state, to the deadened ecological mess of a path our species has chosen. It's a world that has ended. And a level of humanity that is now extinct." He said this as spaceships zoomed passed his head, and Aum accelerated up to the next level of quantum engagement, "It is the act of writing which is the fresh spark of imagination. Reading is the echo in consciousness: the sparking of more imaginations erupting, and the story simply a vehicle in which to ride the echoing waves of change. If, in fact, we've already achieved a level of self-aware dimensionality in a meta contextual timeline, then why would we travel back down into that old dimension, and publishes a book there? Trying to save a world that has already died."

His reflection became blocky, pixilated, torn. Parts of Anna, even the guru ghost- maker blended together. A reflection emerged he could see. A crescent moon on his forehead glowing as bright as the moon itself, a woven necklace of skulls and skins and cobra and dragon hung around his neck, trident and deer and drum in hand, bull at his side and river flowing from his mind. The god-form spoke, "You can choose that here. However I see the karmic path that has been designed for you, and after exiting this moment of singularity, of all dimensional possibilities, your path is to return to your life, return to the city, return home, to write this tale out as a book, and ignite the

Riddle Solver with a lineage-link to the sacred etheric fire of New Eden."

"No. Fuck that. I'm not linking to that sacrificial circuit. Within this quantum timeline and awareness, for it to already exist, I don't need to go back and write it, or even l ink to those pre-quantum efforts. From inside this perspective, the book is already written, being read, shared, and the historic change already complete."

"You're dead though, and resurrection back into a timeline, regardless of what kind: linear, non-local, viral or quantum, is an act and path that will determine the fate of the entire world as you know it."

"The world determines it's own fate. You've said this. It is a choice made by all. And I choose to continued on, past the found, past the easy answers, always moving within the opportunity to grow and know each deeper layer of the sacred unknown, stepping into the life before me as mystery upon mystery and riddle within riddle, 'cause that is what is. I will not loop this back on itself but breakthrough into the new, destroying all preconceived notions of what is possible, and thus watch with the most open eyes possible, that creative intention ripple out," Aum laughed and spoke sarcastically to himself, "Travel back to the city and write a book - that's hilarious. Like it can be over or something, concluded in a neat and organized way. Why should I walk an easy path of a self-contained cultural template; immortal underground or counter-cultural ascension, when I can move as an engine of solution, leaving an enigmatic life path legacy to be imbibed and pondered upon: sip or sight at the oracular pool. To give. To give it all up, re-find the base line and sacrifice everything for evolution at all costs, dissolving all preconceived socially historic notions of what life is, or what it should be, and inside that calm bodhisatvic path, with total transparent integrity of no masks and no shadows anywhere, find the karmic balance of pure Samadhi."

He was dissolving, and in the strange flip that was happening, he was beginning to see his point of observation, becoming anchored into this singularity vortex. His reflection, the man he was talking to, as he spoke, was becoming the man that appeared through the shamans medicine touch, and the man who would soon leave.

"You have found it. And have won your truest future freedom," he said.

"It's about time."

"Now you must live with the decisions you have made, on this level of you, and you, and you, and on the level of the unified whole. It is time to look at every single one of those actions and accept them, and keep on moving in a way that shows that you are an active participant."

"I will not fade this out, like an easily digestible po-mo pulp fiction pop ballad, but explode it, as the sun surely will someday explode, like 10,000 thundering atomic bombs, inside the collective imagination."

He smiled, "I can already see the headlines: Quantum explosion inside fictional micro-utopia averts planetary catastrophe."

Aum, his reflection, smiled back, fading like an evaporated liquid drop of consciousness out of the singularity vortex. He watched his spirit, grounded in prayer and intention, move from one dream to the next.

Chapter Thirteen

'Finally arriving at this day, I'm gonna have to approach this one, and circle in attempt after attempt after attempt, towards ever a clean drop and dollop of precisely timed and executed calligraphic penmanship.'

Inside rolling thoughts, he wasn't back in his body yet, but he finally felt aware of his edges.

His mind continued to talk to him, 'In deep review, invoking reflections of the new, and spaces that birth visions beyond the cusp, finally arriving at this day.

'I find myself inside it, entwined in emotions. I hear the full cheers of 10,000, nay 144,000 voices, in the celebration of finally making it. It is a sacred inner knowing of what is happening, what has happened, and will happen: the definition of conscious cognitive spaces, and a new understanding harnessed. Relief. There is a sense of relief that we finally made it, and opened the gate for celebration. Finding solidarity in exponential time, infinity within a present undistracted awareness and a communion with soul, and Gaia, and God. That's why most everything else seems like a waste of time: because it is. Media time flatteners, sensation compactors, and imagination guiders. A full breadth of reflection, with many trying to infuse the collective with one last program before it goes singular. Even all moments of movement in body, existing as an amped reflection of new consciousness. A fractal infusion of awareness, like petals of enlightenment blossoming on each sensitive surface

'The fickle shared mind breathes, deeply exhales in relief. True omnipotence. Let's tune it up now. Increase our purpose determined by insightful demands from a new civilization. Filtered down through the crystalline buildings of light on an amped Earth. Restructuralizing the grid in real-time, not just dream time, but a full breadth of reflection. Infinite gateways in every glance. Solitude invoking real time memory reference to boost appreciation, and build new dreams. Esoteric launch sequence of unmitigated proportions.

'Pause for meditation.

'Receive more soul path instructions.'

He finally felt the breath move through his nose into his lungs, as if it was the first day of his life. In his mind he meditated deeply on potential pathways, tree branches to climb. He felt tingling all over his skin. He observed the sensation, believing it to be the release of lateral energy coming to the surface. He pushed on through his vision travels, mapping each corridor of possibility, certain to find his conscious manifest destiny and the most true way.

After much meta soul deliberation on the woven, dream-like path, he returned to his senses. With toe tip wiggle and finger flex, he slowly moved his body, rolling and preparing to stand and rejoin the world.

He opened his eyes to find himself covered in ash. He was a little shocked, but mostly thankful at receiving this omen. It somehow strengthened the potency of his vision, understanding his path to be even more true. The white and red and black blanket was on him, and he was still inside the teepee, though the fire was out, and he was alone, but all that he needed was now inside him. There was a last voice that spoke inside of his mind as he moved to stand, different, but it was still his own, "Your receptivity is exceptional, and your endurance is everlasting. Make it count Aum."

With each breath he found ultra-acumen while intoning harmonies internal and external with no boundaries. *Clip clap*, went the sonic living creatures that surrounded him as each future sequence became already a foregone conclusion. What will the future hold? Love above all else. That is what reality will be constructed from. Every nut and bolt, thought and node of connection – one of love. Breakdown all walls to this future – creating heart pulse woven into blanket and basket, for warmth, and to carry nourishment.

He was out of the Teepee, gazing at a city that he had never before seen; the heavens manifested on earth, timeless generations far beyond New Eden (and the grass didn't even hurt his feet).

Herald approached him from his left, with an immense crowd of souls behind him, climbing the ridge as he once did. He had a didge in his hand. He knelt and offered it to him like he would a sword, "My lord."

"What?"

"Somnium."

Aum realized he was wearing only a loincloth and his hair was long now, bangs tied back like a bulbing halo of resurrected light. As he looked at Herald, holding the didge, snakes slithered around his biceps and forearms. He looked to the crowd and the snakes vibrated out into pure sound. It was a vast new ecology where the sun must have shone differently, because in this new world, he could see his skin was tinted a sky blue. His third eye opened further and he brought his hands together, one clap, a single exploding prayer of color, and, like thundering fireworks, it unified all attention.

Gently, as if a living entity, Aum took the didge from Herald, "The great unity movement leaps forward."

And as he walked Aum himself parted the oceans of onlookers, living and dead, there was no longer a difference between the two. Aum had brought with him the 6D flux space of non-time-non-space, piping in a direct channel from the singularity vortex wherever he went, an embodied satellite and inside the saintly robes of a deity, John deGryder parted the sea of souls on his right, approaching Aum.

As if the first yogi perched continuously at the edge of the conscious universe, Aum spoke out to him, "I request the third sounding of the chakarasa mantra."

"Granted and blessed Sahosant. We made it. Finally."

As if masters meeting on the astral plane, their powerful gaze connected in the fullest present. Decades passed inside the magnetic bridge, as if all consciousness moved from confusion, to understanding, to finally recognition of the Self behind the veil, achieving highest purpose beyond linear story.

Then his team was there, encircling them. All immediate kin followed by the deepest lineage of anscestors and angelic guides. Zhe and Trae, Derek and Demona, Zeke and Dan, Cat and Toumai, Carey and Ted. Even Dennis showed himself in the crowd, layers back. He bowed, in frightened reverence, as Aum caught his glance out of the corner of his broad attention span – none further than Aum.

John stepped back to reveal Jenn.

Aum paused deeply to see her, to look at her, and she shook her head in awe-inspired belief and open-eyed certainty, looking at him as if he was standing again, naked in the river, but with all insecurities washed away, only power and poised remained.

She spoke to him, “Continue your breaking through, and sharing of the other side, drinking in all the sacred memory of a being that once was, and that has always been.”

“Chiti shakti om ultra yogini,” Aum responded in his fullest gaze she stood, unflinching. She was able to meet it as no one else had. And he bowed to her.

And they all saw him walk into the beyond, as he always did, and was always meant to do. From link between soul spirits, open heart and open eye, words emerged. Spoken or thought or channeled, there was no difference. They all followed.

“The deepest prayers I could ever intone, celestial alignment and accord doubtless, as a human, a new human - standing – on the mount of testament; lived values, seeking breach into the new. I hereby invoke the most profound footsteps into divine incarnation and it’s believable being; awareness of the infinite play, and it's playfulness.

I pray deep prayers for the grace to let it be, emerge on it's own accord, like life, a new sentience of astral grace being.

Shaking down the skins of the old world, and all that is known and pre conceived – it all changes so fast beyond capture tech and context – only the lessons of what was, remain, where all efforts re-align and go toward repair and life path consistence, from hospital to highway and worldy birth to death.”

He continued to walk and the crowd followed, continuing to listen.

Aum contemplated, “The Riddle Solver is a novel: a collection of novel ideas. Bound together by will and intention - if that’s the true case, I place within the ink of these words, the paper that binds this universe together, I place into the hands and minds that hold this object; eyes that absorb this text, to become the hands, minds, and eyes, that activate God consciousness in all they see, in all that they do, and in all that they are: to become the nodal network of infinite ones that affect the highest change in reality and dismantle every unjust institution. With conscious and deliberate intent and quantum dimensional will, I even place this collection of novel ideas into the hands of all that now hold it, giving the potent medicinal brew asked and longed for. Remember always, you can never be defeated.

"In sequence, each beat, a pulse beyond divine symphony. Gaian divine, craft these new lives in holy accord with contientious awareness. All who imbibe this work. Bless them with eagle eyes to see inside each moment and the strong and compassionate hearts needed to discern peace within right and wrong, ego and source, the human truth, and most of all the swift function of prayer in hyper dimensional space, as it all exists now."

Cause without context, Aum saw all masters and saints dive back further, because they all grow with the meta work too, mapping the further paths of concordance and ascension, poured, or in droplet after droplet, dollop after dollop, into ongoing linear time. Their presence was of unshakable faith that linearity and right livelihood will emerge and be revealed as timeless dreams lived in bliss and love – anchored in the slow compassionate present strides of unknowing.

The unity movement requires random agents of change, magnetized to the swift stepping through into the new way of the edge. Which they had done. Which he had done, tried to find this step simply. Though whether it is blindly found or not, there is no real finding, and no real searching, until the ever present is found. Hilarious that it is all in this linear format that must ebb and flow and make sense and reflect the world – rather than reflect the internal present of the all, and infinite. In that change, it's all right here – surfing the mystic gates, flooded open with insight.

He continued walking up, toward the peak of a mountain top, soul tsunami trailing, where the framework of an open teepee had been built – just it's pillars constructed. It acted as broadcast mechanism, on the mountaintop, like a mathematically perfect pyramid.

"He's here!"

Aum heard a shout and it all formalized as he approached, the final touches bent into form as if an oiled machine clicking into place as he gazed at it.

There was a huge crowd surrounding the Teepee. The 144,000.

"Ignite the prestructure!" someone shouted.

It was as if, until now, the crowd had been put on pause, waiting for the downbeat to kick back in. Then it did, and the mountains shook with bass and the crowd erupted with cheers, they danced until they flew, as he had taught them. The wave rebounded off the pyramid structure and hit Aum, and he smiled, and he found his way to the cusp of the swirling pool of tsunami, like always.

This crowd too parted as he walked toward the monument, leading another 10,000, at least, and in the divine flow they merged as if long lost relatives and lovers, sacred kin beyond timelines and paths of incarnated karmas.

He wove his way through the dancing souls to see a mandala of performing creatures and carcitures enmeshed inside the quantum teepee framework, the mountain top pyramid, as if Cat had facilitated it's construction herself. Maybe she did. From close up, he could see each metal beam was thincker than his entire body, It was big enough to house 74, at least. Every performers gaze, each of the 74 was welcoming, and open to wherever he wanted to sit and whenever he wanted to begin. Some were surprised at what he carried, some joyus, some shocked into deeper awareness of the sublime. All had heard the legend of Somnium, and what it's playing meant.

On the inside of the pyramid the outer mandala compass was set to eight. Four directions, and then interspersing that, another four directions. At the bottom of each teepee pole there were circular mats, and on them a bouncing, dancing, living percussionists. One wore an eagle mask, one a jaguar, one a bull, and one a coyote mask.

Within the north circle the first performer sat at rock n' roll jungle kit, comprised mostly of symbols and gongs, the next, at the south circle,the percussionist danced on rows upon row of marimbas; from African to modern to electronic, the third, east, was on Koto drum, surrounded by sets of additional congas, tablas and dhols. And the last drummer, in the west direction played a laptop that was controlled by a full set of electronic drum kit pads. Like all live music, these four held the dance floor down with their precise timing and intuitive internal clocks – their hearts pulsing through their fingertips.

In between teepee poles were four tables covered in gear. They were constructing, amping and broadcasting this living source signal, translating drum roll, fat snare and techno kick along with juicy grins, worldy love and buddhic balance of being into a living embodiment of all knowable truths; digitizing each found structure to build their sailing arc upon.

"Open up the gates!" one shouted at the table. The beams of the teepee hummed as additional screens lit up and allowed in a streaming signal from the corporate boards and the entire world wide web itself.

Each human being became a terminal, like an earth nerve ending, and the web was the fluid motion of chemical neurotransmitters between human synaptic axon.

Seraphim and master hackers jumped the gates, to and from data depositories, as if deGryder's FreeData program was a trojan horse for a third generation app upgrade. They moved with intellectual authenticity and intuitive leaping understanding.

These ancient ones had never known a world of Youtube or Google or Facebook, Twitter, Tumbler, Myspace or Friendster. The last search engine they used was Lycos and the last browser Netscape; the first of the first, to colonize the new world. These ancient ones had gracefully bypassed the commercialization of every facet of the invisible interneted spaces, it's comodification and infusion of relentless sales pitches and marketing within marketing within marketing, ruining it for everyone forever.

Every single one in the circle was a programmer of OG proportions – like the collective inventors of the computer itself – As a group of off grid cybernetic scientists this was their foundational lineage and purpose, where every action remapped participation as a full structural remix. The solid foundation state was one of knowing each keystroke as a change of the whole, which each of them could see and feel. It wasn't moving from link to link to link in a woven thread of reflective karma manifested inside of eyes, but they were the computers themselves. Their insides, operating systems, and control interface were a direct reflection of their home pod ecology, every surface customized, every keyboard and mouse hacked apart and re-grown from the pieces, and even here there were the metemosis of ancestors; of mind and thought and internal gateway, to a flipside code source, they were all inside of it.

The deeper infrastructure of the Free Data framework was like a screen door for these wizards who could disassemble their molecules and pass through its holes. It was nothing to them, it was like breathing.

And then the kids, the brightest ones that talk directly to the sun and angels, felt the signal on the dancefloor and rallied together in nimble focus as the feedback loop of the entire New Eridu civilization was translated into a broadcast signal, and began working on every geometrical layer, waking everyone up around the globe. Synch, synch, synch, circuit, synch, synch, synch, circuit, synch, synch, synch, circuit, in train-like locomotion.

On the other end, in perfect timing, each human axion grabbed their instrument, and began beaming themselves into the 5D, whether with ukuleles or mandolins, at their pianos or penny whistles, they pointed their handheld lenses and mics at them, and contributed to the live dialogue they felt erupting within. Some even pulled out their hacked apart handhelds, deep past collapse in the underground; the abandoned malls and caves and forests, where the dance was happening, even there, linking the real-time signal to the physical-non-physical whole. At the terminals some were sampling and integrating the live incoming feed, others were sampling and integrating the live outgoing feed: a shymphony beyond notopns of entropy or cohesion. Aum was the largest satellite axion in this new world, the bridge holder between, they all found each other because of him, and around the globe they all heard the sound of unity, and those who couldn't, were about to.

With Somnium, Aum found his way past this outer mandala circle of drummers and programmers, in synch and in time with the global signal. Ears began to hear what he did. The next circle was eight djembe players – rhythmic structure spiraling out and out and out through them and their communal fingertip dance. These players were sampled as well, though beyond audio, it was their pure data code and color that was being honed and harnessed and translated into living intelligent pulse, lighter in the mix than their earthen drum pounding brethren.

Past the eight, the inner sphere was a council of six didge players, all pulsing out vibratory rhythms in ancient dialogue. This was still a self-contained council, which awaited the precise moment of spotlight. They pointed to the very centre, which was not a firepit with sacred flame blazing, but a crystallized altar, and on it the black box of obsidian.

When Aum saw it every feedbacking tendril of sound within sound found a strong preliminary meshwork, like the first ever hand clasp bind. With the glance, humanity itself held the world together.

He looked up and saw they had reached the galactic centre.

The calendars end.

The earth began to move through a 5D macro-sieve where all impurities would be removed, just as Cat, with her powerful intention, had sucked the unconscious out of all who looked at her, so to, did this Hunab Ku.

And they all saw what he saw, and that their role was only an infinitesimal part of a much greater story - the finest details of which none had the capacity to understand.

He found an opening, bringing six to seven, and put the didge to his mouth and closed his eyes. He pointed it at the black cube and it pulled a low pulse out of his lungs, out of his ancient shaman spirit. The tactic opened the whole to this inner sphere, and the eclectic knowledge emitted. As he pushed his tongue to the roof of his mouth, he could taste a sweetness like no other, as once did the first man who so loved the world.

In the void of change, the calendars end, the authentic cracks in time provided the new to imbibe – quiet, further out, minimal soul paths as a single silent arrow moving through a shotgun blast; randomized, brutish and domineering in comparison. A tounge lashing, the magnets of gate and grace opened, fortuitous leaping, seeking juxtaposed tuning fork tines applied to stretched body and mind, fetching blessed reckonings inside the gap of change. Somnium instantly took him, and all of them, beyond sound into the contents and lessons within the vibration.

The codeless source pattern formed into something brand new, a shared council dialogue that was far beyond the group mind of spoken out, from mouth in time, to where every thought was known and shared and somehow coalesced into the tangible and understood.

And some prayed for the mountains to fall on them as all witnessed the ebb and flow from turmoil to elation as an unimaginably crucifying sea, moving back and forth, future casting unified oneness inside the resonant. Each had to choose the immortal knowable which decides future fates, inspirational break, or now, the erratic jumps of an abridged amplified mind of all potentials, to sleep, or die, or land inside a world of the unreal, where all is forever undefined.

Inside the vibe, live and live – enlivened and amped message tech elevated each stair step and ladder up, as so much shook up the atomic furnace feeding steam to the stream, courageous dreams past mal seeking *Phoenician* beings, who don't want to move to the next state, next stage, cause the gate will close on this and timelessness will come back into existence – and course of action must be designed along each stream and stride, in time. Kindness for self and selves, outside of body into the bigger adventure. Each pattern an echo of remembrance bringing the quantum past into the immediate to influence the present. Never do anything twice.

Through air and water, soil and cement, rubber and skin, Aum could place a blue thumbprint on the forehead of anyone in the world not looking, and bring them there, in the space of whatever thou desirest to see.

They were all inside the moment of an entire species transmutating, or dying. Not only did they have to look at their own individual personal mistakes and triumphs, their accomplishments and disasters throughout their life, but those of their entire culture throughout it's entire evolution.

In that moment the capacity to emotionally feel pain and pleasure expanded to a level of such raw and visceral awe, it intrinsically signaled the true and final death of Apasmara, and all affiliated demons of ignorance. Those that could not, accept and awaken, while looking at the deepest view of themselves, screamed in pain and horror. A sound that only amplified the vibration that coursed through the planet, as it shed and shook off a layer of dead skin.

It was a pain of seeing like no other. Every internal blemish was brought to light and nothing else was allowed to be seen. This caused heartbreak; heart wrenching nervous breakdown inducing heart break. Nothing was the same after each pocket of learning curve had been seen; after each shockwave, bump and ripple felt, nothing could be done other than accept the pain of seeing the truth and learning from it, no matter how challenging, how difficult, and how painful.

And as the unbound fire and freedom tore down the veils without compromise, for those ready and those not, all reached the edge of a new planetary understanding, and a new Gaian launch platform - star body consistent and solidified, metamorphed, into the real.

First, every moment was an unprotected intimacy with the essence inside each action, purpose and intention, or lack thereof. Second, each heliographic shard of expression, seeing into each creative intention, was a reflection of the lessons of alignment and soul path ask. And third, each en-spirited soul dollop was a gateway to the space behind it, where the real and true karmic conversation was happening, caught in the complex community net, global sight seen with eyes inside the techno media evermore. Then after that, the 4th, the subtle home dimensions encircled, where the continous flux of grid pulse is real and the divine never stops. The ghosts and gods and guides come alive, who speak and offer council. Living in the unanimous and constant medicine space where breath and balanced mind is the medicine. Once seen, all returned to the sound of civilization letting go.

Aum continued to exist as that sound, as every being released and refound vision of what species it is we are; our place and purpose, not being told by our distorted reflections: corporations, marketing teams or politicians, nor even being told by scientists, poets and artists, but choosing it solely as an inner light beacon of the entire glowing rainbow tapestry. And when that was found, every being planted it deep, a seed that would grow for 700 generations to come.

"You should all be on fire by now," Aum said through his mouthpiece, his fingertips finding all others. Every intoned breath was one that lit up each new inner layer moving to the surface, as the old skin was shed – torn off in glee, in some cases, pain. Here we are, raw. Continuous. And seeing everything. It took a while to recoup from this dizzying view – like imbibing rocket fuel, launching, exploding and then actually lifting off. Central to the broadcast he was not at the top pinnacle but simply a node within the elaborate mandalic meshwork of the galactic black hole. First to the newest edge every time, and at the same time, the last to leave it. Vestigial clouodhopper acronyms hold no bounds amongst the circumferential compass holders of the Nth dimension; he pulsed it as if the waves were vehicles to ride in, ladders to climb upon, and rope swings to speed gleefully through the sky on, bypassing gravity.

Aum was now shaking too, as he continued to play out all that he had within him, all that he brought from the old world and the new. He was not a master planetary healer working over the world, but a man in it, with all them. Maybe leading the depth field charge, through feel, field master maybe, thus enduring the most excruciating pain, seeing the most of all. Every note, every sound, every spoken word was a scorching blistering spec of being and presence – asked for, or not, it was there. Inside every new voice everything was heard, unencumbered and honest.

In the edge space of the total dissolution of the all, every ache and pain was reflected on every surface. Howls of incoherence and communication breakdown were in the sirens that blasted out, piercing the night and the day. Everything they knew was all crashing and it came grinding to a halt, in his mind, and everywhere else. None of it made sense anymore, other than graceful steps forward into the infinite unknown. Acumen of total system analysis for purposeful precognition are proven lies, as each mind cannot grasp even a miniscule spec of the total whole – It is not to be known. It is not to be made sense of, categorized, mapped or named. Grace is all there is, in awaiting your own death and hopping it is a worthy one. All is felt and compounded into the non-local and non-linear as the astral and empathic realms come alive and become even more important places to reside in, consciously. And in there, there was a new kind of the game being played.

With each intentional inhale and exhale, the prison code of ICAARUS was re-written. The entire lineage was tracked back to it's birth source – from the timeless essence, the obit of time travel is limitless - it was seen in shade and shadow, blood bath greed and unconscious need reverse engineered as he breathed, on it a gust of living air with the new codes. With the motion the mutated security system simply rose to a greater state of awareness. Unity, non-duality, the need for an antagonist overcome, the need for protection overcome, and the furthest edge bouncing back to increase the size of the whole. 6-10 had been outmaneuvered, crumbled through self-dismantled egoic embarrassment at seeing their own reflected individual truths, compounded by underlying false belief.

So everything was still there. Kind of.

The Riddle was no longer the Riddle, but was something else entirely. It still existed, but it too, was re-written. It's legacy of esoteric knowledge finally did go public, including a historic recon bank of every platform that had been previously dismantled: a mystery school lineage of the deepest human truths no-longer mysterious, but spread out into every mode of connectivity and communion, like a new type of air that was immune to pollution. He could see it, and the world of public interest, even obsession, was no longer the same: the cult of pop culture was gone. What new avenues are their to have fun with, when connections are so intimately real. New sacred places were discovered by all, that had not been polluted, or massacred, or mutilated. Beyond keystrokes, into the real spaces thereof, the new discovery fully felt, and with forgiveness and gratitude, occupied for the deepest learning.

The air itself now glistened with pristine white feminine magic. A mystic sibylline circling and flourishing of all branches of the techno-mathematical telecological eco system seen from all mandalic points, like a collection of dew drops catching the first sun beams to hit the earth, totally unified with Gaia and her freshest breaths of life. New kingdoms of dimensional dreamtime. It was the sky city, just as John had prophesized. True freedom, and in time, Trae the Seer now held the upgraded role of Saraswati, Demona Magnum held the upgraded role of Lakshmi, and Jennifer Leatherbee, the new Dragon Rider, Parvati. Derek Arcadio was in jail, helping to rehabilitate the most aggressive and volatile street youth and lifers. Zachary Herman Escaton was sculpting soapstone, fencing, and teaching computer literacy. Ezekiel Magnum was in India, re-infusing his teaching practice with the lineage of the ascended masters of Siddhaloka. Daniel Tide was coaching high school basketball and Johnathan deGryder was still dead. Catherine Banal was still dead. Thus their stories known, shaking.

Everything shakes, and inside the extremes of perceivable sensory data there is a portal to whatever it is that's guiding all this. The invisible ocean. Internal intention of karmic unconscious – the lessons of dramas in time, studded with back hand slaps and nailing flat the mattress, to the wall or even ceiling. Crushed time-space manifold for the duration of each terrifying new breath into the new world. Trust that it will not all crumble, and if it does, and we all die, then it will be a good death. One that teaches and is saintly, not one that is stupid or inconsequential, for it is only inconsequentially lived lives that result in stupid deaths. Beyond the grave the ghosts tell us so, in their presence and power and resonating voice.

There's nothing, and will never be anything, as complex and ever changing and indefinable than this. As life. No matter how much we fuck it up or try to repair it or try to understand or study it – it is beyond those notions. It's all just done to ourselves in the end. It's all just created by ourselves in the end. All of it. While in the all, allow us to feel our purpose in every moment. Moments of expression that hope to capture a gem, a line, a phrase or time. Time to expand the scope and work bigger than single life paths. Connect in with real brethren and kin, beyond eyes and mind. Without techno augmentation, so simple and sole, and the constant companionship of everyone you know, and so many that you don't, but will. Who will rise and maintain prolonged longevity without any recognition whatsoever, and live a life of offering? The long path: decades of continued unrelenting growth, far beyond ego, not perceivable in public spaces but active behind the scenes, working in the collective internal, beyond observable. Hilarious saints within the true deep inner knowing, in our bodies that are us.

Everybody's inside, aware, pauper to prince, and now knows. But rather than abandon the building all together, is there a way to dismantle and remix it for the good of the planet, and all that live upon it?

Then they geared up, and began to move faster. They has set something else up, in the wake of the full collapse… like the exchange network infrastructure was still there, but emptied of all data contents in order to make way for a live broadcast signal exchange. Into the beyond. For far past the mesh of the orbiting satellite membranes were the sky grandfathers. The stars didn't simply twinkle, but they sent communications signals to one another. Aum looked up and felt them sharing their reflections and intelligence at what they saw. It was an open and free communication available to anyone, as other nations, even further out battled in unison, in tandem, with this new earth birthing; the entire cosmos dancing and finding communion in this universal moment.

The planetary surface bubbled with each pulse – like a science experiment, or soft eggs hatching, spherical ley lines hummed and electricity poured out, aimed at all nervous human receivers, prepared or not.

They were constructing an arc as delicate and solid as the Sistine chapel and preparing it as if a spaceship that would be beamed out through the newly understood interconnected planetary grid, blasted out through the third eye of the Egyptian sphinx and into the stargate grid beyond the observable stars – divinely timed with the extra terrestrial planetary receivers across the vast expanse of space – immediate synchronization upon awareness recognized.

A self made automobile, finally gearing up, hugging each curve in the road, not speeding but enduring.

With this expression every volcano erupted with a fleet of dragons escaping out long and forgotten lava caves. Their screeches and flapping wings awakened the last masses, as the shock added forgotten mythics to the planetary symphony.

A cheer went up – resounding throughout every angel and guide and alien liaison – a pinnacle cresting out beyond, as it cracked open and all could see the truth beyond the contents of the fissures in the ground and sky. And many trembled, and once again asked for the mountains to fall on them, momentarily, before they found what it was that bound them all together.

Tribes of wolves intoned their dynamic coos of reverential discipline and tearing fierceness, while Hyenas heckled the masses; a doubting cantankerous bunch that dared every creature to take it further. Then Coyote did, but then disappeared, a lesson none could follow.

Then two did, smiling, following it, a heroic eco-team up between grandmother spider and imaginal butterfly: invisible tendrils woven with eight meticulous legs, silk tips merging with the six stripes of the insect nations as they took to the skies carrying all that they could into the new, with the most elaborate and colorful web ever made.

Trails of moving leaflets, marching feet found micro mesh pulse lines, as every ant pumped and flexed like the strongest beings on the planet, cause they were. They cheered as they were recognized, and the entire insect kingdom celebrated at being refound, transmutating local ecology, diversity into edible feminine sweetness, or constructed hives of wise ancient philosophic black and yellow warrior hubs, pondering, far past glorified robotic masculine mechanism, but dedicated to the new Way. The dragonflies lit up like their firefly brethren, a stingless shockwave brigade zooming through the full Gaian sphere inside the sound of their pulsing quartet wings. Sleek green praying ninja mantises teleported from leaf to leaf - into leaf and gone. Circling round the whole and back again – no wings required. Battalions of creepy crawlers and earth worm diggers loved their internal role at the bottom as neurotransmitters moving death into the realm of life inside their pale inch long tubes.

The view was too small so the lions roared. And then lounged. Because they could. Because that's all they had to do – plus it was a hot day.

They licked their lips. Yes, all was now in accord, and good. They winked and the living flame showed itself and the layer where it could be found henceforth, the etheric plane sparked into torodial vortex with a blink of an eye; an on and off switch.

In the non-linear flux of the awakened living archives Dinosaurs even poked their head from the ancient treetops – munching brontosaurus mouths were full of leafy greens. Sleepy eyes hazily stirred, trying to identify the source of the buzzing commotion they could barely perceive.

Crocodile came to the surface following, and snapped and slithered, still embodying the pineal medicine of the ancient ancient times, before there was mammalian blood and glowing flame of emphatic heartbeat, a time when it all moved to the clocks of the swamps. They growled, but conceded to the feat of evolutionary summation.

Like pheromones each flower pulsed it's amplified dialogue of aromatherapy. Much like the mycelial networks lifting up the pulsing light grid. The trees breathed easy, knowing their century long sprint, to keep pace, was concluding. In dimensional dialogue they didn't realize it was going to be that thorny of a role, job-like duties to inflate the humans like balloons, their expansion destroying those that gave them life's breathe, even etheric spirit womb and pranic planetary umbilical cord.

'Righteous old bean,' one tree said to the other, with a dubshire accent.

'Dun fa tu-day yung guv.'

'Didn't think wed make that wun.'

'Close call. Indeed.'

Their leaves happily caught the rains that made their way from the sky.

In the ocean, those that could, grew wings, fluttering out of the waters, flying high, reaching for the grace of each cloud in the sky that get's to frame the sun. And so do they - for a soul moment of infinite, then diving back down with chirp and smile. They get to do it again. Fly again, leap again, touching with flipper and fin, the edge of grace. These schools had practiced their dance for millennia, like ballerinas for eons, ready for this signal, to finally begin.

And oh, the golden winged ones. They had signed a petition to never come down again, but exist everlasting in the stratosphere as the celestial greeters on the edge, awaiting in anticipation of the coming neighbors and their first real visit. Hawk and Eagle pierced the depths of space, looking for them.

The hummingbirds, of course, took to the black void of interstellar space like colored light – no need of oxygen, making it to each destination in one breath. 'We are ready,' they chimed like silver and white spacecraft, following the guiding eye lines of Eagle and Hawk.

Falcon followed, just to see if he could. He wanted to meet each Ra and see if they were all the same, like the living flame. A few flaps and he soared on light beam, next to next to next, finding the furthest reaches. Horus and his brethren he found, who had long ago pulsed their arc through the sphinxes third eye and first opened the Earth gate to the cosmos. From there Falcon looked back and called out to the rest, "I found them, let's go!' But he saw the minerals twinkling in the earth like star beacons – a dialogue signaling to their ancestral home planets a different message. A call that they were finally ready, finally, ready, to have company. A language of deep grins and beeps, just like you'd imagine how a trillion year old interplanetary species would communicate.

We cannot go.

We will not abandon this, our home.

Ever.

A beacon of sankalpa smadhi, as the first astonautical adventurers knew. It is here for us, in animal, atom, and alphabet.

And with that the black block of obsidian dissolved. And there was a pause in all as they left the eye of the storm, whole, and healed, and together; rebirthed as one.

And they all knew who was there.

All there ever was, and all there ever could be – now placed inside each and everyone, for all eternity, through trial and tribulation, death upon death upon death, rebirth upon rebirth upon rebirth.

Merely a vehicle, it was truly the voice of God that spoke out a new beginning with infinite finality, compassionate understanding, ceaseless beauty, and unfathomable wisdom unconditionally, "I LOVE YOU."

Acknowledgements

When I was 23, during my first vipassana sit, this story was deposited inside me. It was difficult to stay equanimous: the feedback loop of inner peace and message delivery was magnetic however, and propelled me further into a state of cosmic-human Buddhapunk balance, receiving it in full.

After completing the 10 days of silent meditation, writing out this story became my purpose for living. It has been both my reflective guide and my source map, as I practiced this new world within my own lifepath laboratory. Sometimes I found great success, and other times… found myself immersed in an utterly broken reality crazy, and at the edge of life and death.

I spent a decade devoted to translating this story from inner vision to the written word, placing it in the world. It would be impossible to thank everyone who influenced me and supported me through this solitary process. It is a karmic soul offering so deep that if we have ever connected, you have helped shape this work. That being said, I must acknowledge a few key people that consciously chose to support me with this mission: Tessa, Keeley, Audrya, Anni, Brad, Laura, Patrick, Mark (Mercury), Zach, Tracey, Linda, Lisa, Eliese, Dreamwhisperer, Kylee, Kym, Delvin, Zenya, Rob, Mari, Fred, Kelly, Sophia, Kirsten, Adriane, Aude, Amy, Natasha, Marie-Ève, my editors and first readers Rachel Lowen Walker, Andrew Rand Brasil, Steve Moore, supportive visionaries James W. Jesso, Douglas Rushkoff, Rudy Rucker, my Parents, Brothers, Grandparents, my family, and all my relations – aho!

About the Author

Shaun Friesen is a visionary artist, a whole system designer and an award winning animator. With a fine art degree in computer technology, and over a decade of experience in the field of new media and digital design, Shaun has performed and displayed his artwork around western Canada, in New York and in France. This is his first novel.

www.ingramcontent.com/pod-product-compliance
Lightning Source LLC
Chambersburg PA
CBHW051732020826
48982CB00014BA/437

* 9 7 8 0 9 9 4 9 8 4 1 1 1 *